JEFFREY ARCHER

THE FOURTH ESTATE

PAN BOOKS

First published in Great Britain 1996 by HarperCollins*Publishers*

This edition published 2010 by Pan Books
an imprint of Pan Macmillan
20 New Wharf Road, London N1 9RR
Associated companies throughout the world
www.panmacmillan.com

ISBN 978-0-330-41908-6

15

A CIP catalogue record for this book is available from
the British Library.

Typeset by SetSystems Ltd, Saffron Walden, Essex
Printed and bound by CPI Group (UK) Ltd, Croydon, CR0 4YY

Visit www.panmacmillan.com to read more about all our books
and to buy them. You will also find features, author interviews and
news of any author events, and you can sign up for e-newsletters
so that you're always first to hear about our new releases.

TO MICHAEL AND JUDITH

AUTHOR'S NOTE

In May 1789, Louis XVI summoned to Versailles a full meeting of the 'Estates General'.

The First Estate consisted of three hundred nobles.

The Second Estate, three hundred clergy.

The Third Estate, six hundred commoners.

Some years later, after the French Revolution, Edmund Burke, looking up at the Press Gallery of the House of Commons, said, 'Yonder sits the Fourth Estate, and they are more important than them all.'

Media Moguls Battle to Save Their Empires

1

The GLOBE

5 NOVEMBER 1991

Armstrong Faces Bankruptcy

The odds were stacked against him. But the odds had never worried Richard Armstrong in the past.

'*Faites vos jeux, mesdames et messieurs.* Place your bets.'

Armstrong stared down at the green baize. The mountain of red chips that had been placed in front of him twenty minutes earlier had dwindled to a single stack. He had already lost forty thousand francs that evening – but what was forty thousand francs when you had squandered a billion dollars in the past twelve months?

He leaned over and deposited all his remaining chips on zero.

'*Les jeux sont faits. Rien ne va plus,*' the croupier said as he flicked his wrist and set the wheel in motion. The little white ball sped around the wheel, before falling and jumping in and out of the tiny black and red slots.

Armstrong stared into the distance. Even after the ball had finally settled he refused to lower his eyes.

'*Vingt-six,*' declared the croupier, and immediately began scooping up the chips that littered every number other than twenty-six.

Armstrong walked away from the table without even glancing in the direction of the croupier. He moved slowly past the crowded backgammon and roulette tables until he reached the double doors that led out into the real world. A tall man in a long blue coat pulled one of them open for him, and smiled at the well-known gambler, anticipating his usual hundred-franc tip. But that wouldn't be possible tonight.

Armstrong ran a hand through his thick black hair as he walked down through the lush terraced gardens of the casino and on past the fountain. It had been fourteen hours since the emergency board meeting in London, and he was beginning to feel exhausted.

Despite his bulk – Armstrong hadn't consulted a set of scales for several years – he kept up a steady pace along the promenade, only stopping when he reached his favourite restaurant overlooking the bay. He knew every table would have been booked at least a week in advance, and the thought of the trouble he was about to cause brought a smile to his face for the first time that evening.

He pushed open the door of the restaurant. A tall, thin waiter swung round and tried to hide his surprise by bowing low.

'Good evening, Mr Armstrong,' he said. 'How nice to see you again. Will anyone be joining you?'

'No, Henri.'

The head waiter quickly guided his unexpected customer through the packed restaurant to a small alcove table. Once Armstrong was seated, he presented him with a large leather-bound menu.

Armstrong shook his head. 'Don't bother with that, Henri. You know exactly what I like.'

The head waiter frowned. European royalty, Hollywood stars, even Italian footballers didn't unnerve him, but whenever Richard Armstrong was in the restaurant he was constantly on edge. And now he was expected to select Armstrong's meal for him. He was relieved that his famous customer's usual table had been free. If Armstrong had arrived a few minutes later, he would have had to wait at the bar while they hastily set up a table in the centre of the room.

By the time Henri placed a napkin on Armstrong's lap the

wine waiter was already pouring a glass of his favourite champagne. Armstrong stared out of the window into the distance, but his eyes did not focus on the large yacht moored at the north end of the bay. His thoughts were several hundred miles away, with his wife and children. How would they react when they heard the news?

A lobster bisque was placed in front of him, at a temperature that would allow him to eat it immediately. Armstrong disliked having to wait for anything to cool down. He would rather be burned.

To the head waiter's surprise, his customer's eyes remained fixed on the horizon as his champagne glass was filled for a second time. How quickly, Armstrong wondered, would his colleagues on the board – most of them placemen with titles or connections – begin to cover their tracks and distance themselves from him once the company's accounts were made public? Only Sir Paul Maitland, he suspected, would be able to salvage his reputation.

Armstrong picked up the dessert spoon in front of him, lowered it into the bowl and began to scoop up the soup in a rapid cyclical movement.

Customers at surrounding tables occasionally turned to glance in his direction, and whispered conspiratorially to their companions.

'One of the richest men in the world,' a local banker was telling the young woman he was taking out for the first time. She looked suitably impressed. Normally Armstrong revelled in the thought of his fame. But tonight he didn't even notice his fellow-diners. His mind had moved on to the boardroom of a Swiss bank, where the decision had been taken to bring down the final curtain – and all for a mere $50 million.

The empty soup bowl was whisked away as Armstrong touched his lips with the linen napkin. The head waiter knew only too well that this man didn't like to pause between courses.

A Dover sole, off the bone – Armstrong couldn't abide unnecessary activity – was deftly lowered in front of him; by its side was a bowl of his favourite large chips and a bottle of HP

Sauce – the only one kept in the kitchen, for the only customer who ever demanded it. Armstrong absent-mindedly removed the cap from the bottle, turned it upside down and shook vigorously. A large brown blob landed in the middle of the fish. He picked up a knife and spread the sauce evenly over the white flesh.

◄○►

That morning's board meeting had nearly got out of control after Sir Paul had resigned as chairman. Once they had dealt with 'Any Other Business', Armstrong had quickly left the boardroom and taken the lift to the roof where his helicopter was waiting for him.

His pilot was leaning on the railing, enjoying a cigarette, when Armstrong appeared. 'Heathrow,' he barked, without giving a thought to clearance by air-traffic control or the availability of take-off slots. The pilot quickly stubbed out his cigarette and ran towards the helicopter landing pad. As they flew over the City of London, Armstrong began to consider the sequence of events that would take place during the next few hours unless the $50 million were somehow miraculously to materialise.

Fifteen minutes later, the helicopter landed on the private apron known to those who can afford to use it as Terminal Five. He lowered himself onto the ground and walked slowly over to his private jet.

Another pilot, this one waiting to receive his orders, greeted him at the top of the steps.

'Nice,' said Armstrong, before making his way to the back of the cabin. The pilot disappeared into the cockpit, assuming that 'Captain Dick' would be joining his yacht in Monte Carlo for a few days' rest.

The Gulfstream took off to the south. During the two-hour flight Armstrong made only one phone call, to Jacques Lacroix in Geneva. But however much he pleaded, the answer remained the same: 'Mr Armstrong, you have until close of business today to repay the $50 million, otherwise I will be left with no choice but to place the matter in the hands of our legal department.'

The only other action he took during the flight was to tear up the contents of the files Sir Paul had left behind on the boardroom table. He then disappeared into the lavatory and flushed the little pieces down the bowl.

When the plane taxied to a halt at Nice airport, a chauffeur-driven Mercedes drew up beside the steps. No words were exchanged as Armstrong climbed into the back: the chauffeur didn't need to ask where his master wished to be taken. In fact Armstrong didn't utter a word during the entire journey from Nice to Monte Carlo; after all, his driver was not in a position to lend him $50 million.

As the car swung into the marina, the captain of Armstrong's yacht stood to attention and waited to welcome him on board. Although Armstrong had not warned anyone of his intentions, others had phoned ahead to alert the thirteen-man crew of *Sir Lancelot* that the boss was on the move. 'But God knows to where,' had been his secretary's final comment.

Whenever Armstrong decided that the time had come for him to head back to the airport, his secretary would be informed immediately. It was the only way any of his staff around the world could hope to survive for more than a week.

The captain was apprehensive. The boss hadn't been expected on board for another three weeks, when he was due to take a fortnight's holiday with the rest of the family. When the call had come through from London that morning, the skipper had been at the local shipyard, supervising some minor repairs to *Sir Lancelot*. No one had any idea where Armstrong was heading, but he wasn't willing to take risks. He had, at considerable expense, managed to get the yacht released from the shipyard and tied up at the quayside only minutes before the boss had set foot in France.

Armstrong strode up the gangplank and past four men in crisp white uniforms, all standing to attention and saluting. He slipped off his shoes and went below to the private quarters.

When he pushed open the door of his stateroom, he discovered that others had anticipated his arrival: there were several faxes already piled up on the table beside his bed.

Could Jacques Lacroix possibly have changed his mind? He dismissed the idea instantly. After years of dealing with the Swiss, he knew them only too well. They remained an unimaginative, one-dimensional nation whose bank accounts always had to be in the black, and in whose dictionary the word 'risk' wasn't to be found.

He began to flick through the sheets of curling fax paper. The first was from his New York bankers, informing him that when the market had opened that morning, the price of shares in Armstrong Communications had continued to drop. He skimmed the page until his eyes settled on the one line he had been dreading. 'No buyers, only sellers,' it stated clinically. 'If this trend continues for much longer, the bank will be left with no choice but to consider its position.'

He swept all the faxes onto the floor, and headed for the little safe hidden behind a large framed photograph of himself shaking hands with the Queen. He swivelled the disk backwards and forwards, stopping at 10–06–23. The heavy door swung open and Armstrong placed both his hands inside, quickly removing all the bulky wads of cash. Three thousand dollars, twenty-two thousand French francs, seven thousand drachma and a thick bundle of Italian lire. Once he had pocketed the money, he left the yacht and headed straight for the casino, without telling any of the crew where he was going, how long he would be or when he might return. The captain ordered a junior rating to shadow him, so that when he made his way back towards the harbour they wouldn't be taken by surprise.

—◇—

A large vanilla ice cream was placed in front of him. The head waiter began to pour hot chocolate sauce over it; as Armstrong never suggested that he should stop, he carried on until the silver sauce-boat was empty. The cyclical movement of the spoon began again, and didn't cease until the last drop of chocolate had been scraped off the side of the bowl.

A steaming black coffee replaced the empty bowl. Armstrong continued to gaze out over the bay. Once the word was out that he couldn't cover a sum as small as $50 million, there wouldn't be a bank on earth that would consider doing business with him.

The head waiter returned a few minutes later, and was surprised to find the coffee untouched. 'Shall we bring you another cup, Mr Armstrong?' he asked in a deferential whisper.

Armstrong shook his head. 'Just the check, Henri.' He drained his champagne glass for the last time. The head waiter scurried away and returned immediately with a folded slip of white paper on a silver salver. This was one customer who couldn't abide waiting for anything, even the bill.

Armstrong flicked open the folded slip but showed no interest in its contents. Seven hundred and twelve francs, *service non compris*. He signed it, rounding it up to a thousand francs. A smile appeared on the head waiter's face for the first time that evening – a smile that would disappear when he discovered that the restaurant was the last in a long queue of creditors.

Armstrong pushed back his chair, threw his crumpled napkin on the table and walked out of the restaurant without another word. Several pairs of eyes followed him as he left, and another was watching as he stepped onto the pavement. He didn't notice the young rating scamper off in the direction of the *Sir Lancelot*.

Armstrong belched as he strode down the promenade, past dozens of boats huddled close together, tied up for the night. He usually enjoyed the sensation of knowing that the *Sir Lancelot* was almost certain to be the largest yacht in the bay, unless of course the Sultan of Brunei or King Fahd had sailed in during the evening. His only thought tonight was how much she might fetch when she was put up for sale on the open market. But once the truth was known, would anyone want to buy a yacht that had been owned by Richard Armstrong?

With the help of the ropes, Armstrong yanked himself up

the gangway to find the captain and the first officer awaiting him.

'We'll sail immediately.'

The captain was not surprised. He knew Armstrong would not want to be tied up in port any longer than was necessary: only the gentle swaying of the boat could lull him to sleep, even in the darkest hours. The captain began issuing the orders to get under way as Armstrong slipped off his shoes and disappeared below.

When Armstrong opened the door of his stateroom he was met by yet another pile of faxes. He grabbed them, still hoping for a lifeline. The first was from Peter Wakeham, the deputy chairman of Armstrong Communications, who, despite the late hour, was obviously still at his desk in London. 'Please call urgently,' read the message. The second was from New York. The company's stock had plummeted to a new low, and his bankers had 'reluctantly found it necessary' to place their own shares on the market. The third was from Jacques Lacroix in Geneva to confirm that as the bank had not received the $50 million by close of business, they had been left with no choice but to . . .

It was twelve minutes past five in New York, twelve minutes past ten in London, and twelve minutes past eleven in Geneva. By nine o'clock the following morning he wouldn't be able to control the headlines in his own newspapers, let alone those owned by Keith Townsend.

Armstrong undressed slowly and allowed his clothes to fall in a heap on the floor. He then took a bottle of brandy from the sideboard, poured himself a large glass and collapsed onto the double bed. He lay still as the engines roared into life, and the ship began to manoeuvre itself out of the harbour.

Hour after hour slipped by, but Armstrong didn't stir, except to refill the brandy balloon from time to time, until he heard four chimes on the little clock by the side of his bed. He pushed himself up, waited for a few moments and then lowered his feet onto the thick carpet. He rose unsteadily, and made his way across the unlit stateroom towards the bathroom. When he reached the open door, he unhooked a large cream dressing-gown with the words *Sir Lancelot* emblazoned in gold on its pocket. He padded back towards the door of the cabin, opened it cautiously and stepped barefoot into the dimly-lit corridor. He hesitated before locking the door behind him and slipping the key into his dressing-gown pocket. He didn't move again until he was sure he could hear nothing except the familiar sound of the ship's engine droning below him.

He lurched from side to side as he stumbled down the narrow corridor, pausing when he reached the staircase which led up onto the deck. He then slowly began to climb the steps, clutching firmly onto the rope on both sides. When he reached the top he stepped out onto the deck, checking quickly in both directions. There was no one to be seen. It was a clear, cool night, no different from ninety-nine in every hundred at that time of year.

Armstrong padded silently on until he was above the engine room – the noisiest part of the ship.

He waited only for a moment before untying the cord of his dressing-gown and allowing it to fall to the deck.

Naked in the warm night, he stared out into the still black sea and thought: isn't your whole life meant to flash before you at a time like this?

2

The Citizen

Townsend Faces Ruin

'Messages?' was all Keith Townsend said as he passed his secretary's desk and headed towards his office.

'The President called from Camp David just before you boarded the plane,' Heather said.

'Which of my papers has annoyed him this time?' Townsend asked as he sat down.

'The *New York Star*. He's heard a rumour that you're going to print his bank statement on tomorrow's front page,' Heather replied.

'It's more likely to be my own bank statement that makes the front pages tomorrow,' said Townsend, his Australian accent more pronounced than usual. 'Who else?'

'Margaret Thatcher has sent a fax from London. She's agreed to your terms for a two-book contract, even though Armstrong's bid was higher.'

'Let's hope someone offers me $6 million when I write *my* memoirs.'

Heather gave him a weak smile.

'Anyone else?'

'Gary Deakins has had another writ served on him.'

'What for this time?'

'He accused the Archbishop of Brisbane of rape, on the front page of yesterday's *Truth*.'

'The truth, the whole truth, and anything but the truth,' said Townsend, smiling. 'Just as long as it sells papers.'

'Unfortunately it turns out that the woman in question is a well-known lay preacher, and has been a friend of the arch-bishop's family for years. It seems that Gary suggested a different meaning each time he used the word "lay".'

Townsend leaned back in his chair and continued to listen to the myriad problems other people were facing all around the world: the usual complaints from politicians, businessmen and so-called media personalities who expected him to intervene immediately to save their precious careers from ruin. By this time tomorrow, most of them would have calmed down and been replaced by another dozen or so equally irate, equally demanding prima donnas. He knew that every one of them would be only too delighted to discover that it was his own career which really was on the verge of collapse – and all because the president of a small bank in Cleveland had demanded that a loan of $50 million be repaid by the close of business tonight.

As Heather continued to go through the list of messages – most of them from people whose names meant nothing to him – Townsend's mind drifted back to the speech he'd given the previous evening. A thousand of his top executives from all over the world had gathered in Honolulu for a three-day conference. In his closing address he'd told them that Global Corp couldn't be in better shape to face the challenges of the new media revolution. He had ended by saying: 'We are the one company that is qualified to lead this industry into the twenty-first century.' They had stood and cheered him for several minutes. As he looked down into the packed audience full of confident faces, he had wondered just how many of them suspected that Global was actually only hours away from going bankrupt.

'What shall I do about the President?' Heather asked for the second time.

Townsend snapped back into the real world. 'Which one?'

'Of the United States.'

'Wait until he calls again,' he said. 'He may have calmed

down a bit by then. Meanwhile, I'll have a word with the editor of the *Star*.'

'And Mrs Thatcher?'

'Send her a large bunch of flowers and a note saying, "We'll make your memoirs number one from Moscow to New York".'

'Shouldn't I add London?'

'No, she knows it will be number one in London.'

'And what should I do about Gary Deakins?'

'Phone the archbishop and tell him I'm going to build that new roof his cathedral so desperately needs. Wait a month, then send him a cheque for $10,000.'

Heather nodded, closed her notebook and asked, 'Do you want to take any calls?'

'Only Austin Pierson.' He paused. 'The moment he phones, put him straight through.'

Heather turned and left the room.

Townsend swivelled his chair round and stared out of the window. He tried to recall the conversation he'd had with his financial adviser when she had phoned him in the private jet on his way back from Honolulu.

'I've just come out of my meeting with Pierson,' she'd said. 'It lasted over an hour, but he still hadn't made up his mind by the time I left him.'

'Hadn't made up his mind?'

'No. He still needs to consult the bank's finance committee before he can come to a final decision.'

'But surely now that all the other banks have fallen into place, Pierson can't – '

'He can and he may well. Try to remember that he's the president of a small bank in Ohio. He's not interested in what other banks have agreed to. And after all the bad press coverage you've been getting in the past few weeks, he only cares about one thing right now.'

'What's that?' he'd asked.

'Covering his backside,' she'd replied.

'But doesn't he realise that all the other banks will renege if he doesn't go along with the overall plan?'

'Yes, he does, but when I put that to him he shrugged his shoulders and said, "In which case I'll just have to take my chance along with all the others."'

Townsend had begun to curse, when E.B. added, 'But he did promise me one thing.'

'What was that?'

'He'll call the moment the committee has reached its decision.'

'That's big of him. So what am I expected to do if it goes against me?'

'Release the press statement we agreed on,' she'd said.

Townsend had felt sick. 'Is there nothing left that I can do?'

'No, nothing,' Ms Beresford had replied firmly. 'Just sit and wait for Pierson to call. If I'm going to make the next flight to New York, I'll have to dash. I should be with you around midday.' The line had gone dead.

Townsend continued to think about her words as he rose from his chair and began pacing around the room. He stopped to check his tie in the mirror above the mantelpiece – he hadn't had time to change his clothes since getting off the plane, and it showed. For the first time, he couldn't help thinking that he looked older than his sixty-three years. But that wasn't surprising after what E.B. had put him through over the past six weeks. He would have been the first to admit that had he sought her advice a little earlier, he might not now be so dependent on a call from the president of a small bank in Ohio.

He stared at the phone, willing it to ring. But it didn't. He made no attempt to tackle the pile of letters Heather had left for him to sign. His thoughts were interrupted when the door opened, and Heather came in. She handed him a single sheet of paper; on it was a list of names arranged in alphabetical order. 'I thought you might find this useful,' she said. After thirty-five years of working for him, she knew he was the last man on earth who could be expected to just sit and wait.

Townsend ran his finger down the list of names unusually slowly. Not one of them meant anything to him. Three had an asterisk against them, indicating that they had worked for Global

Corp in the past. He currently employed thirty-seven thousand people, thirty-six thousand of whom he hadn't ever met. But three of those who had worked for him at some point in their careers were now on the staff of the *Cleveland Sentinel*, a paper he'd never heard of.

'Who owns the *Sentinel*?' he asked, hoping that he might be able to put some pressure on the proprietor.

'Richard Armstrong,' Heather replied flatly.

'That's all I need.'

'In fact you don't control a paper within a hundred miles of Cleveland,' continued Heather. 'Just a radio station to the south of the city that pumps out country and western.'

At that moment Townsend would happily have traded the *New York Star* for the *Cleveland Sentinel*. He glanced again at the three asterisked names, but they still meant nothing to him. He looked back up at Heather. 'Do any of them still love me?' he asked, trying to force a smile.

'Barbara Bennett certainly doesn't,' Heather replied. 'She's the fashion editor on the *Sentinel*. She was sacked from her local paper in Seattle a few days after you took it over. She sued for wrongful dismissal, and claimed her replacement was having an affair with the editor. We ended up having to settle out of court. In the preliminary hearings she described you as "nothing more than a peddler of pornography whose only interest is the bottom line". You gave instructions that she was never to be employed by any of your papers again.'

Townsend knew that that particular list probably had well over a thousand names on it, every one of whom would be only too happy to dip their pens in blood as they composed his obituary for tomorrow's first editions.

'Mark Kendall?' he queried.

'Chief crime reporter,' said Heather. 'Worked on the *New York Star* for a few months, but there's no record of your ever coming across him.'

Townsend's eyes settled on another unfamiliar name, and he waited for Heather to supply the details. He knew she would be saving the best for last: even she enjoyed having some hold over him.

'Malcolm McCreedy. Features editor at the *Sentinel*. He worked for the corporation on the *Melbourne Courier* between 1979 and 1984. In those days he used to tell everyone on the paper that you and he were drinking mates from way back. He was sacked for continually failing to get his copy in on time. It seems that malt whisky was the first thing to gain his attention after the morning conference, and anything in a skirt soon after lunch. Despite his claims, I can't find any proof that you've even met him.'

Townsend marvelled at how much information Heather had come up with in so short a time. But he accepted that after working for him for so long, her contacts were almost as good as his.

'McCreedy's been married twice,' she continued. 'Both times it ended in divorce. He has two children by the first marriage: Jill, who's twenty-seven, and Alan, twenty-four. Alan works for the corporation on the *Dallas Comet*, in the classifieds department.'

'Couldn't be better,' said Townsend. 'McCreedy's our man. He's about to get a call from his long-lost mate.'

Heather smiled. 'I'll get him on the phone right away. Let's hope he's sober.'

Townsend nodded, and Heather returned to her office. The proprietor of 297 journals, with a combined readership of over a billion people around the world, waited to be put through to the features editor on a local paper in Ohio with a circulation of less than thirty-five thousand.

Townsend stood up and began to pace around the office, formulating the questions he needed to ask McCreedy, and thinking about the order he should put them in. As he circled the room, his eyes passed over the framed copies of his newspapers displayed on the walls, bearing their most famous headlines.

The *New York Star*, 23 November 1963: 'Kennedy Assassinated in Dallas'.

The *Continent*, 30 July 1981: 'Happily Ever After', above a picture of Charles and Diana on their wedding day.

The *Globe*, 17 May 1991: 'Richard Branson Deflowered Me, Claims Virgin'.

He would happily have paid half a million dollars to be able to read the headlines on tomorrow's papers.

The phone on his desk gave out a shrill blast, and Townsend quickly returned to his chair and grabbed the receiver.

'Malcolm McCreedy is on line one,' said Heather, putting him through.

As soon as he heard the click, Townsend said, 'Malcolm, is that you?'

'Sure is, Mr Townsend,' said a surprised-sounding voice with an unmistakable Australian accent.

'It's been a long time, Malcolm. Too long, in fact. How are you?'

'I'm fine, Keith. Just fine,' came back a more confident reply.

'And how are the children?' asked Townsend, looking down at the piece of paper Heather had left on his desk. 'Jill and Alan, isn't it? In fact, isn't Alan working for the company out of Dallas?'

A long silence followed, and Townsend began to wonder if he'd been cut off. Eventually McCreedy said, 'That's right, Keith. They're both doing just fine, thanks. And yours?' He was obviously unable to remember how many there were, or their names.

'They're doing just fine too, thank you, Malcolm,' said Townsend, purposely mimicking him. 'And how are you enjoying Cleveland?'

'It's OK,' said McCreedy. 'But I'd rather be back in Oz. I miss being able to watch the Tigers playing on a Saturday afternoon.'

'Well, that was one of the things I was calling you about,' said Townsend. 'But first I need to ask you for some advice.'

'Of course, Keith, anything. You can always rely on me,' said McCreedy. 'But perhaps I'd better close the door to my office,' he added, now that he was certain every other journalist on the floor realised who it was on the other end of the line.

Townsend waited impatiently.

'So, what can I do for you, Keith?' asked a slightly out-of-breath voice.

'Does the name Austin Pierson mean anything to you?'

Another long silence followed. 'He's some big wheel in the financial community, isn't he? I think he heads up one of our banks or insurance companies. Give me a moment, and I'll just check him out on my computer.'

Townsend waited again, aware that if his father had asked the same question forty years before it might have taken hours, perhaps even days, before someone could have come up with an answer.

'Got him,' said the man from Cleveland a few moments later. He paused. 'Now I remember why I recognised the name. We did a feature on him about four years ago when he took over as president at Manufacturers Cleveland.'

'What can you tell me about him?' asked Townsend, unwilling to waste any more time on banalities.

'Not a great deal,' replied McCreedy as he studied the screen in front of him, occasionally pressing more keys. 'He appears to be a model citizen. Rose through the ranks at the bank, treasurer of the local Rotary Club, Methodist lay preacher, married to the same woman for thirty-one years. Three children, all residing in the city.'

'Anything known about the kids?'

McCreedy pressed some more keys before he replied. 'Yes. One teaches biology in the local high school. The second's a staff nurse at Cleveland Metropolitan, and the youngest has just been made a partner in the most prestigious law firm in the state. If you're hoping to do a deal with Mr Austin Pierson, Keith, you'll be pleased to know that he seems to have an unblemished reputation.'

Townsend was not pleased to know. 'So there's nothing in his past that . . .'

'Not that I know of, Keith,' said McCreedy. He quickly read through his five-year-old notes, hoping to find a titbit that would please his former boss. 'Yes, now it all comes back. The man was as tight as a gnat's arse. He wouldn't even allow me to interview him during office hours, and when I turned up at his place in the evening, all I got for my trouble was a watered-down pineapple juice.'

Townsend decided that he'd come to a dead end with Pierson and McCreedy, and that there wasn't any purpose in continuing with the conversation. 'Thank you, Malcolm,' he said. 'You've been most helpful. Call me if you come up with anything on Pierson.'

He was just about to put the phone down when his former employee asked, 'What was the other thing you wanted to discuss, Keith? You see, I was rather hoping that there might be an opening in Oz, perhaps even at the *Courier*.' He paused. 'I can tell you, Keith, I'd be willing to take a drop in salary if it meant I could work for you again.'

'I'll bear that in mind,' said Townsend, 'and you can be sure I'll get straight back to you, Malcolm, if anything should ever cross my desk.'

Townsend put the phone down on a man he felt sure he would never speak to again in his life. All that McCreedy had been able to tell him was that Mr Austin Pierson was a paragon of virtue – not a breed with whom Townsend had a lot in common, or was at all certain he knew how to handle. As usual, E.B.'s advice was proving to be correct. He could do nothing except sit and wait. He leaned back in his chair and tucked one leg under the other.

It was twelve minutes past eleven in Cleveland, twelve minutes past four in London and twelve minutes past three in Sydney. By six o'clock that evening he probably wouldn't be able to control the headlines in his own papers, let alone those of Richard Armstrong.

The phone on his desk rang again – was it possible that McCreedy had found out something interesting about Austin Pierson? Townsend always assumed that everyone had at least one skeleton they wanted to keep safely locked up in the cupboard.

He grabbed the phone.

'I have the President of the United States on line one,' said Heather, 'and a Mr Austin Pierson from Cleveland, Ohio on line two. Which one will you take first?'

FIRST EDITION

Births, Marriages and Deaths

3

THE TIMES

6 JULY 1923

Communist Forces at Work

There are some advantages and many disadvantages in being born a Ruthenian Jew, but it was to be a long time before Lubji Hoch discovered any of the advantages.

Lubji was born in a small stone cottage on the outskirts of Douski, a town that nestled on the Czech, Romanian and Polish borders. He could never be certain of the exact date of his birth, as the family kept no records, but he was roughly a year older than his brother and a year younger than his sister.

As his mother held the child in her arms she smiled. He was perfect, right down to the bright red birthmark below his right shoulderblade – just like his father's.

The tiny cottage in which they lived was owned by his great-uncle, a rabbi. The rabbi had repeatedly begged Zelta not to marry Sergei Hoch, the son of a local cattle trader. The young girl had been too ashamed to admit to her uncle that she was pregnant with Sergei's child. Although she went against his wishes, the rabbi gave the newly married couple the little cottage as a wedding gift.

When Lubji entered the world the four rooms were already overcrowded; by the time he could walk, he had been joined by another brother and a second sister.

His father, of whom the family saw little, left the house soon after the sun had risen every morning and did not return until nightfall.

Lubji's mother explained that he was going about his work.

'And what is that work?' asked Lubji.

'He is tending the cattle left to him by your grandfather.' His mother made no pretence that a few cows and their calves constituted a herd.

'And where does Father work?' asked Lubji.

'In the fields on the other side of town.'

'What is a town?' asked Lubji.

Zelta went on answering his questions until the child finally fell asleep in her arms.

The rabbi never spoke to Lubji about his father, but he did tell him on many occasions that in her youth his mother had been courted by numerous admirers, as she was considered not only the most beautiful, but also the brightest girl in the town. With such a start in life she should have become a teacher in the local school, the rabbi told him, but now she had to be satisfied with passing on her knowledge to her ever-increasing family.

But of all her children, only Lubji responded to her efforts, sitting at his mother's feet, devouring her every word and the answers to any question he posed. As the years passed, the rabbi began to show interest in Lubji's progress – and to worry about which side of the family would gain dominance in the boy's character.

His fears had first been aroused when Lubji began to crawl, and had discovered the front door: from that moment his attention had been diverted from his mother, chained to the stove, and had focused on his father and on where he went when he left the house every morning.

Once Lubji could stand up, he turned the door handle, and the moment he could walk he stepped out onto the path and into the larger world occupied by his father. For a few weeks he was quite content to hold his hand as they walked through the cobbled streets of the sleeping town until they reached the fields where Papa tended the cattle.

But Lubji quickly became bored by the cows that just stood around, waiting first to be milked and later to give birth. He wanted to find out what went on in the town that was just waking as they passed through it every morning.

To describe Douski as a town might in truth be to exaggerate its importance, for it consisted of only a few rows of stone houses, half a dozen shops, an inn, a small synagogue – where Lubji's mother took the whole family every Saturday – and a town hall he had never once entered. But for Lubji it was the most exciting place on earth.

One morning, without explanation, his father tied up two cows and began to lead them back towards the town. Lubji trotted happily by his side, firing off question after question about what he intended to do with the cattle. But unlike the questions he asked his mother, answers were not always forthcoming, and were rarely illuminating.

Lubji gave up asking any more questions, as the answer was always 'Wait and see.' When they reached the outskirts of Douski the cattle were coaxed through the streets towards the market.

Suddenly his father stopped at a less than crowded corner. Lubji decided that there was no purpose in asking him why he had chosen that particular spot, because he knew he was unlikely to get an answer. Father and son stood in silence. It was some time before anyone showed any interest in the two cows.

Lubji watched with fascination as people began to circle the cattle, some prodding them, others simply offering opinions as to their worth, in tongues he had never heard before. He became aware of the disadvantage his father laboured under in speaking only one language in a town on the borders of three countries. He looked vacantly at most of those who offered an opinion after examining the scrawny beasts.

When his father finally received an offer in the one tongue he understood, he immediately accepted it without attempting to bargain. Several pieces of coloured paper changed hands, the cows were handed to their new owner, and his father marched off into the market, where he purchased a sack of grain, a box of potatoes, some gefilte fish, various items of clothing, a pair of second-hand shoes which badly needed repairing and a few other items, including a sleigh and a large brass buckle that he must have felt someone in the family needed. It struck Lubji as strange that while others bargained with the stallholders, Papa always handed over the sum demanded without question.

On the way home his father dropped into the town's only inn, leaving Lubji sitting on the ground outside, guarding their purchases. It was not until the sun had disappeared behind the town hall that his father, having downed several bottles of slivovice, emerged swaying from the inn, happy to allow Lubji to struggle with the sleigh full of goods with one hand and to guide him with the other.

When his mother opened the front door, Papa staggered past her and collapsed onto the mattress. Within moments he was snoring.

Lubji helped his mother drag their purchases into the cottage. But however warmly her eldest son spoke about them, she didn't seem at all pleased with the results of a year's labour. She shook her head as she decided what needed to be done with each of the items.

The sack of grain was propped up in a corner of the kitchen, the potatoes left in their wooden box and the fish placed by the window. The clothes were then checked for size before Zelta decided which of her children they should be allocated to. The shoes were left by the door for whoever needed them. Finally, the buckle was deposited in a small cardboard box which Lubji watched his mother hide below a loose floorboard on his father's side of the bed.

That night, while the rest of the family slept, Lubji decided that he had followed his father into the fields for the last time. The next morning, when Papa rose, Lubji slipped into the shoes left by the door, only to discover that they were too large for him. He followed his father out of the house, but this time he went only as far as the outskirts of the town, where he hid behind a tree. He watched as Papa disappeared out of sight, never once looking back to see if the heir to his kingdom was following.

Lubji turned and ran back towards the market. He spent the rest of the day walking around the stalls, finding out what each of them had to offer. Some sold fruit and vegetables, while others specialised in furniture or household necessities. But most of them were willing to trade anything if they thought they could make a profit. He enjoyed watching the different techniques the traders used when bargaining with their customers: some bullying, some cajoling, almost all lying about the provenance of their wares. What made it more exciting for Lubji was the different languages they conversed in. He quickly discovered that most of the customers, like his father, ended up with a poor bargain. During the afternoon he listened more carefully, and began to pick up a few words in languages other than his own.

By the time he returned home that night, he had a hundred questions to ask his mother, and for the first time he discovered that there were some even she couldn't answer. Her final comment that night to yet another unanswered question was simply, 'It's time you went to school, little one.' The only problem was that there wasn't a school in Douski for anyone so young. Zelta resolved to speak to her uncle about the problem as soon as the opportunity arose. After all, with a brain as good as Lubji's, her son might even end up as a rabbi.

The following morning Lubji rose even before his father had stirred, slipped into the one pair of shoes, and crept out of the house without waking his brothers or sisters. He ran all the way to the market, and once again began to walk around the stalls, watching the traders as they set out their wares in preparation for the day ahead. He listened as they bartered, and he began to understand more and more of what they were saying. He also started to realise what his mother had meant when she had told him that he had a God-given gift for languages. What she couldn't have known was that he had a genius for bartering.

Lubji stood mesmerised as he watched someone trade a

dozen candles for a chicken, while another parted with a chest of drawers in exchange for two sacks of potatoes. He moved on to see a goat being offered in exchange for a worn-out carpet and a cartful of logs being handed over for a mattress. How he wished he could have afforded the mattress, which was wider and thicker than the one his entire family slept on.

Every morning he would return to the marketplace. He learned that a barterer's skill depended not only on the goods you had to sell, but in your ability to convince the customer of his need for them. It took him only a few days to realise that those who dealt in coloured notes were not only better dressed, but unquestionably in a stronger position to strike a good bargain.

—<o>—

When his father decided the time had come to drag the next two cows to market, the six-year-old boy was more than ready to take over the haggling. That evening the young trader once again guided his father home. But after the drunken man had collapsed on the mattress, his mother just stood staring at the large pile of wares her son placed in front of her.

Lubji spent over an hour helping her distribute the goods among the rest of the family, but didn't tell her that he still had a piece of coloured paper with a 'ten' marked on it. He wanted to find out what else he could purchase with it.

The following morning, Lubji did not head straight for the market, but for the first time he ventured into Schull Street to study what was being sold in the shops his great-uncle occasionally visited. He stopped outside a baker, a butcher, a potter, a clothes shop, and finally a jeweller – Mr Lekski – the only establishment that had a name printed in gold above the door. He stared at a brooch displayed in the centre of the window. It was even more beautiful than the one his mother wore once a year at Rosh Hashanah, and which she had once told him was a family heirloom. When he returned home that night, he stood by the fire while his mother prepared their one-course meal.

He informed her that shops were nothing more than stationary stalls with windows in front of them, and that when he had pushed his nose up against the pane of glass, he had seen that nearly all of the customers inside traded with pieces of paper, and made no attempt to bargain with the shopkeeper.

The next day, Lubji returned to Schull Street. He took the piece of paper out of his pocket and studied it for some time. He still had no idea what anyone would give him in exchange for it. After an hour of staring through windows, he marched confidently into the baker's shop and handed the note to the man behind the counter. The baker took it and shrugged his shoulders. Lubji pointed hopefully to a loaf of bread on the shelf behind him, which the shopkeeper passed over. Satisfied with the transaction, the boy turned to leave, but the shop-keeper shouted after him, 'Don't forget your change.'

Lubji turned back, unsure what he meant. He then watched as the shopkeeper deposited the note in a tin box and extracted some coins, which he handed across the counter.

Once he was back on the street, the six-year-old studied the coins with great interest. They had numbers stamped on one side, and the head of a man he didn't recognise on the other.

Encouraged by this transaction, he moved on to the potter's shop, where he purchased a bowl which he hoped his mother would find some use for in exchange for half his coins.

Lubji's next stop was at Mr Lekski's, the jeweller, where his eyes settled on the beautiful brooch displayed in the centre of the window. He pushed open the door and marched up to the counter, coming face to face with an old man who wore a suit and tie.

'And how can I help you, little one?' Mr Lekski asked, leaning over to look down at him.

'I want to buy that brooch for my mother,' he said, pointing back towards the window and hoping that he sounded confident. He opened his clenched fist to reveal the three small coins left over from the morning's bargaining.

The old man didn't laugh, but gently explained to Lubji that he would need many more coins than that before he could hope to purchase the brooch. Lubji's cheeks reddened as he curled up his fingers and quickly turned to leave.

'But why don't you come back tomorrow,' suggested the old man. 'Perhaps I'll be able to find something for you.' Lubji's face was so red that he ran onto the street without looking back.

Lubji couldn't sleep that night. He kept repeating over and over to himself the words Mr Lekski had said. The following morning he was standing outside the shop long before the old man had arrived to open the front door. The first lesson Lubji learned from Mr Lekski was that people who can afford to buy jewellery don't rise early in the morning.

Mr Lekski, an elder of the town, had been so impressed by the sheer *chutzpah* of the six-year-old child in daring to enter his shop with nothing more than a few worthless coins, that over the next few weeks he indulged the son of the cattle trader by answering his constant stream of questions. It wasn't long before Lubji began to drop into the shop for a few minutes every afternoon. But he would always wait outside if the old man was serving someone. Only after the customer had left would he march in, stand by the counter and rattle off the questions he'd thought up the previous night.

Mr Lekski noted with approval that Lubji never asked the same question twice, and that whenever a customer entered the shop he would quickly retreat into the corner and hide behind the old man's daily newspaper. Although he turned the pages, the jeweller couldn't be sure if he was reading the words or just looking at the pictures.

One evening, after Mr Lekski had locked up for the night, he took Lubji round to the back of the shop to show him his motor vehicle. Lubji's eyes opened wide when he was told that this magnificent object could move on its own without being pulled by a horse. 'But it has no legs,' he shouted in disbelief. He opened the car door and climbed in beside Mr Lekski. When the old man pressed a button to start the engine, Lubji felt both sick and frightened at the same time. But despite the fact that he could only just see over the dashboard, within moments he wanted to change places with Mr Lekski and sit in the driver's seat.

Mr Lekski drove Lubji through the town, and dropped him outside the front door of the cottage. The child immediately ran into the kitchen and shouted to his mother, 'One day I will own a motor vehicle.' Zelta smiled at the thought, and didn't mention that even the rabbi only had a bicycle. She went on feeding her youngest child – swearing once again it would be the last. This new addition had meant that the fast-growing Lubji could no longer squeeze onto the mattress with his sisters and brothers. Lately he had had to be satisfied with copies of the rabbi's old newspapers laid out in the fireplace.

Almost as soon as it was dusk, the children would fight for a place on the mattress: the Hochs couldn't afford to waste their small supply of candles on lengthening the day. Night after night, Lubji would lie in the fireplace thinking about Mr Lekski's motor car, trying to work out how he could prove his mother wrong. Then he remembered the brooch she only wore at Rosh Hashanah. He began counting on his fingers, and calculated that he would have to wait another six weeks before he could carry out the plan already forming in his mind.

◄o►

Lubji lay awake for most of the night before Rosh Hashanah. Once his mother had dressed the following morning, his eyes rarely left her – or, to be more accurate, the brooch she wore. After the service she was surprised that when they left the synagogue he clung to her hand on the way back home, something she couldn't recall him doing since his third birthday. Once they were inside their little cottage, Lubji sat cross-legged in the corner of the fireplace and watched his mother unclip the tiny piece of jewellery from her dress. For a moment Zelta stared at the heirloom, before kneeling and removing the loose plank from the floor beside the mattress, and putting the brooch carefully in the old cardboard box before replacing the plank.

Lubji remained so still as he watched her that his mother became worried, and asked him if he wasn't feeling well.

'I'm all right, Mother,' he said. 'But as it's Rosh Hashanah, I was thinking about what I ought to be doing in the new year.' His mother smiled, still nurturing the hope that she had produced one child who might become a rabbi. Lubji didn't speak again as he considered the problem of the box. He felt no guilt about committing what his mother would have described as a sin, because he had already convinced himself that long before the year was up he would return everything, and no one would be any the wiser.

That night, after the rest of the family had climbed onto the mattress, Lubji huddled up in the corner of the fireplace and pretended to be asleep until he was sure that everyone else was. He knew that for the six restless, cramped bodies, two heads at the top, another two at the bottom, with his mother and father at the ends, sleep was a luxury that rarely lasted more than a few minutes.

Once Lubji was confident that no one else was awake, he began to crawl cautiously round the edge of the room, until he reached the far side of the mattress. His father's snoring was so thunderous that Lubji feared that at any moment one of his brothers or sisters must surely wake and discover him.

Lubji held his breath as he ran his fingers across the floorboards, trying to discover which one would prise open.

The seconds turned into minutes, but suddenly one of the planks shifted slightly. By pressing on one end with the palm of his right hand Lubji was able to ease it up slowly. He lowered his left hand into the hole, and felt the edge of something. He gripped it with his fingers, and slowly pulled out the cardboard box, then lowered the plank back into place.

Lubji remained absolutely still until he was certain that no one had witnessed his actions. One of his younger brothers turned over, and his sisters groaned and followed suit. Lubji took advantage of the fuddled commotion and scurried back around the edge of the room, only stopping when he reached the front door.

He pushed himself up off his knees, and began to search for

the doorknob. His sweaty palm gripped the handle and turned it slowly. The old spindle creaked noisily in a way he had never noticed before. He stepped outside into the path and placed the cardboard box on the ground, held his breath and slowly closed the door behind him.

Lubji ran away from the house clutching the little box to his chest. He didn't look back; but had he done so, he would have seen his great-uncle staring at him from his larger house behind the cottage. 'Just as I feared,' the rabbi muttered to himself. 'He takes after his father's side of the family.'

Once Lubji was out of sight, he stared down into the box for the first time, but even with the help of the moonlight he was unable to make out its contents properly. He walked on, still fearful that someone might spot him. When he reached the centre of the town, he sat on the steps of a waterless fountain, trembling and excited. But it was several minutes before he could clearly make out all the treasures that were secreted in the box.

There were two brass buckles, several unmatching buttons, including a large shiny one, and an old coin which bore the head of the Czar. And there, in the corner of the box, rested the most desirable prize of all: a small circular silver brooch surrounded by little stones which sparkled in the early morning sunlight.

When the clock on the town hall struck six, Lubji tucked the box under his arm and headed in the direction of the market. Once he was back among the traders, he sat down between two of the stalls and removed everything from the box. He then turned it upside down and set out all the objects on the flat, grey surface, with the brooch taking pride of place in the centre. No sooner had he done this than a man carrying a sack of potatoes over his shoulder stopped and stared down at his wares.

'What do you want for that?' the man asked in Czech, pointing at the large shiny button.

The boy remembered that Mr Lekski never replied to a question with an answer, but always with another question.

'What do you have to offer?' he enquired in the man's native tongue.

The farmer lowered his sack onto the ground. 'Six spuds,' he said.

Lubji shook his head. 'I would need at least twelve potatoes for something as valuable as that,' he said, holding the button up in the sunlight so that his potential customer could take a closer look.

The farmer scowled.

'Nine,' he said finally.

'No,' replied Lubji firmly. 'Always remember that my first offer is my best offer.' He hoped he sounded like Mr Lekski dealing with an awkward customer.

The farmer shook his head, picked up the sack of potatoes, threw it over his shoulder and headed off towards the centre of the town. Lubji wondered if he had made a bad mistake by not accepting the nine potatoes. He cursed, and rearranged the objects on the box to better advantage, leaving the brooch in the centre.

'And how much are you expecting to get for that?' asked another customer, pointing down at the brooch.

'What do you have to offer in exchange?' asked Lubji, switching to Hungarian.

'A sack of my best grain,' said the farmer, proudly removing a bag from a laden donkey and dumping it in front of Lubji.

'And why do you want the brooch?' asked Lubji, remembering another of Mr Lekski's techniques.

'It's my wife's birthday tomorrow,' he explained, 'and I forgot to give her a present last year.'

'I'll trade this beautiful heirloom, which has been in my family for several generations,' Lubji said, holding up the brooch for him to study, 'in exchange for that ring on your finger . . .'

'But my ring is gold,' said the farmer, laughing, 'and your brooch is only silver.'

'. . . *and* a bag of your grain,' said Lubji, as if he hadn't been given the chance to complete his sentence.

'You must be mad,' replied the farmer.

'This brooch was once worn by a great aristocrat before she fell on hard times, so I'm bound to ask: is it not worthy of the woman who has borne your children?' Lubji had no idea if the man had any children, but charged on: 'Or is she to be forgotten for another year?'

The Hungarian fell silent as he considered the child's words. Lubji replaced the brooch in the centre of the box, his eyes resting fixedly on it, never once looking at the ring.

'The ring I agree to,' said the farmer finally, 'but not the bag of grain as well.'

Lubji frowned as he pretended to consider the offer. He picked up the brooch and studied it again in the sunlight. 'All right,' he said with a sigh. 'But only because it's your wife's birthday.' Mr Lekski had taught him always to allow the customer to feel he had the better of the bargain. The farmer quickly removed the heavy gold ring from his finger and grabbed the brooch.

No sooner had the bargain been completed than Lubji's first customer returned, carrying an old spade. He dropped his half-empty sack of potatoes onto the ground in front of the boy.

'I've changed my mind,' said the Czech. 'I will give you twelve spuds for the button.'

But Lubji shook his head. 'I now want fifteen,' he said without looking up.

'But this morning you only wanted twelve!'

'Yes, but since then you have traded half of your potatoes – and I suspect the better half – for that spade,' Lubji said.

The farmer hesitated.

'Come back tomorrow,' said Lubji. 'By then I'll want twenty.'

The scowl returned to the Czech's face, but this time he didn't pick up his bag and march off. 'I accept,' he said angrily and began to remove some potatoes from the top of the sack.

Lubji shook his head again.

'What do you want now?' he shouted at the boy. 'I thought we had a bargain.'

'You have seen my button,' said Lubji, 'but I haven't seen your potatoes. It's only right that I should make the choice, not you.'

The Czech shrugged his shoulders, opened the sack and allowed the child to dig deep and to select fifteen potatoes.

Lubji did not close another deal that day, and once the traders began to dismantle their stalls, he gathered up his possessions, old and new, put them in the cardboard box, and for the first time began to worry about his mother finding out what he had been up to.

He walked slowly through the market towards the far side of the town, stopping where the road forked into two narrow paths. One led to the fields where his father would be tending the cattle, the other into the forest. Lubji checked the road that led back into the town to be certain no one had followed him, then disappeared into the undergrowth. After a short time he stopped by a tree that he knew he could not fail to recognise whenever he returned. He dug a hole near its base with his bare hands and buried the box, and twelve of the potatoes.

When he was satisfied there was no sign that anything had been hidden, he walked slowly back to the road, counting the paces as he went. Two hundred and seven. He glanced briefly back into the forest and then ran through the town, not stopping until he reached the front door of the little cottage. He waited for a few moments to catch his breath and then marched in.

His mother was already ladling her watered-down turnip soup into bowls, and there might have been many more questions about why he was so late if he hadn't quickly produced the three potatoes. Screeches of delight erupted from his brothers and sisters when they saw what he had to offer.

His mother dropped the ladle in the pot and looked directly at him. 'Did you steal them, Lubji?' she asked, placing her hands on her hips.

'No, Mother,' he replied, 'I did not.' Zelta looked relieved and took the potatoes from him. One by one she washed them in a bucket that leaked whenever it was more than half full. Once she had removed all the earth from them, she began to peel them efficiently with her thumbnails. She then cut each of them into segments, allowing her husband an extra portion. Sergei didn't even think of asking his son where he had got the best food they had seen in days.

That night, long before it was dark, Lubji fell asleep exhausted from his first day's work as a trader.

The following morning he left the house even before his father woke. He ran all the way to the forest, counted two hundred and seven paces, stopped when he came to the base of the tree and began digging. Once he had retrieved the cardboard box, he returned to the town to watch the traders setting up their stalls.

On this occasion he perched himself between two stalls at the far end of the market, but by the time the straggling customers had reached him, most of them had either completed their deals or had little of interest left to trade. That evening, Mr Lekski explained to him the three most important rules of trading: position, position and position.

The following morning Lubji set up his box near the entrance to the market. He quickly found that many more people stopped to consider what he had to offer, several of them enquiring in different languages about what he would be willing to exchange for the gold ring. Some even tried it on for size, but despite several offers, he was unable to close a deal that he considered to his advantage.

Lubji was trying to trade twelve potatoes and three buttons for a bucket that didn't leak when he became aware of a distinguished gentleman in a long black coat standing to one side, patiently waiting for him to complete the bargain.

The moment the boy looked up and saw who it was, he rose and said, 'Good morning, Mr Lekski,' and quickly waved away his other customer.

The old man took a pace forward, bent down and began picking up the objects on the top of the box. Lubji couldn't believe that the jeweller might be interested in his wares. Mr Lekski first considered the old coin with the head of the Czar. He studied it for some time. Lubji realised that he had no real interest in the coin: this was simply a ploy he had seen him carry out many times before asking the price of the object he really wanted. 'Never let them work out what you're after,' he must have told the boy a hundred times.

Lubji waited patiently for the old man to turn his attention to the centre of the box.

'And how much do you expect to get for this?' the jeweller asked finally, picking up the gold ring.

'What are you offering?' enquired the boy, playing him at his own game.

'One hundred korunas,' replied the old man.

Lubji wasn't quite sure how to react, as no one had ever offered him more than ten korunas for anything before. Then he remembered his mentor's maxim: 'Ask for triple and settle for double.' He stared up at his tutor. 'Three hundred korunas.'

The jeweller bent down and placed the ring back on the centre of the box. 'Two hundred is my best offer,' he replied firmly.

'Two hundred and fifty,' said Lubji hopefully.

Mr Lekski didn't speak for some time, continuing to stare at the ring. 'Two hundred and twenty-five,' he eventually said. 'But only if you throw in the old coin as well.'

Lubji nodded immediately, trying to mask his delight at the outcome of the transaction.

Mr Lekski extracted a purse from the inside pocket of his coat, handed over two hundred and twenty-five korunas and pocketed the ancient coin and the heavy gold ring. Lubji looked up at the old man and wondered if he had anything left to teach him.

Lubji was unable to strike another bargain that afternoon, so he packed up his cardboard box early and headed into the centre of the town, satisfied with his day's work. When he reached Schull Street he purchased a brand-new bucket for twelve korunas, a chicken for five and a loaf of fresh bread from the bakery for one.

The young trader began to whistle as he walked down the main street. When he passed Mr Lekski's shop he glanced at the window to check that the beautiful brooch he intended to purchase for his mother before Rosh Hashanah was still on sale.

Lubji dropped his new bucket on the ground in disbelief. His eyes opened wider and wider. The brooch had been replaced by an old coin, with a label stating that it bore the head of Czar Nicholas I and was dated 1829. He checked the price printed on the card below.

'One thousand five hundred korunas'.

4

MELBOURNE COURIER

25 OCTOBER 1929

Wall Street Crisis: Stock Market Collapses

There are many advantages and some disadvantages in being born a second-generation Australian. It was not long before Keith Townsend discovered some of the disadvantages.

Keith was born at 2.37 p.m. on 9 February 1928 in a large colonial mansion in Toorak. His mother's first telephone call from her bed was to the headmaster of St Andrew's Grammar School to register her first-born son for entry in 1941. His father's, from his office, was to the secretary of the Melbourne Cricket Club to put his name down for membership, as there was a fifteen-year waiting list.

Keith's father, Sir Graham Townsend, was originally from Dundee in Scotland, but at the turn of the century he and his parents had arrived in Australia on a cattle boat. Despite Sir Graham's position as the proprietor of the *Melbourne Courier* and the *Adelaide Gazette*, crowned by a knighthood the previous year, Melbourne society – some members of which had been around for nearly a century, and never tired of reminding you that they were not the descendants of convicts – either ignored him or simply referred to him in the third person.

Sir Graham didn't give a damn for their opinions; or if he did, he certainly never showed it. The people he liked to mix with worked on newspapers, and the ones he numbered among his friends also tended to spend at least one afternoon a week at the racecourse. Horses or greyhounds, it made no difference to Sir Graham.

But Keith had a mother whom Melbourne society could not dismiss quite so easily, a woman whose lineage stretched back to a senior naval officer in the First Fleet. Had she been born a generation later, this tale might well have been about her, and not her son.

As Keith was his only son – he was the second of three children, the other two being girls – Sir Graham assumed from his birth that the boy would follow him into the newspaper business, and to that end he set about educating him for the real world. Keith paid his first visit to his father's presses at the *Melbourne Courier* at the age of three, and immediately became intoxicated by the smell of ink, the pounding of type-writers and the clanging of machinery. From that moment on he would accompany his father to the office whenever he was given the chance.

Sir Graham never discouraged Keith, and even allowed him to tag along whenever he disappeared off to the racetrack on a Saturday afternoon. Lady Townsend did not approve of such goings on, and insisted that young Keith should always attend church the following morning. To her disappointment, their only son quickly revealed a preference for the bookie rather than the preacher.

Lady Townsend became so determined to reverse this early decline that she set about a counter-offensive. While Sir Graham was away in Perth on a long business trip, she appointed a nanny called Florrie whose simple job description was: take the children in hand. But Florrie, a widow in her fifties, proved no match for Keith, aged four, and within weeks she was promising not to let his mother know when he was taken to the racecourse. When Lady Townsend eventually discovered this subterfuge, she waited for her husband to make his annual trip to New Zealand, then placed an advertisement on the front page of the London *Times*. Three months later, Miss Steadman disembarked at Station Pier and reported to Toorak for duty. She turned out to be everything her references had promised.

The second daughter of a Scottish Presbyterian minister, educated at St Leonard's, Dumfries, she knew exactly what was expected of her. Florrie remained as devoted to the children as they were to her, but Miss Steadman seemed devoted to nothing other than her vocation and the carrying out of what she considered to be her bounden duty.

She insisted on being addressed at all times and by everyone, whatever their station, as Miss Steadman, and left no one in any doubt where they fitted into her social scale. The chauffeur intoned the words with a slight bow, Sir Graham with respect.

From the day she arrived, Miss Steadman organised the nursery in a fashion that would have impressed an officer in the Black Watch. Keith tried everything, from charm to sulking to bawling, to bring her into line, but he quickly discovered that she could not be moved. His father would have come to the boy's rescue had his wife not continued to sing Miss Steadman's praises – especially when it came to her valiant attempts to teach the young gentleman to speak the King's English.

At the age of five Keith began school, and at the end of the first week he complained to Miss Steadman that none of the other boys wanted to play with him. She did not consider it her place to tell the child that his father had made a great many enemies over the years.

The second week turned out to be even worse, because Keith was continually bullied by a boy called Desmond Motson, whose father had recently been involved in a mining scam which had made the front page of the *Melbourne Courier* for several days. It didn't help that Motson was two inches taller and half a stone heavier than Keith.

Keith often considered discussing the problem with his father. But as they only ever saw each other at weekends, he contented himself with joining the old man in his study on a Sunday morning to listen to his views on the contents of the previous week's *Courier* and *Gazette*, before comparing their efforts with those of his rivals.

'"Benevolent Dictator" – weak headline,' his father declared one Sunday morning as he glanced at the front page of the previous day's *Adelaide Gazette*. A few moments later he added, 'And an even weaker story. Neither of these people should ever be allowed near a front page again.'

'But there's only one name on top of the column,' said Keith, who had been listening intently to his father.

Sir Graham chuckled. 'True, my boy, but the headline would have been set up by a sub-editor, probably long after the journalist who wrote the piece had left for the day.'

Keith remained puzzled until his father explained that headlines could be changed only moments before the paper was put to bed. 'You must grab the readers' attention with the headline, otherwise they will never bother to read the story.'

Sir Graham read out loud an article about the new German leader. It was the first time Keith had heard the name of Adolf Hitler. 'Damned good photograph, though,' his father added, as he pointed to the picture of a little man with a toothbrush moustache, striking a pose with his right hand held high in the air. 'Never forget the hoary old cliché, my boy: "A picture's worth a thousand words".'

There was a sharp rap on the door that both of them knew could only have been administered by the knuckle of Miss Steadman. Sir Graham doubted if the timing of her knock each Sunday had varied by more than a few seconds since the day she had arrived.

'Enter,' he said in his sternest voice. He turned to wink at his son. Neither of the male Townsends ever let anyone else know that behind her back they called Miss Steadman 'Gruppenführer'.

Miss Steadman stepped into the study and delivered the same words she had repeated every Sunday for the past year: 'It's time for Master Keith to get ready for church, Sir Graham.'

'Good heavens, Miss Steadman, is it that late already?' he

would reply before shooing his son towards the door. Keith reluctantly left the safe haven of his father's study and followed Miss Steadman out of the room.

'Do you know what my father has just told me, Miss Steadman?' Keith said, in a broad Australian accent that he felt sure would annoy her.

'I have no idea, Master Keith,' she replied. 'But whatever it was, let us hope that it will not stop you concentrating properly on the Reverend Davidson's sermon.' Keith fell into a gloomy silence as they continued their route march up the stairs to his bedroom. He didn't utter a sound again until he had joined his father and mother in the back of the Rolls.

Keith knew that he would have to concentrate on the minister's every word, because Miss Steadman always tested him and his sisters on the most minute details of the text before they went to bed. Sir Graham was relieved that she never subjected him to the same examination.

Three nights in the treehouse – which Miss Steadman had constructed within weeks of her arrival – was the punishment for any child who obtained less than 80 per cent in the sermon test. 'Good for character-building,' she would continually remind them. What Keith never told her was that he occasionally gave the wrong answer deliberately, because three nights in the treehouse was a blessed escape from her tyranny.

—◦—

Two decisions were made when Keith was eleven which were to shape the rest of his life, and both of them caused him to burst into tears.

Following the declaration of war on Germany, Sir Graham was given a special assignment by the Australian government which, he explained to his son, would require him to spend a considerable amount of time abroad. That was the first.

The second came only days after Sir Graham had departed for London, when Keith was offered, and on his mother's insistence took up, a place at St Andrew's Grammar – a boys' boarding school on the outskirts of Melbourne.

Keith wasn't sure which of the decisions caused him more anguish.

Dressed in his first pair of long trousers, the tearful boy was driven to St Andrew's for the opening day of the new term. His mother handed him over to a matron who looked as if she had been chiselled out of the same piece of stone as Miss Steadman. The first boy Keith set eyes on as he entered the front door was Desmond Motson, and he was later horrified to discover that they were not only in the same house, but the same dormitory. He didn't sleep the first night.

The following morning, Keith stood at the back of the school hall and listened to an address from Mr Jessop, his new headmaster, who hailed from somewhere in England called Winchester. Within days the new boy discovered that Mr Jessop's idea of fun was a ten-mile cross-country run followed by a cold shower. That was for the good boys who, once they had changed and were back in their rooms, were expected to read Homer in the original. Keith's reading had lately concentrated almost exclusively on the tales of 'our gallant war heroes' and their exploits in the front line, as reported in the *Courier*. After a month at St Andrew's he would have been quite willing to change places with them.

During his first holiday Keith told his mother that if schooldays were the happiest days of your life, there was no hope for him in the future. Even she had been made aware that he had few friends and was becoming something of a loner.

The only day of the week Keith looked forward to was Wednesday, when he could escape from St Andrew's at midday and didn't have to be back until lights out. Once the school bell had rung he would cycle the seven miles to the nearest racetrack, where he would spend a happy afternoon moving between the railings and the winners' enclosure. At the age of twelve he thought of himself as something of a wizard of the turf, and only wished he had some more money of his own so he could start placing serious bets. After the last race he would cycle to the offices of the *Courier* and watch the first edition coming off the stone, returning to school just before lights out.

Like his father, Keith felt much more at ease with journalists and the racing fraternity than he ever did with the sons of Melbourne society. How he longed to tell the careers master that all he really wanted to do when he left school was be the racing correspondent for the *Sporting Globe*, another of his father's papers. But he never let anyone into his secret for fear that they might pass the information on to his mother, who had already hinted that she had other plans for his future.

When his father had taken him racing – never informing his mother or Miss Steadman where they were going – Keith would watch as the old man placed large sums of money on every race, occasionally passing over sixpence to his son so he could also try his luck. To begin with Keith's bets did no more than reflect his father's selections, but to his surprise he found that this usually resulted in his returning home with empty pockets.

After several such Wednesday-afternoon trips to the race-track, and having discovered that most of his sixpences ended up in the bookmaker's bulky leather bag, Keith decided to invest a penny a week in the *Sporting Globe*. As he turned the pages, he learned the form of every jockey, trainer and owner recognised by the Victoria Racing Club, but even with this new-found knowledge he seemed to lose just as regularly as before. By the third week of term he had often gambled away all his pocket money.

Keith's life changed the day he spotted a book advertised in the *Sporting Globe* called *How to Beat the Bookie*, by 'Lucky Joe'. He talked Florrie into lending him half a crown, and sent a postal order off to the address at the bottom of the advertisement. He greeted the postman every morning until the book appeared nineteen days later. From the moment Keith opened the first page, Lucky Joe replaced Homer as his compulsory reading during the evening prep period. After he had read the book twice, he was confident that he had found a system which would ensure that he always won. The following Wednesday he returned to the racecourse, puzzled as to why his father hadn't taken advantage of Lucky Joe's infallible method.

Keith cycled home that night having parted with a whole

term's pocket money in one afternoon. He refused to blame Lucky Joe for his failure, and assumed that he simply hadn't fully understood the system. After he had read the book a third time, he realised his mistake. As Lucky Joe explained on page seventy-one, you must have a certain amount of capital to start off with, otherwise you can never hope to beat the bookie. Page seventy-two suggested that the sum required was £10, but as Keith's father was still abroad, and his mother's favourite maxim was 'neither a borrower nor a lender be', he had no immediate way of proving that Lucky Joe was right.

He therefore came to the conclusion that he must somehow make a little extra cash, but as it was against school rules to earn any money during term time, he had to satisfy himself with reading Lucky Joe's book yet again. He would have received 'A' grades in the end-of-term exams if *How to Beat the Bookie* had been the set text.

Once term was over, Keith returned to Toorak and discussed his financial problems with Florrie. She told him of several ways that her brothers had earned pocket money during their school holidays. After listening to her advice, Keith returned to the racecourse the following Saturday, not this time to place a bet – he still didn't have any spare cash – but to collect manure from behind the stables, which he shovelled into a sugarbag that had been supplied by Florrie. He then cycled back to Melbourne with the heavy sack on his handlebars, before spreading the muck over his relatives' flowerbeds. After forty-seven such journeys back and forth to the racecourse in ten days, Keith had pocketed thirty shillings, satisfied the needs of all his relatives, and had moved on to their next-door neighbours.

By the end of the holiday he had amassed £3 7s. 4d. After his mother had handed over his next term's pocket money of a pound, he couldn't wait to return to the racetrack and make himself a fortune. The only problem was that Lucky Joe's foolproof system stated on page seventy-two, and repeated on page seventy-three: 'Don't attempt the system with less than £10.'

Keith would have read *How to Beat the Bookie* a ninth time

if his housemaster, Mr Clarke, had not caught him thumbing through it during prep. Not only was his dearest treasure confiscated, and probably destroyed, but he had to face the humiliation of a public beating meted out by the headmaster in front of the whole school. As he bent over the table he stared down at Desmond Motson in the front row, who was unable to keep the smirk off his face.

Mr Clarke told Keith before lights out that night that if he hadn't intervened on his behalf, Keith would undoubtedly have been expelled. He knew this would not have pleased his father – who was on his way back from a place called Yalta in the Crimea – or his mother, who had begun talking about him going to a university in England called Oxford. But Keith remained more concerned by how he could convert his £3 7s. 4d. into £10.

It was during the third week of term that Keith came up with an idea for doubling his money which he felt sure the authorities would never latch on to.

The school tuck shop opened every Friday between the hours of five and six, and then remained closed until the same time the following week. By Monday morning most of the boys had devoured all their Cherry Ripes, munched their way through several packets of chips and happily guzzled countless bottles of Marchants' lemonade. Although they were temporarily sated, Keith was in no doubt that they still craved more. He considered that, in these circumstances, Tuesday to Thursday presented an ideal opportunity to create a seller's market. All he needed to do was stockpile some of the most popular items from the tuck shop, then flog them off at a profit as soon as the other boys had consumed their weekly supplies.

When the tuck shop opened the following Friday, Keith was to be found at the front of the queue. The duty master was surprised that young Townsend spent £3 purchasing a large carton of Minties, an even larger one of thirty-six packets of chips, two dozen Cherry Ripes and two wooden boxes containing a dozen bottles of Marchants' lemonade. He reported the incident to Keith's housemaster. Mr Clarke's only observation was, 'I'm surprised that Lady Townsend indulges the boy with so much pocket money.'

Keith dragged his spoils off to the changing room, where he hid everything at the back of his games locker. He then waited patiently for the weekend to pass.

On the Saturday afternoon Keith cycled off to the race-course, although he was meant to be watching the first eleven play their annual match against Geelong Grammar. He had a frustrating time, unable to place any bets. Strange, he reflected, how you could always pick winner after winner when you had no money.

After chapel on Sunday, Keith checked the senior and junior common rooms, and was delighted to discover that food and drink supplies were already running low. During the Monday morning break he watched his classmates standing around in the corridor, swapping their last sweets, unwrapping their final chocolate bars and swigging their remaining gulps of lemonade.

On Tuesday morning he saw the rows of empty bottles being lined up by the dustbins in the corner of the quad. By the afternoon he was ready to put his theory into practice.

During the games period he locked himself into the school's small printing room, for which his father had supplied the equipment the previous year. Although the press was fairly ancient and could only be worked by hand, it was quite adequate for Keith's needs.

An hour later he emerged clutching thirty copies of his first tabloid, which announced that an alternative tuck shop would be open every Wednesday between the hours of five and six, outside locker number nineteen in the senior changing room. The other side of the page showed the range of goods on offer and their 'revised' prices.

Keith distributed a copy of the news sheet to every member of his class at the beginning of the final lesson that afternoon, completing the task only moments before the geography master entered the room. He was already planning a bumper edition for the following week if the exercise turned out to be a success.

When Keith appeared in the changing room a few minutes

before five the following afternoon, he found a queue had already formed outside his locker. He quickly unbolted the tin door and tugged the boxes out onto the floor. Long before the hour was up, he had sold out of his entire stock. A mark-up of at least 25 per cent on most items showed him a clear profit of just over a pound.

Only Desmond Motson, who had stood in a corner watching the money changing hands, grumbled about Townsend's extortionate prices. The young entrepreneur simply told him, 'You have a choice. You can join the queue or wait till Friday.' Motson had stalked out of the changing room, muttering veiled threats under his breath.

On Friday afternoon Keith was back at the front of the tuck shop queue and, having made a note of which items had sold out first, purchased his new stock accordingly.

When Mr Clarke was informed that Townsend had spent £4 10s. on tuck that Friday, he admitted to being puzzled, and decided to have a word with the headmaster.

That Saturday afternoon Keith didn't go to the racecourse, using the time to print up a hundred pages of the second edition of his sales sheet, which he distributed the following Monday – not only to his own classmates, but also to those in the two forms below him.

On Tuesday morning, during a lesson on British History 1815–1867, he calculated on the back of a copy of the 1832 Reform Bill that at this rate it would take him only another three weeks to raise the £10 he needed to test Lucky Joe's infallible system.

It was in a Latin lesson on Wednesday afternoon that Keith's own infallible system began to falter. The headmaster entered the classroom unannounced, and asked Townsend to join him in the corridor immediately. 'And bring your locker key with you,' he added ominously. As they marched silently down the long grey corridor Mr Jessop presented him with a single sheet of paper. Keith studied the list he could have recited far more fluently than any of the tables in *Kennedy's Latin Primer*. 'Minties 8d, Chips 4d, Cherry Ripes 4d, Marchants' Lemonade one shilling. Be outside Locker 19 in the senior changing room on Thursday at five o'clock sharp. Our slogan is "First come, first served".'

Keith managed to keep a straight face as he was frogmarched down the corridor.

When they entered the changing room, Keith found his housemaster and the sports master already stationed by his locker.

'Unlock the door, Townsend,' was all the headmaster said.

Keith placed the little key in the lock and turned it slowly. He pulled open the door and the four of them peered inside. Mr Jessop was surprised to discover that there was nothing to be seen other than a cricket bat, a pair of old pads, and a crumpled white shirt that looked as if it hadn't been worn for several weeks.

The headmaster looked angry, his housemaster puzzled, and the sports master embarrassed.

'Could it be that you've got the wrong boy?' asked Keith, with an air of injured innocence.

'Lock the door and return to your class immediately, Townsend,' said the headmaster. Keith obeyed with an insolent nod of the head and strolled slowly back down the corridor.

Once he was seated at his desk, Keith realised that he had to decide on which course of action to take. Should he rescue his wares and save his investment, or drop a hint as to where the tuck might be found and settle an old score once and for all?

Desmond Motson turned round to stare at him. He looked surprised and disappointed to find Townsend back in his place.

Keith gave him a huge smile, and immediately knew which of the two options he should take.

5

THE TIMES

9 MARCH 1936

German Troops in the Rhineland

It was not until after the Germans had remilitarised the Rhineland that Lubji first heard the name of Adolf Hitler.

His mother winced when she read about the Führer's exploits in the rabbi's weekly paper. As she finished each page she handed it on to her eldest son. She stopped only when it became too dark for her to see the words. Lubji was able to go on reading for a few more minutes.

'Will we all have to wear a yellow star if Hitler crosses our border?' he asked.

Zelta pretended to have fallen asleep.

For some time his mother had been unable to hide from the rest of her family the fact that Lubji had become her favourite – even though she suspected that he was responsible for the disappearance of her precious brooch – and she had watched with pride as he grew into a tall, handsome youth. But she remained adamant that despite his success as a trader, from which she acknowledged the whole family had benefited, he was still destined to be a rabbi. She might have wasted her life, but she was determined that Lubji wouldn't waste his.

For the past six years Lubji had spent each morning being tutored by her uncle in the house on the hill. He was released at midday so that he could return to the market, where he had recently purchased his own stall. A few weeks after his bar mitzvah the old rabbi had handed Lubji's mother the letter informing him that Lubji had been awarded a scholarship to the academy in Ostrava. It was the happiest day of Zelta's life. She knew her son was clever, perhaps exceptional, but she also realised that such an offer could only have been secured by her uncle's reputation.

When Lubji was first told the news of his scholarship, he tried not to show his dismay. Although he was only allowed to go to the market in the afternoon, he was already making enough money to have provided every member of the family with a pair of shoes and two meals a day. He wanted to explain to his mother that there was no point in being a rabbi if all you really wanted to do was to build a shop on the vacant plot next to Mr Lekski's.

Mr Leksi shut the shop and took the day off to drive the young scholar to the academy, and on the long journey to Ostrava he told him that he hoped he would take over his shop once he had completed his studies. Lubji wanted to return home immediately, and it was only after considerable persuasion that he picked up his little leather bag – the last barter he had made the previous day – and passed under the massive stone archway that led to the academy. If Mr Lekski hadn't added that he wouldn't consider taking Lubji on unless he completed his five years at the academy, he would have jumped back into the car.

It wasn't long before Lubji discovered that there were no other children at the academy who had come from such a humble background as himself. Several of his classmates made it clear, directly or indirectly, that he was not the sort of person they had expected to mix with. As the weeks passed, he also discovered that the skills he had picked up as a market trader were of little use in such an establishment – though even the most prejudiced could not deny that he had a natural flair for languages. And certainly long hours, little sleep, and rigorous discipline held no fears for the boy from Douski.

At the end of his first year at Ostrava, Lubji finished in the upper half of his class in most subjects. He was top in mathematics and third in Hungarian, which was now his second language. But even the principal of the academy could not fail to notice that the gifted child had few friends, and had become something of a loner. He was relieved at least that no one bullied the young ruffian – the only boy who ever tried had ended up in the sanatorium.

When Lubji returned to Douski, he was surprised to find how small the town was, just how impoverished his family were, and how much they had grown to depend on him.

Every morning after his father had left for the fields, Lubji would walk up the hill to the rabbi's house and continue his studies. The old scholar marvelled at the boy's command of languages, and admitted that he was no longer able to keep up with him in mathematics. In the afternoons Lubji returned to the market, and on a good day he could bring home enough supplies to feed the entire family.

He tried to teach his brothers how to trade, so that they could run the stall in the mornings and while he was away. He quickly concluded it was a hopeless task, and wished his mother would allow him to stay at home and build up a business they could all benefit from. But Zelta showed no interest in what he got up to at the market, and only questioned him about his studies. She read his report cards again and again, and by the end of the holiday must have known them off by heart. It made Lubji even more determined that when he presented her with his next year's reports, they would please her even more.

When his six-week break came to an end, Lubji reluctantly packed his little leather bag and was driven back to Ostrava by Mr Lekski. 'The offer to join me is still open,' he reminded the young man, 'but not until you've completed your studies.'

During Lubji's second year at the academy the name of Adolf Hitler came up in conversation almost as often as that of Moses. Jews were fleeing across the border every day reporting the horrors taking place in Germany, and Lubji could only wonder what the Führer might have planned next. He read every newspaper he could lay his hands on, in whatever language and however out of date.

'Hitler Looks East' read a headline on page one of *The Ostrava*. When Lubji turned to page seven to read the rest of the story he found it was missing, but that didn't stop him wondering how long it would be before the Führer's tanks rolled into Czechoslovakia. He was certain of one thing: Hitler's master race wouldn't include the likes of him.

Later that morning he expressed these fears to his history master, but he seemed incapable of stretching his mind beyond Hannibal, and the question of whether he would make it across the Alps. Lubji closed his old history book and, without considering the consequences, marched out of the classroom and down the corridor towards the principal's private quarters. He stopped in front of a door he had never entered, hesitated for a moment and then knocked boldly.

'Come,' said a voice.

Lubji opened the door slowly and entered the principal's study. The godly man was garbed in full academic robes of red and grey, and a black skullcap rested on top of his long black ringlets. He looked up from his desk. 'I presume this is something of vital importance, Hoch?'

'Yes, sir,' said Lubji confidently. Then he lost his nerve.

'Well?' prompted the principal, after some time had elapsed.

'We must be prepared to leave at a moment's notice,' Lubji finally blurted out. 'We have to assume that it will not be long before Hitler . . .'

The old man smiled up at the fifteen-year-old boy and waved a dismissive hand. 'Hitler has told us a hundred times that he has no interest in occupying any other territory,' he said, as if he were correcting a minor error Lubji had made in a history exam.

'I'm sorry to have bothered you, sir,' Lubji said, realising that however well he presented his case, he wasn't going to persuade such an unworldly man.

But as the weeks passed, first his tutor, then his housemaster, and finally the principal, had to admit that history was being written before their eyes.

It was on a warm September evening that the principal,

carrying out his rounds, began to alert the pupils that they should gather together their possessions, as they would be leaving at dawn the following day. He was not surprised to find Lubji's room already empty.

A few minutes after midnight, a division of German tanks crossed the border and advanced unchallenged towards Ostrava. The soldiers ransacked the academy even before the breakfast bell had rung, and dragged all the students out into waiting lorries. There was only one pupil who wasn't present to answer the final roll-call. Lubji Hoch had left the previous night. After cramming all his possessions into the little leather case, he had joined the stream of refugees heading towards the Hungarian border. He prayed that his mother had read not only the papers, but Hitler's mind, and would somehow have escaped with the rest of the family. He had recently heard rumours about the Germans rounding up Jews and placing them in internment camps. He tried not to think of what might happen to his family if they were captured.

When Lubji slipped out of the academy gates that night he didn't stop to watch the local people rushing from house to house searching for their relatives, while others loaded their possessions onto horse-drawn carts that would surely be overtaken by the slowest armed vehicle. This was not a night to spend fussing about personal possessions: you can't shoot a possession, Lubji wanted to tell them. But no one stood still long enough to listen to the tall, powerfully built young man with long black ringlets, dressed in his academy uniform. By the time the German tanks had surrounded the academy, he had already covered several miles on the road that led south to the border.

Lubji didn't even consider sleeping. He could already hear the roar of guns as the enemy advanced into the city from the west. On and on he strode, past those who were slowed by the burden of pushing and pulling their lives' possessions. He overtook laden donkeys, carts that needed their wheels repaired and families with young children and ageing relatives, held up by the pace of the slowest. He watched as mothers cut the locks from their sons' hair and began to abandon anything that might identify them as Jewish. He would have stopped to remonstrate with them but didn't want to lose any precious time. He swore that nothing would ever make him abandon his religion.

The discipline that had been instilled in him at the academy over the previous two years allowed Lubji to carry on without food or rest until daybreak. When he eventually slept, it was on the back of a cart, and then later in the front seat of a lorry. He was determined that nothing would stop his progress towards a friendly country.

Although freedom was a mere 180 kilometres away, Lubji saw the sun rise and set three times before he heard the cries from those ahead of him who had reached the sovereign state of Hungary. He came to a halt at the end of a straggling queue of would-be immigrants. Three hours later he had travelled only a few hundred yards, and the queue of people ahead of him began to settle down for the night. Anxious eyes looked back to see smoke rising high into the sky, and the sound of guns could be heard as the Germans continued their relentless advance.

Lubji waited until it was pitch dark, and then silently made his way past the sleeping families, until he could clearly see the lights of the border post ahead of him. He lay down in a ditch as inconspicuously as possible, his head resting on his little leather case. As the customs officer raised the barrier the following morning, Lubji was waiting at the front of the queue. When those behind him woke and saw the young man in his academic garb chanting a psalm under his breath, none of them considered asking him how he had got there.

The customs officer didn't waste a lot of time searching Lubji's little case. Once he had crossed the border, he never strayed off the road to Budapest, the only Hungarian city he had heard of. Another two days and nights of sharing food with generous families, relieved to have escaped from the wrath of the Germans, brought him to the outskirts of the capital on 23 September 1939.

Lubji couldn't believe the sights that greeted him. Surely this must be the largest city on earth? He spent his first few hours just walking through the streets, becoming more and more intoxicated with each pace he took. He finally collapsed on the steps of a massive synagogue, and when he woke the following morning, the first thing he did was to ask for directions to the marketplace.

Lubji stood in awe as he stared at row upon row of covered stalls, stretching as far as the eye could see. Some only sold vegetables, others just fruit, while a few dealt in furniture, and one simply in pictures, some of which even had frames.

But despite the fact that he spoke their language fluently, when he offered his services to the traders their only question was, 'Do you have anything to sell?' For the second time in his life, Lubji faced the problem of having nothing to barter with. He stood and watched as refugees traded priceless family heirlooms, sometimes for no more than a loaf of bread or a sack of potatoes. It quickly became clear to him that war allowed some people to amass a great fortune.

Day after day Lubji searched for work. At night he would collapse onto the pavement, hungry and exhausted, but still determined. After every trader in the market had turned him down, he was reduced to begging on street corners.

Late one afternoon, on the verge of despair, he passed an old woman in a newspaper kiosk on the corner of a quiet street, and noticed that she wore the Star of David on a thin gold chain around her neck. He gave her a smile, hoping she might take pity on him, but she ignored the filthy young immigrant and carried on with her work.

Lubji was just about to move on when a young man, only a few years older than him, strolled up to the kiosk, selected a packet of cigarettes and a box of matches, and then walked off without paying the old lady. She jumped out of the kiosk, waving her arms and shouting, 'Thief! Thief!' But the young man simply shrugged his shoulders and lit one of the cigarettes. Lubji ran down the road after him and placed a hand on the man's shoulder. When he turned round, Lubji said, 'You haven't paid for the cigarettes.'

'Get lost, you bloody Slovak,' the man said, pushing him

away before continuing down the street. Lubji ran after him again and this time grabbed his arm. The man turned a second time, and without warning threw a punch at his pursuer. Lubji ducked, and the clenched fist flew over his shoulder. As the man rocked forward, Lubji landed an uppercut in his solar plexus with such force that the man staggered backwards and collapsed in a heap on the ground, dropping the cigarettes and matches. Lubji had discovered something else he must have inherited from his father.

Lubji had been so surprised by his own strength that he hesitated for a moment before bending down to pick up the cigarettes and matches. He left the man clutching his stomach and ran back to the kiosk.

'Thank you,' the old woman said when he handed back her goods.

'My name is Lubji Hoch,' he told her, and bowed low.

'And mine is Mrs Cerani,' she said.

When the old lady went home that night, Lubji slept on the pavement behind the kiosk. The following morning she was surprised to find him still there, sitting on a stack of unopened newspapers.

The moment he saw her coming down the street, he began to untie the bundles. He watched as she sorted out the papers and placed them in racks to attract the early-morning workers. During the day Mrs Cerani started to tell Lubji about the different papers, and was amazed to find how many languages he could read. It wasn't long before she discovered that he could also converse with any refugee who came in search of news from his own country.

The next day Lubji had all the papers set out in their racks long before Mrs Cerani arrived. He had even sold a couple of them to early customers. By the end of the week she could often be found snoozing happily in the corner of her kiosk, needing only to offer the occasional piece of advice if Lubji was unable to answer a customer's query.

After Mrs Cerani locked up the kiosk on the Friday evening, she beckoned Lubji to follow her. They walked in silence for some time, before stopping at a little house about a mile from the kiosk. The old lady invited him to come inside, and ushered him through to the front room to meet her husband. Mr Cerani was shocked when he first saw the filthy young giant, but softened a little when he learned that Lubji was a Jewish refugee from Ostrava. He invited him to join them for supper. It was the first time Lubji had sat at a table since he had left the academy.

Over the meal Lubji learned that Mr Cerani ran a paper shop that supplied the kiosk where his wife worked. He began to ask his host a series of questions about returned copies, loss leaders, margins and alternative stock. It was not long before the newsagent realised why the profits at the kiosk had shot up that week. While Lubji did the washing up, Mr and Mrs Cerani conferred in the corner of the kitchen. When they had finished speaking, Mrs Cerani beckoned to Lubji, who assumed the time had come for him to leave. But instead of showing him to the door, she began to climb the stairs. She turned and beckoned again, and he followed in her wake. At the top of the stairs she opened a door that led into a tiny room. There was no carpet on the floor, and the only furniture was a single bed, a battered chest of drawers and a small table. The old lady stared at the empty bed with a sad look on her face, gestured towards it and quickly left without another word.

◆

So many immigrants from so many lands came to converse with the young man – who seemed to have read every paper – about what was taking place in their own countries, that by the end of the first month Lubji had almost doubled the takings of the little kiosk. On the last day of the month Mr Cerani presented Lubji with his first wage packet. Over supper that night he told the young man that on Monday he was to join him at the shop, in order to learn more about the trade. Mrs Cerani looked disappointed, despite her husband's assurance that it would only be for a week.

At the shop, the boy quickly learnt the names of the regular customers, their choice of daily paper and their favourite brand of cigarettes. During the second week he became aware of a Mr Farkas, who ran the rival shop on the other side of the road, but as neither Mr nor Mrs Cerani ever mentioned him by name, he didn't raise the subject. On the Sunday evening, Mr Cerani told his wife that Lubji would be joining him at the shop permanently. She didn't seem surprised.

Every morning Lubji would rise at four and leave the house to go and open the shop. It was not long before he was delivering the papers to the kiosk and serving the first customers before Mr or Mrs Cerani had finished their breakfast. As the weeks passed, Mr Cerani began coming into the shop later and later each day, and after he had counted up the cash in the evening, he would often slip a coin or two into Lubji's hand.

Lubji stacked the coins on the table by the side of his bed, converting them into a little green note every time he had acquired ten. At night he would lie awake, dreaming of taking over the paper shop and kiosk when Mr and Mrs Cerani eventually retired. Lately they had begun treating him as if he were their own son, giving him small presents, and Mrs Cerani even hugged him before he went to bed. It made him think of his mother.

Lubji began to believe his ambition might be realised when Mr Cerani took a day off from the shop, and later a weekend, to find on his return that the takings had risen slightly.

—◆—

One Saturday morning on his way back from synagogue, Lubji had the feeling he was being followed. He stopped and turned to see Mr Farkas, the rival newsagent from across the road, hovering only a few paces behind him.

'Good morning, Mr Farkas,' said Lubji, raising his wide-rimmed black hat.

'Good morning, Mr Hoch,' he replied. Until that moment Lubji had never thought of himself as Mr Hoch. After all, he had only recently celebrated his seventeenth birthday.

'Do you wish to speak to me?' asked Lubji.

'Yes, Mr Hoch, I do,' he said, and walked up to his side. He began to shift uneasily from foot to foot. Lubji recalled Mr Lekski's advice: 'Whenever a customer looks nervous, say nothing.'

'I was thinking of offering you a job in one of my shops,' said Mr Farkas, looking up at him.

For the first time Lubji realised Mr Farkas had more than one shop. 'In what capacity?' he asked.

'Assistant manager.'

'And my salary?' When Lubji heard the amount he made no comment, although a hundred pengös a week was almost double what Mr Cerani was paying him.

'And where would I live?'

'There is a room above the premises,' said Mr Farkas, 'which I suspect is far larger than the little attic you presently occupy at the top of the Ceranis' house.'

Lubji looked down at him. 'I'll consider your offer, Mr Farkas,' he said, and once again raised his hat. By the time he had arrived back at the house, he had decided to report the entire conversation to Mr Cerani before someone else did.

The old man touched his thick moustache and sighed when Lubji came to the end of his tale. But he did not respond.

'I made it clear, of course, that I was not interested in working for him,' said Lubji, waiting to see how his boss would react. Mr Cerani still said nothing, and did not refer to the subject again until they had all sat down for supper the following evening. Lubji smiled when he learned that he would be getting a rise at the end of the week. But on Friday he was disappointed when he opened his little brown envelope and discovered how small the increase turned out to be.

When Mr Farkas approached him again the following Saturday and asked if he had made up his mind yet, Lubji simply replied that he was satisfied with the remuneration he was presently receiving. He bowed low before walking away, hoping he had left the impression that he was still open to a counter-offer.

As he went about his work over the next few weeks, Lubji occasionally glanced up at the large room over the paper shop on the other side of the road. At night as he lay in bed, he tried to envisage what it might be like inside.

◄○►

After he had been working for the Ceranis for six months, Lubji had managed to save almost all his wages. His only real outlay had been on a second-hand double-breasted suit, two shirts and a spotted tie which had recently replaced his academic garb. But despite his new-found security, he was becoming more and more fearful about where Hitler would attack next. After the Führer had invaded Poland, he had continued to make speeches assuring the Hungarian people that he considered them his allies. But judging by his past record, 'ally' was not a word he had looked up in the Polish dictionary.

Lubji tried not to think about having to move on again, but as each day passed he was made painfully aware of people pointing out that he was Jewish, and he couldn't help noticing that some of the local inhabitants seemed to be preparing to welcome the Nazis.

One morning when he was walking to work, a passer-by hissed at Lubji. He was taken by surprise, but within days this became a regular occurrence. Then the first stones were thrown at Mr Cerani's shop window, and some of the regular customers began to cross the road to transfer their custom to Mr Farkas. But Mr Cerani continued to insist that Hitler had categorically stated he would never infringe the territorial integrity of Hungary.

Lubji reminded his boss that those were the exact words the Führer had used before he invaded Poland. He went on to tell him about a British gentleman called Chamberlain, who had handed in his resignation as prime minister only a few months before.

Lubji knew that he hadn't yet saved enough money to cross another border, so the following Monday, long before the

Ceranis came down for breakfast, he walked boldly across the road and into his rival's shop. Mr Farkas couldn't hide his surprise when he saw Lubji come through the door.

'Is your offer of assistant manager still open?' Lubji asked immediately, not wanting to be caught on the wrong side of the road.

'Not for a Jewboy it isn't,' replied Mr Farkas, looking straight at him. 'However good you think you are. In any case, as soon as Hitler invades I'll be taking over your shop.'

Lubji left without another word. When Mr Cerani came into the shop an hour later, he told him that Mr Farkas had made him yet another offer, 'But I told him I couldn't be bought.' Mr Cerani nodded but said nothing. Lubji was not surprised to find, when he opened his pay packet on Friday, that it contained another small rise.

Lubji continued to save almost all his earnings. When Jews started being arrested for minor offences, he began to consider an escape route. Each night after the Ceranis had retired to bed, Lubji would creep downstairs and study the old atlas in Mr Cerani's little study. He went over the alternatives several times. He would have to avoid crossing into Yugoslavia: surely it would be only a matter of time before it suffered the same fate as Poland and Czechoslovakia. Italy was out of the question, as was Russia. He finally settled on Turkey. Although he had no official papers, he decided that he would go to the railway station at the end of the week and see if he could somehow get on a train making the journey through Romania and Bulgaria to Istanbul. Just after midnight, Lubji closed the old maps of Europe for the last time and returned to his tiny room at the top of the house.

He knew the time was fast approaching when he would have to tell Mr Cerani of his plans, but decided to put it off until he had received his pay packet on the following Friday. He climbed into bed and fell asleep, trying to imagine what life would be like in Istanbul. Did they have a market, and were the Turks a race who enjoyed bargaining?

He was woken from a deep sleep by a loud banging. He

leapt out of bed and ran to the little window that overlooked the street. The road was full of soldiers carrying rifles. Some were banging on doors with the butts of their rifles. It would be only moments before they reached the Ceranis' house. Lubji quickly threw on yesterday's clothes, removed the wad of money from under his mattress and tucked it into his waist, tightening the wide leather belt that held up his trousers.

He ran downstairs to the first landing, and disappeared into the bathroom that he shared with the Ceranis. He grabbed the old man's razor, and quickly cut off the long black ringlets that hung down to his shoulders. He dropped the severed locks into the lavatory and flushed them away. Then he opened the small medicine cabinet and removed Mr Cerani's hair cream, plastering a handful on his head in the hope that it would disguise the fact that his hair had been so recently cropped.

Lubji stared at himself in the mirror and prayed that in his light grey double-breasted suit with its wide lapels, white shirt and spotted blue tie, the invaders just might believe he was nothing more than a Hungarian businessman visiting the capital. At least he could now speak the language without any trace of an accent. He paused before stepping back out onto the landing. As he moved noiselessly down the stairs, he could hear someone already banging on the door of the next house. He quickly checked in the front room, but there was no sign of the Ceranis. He moved on to the kitchen, where he found the old couple hiding under the table, clinging on to each other. While the seven candles of David stood in the corner of the room, there wasn't going to be an easy way of concealing the fact that they were Jewish.

Without saying a word, Lubji tiptoed over to the kitchen window, which looked out onto the back yard. He eased it up cautiously and stuck his head out. There was no sign of any soldiers. He turned his gaze to the right and saw a cat scampering up a tree. He looked to the left and stared into the eyes of a soldier. Standing next to him was Mr Farkas, who nodded and said, 'That's him.'

Lubji smiled hopefully, but the soldier brutally slammed the butt of his rifle into his chin. He fell head first out of the window and crashed down onto the path.

He looked up to find a bayonet hovering between his eyes. 'I'm not Jewish!' he screamed. 'I'm not Jewish!'

The soldier might have been more convinced if Lubji hadn't blurted out the words in Yiddish.

6

Daily Mail

8 FEBRUARY 1945

Yalta: Big Three Confer

When Keith returned for his final year at St Andrew's Grammar, no one was surprised that the headmaster didn't invite him to become a school prefect.

There was, however, one position of authority that Keith did want to hold before he left, even if none of his contemporaries gave him the slightest chance of achieving it.

Keith hoped to become the editor of the *St Andy*, the school magazine, like his father before him. His only rival for the post was a boy from his own form called 'Swotty' Tomkins, who had been the deputy editor during the previous year and was looked on by the headmaster as 'a safe pair of hands'. Tomkins, who had already been offered a place at Cambridge to read English, was considered to be odds-on favourite by the sixty-three sixth formers who had a vote. But that was before anyone realised how far Keith was willing to go to secure the position.

Shortly before the election was due to take place, Keith discussed the problem with his father as they took a walk around the family's country property.

'Voters often change their minds at the last moment,' his father told him, 'and most of them are susceptible to bribery or fear. That has always been my experience, both in politics and business. I can't see why it should be any different for the sixth form at St Andrew's.' Sir Graham paused when they reached the top of the hill that overlooked the property. 'And never forget,' he continued, 'you have an advantage over most candidates in other elections.'

'What's that?' asked the seventeen-year-old as they strolled down the hill on their way back to the house.

'With such a tiny electorate, you know all the voters personally.'

'That might be an advantage if I were more popular than Tomkins,' said Keith, 'but I'm not.'

'Few politicians rely solely on popularity to get elected,' his father assured him. 'If they did, half the world's leaders would be out of office. No better example than Churchill.'

Keith listened intently to his father's words as they walked back to the house.

-<o>-

When Keith returned to St Andrew's, he had only ten days in which to carry out his father's recommendations before the election took place. He tried every form of persuasion he could think of: tickets at the MCG, bottles of beer, illegal packets of cigarettes. He even promised one voter a date with his elder sister. But whenever he tried to calculate how many votes he had secured, he still didn't feel confident that he would have a majority. There was simply no way of telling how anyone would cast his vote in a secret ballot. And Keith wasn't helped by the fact that the headmaster didn't hesitate to make it clear who his preferred candidate was.

With forty-eight hours to go before the ballot, Keith began to consider his father's second option – that of fear. But however long he lay awake at night pondering the idea, he still couldn't come up with anything feasible.

The next afternoon he received a visit from Duncan Alexander, the newly appointed head boy.

'I need a couple of tickets for Victoria against South Australia at the MCG.'

'And what can I expect in return?' asked Keith, looking up from his desk.

'My vote,' replied the head boy. 'Not to mention the influence I could bring to bear on other voters.'

'In a secret ballot?' replied Keith. 'You must be joking.'

'Are you suggesting that my word is not good enough for you?'

'Something like that,' replied Keith.

'And what would your attitude be if I could supply you with some dirt on Cyril Tomkins?'

'It would depend on whether the dirt would stick,' said Keith.

'It will stick long enough for him to have to withdraw from the contest.'

'If that's the case, I'll not only supply you with two seats in the members' stand, but will personally introduce you to any member of the teams you want to meet. But before I even consider parting with the tickets, I'll need to know what you have on Tomkins.'

'Not until I've seen the tickets,' said Alexander.

'Are you suggesting my word is not good enough for you?' Keith enquired with a grin.

'Something like that,' replied Alexander.

Keith pulled open the top drawer of his desk and removed a small tin box. He placed the smallest key on his chain in the lock and turned it. He lifted up the lid and rummaged around, finally extracting two long, thin tickets.

He held them up so that Alexander could study them closely.

After a smile had appeared on the head boy's face, Keith said, 'So what have you got on Tomkins that's so certain to make him scratch?'

'He's a homosexual,' said Alexander.

'Everyone knows that,' said Keith.

'But what they don't know,' continued Alexander, 'is that he came close to being expelled last term.'

'So did I,' said Keith, 'so that's hardly newsworthy.' He placed the two tickets back in the tin.

'But not for being caught in the bogs with young Julian Wells from the lower school,' he paused. 'And both of them with their trousers down.'

'If it was that blatant, why wasn't he expelled?'

'Because there wasn't enough proof. I'm told the master who discovered them opened the door a moment too late.'

'Or a moment too early?' suggested Keith.

'And I'm also reliably informed that the headmaster felt it wasn't the sort of publicity the school needed right now. Especially as Tomkins has won a scholarship to Cambridge.'

Keith's smile broadened as he put his hand back into the tin and removed one of the tickets.

'You promised me both of them,' said Alexander.

'You'll get the other one tomorrow – if I win. That way I can feel fairly confident that your cross will be placed in the right box.'

Alexander grabbed the ticket and said, 'I'll be back tomorrow for the other one.'

When Alexander closed the door behind him, Keith remained at his desk and began typing furiously. He knocked out a couple of hundred words on the little Remington his father had given him for Christmas. After he had completed his copy he checked the text, made a few emendations, and then headed for the school's printing press to prepare a limited edition.

Fifty minutes later he re-emerged, clutching a dummy front page hot off the press. He checked his watch. Cyril Tomkins was one of those boys who could always be relied on to be in his study between the hours of five and six, going over his prep. Today was to prove no exception. Keith strolled down the corridor and knocked quietly on his door.

'Come in,' responded Tomkins.

The studious pupil looked up from his desk as Keith entered the room. He was unable to hide his surprise: Townsend had never visited him in the past. Before he could ask what he wanted, Keith volunteered, 'I thought you might like to see the first edition of the school magazine under my editorship.'

Tomkins pursed his podgy lips. 'I think you'll find,' he said, 'to adopt one of your more overused expressions, that when it comes to the vote tomorrow, I shall win in a canter.'

'Not if you've already scratched, you won't,' said Keith.

'And why should I do that?' asked Tomkins, taking off his spectacles and cleaning them with the end of his tie. 'You certainly can't bribe me, the way you've been trying to do with the rest of the sixth.'

'True,' said Keith. 'But I still have a feeling you'll want to withdraw from the contest once you've read this.' He passed over the front page.

Tomkins replaced his glasses, but did not get beyond the headline and the first few words of the opening paragraph before he was sick all over his prep.

Keith had to admit that this was a far better response than he had hoped for. He felt his father would have agreed that he had grabbed the reader's attention with the headline.

'Sixth Former Caught in Bogs with New Boy. Trousers Down Allegation Denied.'

Keith retrieved the front page and began tearing it up while a white-faced Tomkins tried to regain his composure. 'Of course,' he said, as he dropped the little pieces into the wastepaper basket at Tomkins's side, 'I'd be happy for you to hold the position of deputy editor, as long as you withdraw your name before the voting takes place tomorrow.'

-◦-

'The Case for Socialism' turned out to be the banner headline in the first edition of the *St Andy* under its new editor.

'The quality of the paper and printing are of a far higher standard than I can ever recall,' remarked the headmaster at the staff meeting the following morning. 'However, that is more than can be said for the contents. I suppose we must be thankful that we only have to suffer two editions a term.' The rest of the staff nodded their agreement.

Mr Clarke then reported that Cyril Tomkins had resigned from his position as deputy editor only hours after the first edition of the magazine had been published. 'Pity he didn't get the job in the first place,' the headmaster commented. 'By the way, did anyone ever find out why he withdrew from the contest at the last minute?'

Keith laughed when this piece of information was relayed to him the following afternoon by someone who had overheard it repeated at the breakfast table.

'But will he try to do anything about it?' Keith asked as she zipped up her skirt.

'My father didn't say anything else on the subject, except that he was only thankful you hadn't called for Australia to become a republic.'

'Now there's an idea,' said Keith.

'Can you make the same time next Saturday?' Penny asked, as she pulled her polo-neck sweater over her head.

'I'll try,' said Keith. 'But it can't be in the gym next week because it's already booked for a house boxing match – unless of course you want us to do it in the middle of the ring, surrounded by cheering spectators.'

'I think it might be wise to leave others to end up lying flat on their backs,' said Penny. 'What other suggestions do you have?'

'I can give you a choice,' said Keith. 'The indoor rifle range or the cricket pavilion.'

'The cricket pavilion,' said Penny without hesitation.

'What's wrong with the rifle range?' asked Keith.

'It's always so cold and dark down there.'

'Is that right?' said Keith. He paused. 'Then it will have to be the cricket pavilion.'

'But how will we get in?' she asked.

'With a key,' he replied.

'That's not possible,' she said, rising to the bait. 'It's always locked when the First Eleven are away.'

'Not when the groundsman's son works on the *Courier*, it isn't.'

Penny took him in her arms, only moments after he had finished doing up his fly buttons. 'Do you love me, Keith?'

Keith tried to think of a convincing reply that didn't commit him. 'Haven't I sacrificed an afternoon at the races to be with you?'

Penny frowned as he released himself from her grip. She was just about to press him when he added, 'See you next week.' He unlocked the gym door and peeked out into the corridor. He turned back, smiled and said, 'Stay put for at least another five minutes.'

He took a circuitous route back to his dormitory and let himself in through the kitchen window.

When he crept into his study, he found a note on his desk from the headmaster asking to see him at eight o'clock. He checked his watch. It was already ten to eight. He was relieved that he hadn't succumbed to Penny's charms and stayed a little longer in the gymnasium. He began to wonder what the headmaster was going to complain about this time, but suspected that Penny had already pointed him in the right direction.

He checked the mirror above his washbasin, to be sure there were no outward signs of the extra-curricular activities of the past two hours. He straightened his tie and removed a touch of pink lipstick from his cheek.

As he crunched across the gravel to the headmaster's house, he began to rehearse his defence against the reprimand he had been anticipating for some days. He tried to put his thoughts into a coherent order, and felt more and more confident that he could answer every one of the headmaster's possible admonitions. Freedom of the press, the exercise of one's democratic rights, the evils of censorship – and if the headmaster still rebuked him after that lot, he would remind him of his address to the parents on Founder's Day the previous year when he had condemned Hitler for carrying out exactly the same gagging tactics on the German press. Most of these arguments had been picked up from his father at the breakfast table since he had returned from Yalta.

Keith arrived outside the headmaster's house as the clock

on the school chapel struck eight. A maid answered his knock on the door and said, 'Good evening, Mr Townsend.' It was the first time anyone had ever called him 'Mr'. She ushered him straight through to the headmaster's study. Mr Jessop looked up from behind a desk littered with papers.

'Good evening, Townsend,' he said, dispensing with the usual custom of addressing a boy in his final year by his Christian name. Keith was obviously in deep trouble.

'Good evening, sir,' he replied, somehow managing to make the word 'sir' sound condescending.

'Do have a seat,' said Mr Jessop, waving an arm towards the chair opposite his desk.

Keith was surprised: if you were offered a seat, that usually meant you were *not* in any trouble. Surely he wasn't going to offer him . . .

'Would you care for a sherry, Townsend?'

'No, thank you,' replied Keith in disbelief. The sherry was normally offered only to the head boy.

Ah, thought Keith, bribery. He's going to tell me that perhaps it might be wise in future to temper my natural tendency to be provocative by . . . etc., etc. Well, I already have a reply prepared for that one. You can go to hell.

'I am of course aware, Townsend, of just how much work is involved in trying to gain a place at Oxford while at the same time attempting to edit the school magazine.'

So that's his game. He wants me to resign. Never. He'll have to sack me first. And if he does, I'll publish an underground magazine the week before the official one comes out.

'Nevertheless, I was hoping that you might feel able to take on a further responsibility.'

He's not going to make me a prefect? I don't believe it.

'You may be surprised to learn, Townsend, that I consider the cricket pavilion to be unsuitable . . .' continued the headmaster. Keith turned scarlet.

'Unsuitable, Headmaster?' he blurted out.

'. . . for the first eleven of a school of our reputation. Now, I realise that you have not made your mark at St Andrew's as a sportsman. However, the School Council has decided that this year's appeal should be in aid of a new pavilion.'

Well, they needn't expect any help from me, thought Keith. But I may as well let him go on a bit before I turn him down.

'I know you will be glad to learn that your mother has agreed to be president of the appeal.' He paused. 'With that in mind, I hoped you'd agree to be the student chairman.'

Keith made no attempt to respond. He knew only too well that once the old man got into his full stride, there was little point in interrupting him.

'And as you don't have the arduous responsibility of being a prefect, and do not represent the school in any of its teams, I felt you might be interested in taking up this challenge . . .'

Keith still said nothing.

'The amount the governors had in mind for the appeal was £5,000, and were you to succeed in raising that magnificent sum, I would feel able to inform the college you've applied to at Oxford of your stalwart efforts.' He paused to check some notes in front of him. 'Worcester College, if I remember correctly. I feel that I can safely say that were your application to receive my personal blessing, it would count greatly in your favour.'

And this, thought Keith, from a man who happily climbed the steps of the pulpit every Sunday to rail against the sins of bribery and corruption.

'I therefore hope, Townsend, that you will give the idea your serious consideration.'

As there followed a silence of over three seconds, Keith assumed the headmaster must have come to an end. His first reaction was to tell the old man to think again and to look for some other sucker to raise the money – not least because he had absolutely no interest in either cricket or in going to Oxford. He was determined that the moment he had left school, he would join the *Courier* as a trainee reporter. However, he accepted that for the moment his mother was still winning that particular argument, although if he deliberately failed the entrance exam, she wouldn't be able to do anything about it.

Despite this, Keith could think of several good reasons to

fall in with the headmaster's wishes. The sum was not that large, and collecting it on behalf of the school might open some doors that had previously been slammed in his face. And then there was his mother: she would need a great deal of placating after he had failed to be offered a place at Oxford.

'It's unlike you to take so long to come to a decision,' said the headmaster, breaking into his thoughts.

'I was giving serious consideration to your proposal, Headmaster,' said Keith gravely. He had absolutely no intention of allowing the old man to believe he could be bought off quite that easily. This time it was the headmaster who remained silent. Keith counted to three. 'I'll come back to you on this one if I may, sir,' he said, hoping he sounded like a bank manager addressing a customer requesting a small overdraft.

'And when might that be, Townsend?' enquired the headmaster, sounding a little irritated.

'Two or three days at the most, sir.'

'Thank you, Townsend,' said the headmaster, rising from his chair to indicate that the interview was over. Keith turned to leave, but before he reached the door, the headmaster added, 'Do have a word with your mother before you make your decision.'

⟨◦⟩

'Your father wants me to be the student rep for the annual appeal,' said Keith, as he searched round for his pants.

'What do they want to build this time?' asked Penny, still looking up at the ceiling.

'A new cricket pavilion.'

'Can't see what's wrong with this one.'

'It has been known to be used for other purposes,' said Keith, as he pulled on his trousers.

'Can't think why.' She pulled at a trouser leg. He stared down at her thin naked body. 'So, what are you going to tell him?'

'I'm going to say yes.'

'But why? It could take up all your spare time.'

'I know. But it will keep him off my back, and in any case it might act as an insurance policy.'

'An insurance policy?' said Penny.

'Yes, if I were ever spotted at the racecourse – or worse . . .' He looked down at her again.

'. . . in the slips cradle with the headmaster's daughter?' She pushed herself up and began kissing him again.

'Have we time?' he asked.

'Don't be so wet, Keith. If the First Eleven are playing at Wesley today and the game doesn't end until six, they won't be back much before nine, so we have all the time in the world.' She fell to her knees and began to undo his fly buttons.

'Unless it's raining,' said Keith.

Penny had been the first girl Keith had made love to. She had seduced him one evening when he was meant to be attending a concert by a visiting orchestra; he would never have thought there was enough room in the ladies' loo. He was relieved that there was no way of showing the fact that he had lost his virginity. He was certain it hadn't been Penny's first sexual experience, because to date he hadn't taught her a thing.

But all that had taken place at the beginning of the previous term, and now he had his eye on a girl called Betsy who served behind the counter in the local post office. In fact lately his mother had been surprised by how regularly Keith had been writing home.

Keith lay on a neatly laid-out mattress of old pads in the slips cradle, and began to wonder what Betsy would look like in the nude. He decided that this was definitely going to be the last time.

As she clipped on her bra, Penny asked casually, 'Same time next week?'

'Sorry, can't make it next week,' said Keith. 'Got an appointment in Melbourne.'

'Who with?' asked Penny. 'You're surely not playing for the First Eleven.'

'No, they're not quite that desperate,' said Keith, laughing. 'But I do have to attend an Interview Board for Oxford.'

'Why bother?' said Penny. 'If you were to end up there, it would only confirm your worst fears about the English.'

'I know that, but my . . .' he began, as he pulled up his trousers for a second time.

'And in any case, I heard my father tell Mr Clarke that he only added your name to the final list to please your mother.'

Penny regretted the words the moment she had said them.

Keith's eyes narrowed as he stared down at a girl who didn't normally blush.

‑‑◇►

Keith used the second edition of the school magazine to air his opinions on private education.

'As we approach the second half of the twentieth century, money alone should not be able to guarantee a good education,' the leader declared. 'Attendance at the finest schools should be available to any child of proven ability, and not decided simply by which cot you were born in.'

Keith waited for the wrath of the headmaster to descend upon him, but only silence emanated from that quarter. Mr Jessop did not rise to the challenge. He might have been influenced by the fact that Keith had already banked £1,470 of the £5,000 needed to build a new cricket pavilion. Most of the money had, admittedly, been extracted from his father's contacts, who, Keith suspected, paid up in the hope that it would keep their names off the front pages in future.

In fact, the only result of publishing the article was not a complaint, but an offer of £10 from the *Melbourne Age*, Sir Graham's main rival, who wanted to reproduce the five-hundred-word piece in full. Keith happily accepted his first fee as a journalist, but managed to lose the entire amount the following Wednesday, thus finally proving that Lucky Joe's system was not infallible.

Nevertheless, Keith looked forward to the chance of impressing his father with the little coup. On Saturday he read through his prose, as reproduced in the *Melbourne Age*. They hadn't changed a single word – but they had edited the piece down drastically, and given it a very misleading headline: 'Sir Graham's Heir Demands Scholarships for Aborigines'.

Half the page was given over to Keith's radical views; the other half was taken up by an article from the paper's chief educational correspondent, cogently arguing the case for private education. Readers were invited to respond with their opinions, and the following Saturday the *Age* had a field day at Sir Graham's expense.

Keith was relieved that his father never raised the subject, although he did overhear him telling his mother, 'The boy will have learnt a great deal from the experience. And in any case, I agreed with a lot of what he had to say.'

His mother wasn't quite so supportive.

—◄o►—

During the holidays Keith spent every morning being tutored by Miss Steadman in preparation for his final exams.

'Learning is just another form of tyranny,' he declared at the end of one demanding session.

'It's nothing compared with the tyranny of being ignorant for the rest of your life,' she assured him.

After Miss Steadman had set him some more topics to revise, Keith went off to spend the rest of the day at the *Courier*. Like his father, he found he was more at ease among journalists than with the rich and powerful old boys of St Andrew's from whom he continued to try to coax money for the pavilion appeal.

For his first official assignment at the *Courier*, Keith was attached to the paper's crime reporter, Barry Evans, who sent him off every afternoon to cover court proceedings – petty theft, burglary, shoplifting and even the occasional bigamy. 'Search for names that just might be recognised,' Evans told him. 'Or better still, for those who might be related to people who are well known. Best of all, those who *are* well known.' Keith worked diligently, but without a great deal to show for his efforts. Whenever he did manage to get a piece into the paper, he often found it had been savagely cut.

'I don't want to know your opinions,' the old crime reporter would repeat. 'I just want the facts.' Evans had done his training on the *Manchester Guardian*, and never tired of repeating the words of C. P. Scott: 'Comment is free, but facts are sacred.' Keith decided that if he ever owned a newspaper, he would never employ anyone who had worked for the *Manchester Guardian*.

He returned to St Andrew's for the second term, and used the leader in the first edition of the school magazine to suggest that the time had come for Australia to sever its ties with Britain. The article declared that Churchill had abandoned Australia to its fate, while concentrating on the war in Europe.

Once again the *Melbourne Age* offered Keith the chance to disseminate his views to a far wider audience, but this time he refused – despite the tempting offer of £20, four times the sum he had earned in his fortnight as a cub reporter on the *Courier*. He decided to offer the article to the *Adelaide Gazette*, one of his father's papers, but the editor spiked it even before he had reached the second paragraph.

By the second week of term, Keith realised that his biggest problem had become how to rid himself of Penny, who no longer believed his excuses for not seeing her, even when he was telling the truth. He had already asked Betsy to go to the cinema with him the following Saturday afternoon. However, there remained the unsolved problem of how you dated the next girl before you had disposed of her predecessor.

At their most recent meeting in the gym, when he suggested that perhaps the time had come for them to ... Penny had hinted that she would tell her father how they had been spending Saturday afternoons. Keith didn't give a damn who she told, but he did care about embarrassing his mother. During the week he stayed in his study, working unusually hard and avoiding going anywhere he might bump into Penny.

On Saturday afternoon he took a circuitous route into town, and met up with Betsy outside the Roxy cinema. Nothing like breaking three school rules in one day, he thought. He purchased two tickets for Chips Rafferty in *The Rats of Tobruk*, and guided Betsy into a double seat in the back row. By the time 'The End' flashed up on the screen, he hadn't seen much of the film and his tongue ached. He couldn't wait for next Saturday, when the First Eleven were playing away and he could introduce Betsy to the pleasures of the cricket pavilion.

He was relieved to find that Penny didn't try to contact him during the following week. So on Thursday, when he went to post another letter to his mother, he fixed a date to see Betsy on Saturday afternoon. He promised to take her somewhere she had never been before.

Once the first team's bus was out of sight, Keith hung around behind the trees on the north side of the sports ground, waiting for Betsy to appear. After half an hour he began to wonder if she was going to turn up, but a few moments later he spotted her strolling across the fields, and immediately forgot his impatience. Her long fair hair was done up in a ponytail, secured by an elastic band. She wore a yellow sweater which clung so tightly to her body that it reminded him of Lana Turner, and a black skirt so restricting that when she walked she had no choice but to take extremely short steps.

Keith waited for her to join him behind the trees, then took her by the arm and guided her quickly in the direction of the pavilion. He stopped every few yards to kiss her, and had located the zip on her skirt with at least twenty-two yards still to cover.

When they reached the back door, Keith removed a large key from his jacket pocket and inserted it into the lock. He turned it slowly and pushed the door open, fumbling around for the light switch. He flicked it on, and then heard the groans. Keith stared down in disbelief at the sight that greeted him. Four eyes blinked back up at him. One of the two was shielding herself from the naked lightbulb, but Keith could recognise those legs, even if he couldn't see her face. He turned his attention to the other body lying on top of her.

Duncan Alexander would certainly never forget the day he lost his virginity.

7

THE TIMES

21 NOVEMBER 1940

Hungary Drawn into Axis Net: Ribbentrop's Boast that 'Others Will Follow'

Lubji lay on the ground, doubled up, clutching his jaw. The soldier kept the bayonet pointing between his eyes, and with a flick of the head indicated that he should join the others in the waiting lorry.

Lubji tried to continue his protest in Hungarian, but he knew it was too late. 'Save your breath, Jew,' hissed the soldier, 'or I'll kick it out of you.' The bayonet ripped into his trousers and tore open the skin of his right leg. Lubji hobbled off as quickly as he could to the waiting lorry, and joined a group of stunned, helpless people who had only one thing in common: they were all thought to be Jews. Mr and Mrs Cerani were thrown on board before the lorry began its slow journey out of the city. An hour later they reached the compound of the local prison, and Lubji and his fellow-passengers were unloaded as if they were nothing more than cattle.

The men were lined up and led across the courtyard into a large stone hall. A few minutes later an SS sergeant marched in, followed by a dozen German soldiers. He barked out an order in his native tongue. 'He's saying we must strip,' whispered Lubji, translating the words into Hungarian.

They all took off their clothes, and the soldiers began herding the naked bodies into lines – most of them shivering, some of them crying. Lubji's eyes darted around the room trying to see if there was any way he might escape. There was only one door – guarded by soldiers – and three small windows high up in the walls.

A few minutes later a smartly-dressed SS officer marched in, smoking a thin cigar. He stood in the centre of the room and, in a brief perfunctory speech, informed them that they were now prisoners of war. 'Heil Hitler,' he said, and turned to leave.

Lubji took a pace forward and smiled as the officer passed him. 'Good afternoon, sir,' he said. The officer stopped, and stared with disgust at the young man. Lubji began to claim in pidgin German that they had made a dreadful mistake, and then opened his hand to reveal a wad of Hungarian pengös.

The officer smiled at Lubji, took the notes and set light to them with his cigar. The flame grew until he could hold the wad no longer, when he dropped the burning paper on the floor at Lubji's feet and marched off. Lubji could only think of how many months it had taken him to save that amount of money.

The prisoners stood shivering in the stone hall. The guards ignored them; some smoked, while others talked to each other as if the naked men simply didn't exist. It was to be another hour before a group of men in long white coats wearing rubber gloves entered the hall. They began walking up and down the lines, stopping for a few seconds to check each prisoner's penis. Three men were ordered to dress and told they could return to their homes. That was all the proof needed. Lubji wondered what test the women were being subjected to.

After the men in white coats had left, the prisoners were ordered to dress and then led out of the hall. As they crossed the courtyard Lubji's eyes darted around, looking for any avenue of escape, but there were always soldiers with bayonets no more than a few paces away. They were herded into a long corridor and coaxed down a narrow stone staircase with only an occasional gas lamp giving any suggestion of light. On both sides Lubji passed cells crammed with people; he could hear screaming and pleading in so many different tongues that he didn't dare to turn round and look. Then, suddenly, one of the cell doors was opened and he was grabbed by the collar and hurled in, head first. He would have hit the stone floor if he hadn't landed on a pile of bodies.

He lay still for a moment and then stood up, trying to focus on those around him. But as there was only one small barred window, it was some time before he could make out individual faces.

A rabbi was chanting a psalm – but the response was muted. Lubji tried to stand to one side as an elderly man was sick all over him. He moved away from the stench, only to bump into another prisoner with his trousers down. He sat in the corner with his back to the wall – that way no one could take him by surprise.

When the door was opened again, Lubji had no way of knowing how long he had been in that stench-ridden cell. A group of soldiers entered the room with torches, and flashed their lights into blinking eyes. If the eyes didn't blink, the body was dragged out into the corridor and never seen again. It was the last time he saw Mr Cerani.

Other than watching light followed by darkness through the slit in the wall, and sharing the one meal that was left for the prisoners every morning, there was no way of counting the days. Every few hours the soldiers returned to remove more bodies, until they were confident that only the fittest had survived. Lubji assumed that in time he too must die, as that seemed to be the only way out of the little prison. With each day that passed, his suit hung more loosely on his body, and he began to tighten his belt, notch by notch.

Without warning, one morning a group of soldiers rushed into the cell and dragged out those prisoners who were still alive. They were ordered to march along the corridor and back up the stone steps to the courtyard. When Lubji stepped out into the morning sun, he had to hold his hand up to protect his eyes. He had spent ten, fifteen, perhaps twenty days in that dungeon, and had developed what the prisoners called 'cat's eyes'.

And then he heard the hammering. He turned his head to the left, and saw a group of prisoners erecting a wooden scaffold. He counted eight nooses. He would have been sick, but there was nothing in his stomach to bring up. A bayonet touched his hip and he quickly followed the other prisoners clambering into line, ready to board the crowded lorries.

A laughing guard informed them on the journey back into the city that they were going to honour them with a trial before they returned to the prison and hanged every one of them. Hope turned to despair, as once again Lubji assumed he was about to die. For the first time he wasn't sure if he cared.

The lorries came to a standstill outside the courthouse, and the prisoners were led into the building. Lubji became aware that there were no longer any bayonets, and that the soldiers kept their distance. Once inside the building, the prisoners were allowed to sit on wooden benches in the well-lit corridor, and were even given slices of bread on tin plates. Lubji became suspicious, and began to listen to the guards as they chatted to each other. He picked up from different conversations that the Germans were going through the motions of 'proving' that all the Jews were criminals, because a Red Cross observer from Geneva was present in court that morning. Surely, Lubji thought, such a man would find it more than a coincidence that every one of them was Jewish. Before he could think how to take advantage of this information, a corporal grabbed him by the arm and led him into the courtroom. Lubji stood in the dock, facing an elderly judge who sat in a raised chair in front of him. The trial – if that's how it could be described – lasted for only a few minutes. Before the judge passed the death sentence, an official even had to ask Lubji to remind them of his name.

The tall, thin young man looked down at the Red Cross observer seated on his right. He was staring at the ground in front of him, apparently bored, and only looked up when the death sentence was passed.

Another soldier took Lubji's arm and started to usher him out of the dock so that the next prisoner could take his place. Suddenly the observer stood up and asked the judge a question in a language Lubji couldn't understand.

The judge frowned, and turned his attention back to the prisoner in the dock.

'How old are you?' he asked him in Hungarian.

'Seventeen,' replied Lubji. The prosecuting counsel came forward to the bench and whispered to the judge.

The judge looked at Lubji, scowled, and said, 'Sentence commuted to life imprisonment.' He paused and smiled, then said, 'Retrial in twelve months' time.' The observer seemed satisfied with his morning's work, and nodded his approval.

The guard, who obviously felt Lubji had been dealt with far too leniently, stepped forward, grabbed him by the shoulder and led him back to the corridor. He was handcuffed, marched out into the courtyard and hurled onto an open lorry. Other prisoners sat silently waiting for him, as if he were the last passenger joining them on a local bus.

The tailboard was slammed closed, and moments later the lorry lurched forward. Lubji was thrown onto the floorboards, quite unable to keep his balance.

He remained on his knees and looked around. There were two guards on the truck, seated opposite each other next to the tailboard. Both were clutching rifles, but one of them had lost his right arm. He looked almost as resigned to his destiny as the prisoners.

Lubji crawled back towards the rear of the lorry and sat on the floorboards next to the guard with two arms. He bowed his head and tried to concentrate. The journey to the prison would take about forty minutes, and he felt sure that this would be his last chance if he wasn't to join the others on the gallows. But how could he possibly escape, he pondered, as the lorry slowed to pass through a tunnel. When they re-emerged, Lubji tried to recall how many tunnels there had been between the prison and the courthouse. Three, perhaps four. He couldn't be certain.

As the lorry drove through the next tunnel a few minutes later, he began to count slowly. 'One, two, three.' They were in complete darkness for almost four seconds. He had one advantage over the guards for those few seconds: after his three weeks in a dungeon, they couldn't hope to handle themselves in the dark as well as he could. Against that, he would have two of them to deal with. He glanced across at the other guard. Well, one and a half.

Lubji stared ahead of him and took in the passing terrain. He calculated that they must be about halfway between the city and the gaol. On the near side of the road flowed a river. It might be difficult, if not impossible, to cross, as he had no way of knowing how deep it was. On the other side, fields stretched towards a bank of trees that he estimated must have been about three to four hundred yards away.

How long would it take for him to cover three hundred yards, with the movement of his arms restricted? He turned his head to see if another tunnel was coming into sight, but there was none, and Lubji became fearful that they had passed through the last tunnel before the gaol. Could he risk attempting an escape in broad daylight? He came to the conclusion that he had little choice if there was no sign of a tunnel in the next couple of miles.

Another mile passed, and he decided that once they drove round the next bend, he would have to make a decision. He slowly drew his legs up under his chin, and rested his handcuffs on his knees. He pressed his spine firmly against the back of the lorry and moved his weight to the tips of his toes.

Lubji stared down the road as the lorry careered round the bend. He almost shouted 'Mazeltov!' when he saw the tunnel about five hundred yards away. From the tiny pinprick of light at the far end, he judged it to be at least a four-second tunnel.

He remained on the tips of his toes, tensed and ready to spring. He could feel his heart beating so strongly that the guards must surely sense some imminent danger. He glanced up at the two-armed guard as he removed a cigarette from an inside pocket, lazily placed it in his mouth and began searching for a match. Lubji turned his attention in the direction of the tunnel, now only a hundred yards away. He knew that once they had entered the darkness he would have only a few seconds.

Fifty yards . . . forty . . . thirty . . . twenty . . . ten. Lubji took a deep breath, counted one, then sprang up and threw his handcuffs around the throat of the two-armed guard, twisting with such force that the German fell over the side of the lorry, screaming as he hit the road.

The lorry screeched to a halt as it skidded out of the far end of the tunnel. Lubji leapt over the side and immediately ran back into the temporary safety of the darkness. He was followed by two or three other prisoners. Once he emerged from the other end of the tunnel, he swung right and charged into the fields, never once looking back. He must have covered a hundred yards before he heard the first bullet whistle above his head. He tried to cover the second hundred without losing any speed, but every few paces were now accompanied by a volley of bullets. He swerved from side to side. Then he heard the scream. He looked back and saw that one of the prisoners who had leapt out after him was lying motionless on the ground, while a second was still running flat out, only yards behind him. Lubji hoped the gun was being fired by the one-armed guard.

Ahead of him the trees loomed, a mere hundred yards away. Each bullet acted like a starting pistol and spurred him on as he forced an extra yard out of his trembling body. Then he heard the second scream. This time he didn't look back. With fifty yards to go, he recalled that a prisoner had once told him that German rifles had a range of three hundred yards, so he guessed he must be six or seven seconds from safety. Then the bullet came crashing into his shoulder. The force of the impact pushed him on for a few more paces, but it was only moments before he collapsed headlong into the mud. He tried to crawl, but could only manage a couple of yards before he finally slumped on his face. He remained head down, resigned to death.

Within moments he felt a rough pair of hands grab at his shoulders. Another yanked him up by the ankles. Lubji's only thought was to wonder how the Germans had managed to reach him so quickly. He would have found out if he hadn't fainted.

—◦—

Lubji had no way of knowing what time it was when he woke. He could only assume, as it was pitch black, that he must be back in his cell awaiting execution. Then he felt the excruciating pain in his shoulder. He tried to push himself up with the palms of his hands, but he just couldn't move. He wriggled his fingers, and was surprised to discover that at least they had removed his handcuffs.

He blinked and tried to call out, but could only manage a whisper that must have made him sound like a wounded animal. Once again he tried to push himself up, once again he failed. He blinked, unable to believe what he saw standing in front of him. A young girl fell on her knees and mopped his brow with a rough wet rag. He spoke to her in several languages, but she just shook her head. When she finally did say something, it was in a tongue he had never heard before. Then she smiled, pointed to herself and said simply, 'Mari.'

He fell asleep. When he woke, a morning sun was shining in his eyes; but this time he was able to raise his head. He was surrounded by trees. He turned to his left and saw a circle of coloured wagons, piled high with a myriad of possessions. Beyond them, three or four horses were cropping grass at the base of a tree. He turned in the other direction, and his eyes settled on a girl who was standing a few paces away, talking to a man with a rifle slung over his shoulder. For the first time he became aware of just how beautiful she was.

When he called out, they both looked round. The man walked quickly over to Lubji's side and, standing above him, greeted him in his own language. 'My name is Rudi,' he said, before explaining how he and his little band had escaped across the Czech border some months before, only to find that the Germans were still following them. They had to keep on the move, as the master race considered gypsies inferior even to Jews.

Lubji began to fire questions at him: 'Who are you? Where am I?' And, most important, 'Where are the Germans?' He stopped only when Mari – who, Rudi explained, was his sister – returned with a bowl of hot liquid and a hunk of bread. She knelt beside him and began slowly spooning the thin gruel into his mouth. She paused between mouthfuls, occasionally offering him a morsel of bread, as her brother continued to tell Lubji how he had ended up with them. Rudi had heard the shots, and had run to the edge of the forest thinking the Germans had discovered his little band, only to see the prisoners sprinting towards him. All of them had been shot, but Lubji had been close enough to the forest for his men to rescue him.

The Germans had not pursued them once they had seen him being carried off into the forest. 'Perhaps they were fearful of what they might come up against, although in truth the nine of us have only two rifles, a pistol, and an assortment of weapons from a pitchfork to a fish knife,' Rudi laughed. 'I suspect they were more anxious about losing the other prisoners if they went in search of you. But one thing was certain: the moment the sun came up, they would return in great numbers. That is why I gave the order that once the bullet had been removed from your shoulder, we must move on and take you with us.'

'How will I ever repay you?' murmured Lubji.

When Mari had finished feeding him, two of the gypsies raised Lubji gently up onto the caravan, and the little train continued its journey deeper into the forest. On and on they went, avoiding villages, even roads, as they distanced themselves from the scene of the shooting. Day after day Mari tended Lubji, until eventually he could push himself up. She was delighted by how quickly he learned to speak their language. For several hours he practised one particular sentence he wanted to say to her. Then, when she came to feed him that evening, he told her in fluent Romany that she was the most beautiful woman he had ever seen. She blushed, and ran away, not to return again until breakfast.

With Mari's constant attention, Lubji recovered quickly, and was soon able to join his rescuers round the fire in the evening.

As the days turned into weeks, he not only began to fill his suit again, but started letting out the notches on his belt.

One evening, after he had returned from hunting with Rudi, Lubji told his host that it would not be long before he had to leave. 'I must find a port, and get as far away from the Germans as possible,' he explained. Rudi nodded as they sat round the fire, sharing a rabbit. Neither of them saw the look of sadness that came into Mari's eyes.

When Lubji returned to the caravan that night, he found Mari waiting for him. He climbed up to join her and tried to explain that as his wound had nearly healed, he no longer required her help to undress. She smiled and began to remove his shirt gently from his shoulder, taking off the bandages and cleaning the wound. She looked in her canvas bag, frowned, hesitated for a moment, and started to tear her dress, using the material to rebandage his shoulder.

Lubji just stared at Mari's long brown legs as she slowly ran her fingers down his chest to the top of his trousers. She smiled at him and began to undo the buttons. He placed a cold hand on her thigh, and turned scarlet as she lifted up her dress to reveal that she was wearing nothing underneath.

Mari waited expectantly for him to move his hand, but he continued to stare. She leaned forward and pulled off his pants, then climbed across him and lowered herself gently onto him. He remained as still as he had when felled by the bullet, until she began to move slowly up and down, her head tossed back. She took his other hand and placed it inside the top of her dress, shuddering when he first touched her warm breast. He just left it there, still not moving, even though her rhythm became faster and faster. Just when he wanted to shout out, he quickly pulled her down, kissing her roughly on the lips. A few seconds later he lay back exhausted, wondering if he had hurt her, until he opened his eyes and saw the expression on her face. She sank on his shoulder, rolled onto one side and fell into a deep sleep.

He lay awake, thinking that he might have died without ever having experienced such pleasure. A few hours passed before he woke her. This time he didn't remain motionless, his hands continually discovering different parts of her body, and he found that he enjoyed the experience even more the second time. Then they both slept.

When the caravans moved on the next day, Rudi told Lubji that during the night they had crossed yet another border, and were now in Yugoslavia.

'And what is the name of those hills covered in snow?' asked Lubji.

'From this distance they may look like hills,' said Rudi, 'but they are the treacherous Dinaric Mountains. My caravans cannot hope to make it across them to the coast.' For some time he didn't speak, then he added, 'But a determined man just might.'

They travelled on for three more days, resting only for a few hours each night, avoiding towns and villages, until they finally came to the foot of the mountains.

That night, Lubji lay awake as Mari slept on his shoulder. He began to think about his new life and the happiness he had experienced during the past few weeks, wondering if he really wanted to leave the little band and be on his own again. But he decided that if he were ever to escape the wrath of the Germans, he must somehow reach the other side of those mountains and find a boat to take him as far away as possible. The next morning he dressed long before Mari woke. After breakfast he walked around the camp, shaking hands and bidding farewell to every one of his compatriots, ending with Rudi.

Mari waited until he returned to her caravan. He leaned forward, took her in his arms and kissed her for the last time. She clung to him long after his arms had fallen to his side. After she had finally released him, she passed over a large bundle of food. He smiled and then walked quickly away from the camp towards the foot of the mountains. Although he could hear her following for the first few paces, he never once looked back.

Lubji travelled on and on up into the mountains until it was too dark to see even a pace in front of him. He selected a large rock to shelter him from the worst of the bitter wind, but even huddled up he still nearly froze. He spent a sleepless night eating Mari's food and thinking about the warmth of her body.

As soon as the sun came up he was on the move again, rarely stopping for more than a few moments. At nightfall he wondered if the harsh, cold wind would freeze him to death while he was asleep. But he woke each morning with the sun shining in his eyes.

By the end of the third day he had no food left, and could see nothing but mountains in every direction he looked. He began to wonder why he had ever left Rudi and his little gypsy band.

On the fourth morning he could barely put one foot in front of the other: perhaps starvation would achieve what the Germans had failed to do. By the evening of the fifth day he was just wandering aimlessly forward, almost indifferent to his fate, when he thought he saw smoke rising in the distance. But he had to freeze for another night before flickering lights confirmed the testimony of his eyes. For there in front of him lay a village and, beyond that, his first sight of the sea.

Coming down the mountains might have been quicker than climbing them, but it was no less treacherous. He fell several times, and failed to reach the flat, green plains before sunset, by which time the moon was darting in and out between the clouds, fitfully lighting his slow progress.

Most of the lamps in the little houses had already been blown out by the time he reached the edge of the village, but he hobbled on, hoping he would find someone who was still awake. When he reached the first house, which looked as if it was part of a small farm, he considered knocking on the door, but as there were no lights to be seen he decided against it. He was waiting for the moon to reappear from behind a cloud when his eyes made out a barn on the far side of the yard. He slowly made his way towards the ramshackle building. Stray chickens squawked as they jumped out of his path, and he nearly walked into a black cow which had no intention of moving for the stranger. The door of the barn was half open. He crept inside, collapsed onto the straw and fell into a deep sleep.

When Lubji woke the next morning he found he couldn't move his neck; it was pinned firmly to the ground. He thought for a moment that he must be back in gaol, until he opened his eyes and stared up at a massive figure towering above him. The man was attached to a long pitchfork, which turned out to be the reason why he couldn't move.

The farmer shouted some words in yet another language. Lubji was only relieved that it wasn't German. He raised his eyes to heaven and thanked his tutors for the breadth of his education. Lubji told the man on the end of the pitchfork that he had come over the mountains after escaping from the Germans. The farmer looked incredulous, until he had examined the bullet scar on Lubji's shoulder. His father had owned the farm before him, and he had never told him of anyone crossing those mountains.

He led Lubji back to the farmhouse, keeping the pitchfork firmly in his hand. Over a breakfast of bacon and eggs, and thick slabs of bread supplied by the farmer's wife, Lubji told them, more with hand gestures than words, what he had been through during the past few months. The farmer's wife looked sympathetic and kept filling his empty plate. The farmer said little, and still looked doubtful.

When Lubji came to the end of his tale, the farmer warned him that despite the brave words of Tito, the partisan leader, he didn't think it would be long before the Germans would invade Yugoslavia. Lubji began to wonder if any country on earth was safe from the ambitions of the Führer. Perhaps he would have to spend the rest of his life just running away from him.

'I must get to the coast,' he said. 'Then if I could get on a boat and cross the ocean . . .'

'It doesn't matter where you go,' said the farmer, 'as long as it's as far away from this war as possible.' He dug his teeth into an apple. 'If they ever catch up with you again, they won't let you escape a second time. Find yourself a ship – any ship.

Go to America, Mexico, the West Indies, even Africa,' said the farmer.

'How do I reach the nearest port?'

'Dubrovnik is two hundred kilometres south-east of us,' said the farmer, lighting up a pipe. 'There you will find many ships only too happy to sail away from this war.'

'I must leave at once,' said Lubji, jumping up.

'Don't be in such a hurry, young man,' said the farmer, puffing away. 'The Germans won't be crossing those mountains for some time yet.' Lubji sat back down, and the farmer's wife cut the crust off a second loaf and covered it in dripping, placing it on the table in front of him.

There was only a pile of crumbs left on his plate when Lubji eventually rose from the table and followed the farmer out of the kitchen. When he reached the door, the farmer's wife loaded him down with apples, cheese and more bread, before he jumped onto the back of her husband's tractor and was taken to the edge of the village. The farmer eventually left him by the side of a road that he assured him led to the coast.

Lubji walked along the road, sticking his thumb in the air whenever he saw a vehicle approaching. But for the first two hours every one of them, however fast or slow, simply ignored him. It was quite late in the afternoon when a battered old Tatra came to a halt a few yards ahead of him.

He ran up to the driver's side as the window was being wound down.

'Where are you going?' asked the driver.

'Dubrovnik,' said Lubji, with a smile. The driver shrugged, wound up the window and drove off without another word.

Several tractors, two cars and a lorry passed him before another car stopped, and to the same question Lubji gave the same answer.

'I'm not going that far,' came back the reply, 'but I could take you part of the way.'

One car, two lorries, three horse-drawn carts and the pillion of a motorcycle completed the three-day journey to Dubrovnik. By that time Lubji had devoured all the food the farmer's wife had supplied, and had gathered what knowledge he could on how to go about finding a ship in Dubrovnik that might help him to escape from the Germans.

Once he had been dropped on the outskirts of the busy port, it only took a few minutes to discover that the farmer's worst fears had been accurate: everywhere he turned he could see citizens preparing for a German invasion. Lubji had no intention of waiting around to greet them a second time as they goose-stepped their way down the streets of yet another foreign town. This was one city he didn't intend to be caught asleep in.

Acting on the farmer's advice, he made his way to the docks. Once he had reached the quayside he spent the next couple of hours walking up and down, trying to work out which ships had come from which ports and where they were bound. He shortlisted three likely vessels, but had no way of knowing when they might be sailing or where they were destined for. He continued to hang around on the quayside. Whenever he spotted anyone in uniform he would quickly disappear into the shadows of one of the many alleys that ran alongside the dock, and once even into a packed bar, despite the fact he had no money.

He slipped into a seat in the farthest corner of the dingy tavern, hoping that no one would notice him, and began to eavesdrop on conversations taking place in different languages at the tables around him. He picked up information on where you could buy a woman, who was paying the best rate for stokers, even where you could get yourself a tattoo of Neptune at a cut price; but among the noisy banter, he also discovered that the next boat due to weigh anchor was the *Arridin*, which would cast off the moment it had finished loading a cargo of wheat. But he couldn't find out where it was bound for.

One of the deckhands kept repeating the word 'Egypt'. Lubji's first thought was of Moses and the Promised Land.

He slipped out of the bar and back onto the quayside. This time he checked each ship carefully until he came to a group of men loading sacks into the hold of a small cargo steamer that bore the name *Arridin* on its bow. Lubji studied the flag hanging limply from the ship's mast. There was no wind, so he couldn't be sure where she was registered. But he was certain of one thing: the flag wasn't a swastika.

Lubji stood to one side and watched as the men humped sacks onto their shoulders, carried them up the gangplank and then dropped them into a hole in the middle of the deck. A foreman stood at the top of the gangplank, making a tick on a clipboard as each load passed him. Every few moments a gap in the line would appear as one of the men returned down the gangplank at a different pace. Lubji waited patiently for the exact moment when he could join the line without being noticed. He ambled forward, pretending to be passing by, then suddenly bent down, threw one of the sacks over his left shoulder and walked towards the ship, hiding his face behind the sack from the man at the top of the gangplank. When he reached the deck, he dropped it into the gaping hole.

Lubji repeated the exercise several times, learning a little more about the layout of the ship with each circle he made. An idea began to form in his mind. After a dozen or so drops, he found he could, by speeding up, be on the heels of the man in front of him and a clear distance from the man following him. As the pile of sacks on the quay diminished, Lubji realised he had little opportunity left. The timing would be critical.

He hauled another sack up onto his shoulder. Within moments he had caught up with the man in front of him, who dropped his bag into the hold and began walking back down the gangplank.

When Lubji reached the deck he also dropped his sack into the hold, but, without daring to look back, he jumped in after it, landing awkwardly on top of the pile. He scampered quickly to the farthest corner, and waited fearfully for the raised voices of men rushing forward to help him out. But it was several seconds before the next loader appeared above the hole. He simply leaned over to deposit his sack, without even bothering to look where it landed.

Lubji tried to position himself so that he would be hidden from anyone who might look down into the hold, while at the same time avoiding having a sack of wheat land on top of him. If he made certain of remaining hidden, he almost suffocated, so after each sack came hurtling down, he shot up for a quick breath of fresh air before quickly disappearing back out of sight. By the time the last sack had been dropped into the hold, Lubji was not only bruised from head to toe, but was gasping like a drowning rat.

Just as he began to think it couldn't get any worse, the cover of the cargo hold was dropped into place and a slab of wood wedged between the iron grids. Lubji tried desperately to work his way to the top of the pile, so that he could press his mouth up against the tiny cracks in the slits above him and gulp in the fresh air.

No sooner had he settled himself on the top of the sacks than the engines started up below him. A few minutes later, he began to feel the slight sway of the vessel as it moved slowly out of the harbour. He could hear voices up on the deck, and occasionally feet walked across the boards just above his head. Once the little cargo ship was clear of the harbour, the swaying and bobbing turned into a lurching and crashing as it ploughed into deeper waters. Lubji positioned himself between two sacks and clung on to each with an outstretched arm, trying not to be flung about.

He and the sacks were continually tossed from side to side in the hold until he wanted to scream out for help, but it was now dark, and only the stars were above him, as the deckhands had all disappeared below. He doubted if they would even hear his cries.

He had no idea how long the voyage to Egypt would take, and began to wonder if he could survive in that hold during a storm. When the sun came up, he was pleased to be still alive. By nightfall he wanted to die.

He could not be sure how many days had passed when they eventually reached calmer waters, though he was certain he had remained awake for most of them. Were they entering a harbour? There was now almost no movement, and the engine was only just turning over. He assumed the vessel must have come to a halt when he heard the anchor being lowered, even though his stomach was still moving around as if they were in the middle of the ocean.

At least another hour passed before a sailor bent down and removed the bar that kept the cover of the hold in place. Moments later Lubji heard a new set of voices, in a tongue he'd never encountered before. He assumed it must be Egyptian, and was again thankful it wasn't German. The cover of the hold was finally removed, to reveal two burly men staring down at him.

'So, what have we got ourselves here?' said one of them, as Lubji thrust his hands up desperately towards the sky.

'A German spy, mark my words,' said his mate, with a gruff laugh. The first one leaned forward, grabbed Lubji's out-stretched arms and yanked him out onto the deck as if he were just another sack of wheat. Lubji sat in front of them, legs outstretched, gulping in the fresh air as he waited to be put in someone else's gaol.

He looked up and blinked at the morning sun. 'Where am I?' he asked in Czech. But the dockers showed no sign of understanding him. He tried Hungarian, Russian and, reluc-tantly, German, but received no response other than shrugs and laughter. Finally they lifted him off the deck and frogmarched him down the gangplank, without making the slightest attempt to converse with him in any language.

Lubji's feet hardly touched the ground as the two men dragged him off the boat and down to the dockside. They then hurried him off towards a white building at the far end of the wharf. Across the top of the door were printed words that meant nothing to the illegal immigrant: DOCKS POLICE, PORT OF LIVERPOOL, ENGLAND.

8

St Andy

Dawn of a New Republic

'Abolish the Honours System' read the banner headline in the third edition of the *St Andy*.

In the editor's opinion, the honours system was nothing more than an excuse for a bunch of clapped-out politicians to award themselves and their friends titles that they didn't deserve. 'Honours are almost always given to the undeserving. This offensive display of self-aggrandisement is just another example of the last remnants of a colonial empire, and ought to be done away with at the first possible opportunity. We should consign this antiquated system to the dustbin of history.'

Several members of his class wrote to the editor, pointing out that his father had accepted a knighthood, and the more historically informed among them went on to add that the last sentence had been plagiarised from a far better cause.

Keith was unable to ascertain the headmaster's view as expressed at the weekly staff meeting, because Penny no longer spoke to him. Duncan Alexander and others openly referred to him as a traitor to his class. To everyone's annoyance, Keith gave no sign of caring what they thought.

As the term wore on, he began to wonder if he was more likely to be called up by the army board than to be offered a place at Oxford. Despite these misgivings, he stopped working for the *Courier* in the afternoons so as to give himself more time to study, redoubling his efforts when his father offered to buy him a sports car if he passed the exams. The thought of both proving the headmaster wrong and owning his own car was irresistible. Miss Steadman, who continued to tutor him through the long dark evenings, seemed to thrive on being expected to double her workload.

By the time Keith returned to St Andrew's for his final term, he felt ready to face both the examiners and the headmaster: the appeal for the new pavilion was now only a few hundred pounds short of its target, and Keith decided he would use the final edition of the *St Andy* to announce its success. He hoped that this would make it hard for the headmaster to do anything about an article he intended to run in the next edition, calling for the abolition of the Monarchy.

'Australia doesn't need a middle-class German family who live over ten thousand miles away to rule over us. Why should we approach the second half of the twentieth century propping up such an élitist system? Let's be rid of the lot of them,' trumpeted the editorial, 'plus the National Anthem, the British flag and the pound. Once the war is over, the time will surely have come for Australia to declare itself a republic.'

Mr Jessop remained tight-lipped, while the *Melbourne Age* offered Keith £50 for the article, which he took a considerable time to turn down. Duncan Alexander let it be known that someone close to the headmaster had told him they would be surprised if Townsend managed to survive until the end of term.

During the first few weeks of his final term, Keith continued to spend most of his time preparing for the exams, taking only an occasional break to see Betsy, and the odd Wednesday afternoon off to visit the racecourse while others participated in more energetic pastimes.

Keith wouldn't have bothered to go racing that particular Wednesday if he hadn't been given a 'sure thing' by one of the lads from a local stable. He checked his finances carefully. He still had a little saved from his holiday job, plus the term's pocket money. He decided that he would place a bet on the first race only and, having won, would return to school and continue with his revision. On the Wednesday afternoon, he picked up his bicycle from behind the post office and pedalled off to the racecourse, promising Betsy he would drop in to see her before going back to school.

The 'sure thing' was called Rum Punch, and was down to run in the two o'clock. His informant had been so confident about her pedigree that Keith placed five pounds on the filly to win at seven to one. Before the barrier had opened, he was already thinking about how he would spend his winnings.

Rum Punch led all the way down the home straight, and although another horse began to make headway on the rails, Keith threw his arms in the air as they flew past the winning post. He headed back towards the bookie to collect his winnings.

'The result of the first race of the afternoon,' came an announcement over the loudspeaker, 'will be delayed for a few minutes, as there is a photo-finish between Rum Punch and Colonus.' Keith was in no doubt that from where he was standing Rum Punch had won, and couldn't understand why they had called for a photograph in the first place. Probably, he assumed, to make the officials look as if they were carrying out their duties. He checked his watch and began to think about Betsy.

'Here is the result of the first race,' boomed out a voice over the P.A. 'The winner is number eleven, Colonus, at five to four, by a short head from Rum Punch, at seven to one.'

Keith cursed out loud. If only he had backed Rum Punch both ways, he would still have doubled his money. He tore up his ticket and strode off towards the exit. As he headed for the bicycle shed he glanced at the form card for the next race. Drumstick was among the runners, and well positioned at the start. Keith's pace slowed. He had won twice in the past backing Drumstick, and felt certain it would be three in a row. His only problem was that he had placed his entire savings on Rum Punch.

As he continued in the direction of the bicycle shed, he remembered that he had the authority to withdraw money from an account with the Bank of Australia that was showing a balance of over £4,000.

He checked the form of the other horses, and couldn't see how Drumstick could possibly lose. This time he would place £5 each way on the filly, so that at three to one he was still sure to get his money back, even if Drumstick came in third. Keith pushed his way through the turnstile, picked up his bike and pedalled furiously for about a mile until he spotted the nearest bank. He ran inside and wrote out a cheque for £10.

There were still fifteen minutes to go before the start of the second race, so he was confident that he had easily enough time to cash the cheque and be back in time to place his bet. The clerk behind the grille looked at the customer, studied the cheque and then telephoned Keith's branch in Melbourne. They immediately confirmed that Mr Townsend had signing power for that particular account, and that it was in credit. At two fifty-three the clerk pushed £10 over to the impatient young man.

Keith cycled back to the course at a speed that would have impressed the captain of athletics, abandoned his bicycle and ran to the nearest bookie. He placed £5 each way on Drumstick with Honest Syd. As the barrier sprang open, Keith walked briskly over to the rails and was just in time to watch the mêlée of horses pass him on the first circuit. He couldn't believe his eyes. Drumstick must have been left at the start, because he was trailing the rest of the field badly as they began the second lap and, despite a gallant effort coming down the home straight, could only manage fourth place.

Keith checked the runners and riders for the third race and quickly cycled back to the bank, his backside never once touching the saddle. He asked to cash a cheque for £20. Another phone call was made, and on this occasion the assistant manager in Melbourne asked to speak to Keith personally. Having established Keith's identity, he authorised that the cheque should be honoured.

Keith fared no better in the third race, and by the time an announcement came over the P.A. to confirm the winner of the sixth, he had withdrawn £100 from the cricket pavilion account. He rode slowly back to the post office, considering the consequences of the afternoon. He knew that at the end of the month the account would be checked by the school bursar, and if he had any queries about deposits or withdrawals he would inform the headmaster, who would in turn seek clarification from the bank. The assistant manager would then inform him that Mr Townsend had telephoned from a branch near the racecourse five times during the Wednesday afternoon in question, insisting each time that his cheque should be honoured. Keith would certainly be expelled – a boy had been removed the previous year for stealing a bottle of ink. But worse, far worse, the news would make the front page of every paper in Australia that wasn't owned by his father.

Betsy was surprised that Keith didn't even drop in to speak to her after he had dumped his bike behind the post office. He walked back to school, aware that he only had three weeks in which to get his hands on £100. He went straight to his study and tried to concentrate on old exam papers, but his mind kept returning to the irregular withdrawals. He came up with a dozen stories that in different circumstances might have sounded credible. But how would he ever explain why the cheques had been cashed at thirty-minute intervals, at a branch so near a racecourse?

By the following morning, he was considering signing up for the army and getting himself shipped off to Burma before anyone discovered what he had done. Perhaps if he died winning the VC they wouldn't mention the missing £100 in his obituary. The one thing he didn't consider was placing a bet the following week, even after he had been given another 'sure thing' by the same stable lad. It didn't help when he read in Thursday morning's *Sporting Globe* that this particular 'sure thing' had romped home at ten to one.

It was during prep the following Monday, as Keith was struggling through an essay on the gold standard, that the hand-written note was delivered to his room. It simply stated, 'The headmaster would like to see you in his study immediately.'

Keith felt sick. He left the half-finished essay on his desk and began to make his way slowly over to the headmaster's house. How could they have found out so quickly? Had the bank decided to cover itself and tell the bursar about several irregular withdrawals? How could they be so certain that the money hadn't been used on legitimate expenses? 'So, Townsend, what were those "legitimate expenses", withdrawn from a bank at thirty-minute intervals, just a mile from a racecourse on a Wednesday afternoon?' he could already hear the headmaster asking sarcastically.

Keith climbed the steps to the headmaster's house, feeling cold and sick. The door was opened for him by the maid even before he had a chance to knock. She led him through to Mr Jessop's study without saying a word. When he entered the room, he thought he had never seen such a severe expression on the headmaster's face. He glanced across the room and saw that his housemaster was seated on the sofa in the corner. Keith remained standing, aware that on this occasion he wouldn't be invited to have a seat or take a glass of sherry.

'Townsend,' the headmaster began, 'I am investigating a most serious allegation, in which I am sorry to report that you appear to be personally involved.' Keith dug his nails into his palms to stop himself from trembling. 'As you can see, Mr Clarke has joined us. This is simply to ensure that a witness is present should it become necessary for this matter to be put in the hands of the police.' Keith felt his legs weaken, and feared he might collapse if he wasn't offered a chair.

'I will come straight to the point, Townsend.' The head paused as if searching for the right words. Keith couldn't stop shaking. 'My daughter, Penny, it seems is ... is ... pregnant,' said Mr Jessop, 'and she informs me that she was raped. It appears that you' – Keith was about to protest – 'were the only witness to the episode. And as the accused is not only in your house, but is also the head boy, I consider it to be of the greatest importance that you feel able to co-operate fully with this inquiry.'

Keith let out an audible sigh of relief. 'I shall do my best, sir,' he said, as the headmaster's eyes returned to what he suspected was a prepared script.

'Did you on Saturday 6 October, at around three o'clock in the afternoon, have cause to enter the cricket pavilion?'

'Yes, sir,' said Keith without hesitation. 'I often have to visit the pavilion in connection with my responsibility for the appeal.'

'Yes, of course,' said the headmaster. 'Quite right and proper that you should do so.' Mr Clarke looked grave, and nodded his agreement.

'And can you tell me in your own words what you encountered when you entered the pavilion on that particular Saturday?'

Keith wanted to smirk when he heard the word 'encountered', but somehow managed to keep a serious look on his face.

'Take your time,' said Mr Jessop. 'And whatever your feelings are, you mustn't regard this as sneaking.'

Don't worry, thought Keith, I won't. He pondered whether this was the occasion to settle two old scores at the same time. But perhaps he would gain more by . . .

'You might also care to consider that several reputations rest on your interpretation of what took place on that unfortunate afternoon.' It was the word 'reputations' that helped Keith to make up his mind. He frowned as if contemplating deeply the implications of what he was about to say, and wondered just how much longer he could stretch out the agony.

'When I entered the pavilion, Headmaster,' he began, trying to sound unusually responsible, 'I found the room in complete darkness, which puzzled me until I discovered that all the blinds had been pulled down. I was even more surprised to hear noises coming from the visitors' changing rooms, as I knew the First Eleven were playing away that day. I fumbled around for the light switch, and when I flicked it on, I was shocked to see . . ' Keith hesitated, trying to make it sound as if he felt too embarrassed to continue.

'There is no need for you to worry that you are letting down a friend, Townsend,' prompted the headmaster. 'You can rely on our discretion.'

Which is more than you can on mine, thought Keith.

'. . . to see your daughter and Duncan Alexander lying naked in the slips cradle.' Keith paused again, and this time the headmaster didn't press him to continue. So he took even longer. 'Whatever had been taking place must have stopped the moment I switched the light on.' He hesitated once more.

'This is not easy for me either, Townsend, as you may well appreciate,' said the headmaster.

'I *do* appreciate it, sir,' said Keith, pleased by the way he was managing to string the whole episode out.

'In your opinion were they having, or had they had, sexual intercourse?'

'I feel fairly confident, Headmaster, that sexual intercourse had already taken place,' said Keith, hoping his reply sounded inconclusive.

'But can you be certain?' asked the headmaster.

'Yes, I think so, sir,' said Keith, after a long pause, 'because . . .'

'Don't feel embarrassed, Townsend. You must understand that my only interest is in getting at the truth.'

But that may not be my only interest, thought Keith, who was not in the slightest embarrassed, although it was obvious that the other two men in the room were.

'You must tell us exactly what you saw, Townsend.'

'It wasn't so much what I saw, sir, as what I heard,' said Keith.

The headmaster lowered his head, and took some time to recover. 'The next question is most distasteful for me, Townsend. Because not only will it be necessary for me to rely on your memory, but also on your judgement.'

'I will do my best, sir.'

It was the headmaster's turn to hesitate, and Keith almost had to bite his tongue to prevent himself from saying, 'Take your time, sir.'

'In your judgement, Townsend, and remember we're speaking in confidence, did it appear to you, in so far as you could tell, that my daughter was, so to speak . . .' he hesitated again, '. . . complying?' Keith doubted if the headmaster had put a more clumsy sentence together in his entire life.

Keith allowed him to sweat for a few more seconds before he replied firmly, 'I am in no doubt, sir, on that particular question.' Both men looked directly at him. 'It was not a case of rape.'

Mr Jessop showed no reaction, but simply asked, 'How can you be so sure?'

'Because, sir, neither of the voices I heard before I turned the light on was raised in anger or fear. They were those of two people who were obviously – how shall I put it, sir? – enjoying themselves.'

'Can you be certain of that beyond reasonable doubt, Townsend?' asked the headmaster.

'Yes, sir. I think I can.'

'And why is that?' asked Mr Jessop.

'Because . . . because I had experienced exactly the same pleasure with your daughter only a fortnight before, sir.'

'In the pavilion?' spluttered the headmaster in disbelief.

'No, to be honest with you, sir, in my case it was in the gymnasium. I have a feeling that your daughter preferred the gymnasium to the pavilion. She always said it was much easier to relax on rubber mats than on cricket pads in the slips cradle.' The housemaster was speechless.

'Thank you, Townsend, for your frankness,' the headmaster somehow managed.

'Not at all, sir. Will you be needing me for anything else?'

'No, not for the moment, Townsend.' Keith turned to leave. 'However, I would be obliged for your complete discretion in this matter.'

'Of course, sir,' said Keith, turning back to face him. He reddened slightly. 'I am sorry, Headmaster, if I have embarrassed you, but as you reminded us all in your sermon last Sunday, whatever situation one is faced with in life, one should always remember the words of George Washington: "I cannot tell a lie." '

—<o>—

Penny was nowhere to be seen during the next few weeks. When asked, the headmaster simply said that she and her mother were visiting an aunt in New Zealand.

Keith quickly put the headmaster's problems to one side and continued to concentrate on his own woes. He still hadn't come up with a solution as to how he could return the missing £100 to the pavilion account.

One morning, after prayers, Duncan Alexander knocked on Keith's study door.

'Just dropped by to thank you,' said Alexander. 'Jolly decent of you, old chap,' he added, sounding more British than the British.

'Any time, mate,' responded Keith in a broad Australian accent. 'After all, I only told the old man the truth.'

'Quite so,' said the head boy. 'Nevertheless, I still owe you a great deal, old chap. We Alexanders have long memories.'

'So do we Townsends,' said Keith, not looking up at him.

'Well, if I can be of any help to you in the future, don't hesitate to let me know.'

'I won't,' promised Keith.

Duncan opened the door and looked back before adding, 'I must say, Townsend, you're not quite the shit everyone says you are.'

As the door closed behind him, Keith mouthed the words of Asquith he'd quoted in an essay he'd been working on: 'You'd better wait and see.'

—<o>—

'There's a call for you in Mr Clarke's study on the house phone,' said the junior on corridor duty.

As the month drew to a close, Keith dreaded even opening his mail, or worse, receiving an unexpected call. He always assumed someone had found out. As each day passed he waited

for the assistant manager of the bank to get in touch, informing him that the time had come for the latest accounts to be
presented to the bursar.

'But I've raised over £4,000,' he repeated out loud again and
again.

'That's not the point, Townsend,' he could hear the headmaster saying.

He tried not to show the junior boy how anxious he
really was. As he left his room and walked into the corridor,
he could see the open door of his housemaster's study. His
strides became slower and slower. He walked in, and Mr Clarke
handed him the phone. Keith wished the housemaster would
leave the room, but he just sat there and continued to mark last
night's prep.

'Keith Townsend,' he said.

'Good morning, Keith. It's Mike Adams.'

Keith immediately recognised the name of the editor of
the *Sydney Morning Herald.* How had he found out about the
missing money?

'Are you still there?' asked Adams.

'Yes,' said Keith. 'What can I do for you?' He was relieved
that Adams couldn't see him trembling.

'I've just read the latest edition of the *St Andy*, and in
particular your piece on Australia becoming a republic. I think
it's first class, and I'd like to reprint the whole article in the
SMH – if we can agree on a fee.'

'It's not for sale,' said Keith firmly.

'I was thinking of offering you £75,' said Adams.

'I wouldn't let you reprint it, if you offered me . . .'

'If we offered you *how* much?'

—◁○▷—

The week before Keith was due to sit his exams for Oxford, he
returned to Toorak for some last-minute cramming with Miss
Steadman. They went over possible questions together and read
model answers she had prepared. She failed on only one thing

– getting him to relax. But he couldn't tell her that it wasn't the exams he was nervous about.

'I'm sure you'll pass,' his mother said confidently over breakfast on the Sunday morning.

'I do hope so,' said Keith, only too aware that the following day the *Sydney Morning Herald* was going to publish his 'Dawn of a New Republic.' But that would also be the morning he began his exams, so Keith just hoped that his father and mother would keep their counsel for at least the next ten days, and by then perhaps . . .

'Well, if it's a close-run thing,' said his father, interrupting his thoughts, 'I'm sure you'll be helped by the headmaster's strong endorsement after your amazing success with the pavilion appeal. By the way, I forgot to mention that your grandmother was so impressed by your efforts that she donated another £100 to the appeal, in your name.'

It was the first time Keith's mother had ever heard him swear.

◄○►

By the Monday morning Keith felt as ready to face the examiners as he believed he would ever be, and by the time he had completed the final paper ten days later, he was impressed by how many of the questions Miss Steadman had anticipated. He knew he'd done well in History and Geography, and only hoped that the Oxford board didn't place too much weight on the Classics.

He phoned his mother to assure her that he thought he had performed as well as he could have hoped, and that if he wasn't offered a place at Oxford he wouldn't be able to complain that he'd been unlucky with the questions.

'Neither will I complain,' came back his mother's immediate reply. 'But I do have one piece of advice for you, Keith. Keep out of your father's way for a few more days.'

The anticlimax that followed the ending of the exams was inevitable. While Keith waited to learn the results, he spent some of his time trying to raise the final few hundred pounds for the pavilion appeal, some of it at the racecourse placing small bets with his own money, and a night with the wife of a banker who ended up donating £50.

On the last Monday of term, Mr Jessop informed his staff at their weekly meeting that St Andrew's would be continuing the great tradition of sending its finest students to Oxford and Cambridge, thus maintaining the link with those two great universities. He read out the names of those who had won places:

Alexander, D. T. L.

Tomkins, C.

Townsend, K. R.

'A shit, a swot, and a star, but not necessarily in that order,' said the headmaster under his breath.

SECOND EDITION

To the Victor the Spoils

9

DAILY MIRROR

7 JUNE 1944

Normandy Landings are Successful

When Lubji Hoch had finished telling the tribunal his story, they just looked at him with incredulous stares. He was either some sort of superman, or a pathological liar – they couldn't decide which.

The Czech translator shrugged his shoulders. 'Some of it adds up,' he told the investigating officer. 'But a lot of it sounds a little far-fetched to me.'

The chairman of the tribunal considered the case of Lubji Hoch for a few moments, and then decided on the easy way out. 'Send him back to the internment camp – and we'll see him again in six months' time. He can then tell us his story again, and we'll just have to see how much of it has changed.'

Lubji had sat through the tribunal unable to understand a word the chairman was saying, but at least this time they had supplied him with an interpreter so he was able to follow the proceedings. On the journey back to the internment camp he made one decision. When they reviewed his case in six months' time, he wouldn't need his words translated.

That didn't turn out to be quite as easy as Lubji had anticipated, because once he was back in the camp among his countrymen they showed little interest in speaking anything but Czech. In fact the only thing they ever taught him was how to play poker, and it wasn't long before he was beating every one of them at their own game. Most of them assumed they would be returning home as soon as the war was over.

Lubji was the first internee to rise every morning, and he persistently annoyed his fellow-inmates by always wanting to outrun, outwork and outstrip every one of them. Most of the Czechs looked upon him as nothing more than a Ruthenian ruffian, but as he was now over six feet in height and still growing, none of them voiced this opinion to his face.

Lubji had been back at the camp for about a week when he first noticed her. He was returning to his hut after breakfast when he saw an old woman pushing a bicycle laden with newspapers up the hill. As she passed through the camp gates he couldn't make out her face clearly, because she wore a scarf over her head as a token defence against the bitter wind. She began to deliver papers, first to the officers' mess and then, one by one, to the little houses occupied by the non-commissioned officers. Lubji walked around the side of the parade ground and began to follow her, hoping she might turn out to be the person to help him. When the bag on the front of her bicycle was empty, she turned back towards the camp gates. As she passed Lubji, he shouted, 'Hello.'

'Good morning,' she replied, mounted her bicycle and rode through the gates and off down the hill without another word.

The following morning Lubji didn't bother with breakfast but stood by the camp gates, staring down the hill. When he saw her pushing her laden bicycle up the slope, he ran out to join her before the guard could stop him. 'Good morning,' he said, taking the bicycle from her.

'Good morning,' she replied. 'I'm Mrs Sweetman. And how are you today?' Lubji would have told her, if he'd had the slightest idea what she had said.

As she did her rounds he eagerly carried each bundle for her. One of the first words he learnt in English was 'newspaper'. After that he set himself the task of learning ten new words every day.

By the end of the month, the guard on the camp gate didn't even blink when Lubji slipped past him each morning to join the old lady at the bottom of the hill.

By the second month, he was sitting on the doorstep of Mrs Sweetman's shop at six o'clock every morning so that he could stack all the papers in the right order, before pushing the laden bicycle up the hill. When she requested a meeting with the camp commander at the beginning of the third month, the major told her that he could see no objection to Hoch's working a few hours each day in the village shop, as long as he was always back before roll-call.

Mrs Sweetman quickly discovered that this was not the first newsagent's shop the young man had worked in, and she made no attempt to stop him when he rearranged the shelves, reorganised the delivery schedule, and a month later took over the accounts. She was not surprised to discover, after a few weeks of Lubji's suggestions, that her turnover was up for the first time since 1939.

Whenever the shop was empty Mrs Sweetman would help Lubji with his English by reading out loud one of the stories from the front page of the *Citizen*. Lubji would then try to read it back to her. She often burst out laughing with what she called his 'howlers'. Just another word Lubji added to his vocabulary.

By the time winter had turned into spring there was only the occasional howler, and it was not much longer before Lubji was able to sit down quietly in the corner and read to himself, stopping to consult Mrs Sweetman only when he came to a word he hadn't come across. Long before he was due to reappear in front of the tribunal, he had moved on to studying the leader column in the *Manchester Guardian*, and one morning, when Mrs Sweetman stared at the word 'insouciant' without attempting to offer an explanation, Lubji decided to save her embarrassment by referring in future to the unthumbed Oxford Pocket Dictionary which had been left to gather dust under the counter.

◄○►

'Do you require an interpreter?' the chairman of the panel asked.

'No, thank you, sir,' came back Lubji's immediate reply.

The chairman raised an eyebrow. He was sure that when he had last interviewed this giant of a man only six months before he hadn't been able to understand a word of English. Wasn't he the one who had held them all spellbound with an unlikely tale of what he had been through before he ended up in Liverpool? Now he was repeating exactly the same story and, apart from a few grammatical errors and a dreadful Liverpudlian accent, it was having an even greater effect on the panel than when they had first interviewed him.

'So, what would you like to do next, Hoch?' he asked, once the young Czech had come to the end of his story.

'I wish to join old regiment and play my part in winning war,' came Lubji's well-rehearsed reply.

'That may not prove quite so easy, Hoch,' said the chairman, smiling benignly down at him.

'If you will not give me rifle I will kill Germans with bare hands,' said Lubji defiantly. 'Just give me chance to prove myself.'

The chairman smiled at him again before nodding at the duty sergeant, who came to attention and marched Lubji briskly out of the room.

Lubji didn't learn the result of the tribunal's deliberations for several days. He was delivering the morning papers to the officers' quarters when a corporal marched up to him and said without explanation, ''Och, the CO wants to see you.'

'When?' asked Lubji.

'Now,' said the corporal, and without another word he turned and began marching away. Lubji dropped the remaining papers on the ground, and chased after him as he disappeared through the morning mist across the parade ground in the direction of the office block. They both came to a halt in front of a door marked 'Commanding Officer'.

The corporal knocked, and the moment he had heard the word 'Come,' opened the door, marched in, stood to attention in front of the colonel's desk and saluted.

''Och reporting as ordered, sir,' he bellowed as if he were still outside on the parade ground. Lubji stopped directly behind the corporal, and was nearly knocked over by him when he took a pace backwards.

Lubji stared at the smartly-dressed officer behind the desk. He had seen him once or twice before, but only at a distance. He stood to attention and threw the palm of his hand up to his forehead, trying to mimic the corporal. The commanding officer looked up at him for a moment, and then back down at the single sheet of paper on his desk.

'Hoch,' he began. 'You are to be transferred from this camp to a training depot in Staffordshire, where you will join the Pioneer Corps as a private soldier.'

'Yes, sir,' shouted Lubji happily.

The colonel's eyes remained on the piece of paper in front of him. 'You will embus from the camp at 0700 hours tomorrow morning.'

'Yes, sir.'

'Before then you will report to the duty clerk who will supply you with all the necessary documentation, including a rail warrant.'

'Yes, sir.'

'Do you have any questions, Hoch?'

'Yes, sir,' said Lubji. 'Do the Pioneer Corps kill Germans?'

'No, Hoch, they do not,' replied the colonel, laughing, 'but you will be expected to give invaluable assistance to those who do.'

Lubji knew what the word 'valuable' meant, but wasn't quite sure about 'invaluable'. He made a note of it the moment he returned to his hut.

That afternoon he reported, as instructed, to the duty clerk, and was issued with a rail warrant and ten shillings. After he had packed his few possessions, he walked down the hill for the last time to thank Mrs Sweetman for all she had done during the past seven months to help him learn English. He looked up the new word in the dictionary under the counter, and told Mrs

Sweetman that her help had been invaluable. She didn't care to admit to the tall young foreigner that he now spoke her language better than she did.

The following morning Lubji took a bus to the station in time to catch the 7.20 to Stafford. By the time he arrived, after three changes and several delays, he had read *The Times* from cover to cover.

There was a jeep waiting for him at Stafford. Behind the wheel sat a corporal of the North Staffordshire Regiment, who looked so smart that Lubji called him 'sir'. On the journey to the barracks the corporal left Lubji in no doubt that the 'coolies' – Lubji was still finding it hard to pick up slang – were the lowest form of life. 'They're nothing more than a bunch of skivers who'll do anything to avoid taking part in real action.'

'I want to take part in real action,' Lubji told him firmly, 'and I am not a skiver.' He hesitated. 'Am I?'

'It takes one to know one,' the corporal said, as the jeep came to a halt outside the quartermaster's stores.

Once Lubji had been issued with a private's uniform, trousers a couple of inches too short, two khaki shirts, two pairs of grey socks, a billycan, knife, fork and spoon, and two blankets, he was escorted to his new barracks. He found himself billeted with twenty recruits from the Staffordshire area who, before they had been called up, had worked mostly as potters or coalminers. It took him some time to realise that they were talking the same language he had been taught by Mrs Sweetman.

During the next few weeks Lubji did little more than dig trenches, clean out latrines and occasionally drive lorry-loads of rubbish to a dump a couple of miles outside the camp. To the displeasure of his comrades, he always worked harder and longer than any of them. He soon discovered why the corporal thought the coolies were nothing more than a bunch of skivers.

Whenever Lubji emptied the dustbins behind the officers' mess, he would retrieve any discarded newspapers, however out of date. Later that night he would lie on his narrow bed, his legs dangling over the end, and slowly turn the pages of each paper. He was mostly interested in stories about the war, but the more he read, the more he feared the action was coming to an end, and the last battle would be over long before he had been given the chance to kill any Germans.

◄◦►

Lubji had been a coolie for about six months when he read in morning orders that the North Staffordshire Regiment was scheduled to hold its annual boxing tournament to select representatives for the national army championships later that year. Lubji's section was given the responsibility of setting up the ring and putting out chairs in the gymnasium so that the entire regiment could watch the final. The order was signed by the duty officer, Lieutenant Wakeham.

Once the ring had been erected in the centre of the gymnasium, Lubji started to unfold the seats and place them in rows around it. At ten o'clock the section was given a fifteen-minute break, and most of them slipped out to share a Woodbine. But Lubji remained inside, watching the boxers go about their training.

When the regiment's sixteen-stone heavyweight champion climbed through the ropes, the instructor was unable to find a suitable sparring partner for him, so the champ had to be satisfied with belting a punch-bag held up for him by the largest soldier available. But no one could hold up the bulky punch-bag for long, and after several men had been exhausted, the champion began to shadow-box, his coach urging him to knock out an invisible opponent.

Lubji watched in awe until a slight man in his early twenties, who wore one pip on his shoulder and looked as if he had just left school, entered the gymnasium. Lubji quickly began to unfold more chairs. Lieutenant Wakeham stopped by the side of the ring, and frowned as he saw the heavyweight champion shadow-boxing. 'What's the problem, sergeant? Can't you find anyone to take on Matthews?'

'No, sir,' came back the immediate reply. 'No one who's the right weight would last more than a couple of minutes with 'im.'

'Pity,' said the lieutenant. 'He's bound to become a little rusty if he doesn't get any real competition. Do try and find someone who would be willing to go a couple of rounds with him.'

Lubji dropped the chair he was unfolding and ran towards the ring. He saluted the lieutenant and said, 'I'll go with him for as long as you like, sir.'

The champion looked down from the ring and began to laugh. 'I don't box with coolies,' he said. 'Or with girls from the Land Army, for that matter.'

Lubji immediately pulled himself up into the ring, put up his fists and advanced towards the champion.

'All right, all right,' said Lieutenant Wakeham, looking up at Lubji. 'What's your name?'

'Private Hoch, sir.'

'Well, go and get changed into some gym kit, and we'll soon find out how long you can last with Matthews.'

When Lubji returned a few minutes later, Matthews was still shadow-boxing. He continued to ignore his would-be opponent as he stepped into the ring. The coach helped Lubji on with a pair of gloves.

'Right, let's find out what you're made of, Hoch,' said Lieutenant Wakeham.

Lubji advanced boldly towards the regimental champion and, when he was still a pace away, took a swing at his nose. Matthews feinted to the right, and then placed a glove firmly in the middle of Lubji's face.

Lubji staggered back, hit the ropes and bounced off them towards the champion. He was just able to duck as the second punch came flying over his shoulder, but was not as fortunate with the next, which caught him smack on the chin. He lasted only a few more seconds before he hit the canvas for the first time. By the end of the round he had a broken nose and a cut eye that elicited howls of laughter from his comrades, who had stopped putting out chairs to watch the free entertainment from the back row of the gymnasium.

When Lieutenant Wakeham finally brought the bout to a halt, he asked if Lubji had ever been in a boxing ring before. Lubji shook his head. 'Well, with some proper coaching you might turn out to be quite useful. Stop whatever duties you've been assigned to for the present, and for the next fortnight report to the gym every morning at six. I'm sure we'll be able to make better use of you than putting out chairs.'

By the time the national championships were held, the other coolies had stopped laughing. Even Matthews had to admit that Hoch was a great deal better sparring partner than a punchbag, and that he might well have been the reason he reached the semi-final.

The morning after the championships were over, Lubji was detailed to return to normal duties. He began to help dismantle the ring and take the chairs back to the lecture theatre. He was rolling up one of the rubber mats when a sergeant entered the gym, looked around for a moment and then bellowed, ''Och!'

'Sir?' said Lubji, springing to attention.

'Don't you read company orders, 'Och?' the sergeant shouted from the other side of the gym.

'Yes, sir. I mean, no, sir.'

'Make your mind up, 'Och, because you were meant to 'ave been in front of the regimental recruiting officer fifteen minutes ago,' said the sergeant.

'I didn't realise . . .' began Lubji.

'I don't want to 'ear your excuses, 'Och,' said the sergeant. 'I just want to see you moving at the double.' Lubji shot out of the gym, with no idea where he was going. He caught up with the sergeant, who only said, 'Follow me, 'Och, pronto.'

'Pronto,' Lubji repeated. His first new word for several days.

The sergeant moved quickly across the parade ground, and two minutes later Lubji was standing breathless in front of the recruiting officer. Lieutenant Wakeham had also returned to his normal duties. He stubbed out the cigarette he had been smoking.

'Hoch,' said Wakeham, after Lubji had come to attention and saluted, 'I have put in a recommendation that you should be transferred to the regiment as a private soldier.'

Lubji just stood there, trying to catch his breath.

'Yes, sir. Thank you, sir,' said the sergeant.

'Yes, sir. Thank you, sir,' repeated Lubji.

'Good,' said Wakeham. 'Do you have any questions?'

'No, sir. Thank you, sir,' responded the sergeant immediately.

'No, sir. Thank you, sir,' said Lubji. 'Except . . .'

The sergeant scowled.

'Yes?' said Wakeham, looking up.

'Does this mean I'll get a chance to kill Germans?'

'If I don't kill you first, 'Och,' said the sergeant.

The young officer smiled. 'Yes, it does,' he said. 'All we have to do now is fill in a recruiting form.' Lieutenant Wakeham dipped his pen into an inkwell and looked up at Lubji. 'What is your full name?'

'That's all right, sir,' said Lubji, stepping forward to take the pen. 'I can complete the form myself.'

The two men watched as Lubji filled in all the little boxes, before signing with a flourish on the bottom line.

'Very impressive, Hoch,' said the lieutenant as he checked through the form. 'But might I be permitted to give you a piece of advice?'

'Yes, sir. Thank you, sir,' said Lubji.

'Perhaps the time has come for you to change your name. I don't think you'll get a long way in the North Staffordshire Regiment with a name like Hoch.'

Lubji hesitated, looked down at the desk in front of him. His eyes settled on the packet of cigarettes with the famous emblem of a bearded sailor staring up at him. He drew a line through the name 'Lubji Hoch', and replaced it with 'John Player'.

◄◦►

As soon as he had been kitted up in his new uniform, the first thing Private Player of the North Staffordshire Regiment did was swagger round the barracks, saluting anything that moved.

The following Monday he was despatched to Aldershot to begin a twelve-week basic training course. He still rose every morning at six, and although the food didn't improve, at least he felt he was being trained to do something worthwhile. To kill Germans. During his time at Aldershot he mastered the rifle, the Sten gun, the hand grenade, the compass, and map reading by night and day. He could march slow and at the double, swim a mile and go three days without supplies. When he returned to the camp three months later, Lieutenant Wakeham couldn't help noticing a rather cocky air about the immigrant from Czechoslovakia, and was not surprised to find, when he read the reports, that the latest recruit had been recommended for early promotion.

Private John Player's first posting was with the Second Battalion at Cliftonville. It was only a few hours after being billeted that he realised that, along with a dozen other regiments, they were preparing for the invasion of France. By the spring of 1944, southern England had become one vast training ground, and Private Player regularly took part in mock battles with Americans, Canadians and Poles.

Night and day he trained with his division, impatient for General Eisenhower to give the final order, so that he could once again come face to face with the Germans. Although he was continually reminded that he was preparing for the decisive battle of the war, the endless waiting almost drove him mad. At Cliftonville he added the regimental history, the coastline of Normandy and even the rules of cricket to everything he had learned at Aldershot, but despite all this preparation, he was still holed up in barracks 'waiting for the balloon to go up'.

And then, without warning in the middle of the night of 4 June 1944 he was woken by the sound of a thousand lorries, and realised the preparations were over. The Tannoy began booming out orders across the parade ground, and Private Player knew that at last the invasion was about to begin.

He climbed onto the transport along with all the other soldiers from his section, and couldn't help recalling the first time he had been herded onto a lorry. As one chime struck on the clock on the morning of the fifth, the North Staffordshires drove out of the barracks in convoy. Private Player looked up at the stars, and worked out that they must be heading south.

They travelled on through the night down unlit roads, gripping their rifles tightly. Few spoke; all of them were wondering if they would still be alive in twenty-four hours' time. When they drove through Winchester, newly-erected signposts directed them to the coast. Others had also been preparing for 5 June. Private Player checked his watch. It was a few minutes past three. They continued on and on, still without any idea of where their final destination would be. 'I only 'ope someone knows where we're going,' piped up a corporal sitting opposite him.

It was another hour before the convoy came to a halt at the dockside in Portsmouth. A mass of bodies piled out of lorry after lorry and quickly formed up in divisions, to await their orders.

Player's section stood in three silent rows, some shivering in the cold night air, others from fear, as they waited to board the large fleet of vessels they could see docked in the harbour in front of them. Division upon division waited for the order to embark. Ahead of them lay the hundred-mile crossing that would deposit them on French soil.

The last time he had been searching for a boat, Private Player remembered, it was to take him as far away from the Germans as possible. At least this time he wouldn't be suffocating in a cramped hold with only sacks of wheat to keep him company.

There was a crackling on the Tannoy, and everyone on the dockside fell silent.

'This is Brigadier Hampson,' said a voice, 'and we are all about to embark on Operation Overlord, the invasion of France. We have assembled the largest fleet in history to take you across the Channel. You will be supported by nine battleships, twenty-three cruisers, one hundred and four destroyers and seventy-one corvettes, not to mention the back-up of countless vessels from the Merchant Navy. Your platoon commander will now give you your orders.'

The sun was just beginning to rise when Lieutenant Wakeham completed his briefing and gave the order for the platoon to board the *Undaunted*. Within moments of their climbing aboard the destroyer, the engines roared into action and they began their tossing and bobbing journey across the Channel, still with no idea where they might end up.

For the first half hour of that choppy crossing – Eisenhower had selected an unsettled night despite the advice of his top meteorologist – they sang, joked and told unlikely tales of even more unlikely conquests. When Private Player regaled them all with the story of how he had lost his virginity to a gypsy girl after she had removed a German bullet from his shoulder, they laughed even louder, and the sergeant said it was the most unlikely tale they had heard so far.

Lieutenant Wakeham, who was kneeling at the front of the vessel, suddenly placed the palm of his right hand high in the air, and everyone fell silent. It was only moments before they would be landing on an inhospitable beach. Private Player checked his equipment. He carried a gas mask, a rifle, two bandoliers of ammunition, some basic rations and a water bottle. It was almost as bad as being handcuffed. When the destroyer weighed anchor, he followed Lieutenant Wakeham off the ship into the first amphibious craft. Within moments they were heading towards the Normandy beach. As he looked around he could see that many of his companions were still groggy with seasickness. A hail of machine-gun bullets and mortars came down on them, and Private Player saw men in other craft being killed or wounded even before they reached the beach.

When the craft landed, Player leapt over the side after Lieutenant Wakeham. To his right and left he could see his mates running up the beach under fire. The first shell fell to his left before they had covered twenty yards. Seconds later he saw a corporal stagger on for several paces after a flurry of bullets went right through his chest. His natural instinct was to take cover, but there was none, so he forced his legs to keep going. He continued to fire, although he had no idea where the enemy were.

On and on up the beach he went, unable now to see how many of his comrades were falling behind him, but the sand was already littered with bodies that June morning. Player couldn't be sure how many hours he was pinned on that beach, but for every few yards he was able to scramble forward, he spent twice as long lying still as the enemy fire passed over his head. Every time he rose to advance, fewer of his comrades joined him. Lieutenant Wakeham finally came to a halt when he reached the protection of the cliffs, with Private Player only a yard behind him. The young officer was trembling so much it was some moments before he could give any orders.

When they finally cleared the beach, Lieutenant Wakeham counted eleven of the original twenty-eight men who had been on the landing craft. The wireless operator told him they were not to stop, as their orders were to continue advancing. Player was the only man who looked pleased. For the next two hours they moved slowly inland towards the enemy fire. On and on they went, often with only hedgerows and ditches for protection, men falling with every stride. It was not until the sun had almost disappeared that they were finally allowed to rest. A camp was hastily set up, but few could sleep while the enemy guns continued to pound away. While some played cards, others rested, and the dead lay still.

But Private Player wanted to be the first to come face to face with the Germans. When he was certain no one was watching, he stole out of his tent and advanced in the direction of the enemy, using only the tracers from their fire as his guide. After forty minutes of running, walking, and crawling, he heard the sound of German voices. He skirted round the outside of what looked like their forward camp until he spotted a German soldier relieving himself in the bushes. He crept up behind him, and just as the man was bending down to pull up his pants Player leapt on him. With one arm around his neck, he twisted and snapped his vertebrae, and left him to slump into the bushes. He removed the German's identity tag and helmet and set off back to his camp.

He must have been about a hundred yards away when a voice demanded, 'Who goes there?'

'Little Red Riding Hood,' said Player, remembering the password just in time.

'Advance and be recognised.'

Player took a few more paces forward, and suddenly felt the tip of a bayonet in his back and a second at his throat. Without another word he was marched off to Lieutenant Wakeham's tent. The young officer listened intently to what Player had to say, only stopping him occasionally to double check some piece of information.

'Right, Player,' said the lieutenant, once the unofficial scout had completed his report. 'I want you to draw a map of exactly where you think the enemy are camped. I need details of the terrain, distance, numbers, anything you can remember that will help us once we begin our advance. When you've completed that, try and get some sleep. You're going to have to act as our guide when we begin the advance at first light.'

'Shall I put him on a charge for leaving the camp without requesting permission from an officer?' asked the duty sergeant.

'No,' said Wakeham. 'I shall be issuing company orders, effective immediately, that Player has been made up to corporal.' Corporal Player smiled, saluted and returned to his tent. But before he went to sleep, he sewed two stripes on each sleeve of his uniform.

◄○►

As the regiment advanced slow mile after slow mile deeper into France, Player continued to lead sorties behind the lines, always returning with vital information. His biggest prize was when he came back accompanied by a German officer whom he had caught with his trousers down.

Lieutenant Wakeham was impressed by the fact that Player

had captured the man, and even more when he began the interrogation, and found that the corporal was able to assume the role of interpreter.

The next morning they stormed the village of Orbec, which they overran by nightfall. The lieutenant sent a despatch to his headquarters to let them know that Corporal Player's information had shortened the battle.

—◦—

Three months after Private John Player had landed on the beach at Normandy, the North Staffordshire Regiment marched down the Champs Élysées, and the newly promoted Sergeant Player had only one thing on his mind: how to find a woman who would be happy to spend his three nights' leave with him or – if he got really lucky – three women who would spend one night each.

But before they were let loose on the city, all non-commissioned officers were told that they must first report to the welcoming committee for Allied personnel, where they would be given advice on how to find their way around Paris. Sergeant Player couldn't imagine a bigger waste of his time. He knew exactly how to take care of himself in any European capital. All he wanted was to be let loose before the American troops got their hands on everything under forty.

When Sergeant Player arrived at the committee headquarters, a requisitioned building in the Place de la Madeleine, he took his place in line waiting to receive a folder of information about what was expected of him while he was on Allied territory – how to locate the Eiffel Tower, which clubs and restaurants were within his price range, how to avoid catching V.D. It looked as if this advice was being dispensed by a group of middle-aged ladies who couldn't possibly have seen the inside of a nightclub for the past twenty years.

When he finally reached the front of the queue, he just stood there mesmerised, quite unable to utter a word in any language. A slim young girl with deep brown eyes and dark curly hair stood behind the trestle table, and smiled up at the tall, shy sergeant. She handed him his folder, but he didn't move on.

'Do you have any questions?' she asked in English, with a strong French accent.

'Yes,' he replied. 'What is your name?'

'Charlotte,' she told him, blushing, although she had already been asked the same question a dozen times that day.

'And are you French?' he asked.

She nodded.

'Get on with it, Sarge,' demanded the corporal standing behind him.

'Are you doing anything for the next three days?' he asked, switching to her own language.

'Not a lot. But I am on duty for another two hours.'

'Then I'll wait for you,' he said. He turned and took a seat on a wooden bench that had been placed against the wall.

During the next 120 minutes John Player's gaze rarely left the girl with curly, dark hair, except to check the slow progress of the minute hand on the large clock which hung on the wall behind her. He was glad that he had waited and not suggested he would return later, because during those two hours he saw several other soldiers lean over to ask her exactly the same question he had. On each occasion she looked across in the direction of the sergeant, smiled and shook her head. When she finally handed over her responsibilities to a middle-aged matron, she walked across to join him. Now it was her turn to ask a question.

'What would you like to do first?'

He didn't tell her, but happily agreed to being shown around Paris.

For the next three days he rarely left Charlotte's side, except when she returned to her little apartment in the early hours. He did climb the Eiffel Tower, walk along the banks of the Seine, visit the Louvre and stick to most of the advice given in the folder, which meant that they were almost always accompanied by at least three regiments of single soldiers who, whenever they passed him, were unable to hide the look of envy on their faces.

They ate in overbooked restaurants, danced in nightclubs so crowded they could only shuffle around on the spot, and talked of everything except a war that might cause them to have only three precious days together. Over coffee in the Hôtel Cancelier he told her of the family in Douski he hadn't seen for four years.

He went on to describe to her everything that had happened to him since he had escaped from Czechoslovakia, leaving out only his experience with Mari. She told him of her life in Lyon, where her parents owned a small vegetable shop, and of how happy she had been when the Allies had reoccupied her beloved France. But now she longed only for the war to be over.

'But not before I have won the Victoria Cross,' he told her.

She shuddered, because she had read that many people who were awarded that medal received it posthumously. 'But when the war is over,' she asked him, 'what will you do then?' This time he hesitated, because she had at last found a question to which he did not have an immediate answer.

'Go back to England,' he said finally, 'where I shall make my fortune.'

'Doing what?' she asked.

'Not selling newspapers,' he replied, 'that's for sure.'

During those three days and three nights the two of them spent only a few hours in bed – the only time they were apart.

When he finally left Charlotte at the front door of her tiny apartment, he promised her, 'As soon as we have taken Berlin, I will return.'

Charlotte's face crumpled as the man she had fallen in love with strode away, because so many friends had warned her that once they had left, you never saw them again. And they were to be proved right, because Charlotte Reville never saw John Player again.

—◇—

Sergeant Player signed in at the guardhouse only minutes before he was due on parade. He shaved quickly and changed his shirt before checking company orders, to find that the commanding officer wanted him to report to his office at 0900 hours.

Sergeant Player marched into the office, came to attention and saluted as the clock in the square struck nine. He could think of a hundred reasons why the CO might want to see him. But none of them turned out to be right.

The colonel looked up from his desk. 'I'm sorry, Player,' he said softly, 'but you're going to have to leave the regiment.'

'Why, sir?' Player asked in disbelief. 'What have I done wrong?'

'Nothing,' he said with a laugh, 'nothing at all. On the contrary. My recommendation that you should receive the King's Commission has just been ratified by High Command. It will therefore be necessary for you to join another regiment so that you are not put in charge of men who have recently served with you in the ranks.'

Sergeant Player stood to attention with his mouth open.

'I am simply complying with army regulations,' the CO explained. 'Naturally the regiment will miss your particular skills and expertise. But I have no doubt that we will be hearing of you again at some time in the future. All I can do now, Player, is wish you the best of luck when you join your new regiment.'

'Thank you, sir,' he said, assuming the interview was over. 'Thank you very much.'

He was about to salute when the colonel added, 'May I be permitted to offer you one piece of advice before you join your new regiment?'

'Please do, sir,' replied the newly promoted lieutenant.

'"John Player" is a slightly ridiculous name. Change it to something less likely to cause the men you are about to command to snigger behind your back.'

―◇―

Second Lieutenant Richard Ian Armstrong reported to the officers' mess of the King's Own Regiment the following morning at 0700 hours.

As he walked across the parade ground in his tailored uniform, it took him a few minutes to get used to being saluted by every passing soldier. When he arrived in the mess and sat down for breakfast with his fellow-officers, he watched carefully to see how they held their knives and forks. After breakfast, of which he ate very little, he reported to Colonel Oakshott, his new commanding officer. Oakshott was a red-faced, bluff, friendly man who, when he welcomed him, made it clear that he had already heard of the young lieutenant's reputation in the field.

Richard, or Dick as he quickly became known by his brother officers, revelled in being part of such a famous old regiment. But he enjoyed even more being a British officer with a clear, crisp accent which belied his origins. He had travelled a long way from those two overcrowded rooms in Douski. Sitting by the fire in the comfort of the officers' mess of the King's Own Regiment, drinking port, he could see no reason why he shouldn't travel a great deal further.

—◦—

Every serving officer in the King's Own soon learned of Lieutenant Armstrong's past exploits, and as the regiment advanced towards German soil he was, by his bravery and example in the field, able to convince even the most sceptical that he had not been making it all up. But even his own section was staggered by the courage he displayed in the Ardennes only three weeks after he had joined the regiment.

The forward party, led by Armstrong, cautiously entered the outskirts of a small village, under the impression that the Germans had already retreated to fortify their position in the hills overlooking it. But Armstrong's platoon had only advanced a few hundred yards down the main street before it was met with a barrage of enemy fire. Lieutenant Armstrong, armed only with an automatic pistol and a hand grenade, immediately identified where the German fire was coming from, and, 'careless of his own life' – as the despatch later described his action – charged towards the enemy dugouts.

He had shot and killed the three German soldiers manning the first dugout even before his sergeant had caught up with him. He then advanced towards the second dugout and lobbed his grenade into it, killing two more soldiers instantly. White flags appeared from the one remaining dugout, and three young soldiers slowly emerged, their hands high in the air. One of them took a pace forward and smiled. Armstrong returned the smile, and then shot him in the head. The two remaining Germans turned to face him, a look of pleading on their faces as their comrade slumped to the ground. Armstrong continued to smile as he shot them both in the chest.

His breathless sergeant came running up to his side. The young lieutenant swung round to face him, the smile firmly fixed on his face. The sergeant stared down at the lifeless bodies. Armstrong replaced the pistol in its holster and said, 'Can't take any risks with these bastards.'

'No, sir,' replied the sergeant quietly.

◄○►

That night, once they had set up camp, Armstrong commandeered a German motorcycle and sped back to Paris on a forty-eight-hour leave, arriving on Charlotte's doorstep at seven the following morning.

When she was told by the concierge that there was a Lieutenant Armstrong asking to see her, Charlotte said that she didn't know anyone by that name, assuming it was just another officer hoping to be shown round Paris. But when she saw who it was, she threw her arms around him, and they didn't leave her room for the rest of the day and night. The concierge, despite being French, was shocked. 'I realise there's a war on,' she told her husband, 'but they hadn't even met before.'

When Dick left Charlotte to return to the front on Sunday evening, he told her that by the time he came back he would have taken Berlin, and then they would be married. He jumped on his motorcycle and rode away. She stood in her nightdress by the window of the little apartment and watched until he was out of sight. 'Unless you are killed before Berlin falls, my darling.'

◄○►

The King's Own Regiment was among those selected for the advance on Hamburg, and Armstrong wanted to be the first officer to enter the city. After three days of fierce resistance, the city finally fell.

The following morning, Field Marshal Sir Bernard Montgomery entered the city and addressed the combined troops from the back of his jeep. He described the battle as decisive, and assured them it would not be long before the war was over and they would be going home. After they had cheered their commanding officer, he descended from his jeep and presented medals for bravery. Among those who were decorated with a Military Cross was Captain Richard Armstrong.

Two weeks later, the Germans' unconditional surrender was signed by General Jodl and accepted by Eisenhower. The next day Captain Richard Armstrong MC was granted a week's leave. Dick powered his motorcycle back to Paris, arriving at Charlotte's old apartment building a few minutes before midnight. This time the concierge took him straight up to her room.

The following morning Charlotte, in a white suit, and Dick, in his dress uniform, walked to the local town hall. They emerged thirty minutes later as Captain and Mrs Armstrong, the concierge having acted as witness. Most of the three-day honeymoon was spent in Charlotte's little apartment. When Dick left her to return to his regiment, he told her that now the war was over he intended to leave the army, take her to England and build a great business empire.

◄◊►

'Do you have any plans now that the war is over, Dick?' asked Colonel Oakshott.

'Yes, sir. I intend to return to England and look for a job,' replied Armstrong.

Oakshott opened the buff file that lay on the desk in front of him. 'It's just that I might have something for you here in Berlin.'

'Doing what, sir?'

'High Command are looking for the right person to head up

the PRISC, and I think you're the ideal candidate for the position.'

'What in heaven's name is . . .'

'The Public Relations and Information Services Control. The job might have been made for you. We're looking for someone who can present Britain's case persuasively, and at the same time make sure the press don't keep getting the wrong end of the stick. Winning the war was one thing, but convincing the outside world that we're treating the enemy even-handedly is proving far more difficult. The Americans, the Russians and the French will be appointing their own representatives, so we need someone who can keep an eye on them as well. You speak several languages and have all the qualifications the job requires. And let's face it, Dick, you don't have a family in England to rush back to.'

Armstrong nodded. After a few moments he said, 'To quote Montgomery, what weapons are you giving me to carry out the job?'

'A newspaper,' said Oakshott. '*Der Telegraf* is one of the city's dailies. It's currently operated by a German called Arno Schultz. He never stops complaining that he can't keep his presses rolling, he has constant worries about paper shortages, and the electricity is always being cut off. We want *Der Telegraf* on the streets every day, pumping out our view of things. I can't think of anyone more likely to make sure that happens.'

'*Der Telegraf* isn't the only paper in Berlin,' said Armstrong.

'No, it isn't,' replied the colonel. 'Another German is running *Der Berliner* out of the American sector – which is an added reason why *Der Telegraf* needs to be a success. At the moment *Der Berliner* is selling twice as many copies as *Der Telegraf* a position which as you can imagine we'd like to see reversed.'

'And what sort of authority would I have?'

'You'd be given a free hand. You can set up your own office and staff it with as many people as you feel are necessary to do the job. There's also a flat thrown in, which means that you could send for your wife.' Oakshott paused. 'Perhaps you'd like a little time to think about it, Dick?'

'I don't need time to think about it, sir.'

The colonel raised an eyebrow.

'I'll be happy to take the job on.'

'Good man. Start by building up contacts. Get to know anyone who might be useful. If you come up against any problems, just tell whoever's involved to get in touch with me. If you're really stymied, the words "Allied Control Commission" usually oil even the most immovable wheels.'

It took Captain Armstrong only a week to requisition the right offices in the heart of the British sector, partly because he used the words 'Control Commission' in every other sentence. It took him a little longer to sign up a staff of eleven to manage the office, because all the best people were already working for the Commission. He began by poaching a Sally Carr, a general's secretary who had worked for the *Daily Chronicle* in London before the war.

Once Sally had moved in, the office was up and running within days. Armstrong's next coup came when he discovered that Lieutenant Wakeham was stationed in Berlin working on transport allocation: Sally told him that Wakeham was bored out of his mind filling out travel documents. Armstrong invited him to be his second in command, and to his surprise his former superior officer happily accepted. It took some days to get used to calling him Peter.

Armstrong completed his team with a sergeant, a couple of corporals and half a dozen privates from the King's Own who had the one qualification he required. They were all former barrow boys from the East End of London. He selected the sharpest of them, Private Reg Benson, to be his driver. His next move was to requisition an apartment in Paulstrasse that had previously been occupied by a brigadier who was returning to England. Once the colonel had signed the necessary papers, Armstrong told Sally to send a telegram to Charlotte in Paris.

'What do you want to say?' she asked, turning a page of her notepad.

'Have found suitable accommodation. Pack up everything and come immediately.'

As Sally wrote down his words, Armstrong rose from his seat. 'I'm off to *Der Telegraf* to check up on Arno Schultz. See that everything runs smoothly until I get back.'

'What shall I do with this?' asked Sally, passing him a letter.

'What's it about?' he asked, glancing at it briefly.

'It's from a journalist in Oxford who wants to visit Berlin and write about how the British are treating the Germans under occupation.'

'Too damn well,' said Armstrong as he reached the door. 'But I suppose you'd better make an appointment for him to see me.'

10

News Chronicle

1 OCTOBER 1946

The Judgement of Nuremberg: Goering's Guilt Unique in its Enormity

When Keith Townsend arrived at Worcester College, Oxford to read Politics, Philosophy and Economics, his first impression of England was everything he had expected it to be: complacent, snobbish, pompous and still living in the Victorian era. You were either an officer or other ranks, and as Keith came from the colonies, he was left in no doubt which category he fell into.

Almost all his fellow-students seemed to be younger versions of Mr Jessop, and by the end of the first week Keith would happily have returned home if it hadn't been for his college tutor. Dr Howard could not have been in greater contrast to his old headmaster, and showed no surprise when the young Australian told him over a glass of sherry in his room how much he despised the British class system still perpetuated by most of the undergraduates. He even refrained from making any comment on the bust of Lenin which Keith had placed on the centre of the mantelpiece, where Lord Salisbury had lodged the previous year.

Dr Howard had no immediate solution to the class problem. In fact his only advice to Keith was that he should attend the Freshers' Fair, where he would learn all about the clubs and societies that undergraduates could join, and perhaps find something to his liking.

Keith followed Dr Howard's suggestion, and spent the next morning being told why he should become a member of the Rowing Club, the Philatelic Society, the Dramatic Society, the Chess Club, the Officer Training Corps and, especially, the student newspaper. But after he had met the newly-appointed editor of *Cherwell* and heard his views on how a paper should be run, he decided to concentrate on politics. He left the Freshers' Fair clutching application forms for the Oxford Union and the Labour Club.

The following Tuesday, Keith found his way to the Bricklayers' Arms, where the barman pointed up the stairs to a little room in which the Labour Club always met.

The chairman of the club, Rex Siddons, was immediately suspicious of Brother Keith, as he insisted on addressing him from the outset. Townsend had all the trappings of a traditional Tory – father with a knighthood, public school education, a private allowance and even a second-hand MG Magnette.

But as the weeks passed, and every Tuesday evening the members of the Labour Club were subjected to Keith's views on the monarchy, private schools, the honours system and the élitism of Oxford and Cambridge, he became known as Comrade Keith. One or two of them even ended up in his room after the meetings, discussing long into the night how they would change the world once they were out of 'this dreadful place'.

During his first term Keith was surprised to find that if he failed to turn up for a lecture, or even missed the odd tutorial at which he was supposed to read his weekly essay to his tutor, he was not automatically punished or even reprimanded. It took him several weeks to get used to a system that relied solely on self-discipline, and by the end of his first term his father was threatening that unless he buckled down, he would stop his allowance and bring him back home to do a good day's work.

During his second term Keith wrote a long letter to his father every Friday, detailing the amount of work he was doing, which seemed to stem the flow of invective. He even made the occasional appearance at lectures, where he concentrated on trying to perfect a roulette system, and at tutorials, where he tried to stay awake.

During the summer term Keith discovered Cheltenham, Newmarket, Ascot, Doncaster and Epsom, thus ensuring that he never had enough money to purchase a new shirt or even a pair of socks.

During the vacation several of his meals had to be taken at the railway station which, because of its close proximity to Worcester, was looked upon by some undergraduates as the college canteen. One night after he had drunk a little too much at the Bricklayers' Arms, Keith daubed on Worcester's eighteenth-century wall: 'C'est magnifique, mais ce n'est pas la gare.'

At the end of his first year Keith had little to show for the twelve months he had spent at the university, other than a small group of friends who, like him, were determined to change the system to benefit the majority just as soon as they went down.

His mother, who wrote regularly, suggested that he should take advantage of his vacation by travelling extensively through Europe, as he might never get another chance to do so. He heeded her advice, and started to plan a route – which he would have kept to if he hadn't bumped into the features editor of the *Oxford Mail* over a drink at the local pub.

Dear Mother
I have just received your letter with ideas about what I should do during the vac. I had originally thought of following your advice and driving round the French coast, perhaps ending up at Deauville – but that was before the features editor of the Oxford Mail *offered me the chance to visit Berlin.*
They want me to write four one-thousand-word articles on life in occupied Germany under the Allied forces, and then to go on to Dresden to report on the rebuilding of the city. They are offering me twenty guineas for each article on delivery. Because of my

precarious financial state – my fault, not yours – Berlin
has taken precedence over Deauville.

If they have such things as postcards in Germany,
I will send you one along with copies of the four articles
for Dad to consider. Perhaps the Courier *might be*
interested in them?

Sorry I won't be seeing you this summer.
Love,
Keith

Once term had ended, Keith started off in the same direction
as many other students. He drove his MG down to Dover and
took the ferry across to Calais. But as the others disembarked
to begin their journeys to the historic cities of the Continent,
he swung his little open tourer north-east, in the direction of
Berlin. The weather was so hot that Keith was able to keep his
soft top down for the first time.

As Keith drove along the winding roads of France and
Belgium, he was constantly reminded of how little time had
passed since Europe had been at war. Mutilated hedges and
fields where tanks had taken the place of tractors, bombed-out
farmhouses that had lain between advancing and retreating
armies, and rivers littered with rusting military equipment.
As he passed each bombed-out building and drove through mile
after mile of devastated landscape, the thought of Deauville, with its casino and racecourse, became more and more
appealing.

When it was too dark to avoid holes in the road, Keith
turned off the highway and drove for a few hundred yards down
a quiet lane. He parked at the side of the road and quickly
fell into a deep sleep. He was woken while it was still dark by
the sound of lorries heading ponderously towards the German
border, and jotted down a note: 'The army seems to rise without
regard for the motion of the sun.' It took two or three turns
of the key before the engine spluttered into life. He rubbed
his eyes, swung the MG round and returned to the main road,
trying to remember to keep to the right-hand side.

After a couple of hours he reached the border, and had to wait in a long queue: each person wishing to enter Germany was meticulously checked. Eventually he came to the front, where a customs officer studied his passport. When he discovered that Keith was an Australian, he simply made a caustic comment about Donald Bradman and waved him on his way.

Nothing Keith had heard or read could have prepared him for the experience of a defeated nation. His progress became slower and slower as the cracks in the road turned into potholes, and the potholes turned into craters. It was soon impossible to travel more than a few hundred yards without having to drive as if he was in a dodgem car at a seaside amusement park. And no sooner had he managed to push the speedometer over forty than he would be forced to pull over to allow yet another convoy of trucks – the latest with stars on their doors – to drive past him down the middle of the road.

He decided to take advantage of one of these unscheduled holdups to eat at an inn he spotted just off the road. The food was inedible, the beer weak, and the sullen looks of the innkeeper and his patrons left him in no doubt that he was unwelcome. He didn't bother to order a second course, but quickly settled his bill and left.

He drove on towards the German capital, slow kilometre after slow kilometre, and reached the outskirts of the city only a few minutes before the gas lights were turned on. He began to search immediately among the back streets for a small hotel. He knew that the nearer he got to the centre, the less likely it would be that he could afford the tariff.

Eventually he found a little guesthouse on the corner of a bombed-out street. It stood on its own, as if somehow unaware of what had taken place all around it. This illusion was dispelled as soon as he pushed open the front door. The dingy hall was lit by a single candle, and a porter in baggy trousers and a grey shirt stood sulkily behind a counter. He made little attempt to respond to Keith's efforts to book a room. Keith knew only a few words of German, so he finally held his hand in the air with his palm open, hoping the porter would understand that he wished to stay for five nights.

The man nodded reluctantly, took a key from a hook behind him and led his guest up an uncarpeted staircase to a corner room on the second floor. Keith put his holdall on the floor and stared at the little bed, the one chair, the chest of drawers with three handles out of eight and the battered table. He walked across the room and looked out of the window onto piles of rubble, and thought about the serene duckpond he could see from his college rooms. He turned to say 'Thank you,' but the porter had already left.

After he had unpacked his suitcase, Keith pulled the chair up to the table by the window, and for a couple of hours – feeling guilty by association – wrote down his first impressions of the defeated nation.

◄○►

Keith woke the next morning as soon as the sun shone through the curtainless window. It took him some time to wash in a basin that had no plug and could only manage a trickle of cold water. He decided against shaving. He dressed, went downstairs and opened several doors, looking for the kitchen. A woman standing at a stove turned round, and managed a smile. She waved him towards the table.

Everything except flour, she explained in pidgin English, was in short supply. She set in front of him two large slices of bread covered with a thin suggestion of dripping. He thanked her, and was rewarded with a smile. After a second glass of what she assured him was milk, he returned to his room and sat on the end of the bed, checking the address at which the meeting would take place and then trying to fix it on an out-of-date road map of the city which he had picked up at Blackwell's in Oxford. When he left the hotel it was only a few minutes after eight, but this was not an appointment he wanted to be late for.

Keith had already decided to organise his time so that he

could spend at least a day in each sector of the divided city; he planned to visit the Russian sector last, so he could compare it with the three controlled by the Allies. After what he had seen so far, he assumed it could only be an improvement, which he knew would please his fellow-members of the Oxford Labour Club, who believed that 'Uncle Joe' was doing a far better job than Attlee, Auriol and Truman put together – despite the fact that the farthest east most of them had ever travelled was Cambridge.

Keith pulled up several times on his way into the city to ask directions to Siemensstrasse. He finally found the headquarters of the British Public Relations and Information Services Control a few minutes before nine. He parked his car, and joined a stream of servicemen and women in different-coloured uniforms as they made their way up the wide stone steps and through the swing doors. A sign warned him that the lift was out of order, so he climbed the five floors to the PRISC office. Although he was early for his appointment, he still reported to the front desk.

'How can I help you, sir?' asked a young corporal standing behind the desk. Keith had never been called 'sir' by a woman before, and he didn't like it.

He took a letter out of an inside pocket and handed it across to her. 'I have an appointment with the director at nine o'clock.'

'I don't think he's in yet, sir, but I'll just check.'

She picked up a telephone and spoke to a colleague. 'Someone will come and see you in a few minutes,' she said once she had put the phone down. 'Please have a seat.'

A few minutes turned out to be nearly an hour, by which time Keith had read both the papers on the coffee table from cover to cover, but hadn't been offered any coffee. *Der Berliner* wasn't a lot better than *Cherwell*, the student paper he so scorned at Oxford, and *Der Telegraf* was even worse. But as the director of PRISC seemed to be mentioned on nearly every page of *Der Telegraf*, Keith hoped he wouldn't be asked for his opinion.

Eventually another woman appeared and asked for Mr Townsend. Keith jumped up and walked over to the desk.

'My name is Sally Carr,' said the woman in a breezy cockney accent. 'I'm the director's secretary. How can I help you?'

'I wrote to you from Oxford,' Keith replied, hoping that he sounded older than his years. 'I'm a journalist with the *Oxford Mail* and I've been commissioned to write a series of articles on conditions in Berlin. I have an appointment to see . . .' he turned her letter round, '. . . Captain Armstrong.'

'Oh, yes, I remember,' Miss Carr said. 'But I'm afraid Captain Armstrong is visiting the Russian sector this morning, and I'm not expecting him in the office today. If you can come back tomorrow morning, I'm sure he'll be happy to see you.' Keith tried not to let his disappointment show, and assured her that he would return at nine the following morning. He might have abandoned his plan to see Armstrong altogether had he not been told that this particular captain knew more about what was really going on in Berlin than all the other staff officers put together.

He spent the rest of the day exploring the British sector, stopping frequently to make notes on anything he considered newsworthy. The way the British behaved towards the defeated Germans; empty shops trying to serve too many customers; queues for food on every street corner; bowed heads whenever you tried to look a German in the eye. As a clock in the distance chimed twelve, he stepped into a noisy bar full of soldiers in uniform and took a seat at the end of the counter. When a waiter finally asked him what he wanted, he ordered a large tankard of beer and a cheese sandwich – at least he thought he ordered cheese, but his German wasn't fluent enough to be certain. Sitting at the bar, he began to scribble down some more notes. As he watched the waiters going about their work, he became aware that if you were in civilian clothes you were served after anyone in uniform. Anyone.

The different accents around the room reminded him that the class system was perpetuated even when the British were occupying someone else's city. Some of the soldiers were complaining – in tones that wouldn't have pleased Miss Steadman – about how long it was taking for their papers to be processed before they could return home. Others seemed resigned to a life in uniform, and only talked of the next war and where it might be. Keith scowled when he heard one of them say, 'Scratch them, and underneath they're all bloody Nazis.' But after lunch, as he continued his exploration of the British sector, he thought that on the surface at least the soldiers were well disciplined, and that most of the occupiers seemed to be treating the occupied with restraint and courtesy.

As the shopkeepers began to put up their blinds and shut their doors, Keith returned to his little MG. He found it surrounded by admirers whose looks of envy quickly turned to anger when they saw he was wearing civilian clothes. He drove slowly back to his hotel. After a plate of potatoes and cabbage eaten in the kitchen, he returned to his room and spent the next two hours writing down all he could remember of the day. Later he climbed into bed, and read *Animal Farm* until the candle finally flickered out.

That night Keith slept well. After another wash in near-freezing water, he made a half-hearted effort to shave before making his way down to the kitchen. Several slabs of bread already covered in dripping awaited him. After breakfast he gathered up his papers and set off for his rearranged meeting. If he had been concentrating more on his driving and less on the questions he wanted to ask Captain Armstrong, he might not have turned left at the roundabout. The tank heading straight for him was incapable of stopping without far more warning, and although Keith threw on his brakes and only clipped the corner of its heavy mudguard, the MG spun in a complete circle, mounted the pavement and crashed into a concrete lamp post. He sat behind the wheel, trembling.

The traffic around him came to a halt, and a young lieutenant jumped out of the tank and ran across to check that Keith wasn't injured. Keith climbed gingerly out of the car, a little shaken, but, after he had jumped up and down and swung his arms, he found that he had nothing more than a slight cut on his right hand and a sore ankle.

When they inspected the tank, it had little to show for the encounter other than the removal of a layer of paint from its mudguard. But the MG looked as if it had been involved in a full-scale battle. It was then that Keith remembered he could get only third-party insurance while he was abroad. However, he assured the cavalry officer that he was in no way to blame, and after the lieutenant had told Keith how to find his way to the nearest garage, they parted.

Keith abandoned his MG and began to jog in the direction of the garage. He arrived at the forecourt about twenty minutes later, painfully aware of how unfit he was. He eventually found the one mechanic who spoke English, and was promised that eventually someone would go and retrieve the vehicle.

'What does "eventually" mean?' asked Keith.

'It depends,' said the mechanic, rubbing his thumb across the top of his fingers. 'You see, it's all a matter of . . . priorities.'

Keith took out his wallet and produced a ten-shilling note.

'You have dollars, yes?' asked the mechanic.

'No,' said Keith firmly.

After describing where the car was, he continued on his journey to Siemensstrasse. He was already ten minutes late for his appointment in a city that boasted few trains and even fewer taxis. By the time he arrived at PRISC headquarters, it was his turn to have kept someone waiting forty minutes.

The corporal behind the counter recognised him immediately, but she was not the bearer of encouraging news. 'Captain Armstrong left for an appointment in the American sector a few minutes ago,' she said. 'He waited for over an hour.'

'Damn,' said Keith. 'I had an accident on my way, and got here as quickly as I could. Can I see him later today?'

'I'm afraid not,' she replied. 'He has appointments in the American sector all afternoon.'

Keith shrugged his shoulders. 'Can you tell me how to get to the French sector?'

As he walked around the streets of another sector of Berlin, he added little to his experience of the previous day, except to be reminded that there were at least two languages in this city he couldn't converse in. This caused him to order a meal he didn't want and a bottle of wine he couldn't afford.

After lunch he returned to the garage to check on the progress they were making with his car. By the time he arrived, the gas lights were back on and the one person who spoke English had already gone home. Keith saw his MG standing in the corner of the forecourt in the same broken-down state he had left it in that morning. All the attendant could do was point at the figure eight on his watch.

Keith was back at the garage by a quarter to eight the following morning, but the man who spoke English didn't appear until 8.13. He walked round the MG several times before offering an opinion. 'One week before I can get it back on the road,' he said sadly. This time Keith passed over a pound.

'But perhaps I could manage it in a couple of days . . . It's all a matter of priorities,' he repeated. Keith decided he couldn't afford to be a top priority.

As he stood on a crowded tram he began to consider his funds, or lack of them. If he was to survive for another ten days, pay his hotel bills and for the repairs to his car, he would have to spend the rest of the trip forgoing the luxury of his hotel and sleep in the MG.

Keith jumped off the tram at the now familiar stop, ran up the steps and was standing in front of the counter a few minutes before nine. This time he was kept waiting for twenty minutes, with the same newspapers to read, before the director's secretary reappeared, an embarrassed look on her face.

'I am so sorry, Mr Townsend,' she said, 'but Captain Armstrong has had to fly to England unexpectedly. His second in command, Lieutenant Wakeham, would be only too happy to see you.'

Keith spent nearly an hour with Lieutenant Wakeham, who kept calling him 'old chap', explained why he couldn't get into Spandau and made more jokes about Don Bradman. By the time he left, Keith felt he had learned more about the state of English cricket than about what was going on in Berlin. He passed the rest of the day in the American sector, and regularly stopped to talk to GIs on street corners. They told him with pride that they never left their sector until it was time to return to the States.

When he called back at the garage later that afternoon, the English-speaking mechanic promised him the car would be ready to pick up the following evening.

The next day, Keith made his way by tram to the Russian sector. He soon discovered how wrong he had been to assume that there would be nothing new to learn from the experience. The Oxford University Labour Club would not be pleased to be told that the East Berliners' shoulders were more hunched, their heads more bowed and their pace slower than those of their fellow-citizens in the Allied sectors, and that they didn't appear to speak even to each other, let alone to Keith. In the main square a statue of Hitler had been replaced by an even bigger one of Lenin, and a massive effigy of Stalin dominated every street corner. After several hours of walking up and down drab streets with shops devoid of people and goods, and being unable to find a single bar or restaurant, Keith returned to the British sector.

He decided that if he drove to Dresden the following morning he might be able to complete his assignment early, and then perhaps he could spend a couple of days in Deauville replenishing his dwindling finances. He began to whistle as he jumped on a tram that would drop him outside the garage.

The MG was waiting on the forecourt, and he had to admit that it looked quite magnificent. Someone had even cleaned it, so its red bonnet gleamed in the evening light.

The mechanic passed him the key. Keith jumped behind the wheel and switched on the engine. It started immediately. 'Great,' he said.

The mechanic nodded his agreement. When Keith stepped out of the car, another garage worker leaned over and removed the key from the ignition.

'So, how much will that be?' asked Keith, opening his wallet.

'Twenty pounds,' said the mechanic.

Keith swung round and stared at him. 'Twenty pounds?' he spluttered. 'But I don't have twenty pounds. You've already pocketed thirty bob, and the damn car only cost me thirty pounds in the first place.'

This piece of information didn't seem to impress the mechanic. 'We had to replace the crankshaft and rebuild the carburettor,' he explained. 'And the spare parts weren't easy to get hold of. Not to mention the bodywork. There's not much call for such luxuries in Berlin. Twenty pounds,' he repeated.

Keith opened his wallet and began to count his notes. 'What's that in Deutschmarks?'

'We don't take Deutschmarks,' said the mechanic.

'Why not?'

'The British have warned us to beware of forgeries.'

Keith decided that the time had come to try some different tactics. 'This is nothing less than extortion!' he bellowed. 'I'll damn well have you closed down!'

The German was unmoved. 'You may have won the war, sir,' he said drily, 'but that doesn't mean you don't have to pay your bills.'

'Do you think you can get away with this?' shouted Keith. 'I'm going to report you to my friend Captain Armstrong of the PRISC. Then you'll find who's in charge.'

'Perhaps it would be better if we called in the police, and we can let *them* decide who's in charge.'

This silenced Keith, who paced up and down the forecourt for some time before admitting, 'I don't have twenty pounds.'

'Then perhaps you'll have to sell the car.'

'Never,' said Keith.

'In which case we'll just have to garage it for you – at the usual daily rate – until you're able to pay the bill.'

Keith turned redder and redder while the two men stood hovering over his MG. They looked remarkably unperturbed. 'How much would you offer me for it?' he asked eventually.

'Well, there's not much call for second-hand right-hand

drive sports cars in Berlin,' he said. 'But I suppose I could manage 100,000 Deutschmarks.'

'But you told me earlier that you didn't deal in Deutschmarks.'

'That's only when we're selling. It's different when we're buying.'

'Is that 100,000 over and above my bill?'

'No,' said the mechanic. He paused, smiled and added, 'but we'll see that you get a good exchange rate.'

'Bloody Nazis,' muttered Keith.

◄○►

When Keith began his second year at Oxford, he was pressed by his friends in the Labour Club to stand for the committee. He had quickly worked out that although the club had over six hundred members, it was the committee who met Cabinet ministers whenever they visited the university, and who held the power to pass resolutions. They even selected those who attended the party conference and so had a chance to influence party policy.

When the result of the ballot for the committee was announced, Keith was surprised by how large a margin he had been elected. The following Monday he attended his first committee meeting at the Bricklayers' Arms. He sat at the back in silence, scarcely believing what was taking place in front of his eyes. All the things he despised most about Britain were being re-enacted by that committee. They were reactionary, prejudiced and, whenever it came to making any real decisions, ultra-conservative. If anyone came up with an original idea, it was discussed at great length and then quickly forgotten once the meeting had adjourned to the bar downstairs. Keith concluded that becoming a committee member wasn't going to be enough if he wanted to see some of his more radical ideas become reality. In his final year he would have to become chairman of the Labour Club. When he mentioned this ambition in a letter to his father, Sir Graham wrote back that he was more interested in Keith's prospects of getting a degree, as becoming chairman of the Labour Club was not of paramount importance for someone who hoped to succeed him as proprietor of a newspaper group.

Keith's only rival for the post appeared to be the vice chairman, Gareth Williams, who as a miner's son with a scholarship from Neath Grammar School certainly had all the right qualifications.

The election of officers was scheduled for the second week of Michaelmas term. Keith realised that every hour of the first week would be crucial if he hoped to become chairman. As Gareth Williams was more popular with the committee than with the rank-and-file members, Keith knew exactly where he had to concentrate his energies. During the first ten days of term he invited several paid-up members of the club, including freshmen, back to his room for a drink. Night after night they consumed crates of college beer and tart, non-vintage wine, all at Keith's expense.

With twenty-four hours to go, Keith thought he had it sewn up. He checked over the list of club members, putting a tick next to those he had already approached, and who he was confident would vote for him, and a cross by those he knew were supporters of Williams.

The weekly committee meeting held on the night before the vote dragged on, but Keith derived considerable pleasure from the thought that this would be the last time he had to sit through resolution after pointless resolution that would only end up in the nearest wastepaper basket. He sat at the back of the room, making no contribution to the countless amendments to subclauses so beloved of Gareth Williams and his cronies. The committee discussed for nearly an hour the disgrace of the latest unemployment figures, which had just topped 300,000. Keith would have liked to have pointed out to the brothers that there were at least 300,000 people in Britain who were, in his opinion, simply unemployable, but he reflected that that might be unwise the day before he was seeking their support at the ballot box.

He had leaned back in his chair and was nodding off when the bombshell fell. It was during 'Any Other Business' that Hugh Jenkins (St Peter's), someone Keith rarely spoke to – not simply because he made Lenin look like a Liberal, but also because he was Gareth Williams's closest ally – rose ponderously from his seat in the front row. 'Brother Chairman,' he began, 'it has been brought to my attention that there has been a violation of Standing Order Number Nine, Subsection c, concerning the election of officers to this committee.'

'Get on with it,' said Keith, who already had plans for Brother Jenkins once he was elected that were not to be found under Subsection c in any rule book.

'I intend to, Brother Townsend,' Jenkins said, turning round to face him, 'especially as the matter directly concerns you.'

Keith rocked forward and began to pay close attention for the first time that evening. 'It appears, Brother Chairman, that Brother Townsend has, during the past ten days, been canvassing support for the post of chairman of this club.'

'Of course I have,' said Keith. 'How else could I expect to get elected?'

'Well, I am delighted that Brother Townsend is so open about it, Brother Chairman, because that will make it unnecessary for you to set up an internal inquiry.'

Keith looked puzzled until Jenkins explained.

'It is,' he continued, 'abundantly clear that Brother Townsend has not bothered to consult the party rule book, which states quite unambiguously that any form of canvassing for office is strictly prohibited. Standing Order Number Nine, Subsection c.'

Keith had to admit that he was not in possession of a rule book, and he had certainly never consulted any part of it, let alone Standing Order Number Nine and its subsections.

'I regret that it is nothing less than my duty to propose a resolution,' continued Jenkins: 'That Brother Townsend be disqualified from taking part in tomorrow's election, and at the same time be removed from this committee.'

'On a point of order, Brother Chairman,' said another

member of the committee, leaping up from the second row, 'I think you will find that that is two resolutions.'

The committee then proceeded to discuss for a further forty minutes whether it was one or two resolutions that they would be required to take a vote on. This was eventually settled by an amendment to the motion: by a vote of eleven to seven it was decided that it should be two resolutions. There followed several more speeches and points of order on the question of whether Brother Townsend should be allowed to take part in the vote. Keith said he was quite content not to vote on the first resolution.

'Most magnanimous,' said Williams, with a smirk.

The committee then passed a resolution by a vote of ten to seven, with one abstention, that Brother Townsend should be disqualified from being a candidate for chairman.

Williams insisted that the result of the vote should be recorded in the minutes of the meeting, in case at some time in the future anyone might register an appeal. Keith made it quite clear that he had no intention of appealing. Williams was unable to remove the smirk from his face.

Keith didn't stay to hear the outcome of the second resolution, and had returned to his room in college long before it had been voted on. He missed a long discussion on whether they should print new ballot papers now that there was only one candidate for chairman.

Several students made it clear the following day that they were sorry to learn of Keith's disqualification. But he had already decided that the Labour Party was unlikely to enter the real world much before the end of the century, and that there was little or nothing he could do about it – even if he had become chairman of the club.

The Provost of the college concurred with his judgement over a glass of sherry that evening in the Lodgings. He went on to say, 'I am not altogether disappointed by the outcome, because I have to warn you, Townsend, that your tutor is of the opinion that should you continue to work in the same desultory fashion as you have for the past two years, it is most unlikely that you will obtain any qualification from this university.'

Before Keith could speak up in his own defence, the Provost continued, 'I am of course aware that an Oxford degree is unlikely to be of great importance in your chosen career, but I beg to suggest to you that it might prove a grave disappointment to your parents were you to leave us after three years with absolutely nothing to show for it.'

When Keith returned to his rooms that night he lay on his bed thinking carefully about the Provost's admonition. But it was a letter that arrived a few days later that finally spurred him into action. His mother wrote to inform him that his father had suffered a minor heart attack, and she could only hope that it would not be too long before he was willing to shoulder some responsibility.

Keith immediately booked a call to his mother in Toorak. When he was eventually put through, the first thing he asked her was if she wanted him to return home.

'No,' she replied firmly. 'But your father hopes that you will now spend some more time concentrating on your degree, otherwise he feels Oxford will have served no purpose.'

Once again Keith resolved to confound the examiners. For the next eight months he attended every lecture and never missed a tutorial. With the help of Dr Howard, he continued to cram right through the two vacations, which only made him aware of how little work he had done in the past two years. He began to wish he had taken Miss Steadman to Oxford with him, instead of an MG.

On the Monday of the seventh week of his final term, dressed in subfusc – a dark suit, collar and white tie – and his undergraduate gown, he reported to the Examination Schools in the High. For the next five days he sat at his allotted desk, head down, and answered as many of the questions in the eleven papers as he could. When he emerged into the sunlight on the afternoon of the fifth day, he joined his friends as they sat on the steps of Schools devouring champagne with any passer-by who cared to join them.

Six weeks later Keith was relieved to find his name among those posted in the examination school as having been awarded a Bachelor of Arts (Honours) degree. From that day on, he never revealed the class of degree he had obtained, although he had to agree with Dr Howard's judgement that it was of little relevance to the career on which he was about to embark.

—◦►

Keith wanted to return to Australia on the day after he learned his exam results, but his father wouldn't hear of it. 'I expect you to go and work for my old friend Max Beaverbrook at the *Express*,' he said over a crackling telephone line. 'The Beaver will teach you more in six months than you picked up at Oxford in three years.'

Keith resisted telling him that that would hardly be a great achievement. 'The only thing that worries me, Father, is your state of health. I don't want to stay in England if coming home means I can take some of the pressure off you.'

'I've never felt better, my boy,' Sir Graham replied. 'The doctor tells me I'm almost back to normal, and as long as I don't overdo things, I should be around for a long time yet. You'll be a lot more useful to me in the long run if you learn your trade in Fleet Street than if you come home now and get under my feet. My next call is going to be to the Beaver. So make sure you drop him a line – today.'

Keith wrote to Lord Beaverbrook that afternoon, and three weeks later the proprietor of the *Express* granted the son of Sir Graham Townsend a fifteen-minute interview.

Keith arrived at Arlington House fifteen minutes early, and walked up and down St James's for several minutes before he entered the impressive block of flats. He was kept waiting another twenty minutes before a secretary took him through to Lord Beaverbrook's large office overlooking St James's Park.

'How is your father keeping?' were the Beaver's opening words.

'He's well, sir,' Keith replied, standing in front of his desk, as he hadn't been offered a seat.

'And you want to follow in his footsteps?' said the old man, looking up at him.

'Yes, sir, I do.'

'Good, then you'll report to Frank Butterfield's office at the *Express* by ten tomorrow morning. He's the best deputy editor in Fleet Street. Any questions?'

'No, sir,' said Keith.

'Good,' replied Beaverbrook. 'Please remember me to your father.' He lowered his head, which appeared to be a sign that the interview was over. Thirty seconds later Keith was back out on St James's, not sure if the meeting had ever taken place.

The next morning he reported to Frank Butterfield in Fleet Street. The deputy editor never seemed to stop running from one journalist to another. Keith tried to keep up with him, and it wasn't long before he fully understood why Butterfield had been divorced three times. Few sane women would have tolerated such a lifestyle. Butterfield put the paper to bed every night, except Saturday, and it was an unforgiving mistress.

As the weeks went by, Keith became bored with just following Frank around, and grew impatient to get a broader view of how a newspaper was produced and managed. Frank, who was aware of the young man's restlessness, devised a programme that would keep him fully occupied. He spent three months in circulation, the next three in advertising, and a further three on the shop floor. There he found countless examples of union members playing cards while they should have been working on the presses, or taking the occasional work break between drinking coffee and placing bets at the nearest bookmaker. Some even clocked in under two or three names, drawing a pay packet for each.

By the time Keith had been at the *Express* for six months, he had begun to question whether the editorial content was all that mattered in producing a successful newspaper. Shouldn't he and his father have spent those Sunday mornings looking just as closely at the advertising space in the *Courier* as they did at the front pages? And when they had sat in the old man's study criticising the headlines in the *Gazette*, shouldn't they instead have been looking to see if the paper was overstaffed, or if the expenses of the journalists were getting out of control?

Surely in the end, however massive a paper's circulation was, the principal aim should be to make as large a return on your investment as possible. He often discussed the problem with Frank Butterfield, who felt that the well-established practices on the shop floor were now probably irreversible.

Keith wrote home regularly and at great length, advancing his theories. Now that he was experiencing many of his father's problems at first hand, he began to fear that the trade union practices which were commonplace on the shop floors of Fleet Street would soon find their way to Australia.

At the end of his first year, Keith sent a long memo to Beaverbrook at Arlington House, despite advice to the contrary from Frank Butterfield. In it he expressed the view that the shop floor at the *Express* was overmanned by a ratio of three to one, and that, while wages made up its largest outgoings, there could be no hope of a modern newspaper group being able to make a profit. In the future someone was going to have to take on the unions. Beaverbrook didn't acknowledge the report.

Undaunted, Keith began his second year at the *Express* by putting in hours he hadn't realised existed when he was at Oxford. This served to reinforce his view that sooner or later there would have to be massive changes in the newspaper industry, and he prepared a long memorandum for his father, which he intended to discuss with him the moment he arrived back in Australia. It set out exactly what changes he believed needed to be made at the *Courier* and the *Gazette* if they were to remain solvent during the second half of the twentieth century.

Keith was on the phone in Butterfield's office, arranging his flight to Melbourne, when a messenger handed him the telegram.

11

THE TIMES

5 JUNE 1945

Setting up Control of Germany: Preliminary Meeting of Allied Commanders

When Captain Armstrong visited *Der Telegraf* for the first time, he was surprised to find how dingy the little basement offices were. He was greeted by a man who introduced himself as Arno Schultz, the editor of the paper.

Schultz was about five foot three, with sullen grey eyes and short-cropped hair. He was dressed in a pre-war three-piece suit that must have been made for him when he was a stone heavier. His shirt was frayed at the collar and cuffs, and he wore a thin, shiny black tie.

Armstrong smiled down at him. 'You and I have something in common,' he said.

Schultz shuffled nervously from foot to foot in the presence of this towering British officer. 'And what is that?'

'We're both Jewish,' said Armstrong.

'I would never have known,' said Schultz, sounding genuinely surprised.

Armstrong couldn't hide a smile of satisfaction. 'Let me make it clear from the outset,' he said, 'that I intend to give you every assistance to ensure that *Der Telegraf* is kept on the streets. I only have one long-term aim: to outsell *Der Berliner*.'

Schultz looked doubtful. 'They currently sell twice as many copies a day as we do. That was true even before the war. They have far better presses, more staff, and the advantage of being in the American sector. I don't think it's a realistic aim, Captain.'

'Then we'll just have to change all that, won't we?' said Armstrong. 'From now on you must look upon me as the proprietor of the newspaper, and I will leave you to get on with the editor's job. Why don't you start by telling me what your problems are?'

'Where do I begin?' said Schultz, looking up at his new boss. 'Our printing presses are out of date. Many of the parts are worn out, and there seems to be no way of getting replacements for them.'

'Make a list of everything you need, and I'll see that you get replacements.'

Schultz looked unconvinced. He began cleaning his pebble glasses with a handkerchief he removed from his top pocket. 'And then there's a continual problem with the electricity. No sooner do I get the machinery to work than the supply is cut off, so at least twice a week we end up with no papers being printed at all.'

'I'll make sure that doesn't happen again,' promised Armstrong, without any idea of how he would go about it. 'What else?'

'Security,' said Schultz. 'The censor always checks every word of my copy, so the stories are inevitably two or three days out of date when they appear, and after he has put his blue pencil through the most interesting paragraphs there isn't much left worth reading.'

'Right,' said Armstrong. 'From now on *I'll* vet the stories. I'll also have a word with the censor, so you won't have any more of those problems in the future. Is that everything?'

'No, Captain. My biggest problem comes when the electricity stays on all week.'

'I don't understand,' said Armstrong. 'How can that be a problem?'

'Because then I always run out of paper.'

'What's your current print run?'

'One hundred, one hundred and twenty thousand copies a day at best.'

'And *Der Berliner*?'

'Somewhere around a quarter of a million copies.' Schultz paused. 'Every day.'

'I'll make sure you're supplied with enough paper to print a quarter of a million copies every day. Give me to the end of the month.'

Schultz, normally a courteous man, didn't even say thank you when Captain Armstrong left to return to his office. Despite the British officer's self-confidence, he simply didn't believe it was possible.

Once he was back behind his desk, Armstrong asked Sally to type up a list of all the items Schultz had requested. When she had completed the task he checked the list, then asked her to make a dozen copies and to organise a meeting of the full team. An hour later they all squeezed into his office.

Sally handed a copy of the list to each of them. Armstrong ran briefly through each item and ended by saying, 'I want everything that's on this list, and I want it pronto. When there's a tick against every single item, you will all get three days' leave. Until then you work every waking hour, including weekends. Do I make myself clear?'

A few of them nodded, but no one spoke.

◄○►

Nine days later Charlotte arrived in Berlin, and Armstrong sent Benson to the station to pick her up.

'Where's my husband?' she asked as her bags were put into the back of the jeep.

'He had an important meeting that he couldn't get out of, Mrs Armstrong. He says he'll join you later this evening.'

When Dick returned to the flat that night, he found that Charlotte had finished unpacking and had prepared dinner for him. As he walked through the door she threw her arms around him.

'It's wonderful to have you in Berlin, darling,' he said. 'I'm sorry I couldn't be at the station to meet you.' He released her and looked into her eyes. 'I'm doing the work of six men. I hope you understand.'

'Of course I do,' said Charlotte. 'I want to hear all about your new job over dinner.'

Dick hardly stopped talking from the moment he sat down until they left the unwashed dishes on the table and went to bed. For the first time since he had arrived in Berlin he was late into the office the following morning.

◄○►

It took Captain Armstrong's barrow boys nineteen days to locate every item on the list, and Dick another eight to requisition them, using a powerful mix of charm, bullying and bribery. When an unopened crate of six new Remington typewriters appeared in the office with no requisition order, he simply told Lieutenant Wakeham to turn a blind eye.

If ever Armstrong came up against an obstacle he simply mentioned the words 'Colonel Oakshott' and 'Control Commission'. This nearly always resulted in the reluctant official involved signing in triplicate for whatever was needed.

When it came to the electricity supply, Peter Wakeham reported that because of overloading, one of the four sectors in the city had to be taken off the grid for at least three hours in every twelve. The grid, he added, was officially under the command of an American captain called Max Sackville, who said he hadn't the time to see him.

'Leave him to me,' said Armstrong.

But Dick quickly found out that Sackville was unmoved by charm, bullying or bribery, partly because the Americans seemed to have a surplus of everything and always assumed the ultimate authority was theirs. What he did discover was that the captain had a weakness, which he indulged every Saturday evening. It took several hours of listening to how Sackville won his purple heart at Anzio before Dick was invited to join his poker school.

For the next three weeks Dick made sure he lost around $50 every Saturday night which, under several different headings, he claimed back as expenses the following Monday morning. That way he ensured that the electricity supply in the British sector was never cut off between the hours of three and midnight, except on Saturdays, when no copies of *Der Telegraf* were being printed.

Arno Schultz's list of requests was completed in twenty-six days, by which time *Der Telegraf* was producing 140,000 copies a night. Lieutenant Wakeham had been put in charge of distribution, and the paper never failed to be on the streets by the early hours of the morning. When he was informed by Dick of *Der Telegraf*'s latest circulation figures, Colonel Oakshott was delighted with the results his protégé was achieving, and agreed that the team should be granted three days' leave.

No one was more delighted by this news than Charlotte. Since she had arrived in Berlin, Dick had rarely been home before midnight, and often left the house before she woke. But that Friday afternoon he turned up outside their apartment behind the wheel of someone else's Mercedes, and once she had loaded up the car with battered cases, they set off for Lyon to spend a long weekend with her family.

It worried Charlotte that Dick seemed quite incapable of relaxing for more than a few minutes at a time, but she was grateful that there wasn't a phone in the little house in Lyon. On the Saturday evening the whole family went to see David Niven in *The Perfect Marriage*. The next morning Dick started growing a moustache.

—◦—

The moment Captain Armstrong returned to Berlin, he took the colonel's advice and began building up useful contacts in each sector of the city – a task which was made easier when people learned he was in control of a newspaper which was read by a million people every day (his figures).

Almost all the Germans he came across assumed, by the way he conducted himself, that he had to be a general; everyone else was left in no doubt that even if he wasn't, he had the backing of the top brass. He made sure certain staff officers were mentioned regularly in *Der Telegraf* and after that they rarely queried his requests, however outrageous. He also took advantage of the endless source of publicity provided by the paper to promote himself, and as he was able to write his own copy, he quickly became a celebrity in a city of anonymous uniforms.

Three months after Armstrong met Arno Schultz for the first time, *Der Telegraf* was regularly coming out six days a week, and he was able to report to Colonel Oakshott that the circulation had passed 200,000 copies, and that at this rate it would not be long before they overtook *Der Berliner*. The colonel simply said, 'You're doing a first-class job, Dick.' He wasn't quite sure what Armstrong was actually doing, but he had noticed that the young captain's expenses had crept up to over £20 a week.

Although Dick reported the colonel's praise to Charlotte, she could sense that he was already becoming bored with the job. *Der Telegraf* was selling almost as many copies as *Der Berliner*, and the senior officers in the three Western sectors were always happy to welcome Captain Armstrong to their messes. After all, you only had to whisper a story in his ear, and it would appear in print the following day. As a result, he always had a surplus of Cuban cigars, Charlotte and Sally were never short of nylons, Peter Wakeham could indulge in his favourite tipple of Gordon's gin, and the barrow boys had enough vodka and cigarettes to run a black market on the side.

But Dick was frustrated by the fact that he didn't seem to be making any progress with his own career. Although promotion had been hinted at often enough, nothing seemed to happen in a city that was already far too full of majors and colonels, most of whom were simply sitting around on their backsides waiting to be sent home.

Dick began discussing with Charlotte the possibility of returning to England, especially since Britain's newly-elected Labour Prime Minister, Clement Attlee, had asked soldiers to come home as soon as possible because there was a surplus of jobs waiting for them. Despite their comfortable lifestyle in Berlin Charlotte seemed delighted by the idea, and encouraged Dick to think about requesting an early discharge. The next day he asked to see the colonel.

'Are you sure that's what you really want to do?' said Oakshott.

'Yes, sir,' replied Dick. 'Now that everything's working smoothly, Schultz is quite capable of running the paper without me.'

'Fair enough. I'll try and speed the process up.'

A few hours later Armstrong heard the name of Klaus Lauber for the first time, and slowed the process down.

~o~

When Armstrong visited the print works later that morning, Schultz informed him that for the first time they had sold more copies than *Der Berliner*, and that he felt perhaps they should start thinking about bringing out a Sunday paper.

'I can't see any reason why you shouldn't,' said Dick, sounding a little bored.

'I only wish we could charge the same price as we did before the war,' Schultz sighed. 'With these sales figures we would be making a handsome profit. I know it must be hard for you to believe, Captain Armstrong, but in those days I was considered a prosperous and successful man.'

'Perhaps you will be again,' said Armstrong. 'And sooner than you think,' he added, looking out of the grimy window on to a pavement crowded with weary-looking people. He was about to tell Schultz that he intended to hand the whole operation over to him and return to England, when the German said, 'I'm not sure that will be possible any longer.'

'Why not?' asked Armstrong. 'The paper belongs to you, and everybody knows that the restrictions on shareholding for German citizens are about to be lifted.'

'That may well be the case, Captain Armstrong, but unfortunately I no longer own any shares in the company.'

Armstrong paused, and began to choose his words carefully. 'Really? What made you sell them?' he asked, still looking out of the window.

'I didn't sell them,' said Schultz. 'I virtually gave them away.'

'I'm not sure I understand,' said Armstrong, turning to face him.

'It's quite simple, really,' said Schultz. 'Soon after Hitler came to power, he passed a law which disqualified Jews from owning newspapers. I was forced to dispose of my shares to a third party.'

'So who owns *Der Telegraf* now?' asked Armstrong.

'An old friend of mine called Klaus Lauber,' said Schultz. 'He was a civil servant with the Ministry of Works. We met at a local chess club many years ago, and used to play every Tuesday and Friday – another thing they wouldn't allow me to continue after Hitler came to power.'

'But if Lauber is so close a friend, he must be in a position to sell the shares back to you.'

'I suppose that's still possible. After all, he only paid a nominal sum for them, on the understanding that he would return them to me once the war was over.'

'And I'm sure he will keep his word,' said Armstrong. 'Especially if he was such a close friend.'

'I'm sure he would too, if we hadn't lost touch during the war. I haven't set eyes on him since December 1942. Like so many Germans, he's become just another statistic.'

'But you must know where he lived,' said Armstrong, tapping his swagger stick lightly on the side of his leg.

'His family were moved out of Berlin soon after the bombing started, which was when I lost contact with him. Heaven knows where he is now,' he added with a sigh.

Dick felt he had gleaned all the information he required. 'So, what's happening about that article on the opening of the new airport?' he asked, changing the subject.

'We already have a photographer out at the site, and I thought I'd send a reporter to interview . . .' Schultz continued dutifully, but Armstrong's mind was elsewhere. As soon as he was back at his desk he asked Sally to call the Allied Control Commission and find out who owned *Der Telegraf*.

'I've always assumed it was Arno,' she said.

'Me too,' said Armstrong, 'but apparently not. He was forced to sell his shares to a Klaus Lauber soon after Hitler came to power. So I need to know: one, does Lauber still own the shares? Two, if he does, is he still alive? And three, if he's still alive, where the hell is he? And Sally, don't mention this to anyone. That includes Lieutenant Wakeham.'

It took Sally three days to confirm that Major Klaus Otto Lauber was still registered with the Allied Control Commission as the legal owner of *Der Telegraf*.

'But is he still alive?' asked Armstrong.

'Very much so,' said Sally. 'And what's more, he's holed up in Wales.'

'In Wales?' echoed Armstrong. 'How can that be?'

'It seems that Major Lauber is presently being held in an internment camp just outside Bridgend, where he's spent the last three years, since being captured while serving with Rommel's Afrika Korps.'

'What else have you been able to find out?' asked Armstrong.

'That's about it,' said Sally. 'I fear the major did not have a good war.'

'Well done, Sally. But I still want to know anything else you can find out about him. And I mean anything: date and place of birth, education, how long he was at the Ministry of Works, right up to the day he arrived in Bridgend. See that you use up every favour we're owed, and pawn a few more if you need to. I'm off to see Oakshott. Anything else I should be worrying about?'

'There's a young journalist from the *Oxford Mail* hoping to see you. He's been waiting for nearly an hour.'

'Put him off until tomorrow.'

'But he wrote to you asking for an appointment, and you agreed to see him.'

'Put him off until tomorrow,' Armstrong repeated.

Sally had come to know that tone of voice, and after getting rid of Mr Townsend she dropped everything and set about researching the undistinguished career of Major Klaus Lauber.

When Dick left the office, Private Benson drove him over to the commanding officer's quarters on the other side of the sector.

'You do come up with the strangest requests,' Colonel Oakshott said after he had outlined his idea.

'I think you will find, sir, that in the long term this can only help cement better relations between the occupying forces and the citizens of Berlin.'

'Well, Dick, I know you understand these things far better than I do, but in this case I can't begin to guess how our masters will react.'

'You might point out to them, sir, that if we can show the Germans that our prisoners of war – their husbands, sons and fathers – are receiving fair and decent treatment at the hands of the British, it could turn out to be a massive public relations coup for us, especially remembering the way the Nazis treated the Jews.'

'I'll do the best I can,' promised the colonel. 'How many camps do you want to visit?'

'I think just one to start with,' said Armstrong. 'And perhaps two or three more at some time in the future, should my first sortie prove successful.' He smiled. 'I hope that will give "our masters" less reason to panic.'

'Do you have anywhere in particular in mind?' asked the colonel.

'Intelligence informs me that the ideal camp for such an exercise is probably the one a few miles outside Bridgend.'

—◇—

It took the colonel a little longer to get Captain Armstrong's request granted than it did Sally to discover all there was to know about Klaus Lauber. Dick read through her notes again and again, searching for an angle.

Lauber had been born in Dresden in 1896. He served in the first war, rising to the rank of captain. After the Armistice he had joined the Ministry of Works in Berlin. Although only on the reserve list, he had been called up in December 1942, and given the rank of major. He was shipped out to North Africa and put in charge of a unit which built bridges and, soon afterwards, of one that was ordered to destroy them. He had been captured in March 1943 during the battle of El-Agheila, was shipped to Britain, and was presently held in an internment camp just outside Bridgend. In Lauber's file at the War Office in Whitehall there was no mention of his owning any shares in *Der Telegraf*.

When Armstrong had finished reading the notes yet again, he asked Sally a question. She quickly checked in the Berlin Officers' Handbook and gave him three names.

'Any of them serving with the King's Own or the North Staffs?' asked Armstrong.

'No,' replied Sally, 'but one is with the Royal Rifle Brigade, who use the same messing facilities as we do.'

'Good,' said Dick. 'Then he's our man.'

'By the way,' said Sally, 'what shall I do about the young journalist from the *Oxford Mail*?'

Dick paused. 'Tell him I had to visit the American sector, and that I'll try and catch up with him some time tomorrow.'

It was unusual for Armstrong to dine in the British officers' mess, because with his influence and freedom to roam the city he was always welcome in any dining hall in Berlin. In any case, every officer knew that when it came to eating, you always tried to find some excuse to be in the French sector. However, on that particular Tuesday evening Captain Armstrong arrived at the mess a few minutes after six, and asked the corporal serving behind the bar if he knew a Captain Stephen Hallet.

'Oh yes, sir,' the corporal replied. 'Captain Hallet usually comes in around six-thirty. I think you'll find he works in the Legal Department,' he added, telling Armstrong something he already knew.

Armstrong remained at the bar, sipping a whisky and glancing up at the entrance as each new officer came in. He would then look enquiringly towards the corporal, who shook his head each time, until a thin, prematurely balding man who would have made even the smallest uniform look baggy headed towards the bar. He ordered a Tom Collins, and the barman gave Armstrong a quick nod. Armstrong moved across to take the stool beside him.

He introduced himself, and quickly learned that Hallet couldn't wait to be demobbed and get back to Lincoln's Inn Fields to continue his career as a solicitor.

'I'll see if I can help speed the process up,' said Armstrong, knowing full well that when it came to that department he had absolutely no influence at all.

'That's very decent of you, old chap,' replied Hallet. 'Don't hesitate to let me know if there's anything I can do for you in return.'

'Shall we grab a bite?' suggested Armstrong, slipping off his stool and guiding the lawyer towards a quiet table for two in the corner.

After they had ordered from the set menu and Armstrong had asked the corporal for a bottle of wine from his private rack, he guided his companion onto a subject on which he did need some advice.

'I understand only too well the problems some of these Germans are facing,' said Armstrong, as he filled his companion's glass, 'being Jewish myself.'

'You do surprise me,' said Hallet. 'But then, Captain Armstrong,' he added as he sipped the wine, 'you are obviously a man who's full of surprises.'

Armstrong looked at his companion carefully, but couldn't detect any signs of irony. 'You may be able to assist me with an interesting case that's recently landed on my desk,' he ventured.

'I'll be delighted to help if I possibly can,' said Hallet.

'That's good of you,' said Armstrong, not touching his glass. 'I was wondering what rights a German Jew has if he sold his shares in a company to a non-Jew before the war. Can he claim them back now the war is over?'

The lawyer paused for a moment, and this time he did look

a little puzzled. 'Only if the person who purchased the shares is decent enough to sell them to him. Otherwise there's absolutely nothing they can do about it. The Nuremberg Laws of 1935, if I remember correctly.'

'That doesn't seem fair,' was all Armstrong said.

'No,' came back the reply, as the lawyer took another sip from his glass of wine. 'It isn't. But that was the law at the time, and the way things are set up now, there is no civil authority to override it. I must say, this claret is really quite excellent. However did you manage to lay your hands on it?'

'A good friend of mine in the French sector seems to have an endless supply. If you like, I could send you over a dozen bottles.'

–◦–

The following morning, Colonel Oakshott received authority to allow Captain Armstrong to visit an internment camp in Britain at any time during the next month. 'But they have restricted you to Bridgend,' he added.

'I quite understand,' said Armstrong.

'And they have also made it clear,' continued the colonel, reading from a memo pad on the desk in front of him, 'that you cannot interview more than three prisoners, and that none of them may be above the rank of colonel – strict orders from Security.'

'I'm sure I can manage despite those limitations,' said Armstrong.

'Let's hope this all proves worthwhile, Dick. I still have my doubts, you know.'

'I hope to prove you wrong, sir.'

Once Armstrong had returned to his office, he asked Sally to sort out his travel arrangements.

'When do you want to go?' she asked.

'Tomorrow,' he replied.

'Silly question,' she said.

Sally got him on a flight to London the next day, after a

general had cancelled at the last moment. She also arranged for him to be met by a car and driver who would take him straight to Wales.

'But captains aren't entitled to a car and driver,' he said when Sally handed over his travel documents.

'They are if the brigadier wants his daughter's photo on the front page of *Der Telegraf* when she visits Berlin next month.'

'Why should he want that?' said Armstrong.

'My bet is that he can't get her married off in England,' said Sally. 'And as I've discovered, anything in a skirt is jumped on over here.'

Armstrong laughed. 'If I were paying you, Sally, you'd get a rise. Meanwhile, keep me informed on anything else you find out about Lauber, and again, I mean anything.'

Over dinner that night, Dick told Charlotte that one of the reasons he was going to Britain was to see if he could find a job once his demob papers had been processed. Although she forced a smile, lately she wasn't always sure that he was telling her the whole story. If she ever pressed him, he invariably hid behind the words 'top secret', and tapped his nose with his forefinger, just the way he had seen Colonel Oakshott do.

–◦–

Private Benson dropped him at the airport the following morning. A voice came over the Tannoy in the departure lounge and announced: 'Would Captain Armstrong please report to the nearest military phone before he boards the plane.' Armstrong would have taken the call, if his plane hadn't already been taxiing down the runway.

When he landed in London three hours later, Armstrong marched across the tarmac towards a corporal leaning against a shiny black Austin and holding a placard with the name 'Captain Armstrong' printed on it. The corporal sprang to attention and saluted the moment he spotted the officer advancing towards him.

'I need to be driven to Bridgend immediately,' he said, before the man had a chance to open his mouth. They headed down the A40, and Armstrong dozed off within minutes. He didn't wake until the corporal said, 'Only a couple more miles and we'll be there, sir.'

When they drove up to the camp, memories flooded back of his own internment in Liverpool. But this time when the car passed through the gates, the guards sprang to attention and saluted. The corporal brought the Austin to a halt outside the commandant's office.

As he walked in, a captain rose from behind a desk to greet him. 'Roach,' he said. 'Delighted to make your acquaintance.' He thrust out his hand and Armstrong shook it. Captain Roach displayed no medals on his uniform, and looked as if he'd never even crossed the Channel on a day trip, let alone come in contact with the enemy. 'No one has actually explained to me how I can help you,' he said as he ushered Armstrong towards a comfortable chair by the fire.

'I need to see a list of all the prisoners detailed to this camp,' said Armstrong, without wasting any time on banalities. 'I intend to interview three of them for a report I'm preparing for the Control Commission in Berlin.'

'That's easy enough,' said the captain. 'But why did they choose Bridgend? Most of the Nazi generals are locked up in Yorkshire.'

'I'm aware of that,' said Armstrong, 'but I wasn't given a lot of choice.'

'Fair enough. Now, do you have any idea what type of person you want to interview, or shall I just pick a few out at random?' Captain Roach handed over a clipboard, and Armstrong quickly ran his finger down the list of typed names. He smiled. 'I'll see one corporal, one lieutenant and one major,' he said, putting a cross by three names. He handed the clipboard back to the captain.

Roach studied his selection. 'The first two will be easy enough,' he said. 'But I'm afraid you won't be able to interview Major Lauber.'

'I have the full authority of . . .'

'It wouldn't matter if you had the full authority of Mr Attlee himself,' interrupted Roach. 'When it comes to Lauber, there's nothing I can do for you.'

'Why not?' snapped Armstrong.

'Because he died two weeks ago. I sent him back to Berlin in a coffin last Monday.'

12

MELBOURNE COURIER

12 SEPTEMBER 1950

Sir Graham Townsend Dies

The cortège came to a halt outside the cathedral. Keith stepped out of the leading car, took his mother's arm and guided her up the steps, followed by his sisters. As they entered the building, the congregation rose from their seats. A sidesman led them down the aisle to the empty front pew. Keith could feel several pairs of eyes boring into him, all asking the same question: 'Are you up to it?' A moment later the coffin was borne past them and placed on a catafalque in front of the altar.

The service was conducted by the Bishop of Melbourne, and the prayers read by the Reverend Charles Davidson. The hymns Lady Townsend had selected would have made the old man chuckle: 'To be a Pilgrim', 'Rock of Ages' and 'Fight the Good Fight'. David Jakeman, a former editor of the *Courier*, gave the address. He talked of Sir Graham's energy, his enthusiasm for life, his lack of cant, his love of his family, and of how much he would be missed by all those who had known him. He ended his homily by reminding the congregation that Sir Graham had been succeeded by a son and heir.

After the blessing, Lady Townsend took her son's arm once more and followed the pallbearers as they carried the coffin back out of the cathedral and towards the burial plot.

'Ashes to ashes, dust to dust,' intoned the archbishop as the oak casket was lowered into the ground, and the gravediggers began to shovel sods of earth on top of it. Keith raised his head and glanced around at those who circled the grave. Friends, relations, colleagues, politicians, rivals, bookies – even the odd vulture who, Keith suspected, had come simply to pick over the bones – looked down into the gaping hole.

After the archbishop had made the sign of the cross, Keith led his mother slowly back to the waiting limousine. Just before they reached it, she stopped and turned to face those who silently followed behind her. For the next hour she shook hands with every mourner, until the last one had finally departed.

Neither Keith nor his mother spoke on the journey back to Toorak, and as soon as they arrived at the house Lady Townsend climbed the great marble staircase and retired to her bedroom. Keith went off to the kitchen, where Florrie was preparing a light lunch. He laid a tray and carried it up to his mother's room. When he reached her door he knocked quietly before going in. She was sitting in her favourite chair by the window. His mother didn't move as he placed the tray on the table in front of her. He kissed her on the forehead, turned and left her. He then took a long walk around the grounds, retracing the steps he had so often taken with his father. Now that the funeral was over, he knew he would have to broach the one subject she had been avoiding.

Lady Townsend reappeared just before eight that evening, and together they went through to the dining room. Again she spoke only of his father, often repeating the same sentiments she had voiced the previous night. She only picked at her food, and after the main course had been cleared away she rose without warning and walked through to the drawing room.

When she took her usual place by the fire, Keith remained standing for a moment before sitting in his father's chair. Once the maid had served them with coffee, his mother leaned forward, warmed her hands and asked him the question he had waited so patiently to hear.

'What do you intend to do now you're back in Australia?'

'First thing tomorrow I'll go in and see the editor of the

Courier. There are several changes that need to be made quickly if we're ever going to challenge the *Age*.' He waited for her response.

'Keith,' she said eventually, 'I'm sorry to have to tell you that we no longer own the *Courier*.'

Keith was so stunned by this piece of information that he didn't respond.

His mother continued to warm her hands. 'As you know, your father left everything to me in his will, and I have always had an abhorrence of debt in any form. Perhaps if he had left the newspapers to you . . .'

'But Mother, I . . .' began Keith.

'Try not to forget, Keith, that you've been away for nearly five years. When I last saw you, you were a schoolboy, reluctantly boarding the SS *Stranthedan*. I had no way of knowing if . . .'

'But Father wouldn't have wanted you to sell the *Courier*. It was the first paper he was ever associated with.'

'And it was losing money every week. When the Kenwright Corporation offered me the chance to get out, leaving us without any liabilities, the board recommended I accept their offer.'

'But you didn't even give me the chance to see if I could turn it round. I'm well aware that both papers have been losing circulation for years. That's why I've been working on a plan to do something about it, a plan which Father seemed to be coming round to.'

'I'm afraid that won't be possible,' said his mother. 'Sir Colin Grant, the chairman of the *Adelaide Messenger*, has just made me an offer of £150,000 for the *Gazette*, and the board will be considering it at our next meeting.'

'But why would we want to sell the *Gazette*?' said Keith in disbelief.

'Because we've been fighting a losing battle with the *Messenger* for several years, and their offer appears to be extremely generous in the circumstances.'

'Mother,' said Keith, standing up to face her. 'I didn't return home to sell the *Gazette*, in fact exactly the reverse. It's my long-term aim to take over the *Messenger*.'

'Keith, that's just not realistic in our current financial situation. In any case, the board would never go along with it.'

'Not at the moment, perhaps, but it will once we're selling more copies than they are.'

'You're so like your father, Keith,' said his mother, looking up at him.

'Just give me an opportunity to prove myself,' said Keith. 'You'll find that I've learned a great deal during my time in Fleet Street. I've come home to put that knowledge to good use.'

Lady Townsend stared into the fire for some time before she replied. 'Sir Colin has given me ninety days to consider his offer.' She paused again. 'I will give you exactly the same time to convince me that I should turn him down.'

◄◦►

When Townsend stepped off the plane at Adelaide the following morning, the first thing he noticed as he entered the arrivals hall was that the *Messenger* was placed above the *Gazette* in the newspaper rack. He dropped his bags and switched the papers round, so that the *Gazette* was on top, then purchased a copy of both.

While he stood in line waiting for a taxi, he noted that of the seventy-three people who walked out of the airport, twelve were carrying the *Messenger* while only seven had the *Gazette*. As the taxi drove him into the city, he wrote down these findings on the back of his ticket, with the intention of briefing Frank Bailey, the editor of the *Gazette*, as soon as he reached the office. He spent the rest of the journey flicking through both papers, and had to admit that the *Messenger* was a more interesting read. However, he didn't feel that was an opinion he could express on his first day in town.

Townsend was dropped outside the offices of the *Gazette*. He left his bags in reception and took the lift to the third floor.

No one gave him a second look as he headed through the rows of journalists seated at their desks, tapping away on their typewriters. Without knocking on the editor's door, he walked straight into the morning conference.

A surprised Frank Bailey rose from behind his desk, held out his hand and said, 'Keith, it's great to see you after all this time.'

'And it's good to see you,' said Townsend.

'We weren't expecting you until tomorrow.' Bailey turned to face the horseshoe of journalists seated round his desk. 'This is Sir Graham's son, Keith, who will be taking over from his father as publisher. Those of you who have been around a few years will remember when he was last here as . . .' Frank hesitated.

'As my father's son,' said Townsend.

The comment was greeted with a ripple of laughter.

'Please carry on as if I weren't here,' said Townsend. 'I don't intend to be the sort of publisher who interferes with editorial decisions.' He walked over to the corner of the room, sat on the window ledge and watched as Bailey continued to conduct the morning conference. He hadn't lost any of his skills, or, it seemed, his desire to use the paper to campaign on behalf of any underdog he felt was getting a rough deal.

'Right, what's looking like the lead story tomorrow?' he asked. Three hands shot up.

'Dave,' said the editor, pointing a pencil at the chief crime reporter. 'Let's hear your bid.'

'It looks as if we might get a verdict on the Sammy Taylor trial today. The judge is expected to finish his summing-up later this afternoon.'

'Well, if the way he's conducted the trial so far is anything to go by, the poor bastard hasn't a hope in hell. That man would string Taylor up given the slightest excuse.'

'I know,' said Dave.

'If it's a guilty verdict, I'll give the front page over to it and write a leader on the travesty of justice any Aboriginal can expect in our courts. Is the courthouse still being picketed by Abo protesters?'

'Sure is. It's become a night-and-day vigil. They've taken to sleeping on the pavement since we published those pictures of their leaders being dragged off by the police.'

'Right, if we get a verdict today, and it's guilty, you get the front page. Jane,' he said, turning to the features editor, 'I'll need a thousand words on Abos' rights and how disgracefully this trial has been conducted. Travesty of justice, racial prejudice, you know the sort of thing I want.'

'What if the jury decides he's not guilty?' asked Dave.

'In that unlikely event, you get the right-hand column on the front page and Jane can give me five hundred words for page seven on the strength of the jury system, Australia at last coming out of the dark ages, etc., etc.'

Bailey turned his attention to the other side of the room, and pointed his pencil at a woman whose hand had remained up. 'Maureen,' he said.

'We may have a mystery illness at the Royal Adelaide Hospital. Three young children have died in the last ten days and the hospital's chief administrator, Gyles Dunn, is refusing to make a statement of any kind, however hard I push him.'

'Are all the children local?'

'Yep,' replied Maureen. 'They all come from the Port Adelaide area.'

'Ages?' said Frank.

'Four, three and four. Two girls, one boy.'

'Right, get hold of their parents, especially the mothers. I want pictures, history of the families, everything you can find out about them. Try and discover if the families have any connection with each other, however remote. Are they related? Do they know each other or work at the same place? Do they have any shared interests, however remote, that could just connect the three cases? And I want some sort of statement out of Gyles Dunn, even if it's "No comment."'

Maureen gave Bailey a quick nod before he turned his attention to the picture editor. 'Get me a picture of Dunn looking harassed that will be good enough to put on the front page. You'll have the front-page lead, Maureen, if the Taylor verdict is not guilty, otherwise I'll give you page four with a possible run-on to page five. Try and get pictures of all three children. Family albums is what I'm after – happy, healthy children, preferably on holiday. And I want you to get inside that hospital. If Dunn still refuses to say anything, find someone who will. A doctor, a nurse, even a porter, but make sure the statement is either witnessed or recorded. I don't want another fiasco like the one we had last month with that Mrs Kendal and her complaints against the fire brigade. And Dave,' the editor said, turning his attention back to the chief crime reporter, 'I'll need to know as soon as possible if the verdict on Taylor is likely to be held up, so we can get to work on the layout of the front page. Anyone else got anything to offer?'

'Thomas Playford will be making what's promised to be an important statement at eleven o'clock this morning,' said Jim West, a political reporter. Groans went up around the room.

'I'm not interested,' said Frank, 'unless he's going to announce his resignation. If it's the usual photo call and public relations exercise, producing more bogus figures about what he's supposed to have achieved for the local community, relegate it to a single column on page eleven. Sport, Harry?'

A rather overweight man, seated in the corner opposite Townsend, blinked and turned to a young associate who sat behind him. The young man whispered in his ear.

'Oh, yes,' the sports editor said. 'Some time today the selectors will be announcing our team for the first Test against England, starting on Thursday.'

'Are there likely to be any Adelaide lads in the side?'

Townsend sat through the hour-long conference but didn't say anything, despite feeling that several questions had been left unanswered. When the conference finally broke up, he waited until all the journalists had left before he handed Frank the notes he had written earlier in the back of the taxi. The editor glanced at the scribbled figures, and promised he would study them more carefully just as soon as he had a minute. Without thinking, he deposited them in his out tray.

'Do drop in whenever you want to catch up on anything,

Keith,' he said. 'My door is always open.' Townsend nodded. As he turned to leave, Frank added, 'You know, your father and I always had a good working relationship. Until quite recently he used to fly over from Melbourne to see me at least once a month.'

Townsend smiled and closed the editor's door quietly behind him. He walked back through the tapping typewriters, and took the lift to the top floor.

He felt a shiver as he entered his father's office, conscious for the first time that he would never have the chance to prove to him that he would be a worthy successor. He glanced around the room, his eyes settling on the picture of his mother on the corner of the desk. He smiled at the thought that she was the one person who need have no fear of being replaced in the near future.

He heard a little cough, and turned round to find Miss Bunting standing by the door. She had served as his father's secretary for the past thirty-seven years. As a child Townsend had often heard his mother describe Bunty as 'a wee slip of a girl'. He doubted if she was five feet tall, even if you measured to the top of her neatly tied bun. He had never seen her hair done in any other way, and Bunty certainly made no concession to fashion. Her straight skirt and sensible cardigan allowed only a glimpse of her ankles and neck, she wore no jewellery, and apparently no one had ever told her about nylons. 'Welcome home, Mr Keith,' she said, her Scottish accent undiminished by nearly forty years of living in Adelaide. 'I've just been getting things in order, so that everything would be ready for your return. I am of course due for retirement soon, but will quite understand if you want to bring in someone new to replace me before then.'

Townsend felt that she must have rehearsed every word of that little speech, and had been determined to deliver it before he had a chance to say anything. He smiled at her. 'I shall not be looking for anyone to replace you, Miss Bunting.' He had no idea what her first name was, only that his father called her

'Bunty'. 'The one change I would appreciate is if you went back to calling me Keith.'

She smiled. 'Where would you like to begin?'

'I'll spend the rest of the day going over the files, then I'll start first thing tomorrow morning.'

Bunty looked as if she wanted to say something, but bit her lip. 'Will first thing mean the same as it did for your father?' she asked innocently.

'I'm afraid it will,' replied Townsend with a grin.

—◦—

Townsend was back at the *Gazette* by seven the following morning. He took the lift to the second floor, and walked around the empty desks of the advertising and small ads department. Even with nobody around, he could sense the floor was inefficiently run. Papers were strewn all over desks, files had been left open, and several lights had obviously been burning all through the night. He began to realise just how long his father must have been away from the office.

The first employee strolled in at ten past nine.

'Who are you?' asked Townsend, as she walked across the room.

'Ruth,' she said. 'And who are you?'

'I'm Keith Townsend.'

'Oh, yes, Sir Graham's son,' she said flatly, and walked over to her desk.

'Who runs this department?' asked Townsend.

'Mr Harris,' she replied, sitting down and taking a compact out of her bag.

'And when can I expect to see him?'

'Oh, he usually gets in around nine-thirty, ten.'

'Does he?' said Townsend. 'And which is his office?' The young woman pointed across the floor to the far corner of the room.

Mr Harris appeared in his office at 9.47, by which time Townsend had been through most of his files. 'What the hell do you think you're doing?' were Harris's first words when he found Townsend sitting behind his desk, studying a sheaf of papers.

'Waiting for you,' said Townsend. 'I don't expect my advertising manager to be strolling in just before ten o'clock.'

'Nobody who works for a newspaper starts work much before ten. Even the tea boy knows that,' said Harris.

'When I was the tea boy on the *Daily Express*, Lord Beaverbrook was sitting at his desk by eight o'clock every morning.'

'But I rarely get away before six in the evening,' Harris protested.

'A decent journalist rarely gets home before eight, and the backbench staff should consider themselves lucky if they're away much before midnight. Starting tomorrow, you and I will meet in my office every morning at eight-thirty, and the rest of your staff will be at their desks by nine. If anyone can't manage that, they can start studying the Situations Vacant column on the back page of the paper. Do I make myself clear?'

Harris pursed his lips and nodded.

'Good. The first thing I want from you is a budget for the next three months, with a clear breakdown of how our line prices compare with the *Messenger*. I want it on my desk by the time I come in tomorrow.' He rose from Harris's chair.

'It may not be possible to have all those figures ready for you by this time tomorrow,' protested Harris.

'In that case, you can start studying the Situations Vacant column as well,' said Townsend. 'But not in my time.'

He strode out, leaving Harris shaking, and took the lift up one floor to the circulation department, where he wasn't surprised to encounter exactly the same *laissez-faire* attitude. An hour later he left that department with more than one of them shaking, though he had to admit that a young man from Brisbane called Mel Carter, who had recently been appointed as the department's deputy manager, had impressed him.

Frank Bailey was surprised to see 'young Keith' back in the

office so soon, and even more surprised when he returned to his place on the window ledge for the morning conference. Bailey was relieved that Townsend didn't offer any opinions, but couldn't help noticing that he was continuously taking notes.

By the time Townsend reached his own office, it was eleven o'clock. He immediately set about going through his mail with Miss Bunting. She had laid it all out on his desk in separate files with different-coloured markers, the purpose of which, she explained, was to make sure that he dealt with the real priorities when he was running short of time.

Two hours later, Townsend realised why his father had held 'Bunty' in such high regard, and was wondering not when he would replace her, but just how long she would be willing to stay on.

'I've left the most important matter until last,' said Bunty. 'The latest offer from the *Messenger*. Sir Colin Grant called earlier this morning to welcome you home and to make sure that you had received his letter.'

'Did he?' said Townsend with a smile, as he flicked open the file marked 'Confidential' and skimmed through a letter from Jervis, Smith & Thomas, the lawyers who had represented the *Messenger* for as long as he could remember. He stopped when he came across the figure £150,000, and frowned. He then read the minutes of the previous month's board meeting, which clearly showed the directors' complacent attitude to the bid. But that meeting had taken place before his mother had given him a ninety-day stay of execution.

'Dear Sir,' dictated Townsend, as Bunty flicked over the next page of her shorthand pad. 'I have received your letter of the twelfth inst. New paragraph. In order not to waste any more of your time, let me make it clear that the *Gazette* is not for sale, and never will be. Yours faithfully . . .'

Townsend leaned back in his chair and recalled the last time he had met the chairman of the *Messenger*. Like many failed politicians, Sir Colin was pompous and opinionated, particularly with the young. 'The seen-and-not-heard brigade,' was how he described children, if Townsend remembered correctly. He wondered how long it would be before he heard or saw him again.

—◄o►—

Two days later, Townsend was studying Harris's advertising report when Bunty popped her head round the door to say that Sir Colin Grant was on the line. Townsend nodded and picked up the phone.

'Keith, my boy. Welcome home,' the old man began. 'I've just read your letter, and wondered if you were aware that I had a verbal agreement with your mother concerning the sale of the *Gazette*?'

'My mother told you, Sir Colin, that she would be giving your offer her serious consideration. She made no verbal commitment, and anyone who suggests otherwise is . . .'

'Now hold on, young fellow,' interrupted Sir Colin. 'I'm only acting in good faith. As you well know, your father and I were close friends.'

'But my father is no longer with us, Sir Colin, so in future you will have to deal with me. And we are not close friends.'

'Well, if that's your attitude, there seems no point in mentioning that I was going to increase my offer to £170,000.'

'No point at all, Sir Colin, because I still wouldn't consider it.'

'You will in time,' barked the older man, 'because within six months I'll run you off the streets, and then you'll be only too happy to take £50,000 for whatever remains of the bits and pieces.' Sir Colin paused. 'Feel free to call me when you change your mind.'

Townsend put the phone down and asked Bunty to tell the editor that he wanted to see him immediately.

Miss Bunting hesitated.

'Is there some problem, Bunty?'

'Only that your father used to go down and see the editor in his office.'

'Did he really?' said Townsend, remaining seated.

'I'll ask him to come up straight away.'

Townsend turned to the back page, and studied the Flats

for Rent column while he waited. He had already decided that the journey to Melbourne every weekend stole too many precious hours of his time. He wondered how long he'd be able to hold off telling his mother.

Frank Bailey stormed into his office a few minutes later, but Townsend couldn't see the expression on his face; his head remained down as he pretended to be absorbed in the back page. He circled a box, looked up at the editor and passed him a piece of paper. 'I want you to print this letter from Jervis, Smith & Thomas on the front page tomorrow, Frank, and I'll have three hundred words ready for the leader within the hour.'

'But . . .' said Frank.

'And dig out the worst picture you can find of Sir Colin Grant and put it alongside the letter.'

'But I'd planned to lead on the Taylor trial tomorrow,' said the editor. 'He's innocent, and we're known as a campaigning paper.'

'We're also known as a paper that's losing money,' said Townsend. 'In any case, the Taylor trial was yesterday's news. You can devote as much space to him as you like, but tomorrow it won't be on the front page.'

'Anything else?' asked Frank sarcastically.

'Yes,' said Townsend calmly. 'I expect to see the page-one layout on my desk before I leave this evening.'

Frank strode angrily out of the office, without uttering another word.

'Next I want to see the advertising manager,' Townsend told Bunty when she reappeared. He opened the file Harris had delivered a day late, and stared down at the carelessly compiled figures. That meeting turned out to be even shorter than Frank's, and while Harris was clearing his desk, Townsend called for the deputy circulation manager, Mel Carter.

When the young man entered the room, the look on his face indicated that he too was expecting to be told that his desk should be cleared by the end of the morning.

'Have a seat, Mel,' said Townsend. He looked down at his file. 'I see you've recently joined us on a three-month trial. Let me make it clear from the outset that I'm only interested in results: you've got ninety days, starting today, to prove yourself as advertising manager.'

The young man looked surprised but relieved.

'So tell me,' said Townsend, 'if you could change one thing about the *Gazette*, what would it be?'

'The back page,' said Mel without hesitation. 'I'd move the small ads to an inside page.'

'Why?' asked Townsend. 'It's the page which generates our largest income: a little over £3,000 a day, if I remember correctly.'

'I realise that,' said Mel. 'But the *Messenger* has recently put sport on the back page and taken another 10,000 readers away from us. They've worked out that you can put the small ads on any page, because people are far more interested in circulation figures than they are in positioning when they decide where to place an advertisement. I could give you a more detailed breakdown of the figures by six o'clock tonight if that would help convince you.'

'It certainly would,' said Townsend. 'And if you have any other bright ideas, Mel, don't hesitate to share them with me. You'll find my door is always open.'

It was a change for Townsend to see someone leaving his office with a smile on their face. He checked his watch as Bunty walked in.

'Time for you to be leaving for your lunch with the circulation manager of the *Messenger*.'

'I wonder if I can afford it,' said Townsend, checking his watch.

'Oh yes,' she said. 'Your father always thought the Caxton Grill very reasonable. It's Pilligrini's he considered extravagant, and he only ever took your mother there.'

'It's not the price of the meal I'm worried about, Bunty. It's how much he'll demand if he agrees to leave the *Messenger* and join us.'

—◇—

Townsend waited for a week before he called for Frank Bailey and told him that the small ads would no longer be appearing on the back page.

'But the small ads have been on the back page for over seventy years,' was the editor's first reaction.

'If that's true, I can't think of a better argument for moving them,' said Townsend.

'But our readers don't like change.'

'And the *Messenger's* do?' said Townsend. 'That's one of the many reasons they're selling far more copies than we are.'

'Are you willing to sacrifice our long tradition simply to gain a few more readers?'

'I can see you've got the message at last,' said Townsend, not blinking.

'But your mother assured me that . . .'

'My mother is not in charge of the day-to-day running of this paper. She gave me that responsibility.' He didn't add, but only for ninety days.

The editor held his breath for a moment before he said calmly, 'Are you hoping I'll resign?'

'Certainly not,' said Townsend firmly. 'But I am hoping you'll help me run a profitable newspaper.'

He was surprised by the editor's next question.

'Can you hold the decision off for another two weeks?'

'Why?' asked Townsend.

'Because my sports editor isn't expected back from holiday until the end of the month.'

'A sports editor who takes three weeks off in the middle of the cricket season probably wouldn't even notice if his desk had been replaced when he came back,' snapped Townsend.

The sports editor handed in his resignation on the day he returned, which deprived Townsend of the pleasure of sacking him. Within hours he had appointed the twenty-five-year-old cricket correspondent to take his place.

Frank Bailey came charging up to Townsend's room a few moments after he heard the news. 'It's the editor's job to make appointments,' he began, even before he had closed the door to Townsend's office, 'not . . .'

'Not any longer it isn't,' said Townsend.

The two men stared at each other for some time before Frank tried again. 'In any case, he's far too young to take on such a responsibility.'

'He's three years older than I am,' said Townsend.

Frank bit his lip. 'May I remind you,' he said, 'that when you visited my office for the first time only four weeks ago, you assured me, and I quote, that "I don't intend to be the sort of publisher who interferes with editorial decisions"?'

Townsend looked up from his desk and reddened slightly.

'I'm sorry, Frank,' he said. 'I lied.'

—<o>—

Long before the ninety days were up, the gap between the circulations of the *Messenger* and the *Gazette* had begun to narrow, and Lady Townsend quite forgot she had ever put a time limit on whether they should accept the *Messenger*'s offer of £150,000.

After looking over several apartments, Townsend eventually found one in an ideal location, and signed the lease within hours. That evening he explained to his mother over the phone that in future, because of the pressure of work, he wouldn't be able to visit her in Toorak every weekend. She didn't seem at all surprised.

When Townsend attended his third board meeting, he demanded that the directors make him chief executive, so no one would be left in any doubt that he was not there simply as the son of his father. By a narrow vote they turned him down. When he rang his mother that night and asked why she thought they had done so, she told him that the majority had considered that the title of publisher was quite enough for anyone who had only just celebrated his twenty-third birthday.

The new circulation manager reported – six months after he had left the *Messenger* to join the *Gazette* – that the gap between the two papers had closed to 32,000. Townsend was delighted by the news, and at the next board meeting he told the directors that the time had come for them to make a takeover bid for the *Messenger*. One or two of the older members only just managed to stop themselves laughing, but then Townsend presented them with the figures, produced something he called trend graphs, and was able to show that the bank had agreed to back him.

Once he had persuaded the majority of his colleagues to go along with the bid, Townsend dictated a letter to Sir Colin, making him an offer of £750,000 for the *Messenger*. Although he received no official acknowledgement of the bid, Townsend's lawyers informed him that Sir Colin had called an emergency board meeting, which would take place the following afternoon.

The lights on the executive floor of the *Messenger* burned late into the night. Townsend, who had been refused entry to the building, paced up and down the pavement outside, waiting to learn the board's decision. After two hours he grabbed a hamburger from a café in the next street, and when he returned to his beat he found the lights on the top floor were still burning. Had a passing policeman spotted him, he might have been arrested for loitering with intent.

The lights on the executive floor were finally switched off just after one, and the directors of the *Messenger* began to stream out of the building. Townsend looked hopefully at each one of them, but they walked straight past him without giving him so much as a glance.

Townsend hung around until he was certain that there was no one other than the cleaners left in the building. He then walked slowly back to the *Gazette* and watched the first edition come off the stone. He knew he wouldn't be able to sleep that night, so he joined the early-morning vans and helped to deliver the first editions around the city. It gave him the chance to make sure the *Gazette* was put above the *Messenger* in the racks.

◄○►

Two days later Bunty placed a letter in the priority file:

> *Dear Mr Townsend,*
> *I have received your letter of the twenty-sixth inst.*
> *In order not to waste any more of your time, let me make it clear the* Messenger *is not for sale, and never will be.*
> *Yours faithfully,*
> *Colin Grant*

Townsend smiled and dropped the letter in the wastepaper basket.

—◇—

Over the next few months Townsend pushed his staff night and day in a relentless drive to overtake his rival. He always made it clear to every one of his team that no one's job was safe – and that included the editor's. Resignations from those who were unable to keep up with the pace of the changes at the *Gazette* were outnumbered by those who left the *Messenger* to join him once they realised it was going to be 'a battle to the death' – a phrase Townsend used whenever he addressed the monthly staff meeting.

A year after Townsend had returned from England, the two papers' circulations were running neck and neck, and he felt the time had come for him to make another call to the chairman of the *Messenger*.

When Sir Colin came on the line, Townsend didn't bother with the normal courtesies. His opening gambit was, 'If £750,000 isn't enough, Sir Colin, what do you consider the paper's actually worth?'

'Far more than you can afford, young man. In any case,' he added, 'as I've already explained, the *Messenger*'s not for sale.'

'Well, not for another six months,' said Townsend.

'Not ever!' shouted Sir Colin down the line.

'Then I'll just have to run you off the streets,' said Townsend. 'And then you'll be only too happy to take £50,000 for whatever remains of the bits and pieces.' He paused. 'Feel free to call me when you change your mind.'

It was Sir Colin's turn to slam the phone down.

◄◊►

On the day the *Gazette* outsold the *Messenger* for the first time, Townsend held a celebration party on the fourth floor, and announced the news in a banner headline above a picture of Sir Colin taken the previous year at his wife's funeral. As each month passed, the gap between the two papers widened, and Townsend never missed an opportunity to inform his readers of the latest circulation figures. He was not surprised when Sir Colin rang and suggested that perhaps the time had come for them to meet.

After weeks of negotiations, it was agreed that the two papers should merge, but not before Townsend had secured the only two concessions he really cared about. The new paper would be printed on his presses, and called the *Gazette Messenger*.

When the newly-designated board met for the first time, Sir Colin was appointed chairman and Townsend chief executive.

Within six months the word *Messenger* had disappeared from the masthead, and all major decisions were being taken without any pretence of consulting the board or its chairman. Few were shocked when Sir Colin offered his resignation, and no one was surprised when Townsend accepted it.

When his mother asked what had caused Sir Colin to resign, Townsend replied that it had been by mutual agreement, because he felt the time had come to make way for a younger man. Lady Townsend wasn't altogether convinced.

THIRD EDITION

Where There's a Will . . .

13

𝕯𝖊𝖗 𝕿𝖊𝖑𝖊𝖌𝖗𝖆𝖋

31 AUGUST 1947

Berlin Food Shortages to Continue

'If Lauber made a will, I need to get my hands on it.'

'Why is getting hold of this will so important?' asked Sally.

'Because I want to know who inherits his shares in *Der Telegraf*.'

'I assume his wife does.'

'No, it's more likely to be Arno Schultz. In which case I'm wasting my time – so the sooner we find out, the better.'

'But I wouldn't know where to begin.'

'Try the Ministry of the Interior. Once Lauber's body was returned to Germany, it became their responsibility.'

Sally looked doubtful.

'Use up every favour we're owed,' said Armstrong, 'and promise anything in return, but find me that will.' He turned to leave. 'Right, I'm off to see Hallet.'

Armstrong left without another word, and was driven to the British officers' mess by Benson. He took the stool at the corner of the bar and ordered a whisky, checking his watch every few minutes.

Stephen Hallet strolled in a few moments after six-thirty had chimed on the grandfather clock in the hall. When he saw Armstrong, he smiled broadly and joined him at the bar.

'Dick. Thank you so much for that case of the Mouton-

Rothschild '29. It really is quite excellent. I must confess I'm trying to ration it until my demob papers come through.'

Armstrong smiled. 'Then we'll just have to see if we can't somehow arrange a more regular supply. Why don't you join me for dinner? Then we can find out why they're making such a fuss about the Chateau Beychevelle '33.'

Over a burnt steak, Captain Hallet experienced the Beychevelle for the first time, while Armstrong found out all he needed to know about probate, and why Lauber's shares would automatically go to Mrs Lauber, as his next of kin, if no will was discovered.

'But what if she's dead too?' asked Armstrong as the steward uncorked a second bottle.

'If she's dead, or can't be traced – ' Hallet sipped his refilled glass, and the smile returned to his lips ' – the original owner would have to wait five years. After that he would probably be able to put in a claim for the shares.'

Because Armstrong was unable to take notes, he found himself repeating questions to make sure he had all the salient information committed to memory. This didn't seem to worry Hallet, who, Armstrong suspected, knew exactly what he was up to but wasn't going to ask too many questions as long as someone kept on filling his glass. Once Armstrong was sure he fully understood the legal position, he made some excuse about having promised his wife he wouldn't be home late, and left the lawyer with a half-full bottle.

After he left the mess, Armstrong made no attempt to return home. He didn't feel like spending another evening explaining to Charlotte why it was taking so long for his demob papers to be processed when several of their friends had already returned to Blighty. Instead he ordered a tired-looking Benson to drive him to the American sector.

His first call was on Max Sackville, with whom he stopped to play a couple of hours of poker. Armstrong lost a few dollars but gained some useful information about American troop movements, which he knew Colonel Oakshott would be grateful to hear about.

He left Max soon after he had lost enough to ensure that he would be invited back again, and strolled across the road and down an alley before dropping into his favourite bar in the American sector. He joined a group of officers who were celebrating their imminent return to the States. A few whiskies later he left the bar, having added to his store of information. But he would happily have traded everything he'd picked up for one glance at Lauber's will. He didn't notice a sober man, wearing civilian clothes, get up and follow him out onto the street.

He was heading back towards his jeep when a voice behind him said, 'Lubji.'

Armstrong stopped dead in his tracks, feeling slightly sick. He swung round to face a man who must have been about his own age, though much shorter and stockier than he was. He was dressed in a plain grey suit, white shirt and dark blue tie. In the unlit street Armstrong couldn't make out the man's features.

'You must be a Czech,' said Armstrong quietly.

'No, Lubji, I am not.'

'Then you're a bloody German,' said Armstrong, clenching his fists and advancing towards him.

'Wrong again,' said the man, not flinching.

'Then who the hell are you?'

'Let's just say I'm a friend.'

'But I don't even know you,' said Armstrong. 'Why don't you stop playing games and tell me what the hell you want.'

'Just to help you,' said the man quietly.

'And how do you propose doing that?' snarled Armstrong.

The man smiled. 'By producing the will you seem so determined to get your hands on.'

'The will?' said Armstrong nervously.

'Ah, I see I have finally touched what the British describe as a "raw nerve".' Armstrong stared down at the man as he placed a hand in his pocket and took out a card. 'Why don't you visit me when you're next in the Russian sector?' he said, handing over his card.

In the dim light, Armstrong couldn't read the name on the card. When he looked up, the man had disappeared into the night.

He walked on a few paces until he came to a gas light, then looked down at the card again.

MAJOR S. TULPANOV

Diplomatic Attaché

Leninplatz, Russian sector

When Armstrong saw Colonel Oakshott the following morning, he reported everything that had happened in the American sector the previous evening and handed over Major Tulpanov's card. The only thing he didn't mention was that Tulpanov had addressed him as Lubji. Oakshott jotted down some notes on the pad in front of him. 'Don't mention this to anyone until I've made one or two enquiries,' he said.

Armstrong was surprised to receive a call soon after he returned to his office: the colonel wanted him to return to headquarters immediately. He was quickly driven back across the sector by Benson. When he walked into Oakshott's room for the second time that morning, he found his commanding officer flanked by two men he had never seen before, in civilian clothes. They introduced themselves as Captain Woodhouse and Major Forsdyke.

'It looks as if you've hit the jackpot with this one, Dick,' said Oakshott, even before Armstrong had sat down. 'It seems your Major Tulpanov is with the KGB. In fact we think he's their number three in the Russian sector. He's considered to be a rising star. These two gentlemen,' he said, 'are with the security service. They would like you to take up Tulpanov's suggestion of a visit, and report back everything you can find out, right down to the brand of cigarettes he smokes.'

'I could go across this afternoon,' said Armstrong.

'No,' said Forsdyke firmly. 'That would be far too obvious. We would prefer you to wait a week or two and make it look more like a routine visit. If you turn up too quickly, he's bound to become suspicious. It's his job to be suspicious, of course, but why make it easy for him? Report to my office on Franklinstrasse at eight tomorrow morning, and I'll see that you're fully briefed.'

Armstrong spent the next ten mornings being taken through routine procedures by the security service. It quickly became clear that they didn't consider him a natural recruit. After all, his knowledge of England was confined to a transit camp in Liverpool, a period as a private soldier in the Pioneer Corps, graduation to the ranks of the North Staffordshire Regiment and a journey through the night to Portsmouth, before being shipped to France. Most of the officers who briefed him would have considered Eton, Trinity and the Guards a more natural qualification for the career they had chosen. 'God is not on our side with this one,' Forsdyke sighed over lunch with his colleague. They hadn't even considered inviting Armstrong to join them.

Despite these misgivings, ten days later Captain Armstrong visited the Russian sector on the pretext of trying to find some spare parts for *Der Telegraf*'s printing presses. Once he had confirmed that his contact didn't have the equipment he needed – as he knew only too well he wouldn't – he walked briskly over to Leninplatz and began to search for Tulpanov's office.

The entrance to the vast grey building through an archway on the north side of the square was not at all imposing, and the secretary who sat alone in a dingy outer office on the third floor didn't make Armstrong feel that her boss was a rising star. She checked his card, and didn't seem at all surprised that a captain in the British Army would drop in without an appointment. She led Armstrong silently down a long grey corridor, its peeling walls lined with photographs of Marx, Engels, Lenin and Stalin, and stopped outside a door with no name on it. She knocked, opened the door and stood aside to allow Captain Armstrong to enter Tulpanov's office.

Armstrong was taken by surprise as he walked into a luxuriously appointed room, full of fine paintings and antique furniture. He had once had to brief General Templer, the military governor of the British sector, and his office was far less imposing.

Major Tulpanov rose from behind his desk and walked across the carpeted room to greet his guest. Armstrong couldn't help noticing that the major's uniform was far better tailored than his.

'Welcome to my humble abode, Captain Armstrong,' said the Russian officer. 'Isn't that the correct English expression?' He made no attempt to hide a smirk. 'Your timing is perfect. Would you care to join me for lunch?'

'Thank you,' replied Armstrong in Russian. Tulpanov showed no surprise at the switch in tongues, and led his guest through to a second room where a table had been set for two. Armstrong couldn't help wondering if the major hadn't anticipated his visit.

As Armstrong took his place opposite Tulpanov, a steward appeared carrying two plates of caviar, and a second followed with a bottle of vodka. If this was meant to put him at his ease, it didn't.

The major raised his brimming glass high in the air and toasted 'Our future prosperity.'

'Our future prosperity,' repeated Armstrong as the major's secretary entered the room. She placed a thick brown envelope on the table by Tulpanov's side.

'And when I say "our", I mean "our",' said the major. He put his glass down, ignoring the envelope.

Armstrong also placed his drink back on the table, but said nothing in response. One of his instructions from the security service briefings was to make no attempt to lead the conversation.

'Now, Lubji,' said Tulpanov, 'I will not waste your time by lying about my role in the Russian sector, not least because you have just spent the last ten days being briefed on exactly why I'm stationed in Berlin and the role I play in this new "cold war" – isn't that how your lot describe it? – and by now I suspect you know more about me than my secretary does.'

He smiled and spooned a large lump of caviar into his mouth. Armstrong toyed uncomfortably with his fork but made no attempt to eat anything.

'But the truth is, Lubji – or would you prefer me to call you John? Or Dick? – that I certainly know more about you than your secretary, your wife and your mother put together.'

Armstrong still didn't speak. He put down his fork and left the caviar untouched in front of him.

'You see, Lubji, you and I are two of a kind, which is why I feel confident we can be of great assistance to each other.'

'I'm not sure I understand you,' said Armstrong, looking directly across at him.

'Well, for example, I can tell you exactly where you will find Mrs Klaus Lauber, and that she doesn't even know that her husband was the owner of *Der Telegraf.*'

Armstrong took a sip of vodka. He was relieved that his hand didn't shake, even if his heart was beating at twice its normal rate.

Tulpanov picked up the thick brown envelope by his side, opened it and removed a document. He slid it across the table. 'And there's no reason to let her know, if we're able to come to an agreement.'

Armstrong unfolded the heavy parchment and read the first paragraph of Major Klaus Otto Lauber's will, while Tulpanov allowed the steward to serve him a second plate of caviar.

'But it says here . . .' said Armstrong, as he turned the third page.

The smile reappeared on Tulpanov's face. 'Ah, I see you have come to the paragraph which confirms that Arno Schultz has been left all the shares in *Der Telegraf.*'

Armstrong looked up and stared at the major, but said nothing.

'That of course is relevant only so long as the will is still in existence,' said Tulpanov. 'If this document were never to see the light of day, the shares would go automatically to Mrs Lauber, in which case I can see no reason . . .'

'What do you expect of me in return?' asked Armstrong.

The major didn't reply immediately, as if he were considering the question. 'Oh, a little information now and then, perhaps. After all, Lubji, if I made it possible for you to own your first newspaper before you were twenty-five, I would surely be entitled to expect a little something in return.'

'I don't quite understand,' said Armstrong.

'I think you understand only too well,' said Tulpanov with a smile, 'but let me spell it out for you.'

Armstrong picked up his fork and experienced his first taste of caviar as the major continued.

'Let us start by acknowledging the simple fact, Lubji, that you are not even a British citizen. You just landed there by chance. And although they may have welcomed you into their army – ' he paused to take a sip of vodka ' – I feel sure you've already worked out that that doesn't mean they've welcomed you into their hearts. The time has therefore come for you to decide which team you are playing for.'

Armstrong took a second mouthful of caviar. He liked it.

'I think you would find that membership of our team would not be too demanding, and I am sure that we could, from time to time, help each other advance in what the British still insist on calling "the great game".'

Armstrong scooped up the last mouthful of caviar, and hoped he would be offered more.

'Why don't you think it over, Lubji?' Tulpanov said as he leaned across the table, retrieved the will and placed it back in the envelope.

Armstrong said nothing as he stared down at his empty plate.

'In the meantime,' said the KGB major, 'let me give you a little piece of information to take back to your friends in the security service.' He removed a sheet of paper from his inside pocket and pushed it across the table. Armstrong read it, and was pleased to find he could still think in Russian.

'To be fair, Lubji, you should know that your people are already in possession of this document, but they will still be pleased to have its contents confirmed. You see, the one thing all secret service operatives have in common is a love of paperwork. It's how they are able to prove that their job is necessary.'

'How did I get my hands on this?' asked Armstrong, holding up the sheet of paper.

'I fear I have a temporary secretary today, who will keep leaving her desk unattended.'

Dick smiled as he folded up the sheet of paper and slipped it into his inside pocket.

'By the way, Lubji, those fellows back in your security service are not quite as dumb as you may think. Take my advice: be wary of them. If you decide to join the game, you will in the end have to be disloyal to one side or the other, and if they ever find out you are double-crossing them, they will dispose of you without the slightest remorse.'

Armstrong could now hear his heart thumping away.

'As I have already explained,' continued the major, 'there's no need for you to make an immediate decision.' He tapped the brown envelope. 'I can easily wait for a few more days before I inform Mr Schultz of his good fortune.'

◄○►

'I've some good news for you, Dick,' said Colonel Oakshott when Armstrong reported to HQ the following morning. 'Your demob papers have been processed at last, and I can see no reason why you shouldn't be back in England within a month.'

The colonel was surprised that Armstrong's reaction was so muted, but he assumed he must have other things on his mind. 'Not that Forsdyke will be pleased to learn you're leaving us so soon after your triumph with Major Tulpanov.'

'Perhaps I shouldn't rush back quite so quickly,' said Armstrong, 'now that I have a chance to build up a relationship with the KGB.'

'That's damned patriotic of you, old chap,' said the colonel. 'Shall we just leave it that I won't hurry the process along until you tip me the wink?' Armstrong's English was as fluent as that of most officers in the British Army, but Oakshott was still able to add the occasional new expression to his vocabulary.

Charlotte continued to press him on when they might hope to leave Berlin, and that evening she explained why it was suddenly so important. When he heard the news, Dick realised that he could not prevaricate much longer. He didn't go out that night, but sat in the kitchen with Charlotte, telling her all about his plans once they had set up home in England.

The next morning he found an excuse to visit the Russian sector, and following a long briefing from Forsdyke, he arrived outside Tulpanov's office a few minutes before lunch.

'How are you, Lubji?' asked the KGB man as he rose from behind his desk. Armstrong nodded curtly. 'And more importantly, my friend, have you come to a decision as to which side you are going to open the batting for?'

Armstrong looked puzzled.

'To appreciate the English,' said Tulpanov, 'you must first understand the game of cricket, which cannot commence until after the toss of a coin. Can you imagine anything more stupid than giving the other side a chance? But have you tossed the coin yet, Lubji, I keep asking myself. And if so, have you decided whether to bat or bowl?'

'I want to meet Mrs Lauber before I make a final decision,' said Dick.

The major walked around the room, his lips pursed, as if he were giving serious thought to Armstrong's request.

'There is an old English saying, Lubji. Where there's a will . . .'

Armstrong looked puzzled.

'Another thing you must understand about the English is that their puns are dreadful. But for all their sense of what they call fair play, they are deadly when it comes to defending their position. Now, if you wish to visit Mrs Lauber, it will be necessary for us to make a journey to Dresden.'

'Dresden?'

'Yes. Mrs Lauber is safely ensconced deep in the Russian

zone. That can only be to your advantage. But I don't think we should visit her for a few days.'

'Why not?' asked Armstrong.

'You still have so much to learn about the British, Lubji. You must not imagine that conquering their language is the same as knowing how their minds work. The English love routine. You return tomorrow and they will become suspicious. You return some time next week and they won't give it a second thought.'

'So what do I tell them when I report back?'

'You say I was cagey, and that you're "still testing the water".' Tulpanov smiled again. 'But you can tell them that I asked you about a man called Arbuthnot, Piers Arbuthnot, and whether it's true that he's about to take up a post in Berlin. You told me that you'd never heard of him, but that you would try to find out.'

Armstrong returned to the British sector later that afternoon and reported most of the conversation to Forsdyke. He expected to be told who Arbuthnot was and when he would be arriving in Berlin, but all Forsdyke said was, 'He's just trying you out for size. He knows exactly who Arbuthnot is and when he's taking up his post. How soon can you find a convincing excuse to visit the Russian sector again?'

'Next Wednesday or Thursday I've got my usual monthly meeting with the Russians on paper supplies.'

'Right, if you just happen to drop in and see Tulpanov, tell him you couldn't get a word out of me on Arbuthnot.'

'But won't that make him suspicious?'

'No, he would be more suspicious if you were able to tell him anything about that particular man.'

—◦—

Over breakfast the following morning, Charlotte and Dick had another row about when he expected to return to Britain.

'How many new excuses can you come up with to keep putting it off?' she asked.

Dick made no attempt to answer. Without giving her a

second look he picked up his swagger stick and peaked hat, and stormed out of the apartment.

Private Benson drove him straight to the office, and once he was at his desk he immediately buzzed Sally. She came through with a pile of mail for signing and greeted him with a smile. When she left an hour later, she looked drained. She warned everyone to keep out of the captain's way for the rest of the day because he was in a foul mood. His mood hadn't improved by Wednesday, and on Thursday the whole team was relieved to learn that he would be spending most of the day out of the office.

Benson drove him into the Russian sector a few minutes before ten. Armstrong stepped out of the jeep, carrying his Gladstone bag, and told his driver to return to the British sector. He walked through the great archway off Leninplatz that led to Tulpanov's office, and was surprised to find the major's secretary waiting for him in the outer courtyard.

Without a word she guided him across the cobbled yard to a large black Mercedes. She held open the door and he slid onto the back seat beside Tulpanov. The engine was already running, and without waiting for instructions the driver drove out into the square and began following the signs for the autobahn.

The major showed no surprise when Armstrong reported the conversation he'd had with Forsdyke, and his failure to find out anything about Arbuthnot.

'They don't trust you yet, Lubji,' said Tulpanov. 'You see, you're not one of them. Perhaps you never will be.' Armstrong pouted and turned to look out of the window.

Once they had reached the outskirts of Berlin, they headed south towards Dresden. After a few minutes, Tulpanov bent down and handed Armstrong a small, battered suitcase stamped with the initials 'K.L.'.

'What's this?' he asked.

'All the good major's worldly possessions,' Tulpanov replied. 'Or at least, all the ones his widow can expect to inherit.' He passed Armstrong a thick brown envelope.

'And this? More worldly goods?'

'No. That's the 40,000 marks Lauber paid Schultz for his original shares in *Der Telegraf*. You see, whenever the British are involved, I do try to stick to the rules. "Play up, play up and play the game,"' said Tulpanov. He paused. 'I believe you are in possession of the only other document that is required.'

Armstrong nodded, and placed the thick envelope in his Gladstone bag. He gazed back out of the window and watched the passing countryside, horrified at how little rebuilding had been carried out since the war had ended. He tried to concentrate on how he would handle Mrs Lauber, and didn't speak again until they reached the outskirts of Dresden.

'Does the driver know where to go?' asked Armstrong as they passed a 40-kilometre speed warning.

'Oh yes,' said Tulpanov. 'You're not the first person he's taken to visit this particular old lady. He has "the knowledge".'

Armstrong looked puzzled.

'When you settle down in London, Lubji, someone will explain that one to you.'

A few minutes later they came to a halt outside a drab concrete block of flats in the centre of a park which looked as if it had been bombed the previous day.

'It's number sixty-three,' said Tulpanov. 'I'm afraid there's no lift, so you'll have to do a little climbing, my dear Lubji. But then, that's something you're rather good at.'

Armstrong stepped out of the car, carrying his Gladstone bag and the major's battered suitcase. He made his way down a weed-infested path to the entrance of the pre-war ten-storey block. He began to climb the concrete staircase, relieved that Mrs Lauber didn't live on the top floor. When he reached the sixth floor, he continued around a narrow, exposed walkway until he reached a door with '63' daubed in red on the wall next to it.

He tapped his swagger stick on the glass, and the door was opened a few moments later by an old woman who showed no surprise at finding a British officer standing on her doorstep. She led him down a mean, unlit corridor to a tiny, cold room overlooking an identical ten-storey block. Armstrong took the seat opposite her next to a two-bar electric heater; only one of the bars was glowing.

He shivered as he watched the old woman shrink into her chair and pull a threadbare shawl around her shoulders.

'I visited your husband in Wales just before he died,' he began. 'He asked me to give you this.' He passed over the battered suitcase.

Mrs Lauber complimented him on his German, then opened the suitcase. Armstrong watched as she removed a framed picture of her husband and herself on their wedding day, followed by a photograph of a young man he assumed was their son. From the sad look on her face, Armstrong felt he must also have lost his life in the war. There followed several items, including a book of verse by Rainer Maria Rilke and an old wooden chess set.

When she had finally removed her husband's three medals, she looked up and asked hopefully, 'Did he leave you any message for me?'

'Only that he missed you. And he asked if you would give the chess set to Arno.'

'Arno Schultz,' she said. 'I doubt if he's still alive.' She paused. 'You see, the poor man was Jewish. We lost contact with him during the war.'

'Then I will make it my responsibility to try and find out if he survived,' said Armstrong. He leaned forward and took her hand.

'You are kind,' she said, clinging on to him with her bony fingers. It was some time before she released his hand. She then picked up the chess set and passed it over to him. 'I do hope he's still alive,' she said. 'Arno was such a good man.'

Armstrong nodded.

'Did my husband leave any other message for me?'

'Yes. He told me that his final wish was that you should also return Arno's shares to him.'

'What shares did he mean?' she asked, sounding anxious for the first time. 'They didn't mention any shares when they came to visit me.'

'It seems that Arno sold Herr Lauber some shares in a publishing company not long after Hitler came to power, and your husband promised he would return them as soon as the war was over.'

'Well, of course I would be only too happy to do so,' the old woman said, shivering again. 'But sadly I am not in possession of any shares. Perhaps Klaus made a will . . .'

'Unfortunately not, Mrs Lauber,' Armstrong said. 'Or if he did, we haven't been able to find it.'

'How unlike Klaus,' she said. 'He was always so meticulous. But then, perhaps it has disappeared somewhere in the Russian zone. You can't trust the Russians you know,' she whispered.

Armstrong nodded his agreement. 'That doesn't present a problem,' he said, taking her hand again. 'I am in possession of a document which invests me with the authority to ensure that Arno Schultz, if he is still alive and we can find him, will receive the shares he's entitled to.'

Mrs Lauber smiled. 'Thank you,' she said. 'It's a great relief to know that the matter is in the hands of a British officer.'

Armstrong opened his briefcase and removed the contract. Turning to the last of its four pages, he indicated two pencilled crosses, and handed Mrs Lauber his pen. She placed her spidery signature between the crosses, without having made any attempt to read a single clause or paragraph of the contract. As soon as the ink was dry, Armstrong placed the document back in his Gladstone bag and clipped it shut. He smiled across at Mrs Lauber.

'I must return to Berlin now,' he said, rising from his chair, 'where I shall make every effort to locate Herr Schultz.'

'Thank you,' said Mrs Lauber, who slowly rose to her feet and led him back down the passage to the front door. 'Goodbye,' she said, as he stepped out onto the landing, 'it was most kind of you to come all this way on my behalf.' She smiled weakly and closed the door without another word.

'Well?' said Tulpanov when Armstrong rejoined him in the back of the car.

'She signed the agreement.'

'I thought she might,' said Tulpanov. The car swung round in a circle and began its journey back to Berlin.

'So what happens next?' asked Armstrong.

'Now you have spun the coin,' said the KGB major. 'You have won the toss, and decided to bat. Though I must say that what you've just done to Mrs Lauber could hardly be described as cricket.'

Armstrong looked quizzically at him.

'Even I thought you'd give her the 40,000 marks,' said Tulpanov. 'But no doubt you plan to give Arno –' he paused ' – the chess set.'

–◦–

The following morning, Captain Richard Armstrong registered his ownership of *Der Telegraf* with the British Control Commission. Although one of the officials raised an eyebrow, and he was kept waiting for over an hour by another, eventually the duty clerk stamped the document authorising the transaction, and confirmed that Captain Armstrong was now the sole owner of the paper.

Charlotte tried to disguise her true feelings when she was told the news of her husband's 'coup'. She was certain it could only mean that their departure for England would be postponed yet again. But she was relieved when Dick agreed that she could return to Lyon to be with her parents for the birth of their firstborn, as she was determined that any child of hers would begin its life as a French citizen.

Arno Schultz was surprised by Armstrong's sudden renewed commitment to *Der Telegraf*. He started making contributions at the morning editorial conference, and even took to riding on the delivery vans on their midnight sojourns around the city. Arno assumed that his boss's new enthusiasm was directly related to Charlotte's absence in Lyon.

Within a few weeks they were selling 300,000 copies of the paper a day for the first time, and Arno accepted that the pupil had become the master.

A month later, Captain Armstrong took ten days' compassionate leave so he could be in Lyon for the birth of his first child. He was delighted when Charlotte presented him with a boy, whom they christened David. As he sat on the bed holding the child in his arms, he promised Charlotte that it would not be long before they left for England, and the three of them would embark on a new life.

He arrived back in Berlin a week later, resolved to tell Colonel Oakshott that the time had come for him to resign his commission and return to England.

He would have done so if Arno Schultz hadn't held a party to celebrate his sixtieth birthday.

14

Adelaide Gazette

13 MARCH 1956

Menzies Stays Put

The first time Townsend noticed her was on a flight up to Sydney. He was reading the *Gazette*: the lead story should have been relegated to page three and the headline was weak. The *Gazette* now had a monopoly in Adelaide, but the paper was becoming increasingly slack. He should have removed Frank Bailey from the editor's chair after the merger, but he had to satisfy himself with getting rid of Sir Colin first. He frowned.

'Would you like your coffee topped up, Mr Townsend?' she asked. Townsend glanced up at the slim girl who was holding a coffee pot, and smiled. She must have been about twenty-five, with curly fair hair and blue eyes which made you go on staring at them.

'Yes,' he replied, despite not wanting any more. She returned his smile – an air hostess's smile, a smile that didn't vary for the fat or the thin, the rich or the poor.

Townsend put the *Gazette* to one side and tried to concentrate on the meeting that was about to take place. He had recently purchased, at a cost of half a million pounds, a small print group which specialised in giveaway papers distributed in the western suburbs of Sydney. The deal had done no more than give him a foothold in Australia's largest city.

It had been at the Newspapers and Publishers Annual Dinner at the Cook Hotel that a man of about twenty-seven or twenty-eight, five foot eight, square-jawed with bright red hair and the shoulders of a prop forward, came up to his table after the speeches were over and whispered in his ear, 'I'll see you in the men's room.' Townsend wasn't sure whether to laugh or just to ignore the man. But curiosity got the better of him, and a few minutes later he rose from his place and made his way through the tables to the men's room. The man with the red hair was washing his hands in the corner basin. Townsend walked across, stood at the basin next to him and turned on the tap.

'What hotel are you staying at?' he asked.

'The Town House,' Keith replied.

'And what's your room number?'

'I have no idea.'

'I'll find out. I'll come to your room around midnight. That is, if you're interested in getting your hands on the *Sydney Chronicle*.' The red-headed man turned off the tap, dried his hands and left.

Townsend learned in the early hours of the morning that the man who had accosted him at the dinner was Bruce Kelly, the *Chronicle*'s deputy editor. He wasted no time in telling Townsend that Sir Somerset Kenwright was considering selling the paper, as he felt it no longer fitted in with the rest of his group.

'Was there something wrong with your coffee?' she asked.

Townsend looked up at her, and then down at his untouched coffee. 'No, it was fine, thank you,' he said. 'I'm just a little preoccupied at the moment.' She gave him that smile again, before removing the cup and continuing on to the row behind. Once again he tried to concentrate.

When he had first discussed the idea with his mother, she had told him that it had been his father's lifelong ambition to own the *Chronicle*, though her own feelings were ambivalent. The reason he was travelling to Sydney for the third time in as many weeks was for another meeting with Sir Somerset's top management team, so he could go over the terms of a possible deal. And one of them still owed him a favour.

Over the past few months Townsend's lawyers had been working in tandem with Sir Somerset's, and both sides now felt they were at last coming close to an agreement. 'The old man thinks you're the lesser of two evils,' Kelly had warned him. 'He's faced the fact that his son isn't up to the job, but he doesn't want the paper to fall into the hands of Wally Hacker, who he's never liked, and certainly doesn't trust. He's not sure about you, although he has fond memories of your father.' Since Kelly had given him that piece of invaluable information, Townsend had mentioned his father whenever he and Sir Somerset met.

When the plane taxied to a halt at Kingsford-Smith airport, Townsend unfastened his seatbelt, picked up his briefcase and began to walk towards the forward exit. 'Have a good day, Mr Townsend,' she said. 'I do hope you'll be flying Austair again.'

'I will,' he promised. 'In fact I'm coming back tonight.' Only an impatient line of passengers who were pressing forward stopped him from asking if she would be on that flight.

When his taxi came to a halt in Pitt Street, Townsend checked his watch and found he still had a few minutes to spare. He paid the fare and darted through the traffic to the other side of the road. When he had reached the far pavement, he turned round and stared up at the building which housed the biggest-selling newspaper in Australia. He only wished his father was still alive to witness him closing the deal.

He walked back across the road, entered the building and paced around the reception area until a well-dressed middle-aged woman appeared out of one of the lifts, walked over to him and said, 'Sir Somerset is expecting you, Mr Townsend.'

When Townsend walked into the vast office overlooking the harbour, he was greeted by a man he had regarded with awe and admiration since his childhood. Sir Somerset shook him warmly by the hand. 'Keith. Good to see you. I think you were at school with my chief executive, Duncan Alexander.' The two men shook hands, but said nothing. 'But I don't believe you've met the *Chronicle*'s editor, Nick Watson.'

'No, I haven't had that pleasure,' said Townsend, shaking Watson by the hand. 'But of course I know of your reputation.'

Sir Somerset waved them to seats around a large boardroom table, taking his place at the top. 'You know, Keith,' began the old man, 'I'm damn proud of this paper. Even Beaverbrook tried to buy it from me.'

'Understandably,' said Townsend.

'We've set a standard of journalism in this building that I like to think even your father would have been proud of.'

'He always spoke of your papers with the greatest respect. Indeed, when it came to the *Chronicle*, I think the word "envy" would be more appropriate.'

Sir Somerset smiled. 'It's kind of you to say so, my boy.' He paused. 'Well, it seems that during the past few weeks our teams have been able to agree most of the details. So, as long as you can match Wally Hacker's offer of £1.9 million and – just as important to me – you agree to retain Nick as editor and Duncan as chief executive, I think we might have ourselves a deal.'

'It would be foolish of me not to rely on their vast knowledge and expertise,' said Townsend. 'They are two highly respected professionals, and I shall naturally be delighted to work with them. Though I feel I should let you know that it's not my policy to interfere in the internal working of my papers, especially when it comes to the editorial content. That's just not my style.'

'I see that you've learned a great deal from your father,' said Sir Somerset. 'Like him, and like you, I don't involve myself in the day-to-day running of the paper. It always ends in tears.'

Townsend nodded his agreement.

'Well, I don't think there's much more for us to discuss at this stage, so I suggest we adjourn to the dining room and have some lunch.' The old man put his arm round Townsend's shoulder and said, 'I only wish your father were here to join us.'

◄o►

The smile never left Townsend's face on the journey back to the airport. If she were on the return flight, that would be a bonus. His smile became even wider as he fastened his seatbelt and began to rehearse what he would say to her.

'I hope you had a worthwhile trip to Sydney, Mr Townsend,' she said as she offered him an evening paper.

'It couldn't have turned out better,' he replied. 'Perhaps you'd like to join me for dinner tonight and help me celebrate?'

'That's very kind of you, sir,' she said, emphasising the word 'sir', 'but I'm afraid it's against company policy.'

'Is it against company policy to know your name?'

'No, sir,' she said. 'It's Susan.' She gave him that same smile, and moved on to the next row.

The first thing he did when he got back to his flat was to make himself a sardine sandwich. He had only taken one bite when the phone rang. It was Clive Jervis, the senior partner at Jervis, Smith & Thomas. Clive was still anxious about some of the finer details of the contract, including compensation agreements and stock write-offs.

No sooner had Townsend put the phone down than it rang again, and he took an even longer call from Trevor Meacham, his accountant, who still felt that £1.9 million was too high a price.

'I don't have a lot of choice,' Townsend told him. 'Wally Hacker has already offered the same amount.'

'Hacker is also capable of paying too much,' came back the reply. 'I think we should still demand staged payments, based on this year's circulation figures, and not aggregated over the past ten years.'

'Why?' asked Townsend.

'Because the *Chronicle* has been losing 2 to 3 per cent of its readers year on year. Everything ought to be based on the latest figures available.'

'I agree with you on that, but I don't want it to be the reason I lose this deal.'

'Neither do I,' said his accountant. 'But I also don't want you to end up bankrupt simply because you paid far too much for sentimental reasons. Every deal must stack up in its own right, and not be closed just to prove you're as good as your father.'

Neither man spoke for several moments.

'You needn't worry about that,' said Townsend eventually. 'I already have plans to double the circulation of the *Chronicle*. In a year's time £1.9 million will look cheap. And what's more, my father would have backed me on this one.' He put the phone down before Trevor could say another word.

The final call came from Bruce Kelly just after eleven, by which time Townsend was in his dressing-gown, and the half-eaten sardine sandwich was stale.

'Sir Somerset is still nervous,' he warned him.

'Why?' asked Townsend. 'I felt today's meeting couldn't have gone better.'

'The meeting wasn't the problem. After you left, he had a call from Sir Colin Grant which lasted nearly an hour. And Duncan Alexander isn't exactly your closest mate.'

Townsend thumped his fist on the table. 'Damn the man,' he said. 'Now listen carefully, Bruce, and I'll tell you exactly what line you should take. Whenever Sir Colin's name comes up, remind Sir Somerset that as soon as he became chairman of the *Messenger*, it began losing sales every week. As for Alexander, you can leave him to me.'

◄○►

Townsend was disappointed to find that on his next flight up to Sydney, Susan was nowhere to be seen. When a steward served him with coffee, he asked if she was working on another flight.

'No, sir,' he replied. 'Susan left the company at the end of last month.'

'Do you know where she's working now?'

'I've no idea, sir,' he replied, before moving on to the next passenger.

Townsend spent the morning being shown round the *Chronicle*'s offices by Duncan Alexander, who kept the conversation businesslike, making no attempt to be friendly. Townsend waited until they were alone in the lift before he turned to him and said, 'You once told me many years ago, "We Alexanders have long memories. Call on me when you need me."'

'Yes, I did,' Duncan admitted.

'Good, because the time has come for me to call in my marker.'

'What do you expect from me?'

'I want Sir Somerset to be told what a good man I am.'

The lift came to a halt, and the doors opened.

'If I do that, will you guarantee I'll keep my job?'

'You have my word on it,' said Townsend as he stepped out into the corridor.

After lunch, Sir Somerset – who seemed a little more restrained than when they had first met – accompanied Townsend around the editorial floor, where he was introduced to the journalists. All of them were relieved to find that the new proprietor just nodded and smiled at them, making himself agreeable to even the most junior staff. Everyone who came in contact with Townsend that day was pleasantly surprised, especially after what they had been told by reporters who had worked for him on the *Gazette*. Even Sir Somerset began to wonder if Sir Colin hadn't exaggerated about Townsend's behaviour in the past.

'Don't forget what happened to the sales of the *Messenger* when Sir Colin took over as chairman,' Bruce Kelly whispered into several ears, including his editor's, soon after Townsend had left.

The staff on the *Chronicle* would not have given Townsend the benefit of the doubt if they had seen the notes he was compiling on the flight back to Adelaide. It was clear to him that if he hoped to double the paper's profits, there was going to have to be some drastic surgery, with cuts from top to bottom.

Townsend found himself looking up from time to time and thinking about Susan. When another steward offered him a copy of the evening paper, he asked if he had any idea where she was now working.

'Do you mean Susan Glover?' he asked.

'Blonde, curly hair, early twenties,' said Townsend.

'Yes, that's Susan. She left us when she was offered a job at Moore's. Said she couldn't take the irregular hours any longer, not to mention being treated like a bus conductor. I know just how she feels.'

Townsend smiled. Moore's had always been his mother's favourite store in Adelaide. He was sure it wouldn't take him long to discover which department Susan worked in.

The following morning, after he had finished going through the mail with Bunty, he dialled Moore's number the moment she had closed the door behind her.

'Can you put me through to Miss Glover, please?'

'Which department does she work in?'

'I don't know,' said Townsend.

'Is it an emergency?'

'No, it's a personal call.'

'Are you a relative?'

'No, I'm not,' he said, puzzled by the question.

'Then I'm sorry, but I can't help. It's against company policy for staff to take private calls during office hours.' The line went dead.

Townsend replaced the phone, rose from his chair and walked into Bunty's office. 'I'll be away for about an hour, maybe a little longer, Bunty. I've got to pick up a birthday present for my mother.'

Miss Bunting was surprised, as she knew his mother's birthday was four months away. But at least he was an improvement on his father, she thought. She'd always had to remind Sir Graham the day before.

When Townsend stepped out of the building it was such a warm day that he told his driver, Sam, he would walk the dozen or so blocks to Moore's, which would give him a chance to check all the paper stands on the way. He was not pleased to find that the first one he came across, on the corner of King William Street, had already sold out of the *Gazette*, and it was only a few minutes past ten. He made a note to speak to the distribution manager as soon as he returned to the office.

As he approached the massive department store on Rundle Street, he wondered just how long it would take him to find Susan. He pushed his way through the revolving door and walked up and down between the counters on the ground floor: jewellery, gloves, perfume. But he could see no sign of her. He took the escalator to the second floor, where he repeated the process: crockery, bedding, kitchenware. Still no success. The third floor turned out to be menswear, which reminded him that he needed a new suit. If she worked there he could order one immediately, but there wasn't a woman in sight.

As he stepped onto the escalator to take him up to the fourth floor, Townsend thought he recognised the smartly-dressed man standing on the step above him.

When he turned round and saw Townsend, he said, 'How are you?'

'I'm fine,' replied Townsend, trying desperately to place him.

'Ed Scott,' the man said, solving the problem. 'I was a couple of years below you at St Andrew's, and still remember your editorials in the school magazine.'

'I'm flattered,' said Townsend. 'So, what are you up to now?'

'I'm the assistant manager.'

'You've done well then,' said Townsend, looking round at the huge store.

'Hardly,' said Ed. 'My father's the managing director. But then, that's something I don't have to explain to you.'

Townsend scowled.

'Were you looking for anything in particular?' asked Ed as they stepped off the escalator.

'Yes,' replied Townsend. 'A present for my mother. She's already chosen something, and I've just come to pick it up. I can't remember which floor it's on, but I do have the name of the assistant who served her.'

'Tell me the name, and I'll find out the department.'

'Susan Glover,' said Townsend, trying not to blush.

Ed stood to one side, dialled a number on his intercom and

repeated the name. A few moments later a look of surprise crossed his face. 'It seems she's in the toy department,' he said. 'Are you certain you've been given the right name?'

'Oh yes,' said Townsend. 'Puzzles.'

'Puzzles?'

'Yes, my mother can't resist jigsaw puzzles. But none of the family is allowed to choose them for her, because whenever we do, it always turns out to be one she already has.'

'Oh, I see,' said Ed. 'Well, take the escalator back down to the basement. You'll find the toy department on your right-hand side.' Townsend thanked him, and the assistant manager disappeared off in the direction of luggage and travel.

Townsend took the escalator all the way down to 'The World of Toys'. He looked round the counters, but there was no sign of Susan, and he started to wonder if it might be her day off. He wandered slowly around the department, and decided against asking a rather officious-looking woman, who wore a badge on her ample chest declaring she was the 'Senior Sales Assistant', if a Susan Glover worked there.

He thought he would have to come back the following day, and was about to leave when a door behind one of the counters opened and Susan came through it, carrying a large Meccano set. She went over to a customer who was leaning on the counter.

Townsend stood transfixed on the spot. She was even more captivating than he had remembered.

'Can I help you, sir?'

Townsend jumped, turned round and came face to face with the officious-looking woman.

'No, thank you,' he said nervously. 'I'm just looking for a present for . . . for my . . . nephew.' The woman glared at him, and Townsend moved away and selected a spot where he could be hidden from her view but still keep Susan in his sights.

The customer she was serving took an inordinate amount of time making up her mind if she wanted the Meccano set. Susan was made to open up the box to prove that the contents fulfilled the promise on the lid. She picked up some of the red and yellow pieces and tried to put them together, but the customer left a few minutes later, empty-handed.

Townsend waited until the officious woman began to serve another customer before he strolled over to the counter. Susan looked up and smiled. This time it was a smile of recognition.

'How may I help you, Mr Townsend?' she asked.

'Will you have dinner with me tonight?' he replied. 'Or is it still against company policy?'

She smiled and said, 'Yes, it is Mr Townsend, but . . .'

The senior sales assistant reappeared at Susan's side, looking more suspicious than ever.

'It must be over a thousand pieces,' said Townsend. 'My mother needs the sort of puzzle that will keep her going for at least a week.'

'Of course, sir,' said Susan, and led him over to a table which displayed several different jigsaw puzzles.

He began picking them up and studying them closely, without looking at her. 'How about Pilligrini's at eight o'clock?' he whispered, just as the officious woman was approaching.

'That's perfect. I've never been there, but I've always wanted to,' she said, taking the puzzle of Sydney Harbour from his hands. She walked back to the counter, rang up the bill and dropped the large box into a Moore's bag. 'That will be £2 10s. please, sir.'

Townsend paid for his purchase, and would have confirmed their date if the officious lady hadn't stuck close to Susan and said, 'I do hope your nephew enjoys the puzzle.'

Two sets of eyes followed his progress out of the store.

When he returned to the office, Bunty was a little surprised to discover the contents of the shopping bag. In the thirty-two years she had worked for Sir Graham, she couldn't once remember him giving his wife a jigsaw puzzle.

Townsend ignored her enquiring look, and said, 'Bunty, I want to see the circulation manager immediately. The news stand on the corner of King William Street had run out of the

Gazette by ten o'clock.' As she turned to leave he added, 'Oh, and could you book me a table for two tonight at Pilligrini's?'

⊰◦⊱

As Susan entered the restaurant, several men in the room turned to watch her walk across to the corner table. She was wearing a pink suit that emphasised her slim figure, and although her skirt fell an inch below the knee, Townsend's eyes were still looking down when she arrived at the table. When she took the seat opposite him, some of his fellow-diners' looks turned to envy.

One voice, which was intended to carry, said, 'That bloody man gets everything he wants.'

They both laughed, and Townsend poured her a glass of champagne. He soon found how easy it was to be in her company. They began to swap stories of what they had both been doing for the past twenty years as if they were old friends just catching up. Townsend explained why he had been making so many journeys to Sydney recently, and Susan told him why she wasn't enjoying working in the toy department of Moore's.

'Is she always that awful?' asked Townsend.

'You caught her in a good mood. After you left, she spent the rest of the morning being sarcastic about whether it was your mother or your nephew or perhaps someone else that you'd come in for. And when I was a couple of minutes late getting back from lunch, she said, "You're one hundred and twenty seconds late, Miss Glover. One hundred and twenty seconds of the company's time. If it happens again, we'll have to think about deducting the appropriate sum from your wages."' It was an almost perfect imitation, and caused Townsend to burst out laughing.

'What's her problem?'

'I think she wanted to be an air hostess.'

'I fear she lacks one or two of the more obvious qualifications,' suggested Townsend.

'So, what have you been up to today?' Susan asked. 'Still trying to pick up air hostesses on Austair?'

'No,' he smiled. 'That was last week – and I failed. Today I satisfied myself with trying to work out if I could afford to pay £1.9 million for the *Sydney Chronicle*.'

'One point nine million?' she said incredulously. 'Then the least I can do is pick up the tab for dinner. Last time I bought a copy of the *Sydney Chronicle* it was sixpence.'

'Yes, but I want all the copies,' said Townsend.

Although their coffee cups had been cleared away, they continued to talk until long after the kitchen staff had left. A couple of bored-looking waiters lounged against a pillar, occasionally glancing at them hopefully. When he caught one of them stifling a yawn, Townsend called for the bill and left a large tip. As they stepped out onto the pavement, he took Susan's hand. 'Where do you live?'

'In the northern suburbs, but I'm afraid I've missed the last bus. I'll have to get a taxi.'

'It's such a glorious evening, why don't we walk?'

'Suits me,' she said, smiling.

They didn't stop talking until they arrived outside her front door an hour later. Susan turned to him and said, 'Thank you for a lovely evening, Keith. You've brought a new meaning to the words "walking it off".'

'Let's do it again soon,' he said.

'I'd like that.'

'When would suit you?'

'I would have said tomorrow, but it depends on whether I'm going to be expected to walk home every time. If I am, I might have to suggest a local restaurant, or at least wear more sensible shoes.'

'Certainly not,' said Townsend. 'I promise you tomorrow I'll drive you home. But I have to be in Sydney to sign a contract earlier in the day, so I don't expect to be back much before eight.'

'That's perfect. It will give me enough time to go home and change.'

'Would L'Étoile suit you?'

'Only if you have something to celebrate.'

'There will be something to celebrate, that I promise you.'

'Then I'll see you at L'Étoile at nine.' She leaned over and kissed him on the cheek. 'You know, you'll never get a taxi out here at this time of night, Keith,' she said, looking rather concerned. 'I'm afraid you're going to have a long walk back.'

'It will be worth it,' said Townsend, as Susan disappeared down the short drive to her front door.

A car drove up and came to a halt by his side. The driver jumped out and opened the door for him.

'Where to, boss?'

'Home, Sam,' he said to his driver. 'But let's go via the station, so I can pick up the early morning edition.'

◄○►

Townsend took the first flight to Sydney the following morning. His lawyer, Clive Jervis, and his accountant, Trevor Meacham, were sitting on either side of him.

'I'm still not altogether happy with the rescission clause,' said Clive.

'And the payment schedule needs a little fine tuning, that's for sure,' added Trevor.

'How long is it going to take to sort out these problems?' asked Townsend. 'I have a dinner appointment in Adelaide tonight, and I must catch an afternoon flight.' Both men looked doubtful.

Their fears were to prove justified. The two companies' lawyers spent the morning going over the fine print, and the two accountants took even longer checking the figures. Nobody stopped for lunch, and by three o'clock Townsend was checking his watch every few minutes. Despite his pacing up and down the room, delivering monosyllabic replies to lengthy questions, the final document wasn't ready for signing until a few minutes after five.

Townsend breathed a sigh of relief when the lawyers finally rose from the boardroom table and began to stretch themselves. He checked his watch again, and was confident he could still catch a plane that would get him back to Adelaide in time. He thanked both his advisers for their efforts, and was shaking hands with their opposite numbers when Sir Somerset walked into the room, followed by his editor and chief executive.

'I'm told we have an agreement at last,' said the old man with a broad grin.

'I think so,' said Townsend, trying not to show how anxious he was to escape. If he called Moore's to warn her he might be late, he knew they wouldn't put him through.

'Well, let's have a drink to celebrate before we put our signatures to the final document,' said Sir Somerset.

After the third whisky, Townsend suggested that perhaps the time had come to sign the contract. Nick Watson agreed, and reminded Sir Somerset that he still had a paper to bring out that night. 'Quite right,' said the proprietor, removing a fountain pen from his inside pocket. 'And as I will still own the *Chronicle* for another six weeks, we can't allow standards to drop. By the way, Keith, I do hope you'll be able to join me for dinner?'

'I'm afraid I can't tonight,' replied Townsend. 'I already have a dinner appointment in Adelaide.'

Sir Somerset swung round to face him. 'It had better be a beautiful woman,' he said, 'because I'm damned if I'll be stood up for another business deal.'

'I promise you she's beautiful,' said Townsend, laughing. 'And it's only our second date.'

'In that case, I won't hold you up,' said Sir Somerset, heading towards the boardroom table where two copies of the agreement had been laid out. He stopped for a moment, staring down at the contract, and seemed to hesitate. Both sides looked a little nervous, and one of Sir Somerset's lawyers began to fidget.

The old man turned to Townsend and winked. 'I must tell you that it was Duncan who finally convinced me I should go with you, and not Hacker,' he said. He bent down and put his signature to both contracts, then passed the pen over to Townsend, who scribbled his name by the side of Sir Somerset's.

The two men shook hands rather formally. 'Just time for

another drink,' said Sir Somerset, and winked at Townsend. 'You run along, Keith, and we'll see how much of the profits we can consume in your absence. I must say, my boy, I couldn't be more delighted that the *Chronicle* will be passing into the hands of Sir Graham Townsend's son.'

Nick Watson stepped forward and put his arm round Townsend's shoulder as he turned to leave. 'I must say, as editor of the *Chronicle*, how much I'm looking forward to working with you. I hope we'll be seeing you back in Sydney before too long.'

'I'm looking forward to working with you as well,' said Townsend, 'and I'm sure we'll bump into each other from time to time.' He turned to shake hands with Duncan Alexander. 'Thank you,' he said. 'We're all square.' Duncan thrust out his hand, but Townsend was already rushing out of the door. He saw the lift doors close seconds before he could stab the down arrow on the wall. When he finally flagged a taxi, the driver refused to break the speed limit despite coaxing, bribing and finally shouting. As he was being driven into the terminal, Townsend was able to watch the Douglas DC4 rise into the air above him, oblivious of its final passenger stranded in a taxi below.

'It must have left on time for a change,' said the taxi driver with a shrug of the shoulders. That was more than could be said for the next flight, which was scheduled to take off an hour later, but ended up being delayed by forty minutes.

Townsend checked his watch, walked slowly over to the phone booth, and looked up Susan's number in the Adelaide directory. The operator told him that the number was engaged. When he rang again a few minutes later, there was no reply. Perhaps she was taking a shower. He tried to imagine the scene as the Tannoy announced, 'This is a final call for all passengers travelling to Adelaide.'

He asked the operator to try once more, only to find the number was engaged again. He cursed, replaced the phone and ran all the way to the aircraft, boarding just before they closed the door. He continually thumped his armrest throughout the flight, but it didn't make the plane go any faster.

Sam was standing by the car looking anxious when his master came charging out of the terminal. He drove into Adelaide, ignoring every known speed limit, but by the time he dropped his boss outside L'Étoile, the head waiter had already taken the last orders.

Townsend tried to explain what had happened, but Susan seemed to understand even before he had opened his mouth. 'I phoned you from the airport, but it was either engaged or just went on ringing.' He looked at the untouched cutlery on the table in front of her. 'Don't tell me you haven't eaten.'

'No, I didn't feel that hungry,' she said, and took his hand. 'But you must be famished, and I'll bet you still want to celebrate your triumph. So, if you had a choice, what would you like to do most?'

---◦---

When Townsend walked into his office the following morning, he found Bunty hovering by his desk clutching a sheet of paper. She looked as if she had been standing there for some time.

'Problem?' Townsend asked as he closed the door.

'No. It's just that you seem to have forgotten that I'm due to retire at the end of this month.'

'I hadn't forgotten,' said Townsend, as he took the seat behind his desk. 'I just didn't think . . .'

'The rules of the company are quite clear on this matter,' said Bunty. 'When a female employee reaches the age of sixty . . .'

'You're never sixty, Bunty!'

'. . . she qualifies for retirement on the last Friday of that calendar month.'

'Rules are there to be broken.'

'Your father said that there should be no exceptions to that particular rule, and I agree with him.'

'But I haven't got the time to look for anyone else at the moment, Bunty. What with the takeover of the *Chronicle* and . . .'

'I had anticipated that problem,' she said, not flinching, 'and I have found the ideal replacement.'

'But what are her qualifications?' demanded Townsend, ready to dismiss them immediately as inadequate.

'She's my niece,' came back the reply, 'and more importantly, she comes from the Edinburgh side of the family.'

Townsend couldn't think of a suitable reply. 'Well, you'd better make an appointment for her to see me.' He paused. 'Some time next month.'

'She is at this moment sitting in my office, and can see you right now,' said Bunty.

'You know how busy I am,' said Townsend, looking down at the blank page in his diary. Bunty had obviously made certain he had no appointments that morning. She handed over the piece of paper she had been holding.

He began studying Miss Younger's curriculum vitae, searching for any excuse not to have to see her. When he reached the bottom of the page, he said reluctantly, 'I'll see her now.'

When Heather Younger entered the room, Townsend stood and waited until she had taken the seat on the opposite side of the desk. Miss Younger was about five foot nine, and Townsend knew from her curriculum vitae that she was twenty-eight, though she looked considerably older. She was dressed in a green pullover and tweed skirt. Her brown stockings brought back memories for Townsend of ration books, and she wore a pair of shoes that his mother would have described as sensible.

Her auburn hair was done up in a bun, with not a hair out of place. Townsend's first impression was of being revisited by Miss Steadman, an illusion that was reinforced when Miss Younger began to answer his questions crisply and efficiently.

The interview lasted for eleven minutes, and Miss Younger began work the following Monday.

—◇—

Townsend had to wait another six weeks before the *Chronicle* was legally his. During that time he saw Susan almost every day.

Whenever she asked him why he remained in Adelaide when he felt the *Chronicle* needed so much of his time and attention, he told her simply, 'Until I own the paper I can't do anything about it. And if they had any idea what I have in mind for them, they would tear up the contract long before the six weeks was up.'

If it hadn't been for Susan, those six weeks would have seemed interminable, even though she still regularly teased him about how rarely he was on time for a date. He finally solved the problem by suggesting, 'Perhaps it would be easier if you moved in with me.'

On the Sunday evening before Townsend was officially due to take over the *Chronicle*, he and Susan flew up to Sydney together. Townsend asked the taxi driver to stop outside the paper's offices before going on to the hotel. He took Susan by the elbow and guided her across the road. Once they had reached the pavement on the far side, he turned to look up at the *Chronicle* building. 'At midnight it belongs to me,' he said, with a passion she had never heard before.

'I was rather hoping you'd belong to me at midnight,' she teased.

When they arrived at the hotel, Susan was surprised to find Bruce Kelly waiting for them in the foyer. She was even more surprised when Keith asked him to join them for dinner.

She found her attention drifting while Keith went over his plans for the future of the newspaper as if she wasn't there. She was puzzled as to why the *Chronicle*'s editor hadn't also been invited to join them. When Bruce eventually left, she and Keith took the lift to the top floor and disappeared into their separate rooms. Keith was sitting at the desk, going over some figures, when she slipped through the connecting door to join him.

◄◦►

The proprietor of the *Chronicle* rose at a few minutes before six the following morning, and had left the hotel long before Susan was awake. He walked to Pitt Street, stopping to check every news stand on the way. Not as bad as his first experience with the *Gazette*, he thought, as he arrived outside the *Chronicle* building, but it could still be a lot better.

As he walked into the lobby, he told the security man on the front desk that he wanted to see the editor and the chief executive the moment they came in, and that he required a locksmith immediately. This time as he walked through the building no one asked who he was.

Townsend sat in Sir Somerset's chair for the first time and began reading the final edition of that morning's *Chronicle*. He jotted down some notes, and when he had read the paper from cover to cover he rose from his chair and began to pace around the office, occasionally stopping to look out over Sydney Harbour. When the locksmith appeared a few minutes later, he told him exactly what needed to be done.

'When?' asked the locksmith.

'Now,' said Townsend. He returned to his desk, wondering which of the two men would arrive first. He had to wait another forty minutes before there was a knock on the door. Nick Watson, the editor of the *Chronicle*, walked in to find Townsend, head down, reading through a bulky file.

'I'm so sorry, Keith,' he began. 'I had no idea that you would be in so early on your first day.' Townsend looked up as Watson added, 'Can we make this quick? I'm chairing morning conference at ten.'

'You won't be taking morning conference today,' said Townsend. 'I've asked Bruce Kelly to.'

'What? But I'm the editor,' said Nick.

'Not any longer you aren't,' said Townsend. 'I'm promoting you.'

'Promoting me?' said Nick.

'Yes. You'll be able to read the announcement in tomorrow's paper. You're to be the *Chronicle*'s first Editor Emeritus.'

'What does that mean?'

'"E" means ex, and "meritus" means you deserve it.' Townsend paused as he watched the realisation sink in. 'Don't worry, Nick. You've got a grand title and a year's fully-paid leave.'

'But you told Sir Somerset, in my presence, that you were looking forward to working with me.'

'I know I did, Nick,' he said, and reddened slightly. 'I'm sorry, I . . .' He would have completed the sentence if there hadn't been another knock at the door.

Duncan Alexander walked in and said, 'I apologise for bothering you, Keith, but someone's changed the lock on my office door.'

15

Evening Chronicle

20 NOVEMBER 1947

This Happy Day
Radiant Princess Elizabeth Weds
her Sailor Duke

Charlotte decided that she wouldn't attend Arno Schultz's sixtieth birthday party because she didn't feel confident enough yet to leave David with their German nanny. Since she had returned from Lyon, Dick had become more attentive, and sometimes he even got home in time to see their firstborn before he was put to bed.

That evening Armstrong left the flat for Arno's house just after seven. He assured Charlotte that he only intended to drop in and drink Arno's health, and then return home. She smiled and promised his dinner would be ready by the time he came back.

He hurried across the city in the hope that if he arrived before they sat down for dinner, he would be able to get away after just a quick drink. Then he might even have time to join Max Sackville for a couple of games of poker before going home.

It was a few minutes before eight when Armstrong knocked on Arno's front door. As soon as his host had escorted him into the packed drawing room, it became clear that they had all been waiting for him before sitting down to dinner. He was introduced to Arno's friends, who greeted him as if he was the guest of honour.

Once Arno had placed a glass of white wine in his hand – from a bottle that Armstrong realised the moment he sipped it had not come from the French sector – he was led into the small dining room and placed next to a man who introduced himself as Julius Hahn, and who Arno described as 'my oldest friend and greatest rival'.

Armstrong had heard the name before, but couldn't immediately place it. At first he ignored Hahn, and concentrated on the food that was set in front of him. He had started on his bowl of thin soup, uncertain which animal it had originated from, when Hahn began to question him about how things were back in London. It quickly became clear to Armstrong that this particular German had a far greater knowledge of the British capital than he did.

'I do hope it won't be too long before foreign travel restrictions are lifted,' said Hahn. 'I desperately need to visit your country again.'

'I can't see the Allies agreeing to that for some time yet,' said Armstrong, as Mrs Schultz replaced his empty soup bowl with a plate of rabbit pie.

'That distresses me,' said Hahn. 'I am finding it increasingly difficult to keep track of some of my business interests in London.' And then the name clicked, and for the first time Armstrong rested his knife and fork on the plate. Hahn was the proprietor of *Der Berliner*, the rival paper, published in the American sector. But what else did he own?

'I've been wanting to meet you for some time,' said Armstrong. Hahn looked surprised, because up until that moment Captain Armstrong had shown no interest in him at all. 'How many copies of *Der Berliner* are you printing?' Armstrong asked, already knowing, but wanting to keep Hahn talking before he asked the one question to which he really needed an answer.

'Around 260,000 copies a day,' replied Hahn. 'And our other daily in Frankfurt is, I'm happy to say, back to selling well over two hundred thousand.'

'And how many papers do you have in all?' asked Armstrong casually, picking up his knife and fork again.

'Just the two. It used to be seventeen before the war, as well as several specialist scientific magazines. But I can't hope to return to those sorts of numbers again until all the restrictions are lifted.'

'But I thought Jews – and I am a Jew myself – ' once again Hahn looked surprised ' – weren't allowed to own newspapers before the war.'

'That's true, Captain Armstrong. But I sold all my shares in the company to my partner, who was not Jewish, and he returned them to me at the price he had paid for them within days of the war ending.'

'And the magazines?' asked Armstrong, picking at his rabbit pie. 'Could they make a profit during these hard times?'

'Oh, yes. Indeed, in the long run they may well prove to be a more reliable source of income than the newspapers. Before the war, my company had the lion's share of Germany's scientific publications. But from the moment Hitler marched into Poland, we were forbidden to publish anything that might prove useful to enemies of the Third Reich. I am presently sitting on eight years of unpublished research, including most of the scientific papers produced in Germany during the war. The publishing world would pay handsomely for such material if only I could find an outlet for it.'

'What's stopping you from publishing it now?' asked Armstrong.

'The London publishing house which had an arrangement with me is no longer willing to distribute my work.'

The lightbulb hanging from the ceiling was suddenly switched off, and a small cake boasting a single candle was placed in the centre of the table.

'And why is that?' asked Armstrong, determined not to let the conversation be interrupted, as Arno Schultz blew out his candle to a round of applause.

'Sadly, because the only son of the chairman was killed on the beaches of Dunkirk,' said Hahn, as the largest slice of cake was placed on Armstrong's plate. 'I have written to him often to express my condolences, but he simply doesn't reply.'

'There are other publishing houses in England,' said Armstrong, picking up the cake and stuffing it into his mouth.

'Yes, but my contract doesn't allow me to approach anyone else at the present time. I only have to wait a few more months now. I've already decided which London publishing house would best represent my interests.'

'Have you?' said Armstrong, wiping the crumbs off his mouth.

'If you could find the time, Captain Armstrong,' the German publisher said, 'I would consider it an honour to show you round my presses.'

'My schedule is fairly hectic at the moment.'

'Of course,' said Hahn. 'I quite understand.'

'But perhaps when I'm next visiting the American sector I could drop by.'

'Please do,' said Hahn.

Once dinner was over, Armstrong thanked his host for a memorable evening, and timed his departure so that he left at the same time as Julius Hahn.

'I hope we will meet again soon,' said Hahn as they stepped out onto the pavement.

'I'm sure we will,' said Armstrong, shaking hands with Arno Schultz's closest friend.

When Dick arrived back at the apartment a few minutes before midnight, Charlotte was already asleep. He undressed, threw on a dressing-gown and crept upstairs to David's room. He stood by the side of the cot for some time, staring down at his son.

'I shall build you an empire,' he whispered, 'which one day you will be proud to take over.'

◄◦►

The next morning, Armstrong reported to Colonel Oakshott that he had attended Arno Schultz's sixtieth birthday party, but not that he had met Julius Hahn. The only piece of news

Oakshott had for Dick was that Major Forsdyke had phoned to say he wanted him to make another trip to the Russian sector. Armstrong promised he would contact Forsdyke, but didn't add that he planned to visit the American sector first.

'By the way, Dick,' said the colonel. 'I never did see your article about the way we're treating the Germans in our internment camps.'

'No, sir. I'm sorry to say that the bloody Krauts just wouldn't co-operate. I'm afraid it all turned out to be a bit of a waste of time.'

'I'm not that surprised,' said Oakshott. 'I did warn you . . .'

'And you have been proved right, sir.'

'I'm sorry to hear it, though,' replied the colonel, 'because I still believe it's important to build bridges with these people and to regain their confidence.'

'I couldn't agree with you more, sir,' said Armstrong. 'And I can assure you that I'm trying to play my part.'

'I know you are, Dick. How's *Der Telegraf* faring in these difficult times?'

'Never better,' he replied. 'Starting next month we'll have a Sunday edition on the streets, and the daily is still breaking records.'

'That's tremendous news,' said the colonel. 'By the way, I've just been told that the Duke of Gloucester may be making an official visit to Berlin next month. Could make a good story.'

'Would you like to see it on the front page of *Der Telegraf?*' Armstrong asked.

'Not until I get the all-clear from Security. Then you can have – what do you call it? – an exclusive.'

'How exciting,' said Armstrong, remembering the colonel's penchant for visiting dignitaries, especially members of the royal family. He rose to leave.

'Don't forget to report to Forsdyke,' were the colonel's final words before Armstrong saluted and was driven back to his office.

Armstrong had more pressing considerations on his mind than a major from the security service. As soon as he had cleared the mail from his desk, he warned Sally that he intended to spend the rest of the day in the American sector. 'If Forsdyke calls,' he said, 'make an appointment for me to see him some time tomorrow.'

As Private Benson drove him across the city towards the American sector, Armstrong went through the sequence of events that would be necessary if everything were to appear unplanned. He told Benson to stop off at Holt & Co, where he withdrew £100 from his account, almost clearing his entire balance. He left a token sum, as it was still a court-martial offence for a British officer to have an overdraft.

Once he had crossed into the American sector, Benson drew up outside another bank, where Armstrong exchanged the sterling for $410, which he hoped would be a large enough stake to ensure that Max Sackville would fall in with his plans. The two of them had a leisurely lunch in the American mess, and Armstrong agreed to join the captain later that evening for their usual game of poker. When he jumped back into his jeep, he ordered Benson to drive him to the offices of *Der Berliner*.

Julius Hahn was surprised to see Captain Armstrong so soon after their first meeting, but he immediately dropped what he was doing to show his distinguished visitor round the plant. It took Armstrong only a few minutes to realise the size of the empire Hahn controlled, even if he did keep repeating in a self-deprecating way, 'It's nothing like the old days.'

By the time Armstrong had completed his tour, including the twenty-one presses in the basement, he was aware of just how insignificant *Der Telegraf* was by comparison with Hahn's outfit, especially when his host mentioned that he had seven other printing presses of roughly the same size in other parts of Germany, including one in the Russian sector of Berlin.

When Armstrong finally left the building a few minutes after five, he thanked Julius, as he had started to call him, and said, 'We must meet again soon, my friend. Perhaps you'd care to join me for lunch some time?'

'That's most kind of you,' said Hahn. 'But as I'm sure you

know, Captain Armstrong, I'm not allowed to visit the British sector.'

'Then I will simply have to come to you,' said Armstrong with a smile.

Hahn accompanied his visitor to the door and shook him warmly by the hand. Armstrong crossed the road and walked down one of the side streets, ignoring his driver. He stopped when he came to a bar called Joe's, and wondered what it had been known as before the war. He stepped inside as Benson brought the jeep to a halt a few yards further down the road.

Armstrong ordered a Coca-Cola and took a seat in the corner of the bar. He was relieved that no one recognised him or made any attempt to join him. After a third Coke, he checked that the $410 was in place. It was going to be a long night.

—◦—

'Where the hell is he?' demanded Forsdyke.

'Captain Armstrong had to go over to the American sector just before lunch, sir,' said Sally. 'Something urgent came up following his meeting with Colonel Oakshott. But before he left, he did ask me to make an appointment if you called.'

'That was most thoughtful of him,' said Forsdyke sarcastically. 'Something urgent has come up in the British sector, and I'd be obliged if Captain Armstrong would report to my office at nine o'clock tomorrow morning.'

'I'll see that he gets your message just as soon as he returns, Major Forsdyke,' said Sally. She would have tried to contact Dick immediately, but she had absolutely no idea where he was.

—◦—

'Five card stud as usual?' said Max, pushing a bottle of beer and an opener across the green baize table.

'Suits me,' said Armstrong as he began to shuffle the deck.

'I have a feeling about tonight, old buddy,' said Max, removing his jacket and hanging it on the arm of his chair. 'I hope you've got a lot of money to burn.' He poured his beer slowly into a glass.

245

'Enough,' said Armstrong. He only sipped at his beer, aware that he would need to remain stone cold sober for several hours. When he had finished shuffling, Max cut the deck and lit a cigarette.

By the end of the first hour, Armstrong was $70 ahead, and the word 'lucky' kept floating across from the other side of the table. He began the second hour with a cushion of nearly $500. 'You've been on a lucky run so far,' said Max, flicking the top off his fourth bottle of beer. 'But the night is far from over.'

Armstrong smiled and nodded, as he tossed another card across to his opponent and dealt himself a second one. He checked his cards: the four and nine of spades. He placed $5 on the table and dealt two more cards.

Max countered the bid with $5 of his own, and turned the corner of his card to see what Dick had dealt him. He tried not to smile, and placed another $5 on top of Armstrong's stake.

Armstrong dealt himself a fifth card, and studied his hand for some time before placing a $10 bill in the kitty. Max didn't hesitate to remove $10 from a wad in an inside pocket and drop it on the pile of notes in the centre of the table. He licked his lips and said, 'See you, old buddy.'

Armstrong turned his cards over to reveal a pair of fours. Max's smile became even broader as he produced a pair of tens. 'You can't bluff me,' said the American, and clawed the money back to his side of the table.

By the end of the second hour Max was slightly ahead. 'I did warn you that it was going to be a long night,' he said. He had dispensed with the glass some time ago, and was now drinking straight from the bottle.

It was during the third hour, after Max had won three hands in a row, that Dick brought the name of Julius Hahn into the conversation. 'Claims he knows you.'

'Yeah, sure does,' said Max. 'He's responsible for bringing out the paper in this sector. Not that I ever read it.'

'He seems pretty successful,' said Armstrong, dealing another hand.

'Certainly is. But only thanks to me.' Armstrong placed $10

in the centre of the table, despite having nothing more than ace high. Max immediately dropped $10 on top of his, and demanded another card.

'What do you mean "because of you"?' Armstrong asked, placing $20 on the growing pile.

Max hesitated, checked his cards, looked at the pile and said, 'Was that $20 you just put in?' Armstrong nodded, and the American extracted $20 from the pocket of his jacket.

'He couldn't even wipe his ass in the morning if I didn't hand him the paper,' said Max, studying his hand intently. 'I issue his monthly permit. I control his paper supply. I decide how much electricity he gets. I decide when it will be turned on and off. As you and Arno Schultz know only too well.'

Max looked up, and was surprised to see Armstrong removing a stack of notes from his wallet. 'You're bluffing, kid,' said Max. 'I can smell it.' He hesitated. 'How much did you put up that time?'

'Fifty dollars,' said Armstrong casually.

Max dug into his jacket pocket and extracted two tens and six fives, placing them gingerly on the table. 'So let's see what you've come up with this time,' he said apprehensively.

Armstrong revealed a pair of sevens. Max immediately burst out laughing, and flicked over three jacks.

'I knew it. You're full of shit.' He took another swig from his bottle. As he started dealing the next hand the smile never left his face. 'I'm not sure which one would be easier to polish off, you or Hahn,' he said, beginning to slur his words.

'Are you sure that's not the drink talking?' said Dick, studying his hand with little interest.

'You'll see who's doing the talking,' replied Max. 'Within an hour I'll have wiped you out.'

'I wasn't referring to me,' said Armstrong, dropping another $5 into the centre of the table. 'I was talking about Hahn.'

There was a long pause while Max took another swig from the bottle. He then studied his cards before putting them face down on the table. Armstrong drew another card and deposited $10 with the bank. Max demanded a further card, and when he saw it he began licking his lips. He returned to his wad and extracted a further $10.

'Let's see what you've got this time, old buddy,' Max said, confident he must win with two pairs, aces and jacks.

Armstrong turned over three fives. Max scowled as he watched his winnings return across the table. 'Would you be willing to put real money in place of that big mouth of yours?' he asked.

'I just have,' said Dick, pocketing the money.

'No, I meant when it comes to Hahn.'

Dick said nothing.

'You're full of chickenshit,' said Max, after Dick had remained silent for some time.

Dick placed the deck back on the table, looked across at his opponent and said coolly, 'I'll bet you a thousand dollars you can't put Hahn out of business.'

Max put down his bottle and stared across the table as if he couldn't believe what he'd just heard. 'How long will you give me?'

'Six weeks.'

'No, that's not long enough. Don't forget I have to make it look as if it's nothing to do with me. I'll need at least six months.'

'I haven't got six months,' said Armstrong. 'I could always close down *Der Telegraf* in six weeks if you want to reverse the bet.'

'But Hahn's running a far bigger operation than Arno Schultz,' said Max.

'I realise that. So I'll give you three months.'

'Then I'd expect you to offer me odds.'

Once again, Armstrong pretended he needed time to consider the proposition. 'Two to one,' he eventually said.

'Three to one and you're on,' said Max.

'You've got a deal,' said Armstrong, and the two men leaned across the table and shook hands. The American captain then rose unsteadily from his chair, and walked over to a drawing of a scantily dressed woman adorning a calendar on the far wall.

He lifted the pages until he reached October, removed a pen from his hip pocket, counted out loud and drew a large circle around the seventeenth. 'That'll be the day when I collect my thousand dollars,' he said.

'You haven't a hope in hell,' said Armstrong. 'I've met Hahn, and I can tell you he won't be that easy to roll over.'

'Just watch me,' said Max as he returned to the table. 'I'm going to do to Hahn exactly what the Germans failed to do.'

Max began to deal a new hand. For the next hour, Dick continued to win back most of what he had lost earlier in the evening. But when he left to return home just before midnight, Max was still licking his lips.

—◦—

When Dick came out of the bathroom the following morning he found Charlotte sitting up in bed wide awake.

'And what time did you get home last night?' she asked coldly, as he pulled open a drawer in search of a clean shirt.

'Twelve,' said Dick, 'maybe one. I ate out so you didn't have to worry about me.'

'I'd rather you came home at a civilised hour, and then perhaps we could eat one of the meals I prepare for you every night.'

'As I keep trying to tell you, everything I do is in your best interests.'

'I'm beginning to think you don't know what is in my best interests,' said Charlotte.

Dick studied her reflection in the mirror, but said nothing.

'If you're never going to make the effort to get us out of this hellhole, perhaps the time has come for me to go back to Lyon.'

'My demob papers should be through fairly soon,' Dick said as he checked his Windsor knot in the mirror. 'Three months at the most, Colonel Oakshott assured me.'

'Three more months?' said Charlotte in disbelief.

'Something's come up that could turn out to be very important for our future.'

'And as usual I suppose you can't tell me what it is.'

'No. It's top secret.'

'How very convenient,' said Charlotte. 'Every time I want to discuss what's happening in our life, all you say is "Something's come up." And when I ask you for details, you always tell me it's top secret.'

'That's not fair,' said Dick. 'It *is* top secret. And everything I am trying to achieve will in the end be for you and David.'

'How would you know? You're never here when I put David to bed, and you've left for the office long before he wakes up in the morning. He sees so little of you nowadays that he's not sure if it's you or Private Benson who's his father.'

'I have responsibilities,' said Dick, his voice rising.

'Yes,' said Charlotte. 'Responsibilities to your family. And the most important one must surely be to get us out of this godforsaken city as soon as possible.'

Dick put on his khaki jacket and turned round to face her. 'I'm still working on it. It's not easy at the moment. You must try to understand.'

'I think I understand only too well, because it seems remarkably easy for a lot of other people I know. And as *Der Telegraf* keeps reminding us, trains are now leaving Berlin at least twice a day. Perhaps David and I should catch one.'

'What do you mean by that?' shouted Dick, advancing towards her.

'Quite simply that you might just come home one night and find you no longer have a wife and child.'

Dick took another step towards her and raised his fist, but she didn't flinch. He stopped and stared down into her eyes.

'Going to treat me the same way you treat anyone below the rank of captain, are you?'

'I don't know why I bother,' said Dick, lowering his fist. 'You don't give me any support when I most need it, and whenever I try to do something for you, you just complain all the time.' Charlotte didn't blanch. 'Go back to your family if you want to, you stupid bitch, but don't think I'll come running after you.' He stormed out of the bedroom, grabbed his peaked hat and swagger stick from the hall stand, ran down the stairs and strode out of the front door. Benson was sitting in the jeep, engine running, waiting to drive him to the office.

'And where the bloody hell do you imagine you'd end up if you left me?' Armstrong said as he climbed into the front seat.

'I beg your pardon, sir?' said Benson.

Armstrong turned to face his driver and said, 'Are you married, Reg?'

'No, sir. Hitler saved me just in time.'

'Hitler?'

'Yes, sir, I was called up three days before the wedding.'

'Is she still waiting for you?'

'No, sir. She married my best mate.'

'Do you miss her?'

'No, but I miss him.'

Armstrong laughed as Benson drew up outside the office.

The first person he came across as he walked into the building was Sally. 'Did you get my message?' she asked.

Armstrong stopped immediately. 'What message?'

'I phoned you at home yesterday and asked Charlotte to tell you that Major Forsdyke expects to see you in his office at nine this morning.'

'Damn the woman,' said Armstrong, heading back past Sally and towards the front door. 'What else have I got on today?' he shouted on the move.

'The diary is fairly clear,' she replied, chasing after him, 'except for a dinner this evening in honour of Field Marshal Auchinleck. Charlotte's been invited too. You have to be in the officers' mess at seven for seven-thirty. All the top brass is going to be on parade.'

As Armstrong reached the front door he said, 'Don't expect me back much before lunch.'

Benson hastily stubbed out the cigarette he had just lit and said, 'Where to this time, sir?' as Armstrong jumped in beside him.

'Major Forsdyke's office, and I need to be there by nine o'clock.'

'But, sir . . .' began Benson as he pressed the starter, and decided against telling the captain that even Nuvolari would be hard-pressed to get to the other side of the sector in seventeen minutes.

Armstrong was dropped outside Forsdyke's office with sixty seconds to spare. Benson was only relieved that they hadn't been stopped by the military police.

'Good morning, Armstrong,' said Forsdyke as Dick entered his office. He waited for him to salute, but he didn't. 'Something urgent has come up. We need you to deliver a package to your friend Major Tulpanov.'

'He's not my friend,' Armstrong replied curtly.

'No need to be so sensitive, old fellow,' said Forsdyke. 'You should know by now that you can't afford to be when you work for me.'

'I don't work for you,' barked Armstrong.

Forsdyke looked up at the man standing on the other side of his desk. His eyes narrowed and his lips tightened in a straight line. 'I am aware of the influence you have in the British sector, Captain Armstrong, but I would remind you that however powerful you imagine you are, I still outrank you. And perhaps more importantly, I have absolutely no interest in appearing on the front page of your frightful little rag. So can we stop fussing about your over-inflated ego, and get on with the job in hand.'

A long silence followed. 'You wanted me to make a delivery,' Armstrong eventually managed.

'Yes, I do,' the major replied. He pulled open a drawer in his desk, took out a package the size of a shoebox and handed it across to Armstrong. 'Please see that Major Tulpanov gets this as soon as possible.'

Armstrong took the package, placed it under his left arm, saluted in an exaggerated manner, and marched out of the major's office.

'The Russian sector,' he barked as he climbed back into the jeep.

'Yes, sir,' said Benson, pleased that on this occasion he had at least had time to have a couple of drags on his cigarette.

A few minutes after they had crossed into the Russian sector, Armstrong ordered him to pull in to the kerb.

'Wait here, and don't move until I return,' he said as he stepped out of the jeep and made off in the direction of Leninplatz.

'Excuse me, sir,' said Benson, jumping out of the jeep and running after him.

Armstrong swung round and glared at his driver. 'What the hell do you think you're doing?'

'Won't you be needing this, sir?' he asked, holding out the brown paper parcel.

Armstrong grabbed the package and walked away without saying another word. Benson wondered if his boss was visiting a mistress, although the cathedral clock had only just struck ten.

When Armstrong reached Leninplatz a few minutes later, his temper had hardly cooled. He charged straight into the building and up the stairs, through the room where the secretary sat and on towards Tulpanov's office.

'Excuse me, sir,' said the secretary, shooting out of her chair. But it was too late. Armstrong had reached the door of Tulpanov's office long before she could catch up with him. He pushed it open and strode in.

He stopped in his tracks the moment he saw who Tulpanov was speaking to. 'I'm sorry, sir,' he stammered, and quickly turned to leave, nearly knocking over the advancing secretary.

'No, Lubji, please don't go,' said Tulpanov. 'Won't you join us?'

Armstrong swung back, came to attention and gave a crisp salute. He felt his face going redder and redder. 'Marshal,' the KGB man said, 'I don't think you've met Captain Armstrong, who's in charge of public relations for the British sector.'

Armstrong shook hands with the officer commanding the Russian sector and apologised once again for interrupting him, but this time in Russian. 'I am delighted to meet you,' said Marshal Zhukov in his own tongue. 'If I'm not mistaken, I believe I shall be joining you for dinner tonight.'

Armstrong looked surprised. 'I don't think so, sir.'

'Oh, yes,' said Zhukov. 'I checked the guest list only this morning. I have the pleasure of being seated next to your wife.'

There followed an uneasy silence in which Armstrong decided not to venture any more opinions. 'Thank you for dropping by, sir,' said Tulpanov, breaking the silence. 'And for clearing up that little misunderstanding.'

Major Tulpanov gave a half-hearted salute. Zhukov responded in kind, and left them without another word. When the door had closed behind him, Armstrong asked, 'Do marshals usually visit majors in your army?'

'Only when the majors are in the KGB,' said Tulpanov with a smile. His eyes settled on the parcel. 'I see you come bearing gifts.'

'I've no idea what it is,' said Armstrong, handing over the parcel. 'All I know is that Forsdyke asked me to make sure it was delivered to you immediately.'

Tulpanov took the parcel and slowly undid the string, like a child unwrapping an unexpected Christmas present. Once he had removed the brown paper, he lifted the lid of the box to reveal a pair of brown Church's brogues. He tried them on. 'A perfect fit,' he said, looking down at the highly polished toecaps. 'Forsdyke may well be what your friend Max would call an arrogant son of a bitch, but you can always rely on the English to supply one with the finer things in life.'

'So, am I nothing more than a messenger boy?' asked Armstrong.

'In our service, Lubji, I can assure you there is no higher calling.'

'I told Forsdyke, and I'll tell you . . .' began Armstrong, his voice rising. But he stopped in mid-sentence.

'I can see,' said the KGB major, 'that – to use another English expression – you got out of the wrong side of the bed this morning.'

Armstrong stood before him, almost shaking with anger.

'No, no, do go on, Lubji. Please tell me what you said to Forsdyke.'

'Nothing,' said Armstrong. 'I said nothing.'

'I'm glad to hear that,' said the major. 'Because you must understand that I am the only person to whom you can afford to tell anything.'

'What makes you so sure of that?' said Armstrong.

'Because, Lubji, like Faust, you have signed a contract with the devil.' He paused. 'And perhaps also because I already know about your little plot to destabilise – a uniquely British word, that admirably expresses your intentions – Mr Julius Hahn.'

Armstrong looked as if he was about to protest. The major raised an eyebrow, but Armstrong said nothing.

'You should have let me in on your little secret from the start, Lubji,' Tulpanov continued. 'Then we could have played our part. We would have stopped the flow of electricity, not to mention the supply of paper to Hahn's plant in the Russian sector. But then, you were probably unaware that he prints all his magazines in a building a mere stone's throw from where we are now standing. If you had only confided in us, we could have lengthened the odds on Captain Sackville collecting his thousand dollars . . . quite considerably.'

Armstrong still said nothing.

'But perhaps that is exactly what you had planned. Three to one is good odds, Lubji, just as long as I am one of the three.'

'But how did you . . .'

'Once again you have underestimated us, Lubji. But be assured, we still have your best interests at heart.' Tulpanov began walking towards the door. 'And do tell Major Forsdyke, when you next see him, a perfect fit.'

It was clear that he had no intention of inviting him to lunch on this occasion. Armstrong saluted, left Tulpanov's office and returned sulkily to his jeep.

'*Der Telegraf*,' he said quietly to Benson.

They were held up for only a few minutes at the checkpoint before being allowed to enter the British sector. As Armstrong walked into the print room of *Der Telegraf*, he was surprised to find the presses running flat out. He headed straight over to Arno, who was overseeing the bundling of each new stack of papers.

'Why are we still printing?' Armstrong shouted, trying to make himself heard above the noise of the presses. Arno pointed in the direction of his office, and neither of them spoke again until he had closed the door behind them.

'Haven't you heard?' Arno asked, waving Armstrong into his chair.

'Heard what?'

'We sold 350,000 copies of the paper last night, and they still want more.'

'Three hundred and fifty thousand? And they want more? Why?'

'*Der Berliner* hasn't been on the streets for the last two days. Julius Hahn rang this morning to tell me that for the past forty-eight hours his electricity has been cut off.'

'What extraordinary bad luck,' said Armstrong, trying to look sympathetic.

'And to make matters worse,' added Arno, 'he's also lost his usual supply of paper from the Russian sector. He wanted to know if we'd been having the same problems.'

'What did you tell him?' asked Armstrong.

'That we haven't had any trouble since you took over,' Arno replied. Armstrong smiled and rose from his chair.

'If they're off the streets again tomorrow,' said Arno as Armstrong began walking towards the door, 'we'll have to print at least 400,000 copies.'

Armstrong closed the door behind him and repeated, 'What extraordinary bad luck.'

16

SYDNEY
Morning Herald

30 JANUARY 1957

Dane's Controversial Design
Wins Opera House Contest

'But I've hardly seen you since we announced our engagement,' Susan said.

'I'm trying to bring out one newspaper in Adelaide and another in Sydney,' said Keith, turning over to face her. 'It's just not possible to be in two places at once.'

'It's never possible for you to be in one place at once nowadays,' said Susan. 'And if you get your hands on that Sunday paper in Perth, as I keep reading you're trying to, I won't even see you at the weekends.'

Keith realised that this wasn't the time to tell her that he had already closed the deal with the owner of the *Perth Sunday Monitor*. He slipped out of bed without making any comment.

'And where are you off to now?' she asked as he disappeared into the bathroom.

'I've got a breakfast meeting in the city,' shouted Keith from behind a closed door.

'On a Sunday morning?'

'It was the only day he could see me. The man's flown down from Brisbane specially.'

'But we're meant to be spending the day sailing. Or had you forgotten that as well?'

'Of course I hadn't forgotten,' said Keith as he came out of the bathroom. 'That's exactly why I agreed to a breakfast meeting. I'll be home long before you're ready to leave.'

'Like you were last Sunday?'

'That was different,' said Keith. 'The *Perth Monitor* is a Sunday paper, and if I'm buying it, how can I find out what it's like except by being there on the one day it comes out?'

'So you have bought it?' said Susan.

Keith pulled on his trousers, then turned to face her sheepishly. 'Yes, subject to legal agreement. But it's got a first-class management team, so there should be no reason for me to have to go to Perth that often.'

'And the editorial staff?' asked Susan as Keith slipped on a sports jacket. 'If this one follows the same pattern as every other paper you've taken over, you'll be living on top of them for the first six months.'

'No, it won't be that bad,' said Keith. 'I promise you. Just be sure you're ready to leave the moment I get back.' He leaned down and kissed her on the cheek. 'I shouldn't be more than an hour, two at the most.' He closed the bedroom door before she had a chance to comment.

As Townsend climbed into the front of the car, his driver turned on the ignition.

'Tell me, Sam, does your wife give you a hard time about the hours you have to work for me?'

'Hard to tell, sir. Lately she's stopped talking to me altogether.'

'How long have you been married?'

'Eleven years.'

He decided against asking Sam any further questions about matrimony. As the car sped towards the city, he tried to dismiss Susan from his thoughts and to concentrate on the meeting he was about to have with Alan Rutledge. He had never met the man before, but everyone in the newspaper world knew of Rutledge's reputation as an award-winning journalist and a man who could drink anyone under the table. If Townsend's latest idea was to have any chance of succeeding, he needed someone of Rutledge's ability to get it off the ground.

Sam turned off Elizabeth Street and swept up to the entrance of the Town House Hotel. Townsend smiled when he saw the *Sunday Chronicle* on top of the news stand, and remembered its leader that morning. Once again the paper had told its readers that the time had come for Mr Menzies to step down and make way for a younger man more in tune with the aspirations of modern Australians.

As the car drew in to the kerb Townsend said, 'I should be about an hour, two at the most.' Sam smiled to himself as his boss jumped out of the car, pushed his way through the swing doors and disappeared.

Townsend walked quickly through the foyer and on into the breakfast room. He glanced around and spotted Alan Rutledge sitting on his own in a window seat, smoking a cigarette and reading the *Sunday Chronicle*.

He rose as Townsend headed towards the table, and they shook hands rather formally. Rutledge tossed the paper to one side and said, smiling, 'I see you've taken the *Chronicle* even further downmarket.' Townsend glanced at the headline: 'Shrunken Head Found on Top of Sydney Bus.' 'Hardly a headline in the tradition of Sir Somerset Kenwright, I would have thought.'

'No,' said Townsend, 'but then neither is the bottom line. We're selling 100,000 more copies a day than they did when he was the proprietor, and the profits are up by 17 per cent.' He glanced up at the hovering waitress. 'Just a black coffee for me, and perhaps some toast.'

'I hope you weren't thinking of asking me to be the next editor of the *Chronicle*,' said Rutledge, lighting another Turf. Townsend glanced at the ashtray on the table, and saw that this was Rutledge's fourth since he had arrived at the breakfast table.

'No,' said Townsend. 'Bruce Kelly's the right man for the *Chronicle*. What I have in mind for you is far more appropriate.'

'And what might that be?' asked Rutledge.

'A paper that doesn't even exist yet,' said Townsend, 'other than in my imagination. But one I need you to help me create.'

'And which city have you got in your sights?' asked Rutledge. 'Most of them already have too many papers, and those that don't have created a virtual monopoly for themselves. No better example than Adelaide.'

'I can't disagree with that,' said Townsend, as the waitress poured him a cup of steaming black coffee. 'But what this country doesn't have at the moment is a national paper for all Australians. I want to create a paper called the *Continent*, which will sell from Sydney to Perth, and everywhere in between. I want it to be the *Times* of Australia, and regarded by everyone as the nation's number-one quality newspaper. More importantly, I want you to be its first editor.'

Alan inhaled deeply, and didn't speak for some time, 'Where would it be based?'

'Canberra. It has to come out of the political capital, where the nation's decisions are made. Our biggest task will be to sign up the best journalists available. That's where you come in, because they're more likely to come on board if they know you're going to be the editor.'

'How long do you imagine the run-in time will be?' asked Rutledge, stubbing out his fifth cigarette.

'I hope to have it on the streets in six months,' Townsend replied.

'And what circulation are you hoping for?' Rutledge asked, as he lit another cigarette.

'Two hundred to 250,000 in the first year, building up to 400,000.'

'How long will you stay with it if you don't manage those numbers?'

'Two years, perhaps three. But as long as it breaks even, I'll stay with it forever.'

'And what sort of package do you have in mind for me?' asked Alan.

'Ten thousand a year, with all the usual extras.' A smile

appeared on Rutledge's face, but then, Townsend knew it was almost double what he was getting in his present job.

By the time Townsend had answered all his questions and Rutledge had opened another packet of cigarettes, they could have ordered an early lunch. When Townsend finally rose to shake hands again, Rutledge said he would consider his proposition and get back to him by the end of the week.

As Sam drove him back to Darling Point, Townsend wondered how he could make the idea of travelling between Sydney, Canberra, Adelaide and Perth every seven days sound exciting to Susan. He wasn't in much doubt what her reaction would be.

When Sam pulled in to the drive a few minutes before one, the first thing Keith saw was Susan coming down the path, carrying a large hamper in one hand and a bag full of beachwear in the other.

'Close the front door,' was all she said as she passed Keith and continued walking towards the car. Keith's fingers had just touched the door handle when the phone began to ring. He hesitated for a moment, and decided to tell whoever it was that they would have to call back that evening.

'Afternoon, Keith. It's Dan Hadley.'

'Good afternoon, Senator,' Keith replied. 'I'm in a bit of a rush. Would it be possible for you to call me back this evening?'

'You won't be in a rush when you've heard what I've got to tell you,' said the senator.

'I'm listening, Dan, but it will still have to be quick.'

'I've just put the phone down on the postmaster general. He tells me that Bob Menzies is willing to support the state's request for a new commercial radio network. He's also let slip that Hacker and Kenwright wouldn't be in the running, as they already control their own networks. So this time you must be in with a fighting chance of picking it up.'

Keith sat down on the chair by the phone and listened to the senator's proposed plan of campaign. Hadley was aware of the fact that Townsend had already made unsuccessful takeover bids for his rivals' networks. Both approaches had been rebuffed, because Hacker was still angry not to have got his hands on the *Chronicle*, and as for Kenwright, he and Townsend were no longer on speaking terms.

Forty minutes later Townsend put the phone down and ran out, slamming the door behind him. The car was no longer there. He cursed as he walked back up the path and let himself into the house. But now that Susan had left without him, he decided he might as well carry out the senator's first suggestion. He picked up the phone and dialled a number that would put him straight through to the editor's desk.

'Yes,' said a voice that Townsend recognised from the single word.

'Bruce, what's the subject of your leader for tomorrow's paper?' he asked, without bothering to announce who it was.

'Why Sydney doesn't need an opera house, but does need another bridge,' said Bruce.

'Scrap it,' said Townsend. 'I'll have two hundred words ready for you in an hour's time.'

'What's the theme, Keith?'

'I shall be telling our readers what a first-class job Bob Menzies is doing as prime minister, and how foolish it would be to replace a statesman with some inexperienced, wet-behind-the-ears apparatchik.'

—◦—

Townsend spent most of the next six months locked up in Canberra with Alan Rutledge as they prepared to launch the new paper. Everything ran late, from locating the offices to employing the best administrative staff and poaching the most experienced journalists. But Townsend's biggest problem was making enough time to see Susan, because when he wasn't in Canberra he was inevitably in Perth.

The *Continent* had been on the streets for just over a month, and his bank manager was beginning to remind him that its cash flow was only going one way – out. Susan told him that even at weekends, he was always going one way – back.

Townsend was in the newsroom talking to Alan Rutledge

when the phone rang. The editor put his hand over the speaker and warned him that Susan was on the line.

'Oh, Christ, I'd forgotten. It's her birthday, and we're meant to be having lunch at her sister's place in Sydney. Tell her I'm at the airport. Whatever you do, don't let her know I'm still here.'

'Hi, Susan,' said Alan. 'I've just been told that Keith left for the airport some time ago, so I guess he's already on his way to Sydney.' He listened carefully to her reply. 'Yes . . . Fine . . . OK . . . I will.' He put the phone down. 'She says if you leave right away, you might just get to the airport in time to catch the 8.25.'

Townsend left Alan's office without even saying goodbye, jumped into a delivery van and drove himself to the airport, where he had already spent most of the previous night. One of the problems he hadn't considered when choosing Canberra as the paper's base was how many days a week planes would be unable to take off because of fog. During the past four weeks he felt he had spent half his life checking the advance weather forecasts, and the other half standing on the runway, liberally dishing out cash to reluctant pilots, who were fast becoming the most expensive newspaper delivery boys in the world.

He was pleased with the initial reception the *Continent* had received, and sales had quickly reached 200,000 copies. But the novelty of a national paper already seemed to be wearing off, and the figures were now dropping steadily. Alan Rutledge was delivering the paper Townsend had asked for, but the *Continent* wasn't proving to be the paper the Australian people felt they needed.

For the second time that morning Townsend drove in to the airport carpark. But this time the sun was shining and the fog had lifted. The plane for Sydney took off on time, but it wasn't the 8.25. The stewardess offered him a copy of the *Continent*, but only because every plane that left the capital was supplied with a free copy for every passenger. That way the circulation figures held above 200,000, and kept the advertisers happy.

He turned the pages of a paper he felt his father would have been proud of. It was the nearest thing Australia had to *The Times*. And it had something else in common with that distinguished broadsheet – it was losing money fast. Townsend already realised that if they were ever going to make a profit, he would have to take the paper downmarket. He wondered just how long Alan Rutledge would agree to remain as editor once he learned what he had in mind.

He continued to turn the pages until his eyes settled on a column headed 'Forthcoming Events'. His marriage to Susan in six days' time was being billed as 'the wedding of the year'. Everyone who mattered would be attending, the paper predicted, other than the prime minister and Sir Somerset Kenwright. That was one day Keith would have to be in Sydney from morning to night, because he didn't plan to be late for his own wedding.

He turned to the back page to check what was on the radio. Victoria were playing cricket against New South Wales, but none of the networks was covering the game, so he wouldn't be able to follow it. After months of twisting arms, investing in causes he didn't believe in and supporting politicians he despised, Townsend had failed to be awarded the franchise for the new network. He had sat in the visitors' gallery of the House of Representatives to hear the postmaster general announce that the franchise had been awarded to a long-time supporter of the Liberal Party. Later that evening Senator Hadley had told Townsend that the prime minister had personally blocked his application. What with the drop in sales of the *Continent*, the money he had lost trying to secure the radio franchise, and his mother and Susan continually complaining about never seeing him, it wasn't turning out to be a glorious year.

Once the plane had taxied to a halt at Kingsford-Smith airport, Townsend ran down the steps, across the tarmac, through the arrivals terminal and out on to the pavement to find Sam standing by the car, waiting for him. 'What's that?' asked Townsend, pointing to a large, smartly wrapped parcel on the back seat.

'It's a birthday present for Susan. Heather thought you might not have been able to find anything suitable in Canberra.'

'God bless her,' said Townsend.

Although Heather had only been with him for four months, she was already proving a worthy successor to Bunty.

'How much longer is it going to take before we get there?' asked Townsend anxiously, looking at his watch.

'If the traffic stays as light as this, boss, it should be no longer than twenty minutes.' Townsend tried to relax, but he couldn't help reflecting on how much work he had to get through before the wedding. He was already beginning to regret that he had committed himself to a two-week honeymoon.

When the car came to a halt outside a small terraced house in the southern suburbs, Sam leaned back and handed the present over to his boss. Townsend smiled, jumped out of the car and ran up the path. Susan had opened the door even before he had rung the bell. She was about to remonstrate with him when he gave her a long kiss and handed the parcel over to her. She smiled and quickly led him through to the dining room just as the birthday cake was being wheeled in. 'What's inside?' she asked, rattling the parcel like a child.

Townsend just stopped himself saying 'I haven't a clue,' and managed, 'I'm not going to tell you, but I think you'll be pleased with my choice.' He nearly risked 'colour'.

He kissed her on the cheek and took the empty seat between Susan's sister and her mother, and they all watched as she began to unwrap the large box. Keith waited with the same anticipation as everyone else. Susan lifted the lid to reveal a full-length eggshell-blue cashmere coat she had first seen in Farmers over a month before. She could have sworn Keith hadn't been with her at the time.

'How did you know that was my favourite colour?' she asked.

Keith had no idea, but he smiled knowingly, and turned his attention to the slice of birthday cake on the plate in front of him. The rest of the meal was spent going over the wedding plans, and Susan warned him yet again that Bruce Kelly's speech at the reception was definitely not to be in the same vein as the paper's editorials.

After lunch Susan helped her mother and sister clear the table, while the men settled down around the radio in the drawing room. Keith was surprised to find the cricket was on.

'Which station are we listening to?' he asked Susan's father.

'2WW, from Wollongong.'

'But you can't pick up 2WW in Sydney.'

'You can in the southern suburbs,' he replied.

'Wollongong's a one-horse town, isn't it?' said Keith.

'One horse, two coalmines and a hotel when I was a boy. But the population has doubled in the last ten years.'

Keith continued to listen to the ball-by-ball commentary, but his mind was already in Wollongong. As soon as he thought he could get away with it, he strolled into the kitchen to find the women sitting round the table, still discussing the wedding.

'Susan, did you come in your own car?' Keith asked.

'Yes, I drove over yesterday and stayed the night.'

'Fine. I'll get Sam to take me home now. I'm feeling a bit guilty about having him hang about for so long. See you in about an hour?' He kissed her on the cheek and turned to leave. He was halfway down the path before Susan realised that he could have sent Sam off hours ago, because they could have gone home in her car.

'Back to Darling Point, boss?'

'No,' said Keith. 'Wollongong.'

Sam swung the car round in a circle, turning left at the end of the road so that he could join the afternoon traffic leaving Sydney on the Princes Highway. Keith suspected that if he had said 'Wagga Wagga' or 'Broken Hill', Sam still wouldn't have raised an eyebrow.

Within moments Keith had fallen asleep, suspecting the trip was likely to prove a waste of time. When they passed a sign saying 'Welcome to Wollongong', Sam took the next corner sharply, which always woke the boss. 'Anywhere in particular?' he asked. 'Or were you just hoping to buy a coalmine?'

'No, a radio station actually,' said Keith.

'Then my guess,' said Sam, 'is that it has to be pretty near that great aerial sticking out of the ground over there.'

'Bet you got an observation badge when you were in the Cubs.'

A few minutes later Sam dropped him outside a building which had '2WW' written in faded white letters across its corrugated-iron roof.

Townsend got out of the car, ran up the steps, pushed through the door and walked up to a small desk. The young receptionist stopped knitting and looked up.

'Can I help you?' she asked.

'Yes,' said Townsend. 'Do you know who owns this station?'

'Yes, I do,' she replied.

'And who's that?' asked Townsend.

'My uncle.'

'And who is your uncle?'

'Ben Ampthill.' She looked up at him. 'You're not local, are you?'

'No, I'm not,' admitted Townsend.

'I thought I hadn't seen you before.'

'Do you know where he lives?'

'Who?'

'Your uncle.'

'Yes, of course I do.'

'Would it be possible for you to tell me where that is?' said Townsend, trying not to sound too exasperated.

'Sure can. It's the big house on the hill in Woonona, just outside town. Hard to miss it.'

Townsend ran back out of the building, jumped into the car and passed on the directions to Sam.

The young receptionist turned out to be right about one thing: the large white house nestling in the hills was hard to miss. Sam swung off the main road, slowing down as he passed through the wrought-iron gates and up a long drive towards the house. They pulled up outside a smart portico.

Townsend banged on the large black doorknocker and waited patiently, his speech already prepared: I'm sorry to bother you on a Sunday afternoon, but I was rather hoping I might be able to have a word with Mr Ampthill.

The door was opened by a middle-aged woman in a smart floral dress, who looked as if she had been expecting him.

'Mrs Ampthill?'

'Yes. How can I help you?'

'My name is Keith Townsend. I'm sorry to bother you on a Sunday afternoon, but I was rather hoping I might be able to have a word with your husband.'

'My niece was right,' said Mrs Ampthill. 'You're not local, otherwise you would have known that Ben can always be found at the mine office from Monday to Friday, takes the day off on Saturday to play golf, goes to church on Sunday morning and spends the afternoon at the radio station, listening to the cricket. I think that's the only reason he bought the station in the first place.'

Townsend smiled at this piece of information and said, 'Thank you for your help, Mrs Ampthill. I'm sorry to have bothered you.'

'No bother,' she replied, as she watched him run back towards the car.

'Back to the radio station,' Townsend said, unwilling to admit his mistake to Sam.

When Townsend walked up to the reception desk for a second time, he immediately asked, 'Why didn't you tell me that your uncle was here all the time?'

'Because you didn't ask,' the young woman said, not bothering to look up from her knitting.

'So where is he, *exactly*?' asked Townsend slowly.

'In his office.'

'And where is his office?'

'On the third floor.'

'Of this building?'

'Of course,' she said, looking at him as if she were dealing with a moron.

As there was no sign of a lift, Townsend ran up the stairs to the third floor. He looked up and down the corridor, but there was no clue as to where Mr Ampthill's office might be. He had knocked on several doors before someone eventually hollered, 'Come in.'

Townsend pushed open the door to find an overweight, balding man in a sweatshirt with his feet up on the desk. He was listening to the closing overs of the match Townsend had been following earlier in the afternoon. He swung round, took one look at Townsend and said, 'Have yourself a seat, Mr Townsend. But don't say anything just yet, because we only need another eleven runs to win.'

'I support New South Wales too,' said Townsend.

Ben Ampthill smiled as the next ball was hit to the boundary. Still without looking at Townsend, he leaned back and passed him a bottle of Resch's and an opener.

'A couple more balls should do it, and then I'll be with you,' he said.

Neither spoke until the last seven runs had been scored. Then Mr Ampthill leaned forward, punched his fist in the air and said, 'That should wrap up the Sheffield Shield for us.' He removed his feet from the desk, swung round, thrust out his hand and said, 'I'm Ben Ampthill.'

'Keith Townsend.'

Ampthill nodded. 'Yes, I know who you are. My wife rang to tell me you'd been up to the house. She thought you might be a salesman of some sort, in that flashy suit and wearing a tie on a Sunday afternoon.'

Townsend tried not to laugh. 'No, Mr Ampthill, I'm not . . .'

'Call me Ben, everybody else does.'

'No, Ben, I'm not a seller, I'm a buyer.'

'And what are you hoping to buy, young man?'

'Your radio station.'

'It's not for sale, Keith. Not unless you also want the local newspaper, a no-star hotel, and a couple of coalmines thrown in. Because they're all part of the same company.'

'Who owns the company?' asked Townsend. 'It's just possible that the shareholders might consider . . .'

'There are only two shareholders,' Ben explained. 'Pearl and me. So even if I wanted to sell, I'd still have to convince her.'

'But if you own the company – ' Townsend hesitated ' – along with your wife, you have it in your power to sell me the station.'

'Sure do,' said Ben. 'But I'm not going to. If you want the station, you're just going to have to buy everything else that goes with it.'

After several more Resch's and another hour of haggling, Townsend came to realise that Ben's niece had failed to inherit any genes from his side of the family.

When Townsend finally emerged from Ben's office it was pitch dark, and the receptionist had left. He fell into the car, and told Sam to take him back to the Ampthills' house. 'And by the way,' he said, as the car swung round yet again, 'you were right about the coalmines. I'm now the proud owner of two of them, as well as the local paper and a hotel, but most important of all, a radio station. But the deal can't be finally ratified until I've had dinner with the other shareholder, just to be sure she approves of me.'

—◆—

When Keith crept into the house at one o'clock the following morning, he wasn't surprised to find Susan was fast asleep. He quietly closed the bedroom door and went down to his study on the ground floor, where he sat at his desk and began writing some notes. It wasn't long before he started wondering what was the earliest moment that he could possibly call his lawyer. He settled on six thirty-five, and filled in the time by having a shower, putting on a fresh set of clothes, packing a suitcase, making himself some breakfast and reading the first editions of the Sydney papers, which were always delivered to him by five every morning.

At twenty-five to seven he left the kitchen, returned to his study and dialled his lawyer's home number. A sleepy voice answered the phone.

'Good morning, Clive. I thought I ought to let you know I've just bought a coalmine. Two, in fact.'

'And why in heaven's name did you do that, Keith?' a more awake voice asked. It took another forty minutes for Townsend to explain how he had spent the previous afternoon, and the price agreed on. Clive's pen never stopped moving across the pad by the side of his bed, which was always there just in case Townsend phoned.

'My first reaction is that Mr Ampthill looks as if he's got himself a good deal,' said Clive when his client finally stopped talking.

'He sure did,' said Townsend. 'And had he wanted to prove it, he could also have drunk me under the table.'

'Well, I'll call you later this morning to fix an appointment so we can flesh this deal out.'

'Can't do that,' said Townsend. 'I have to catch the first flight to New York if I'm going to make this deal worthwhile. You'll need to sort out the details with Ben Ampthill. He's not the sort of man who'll go back on his word.'

'But I'm still going to need your input.'

'You've just had it,' said Townsend. 'So be sure you have the contract ready for signing the moment I get back.'

'How long will you be away?' asked Clive.

'Four days, five at the most.'

'Can you pick up what you need in five days?'

'If I can't, I'll have to take up coalmining.'

Once he had put the phone down, Townsend returned to the bedroom and picked up his suitcase. He decided not to wake Susan: flying off to New York at such short notice would take a lot of explaining. He scribbled her a note and left it on the hall table.

When he saw Sam standing at the end of the drive, Townsend couldn't help thinking that he looked as if he hadn't had much sleep either. At the airport, he told him that he'd be back some time on Friday.

'Don't forget you're getting married on Saturday, boss.'

'Even I couldn't forget that,' said Townsend. 'No need to worry, I'll be back with at least twenty-four hours to spare.'

In the plane, he fell asleep moments after he had fastened his seatbelt. When he woke several hours later, he couldn't remember where he was going or why. Then it all came back to him. He and his radio team had spent several days in New York during their preparations for the earlier network bid, and he had made three subsequent visits to the city that year, setting up deals with American networks and agencies that would have been immediately turned into a programme schedule had he been awarded the new franchise. Now he intended to take advantage of all that hard work.

A Yellow Cab drove him from the airport to the Pierre. Despite all four windows being down, Townsend had removed his tie and undone his shirt collar long before he was dropped outside the hotel.

The concierge welcomed him as if he had made fifty trips to New York that year, and instructed a bellboy to show Mr Townsend up to 'his usual room'. Another shower, a further change of clothes, a late breakfast and several more phone calls were made before Townsend began shuttling round the city from agent to agent, network to network, studio to studio, in an attempt to close deals at breakfast, lunch, dinner and sometimes in the small hours of the morning.

Four days later he had purchased the Australian rights for most of the top American radio programmes for the coming season, with options on them for a further four years. He signed the final agreement only a couple of hours before his flight was due to leave for Sydney. He packed a suitcase full of dirty clothes – he disapproved of paying unnecessary bills – and took a cab to the airport.

Once the plane had taken off he started drafting a 500-word article, revising paragraphs and changing phrases, until he was satisfied it was good enough for the front page. When they landed in Los Angeles, Townsend went in search of the nearest pay phone and called Bruce Kelly's office. He was surprised that the editor wasn't at his desk. Kelly's deputy assured him that he still had enough time to make the final edition, and quickly transferred him to a copy typist. As Townsend dictated the article, he wondered how long it would be before Hacker and Kenwright were on the phone, begging him to make a deal now that he had broken their cosy cartel wide open.

He heard his name being called out over the loudspeaker, and had to run all the way back to the aircraft. They closed the door as soon as he had stepped on board. Once he had settled into his seat, his eyes didn't open again until the plane touched down at Sydney the following morning.

When he reached the baggage collection area, he called Clive Jervis as he waited for his suitcases to come down the chute. He glanced at his watch when he heard Clive's voice on the other end of the line. 'I hope I didn't get you out of bed,' he said.

'Not at all. I was just putting on my morning dress,' the lawyer replied.

Townsend would have asked whose wedding Clive was attending, but he was only interested in finding out if Ampthill had signed the contract.

'Let me tell you before you ask,' Clive began. 'You are now the proud owner of the *Wollongong Times*, the Wollongong Grand Hotel, two coalmines and a radio station known as 2WW, which can be picked up as far south as Nowra and as far north as the southern outskirts of Sydney. I only hope you know what you're up to, Keith, because I'm damned if I do.'

'Read the front page of this morning's *Chronicle*,' said Townsend. 'It might give you a clue.'

'I never read the papers on a Saturday morning,' said Clive. 'I think I'm entitled to one day off a week.'

'But today's Friday,' said Townsend.

'It may be Friday in New York,' replied Clive, 'but I can assure you it's Saturday here in Sydney. I'll look forward to seeing you at the church in about an hour's time.'

'Oh my God,' cried Townsend. He dropped the phone, ran out of the customs hall without his luggage and emerged onto the pavement to find Sam standing by the car, looking slightly agitated. Townsend leaped into the front seat. 'I thought it was Friday,' he said.

'No, sir, I'm afraid it's Saturday,' said Sam. 'And you're meant to be getting married in fifty-six minutes' time.'

'But that doesn't even leave me enough time to go home and change.'

'Don't worry,' said Sam. 'Heather's put everything you'll need on the back seat.'

Keith turned round to find a pile of clothes, a pair of gold cufflinks and a red carnation all neatly laid out for him. He quickly removed his coat, and began undoing the buttons of his shirt.

'Will we get there on time?' he asked.

'We should make it to St Peter's with about five minutes to spare,' said Sam as Keith threw yesterday's shirt onto the floor in the back of the car. He paused. 'As long as the traffic keeps moving and the lights are all green.'

'What else should I be worrying about?' Keith asked as he forced his right arm into the left sleeve of a starched shirt.

'I think you'll find that Heather and Bruce have thought of everything between them,' said Sam.

Keith finally succeeded in putting his arm in the correct sleeve, then asked if Susan realised that he'd only just returned.

'I don't think so,' said Sam. 'She's spent the last few days at her sister's place in Kogarah, and she's being driven direct to the church from there. She did ring a couple of times this morning, but I told her you were in the shower.'

'I could do with a shower.'

'I would have had to phone her if you hadn't been on that flight.'

'That's for sure, Sam. I suppose we'd better hope the bride will be the traditional few minutes late.' Keith leaned back and grabbed a pair of grey striped trousers with braces already attached, neither of which he had ever seen before.

Sam tried to disguise a yawn.

Keith turned to him. 'Don't tell me you've been waiting outside that airport for the past twenty-four hours?'

'Thirty-six, sir. After all, you did say some time on Friday.'

'I'm sorry,' said Keith. 'Your wife must be livid with me.'

'She won't give a damn, sir.'

'Why not?' asked Keith as the car careered round a sharp bend at fifty miles an hour and he tried to do up his fly buttons.

'Because she left me last month, and has started divorce proceedings.'

'I'm sorry to hear that,' said Keith quietly.

'Don't worry about it, sir. She never really came to terms with the sort of lifestyle a driver has to lead.'

'So it was my fault?'

'Certainly not,' said Sam. 'She was even worse when I was driving the taxi. No, the truth is I enjoy this sort of work, but she just couldn't cope with the hours.'

'And it took you eleven years to discover that,' said Keith, leaning forward so that he could pull on his grey tailcoat.

'I think we've both realised it for some time,' said Sam. 'But in the end I couldn't take any more of her grumbling about never being sure when I was going to be home.'

'Never being sure when you were going to be home?' repeated Keith as they careered round another corner.

'Yes. She couldn't understand why I didn't finish work by five every night, like any normal husband.'

'I understand the problem only too well,' said Keith. 'You're not the only one who has to live with it.' Neither spoke for the rest of the journey, Sam concentrating on choosing the least congested lane, which would save him a few seconds, while Keith thought about Susan as he retied his tie for a third time.

Keith was pinning the carnation to his lapel as the car swung into the road which led up to St Peter's Church. He could hear the bells pealing, and the first person he saw, standing in the middle of the road and peering in their direction, was an anxious-looking Bruce Kelly. A look of relief came over his face when he recognised the car.

'Just as I promised, sir,' said Sam, as he changed down into third gear. 'We've made it with five minutes to spare.'

'Or with eleven years to regret,' said Keith quietly.

'I beg your pardon, sir?' said Sam as he touched the brake, put the gear lever into second and began to slow down.

'Nothing, Sam. It's just that you've made me realise that this is one gamble I'm not willing to take.' He paused for a moment, and just before the car came to a halt, said firmly, 'Don't stop, Sam. Just keep on driving.'

17

THE TIMES

24 MARCH 1948

Western Powers Boycott Berlin Meetings After Russian Withdrawal

'It was extremely kind of you to come and see me at such short notice, Captain Armstrong.'

'Not at all, Julius. In times of trouble we Jews must stick together.' Armstrong slapped the publisher on the shoulder. 'Tell me, how can I help?'

Julius Hahn rose from behind his desk, and paced round the room as he took Armstrong through the catalogue of disasters that had befallen his company during the past two months. Armstrong listened attentively. Hahn returned to his seat and asked, 'Do you think there is anything you can do?'

'I'd like to, Julius. But as you understand better than most, the American and Russian sectors are a law unto themselves.'

'I was afraid that would be your response,' said Hahn. 'But I've often been told by Arno that your influence stretches far beyond the British sector. I wouldn't have considered bothering you if my situation were not desperate.'

'Desperate?' asked Armstrong.

'I'm afraid that's the only word to describe it,' said Hahn. 'If the problem continues for another month, some of my oldest customers will lose confidence in my ability to deliver, and I may have to close down one, possibly two, of my plants.'

'I had no idea it was that bad,' said Armstrong.

'It's worse. Although I can't prove it, I have a feeling the man behind this is Captain Sackville – who you know I've never got on with.' Hahn paused. 'Do you think it's possible that he's simply anti-Semitic?'

'I wouldn't have thought so,' said Armstrong. 'But then, I don't know him that well. I'll see if I can use some of my contacts to find out if anything can be done to help you.'

'That's very thoughtful of you, Captain Armstrong. If you were able to help, I would be eternally grateful.'

'I'm sure you would, Julius.'

--o--

Armstrong left Hahn's office and ordered his driver to take him to the French sector, where he exchanged a dozen bottles of Johnnie Walker Black Label for a case of claret that even Field Marshal Auchinleck hadn't sampled on his recent visit.

On his way back to the British sector, Armstrong decided to drop in on Arno Schultz and find out if Hahn was telling him the whole story. When he walked into *Der Telegraf*'s office, he was surprised to find that Arno was not at his desk. His deputy, whose name Armstrong could never remember, explained that Mr Schultz had been granted a twenty-four-hour permit to visit his brother in the Russian sector. Armstrong didn't even realise that Arno had a brother. 'And, Captain Armstrong,' said the deputy, 'you'll be pleased to know that we had to print 400,000 copies again last night.'

Armstrong nodded and left, feeling confident that everything was falling into place. Hahn would have to agree to his terms within a month if he hoped to remain in business. He checked his watch and instructed Benson to drop by Captain Hallet's office. When he arrived there he placed the dozen bottles of claret on Hallet's desk before the captain had a chance to say anything.

'I don't know how you do it,' said Hallet, opening his top drawer and taking out an official-looking document.

'Each to his own,' said Armstrong, trying out a cliché he had heard Colonel Oakshott use the previous day.

For the next hour Hallet took Armstrong clause by clause through a draft contract, until he was certain that he fully understood its implications, and also that it met his requirements.

'And if Hahn agrees to sign this document,' said Armstrong when they had reached the final paragraph, 'can I be certain that it will stand up in an English court of law?'

'There's no doubt about that,' said Stephen.

'But what about Germany?'

'The same applies. I can assure you, it's absolutely watertight – although I'm still puzzled –' the lawyer hesitated for a moment ' – as to why Hahn would part with such a large slice of his empire in exchange for *Der Telegraf*.'

'Let's just say that I'm also able to sort out one or two of his requirements,' said Armstrong, placing a hand on the case of claret.

'Quite so,' said Hallet as he rose from his chair. 'By the way, Dick, my demob papers have finally come through. I expect to be going home very soon.'

'Congratulations, old chap,' said Armstrong. 'That's marvellous news.'

'Yes, isn't it? And of course, should you ever need a lawyer when you get back to England . . .'

–◁○▷–

When Armstrong returned to his office twenty minutes later, Sally warned him that there was a visitor in his room who claimed he was a close friend, although she had never seen him before.

Armstrong opened the door to find Max Sackville pacing up and down. The first thing he said was, 'The bet's off, old buddy.'

'What do you mean, "off"?' said Armstrong, slipping the contract into the top drawer of his desk and turning the key in the lock.

'What I said – off. My papers have finally come through. They're shipping me back to North Carolina at the end of the month. Isn't that great news?'

'It certainly is,' said Armstrong, 'because with you out of the way, Hahn is bound to survive, and then nothing will stop me collecting my thousand dollars.'

Sackville stared at him. 'You wouldn't hold an old buddy to a bet when the circumstances have changed, would you?'

'I most certainly would, old buddy,' said Armstrong. 'And what's more, if you intend to welch, the whole American sector will know by this time tomorrow.' Armstrong sat at his desk and watched as beads of perspiration appeared on the American's forehead. He waited for a few moments before saying, 'Tell you what I'll do, Max. I'll settle for $750, but only if you pay up today.'

It was almost a full minute before Max began to lick his lips. 'Not a hope,' he said. 'I can still bring Hahn down by the end of the month. I'll just have to speed things up a little – old buddy.'

He stormed out of the room, leaving Armstrong not altogether confident that Max could manage Hahn's downfall on his own. Perhaps the time had come to give him a helping hand. He picked up the phone and told Sally he didn't want to be disturbed for at least an hour.

When he had finished typing the two articles with one finger, he checked them both carefully before making a few small emendations to the texts. He then slipped the first sheet of paper into an unmarked buff envelope and sealed it. The second sheet he folded and placed in the top pocket of his jacket. He picked up the phone and asked Sally to send in his driver. Benson listened carefully as the captain told him what he wanted him to do, making him repeat his orders so as to be certain that he hadn't misunderstood anything – especially the part about changing into civilian clothes.

'And you are never to discuss this conversation with anyone, Reg – and I mean anyone. Do I make myself clear?'

'Yes, sir,' said Benson. He took the envelope, saluted and left the room.

Armstrong smiled, pressed the buzzer on his phone and asked Sally to bring in the post. He knew that the first edition of *Der Telegraf* would not be on sale at the station until shortly before midnight. No copies would reach the American or Russian sectors for at least an hour after that. It was vital that his timing should be perfect.

He remained at his desk for the rest of the day, checking the latest distribution figures with Lieutenant Wakeham. He also called Colonel Oakshott and read over the proposed article to him. The colonel didn't see why a single word should be changed, and agreed that the piece could be published on *Der Telegraf*'s front page the following morning.

At six o'clock Private Benson, back in uniform, drove Armstrong to the flat, where he spent a relaxed evening with Charlotte. She seemed surprised and delighted that he was home so early. After he had put David to bed, they had supper together. He managed three helpings of his favourite stew, and Charlotte decided not to mention that she thought perhaps he was putting on a little weight.

Shortly after eleven, Charlotte suggested it was time to go to bed. Dick agreed, but said, 'I'll just pop out and pick up the first edition of the paper. I'll only be a few minutes.' He checked his watch. It was 11.50. He stepped out onto the pavement and walked slowly in the direction of the station, arriving a few minutes before the first edition of *Der Telegraf* was due to be dropped off.

He checked his watch again: it was almost twelve. They must be running late. But perhaps that was just a consequence of Arno being in the Russian sector, visiting his brother. He had to wait only a few more minutes before the familiar red van swung round the corner and came to a halt by the entrance to the station. He slipped into the shadows behind a large column as a bundle of papers landed on the pavement with a thud, before the van sped off in the direction of the Russian sector.

A man walked out of the station and bent down to untie the string as Armstrong ambled over and stood above him. When he looked up and saw who it was, he nodded in recognition and handed him the top copy.

He quickly read through the front-page article to make sure they hadn't changed a word. They hadn't. Everything, including the headline, was exactly as he'd typed it out.

Distinguished Publisher
Faces Bankruptcy

Julius Hahn, the chairman of the famous publishing house that bears his name, was under increasing pressure last night to make a public statement concerning the company's future.

His flagship paper, *Der Berliner*, has not been seen on the streets of the capital for the past six days, and some of his magazines are reported to be several weeks behind schedule. One leading wholesaler said last night, 'We can no longer rely on Hahn's publications being available from one day to the next, and we are having to consider alternatives.'

Herr Hahn, who spent the day with his lawyers and accountants, was not available for comment, but a spokesman for the company admitted that they would not meet their projected forecasts for the coming year. When contacted last night, Herr Hahn was unwilling to speak on the record about the company's future.

Armstrong smiled and checked his watch. The second edition would just about be coming off the presses, but would not yet be stacked and ready for the returning vans. He strode purposefully in the direction of *Der Telegraf*, arriving seventeen minutes later. He marched in and shouted at the top of his voice that he wanted to see whoever was in charge in Herr Schultz's office immediately. A man whom Armstrong wouldn't have recognised had he passed him in the street hurried in to join him.

'Who's responsible for this?' Armstrong shouted, throwing his copy of the first edition of the paper down on the desk.

'You were, sir,' said the deputy editor, looking surprised.

'What do you mean, I was?' said Armstrong. 'I had nothing to do with it.'

'But the article was sent to us directly from your office, sir.'

'Not by me it wasn't,' said Armstrong.

'But the man said you had told him to deliver it personally.'

'What man? Have you ever seen him before?' asked Armstrong.

'No, sir, but he assured me that he had come straight from your office.'

'How was he dressed?'

The deputy editor remained silent for a few moments. 'In a grey suit, if I remember, sir,' he eventually said.

'But anyone who works for me would have been in uniform,' said Armstrong.

'I know, sir, but . . .'

'Did he give you his name? Did he show you any form of identification or proof of authority?'

'No, sir, he didn't. I just assumed . . .'

'You "just assumed"? Why didn't you pick up a phone and check that I had authorised the article?'

'I didn't realise . . .'

'Good heavens, man. Once you'd read the piece, didn't you consider editing it?'

'No one edits your work, sir,' said the deputy editor. 'It's just put straight on the presses.'

'You never even checked the contents?'

'No, sir,' replied the deputy editor, his head now bowed low.

'So there is no one else to blame?'

'No, sir,' said the deputy editor, shaking.

'Then you're sacked,' shouted Armstrong, staring down at him. 'I want you off the premises immediately. Immediately, do you understand?'

The deputy editor looked as if he was about to protest, but

Armstrong bellowed, 'If your office hasn't been cleared of all your possessions within fifteen minutes, I'll call in the military police.'

The deputy editor crept out of the room without uttering another word.

Armstrong smiled, took off his jacket and hung it on the chair behind Arno's desk. He checked his watch, and was confident that enough time had passed. He rolled up his sleeves, walked out of the office and pressed a red button on the wall. All the presses came to a grinding halt.

Once he was certain he had everyone's attention, he began barking out a series of orders. 'Tell the drivers to get out there and bring me back every copy of the first edition they can lay their hands on.' The transport manager ran out into the yard, and Armstrong turned to the chief printer.

'I want that front-page story about Hahn pulled and this set up in its place,' he said, extracting a sheet of paper from his jacket pocket and handing it over to the bewildered chief printer, who immediately began to set up a new block for the front page, leaving a space in the top right-hand corner for the most recent picture they had of the Duke of Gloucester.

Armstrong turned round to see a group of stackers waiting for the next edition to come off the presses. 'You lot,' he shouted. 'See that every copy of the first edition that's still on the premises is destroyed.' They scattered, and began gathering up every paper they could find, however old.

Forty minutes later, a proof copy of the new front page was hurried up to Schultz's office. Armstrong studied the other story he had written that morning about the proposed visit to Berlin by the Duke of Gloucester.

'Good,' he said, once he had finished checking it through. 'Let's get on with bringing out the second edition.'

When Arno came rushing through the door nearly an hour later, he was surprised to find Captain Armstrong, his sleeves rolled up, helping to load the newly-printed second edition onto the vans. Armstrong waved a finger in the direction of his office.

Once the door was closed, he told him what he had done the moment he had seen the front-page article.

'I've managed to get most of the early copies back and have them destroyed,' he told Schultz. 'But I couldn't do anything about the twenty thousand or so that were distributed in the Russian and American sectors. Once they've crossed the check-point, you can never hope to retrieve them.'

'What a piece of luck that you picked up a first edition as it hit the streets,' said Arno. 'I blame myself for not coming back earlier.'

'You are in no way to blame,' said Armstrong. 'But your deputy far exceeded his responsibility in going ahead and printing the article without even bothering to check with my office.'

'I'm surprised. He's normally so reliable.'

'I had no choice but to sack him on the spot,' said Armstrong, looking directly at Schultz.

'No choice,' said Schultz. 'Of course.' He continued to look distressed. 'Although I fear the damage may be irretrievable.'

'I'm not sure I understand,' said Armstrong. 'I managed to get all but a few of the early copies back.'

'Yes, I realise that. In fact you couldn't have done more. But just before I crossed the checkpoint I picked up a first edition in the Russian sector. I'd only been home for a few minutes when Julius called to say his phone hadn't stopped ringing for the past hour – mostly calls from anxious retailers. I promised I'd come straight over and see how it could possibly have happened.'

'You can tell your friend that I shall instigate a full inquiry in the morning,' promised Armstrong. 'And I'll take charge of it personally.' He rolled down his sleeves and put his jacket back on. 'I was just stacking the second edition for the vans when you walked in, Arno. Perhaps you would be good enough to take over. My wife . . .'

'Of course, of course,' said Arno.

Armstrong left the building with Arno's last words ringing in his ears: 'You couldn't have done more, Captain Armstrong, you couldn't have done more.'

Armstrong had to agree with him.

◄○►

Armstrong was not surprised to receive a call from Julius Hahn early the following morning.

'So sorry about our first edition,' he said, before Hahn had a chance to speak.

'It wasn't your fault,' said Hahn. 'Arno has explained how much worse it might have been without your intervention. But now I fear I need another favour.'

'I'll do anything I can to help, Julius.'

'That's most kind of you, Captain Armstrong. Would it be possible for you to come and see me?'

'Would some time next week suit you?' asked Armstrong, casually flicking over the pages of his diary.

'I'm afraid it's rather more urgent than that,' said Hahn. 'Do you think there might be a chance that we could meet some time today?'

'Well, it's not convenient at the moment,' said Armstrong, looking down at the empty page in his diary, 'but as I have another appointment in the American sector this afternoon, I suppose I could drop in on you around five – but only for fifteen minutes, you understand.'

'I understand, Captain Armstrong. But I would be most grateful if you could manage even fifteen minutes.'

Armstrong smiled as he put the phone down. He unlocked the top drawer of his desk and removed the contract. For the next hour he checked over each clause to make sure that every eventuality was covered. The only interruption he received was a call from Colonel Oakshott, congratulating him on the article about the Duke of Gloucester's forthcoming visit. 'First class,' he said. 'First class.'

After a long lunch in the mess, Armstrong spent the early afternoon clearing his desk of letters Sally had wanted answered for weeks. At half past four he asked Private Benson to drive him over to the American sector; the jeep pulled up outside the offices of *Der Berliner* at a few minutes past five. A nervous Hahn was waiting on the steps of the building, and quickly ushered him through to his office.

'I must apologise again for our first edition last night,' began Armstrong. 'I was having dinner with a general from the American sector, and Arno was unfortunately visiting his brother in the Russian sector, so neither of us had any idea what his deputy was up to. I sacked him immediately, of course, and have set up a full inquiry. If I hadn't been passing the station at midnight . . .'

'No, no, you are not in any way to blame, Captain Armstrong.' Hahn paused. 'However, the few copies that did reach the American and Russian sectors have been more than enough to cause panic among some of my oldest clients.'

'I'm very sorry to hear that,' said Armstrong.

'I fear that they fell into the wrong hands. One or two of my most reliable suppliers have rung today demanding that in future they must be paid in advance, and that won't prove easy after all the extra expense I've had to bear during the past couple of months. We both know it's Captain Sackville who is behind all this.'

'Take my advice, Julius,' said Armstrong. 'Don't even mention his name when referring to this incident. You have no proof, absolutely no proof, and he's the sort of man who wouldn't hesitate to close you down if you gave him the slightest excuse.'

'But he's systematically bringing my company to its knees,' said Hahn. 'And I don't know what I've done to deserve it, or how to stop him.'

'Don't get so upset, my friend. I've been working on your behalf for some time now, and I may just have come up with a solution.'

Hahn forced a smile, but didn't look convinced.

'How would you feel,' continued Armstrong, 'if I were to arrange for Captain Sackville to be posted back to America by the end of the month?'

'That would solve all my problems,' said Hahn, with a deep

sigh. But the look of doubt remained. 'If only he could be sent home . . .'

'By the end of the month,' Armstrong repeated. 'Mind you, Julius, it's going to take a lot of arm-twisting at the very highest levels, not to mention . . .'

'Anything. I'll do anything. Just tell me what you want.'

Armstrong removed the contract from his inside pocket and pushed it across the desk. 'You sign this, Julius, and I'll see that Sackville is sent back to the States.'

Hahn read the four-page document, first quickly and then more slowly, before placing it on the desk in front of him. He looked up and said quietly, 'Let me understand the consequences of this agreement, should I sign it.' He paused again and picked up the contract again. 'You would receive the foreign distribution rights for all my publications.'

'Yes,' said Armstrong quietly.

'I take it by that you mean for Britain.' He hesitated. 'And the Commonwealth.'

'No, Julius. The rest of the world.'

Hahn checked the contract once again. When he came to the relevant clause, he nodded gravely.

'And in return I would receive 50 per cent of the profits.'

'Yes,' said Armstrong. 'After all, you did tell me, Julius, that you would be looking for a British company to represent you once your present contract had come to an end.'

'True, but at the time I didn't realise you were in publishing.'

'I have been all my life,' said Armstrong. 'And once I've been demobbed, I shall be returning to England to carry on running the family business.'

Hahn looked bemused. 'And in exchange for these rights,' he said, 'I would become the sole proprietor of *Der Telegraf*.' He paused again. 'I had no idea that you owned the paper.'

'Neither does Arno, so I must ask you to keep that piece of information in the strictest confidence. I had to pay well above the market price for his shares.'

Hahn nodded, then frowned. 'But if I were to sign this document, you could become a millionaire.'

'And if you don't,' said Armstrong, 'you could be bankrupt by the end of the month.'

Both men stared at each other.

'You have evidently given my problem considerable thought, Captain Armstrong,' said Hahn eventually.

'Only with your best interests in mind,' said Armstrong.

Hahn didn't comment, so Armstrong continued, 'Allow me to prove my good will, Julius. I would not wish you to sign the document if Captain Sackville is still in this country on the first day of next month. If he has been replaced by then, I will expect you to put your signature to it on the same day. For the moment, Julius, a handshake will be good enough for me.'

Hahn remained silent for a few more seconds. 'I can't argue with that,' he said eventually. 'If that man has left the country by the end of the month, I will sign the contract in your favour.'

The two men stood up and shook hands solemnly.

'I'd better be on my way,' said Armstrong. 'There are still quite a number of people I'll have to get in line, and a lot of paperwork to be dealt with if I'm to make sure Sackville is sent back to America in three weeks' time.'

Hahn just nodded.

◄o►

Armstrong dismissed his driver, and strolled the nine blocks to Max's quarters for their usual Friday-night poker session. The cold air cleared his head, and by the time he arrived he was ready to put the second part of his plan into action.

Max was impatiently shuffling the deck. 'Pour yourself a beer, old buddy,' he said as Armstrong took his place at the table, 'because tonight, my friend, you're going to lose.'

Two hours later, Armstrong was about $80 up, and Max hadn't licked his lips all evening. He took a long draught of beer as Dick began shuffling the deck. 'It doesn't help to think,' said Max, 'that if Hahn is still in business at the end of the month

I'll owe you another thousand – which would just about wipe me out.'

'It's looking a pretty good bet for me at the moment, I must admit.' Armstrong paused as he dealt Max his first card. 'Mind you, there are circumstances in which I might agree to waive the wager.'

'Just tell me what I have to do,' said Max, dropping his cards face-up on the table. Armstrong pretended to be concentrating on his hand, and said nothing.

'Anything, Dick. I'll do anything.' Max paused. 'Short of killing the damn Kraut.'

'How about bringing him back to life again?'

'I'm not sure I understand.'

Armstrong placed his hand on the table and looked across at the American. 'I want you to make sure that Hahn gets all the electricity he needs, all the paper he requires, and a helping hand whenever he contacts your office.'

'But why this sudden change of heart?' asked Max, sounding suspicious.

'Simple really, Max. It's just that I've been laying off the bet with several suckers in the British sector. I've been backing Hahn to still be in business in a month's time. So if you were to reverse everything, I'd stand to make a lot more than a thousand dollars.'

'You cunning old bastard,' said Max, licking his lips for the first time that evening. 'You've got yourself a deal, old buddy.' He thrust his hand across the table.

Armstrong shook hands on the second agreement he'd made that day.

◄○►

Three weeks later, Captain Max Sackville boarded a plane for North Carolina. He hadn't had to pay Armstrong more than the few dollars he'd lost in their final poker game. On the first of the month he was replaced by a Major Bernie Goodman.

Armstrong drove over to the American sector that afternoon to see Julius Hahn, who handed him the signed contract.

'I'm not quite sure how you managed it,' said Hahn, 'but I'm bound to admit, from your lips to God's ears.'

They shook hands.

'I look forward to a long and fruitful partnership,' were Armstrong's parting words. Hahn made no comment.

When Armstrong arrived back at the flat early that evening, he told Charlotte that his demob papers had finally come through, and that they would be leaving Berlin before the end of the month. He also let her know that he had been offered the rights to represent Julius Hahn's overseas distribution, which would mean he'd be working flat out from the moment the plane landed in London. He began roaming around the room, blasting off idea after idea, but Charlotte didn't complain because she was only too happy to be leaving Berlin. When he had finally stopped talking, she looked up at him and said, 'Please sit down, Dick, because I also have something to tell you.'

◄○►

Armstrong promised Lieutenant Wakeham, Private Benson and Sally that they could be sure of a job when they left the army, and all of them said they would be in touch just as soon as their discharge papers came through.

'You've done one hell of a job for us here in Berlin, Dick,' Colonel Oakshott told him. 'In fact, I don't know how we're going to replace you. Mind you, after your brilliant suggestion of merging *Der Telegraf* and *Der Berliner*, we may not even have to.'

'It seemed the obvious solution,' said Armstrong. 'May I add how much I've enjoyed being part of your team, sir.'

'It's kind of you to say so, Dick,' the colonel said. He lowered his voice. 'I'm due to be discharged myself fairly shortly. Once you're back in civvy street, do let me know if you hear of anything that might suit an old soldier.'

Armstrong didn't bother to visit Arno Schultz, but Sally told him that Hahn had offered him the job of editor of the new paper.

Armstrong's final call before he handed in his uniform to the quartermaster was to Major Tulpanov's office in the Russian sector, and on this occasion the KGB man did invite him to stay for lunch.

'Your coup with Hahn was a pleasure to observe, Lubji,' said Tulpanov, waving him to a chair, 'even if only from a distance.' An orderly poured them each a vodka, and the Russian raised his glass high in the air.

'Thank you,' said Armstrong, returning the compliment. 'And not least for the part you played.'

'Insignificant,' said Tulpanov, placing his drink back on the table. 'But that may not always be the case, Lubji.' Armstrong raised an eyebrow. 'You may well have secured the foreign distribution rights to the bulk of German scientific research, but it won't be too long before it's out of date, and then you'll need all the latest Russian material. That is, if you wish to remain ahead of the game.'

'And what would you expect in return?' asked Armstrong, scooping up another spoonful of caviar.

'Let us just leave it, Lubji, that I will be in touch from time to time.'

18

Daily Mail

13 APRIL 1961

The Voice from Space: 'How I did it.'
Gagarin Tells Khrushchev of the Blue Earth

Heather placed a cup of black coffee in front of him. Townsend was already regretting that he had agreed to give the interview, especially to a trainee reporter. His golden rule was never to allow a journalist to talk to him on the record. Some proprietors enjoyed reading about themselves in their own papers. Townsend was not among them, but when Bruce Kelly had pressed him in an unguarded moment, saying it would be good for the paper and good for his image, he'd reluctantly agreed.

He had nearly cancelled two or three times that morning, but a series of telephone calls and meetings meant that he'd never got round to doing it. And then Heather walked in to tell him that the young reporter was waiting in the outer hall. 'Shall I send her in?' Heather asked.

'Yes,' he said, checking his watch. 'But I don't want to be too long. There are several things I need to go over with you before tomorrow's board meeting.'

'I'll come back in about fifteen minutes and tell you there's an overseas call on the line.'

'Good idea,' he said. 'But say it's from New York. For some reason that always makes them leave a little quicker. And if you get desperate, use the Andrew Blacker routine.'

Heather nodded and left the room as Townsend ran his finger down the agenda for the board meeting. He stopped at item seven. He needed to be better briefed on the West Riding Group if he was going to convince the board that they should back him on that one. Even if they gave him the go-ahead he still had to close the deal on his trip to England. In fact he would have to travel straight up to Leeds if he felt the deal was worth pursuing.

'Good morning, Mr Townsend.'

Keith looked up, but didn't speak.

'Your secretary warned me that you're extremely busy, so I'll try not to waste too much of your time,' she said rather quickly.

He still didn't say a word.

'I'm Kate Tulloh. I'm a reporter with the *Chronicle*.'

Keith came from behind his desk, shook hands with the young journalist, and ushered her towards a comfortable chair usually reserved for board members, editors or people with whom he expected to close important deals. Once she was seated, he took the chair opposite her.

'How long have you been with the company?' he asked as she extracted a shorthand pad and a pencil from her bag.

She crossed her legs and said, 'Only for a few months, Mr Townsend. I joined the *Chronicle* as a trainee after leaving college. You're my first big assignment.'

Keith felt old for the first time in his life, although he had only recently celebrated his thirty-third birthday.

'What's the accent?' he asked. 'I can't quite place it.'

'I was born in Budapest, but my parents fled from Hungary at the time of the revolution. The only ship we could get on was going to Australia.'

'My grandfather also fled to Australia,' Keith said.

'Because of a revolution?' she asked.

'No. He was Scottish, and just wanted to get as far away from the English as possible.' Kate laughed. 'You recently won a young writers' award, didn't you?' he asked, trying to recall the briefing note Heather had prepared for him.

'Yes. Bruce presented the awards last year, which is how I ended up on the *Chronicle*.'

'So what does your father do?'

'Back in Hungary he was an architect, but over here he's only been able to pick up odd labouring jobs. The government refuses to recognise his qualifications, and the unions haven't been all that sympathetic.'

'They don't like me either,' said Keith. 'And what about your mother?'

'I'm sorry to appear rude, Mr Townsend, but I think I'm meant to be interviewing you.'

'Yes, of course,' said Keith, 'do go ahead.' He stared at the girl, unaware of how nervous he was making her. He had never seen anyone more captivating. She had long, dark hair which fell onto her shoulders, and a perfectly oval face that hadn't yet been savaged by the Australian sun. He suspected that the simple, well-tailored navy-blue suit she wore was more formal than she might normally have chosen. But that was probably because she was interviewing her boss. She crossed her legs again and her skirt rose slightly. He tried not to lower his eyes.

'Shall I repeat the question, Mr Townsend?'

'Err . . . I'm so sorry.'

Heather walked in, and was surprised to find them seated in the directors' corner of the room.

'There's a call for you on line one from New York,' she said. 'Mr Lazar. He needs to have a word about a counterbid he's just received from Channel 7 for one of next season's sitcoms.'

'Tell him I'll call back later,' said Keith, without looking up. 'By the way, Kate,' he said, leaning forward, 'would you like a coffee?'

'Yes, thank you Mr Townsend.'

'Black or white?'

'White, but no sugar. Thank you,' she repeated, looking towards Heather.

Heather turned and left the room without asking Keith if he wanted another coffee.

'Sorry, what was the question?' Keith asked.

'Did you write or publish anything when you were at school?'

'Yes, I was editor of the school magazine in my last year,' he said. Kate began writing furiously. 'As my father was before me.' By the time Heather reappeared with the coffee, he was still telling Kate about his triumph with the pavilion appeal.

'And when you went to Oxford, why didn't you edit the student newspaper, or take over *Isis*, the university magazine?'

'In those days I was far more interested in politics – and in any case, I knew I'd be spending the rest of my life in the news-paper world.'

'Is it true that when you returned to Australia, you were devastated to find that your mother had sold the *Melbourne Courier*?'

'Yes, it is,' admitted Keith, as Heather walked back into the room. 'And I'll get it back one day,' he added under his breath.

'A problem, Heather?' he asked, raising an eyebrow. She was standing only a foot away from him.

'Yes. I'm sorry to interrupt you again, Mr Townsend, but Sir Kenneth Stirling has been trying to get in touch with you all morning. He wants to discuss your proposed trip to the UK.'

'Then I'll have to call him back as well, won't I?'

'He did warn me that he'll be out most of the afternoon.'

'Then tell him I'll call him at home this evening.'

'I can see you're busy,' said Kate. 'I can wait or come back at some other time.'

Keith shook his head, despite Heather remaining fixed on the spot for several seconds. He even began to wonder if Ken really was on the line.

Kate tried once more. 'There are several stories among the clippings about how you took control of the *Adelaide Messenger*, and your coup with the late Sir Colin Grant.'

'Sir Colin was a close friend of my father,' said Keith, 'and a merger was always going to be in the best interests of both papers.' Kate didn't look convinced. 'I'm sure you'll have read in the clippings that Sir Colin was the first chairman of the merged group.'

'But he only chaired one board meeting.'

'I think you'll find it was two.'

'Didn't Sir Somerset Kenwright suffer roughly the same fate when you took over the *Chronicle*?'

'No, that's not quite accurate. I can assure you that no one admired Sir Somerset more than I did.'

'But Sir Somerset once described you,' said Kate, glancing down at her notes, 'as "a man who is happy to lie in the gutter and watch while others climb mountains".'

'I think you'll find that Sir Somerset, like Shakespeare, is often misquoted.'

'It would be hard to prove either way,' said Kate, 'as he's also dead.'

'True,' said Keith, a little defensively. 'But the words of Sir Somerset that I will always recall are: "I couldn't be more delighted that the *Chronicle* will be passing into the hands of Sir Graham Townsend's son."'

'But didn't Sir Somerset say that,' suggested Kate, once again referring to her notes, 'six weeks before you actually took over?'

'What difference does that make?' asked Keith, trying to fight back.

'Simply that on the first day you arrived at the *Chronicle* as its proprietor, you sacked the editor and the chief executive. A week later they issued a joint statement, saying – and this time I quote verbatim . . .'

'Your next appointment has arrived, Mr Townsend,' said Heather, standing by the door as if she was about to show someone in.

'Who is it?' asked Keith.

'Andrew Blacker.'

'Rearrange it.'

'No, no, please,' said Kate. 'I have more than enough.'

'Rearrange it,' repeated Keith firmly.

'As you wish,' said Heather, equally firmly. She walked back out, leaving the door wide open.

'I'm sorry to have taken up so much of your time, Mr Townsend,' said Kate. 'I'll try to speed things up,' she added, before returning to her long list of questions. 'Can I now turn to the launching of the *Continent*?'

'But I haven't finished telling you about Sir Somerset Kenwright, and the state the *Chronicle* was in when I took it over.'

'I'm sorry,' said Kate, 'it's just that I'm concerned about the calls you have to make, and I'm feeling a little guilty about Mr Blacker.'

There was a long silence before Keith admitted, 'There is no Mr Blacker.'

'I'm not sure I understand,' said Kate.

'He's a code name. Heather uses them to let me know how long a meeting has overrun: New York is fifteen minutes, Mr Andrew Blacker is thirty minutes. In a quarter of an hour she'll reappear and tell me I have a conference call with London and Los Angeles. And if she's really cross with me, she throws in Tokyo for good measure.'

Kate began to laugh.

'Let's hope you last the full hour. You'll never believe what she comes up with after an hour.'

'To be honest, Mr Townsend, I wasn't expecting to be given more than fifteen minutes of your time,' Kate said, as she looked back down at her questions.

'You'd begun to ask me about the *Continent*,' prompted Keith.

'Oh, yes,' said Kate. 'It's often reported that you were devastated when Alan Rutledge resigned as editor.'

'Yes, I was,' admitted Keith. 'He was a fine journalist, and had become a close friend. But the paper had fallen below 50,000 copies a day, and we were losing nearly £100,000 a week. Now, under the new editor, we have returned to sales of 200,000 copies a day, and will be launching a *Sunday Continent* early in the new year.'

'But surely you accept that the paper can no longer be described as "the *Times* of Australia"?'

'Yes, and I regret that,' said Keith, admitting the fact for the first time to anyone other than his mother.

'Will the *Sunday Continent* follow the same pattern as the

daily, or are you going to produce the quality national news-paper Australia so desperately needs?'

Keith was beginning to realise why Miss Tulloh had won her award, and why Bruce thought so highly of her. This time he chose his words more carefully. 'I will endeavour to produce a paper that the majority of Australians would like to see on their breakfast tables every Sunday morning. Does that answer your question, Kate?'

'I fear it does, Mr Townsend,' she said with a smile.

Keith returned the smile. It quickly disappeared when he heard her next question.

'May I now turn to an incident in your life that has been widely covered by the gossip columns?' Keith reddened slightly as she waited for his response. His instinct was to end the interview there and then, but he just nodded.

'Is it true that on your wedding day you ordered your chauffeur to drive straight past the church only moments before the bride was due to arrive?'

Keith was relieved when Heather marched into the room and said firmly, 'Your conference call is due in a couple of minutes, Mr Townsend.'

'My conference call?' he asked, brightening up.

'Yes, sir,' said Heather. 'Sir' was a word she resorted to only when she was very cross.

'London and Los Angeles,' she said. She paused before adding, 'and Tokyo.' Very cross, thought Keith. But at least she had given him the chance to escape. Kate had even closed her shorthand pad.

'Rearrange it for this afternoon,' he said quietly. He wasn't sure which of the women looked more surprised. Heather left them without another word, and this time she closed the door behind her.

Neither of them spoke again until Keith said, 'Yes, it's true. But I'd be obliged if you didn't refer to it in your article.'

Kate put her pencil down on the table, as Keith turned and looked out of the window. 'I'm sorry, Mr Townsend,' she said, 'that was insensitive of me.'

'"Just doing my job" is what reporters usually say,' said Keith quietly.

'Perhaps we could move on to your somewhat unusual, if not to say bizarre, takeover of 2WW.'

Keith sat up in his chair and relaxed a little for the first time.

'When the story first broke in the *Chronicle* – on the morning of your wedding, incidentally – Sir Somerset described you as "a pirate".'

'I'm sure he intended it as a compliment.'

'A compliment?'

'Yes. I assume he meant that I was acting in the great tradition of pirates.'

'Who did you have in mind?' asked Kate innocently.

'Walter Raleigh and Francis Drake,' replied Keith.

'I suspect it's more likely to have been Bluebeard or Captain Morgan that Sir Somerset had in mind,' said Kate, returning his smile.

'Perhaps. But I think you'll find that both sides ended up satisfied with that particular deal.'

Kate looked back down at her notes. 'Mr Townsend, you now own, or have the majority shareholding in, seventeen newspapers, eleven radio stations, an aircraft company, a hotel and two coalmines.' She looked back up at him. 'What do you plan to do next?'

'I'd like to sell the hotel and the coalmines, so if you happen to come across anyone who might be interested . . .'

Kate laughed. 'No, seriously,' she said, as Heather marched back into the room.

'The prime minister is on his way up in the lift, Mr Townsend,' she said, her Scottish accent even more pronounced than usual. 'You are, as you will remember, entertaining him for lunch in the boardroom.'

Keith winked at Kate, who burst out laughing. Heather held open the door and stood back to allow a distinguished-looking gentleman with a head of silver hair to enter the room.

'Good morning, Prime Minister,' Keith said, as he rose from

his place and stepped forward to greet Robert Menzies. The two men shook hands before Keith turned round to introduce Kate, who was trying to hide in the corner of the room. 'I don't think you've met Kate Tulloh, Prime Minister. She's one of the *Chronicle*'s most promising young reporters. I know she was hoping to get an interview with you at some point.'

'I should be delighted,' said Menzies. 'Why don't you give my office a call, Miss Tulloh, and we can fix a time?'

—◆—

For the next two days Keith was unable to get Kate out of his mind. One thing was certain: she didn't fit into any of his well-ordered plans.

When they had sat down to lunch, the prime minister had wondered why his host was so preoccupied. Townsend showed little interest in his innovative proposals for curbing the power of the trades unions, despite the fact that his papers had been pressing the government on the subject for several years.

Townsend wasn't a great deal more articulate the following morning, when he chaired the monthly board meeting. In fact, for a man who controlled the largest communications empire in Australia, he was amazingly uncommunicative. One or two of his fellow-directors wondered if he was going down with something. When he addressed the board on item seven, his proposed trip to the UK for the purpose of taking over a small newspaper group in the north of England, few of them could see much point in his making the journey. He totally failed to convince them that anything worthwhile could possibly come out of it.

Once the board meeting was over and the directors had dispersed, Townsend returned to his office and remained at his desk going over papers until Heather finally left for the evening. He checked his watch as the door closed behind her. It was a few minutes past seven, which reminded him how late she normally worked. He didn't pick up the phone until he was sure she wasn't going to return, then he dialled the three digits that would put him straight through to the editor's desk.

'Bruce, this trip I'm about to take to London. I ought to have a journalist along with me to make sure that if the story breaks, you'll be the first to hear about it.'

'What are you hoping to buy this time?' asked Bruce. '*The Times*?'

'No, not on this trip,' replied Townsend. 'I'm looking for something that just might make a profit.'

'Why don't I call Ned Brewer at the London bureau? He's the obvious man to follow up any story.'

'I'm not sure it's a job for the bureau chief,' said Townsend. 'I'm going to be traipsing round the north of England for several days, looking at print works, meeting journalists, trying to decide which editors to retain. I wouldn't want Ned to be away from his desk for that length of time.'

'I suppose I could spare Ed Makins for a week. But I'd need him back for the opening of Parliament – especially if your hunch turns out to be right and Menzies does announce a bill to curb the powers of the trades unions.'

'No, no, I don't need someone that high-powered. In any case, I can't be sure how long I'll be away. A good junior could do the job.' He paused, but Bruce made no helpful suggestions. 'I was impressed by that girl you sent up to interview me the other day,' he said. 'What was her name?'

'Kate Tulloh,' said Bruce. 'But she's far too young and inexperienced for something as big as this.'

'So were you when we first met, Bruce. It didn't stop me from offering you the job as editor.'

There was a moment's silence before Bruce said, 'I'll see if she's available.'

Townsend smiled as he put the phone down. He couldn't pretend that he'd been looking forward to the trip to England, although he knew the time had come to expand his horizons beyond Australia.

He looked back down at the pile of notes that littered his desk. Despite a team of management consultants trawling through the details of every newspaper group in the United Kingdom, they had only come up with one good prospect.

A file had been prepared for him to consider over the weekend. He turned the first page and began to read a profile of the West Riding Group. Its head office was in Leeds. He smiled. The nearest he'd ever been to Leeds was a visit to the Doncaster racecourse when he was at Oxford. On that occasion – if he remembered correctly – he'd backed a winner.

19

News Chronicle

25 OCTOBER 1951

Final Poll Gives Churchill the Lead

'And how will you be paying, Mr Armstrong?' asked the estate agent.

'It's Captain Armstrong, actually.'

'I'm sorry, Captain Armstrong.'

'I'll pay by cheque.'

It had taken Armstrong ten days to find suitable accommodation, and he only signed the short lease on a flat in Stanhope Gardens when the agent mentioned that a retired brigadier was living on the floor above.

The search for an appropriate office took even longer, because it needed to have an address that would convince Julius Hahn that Armstrong had been in publishing all his life.

When John D. Wood asked what price range he had in mind, a very junior agent was handed the assignment.

Two weeks later, Armstrong settled on an office that was even smaller than his flat in Stanhope Gardens. Although he couldn't altogether accept the agent's description of the 308-square-foot room with a lavatory on the floor above as ideal, perfect and unique, it did have two advantages. The Fleet Street address, and a rent he could afford to pay – for the first three months.

'If you'll be kind enough to sign on the bottom line, Captain Armstrong.'

Armstrong unscrewed the top of his new Parker pen and signed the contract.

'Good. Then that's settled,' said the young agent as he waited for the ink to dry. 'The rent for this property is, as you know, Captain Armstrong, £10 a week, payable quarterly in advance. Perhaps you would be kind enough to let me have a cheque for £130.'

'I'll send one of my staff round with a cheque later this afternoon,' said Armstrong, straightening his bow tie.

The agent hesitated for a moment, and then placed the contract in his briefcase. 'I'm sure that will be all right, Captain Armstrong,' he said, handing over the keys to the smallest property on their books.

Armstrong felt confident that Hahn would have no way of knowing, when he rang FLE 6093 and heard the words 'Armstrong Communications', that his publishing house consisted of one room, two desks, a filing cabinet and a recently installed telephone. And as for 'one of my staff', one was correct. Sally Carr had returned to London the week before, and had joined him as his personal assistant earlier that morning.

Armstrong had been unable to give the estate agent a cheque immediately because he had only recently opened an account with Barclays, and the bank was unwilling to issue a chequebook until it received the promised transfer of funds from Holt & Co in Berlin. The fact that he was Captain Armstrong MC, as he kept reminding them, didn't seem to impress the manager.

When the money did eventually come through, the manager confessed to his accounts clerk that after their meeting he had expected a little more than £217 9s. 6d. to be deposited in Captain Armstrong's account.

While he was waiting for the money to be transferred, Armstrong contacted Stephen Hallet at his offices in Lincoln's Inn Fields, and asked him to register Armstrong Communications as a private company. That cost him another £10.

No sooner had the company been formed than another unpayable bill landed on Sally's desk. This time Armstrong didn't have a dozen bottles of claret to settle the account, so he invited Hallet to become company secretary.

Once his funds had been deposited, Armstrong cleared all his debts, which left him with less than £40 in the account. He told Sally that in future she should not pay any bills over £10 until they had received at least three demands for payment.

Charlotte, already six months pregnant with their second child, joined Dick in London a few days after he had signed the lease on the Knightsbridge flat. When she was first shown round the four rooms, she didn't comment on how small they were compared with their spacious apartment in Berlin. She was only too happy to have escaped from Germany.

As Armstrong travelled to and from the office by bus each day, he wondered how long it would be before he had a car and a driver. Once the company had been registered, he flew to Berlin and talked a reluctant Hahn into a loan of £1,000. He returned to London with a cheque and a dozen manuscripts, having promised that they would be translated within days, and that the money would be repaid as soon as he signed the first foreign distribution deal. But he was facing a problem that he couldn't admit to Hahn. Although Sally spent hours on the phone trying to arrange appointments with the chairmen of all the leading scientific publishing houses in London, she quickly discovered that their doors didn't open for Captain Armstrong MC in the way they had done in Berlin.

On those evenings when he got home before midnight, Charlotte would ask him how the business was doing. 'Never better' took the place of 'top secret'. But she couldn't help noticing that thin brown envelopes were regularly dropping through their letterbox, and seemed to get stuffed into the nearest drawer, unopened. When she flew out to Lyon for the birth of their second child, Dick assured her that by the time she returned he would have signed his first big contract.

Ten days later, while Armstrong was dictating an answer to the one letter he'd received that morning, there was a knock on the door. Sally bustled across the room to open it, and came face to face with their first customer. Geoffrey Bailey, a

Canadian who represented a small publisher in Montreal, had actually got out of the lift on the wrong floor. But an hour later he left clutching three German scientific manuscripts. Once he had had them translated, and had realised their commercial potential, he returned with a cheque, and signed a contract for the Canadian and French rights on all three books. Armstrong banked the cheque, but didn't bother to inform Julius Hahn of the transaction.

Thanks to Mr Bailey, by the time Charlotte arrived back at Heathrow six weeks later, carrying Nicole in her arms, Dick had signed two more contracts, with publishers from Spain and Belgium. She was surprised to find that he had acquired a large Dodge automobile, and that Private Benson was behind the wheel. What he didn't tell her was that the Dodge was on the 'never never', and that he couldn't always afford to pay Benson at the end of the week.

'It impresses the customers,' he said, and assured her that business was looking better and better. She tried to ignore the fact that some of his stories had changed since she'd been away, and that the unopened brown envelopes remained in the drawer. But even she was impressed when he told her that Colonel Oakshott was back in London, and had visited Dick and asked him if he knew of anyone who might employ an old soldier.

Armstrong had been the fifth person he had approached, and none of the others had anything to offer someone of his age or seniority. The following day Oakshott had been appointed to the board of Armstrong Communications at a salary of £1,000 a year, although his monthly cheque wasn't always honoured on the first presentation.

Once the first three manuscripts had been published in Canada, France, Belgium and Spain, more and more foreign publishers began to get out of the lift on the right floor, later leaving Armstrong's office carrying long typewritten lists of all the books whose rights were available.

As Armstrong began to close an increasing number of deals, he cut down on his trips to Berlin, sending Colonel Oakshott in his place, and giving him the unenviable task of explaining to Julius Hahn why the cash flow was so slow. Oakshott continued to believe everything Armstrong told him – after all, hadn't they served as officers in the same regiment? – and so, for some time, did Hahn.

But despite the occasional coup with foreign houses, Armstrong was still having no luck in convincing a leading British publisher to take on the rights to his books. After months of being told, 'I'll get back to you, Captain Armstrong,' he began to wonder just how long it was going to take him to push open the door that would allow him to become part of the British publishing establishment.

It was on an October morning when Armstrong was staring across at the massive edifices of the *Globe* and the *Citizen* – the nation's two most popular dailies – that Sally told him a journalist from *The Times* was on the line. Armstrong nodded.

'I'll put you through to Captain Armstrong,' she said.

Armstrong crossed the room and took the receiver from her hand. 'It's Dick Armstrong, chairman of Armstrong Communications. How can I help you?'

'My name is Neville Andrade. I'm the science correspondent of *The Times*. I recently picked up the French edition of one of Julius Hahn's publications, *The Germans and the Atom Bomb*, and was curious to know how many other titles you have in translation.' Armstrong put the phone down an hour later, having told Andrade his life story and promised that his driver would have the complete list of titles on his desk by midday.

When he arrived at the office late the following morning, because of what Londoners described as a pea-souper, Sally told him she had taken seven calls in twenty minutes. As the phone rang again, she pointed to his desk. A copy of *The Times* lay open at the science page. Armstrong sat down and began to read Andrade's long piece about the atom bomb and how, despite losing the war, German scientists still remained far ahead of the rest of the world in many fields.

The phone rang again, but he remained puzzled as to why Sally was being besieged until he came to the final paragraph of the article. 'The key to this information is held by Captain Richard Armstrong MC, who controls the translation rights in all the publications of the prestigious Julius Hahn empire.'

Within days, the phrase 'We'll get back to you, Captain Armstrong,' became 'I'm sure we can match those terms, Dick,' and he began selecting which houses would be allowed to publish his manuscripts and distribute his magazines. People he had never been able to get an appointment with in the past were inviting him to lunch at the Garrick, even if, having met him, they didn't go as far as suggesting he should become a member.

By the end of the year Armstrong had finally returned the £1,000, and it was no longer possible for Colonel Oakshott to convince Hahn that his chairman was still having a tough time getting anyone to sign a contract. Oakshott was glad Hahn couldn't see that the Dodge had been replaced by a Bentley, and that Benson was now wearing a smart grey uniform and a peaked cap. Armstrong's newest problem was to find suitable new offices and qualified staff, so that he could keep up with the rapid expansion. When the floors above and below him fell vacant, he signed new leases for them within hours.

It was at the annual reunion of the North Staffordshire Regiment at the Café Royal that Armstrong bumped into Major Wakeham. He discovered that Peter had just been demobbed, and was about to take up a job in personnel with the Great Western Railway. Armstrong spent the rest of the evening persuading him that Armstrong Communications was a better prospect. Peter joined him as general manager the following Monday.

Once Peter had settled in, Armstrong began to travel all over the world – from Montreal to New York to Tokyo to Christchurch – selling Hahn manuscripts, and always demanding large advances. He began to place the money in several different bank accounts, with the result that even Sally couldn't be quite sure just how much the company had on deposit at any one time, or where it was located. Whenever he was back in England, he found his small staff quite unable to keep up with the demands of an ever-growing order book. And Charlotte had become tired of him commenting on how much the children had grown.

When the lease for the entire building in Fleet Street came on the market, he immediately snapped it up. Now even the most sceptical potential customer who visited him in his new offices accepted that Captain Armstrong was safe to do business with. Rumours reached Berlin of Armstrong's success, but Hahn's letters requesting details of sales figures country by country, sight of all overseas contracts and audited accounts were studiously ignored.

Colonel Oakshott, who was left to report Hahn's growing incredulity at Armstrong's claims that the company was having difficulty in breaking even, was treated more and more like a messenger boy, despite the fact that he had recently been appointed deputy chairman. But even after Oakshott threatened to resign, and Stephen Hallet warned Armstrong that he had received a letter from Hahn's London solicitors threatening to terminate their partnership, Armstrong remained unperturbed. He felt confident that as long as the law prevented Hahn from travelling outside Germany, he had no way of discovering how large his empire had grown, and therefore how much 50 per cent actually represented.

◄○►

Within weeks of Winston Churchill's government being returned to power in 1951, all restrictions on travel for German citizens were lifted. Armstrong was not surprised to learn from the colonel that Hahn's and Schultz's first trip abroad would be to London.

After a long consultation with a KC at Gray's Inn, the two Germans took a taxi to Fleet Street for a meeting with their overseas partner. Hahn's habit of punctuality had not deserted him in old age, and Sally met the two men in reception. She guided them up to Dick's vast new office, and hoped they were suitably impressed by the hustle and bustle of activity that was taking place all around them.

They entered Armstrong's office to be greeted with the expansive smile they both remembered so well. Schultz was shocked by how much weight the captain had put on, and didn't care for his colourful bow tie.

'Welcome, my dear old friends,' Armstrong began, holding out his arms like a large bear. 'It has been far too long.' He appeared surprised to receive a cool response, but he ushered them to the comfortable seats on the other side of his partner's desk, then returned to an elevated chair which allowed him to tower over them. Behind him on the wall hung a large blown-up photograph of Field Marshal Montgomery pinning the Military Cross on the young captain's chest.

Once Sally had poured his guests Brazilian coffee served in bone china cups, Hahn wasted no time in trying to tell Armstrong – as he referred to him – the purpose of their visit. He was just about to embark on his well-prepared speech when one of the four phones on the desk began ringing. Armstrong grabbed it, and Hahn assumed that he would instruct his secretary to hold all further calls. But instead he began an intense conversation in Russian. No sooner had he finished than another phone rang, and he started a fresh dialogue in French. Hahn and Schultz hid their misgivings and waited patiently for Captain Armstrong to complete the calls.

'So sorry,' said Armstrong, after he had finally put the third phone down, 'but as you can see, the damn thing never stops ringing. And 50 per cent of it,' he added with a broad smile, 'is on your behalf.'

Hahn was just about to begin his speech a second time, when Armstrong pulled open his top drawer and took out a box of Havana cigars, a sight neither of his guests had seen for over ten years. He pushed the box across the desk. Hahn waved a hand in dismissal, and Schultz reluctantly followed his chairman's lead.

Hahn tried to begin a third time.

'By the way,' said Armstrong, 'I've booked a table for lunch at the Savoy Grill. Anybody who's anybody eats at the Grill.' He gave them another expansive smile.

'We are not free for lunch,' said Hahn curtly.

'But we have so much to discuss,' insisted Armstrong, 'not least catching up on old times.'

'We have very little to discuss,' said Hahn. 'Especially old times.'

Armstrong was silenced for a moment.

'I am sorry to have to inform you, Captain Armstrong,' Hahn continued, 'that we have decided to terminate our arrangement with you.'

'But that's not possible,' said Armstrong. 'We have a binding legal agreement.'

'You have obviously not read the document for some time,' said Hahn. 'If you had, you would be only too aware of the penalties for failing to fulfil your financial obligations to us.'

'But I intend to fulfil . . .'

'"In the event of non-payment, after twelve months all overseas rights automatically revert to the parent company."' Hahn sounded as if he knew the clause off by heart.

'But I can clear all my obligations immediately,' said Armstrong, not at all certain that he could.

'That would not influence my decision,' said Hahn.

'But the contract stipulates that you must give me ninety days' notice in writing,' said Armstrong, remembering one of the clauses Stephen Hallet had emphasised recently.

'We have done so on eleven separate occasions,' replied Hahn.

'I am not aware of having received any such notice,' said Armstrong. 'Therefore I . . .'

'The last three of which,' continued Hahn, 'were sent to this office, recorded delivery.'

'That doesn't mean we ever received them.'

'Each of them was signed for by your secretary or Colonel Oakshott. Our final demand was hand-delivered to your solicitor, Stephen Hallet, who I understand drew up the original agreement.'

Once again Armstrong was silenced.

Hahn opened his battered briefcase, that Armstrong remembered so well, and removed copies of three documents which he placed on the desk in front of his former partner. He then took out a fourth document.

'I am now serving you with a month's notice, requesting that you return any publications, plates or documents in your possession which have been supplied by us during the past two years, along with a cheque for £170,000 to cover the royalties due to us. Our accountants consider this a conservative estimate.'

'Surely you'll give me one more chance, after all I've done for you?' pleaded Armstrong.

'We have given you far too many chances already,' said Hahn, 'and neither of us,' he nodded towards his colleague, 'is at an age when we can waste any more time hoping you will honour your agreements.'

'But how can you hope to survive without me?' demanded Armstrong.

'Quite simply,' said Hahn. 'We have already signed an agreement this morning to be represented by the distinguished publishing house of Macmillan, with whom I'm sure you are familiar. We will be making an announcement to that effect in next Friday's *Bookseller*, so that our clients in Britain, the United States and the rest of the world are aware that you no longer represent us.'

Hahn rose from his chair, and Armstrong watched as he and Schultz turned to leave without another word. Before they reached the door, he shouted after them, 'You'll be hearing from my lawyers!'

Once the door had been closed, he walked slowly over to the window behind his desk. He stared down at the pavement, and didn't move until he'd seen them climb into a taxi. As they drove away he returned to his chair, picked up the nearest phone and dialled a number. A familiar voice answered. 'For the next seven days, buy every Macmillan share you can lay your hands on.' He slammed the phone down, then made a second call.

Stephen Hallet listened carefully as his client gave him a full report of his meeting with Hahn and Schultz. Hallet wasn't surprised by their attitude, because he'd recently informed Armstrong about the termination order he'd received from Hahn's London solicitors. When Armstrong had finished his version of the meeting, he only had one question: 'How long do you think I can string it out for? I'm due to collect several large payments in the next few weeks.'

'A year, eighteen months perhaps, if you're willing to issue a writ and take them all the way to court.'

—◇—

Two years later, after Armstrong had exhausted everyone, including Stephen Hallet, he settled with Hahn on the court-room steps.

Hallet drew up a lengthy document in which Armstrong agreed to return all of Hahn's property, including publishing material, plates, rights agreements, contracts and over a quarter of a million books from his warehouse in Watford. He also had to pay out £75,000 as a full and final settlement for profits made during the previous five years.

'Thank God we're finally rid of the man,' was all Hahn said as he walked away from the High Court in the Strand.

The day after the settlement had been signed, Colonel Oakshott resigned from the board of Armstrong Communi-cations without explanation. He died of a heart attack three weeks later. Armstrong couldn't find the time to attend the funeral, so he sent Peter Wakeham, the new deputy chairman, to represent him.

Armstrong was in Oxford on the day of Oakshott's funeral, signing a long lease on a large building on the outskirts of the city.

—◇—

During the next two years Armstrong almost spent more time in the air than he did on the ground, as he travelled around the world visiting author after author contracted to Hahn, and trying to persuade them that they should break their agreements and join Armstrong Communications. He realised he might not be able to convince some of the German scientists to come across to him, but that had been more than compensated for by the exclusive entrée into Russia which Colonel Tulpanov had made possible, and the many contacts Armstrong had made in America during the years when Hahn had been unable to travel abroad.

Many of the scientists, who rarely ventured outside their laboratories, were flattered by Armstrong's personal approach and the promise of exposure to a vast new readership around the world. They often had no idea of the true commercial value of their research, and happily signed the proffered contract. Later they would despatch their life's works to Headley Hall, Oxford, often assuming that it was in some way connected to the university.

Once they had signed an agreement, usually committing all their future works to Armstrong in exchange for a derisory advance, they never heard from him again. These tactics made it possible for Armstrong Communications to declare a profit of £90,000 the year after he and Hahn had parted, and a year later the *Manchester Guardian* named Richard Armstrong Young Entrepreneur of the Year. Charlotte reminded him that he was nearer forty than thirty.

'True,' he replied, 'but never forget that all my rivals had a twenty-year start on me.'

—◦—

Once they had settled into Headley Hall, their Oxford home, Dick found that he received many invitations to attend university events. He turned most of them down, because he knew all they wanted was his money. But then Allan Walker wrote. Walker was the president of the Oxford University Labour Club, and he wanted to know if Captain Armstrong would sponsor a dinner to be given by the committee in honour of Hugh Gaitskell, the leader of the opposition. 'Accept it,' said Dick. 'On one condition: that I can sit next to him.' After that he sponsored every visit to the university by a front-bench

Labour spokesman, and within a couple of years he had met every member of the shadow cabinet and several foreign dignitaries, including the prime minister of Israel, David Ben-Gurion, who invited him to Tel Aviv, and suggested he take an interest in the plight of Jews who had not been quite as fortunate as him.

After Allan Walker had taken his degree, his first job application was to Armstrong Communications. The chairman immediately took him onto his personal staff so he could advise him on how he should go about extending his political influence. Walker's first suggestion was for him to take over the ailing university magazine *Isis*, which was, as usual, in financial trouble. For a small investment Armstrong became a hero of the university left, and shamelessly used the magazine to promote his own cause. His face appeared on the cover at least once a term, but as the magazine's editors only ever lasted for a year, and doubted if they would find another source of income, none of them objected.

When Harold Wilson became leader of the Labour Party, Armstrong began to make public statements in his support; cynics suggested it was only because the Tories would have nothing to do with him. He never failed to let visiting front-bench Labour spokesmen know that he was happy to bear any losses on *Isis*, as long as it could in some way encourage the next generation of Oxford students to support the Labour Party. Some politicians found this approach fairly crude. But Armstrong began to believe that if the Labour Party were to form the next government, he would be able to use his influence and wealth to fulfil his new dream – to be the proprietor of a national newspaper.

In fact, he began to wonder just who would be able to stop him.

20

THE TIMES

16 OCTOBER 1964

Khrushchev Gives Up – 'Old and Ill'. Brezhnev and Kosygin to Rule Russia

Keith Townsend unfastened his seatbelt a few minutes after the Comet took off, flicked open his briefcase and removed a bundle of papers. He glanced across at Kate, who was already engrossed in the latest novel by Patrick White.

He began to check through the file on the West Riding Group. Was this his best chance yet of securing a foothold in Britain? After all, his first purchase in Sydney had been a small group of papers, which in time had made it possible for him to buy the *Sydney Chronicle*. He was convinced that once he controlled a regional newspaper group in Britain, he would be in a far stronger position to make a takeover bid for a national paper.

Harry Shuttleworth, he read, was the man who had founded the group at the turn of the century. He had first published an evening paper in Huddersfield as an adjunct to his highly successful textile mill. Townsend recognised the pattern of a local paper being controlled by the biggest employer in the area – that was how he had ended up with a hotel and two coalmines. Each time Shuttleworth opened a factory in a new town, a newspaper would follow a couple of years later. By the time he retired, he had four mills and four newspapers in the West Riding.

Shuttleworth's eldest son, Frank, took over the firm when he returned from the First World War, and although his primary interest remained in textiles, he . . .

'Would you like a drink, sir?'

Townsend nodded. 'A whisky and a little water please.'

. . . he also added local papers to the three factories he built in Doncaster, Bradford and Leeds. At various times these had attracted friendly approaches from Beaverbrook, Northcliffe and Rothermere. Frank had apparently given all three of them the oft-quoted reply: 'There's nowt here for thee, lad.'

But it seemed that the third generation of Shuttleworths were not of the same mettle. A combination of cheap imported textiles from India and an only son who had always wanted to be a botanist meant that though Frank died leaving eight mills, seven dailies, five weeklies and a county magazine, the profits of his company began falling within days of his coffin being lowered into the ground. The mills finally went into liquidation in the late 1940s, and since then the newspaper group had barely broken even. It seemed now to be surviving only on the loyalty of its readers, but the latest figures showed that even that couldn't be sustained much longer.

Townsend looked up as a table was fitted into his armrest and a small linen cloth placed over it. When the stewardess did the same for Kate she put down *Riders in the Chariot* but remained silent, not wanting to interrupt her boss's concentration.

'I'd like you to read this,' he said, passing her the first few pages of the report. 'Then you'll understand why I'm making this trip to England.'

Townsend opened a second file, prepared by Henry Wolstenholme, a contemporary of his at Oxford and now a solicitor in Leeds. He could remember very little about Wolstenholme, except that after a few drinks in the buttery he became unusually loquacious. He would not have been Townsend's first choice to do business with, but as his firm had represented the West Riding Group since its foundation, there wasn't an alternative. It had been Wolstenholme who had first alerted him to the group's potential: he had written to him in Sydney suggesting that although WRG was not on the market – certainly its current chairman would deny it should he be approached – he knew that if John Shuttleworth were ever to consider a sale, he would want the purchaser to come from as far away from Yorkshire as possible. Townsend smiled as a bowl of turtle soup was placed in front of him. As the proprietor of the *Hobart Mail*, he had to be the best-qualified candidate in the world.

Once Townsend had written expressing interest, Wolstenholme had suggested that they meet to discuss terms. Townsend's first stipulation was that he needed to see the group's presses. 'Not a hope,' came back the immediate reply. 'Shuttleworth doesn't want to be the subject of his own front pages until the deal is closed.' Townsend accepted that no negotiations through a third party were ever easy, but with this one he was going to have to rely on Wolstenholme to answer even more questions than usual.

With a fork in one hand, and the next page in the other, he began to go over the figures Clive Jervis had prepared for him. Clive estimated that the company was worth about a hundred to a hundred and fifty thousand pounds, but pointed out that having seen nothing except the balance sheet, he was in no position to commit himself – clearly he wanted a get-out clause in case anything went wrong at a later stage, thought Townsend.

'It's more exciting than *Riders in the Chariot*,' Kate said after she had put down the first file. 'But what part am I expected to play?'

'That will depend on the ending,' replied Keith. 'If I pull this one off, I'll need articles in all my Australian papers, and I'll want a separate piece – slightly less gushing – for Reuters and the Press Association. The important thing is to alert publishers all over the world to the fact that I'm now a serious player outside Australia.'

'How well do you know Wolstenholme?' Kate asked. 'It seems to me that you're going to have to rely a lot on his judgement.'

'Not that well,' admitted Keith. 'He was a couple of years ahead of me at Worcester, and was considered a bit of a hearty.'

'A hearty?' repeated Kate, looking puzzled.

'During Michaelmas he spent most of his time with the college rugby team, and the other two terms standing on the riverbank urging on the college boat. I think he was chosen to coach them because he had a voice that could be heard on the other side of the Thames, and enjoyed the odd pint of ale with the crew, even after they'd sunk. But that was ten years ago; for all I know he's settled down and become a dour Yorkshire solicitor, with a wife and several children.'

'Do you have any idea how much the West Riding Group is really worth?'

'No, but I can always make an offer subject to seeing the six presses, and at the same time try to get a feel of how good the editors and journalists are. But in England the biggest problem is always the trades unions. If this group's controlled by a closed shop, then I'm not interested, because however good the deal is, the unions could still bankrupt me within months.'

'And if it isn't?' said Kate.

'Then I might be willing to go as high as a hundred, even a hundred and twenty thousand. But I won't suggest a figure until they let me know what they have in mind.'

'Well, it beats covering the juvenile courts,' said Kate.

'That's where I started too,' said Keith. 'But the editor didn't think my efforts were award-winning material, unlike yours, and most of my copy was spiked before he'd finished the first paragraph.'

'Perhaps he wanted to prove that he wasn't frightened of your father.'

Keith looked across at her, and could see that she was wondering if she had gone too far. 'Perhaps,' he replied. 'But that was before I took over the *Chronicle* and was able to sack him.'

Kate remained silent as a stewardess cleared away their trays. 'We're just about to dim the cabin lights,' she said, 'but there's a light above your heads if you wish to carry on reading.'

Keith nodded and flicked on his light. Kate stretched and eased her seat back as far as it would go, covered herself in a blanket and closed her eyes. Keith looked at her for a few moments before opening a fourth file. He read on through the night.

-◄◦►-

When Colonel Tulpanov phoned to suggest that he should meet a business associate of his called Yuri Valchek to discuss a matter of mutual interest, Armstrong suggested they have lunch at the Savoy when Mr Valchek was next in London.

For the past decade Armstrong had been making regular trips to Moscow, and in exchange for the exclusive foreign rights to the works of Soviet scientists he had continued to carry out little tasks for Tulpanov, still able to persuade himself that he wasn't doing any real harm to his adopted country. This delusion was helped by always letting Forsdyke know when he was making such trips, and occasionally by delivering messages on his behalf, often to return with unfathomable replies. Armstrong realised that both sides considered him to be their man, and suspected that Valchek was not a messenger on a simple errand, but was being sent to find out just how far he could be pushed. By choosing the Savoy Grill, Armstrong hoped to convince Forsdyke that he was hiding nothing from him.

Armstrong arrived at the Savoy a few minutes early, and was guided to his usual alcove table in the corner. He abandoned his favourite whisky and soda for a vodka, the agreed sign among agents that no English would be spoken. He glanced towards the entrance of the restaurant, and wondered if he would be able to identify Valchek when he walked in. Ten years ago it would have been easy, but he had warned many of the new breed that they stuck out like sore thumbs in their cheap double-breasted suits and thin gravy-stained ties. Since then several of the more regular visitors to London and New York had learned to drop into Savile Row and Fifth Avenue during their visits – though Armstrong suspected that a quick change had to be made on Aeroflot flights when they flew back to Moscow.

Two businessmen strolled into the Grill, deep in conversation. Armstrong recognised one of them, but couldn't recall his name. They were followed by a stunning young woman with another two men in her wake. A woman having lunch in the Grill was an unusual sight, and he followed her progress as they were guided into the adjoining alcove.

The head waiter interrupted him. 'Your guest has arrived, sir.'

Armstrong rose to shake hands with a man who could have passed for a British company director, and who obviously did not need to be told where Savile Row was. Armstrong ordered two vodkas.

'How was your flight?' he asked in Russian.

'Not good, comrade,' replied Valchek. 'Unlike you, I have no choice but to fly Aeroflot. If you ever have to, take a sleeping pill, and don't even think of eating the food.'

Armstrong laughed. 'And how is Colonel Tulpanov?'

'*General* Tulpanov is about to be appointed as the KGB's number two, and he wants you to let Brigadier Forsdyke know he still outranks him.'

'That will be a pleasure,' said Armstrong. 'Are there any other changes at the top that I should know about?'

'Not at the moment,' he paused. 'Though I suspect Comrade Khrushchev will not be sitting at the high table for much longer.'

'Then perhaps even you may have to clear your desk,' Armstrong said, staring at him directly.

'Not as long as Tulpanov is my boss.'

'And who will be Khrushchev's successor?' asked Armstrong.

'Brezhnev would be my bet,' said his visitor. 'But as Tulpanov has files on every possible candidate, no one is going to try to replace him.'

Armstrong smiled at the thought that Tulpanov hadn't lost his touch.

A waiter placed another vodka in front of his guest. 'The general speaks highly of you,' said Valchek once the waiter had disappeared, 'and no doubt your position will become even more influential when his appointment is made official.' Valchek paused while he checked the menu before making his order in

English to a hovering waiter. 'Tell me,' he continued once the waiter had left them alone, 'why does General Tulpanov always refer to you as Lubji?'

'It's as good a code name as any,' said Armstrong.

'But you are not a Russian.'

'No, I am not,' said Armstrong firmly.

'But you are also not English, comrade?'

'I'm more English than the English,' replied Armstrong, which seemed to silence his guest. A plate of smoked salmon was placed in front of him.

Valchek had finished his first course, and was cutting into a rare steak before he began to reveal the real purpose of his visit.

'The National Science Institute want to publish a book commemorating their achievements in space exploration,' he said, after selecting a Dijon mustard. 'The chairman feels that President Kennedy is receiving far too much credit for his NASA programme when, as everyone knows, it was the Soviet Union that put the first man in space. We have prepared a document detailing the achievements of our programme from the founding of the Space Academy to the present day. I am in possession of a 200,000-word manuscript compiled by the leading scientists in the field, over a hundred photographs taken as recently as last month, and detailed diagrams and specifications for Luna IV and V.'

Armstrong made no attempt to stop Valchek's flow. The messenger had to be aware that such a book would be out of date even before it was published. Clearly there had to be another reason why he had travelled all the way from Moscow to have lunch with him. But his guest chatted on, adding more and more irrelevant details. Finally he asked Armstrong for his opinion of the project.

'How many copies does General Tulpanov expect to be printed?'

'One million in hardback, to be distributed through the usual channels.'

Armstrong doubted whether such a book would have a

worldwide readership of even a fraction of that figure. 'But my print costs alone . . .' he began.

'We fully understand the risks you would be taking with such a publication. So we will be advancing you a sum of five million dollars, to be distributed among those countries in which the book will be translated, published and sold. Naturally there will be an agent's commission of 10 per cent. I should add that it will come as no great surprise to General Tulpanov if the book does not appear on any best-seller list. Just as long as you are able to show in your annual report that a million copies were printed, he will be content. It's the distribution of the profits that really matters,' added Valchek, sipping his vodka.

'Is this to be a one-off?' asked Armstrong.

'If you make a success of this – ' Valchek paused before choosing the right word ' – project, we would want a paperback edition to be published a year later, which we of course appreciate would require a further advance of five million. After that there might have to be reprints, revised versions . . .'

'Thus ensuring a continuous flow of currency to your operatives in every country where the KGB has a presence,' said Armstrong.

'And as our representative,' said Valchek, ignoring the comment, 'you will receive 10 per cent of any advance. After all, there is no reason why you should be treated differently from any normal literary agent. And I'm confident that our scientists will be able to produce a new manuscript that is worthy of publication every year.' He paused. 'Just as long as their royalties are always paid on time and in whichever currency we require.'

'When do I get to see the manuscript?' asked Armstrong.

'I have a copy with me,' Valchek replied, lowering his eyes to the briefcase by his side. 'If you agree to be the publisher, the first five million will be paid into your account in Liechtenstein by the end of the week. I understand that is how we've always conducted business with you in the past.'

Armstrong nodded. 'I'll need a second copy of the manuscript to give to Forsdyke.'

Valchek raised an eyebrow as his plate was whisked away.

'He has an agent seated on the far side of the room,' said
Armstrong. 'So you should hand over the manuscript just before
we leave, and I'll walk out with it under my arm. Don't worry,'
he continued, sensing Valchek's anxiety. 'He knows nothing
about publishing, and his department will probably spend
months searching for coded messages among the Sputniks.'

Valchek laughed, but made no attempt to look across the
room as the dessert trolley was wheeled over to their table, but
simply stared at the three tiers of extravagances before him.

In the silence that followed, Armstrong caught a single word
drifting across from the next table – 'presses'. He began to listen
in to the conversation, but then Valchek asked him for his
opinion of a young Czech called Havel, who had recently been
put in gaol.

'Is he a politician?'

'No, he's a . . .'

Armstrong put a finger to his lips to indicate that his
colleague should continue talking but shouldn't expect an
answer. The Russian needed no lessons in this particular deceit.

Armstrong concentrated on the three people seated in the
adjoining alcove. The thin, softly-spoken man with his back to
him could only be an Australian, but although the accent was
obvious, Armstrong could hardly pick up a word he was saying.
Next to him sat the young woman who had so distracted him
when she first entered the room. At a guess, he would have said
she was mid-European, and had probably originated not that far
from his own birthplace. On her right, facing the Australian,
was a man with an accent from the north of England and a
voice that would have delighted his old regimental sergeant
major. The word 'confidential' had obviously never been fully
explained to him.

As Valchek continued talking softly in Russian, Armstrong
removed a pen from his pocket and began to jot down the odd

word on the back of the menu – not an easy exercise, unless you have been taught by a master of the profession. Not for the first time, he was thankful for Forsdyke's expertise.

'John Shuttleworth, WRG chairman' were the first words he scribbled down, and a moment later, 'owner'. Some time passed before he added '*Huddersfield Echo*' and the names of six other papers. He stared into Valchek's eyes and continued to concentrate, then scribbled down four more words: 'Leeds, tomorrow, twelve o'clock'. While his coffee went cold there followed '120,000 fair price'. And finally 'factories closed for some time'.

When the subject at the next table turned to cricket, Armstrong felt that although he had several pieces of a jigsaw in place, he now needed to return to his office as soon as possible if he was to have any hope of completing the picture before twelve o'clock the following day. He checked his watch, and despite having only just been served with a second helping of bread and butter pudding, he called for the bill. When it appeared a few moments later, Valchek removed a thick manuscript from his briefcase and handed it ostentatiously across the table to his host. Once the bill had been settled, Armstrong rose from his place, tucked the manuscript under his arm and talked to Valchek in Russian as they strolled past the next alcove. He glanced at the woman, and thought he detected a look of relief on her face when she heard them speaking in a foreign language.

When they reached the door, Armstrong passed a pound note to the head waiter. 'An excellent lunch, Mario,' he said. 'And thank you for seating such a stunning young woman in the next booth.'

'My pleasure, sir,' said Mario, pocketing the money.

'Dare I ask what name the table was booked in?'

Mario ran a finger down the booking list. 'A Mr Keith Townsend, sir.'

That particular piece of the jigsaw had been well worth a pound, thought Armstrong as he marched out of the restaurant in front of his guest.

When they reached the pavement, Armstrong shook hands with the Russian and assured him that the publication process would be set in motion without delay. 'That is good to hear, comrade,' said Valchek, in the most refined English accent. 'And now,' he said, 'I must hurry if I'm not to be late for an appointment with my tailor.' He quickly melted into the stream of people crossing the Strand, and disappeared in the direction of Savile Row.

As Benson drove him back to the office, Armstrong's mind was not on Tulpanov, Yuri Gagarin, or even Forsdyke. Once he had reached the top floor he ran straight into Sally's office, where he found her talking on the phone. He leaned across the desk and cut the caller off. 'Why should Keith Townsend be interested in something called WRG?'

Sally, still holding the receiver, thought for a moment then suggested, 'Western Railway Group?'

'No, that can't be right – Townsend's only interested in newspapers.'

'Do you want me to try and find out?'

'Yes,' said Armstrong. 'If Townsend's in London to buy something, I want to know what. Allow only the Berlin team to work on this one, and don't let anyone else in on it.'

It took Sally, Peter Wakeham, Stephen Hallet and Reg Benson a couple of hours to supply several more pieces of the jigsaw, while Armstrong called his accountant and banker and warned them to be on twenty-four-hour standby.

By 4.15 Armstrong was studying a report on the West Riding Publishing Group which had been hand-delivered to him by Dunn & Bradstreet a few minutes earlier. After he had been through the figures a second time, he had to agree with Townsend that £120,000 was a fair price. But of course that was before Mr John Shuttleworth knew he would be receiving a counter-offer.

The team were all seated around Armstrong's desk ready to reveal their findings by six o'clock that evening.

Stephen Hallet had discovered who the other man at the table was, and which firm of solicitors he belonged to. 'They've represented the Shuttleworth family for over half a century,' he told Armstrong. 'Townsend has a meeting with John

Shuttleworth, the present chairman, in Leeds tomorrow, but I couldn't find out where or the precise time.' Sally smiled.

'Well done, Stephen. What have you got to offer, Peter?'

'I have Wolstenholme's office and home numbers, the time of the train he'll be catching back to Leeds, and the registration number of the car his wife will be driving when she meets him at the station. I managed to convince his secretary that I'm an old schoolfriend.'

'Good, you've filled in a couple of corners of the jigsaw,' said Armstrong. 'What about you, Reg?' It had taken him years to stop addressing him as Private Benson.

'Townsend's staying at the Ritz, and so is the girl. She's called Kate Tulloh. Twenty-two years old, works on the *Sunday Chronicle*.'

'I think you'll find it's the *Sydney Chronicle*,' interrupted Sally.

'Bloody Australian accent,' said Reg in a cockney twang. 'Miss Tulloh,' he continued, 'the head porter assures me, is not only booked into a separate room from her boss, but is two floors below him.'

'So she's not his mistress,' said Armstrong. 'Sally, what have you come up with?'

'The connection between Townsend and Wolstenholme is that they were undergraduates at Oxford at the same time, as the Worcester College secretary confirmed. But the bad news is that John Shuttleworth is the sole shareholder of the West Riding Group, and virtually a recluse. I can't find out where he lives, and he's not on the telephone. In fact, no one at the group's headquarters has seen him for several years. So the idea of making a counter-offer before twelve o'clock tomorrow is just not realistic.'

Sally's news caused a glum silence, finally broken by Armstrong.

'Right then. Our only hope is somehow to stop Townsend attending the meeting in Leeds, and to take his place.'

'That won't be easy if we don't know where the meeting's going to be held,' said Peter.

'The Queen's Hotel,' said Sally.

'How can you be sure of that?' asked Armstrong.

'I rang all the large hotels in Leeds and asked if they had a reservation in Wolstenholme's name. The Queen's said he'd booked the White Rose Room from twelve to three, and would be serving lunch for a party of four at one o'clock. I can even tell you what's on the menu.'

'I don't know what I'd do without you, Sally,' said Armstrong. 'So now, let's take advantage of the knowledge we have. Where is Wolst . . .'

'Already on his way back to Leeds,' interrupted Peter, 'on the 6.50 from King's Cross. He's expected to be at his desk by nine tomorrow morning.'

'What about Townsend and the girl?' asked Armstrong. 'Reg?'

'Townsend has ordered a car to take them to King's Cross at 7.30 tomorrow, so they can catch the 8.12 which arrives at Leeds Central at 11.47, giving them enough time to reach the Queen's Hotel by midday.'

'So between now and 7.30 tomorrow we somehow have to stop Townsend getting on that train to Leeds.' Armstrong glanced around the room, but none of them looked at all hopeful. 'And we'll have to come up with something good,' he added, 'because I can tell you, Townsend is a lot sharper than Julius Hahn. And I have a feeling Miss Tulloh is no fool either.'

There followed another long silence before Sally said, 'I don't have a particular brainwave, but I did find out that Townsend was in England when his father died.'

'So what?' said Armstrong.

21

DAILY MIRROR

17 OCTOBER 1964

Wilson's First Pledge: 'It's Our Job to Govern, and We Will'

Keith had agreed to meet Kate in the Palm Court for breakfast at seven o'clock. He sat at a table in the corner reading *The Times*. He wasn't surprised that it made so little money, and couldn't understand why the Astors didn't close it down, because no one else would want to buy it. He sipped a black coffee, and stopped concentrating on the lead story as his mind drifted back to Kate. She remained so distant and professional that he began to wonder if there was some other man in her life, and whether he had been foolish to ask her to accompany him.

Just after seven she joined him at the table. She was carrying a copy of the *Guardian*. Not the best way to start the day, Keith thought, although he had to admit he still felt the same excitement as he had the first moment he saw her.

'How are you this morning?' she asked.

'Never better,' said Keith.

'Does it feel like a day for taking something over?' she asked with a grin.

'Yes,' he said. 'I have a feeling that by this time tomorrow, I will own my first paper in England.'

A waiter poured Kate a cup of white coffee. She was

330

impressed that after only one day at the hotel he didn't need to ask whether she took milk.

'Henry Wolstenholme telephoned last night just before I went to bed,' said Keith. 'He'd already spoken to Shuttleworth, and by the time we arrive in Leeds the lawyers will have all the contracts ready to sign.'

'Isn't it all a bit risky? You haven't even seen the presses.'

'No, I'm only signing subject to a ninety-day due diligence clause, so you'd better be prepared to spend some time in the north of England. At this time of year it will be what they call "parky".'

'Mr Townsend, paging Mr Townsend.' A bellboy, carrying a sign with Keith's name on it, walked straight over to them. 'Message for you, sir,' he said, handing him an envelope.

Keith ripped it open to find a note scribbled on a sheet of paper embossed with the crest of the Australian High Commissioner. 'Please call urgently. Alexander Downer.'

He showed it to Kate. She frowned. 'Do you know Downer?' she asked.

'I met him once at the Melbourne Cup,' said Keith, 'but that was long before he became High Commissioner. I don't suppose he'll remember me.'

'What can he want at this time in the morning?' asked Kate.

'No idea. Probably wants to know why I turned down his invitation for dinner this evening,' he said, laughing. 'We can always pay him a visit when we get back from the north. Still, I'd better try and speak to him before we leave for Leeds in case it's something important.' He rose from his chair. 'I look forward to the day when they have phones in cars.'

'I'll pop up to my room and see you back in the foyer just before 7.30,' said Kate.

'Right,' said Keith, and left the Palm Court in search of a phone. When he reached the foyer, the hall porter pointed to a little table opposite the reception desk. Keith dialled the number at the top of the sheet of paper, and a woman's voice answered almost immediately. 'Good morning, Australian High Commission.'

'Can I speak to the High Commissioner?' Keith asked.

'Mr Downer's not in yet, sir,' she replied. 'Would you like to call back after 9.30?'

'It's Keith Townsend. I was asked to phone him urgently.'

'Oh, yes, sir, I was told that if you called, I was to put you through to the residence. Please hold on.'

As Keith waited to be connected, he checked his watch. It was 7.20.

'Alexander Downer speaking.'

'It's Keith Townsend, High Commissioner. You asked me to call urgently.'

'Yes, thank you, Keith. We last met at the Melbourne Cup, but I don't suppose you remember.' His Australian accent sounded far more pronounced than Townsend recalled.

'I do remember actually,' said Townsend.

'I'm sorry to say it's not good news, Keith. It seems that your mother has had a heart attack. She's at the Royal Melbourne Hospital. Her condition's stable, but she's in intensive care.'

Townsend was speechless. He had been out of the country when his father had died, and he wasn't going to . . .

'Are you still there, Keith?'

'Yes, yes,' he said. 'But I had dinner with her the night before I left, and I've never seen her looking better.'

'I'm sorry, Keith. It's damned bad luck that it happened while you're abroad. I've arranged to hold two first-class seats on a Qantas flight to Melbourne that takes off at nine this morning. You can still make it if you leave at once. Or you could catch the same flight tomorrow morning.'

'No, I'll leave immediately,' said Townsend.

'Would you like me to send my car over to the hotel to take you to the airport?'

'No, that won't be necessary. I already have a car booked to drive me to the station. I'll use that one.'

'I've alerted the Qantas staff at Heathrow, so you won't have any delays, but don't hesitate to call me if there's anything else I can do to help. I hope we meet again in happier circumstances.'

'Thank you,' said Townsend. He put the phone down and ran across to the reception desk.

'I'll be checking out immediately,' he said to the man standing behind the counter. 'Please have my bill ready as soon as I come back down.'

'Certainly, sir. Do you still need the car that's waiting outside?'

'Yes, I do,' said Townsend. He turned quickly and ran up the stairs to the first floor, and jogged along the passageway checking the numbers. When he reached 124, he banged on the door with his fist. Kate opened it a few moments later, and immediately saw the anxiety in his face.

'What's happened?' she asked.

'My mother's had a heart attack. Bring your bags straight down. We're leaving in five minutes.'

'I'm so sorry,' she said. 'Would you like me to call Henry Wolstenholme and tell him what's happened?'

'No. We can do that from the airport,' said Townsend, rushing off down the corridor.

A few minutes later he emerged from the lift on the ground floor. While his luggage was being placed in the boot, he settled the bill, walked quickly to the car, tipped the bellboy and joined Kate in the back. He leaned forward and said to the driver, 'Heathrow.'

'Heathrow?' said the driver. 'My day sheet says I'm to take you to King's Cross. There's nothing here about Heathrow.'

'I don't give a damn what your day sheet says,' said Townsend. 'Just get me to Heathrow.'

'I'm sorry, sir, but I've got my instructions. You see, King's Cross is an inner-city booking whereas Heathrow is an outer-city journey, and I can't just . . .'

'If you don't move and move quickly, I'll break your bloody neck,' said Townsend.

'I don't have to listen to language like that from anyone,' said the driver. He got out of the car, unlocked the boot and began unloading their cases onto the kerb.

Townsend was about to leap out after him when Kate took his hand. 'Sit still and let me deal with this,' she said firmly.

Townsend was unable to hear the conversation that was taking place behind the car, but after a few moments he could see the cases being put back into the boot.

When Kate rejoined him, he said, 'Thank you.'

'Don't thank me, thank him,' she whispered.

The driver eased the car away from the kerb, turned left at the lights, and joined the morning traffic. He was relieved that the traffic leaving London at that time in the morning wasn't like the bumper-to-bumper queues that were trying to fight their way into the capital.

'I'll have to call Downer as soon as we get to the airport,' said Townsend quietly.

'Why do you want to speak to him again?' asked Kate.

'I thought I'd try and have a word with my mother's doctor in Melbourne before we take off, but I don't have the number.'

Kate nodded. Townsend began tapping his fingers on the window. He tried to remember the last meeting he had had with his mother. He had briefed her on the possible takeover of the West Riding Group, and she had responded with her usual set of shrewd questions. After dinner he had left, promising her that he would call her from Leeds if he closed the deal.

'And who's the girl going with you?' she had asked. He'd been cagey, but he knew he hadn't fooled her. He glanced across at Kate and wanted to take her hand, but she seemed preoccupied. Neither of them spoke until they arrived at the airport. When the car pulled up outside the terminal, Townsend jumped out and went in search of a trolley while the driver unloaded the cases. The moment they were stacked up, he gave him a large tip, said 'Thank you' several times, then pushed the trolley as fast as he could through the hall to the checking-in counter, with Kate following a pace behind him.

'Are we still in time for the Melbourne flight?' Townsend asked as he placed his passport on the Qantas check-in desk.

'Yes, Mr Townsend,' the booking clerk replied, flicking open his passport. 'The High Commissioner called earlier.' She looked up and said, 'We have reserved two tickets for you, one in your name, the other for Miss Tulloh.'

'That's me,' said Kate, handing over her passport.

'You're both in first class, seats 3D and E. Would you please go straight to gate number seventeen, where boarding is about to commence.'

By the time they arrived in the departure lounge, economy was already boarding, and Townsend left Kate to check them in while he went off in search of a telephone. He had to wait in a queue of three for the one available phone, and when he eventually reached the front of the line, he dialled Henry's home number. It was engaged. He tried three more times, but it continued to give out the same long beeps. As he began dialling the number at the head of the High Commissioner's writing paper, a booking clerk announced that all remaining passengers should take their seats, as the gates were about to close. The High Commissioner's number began to ring, and Townsend glanced round to find that the departure lounge was empty, apart from him and Kate. He waved her in the direction of the aircraft.

Townsend let the phone ring for a few more moments, but no one answered. He gave up and replaced the receiver, then ran down the corridor to find Kate waiting by the door of the plane. Once they had entered it, the doors swung closed behind them.

'Any luck?' asked Kate, as she began strapping herself into the seat.

'No,' said Townsend. 'Henry was constantly engaged, and the High Commission didn't answer the phone.'

Kate remained silent as the plane taxied towards the runway. When it came to a halt, she said, 'While you were on the phone, I began thinking. It just doesn't add up.'

The plane began to accelerate down the runway as Townsend fastened his seatbelt.

'What do you mean, it doesn't add up?'

'The last hour,' said Kate.

'I don't know what you're talking about.'

'Well, to start with, my ticket.'

'Your ticket?' said Keith, puzzled.

'Yes. How did Qantas know what name to book it in?'

'I suppose the High Commissioner told them.'

'But how could he?' said Kate. 'When he sent you the invitation to dinner it didn't include me, because he had no idea that I was with you.'

'He could have asked the hotel manager.'

'Possibly. But something else has been nagging at the back of my mind.'

'And what's that?'

'The bellboy knew exactly which table to go to.'

'So what?'

'You were facing me in the corner of the room looking towards the window, but I just happened to look up when he came into the Palm Court. I remember thinking it was strange that he knew exactly where to go, despite you having your back to him.'

'He could have asked the head waiter.'

'No,' said Kate. 'He walked straight past the head waiter. Didn't even give him a glance.'

'What are you getting at?'

'And Henry's phone – continually engaged even though it was only just after 8.30 in the morning.' The wheels of the plane left the ground. 'And why couldn't you get through to the High Commissioner at 8.30 when you could at 7.20?'

Keith looked straight at her.

'We've been taken, Keith. And by someone who wanted to be certain that you wouldn't be in Leeds at twelve o'clock to sign that contract.'

Keith flicked off his seatbelt, ran up the aisle and barged into the cockpit before the steward could stop him. The captain listened to his story sympathetically, but pointed out that there was nothing he could do now that the plane was on its way to Bombay.

◄◊►

'Flight 009 has taken off for Melbourne with both pieces of cargo on board,' said Benson from a telephone in the airport. 'They will be in the air for at least the next fourteen hours.'

336

'Well done, Reg,' said Armstrong. 'Now get back to the Ritz. Sally's already booked the room Townsend was in, so wait there for Wolstenholme to call. My guess is that it will be soon after twelve. By then I'll have arrived at the Queen's Hotel, and I'll let you know my room number.'

Keith sat in his seat on the plane, banging the armrests with the palms of his hands. 'Who are they, and how did they manage it?'

Kate was fairly certain she knew who, and a great deal of how.

<o>

Three hours later, a call came through to the Ritz for Mr Keith Townsend. The switchboard operator followed the instructions she'd been given by the extremely generous gentleman who'd had a word with her earlier that morning, and put the call through to room 319, where Benson was sitting on the edge of the bed.

'Is Keith there?' asked an anxious voice.

'Who's calling, please?'

'Henry Wolstenholme,' he boomed.

'Good morning, Mr Wolstenholme. Mr Townsend tried to call you this morning, but your line was continually engaged.'

'I know. Someone called me at home around seven, but it turned out to be a wrong number. When I tried to dial out later, the line had gone dead. But where is Keith?'

'He's on a plane to Melbourne. His mother's had a heart attack and the High Commissioner arranged to hold up the flight for him.'

'I'm sorry to hear about Keith's mother, but I fear Mr Shuttleworth may not be willing to hold up the contract. It's been hard enough to get him to agree to see us at all.'

Benson read out the exact words Armstrong had written down for him: 'Mr Townsend instructed me to say that he has sent a representative up to Leeds with the authority to sign any contract, as long as you have no objection.'

'I have no objection,' said Wolstenholme. 'When is he expected to arrive?'

'He should be at the Queen's Hotel by now. He left for Leeds soon after Mr Townsend departed for Heathrow. I wouldn't be surprised if he was already in the hotel looking for you.'

'I'd better go down to the foyer and see if I can find him,' said Wolstenholme.

'By the way,' said Benson, 'our accountant just wanted to check the final figure – £120,000.'

'Plus all the legal expenses,' said Wolstenholme.

'Plus all the legal expenses,' repeated Benson. 'I won't keep you any longer, Mr Wolstenholme.' He put the phone down.

Wolstenholme left the White Rose Room and headed down in the lift, confident that if Keith's lawyer had a money draft for the full amount, he could still have everything settled before Mr Shuttleworth arrived. There was only one problem: he had no idea who he was looking for.

Benson asked the switchboard operator to connect him to a number in Leeds. When the call was answered, he asked to be put through to room 217.

'Well done, Benson,' said Armstrong after he had confirmed the figure of £120,000. 'Now book out of the hotel pay the bill in cash and take the rest of the day off.'

Armstrong left room 217 and took the lift down to the ground floor. As he stepped out into the foyer he saw Hallet talking to the man he had seen at the Savoy. He went straight over to them. 'Good morning,' he said. 'My name is Richard Armstrong, and this is the company lawyer. I think you're expecting us.'

Wolstenholme stared at Armstrong. He could have sworn he'd seen him somewhere before. 'Yes. I've booked us into the White Rose Room so we won't be disturbed.'

The two men nodded and followed him. 'Sad news about Keith's mother,' said Wolstenholme as they stepped into the lift.

'Yes, wasn't it?' said Armstrong, careful not to add anything that might later incriminate him.

Once they had taken their places round the boardroom table in the White Rose Room, Armstrong and Hallet checked over the details of the contract line by line, while Wolstenholme sat in the corner drinking coffee. He was surprised that they were going over the final draft so thoroughly when Keith had already given it his blessing, but he accepted that he would have done the same in their position. From time to time Hallet came up with a question which was invariably followed by a whispered exchange with Armstrong. An hour later they passed the contract back to Wolstenholme and confirmed that everything was in order.

Wolstenholme was about to ask some questions of his own, when a middle-aged man shuffled in, dressed in a pre-war suit that hadn't yet come back into fashion. Wolstenholme introduced John Shuttleworth, who smiled shyly. After they had shaken hands Armstrong said, 'Nothing left for us to do except sign the contract.'

John Shuttleworth nodded his agreement, and Armstrong removed a pen from inside his jacket and bent down to sign where Stephen's trembling finger was poised. He passed the pen over to Shuttleworth, who signed between the pencilled crosses without uttering a word. Stephen then handed over a draft for £120,000 to Wolstenholme. The lawyer nodded when Armstrong reminded him that as it was a draft for cash, it would perhaps be wise to bank it immediately.

'I'll just pop across to the nearest Midland while they're setting up for lunch,' said Wolstenholme. 'I shouldn't be more than a few minutes.'

When Wolstenholme returned, he found Shuttleworth seated at the lunch table on his own. 'Where are the other two?' he asked.

'They were most apologetic, but said they couldn't wait for lunch – had to get back to London.' Wolstenholme looked perplexed. There were still several questions he wanted to ask – and he didn't know where to send his bill. Shuttleworth poured him a glass of champagne and said, 'Congratulations, Henry. You couldn't have done a more professional job. I must say your friend Townsend is obviously a man of action.'

'Not much doubt about that,' said Wolstenholme.

'And generous, too,' said Shuttleworth.

'Generous?'

'Yes – they may have left without saying goodbye, but they threw in a couple of bottles of champagne.'

—◦—

When Wolstenholme arrived home that night, the phone was ringing. He picked it up to find Townsend on the other end of the line.

'I was so sorry to hear about your mother,' were Henry's opening words.

'There's nothing wrong with my mother,' said Townsend sharply.

'What?' said Henry. 'But . . .'

'I'm returning on the next available flight. I'll be in Leeds by tomorrow evening.'

'No need to do that, old chap,' said Henry, slightly bemused. 'Shuttleworth has already signed.'

'But the contract still needs my signature,' said Townsend.

'No it doesn't. Your representative signed everything on your behalf,' said Henry, 'and I can assure you that all the paperwork was in order.'

'My representative?' said Townsend.

'Yes, a Mr Richard Armstrong. I banked his draft for £120,000 just before lunch. There's really no need for you to come all the way back. WRG now belongs to you.'

Townsend slammed the phone down and turned round to find Kate standing behind him. 'I'm going on to Sydney, but I want you to return to London and find out everything you can about a man called Richard Armstrong.'

'So that's the name of the man who was sitting in the next alcove to us at the Savoy.'

'It would seem so,' said Townsend, spitting out the words.

'And he now owns the West Riding Group?'

'Yes, he does.'

'Can't you do anything about it?'

'I could sue him for misrepresentation, even fraud, but

that could take years. In any case, a man who would go to that amount of trouble will have made sure he stayed within the letter of the law. And one thing's for sure: Shuttleworth isn't going to agree to appear in any witness box.'

Kate frowned. 'Well then, I can't see much point in returning to London now. I suspect your battle with Mr Richard Armstrong has only just begun. We may as well spend the night in Bombay,' she suggested. 'I've never been to India.'

Townsend looked at her, but didn't say anything until he spotted a TWA captain heading towards them.

'Which is the best hotel in Bombay?' he asked him.

The captain stopped. 'They tell me the Grand Palace is in a class of its own, but I've never actually stayed there myself,' he replied.

'Thank you,' said Townsend, and began pushing their baggage towards the exit. Just as they stepped out of the terminal it began to rain.

Townsend loaded their bags into a waiting taxi that he felt certain would have been decommissioned in any other country. Once he had joined Kate in the back, they began the long journey into Bombay. Although some of the street lights were working, the taxi's were not, nor were its windscreen wipers. And the driver didn't seem to know how to get out of second gear. But he was able to confirm every few minutes that the Grand Palace was 'in a class of its own'.

When they eventually swept into the driveway, a clap of thunder struck above them. Keith had to admit that the ornate white building was certainly large and palatial, even if the more seasoned traveller might ungraciously have added the word 'faded'.

'Welcome,' said a man in a fashionable dark suit as they entered the marble-floored foyer. 'My name is Mr Baht. I am the general manager.' He bowed low. 'May I ask what name your booking is in?'

'We don't have a reservation. We'll be needing two rooms,' said Keith.

'That is indeed unfortunate,' said Mr Baht, 'because I am

almost certain that we are fully booked for the night. Let me find out.' He ushered them towards the reservation desk and spoke for some time to the booking clerk. The clerk kept shaking his head. Mr Baht studied the reservation sheet himself and finally turned to face them again.

'I'm very very sorry to tell you that we have only one room vacant,' he said, placing his hands together, perhaps in the hope that through the power of prayer one room might miraculously turn into two. 'And I fear . . .'

'You fear . . . ?' said Keith.

'It is the Royal Suite, sahib.'

'How appropriate,' said Kate, 'remembering your views on the monarchy.' She was trying not to laugh. 'Does it have a sofa?' she asked.

'Several,' said a surprised general manager, who had never been asked that question before.

'Then we'll take it,' said Kate.

After they had filled in the booking form, Mr Baht clapped his hands and a porter in a long red tunic, red pantaloons and a red turban came bustling forward.

'Very fine suite,' said the porter as he carried their bags up the wide staircase. This time Kate did laugh. 'Slept in by Lord Mountbatten,' he added with obvious pride, 'and many mahara-jahs. Very fine suite.' He placed the bags by the entrance to the Royal Suite, put a large key in the lock and pushed open the double door, then switched on the lights and stood aside to usher them in.

The two of them walked into an enormous room. Up against the far wall was a vast, opulent double bed, which could have slept half a dozen maharajahs. And to Keith's disappointment there were, as Mr Baht had promised, several large sofas.

'Very fine bed,' said the porter, placing their bags in the centre of the room. Keith handed him a pound note. The porter bowed low, turned and left the room as a flash of lightning shot across the sky and the lights suddenly went out.

'How did you manage that?' asked Kate.

'If you look out of the window, I think you'll find it was

carried out by a far higher authority than me.' Kate turned to see that the whole city was in darkness.

'So, shall we just stand around waiting for the lights to come back on, or shall we go in search of somewhere to sit down?' Keith put out his hand in the darkness, and touched Kate's hip. 'You lead,' she said, taking his hand. He turned in the direction of the bed and began taking small paces towards it, sweeping the air in front of him with his free arm until he eventually hit the corner post. They fell onto the large mattress together, laughing.

'Very fine bed,' said Keith.

'Slept in by many maharajahs,' said Kate.

'And by Lord Mountbatten,' said Keith.

Kate laughed. 'By the way, Keith, you didn't have to buy off the Bombay electricity company just to get me into bed. I've spent the last week thinking you were only interested in my brain.'

FOURTH EDITION

Armstrong and Townsend Battle for the *Globe*

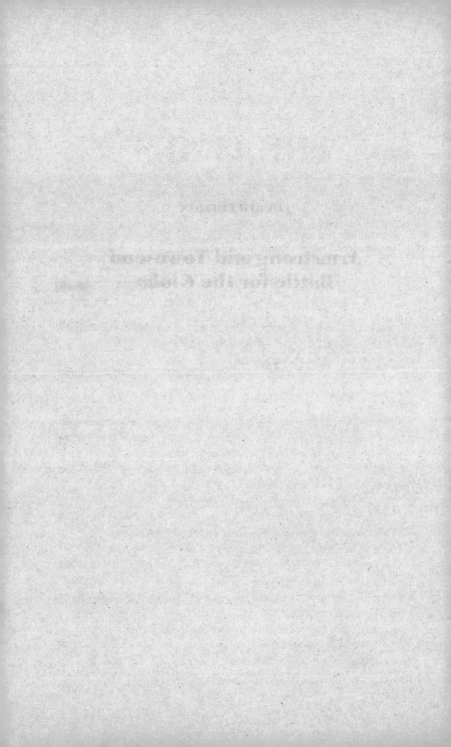

22

THE TIMES

1 APRIL 1966

Labour Sweeps to Power: Majority of 100 Assured

Armstrong glanced at a typist he didn't recognise, and walked on into his office to find Sally on the phone.

'Who's my first appointment?'

'Derek Kirby,' she said, cupping her hand over the mouthpiece.

'And who's he?'

'A former editor of the *Daily Express*. The poor man only lasted eight months, but he claims to have some interesting information for you. Shall I ask him to come in?'

'No, let him wait a little longer,' said Armstrong. 'Who's on the line now?'

'Phil Barker. He's calling from Leeds.'

Armstrong nodded and took the phone from Sally to speak to the new chief executive of the West Riding Group.

'Did they agree to my terms?'

'They settled for £1.3 million, to be paid over the next six years in equal instalments – as long as sales remain constant. But if sales drop during the first year, every succeeding payment will also drop pro rata.'

'They didn't spot the flaw in the contract?'

'No,' said Barker. 'They assumed that you would want to put the circulation up in the first year.'

'Good. Just see that you fix the lowest audited figure possible, then we'll start building them up again in the second year. That way I'll save myself a fortune. How about the *Hull Echo* and the *Grimsby Times*?'

'Early days yet, but now that everybody realises you're a buyer, Dick, my task isn't made any easier.'

'We'll just have to offer more and pay less.'

'And how do you propose to do that?' asked Barker.

'By inserting clauses that make promises we have absolutely no intention of keeping. Never forget that old family concerns rarely sue, because they don't like ending up in court. So always take advantage of the letter of the law. Don't break it, just bend it as far as it will go without snapping. Get on with it.' Armstrong put the phone down.

'Derek Kirby is still waiting,' Sally reminded him.

Armstrong checked his watch. 'How long has he been hanging about?'

'Twenty, twenty-five minutes.'

'Then let's go through the post.'

After twenty-one years, Sally knew which invitations Armstrong would accept, which charities he didn't want to support, which gatherings he was willing to address and whose dinner parties he wanted to be seen at. The rule was to say yes to anything that might advance his career, and no to the rest. When she closed her shorthand pad forty minutes later, she pointed out that Derek Kirby had now been waiting for over an hour.

'All right, you can send him in. But if you get any interesting calls, put them through.'

When Kirby entered the room, Armstrong made no attempt to rise from his place, but simply jabbed a finger at the seat on the far side of the desk.

Kirby appeared nervous; Armstrong had found that keeping someone waiting for any length of time almost always made them on edge. His visitor must have been about forty-five, though the furrows on his forehead and his receding hairline made him look older. His suit was smart, but not of the latest fashion, and although his shirt was clean and well ironed, the collar and cuffs were beginning to fray. Armstrong suspected he had been living on freelance work since leaving the *Express*, and would be missing his expense account. Whatever Kirby had to sell, he could probably offer him half and pay a quarter.

'Good morning, Mr Armstrong,' Kirby said before he sat down.

'I'm sorry to have kept you waiting,' said Armstrong, 'but something urgent came up.'

'I understand,' said Kirby.

'So, what can I do for you?'

'No, it's what I can do for you,' said Kirby, which sounded to Armstrong like a well-rehearsed line.

Armstrong nodded. 'I'm listening.'

'I am privy to confidential information which could make it possible for you to get your hands on a national newspaper.'

'It can't be the *Express*,' said Armstrong, looking out of the window, 'because as long as Beaverbrook is alive . . .'

'No, it's bigger than that.'

Armstrong remained silent for a moment and then said, 'Would you like some coffee, Mr Kirby?'

'I'd prefer tea,' replied the former editor. Armstrong picked up one of the phones on his desk. 'Sally, can we both have some tea?' – a signal that the appointment might go on longer than expected, and that he was not to be interrupted.

'You were editor of the *Express*, if I remember correctly,' said Armstrong.

'Yes, one of seven in the last eight years.'

'I never understood why they sacked you.'

Sally entered the room carrying a tray. She placed one cup of tea in front of Kirby and another in front of Armstrong.

'The man who followed you was a moron, and you were never really given enough time to prove yourself.'

A smile appeared on Kirby's face as he poured some milk into his tea, dropped in two sugarcubes and settled back in his chair. He didn't feel that this was the moment to point out to Armstrong that he had recently employed his replacement to edit one of his own papers.

'Well, if it isn't the *Express*, which paper are we talking about?'

'Before I say anything more, I need to be clear about my own position,' said Kirby.

'I'm not sure I understand.' Armstrong placed his elbows on the table and stared across at him.

'Well, after my experience at the *Express*, I want to be sure my backside is covered.'

Armstrong said nothing. Kirby opened his briefcase and removed a document. 'My lawyers have drawn this up to protect . . .'

'Just tell me what you want, Derek. I'm well known for honouring my pledges.'

'This document states that if you take control of the paper in question, I will be appointed editor, or paid compensation of £100,000.' He handed Armstrong the one-page agreement.

Armstrong read quickly through it. As soon as he realised there was no mention of any salary, only of the appointment as editor, he signed above his name at the bottom of the page. He had got rid of a man in Bradford by agreeing he should be editor and then paying him a pound a year. He would have advised Kirby that cheap lawyers always get you cheap results, but he satisfied himself with passing the signed document back to its eager recipient.

'Thank you,' said Kirby, looking a little more confident.

'So, which paper do you want to edit?'

'The *Globe*.'

For the second time that morning Armstrong was taken by surprise. The *Globe* was one of the icons of Fleet Street. No one had ever suggested it might be up for sale.

'But all the shares are held by one family,' said Armstrong.

'That's correct,' said Kirby. 'Two brothers and a sister-in-law. Sir Walter, Alexander, and Margaret Sherwood. And because Sir Walter is the chairman, everyone imagines he controls the company. But that isn't the case: the shares are split equally between the three of them.'

'I knew that much,' said Armstrong. 'It's been reported in every profile of Sir Walter I've ever read.'

'Yes. But what hasn't been reported is that recently there's been a falling-out between them.'

Armstrong raised an eyebrow.

'They all met for dinner at Alexander's apartment in Paris last Friday. Sir Walter flew in from London, and Margaret from New York, ostensibly to celebrate Alexander's sixty-second birthday. But it didn't turn out to be a celebration, because Alexander and Margaret let Walter know they were fed up with him not paying enough attention to what was happening to the *Globe*, and blamed him personally for the drop in sales. They've gone from over four million to under two million since he became chairman – falling behind the *Daily Citizen*, which is boasting that it's now the paper with the largest daily circulation in the land. They accused him of spending far too much time flitting between the Turf Club and the nearest racecourse. A real shouting match followed, and Alexander and Margaret made it abundantly clear that although they had turned down several offers for their shares in the past, that didn't mean they would do so in the future, as they had no intention of sacrificing their lifestyle simply because of his incompetence.'

'How do you know all this?' asked Armstrong.

'His cook,' replied Kirby.

'His cook?' repeated Armstrong.

'Her name's Lisa Milton. She used to work for Fleet Street Caterers before Alexander offered her the job with him in Paris.' He paused. 'Alexander hasn't been the easiest of employers, and Lisa would resign and return to England if . . .'

'. . . if she could afford to do so?' suggested Armstrong.

Kirby nodded. 'Lisa could hear every word they were saying while she was preparing dinner in the kitchen. In fact, she told me she wouldn't have been surprised if the entire exchange could have been heard on the floors above and below.'

Armstrong smiled. 'You've done well, Derek. Is there any other information you have that might be useful to me?'

Kirby leaned down and removed a bulky file from his briefcase. 'You'll find all the details on the three of them in here. Profiles, addresses, phone numbers, even the name of Alexander's mistress. If you need anything else, you can call me direct.' He pushed a card across the table.

Armstrong took the file and placed it on the blotter in front of him, slipping the card into his wallet. 'Thank you,' he said. 'If the cook comes up with any fresh information or you ever want to get in touch with me, I'm always available. Use my direct line.' He passed his own card over to Kirby.

'I'll call the moment I hear anything,' said Kirby, rising to leave.

Armstrong accompanied him to the door, and when they entered Sally's room he put an arm round his shoulder. As they shook hands he turned to his secretary and said, 'Derek must always be able to get in touch with me, night or day, whoever I'm with.'

As soon as Kirby had left, Sally joined Armstrong in his office. He was already studying the first page of the Sherwood file. 'Did you mean what you just said about Kirby always being able to get in touch with you night and day?'

'For the foreseeable future, yes. But now I need you to clear my diary to make space for a trip to Paris to see a Mr Alexander Sherwood. If that proves successful, I'll need to go on to New York to meet his sister-in-law.'

Sally began flicking over the pages. 'Your diary's jam-packed with appointments,' she said.

'Like a bloody dentist,' snapped Armstrong. 'See they're all cancelled by the time I get back from lunch. And while you're at it, go through every single piece of paper in this file. Then perhaps you'll realise why seeing Mr Sherwood is so important – but don't let anyone else get their hands on it.'

He checked his watch and marched out of the room. As he walked down the corridor, his eyes settled on the new typist he had noticed that morning. This time she looked up and smiled. In the car on the way to the Savoy, he asked Reg to find out all he could about her.

Armstrong found it hard to concentrate during lunch – despite the fact that his guest was a cabinet minister – because he was already imagining what it might be like to be the proprietor of the *Globe*. In any case, he had heard that this particular minister would be returning to the back benches as soon as the prime minister carried out his next reshuffle. He was not at all sorry when the minister said he would have to leave early, as his department was answering questions in the House that afternoon. Armstrong called for the bill.

He watched as the minister was whisked away in a chauffeur-driven car, and hoped the poor man hadn't got too used to it. When he climbed into the back of his own car, his thoughts returned to the *Globe*.

'Excuse me, sir,' said Benson, glancing into the rear-view mirror.

'What is it?' snapped Armstrong.

'You asked me to find out about that girl.'

'Ah, yes,' said Armstrong, softening.

'She's a temp – Sharon Levitt, covering for Mr Wakeham's secretary while she's on holiday. She's only going to be around for a couple of weeks.'

Armstrong nodded. When he stepped out of the lift and walked to his office, he was disappointed to find that she was no longer sitting at the desk in the corner.

Sally followed him into his room, clutching his diary and a bundle of papers. 'If you cancel your speech to SOGAT on Saturday night,' she said on the move, 'and lunch on Sunday with your wife – ' Armstrong waved a dismissive hand. 'It's her birthday,' Sally reminded him.

'Send her a bunch of flowers, go to Harrods and choose a gift, and remind me to call her on the day.'

'In which case the diary's clear for the whole weekend.'

'What about Alexander Sherwood?'

'I called his secretary in Paris just before lunch. To my surprise, Sherwood himself called back a few minutes ago.'

'And?' said Armstrong.

'He didn't even ask why you wanted to see him, but

wondered if you'd care to join him for lunch at one o'clock on Saturday, at his apartment in Montmartre.'

'Well done, Sally. I'll also need to see his cook before I meet him.'

'Lisa Milton,' said Sally. 'She'll join you at the George V for breakfast that morning.'

'Then all that's left for you to do this afternoon is to finish off the post.'

'You've forgotten that I have a dental appointment at four. I've already put it off twice, and my toothache is starting to . . .'

Armstrong was about to tell her to put it off a third time, but checked himself. 'Of course you mustn't cancel your appointment, Sally. Ask Mr Wakeham's secretary to cover for you.'

Sally couldn't hide her surprise, as Dick had never allowed anyone to cover for her since the first day she'd worked for him.

'I think he's using a temp for the next couple of weeks,' she said uneasily.

'That's fine. It's only routine stuff.'

'I'll go and get her,' said Sally, as the private phone on Armstrong's desk began to ring. It was Stephen Hallet, confirming that he had issued a writ for libel against the editor of the *Daily Mail*, and suggesting it might be wise for Dick to keep a low profile for the next few days.

'Have you discovered who leaked the story in the first place?' asked Armstrong.

'No, but I suspect it came out of Germany,' said Hallet.

'But all that was years ago,' said Armstrong. 'In any case, I attended Julius Hahn's funeral, so it can't be him. My bet is still Townsend.'

'I don't know who it is, but someone out there wants to discredit you, and I think we might have to issue a series of gagging writs over the next few weeks. At least that way they'll think twice about what they print in the future.'

'Send me copies of anything and everything that mentions my name,' he said. 'If you need me urgently, I'll be in Paris over the weekend.'

'Lucky you,' said Hallet. 'And do give my love to Charlotte.'

Sally walked back into the room, followed by a tall, slim blonde in a miniskirt that could only have been worn by someone with the most slender legs.

'I'm just about to embark on a very important deal,' said Armstrong in a slightly louder voice.

'I understand,' said Stephen. 'Be assured I'll stay on top of it.'

Armstrong slammed the phone down and smiled sweetly up at the temp.

'This is Sharon. I've told her it will only be run-of-the-mill stuff, and you'll let her go by five,' said Sally. 'I'll be back first thing in the morning.'

Armstrong's eyes settled on Sharon's ankles and then moved slowly up. He didn't even look at Sally as she said, 'See you tomorrow.'

Townsend finished reading the article in the *Daily Mail*, swung round on his chair and stared out over Sydney Harbour. It had been an unflattering portrayal of the rise and rise of Lubji Hoch, and his desire to be accepted in Britain as a press baron. They had used several unattributed quotes from Armstrong's fellow-officers in the King's Own Regiment, from Germans who had come across him in Berlin, and from past employees.

There was little in the article that hadn't been lifted from the profile Kate had written for the *Sunday Continent* some weeks before. Townsend knew that few people in Australia would have any interest in the life of Richard Armstrong. But the article would have landed on the desk of every editor in Fleet Street within days, and then it would be only a matter of time before it was being reproduced in part or in full for dissemination to the British public. He had only wondered which newspaper would publish first.

He knew it wouldn't take long for Armstrong to discover the source of the original article, which gave him even more pleasure. Ned Brewer, his bureau chief in London, had recently told him that stories about Armstrong's private life had stopped appearing quite so frequently since the writs had begun falling like confetti on editors' desks.

Townsend had watched with increasing anger as Armstrong built up WRG into a strong power-base in the north of England. But he was in no doubt where the man's true ambitions lay. Townsend had already infiltrated two people into Armstrong's Fleet Street headquarters, and they reported back on anyone and everyone who made an appointment to see him. The latest visitor, Derek Kirby, the former editor of the *Express*, had left with Armstrong's arm around his shoulder. Townsend's advisers thought Kirby was probably taking over as editor of one of WRG's regional papers. Townsend wasn't quite so sure, and left instructions that he should be told immediately if Armstrong was discovered bidding for anything. He repeated, 'Anything.'

'Is WRG really that important to you?' Kate had asked him.

'No, but a man who would stoop so low as to use my mother as a bargaining chip will get what's coming to him.'

So far Townsend had been briefed on Armstrong's purchases from Stoke-on-Trent to Durham. He now controlled nineteen local and regional papers and five county magazines, and he had certainly pulled off a coup when he captured 25 per cent of Lancashire Television and 49 per cent of the regional radio station, in exchange for preference shares in his own company. His latest venture had been to launch the *London Evening Post*. But Townsend knew that, like himself, what Armstrong most craved was to be the proprietor of a national daily.

Over the past four years Townsend had purchased three more Australian dailies, a Sunday and a weekly news magazine. He now controlled newspapers in every state of Australia, and there wasn't a politician or businessman in the country who wasn't available whenever Townsend picked up a phone. He had also visited America a dozen times in the past year, selecting cities where the main employers were in steel, coal, or automobiles, because he nearly always found that companies involved in those ailing industries also controlled the local newspapers. Whenever he discovered such a company having cash-flow problems he moved in, and was often able to close a deal for the newspaper quickly. In almost every case he then found his new acquisition overstaffed and badly managed, because it was rare for anyone on the main board to have any first-hand experience of running a newspaper. By sacking half the staff and replacing most of the senior management with his own people, he could turn the balance sheet round in a matter of months.

Using this approach he had succeeded in picking up nine city papers, from Seattle to North Carolina, and that in turn had allowed him to build up a company which would be large enough to bid for one of America's flagship newspapers, should the opportunity ever arise.

Kate had accompanied him on several of these trips, and although he was in no doubt that he wanted to marry her, he still wasn't sure, after his experiences with Susan, that he could ask anyone to spend the rest of her life living out of suitcases and never being quite sure where their roots were.

If he ever envied Armstrong anything, it was that he had a son to take over his empire.

23

THE TIMES

29 OCTOBER 1966

Channel Tunnel Target Date 1975. Four Years to Build

'Miss Levitt will be accompanying me to Paris,' said Armstrong. 'Book me two first-class tickets and my usual suite at the George V.'

Sally carried out his orders as if it was a normal business transaction. She smiled at the thought of the promises that would be made over the weekend and then not kept, of the presents that would be offered but never materialise. On Monday morning she would be expected to settle up with the girl, in cash, just like her predecessors – but at a far higher hourly rate than any agency would have dared to charge for even the most experienced temp.

When Armstrong arrived back from Paris on Monday morning, there was no sign of Sharon. Sally assumed she would be hearing from her later that day. 'How did the meeting with Alexander Sherwood go?' she asked after she had placed the morning post on his desk.

'We agreed on a price for his third of the *Globe*,' Armstrong said triumphantly. Before Sally could ask for any details, he added, 'Your next task is to get hold of the catalogue for a sale at Sotheby's in Geneva that's taking place on Thursday morning.'

She didn't bat an eyelid as she flicked over three pages of the diary. 'You've got appointments that morning at ten, eleven and eleven forty-five, and a lunch with William Barnetson, the chairman of Reuters. You've already rearranged it twice.'

'Then you'll just have to rearrange it for a third time,' said Armstrong, not even looking up.

'Including the meeting with the chief secretary to the Treasury?'

'Including everything,' he said. 'Book me two first-class tickets for Geneva on Wednesday evening, and my usual room at Le Richemond overlooking the lake.'

So Sharon whatever-her-name-was must have survived for a second outing.

Sally put a line through the seven appointments in the diary on Thursday, well aware that there had to be a good reason for Dick to postpone a cabinet minister and the chairman of Reuters. But what could he be buying? The only thing he had ever bid for in the past had been newspapers, and you couldn't pick up one of those at an auction house.

Sally returned to her office and asked Benson to drive over to Sotheby's in Bond Street and purchase a copy of their catalogue for the Geneva sale. When he presented it to her an hour later, she was even more surprised. Dick had never shown any interest in collecting eggs in the past. Could it be the Russian connection? Because surely Sharon wasn't expecting a Fabergé for two nights' work?

—◦—

On the Wednesday evening, Dick and Sharon flew into the Swiss capital and checked into Le Richemond. Before dinner they strolled over to the Hôtel de Bergues in the centre of the city, where Sotheby's always conduct their Geneva auctions, to inspect the room where the sale would be taking place.

Armstrong watched as the hotel staff put out the chairs on a floor which he estimated would hold about four hundred people. He walked slowly round the room, deciding where he needed to sit to be sure that he had a clear view of the auctioneer as well as the bank of nine telephones placed on a raised platform at one side of the room. As he and Sharon were about to leave, he stopped to glance round the room once more.

As soon as they arrived back at their hotel, Armstrong marched into the small dining room overlooking the lake and headed straight for the alcove table in the corner. He had sat down long before the head waiter could tell him the table was reserved for another guest. He ordered for himself and then passed the menu to Sharon.

As he waited for the first course, he began to butter the bread roll on the plate by his side. When he had eaten it, he leaned across and took Sharon's roll from her plate. She continued to turn the pages of the Sotheby's catalogue.

'Page forty-nine,' he said between mouthfuls. Sharon quickly flicked over a few more pages. Her eyes settled on an object whose name she couldn't pronounce.

'Is this to be added to a collection?' she asked, hoping it might be a gift for her.

'Yes,' he replied, with his mouth full, 'but not mine. I'd never heard of Fabergé until last week,' he admitted. 'It's just part of a bigger deal I'm involved in.'

Sharon's eyes continued down the page, passing over the detailed description of how the masterpiece had been smuggled out of Russia in 1917, until they settled on the estimated price.

Armstrong reached under the table and put a hand on her thigh.

'How high will you go?' she asked, as a waiter appeared by their side and placed a large bowl of caviar in front of them.

Armstrong quickly removed his hand and switched his attention to the first course.

Since their weekend in Paris they had spent every night together, and Dick couldn't remember how long it was since he had been so obsessed by anyone – if ever. Much to Sally's surprise, he had taken to leaving the office in the early evening, and not reappearing until ten the next day.

Over breakfast each morning he would offer to buy her presents, but she always rejected them, which made him fearful of losing her. He knew it wasn't love, but whatever it was, he hoped it would go on for a long time. He had always dreaded the thought of a divorce, even though he rarely saw Charlotte nowadays other than at official functions and couldn't even remember when they had last slept together. But to his relief Sharon never talked about marriage. The only suggestion she ever made would, she kept reminding him, allow them the best of both worlds. He was slowly coming round to falling in with her wishes.

After the empty caviar bowl had been whisked away, Armstrong began to attack a steak which took up so much of his plate that the extra vegetables he had demanded had to be placed on several other dishes. By using two forks he found he was able to eat from two plates at once, while Sharon contented herself with nibbling a lettuce leaf and toying with some smoked salmon. He would have ordered a second helping of Black Forest gateau if she hadn't started running the tip of her right foot along the inside of his thigh.

He threw his napkin down on the table and headed out of the restaurant towards the lift, leaving Sharon to follow a pace behind. He stepped in and jabbed the button for the seventh floor, and the doors closed just in time to prevent an elderly couple from joining them.

When they reached their floor he was relieved that there was no one else in the corridor, because if there had been, they could not have failed to notice the state he was in.

Once he had kicked the bedroom door closed with his heel, she pulled him down on to the floor and began pulling off his shirt. 'I can't wait any longer,' she whispered.

—◁◦▷—

The following morning, Armstrong sat down at a table laid for two in their suite. He ate both breakfasts while checking the exchange rate for the Swiss franc against the pound in the *Financial Times*.

Sharon was admiring herself in a long mirror at the other end of the room, taking her time to get dressed. She liked what she saw, and smiled before turning round and walking over to the breakfast table. She placed a long, slim leg on the arm of Armstrong's chair. He dropped his butter knife on the carpet as she began pulling on a black stocking. When she changed legs he stood up to face her, sighing as she slipped her arms inside his dressing-gown.

'Have we got time?' he asked.

'Don't worry about time, my darling, the auction doesn't start until ten,' she whispered, unclipping her bra and pulling him back down to the floor.

They left the hotel a few minutes before ten, but as the only item Armstrong was interested in was unlikely to come up much before eleven, they strolled arm in arm along the side of the lake, making their way slowly in the direction of the city centre and enjoying the warmth of the morning sun.

When they entered the foyer of the Hôtel de Bergues, Armstrong felt strangely apprehensive. Despite the fact that he had bargained for everything he had ever wanted in his life, this was the first time he had attended an auction. But he had been carefully briefed on what was expected of him, and he immediately began to carry out his instructions. At the entrance to the ballroom he gave his name to one of the smartly-dressed women seated behind a long table. She spoke in French and he replied in kind, explaining that he was only interested in Lot Forty-three. Armstrong was surprised to find that almost every place in the room had already been taken, including the one he had identified the previous evening. Sharon pointed to two empty chairs on the left-hand side of the room, towards the back. Armstrong nodded and led her down the aisle. As they sat down a young man in an open-necked shirt slipped into a seat behind them.

Armstrong checked that he had a clear view of the auctioneer as well as the bank of temporary phones, each of them manned by an overqualified telephonist. His position wasn't as convenient as his original choice, but he could see no reason why it should prevent him from fulfilling his part of the bargain.

'Lot Seventeen,' declared the auctioneer from his podium at

the front of the ballroom. Armstrong turned to the relevant page in his catalogue, and looked down at a silver-gilt Easter egg supported by four crosses with the blue enamelled cipher of Czar Nicholas II, commissioned in 1907 from Peter Carl Fabergé for the Czarina. He began to concentrate on the proceedings.

'Do I hear 10,000?' asked the auctioneer, looking around the room. He nodded at someone towards the back. 'Fifteen thousand.' Armstrong tried to follow the different bids, although he wasn't quite sure where they were coming from, and when Lot Seventeen eventually sold for 45,000 francs, he had no idea who the purchaser was. It came as a surprise that the auctioneer brought the hammer down without saying 'Going, going, gone.'

By the time the auctioneer had reached Lot Twenty-five, Armstrong felt a little more sure of himself, and by Lot Thirty he thought he could even spot the occasional bidder. By Lot Thirty-five he felt he was an expert, but by Lot Forty, the Winter Egg of 1913, he had begun to feel nervous again.

'I shall start this lot at 20,000 francs,' declared the auctioneer. Armstrong watched as the bidding climbed quickly past 50,000, with the hammer finally coming down at 120,000 francs, to a customer whose anonymity was guaranteed by his being on the other end of a telephone line.

Armstrong felt his hands begin to sweat when Lot Forty-one, the Chanticleer Egg of 1896, encrusted in pearls and rubies, went for 280,000 francs. During the sale of Lot Forty-two, the Yuberov Yellow Egg, he began to fidget, continually looking up at the auctioneer and then down at the open page of his catalogue.

When the auctioneer called Lot Forty-three, Sharon squeezed his hand and he managed a nervous smile. A buzz of conversation struck up around the room.

'Lot Forty-three,' repeated the auctioneer, 'the Fourteenth Imperial Anniversary Egg. This unique piece was commissioned by the Czar in 1910. The paintings were executed by Vasily Zulev, and the craftsmanship is considered to be among the finest examples of Fabergé's work. There has already been considerable interest shown in this lot, so I shall start the bidding at 100,000 francs.'

Everyone in the room fell silent except for the auctioneer. The head of his hammer was gripped firmly in his right hand as he stared down into the audience, trying to place the bidders.

Armstrong remembered his briefing, and the exact price at which he should come in. But he could still feel his pulse rate rise when the auctioneer pronounced 'One hundred and fifty thousand,' then, turning to his left, said, 'The bid is now on the telephone at 150,000 francs, 150,000,' he repeated. He looked intently around the audience, then a smile crossed his lips. 'Two hundred thousand in the centre of the room.' He paused and looked towards the assistant on the end phone. Armstrong watched her whisper into the receiver, and then she nodded in the direction of the auctioneer, who immediately responded with 'Two hundred and fifty thousand.' He turned his attention back to those seated in the room, where there must have been another bid because he immediately switched his gaze back to the assistant on the phone and said, 'I have a bid of 300,000 francs.'

The woman informed her client of the latest bid and, after a few moments, she nodded again. All heads in the room swung back to the auctioneer as if they were watching a tennis match in slow motion. 'Three hundred and fifty thousand,' he said, glancing at the centre of the room.

Armstrong looked down at the catalogue. He knew it was not yet time for him to join in the bidding, but that didn't stop him continuing to fidget.

'Four hundred thousand,' said the auctioneer, nodding to the woman on the end phone. 'Four hundred and fifty thousand in the centre of the room.' The woman on the phone responded immediately. 'Five hundred thousand. Six hundred thousand,' said the auctioneer, his eyes now fixed on the centre aisle. With that one bid Armstrong had learned another of the auctioneer's skills.

Armstrong craned his neck until he finally spotted who it

was bidding from the floor. His eyes moved over to the woman on the phone, who nodded once again. 'Seven hundred thousand,' said the auctioneer calmly.

A man seated just in front of him raised his catalogue. 'Eight hundred thousand,' declared the auctioneer. 'A new bidder towards the back.' He turned to the woman on the phone, who took rather longer telling her customer the latest bid. 'Nine hundred thousand?' he suggested, as if he was trying to woo her. Suddenly she consented. 'I have a bid of 900,000 on the phone,' he said, and looked towards the man at the back of the room. 'Nine hundred thousand,' the auctioneer repeated. But this time he received no response.

'Are there any more bids?' asked the auctioneer. 'Then I'm letting this item go for 900,000 francs. Fair warning,' he said, raising the hammer. 'I'm going to let . . .'

When Armstrong raised his catalogue, it looked to the auctioneer as if he was waving. He wasn't, he was shaking.

'I have a new bidder on the right-hand aisle, towards the back of the room, at one million francs.' The auctioneer once again directed his attention to the woman on the telephone.

'One million one hundred thousand?' said the auctioneer, pointing the handle of his hammer at the assistant on the end phone. Armstrong sat in silence, not sure what he should do next, as a million francs was the figure they had agreed on. People began to turn round and stare in his direction. He remained silent, knowing that the woman on the phone would shake her head.

She shook her head.

'I have a bid of one million on the aisle,' said the auctioneer, pointing towards Armstrong. 'Are there any more bids? Then I'm going to let this go for one million.' His eyes scanned the audience hopefully, but no one responded. He finally brought the hammer down with a thud and, looking at Armstrong, said, 'Sold to the gentleman on the aisle for one million francs.' A burst of applause erupted around the room.

Sharon squeezed his hand again. But before Dick could

catch his breath, a woman was kneeling on the floor beside him. 'If you fill in this form, Mr Armstrong, someone at the reception desk will advise you on collecting your lot.'

Armstrong nodded. But once he had completed the form, he did not head for the desk, but instead went to the nearest telephone in the lobby and dialled an overseas number. When the phone was answered he said, 'Put me straight through to the manager.' He gave the order for a million francs to be sent to Sotheby's Geneva by swift telegraph transfer, as agreed. 'And make it swift,' said Armstrong, 'because I've no desire to hang around here any longer than necessary.'

He replaced the phone and went over to the woman at the reception desk to explain how the account would be settled, just as the young man in the open-necked shirt began dialling an overseas number, despite the fact that he knew he would be waking his boss.

Townsend sat up in bed and listened carefully. 'Why would Armstrong pay a million francs for a Fabergé egg?' he asked.

'I can't work that out either,' said the young man. 'Hang on, he's just going upstairs with the girl. I'd better stick with him. I'll ring back as soon as I find out what he's up to.'

Over lunch in the hotel dining room, Armstrong appeared so preoccupied that Sharon thought it sensible to say nothing unless he started a conversation. It was obvious that the egg had not been purchased for her. When he had put down his empty coffee cup, he asked her to go back to their room and finish packing, as he wanted to leave for the airport in an hour. 'I have one more meeting to attend,' he said, 'but it shouldn't take too long.'

When he kissed her on the cheek at the entrance to the hotel, the young man in the open-necked shirt knew which of them he would have preferred to follow.

'See you in about an hour,' he overheard his quarry say. Then Armstrong turned and almost ran down the wide staircase to the ballroom where the auction had taken place. He went straight to the woman seated behind the long table, checking purchase slips.

'Ah, Mr Armstrong, how nice to see you again,' she said, giving him a million-franc smile. 'Your funds have been cleared by swift telegraphic transfer. If you would be kind enough to join my colleague in the inner office,' she said, indicating a door behind her, 'you will be able to collect your lot.'

'Thank you,' said Armstrong, as she passed over his receipt for the masterpiece. He turned round, nearly bumping into a young man standing directly behind him, walked into the back office and presented his receipt to a man in a black tailcoat who was standing behind the counter.

The official checked the little slip carefully, took a close look at Mr Armstrong, smiled and instructed the security guard to fetch Lot Forty-three, the Imperial Anniversary Egg of 1910. When the guard returned with the egg he was with the auctioneer, who gave the ornate piece one last longing look before holding it up for his customer to inspect. 'Quite magnificent, wouldn't you say?'

'Quite magnificent,' repeated Armstrong, grabbing the egg as if it were a rugby ball coming out of a loose scrum. He turned to leave without uttering another word, so didn't hear the auctioneer whisper to his assistant, 'Strange that none of us has ever come across Mr Armstrong before.'

The doorman of the Hôtel de Bergues touched his cap as Armstrong slid into the back of a taxi, clinging on to the egg with both hands. He instructed the driver to take him to the Banque de Genève just as another empty taxi drew up behind them. The young man hailed it.

When Armstrong walked into the bank, which he had never entered before, he was greeted by a tall, thin, anonymous-looking man in morning dress, who wouldn't have looked out of place proposing a toast to the bride at a society wedding in Hampshire. The man bowed low to indicate that he had been waiting for him. He did not ask Mr Armstrong if he would like him to carry the egg.

'Will you please follow me, sir?' he said in English, leading Armstrong across the marble floor to a waiting lift. How did he know who he was? Armstrong wondered. They stepped into the lift and the doors closed. Neither spoke as they travelled slowly up to the top floor. The doors parted and the tailcoated man preceded him down a wide, thickly-carpeted corridor until he reached the last door. He gave a discreet knock, opened the door and announced, 'Mr Armstrong.'

A man in a pinstripe suit, stiff collar and silver-grey tie stepped forward and introduced himself as Pierre de Mont-iaque, the bank's chief executive. He turned and faced another man seated on the far side of the boardroom table, then indicated that his visitor should take the vacant chair opposite him. Armstrong placed the Fabergé egg in the centre of the table, and Alexander Sherwood rose from his place, leaned across and shook him warmly by the hand.

'Good to see you again,' he said.

'And you,' replied Armstrong, smiling. He took his seat and looked across at the man with whom he had closed the deal in Paris.

Sherwood picked up the Imperial Anniversary Egg of 1910 and studied it closely. A smile appeared on his face. 'It will be the pride of my collection, and there should never be any reason for my brother or sister-in-law to become suspicious.' He smiled again and nodded in the direction of the banker, who opened a drawer and extracted a document, which he passed across to Armstrong.

Dick studied the agreement that Stephen Hallet had drawn up for him before he'd flown to Paris the previous week. Once he had checked that no alterations had been made, he signed at the bottom of the fifth page and then pushed the document across the table. Sherwood showed no interest in checking the contents, but simply turned to the last page and penned his signature next to that of Richard Armstrong.

'Can I therefore confirm that both sides are in agreement?' said the banker. 'I am currently holding $20 million on deposit, and only await Mr Armstrong's instructions to transfer it to Mr Sherwood's account.'

Armstrong nodded. Twenty million dollars was the sum Alexander and Margaret Sherwood had agreed should be paid for Alexander's third share in the *Globe*, with an understanding that she would then part with her third for exactly the same amount. What Margaret Sherwood didn't know was that Alexander had demanded a little reward for setting up the deal: a Fabergé egg, which would not appear as part of the formal contract.

Armstrong might have paid a million more francs than was stated in the contract, but he was now in possession of 33.3 per cent of a national newspaper which had once boasted the largest circulation in the world.

'Then our business is concluded,' said de Montiaque, rising from his place at the head of the table.

'Not quite,' said Sherwood, who remained seated. The chief executive resumed his place uneasily. Armstrong shuffled in his place. He could feel the sweat under his collar.

'As Mr Armstrong has been so co-operative,' said Sherwood, 'I consider it only fair that I should repay him in kind.' From the expression on their faces, it was obvious that neither Armstrong nor de Montiaque was prepared for this intervention. Alexander Sherwood then proceeded to reveal a piece of information concerning his father's will, which brought a smile to Richard Armstrong's lips.

When he left the bank a few minutes later to return to Le Richemond, he believed his million francs had been well spent.

◄○►

Townsend didn't comment when he was woken from a deep sleep for the second time that night. He listened intently and whispered his responses for fear of disturbing Kate. When he eventually put the phone down, he was unable to get back to sleep. Why would Armstrong have paid a million francs for a Fabergé egg, delivered it to a Swiss bank, and left less than an hour later, empty-handed?

The clock by his bed reminded him that it was only 3.30 a.m. He lay watching as Kate slept soundly. His mind drifted from her to Susan; then back to Kate, and how different she was; to his mother, and whether she would ever understand him; and then inevitably back to Armstrong, and how he could find out what he was up to.

When he finally rose later that morning, Townsend was no nearer to solving the little conundrum. He would have remained in the dark if a few days later he had not accepted a reverse-charge call from a woman in London.

24

Daily Telegraph

6 FEBRUARY 1967

Kosygin Sees Wilson in London Today

Armstrong was furious when he returned to the flat and found the note from Sharon. It simply said that she didn't want to see him again until he had come to a decision.

He sank onto the sofa and read her words a second time. He dialled her number; he was certain she was there, but there was no answer. He left it to ring for over a minute before he replaced the handset.

He couldn't recall a happier time in his life, and Sharon's note brought home to him how much she was now a part of it. He had even started having his hair dyed and his hands manicured, so she wouldn't be constantly reminded of the difference in their ages. After several sleepless nights and unacknowledged deliveries of flowers, and dozens of unanswered telephone calls, he realised that the only way he was going to get her back was to fall in with her wishes. He had been trying to convince himself for some time that she was not altogether serious about the whole idea, but it was now clear that those were the only terms on which she would agree to lead a double life. He decided that he would deal with the problem on Friday.

That morning he arrived unusually late at the office, and immediately asked Sally to get his wife on the phone. Once she had put Charlotte through, she began to prepare the papers for the trip to New York and his meeting with Margaret Sherwood.

She was aware that Dick had been on edge all week – at one point he had swept a tray of coffee cups off his desk onto the floor. No one seemed to know what was causing the problem. Benson thought it must be woman trouble; Sally suspected that after getting his hands on 33.3 per cent of the *Globe*, he was becoming increasingly frustrated at having to wait for Margaret Sherwood to return from her annual cruise before he could take advantage of the information he had recently been given by Alexander Sherwood.

'Every day gives Townsend more time to find out what I'm up to,' he muttered irritably.

His mood had caused Sally to postpone their annual discussion about her pay rise, which always made him lose his temper. But she had already started to put off paying certain bills that were long overdue, and she knew she was going to have to face up to him soon, however foul his mood.

Armstrong put the phone down on his wife, and asked Sally to come back in. She had already sorted through the morning post, dealt with all the routine letters, drafted provisional replies to the remainder, and put them all in a folder for his consideration. The majority only required his signature. But before she had even closed the door, he began dictating furiously. As the words came tumbling out, she automatically corrected his grammar, and realised that in some cases she would later have to temper his words.

As soon as he had finished dictating, he stormed out of the office for a lunch appointment, without giving her the chance to say anything. She decided that she would have to raise the subject of her salary as soon as he returned. After all, why should her holiday be postponed simply because of her boss's refusal to consider other people's lives?

By the time Armstrong came back from lunch, Sally had typed up all his dictation and had the letters in a second folder on his desk awaiting signature. She couldn't help noticing that, unusually, there was a smell of whisky on his breath; but she realised she couldn't put it off any longer.

The first question he asked as she stood in front of his desk was, 'Who in hell's name arranged for me to have lunch with the minister of telecommunications?'

'It was at your specific request,' said Sally.

'It most certainly was not,' said Dick. 'On the contrary, I distinctly remember telling you that I never wanted to see the prat again.' His voice rose with every word. 'He's basically unemployable, like half this bloody government.'

Sally clenched her hand. 'Dick, I feel I must . . .'

'What's the latest on Margaret Sherwood?'

'There's still no change,' said Sally. 'She returns from her cruise at the end of the month, and I've arranged for you to see her in New York the following day. The flight is already booked, and I've reserved your usual suite at the Pierre, overlooking Central Park. I'm preparing a file, with reference to Alexander Sherwood's latest piece of information. I understand he's already let his sister-in-law know the price at which he's sold you his shares, and has advised her to do the same as soon as she gets back.'

'Good. So do I have any other problems?'

'Yes. Me,' said Sally.

'You?' said Armstrong. 'Why? What's wrong with you?'

'My annual pay rise is nearly two months overdue, and I'm becoming . . .'

'I wasn't thinking of giving you a rise this year.'

Sally was about to laugh when she caught the expression on her employer's face. 'Oh, come off it, Dick. You know I can't live on what you pay me.'

'Why not? Others seem to manage well enough without complaining.'

'Be reasonable, Dick. Since Malcolm left me . . .'

'I suppose you're going to claim it was my fault he left you?'

'Most probably.'

'What are you suggesting?'

'I'm not suggesting anything, but with the hours I put in . . .'

'Then perhaps the time has come for you to look for a job where the hours aren't quite as demanding.'

Sally couldn't believe what she was hearing. 'After twenty-one years of working for you,' she said, 'I'm not sure anyone else would be willing to take me on.'

'And just what do you mean by that?' shouted Armstrong.

Sally rocked back, wondering what had come over him. Was he drunk, and unaware of what he was saying? Or had he been drinking because he knew exactly what he wanted to say? She stared down at him. 'What's come over you, Dick? I'm only asking for an increase in line with inflation, not even a proper rise.'

'I'll tell you what's come over me,' he replied. 'I'm sick and tired of the inefficiency in this place, plus the fact that you've got into the habit of fixing up private appointments during office hours.'

'It's not the first of April, is it, Dick?' she asked, trying to lighten the mood.

'Don't you get sarcastic with me, or you'll find it's more like the Ides of March. It's exactly that sort of attitude that convinces me the time has come to bring in someone who will carry out this job without always complaining. Someone with fresh ideas. Someone who would bring some much-needed discipline into this office.' He slammed his clenched fist down on the folder of unsigned letters.

Sally stood shaking in front of his desk, and stared at him in disbelief. Benson must have been right all along. 'It's that girl, isn't it?' she said. 'What was her name? Sharon?' Sally paused before adding, 'So that's why she hasn't been in to see me.'

'I don't know what you're talking about,' shouted Armstrong. 'I simply feel that . . .'

'You know exactly what I'm talking about,' snapped Sally. 'You can't fool me after all these years, Dick. You've offered her my job, haven't you? I can hear your exact words. "It will solve all our problems, darling. That way we'll always be together."'

'I said nothing of the sort.'

'Used a different line this time, did you?'

'I just feel that I need a change,' he said lamely. 'I'll see that you're properly compensated.'

'Properly compensated?' shouted Sally. 'You know damn

well that at my age it will be almost impossible for me to find another job. And in any case, how do you propose to "compensate" me for all the sacrifices I've made for you over the years? A dirty weekend in Paris, perhaps?'

'How dare you speak to me like that.'

'I shall speak to you in any way I like.'

'Carry on like this and you'll live to regret it, my girl.'

'I am not your girl,' said Sally. 'In fact I am the one person in this organisation you can neither seduce nor bully. I've known you far too long for that.'

'I agree, far too long. Which is why the time has come for you to leave.'

'To be replaced by Sharon, no doubt.'

'It's none of your god-damned business.'

'I only hope she's good in bed,' said Sally.

'And what do you mean by that?'

'Only that when she temped here for a couple of hours, I had to retype seven of her nine letters because she couldn't spell, and the other two because they were addressed to the wrong person. Unless of course you wanted the prime minister to know your inside-leg measurements.'

'It was her first day. She'll improve.'

'Not if your fly buttons are undone the whole time, she won't.'

'Get out before I have you thrown out.'

'You'll have to do it yourself, Dick, because there's no one on your staff who'd be willing to do it for you,' she said calmly. He rose from his chair, red in the face, placed the palms of his hands on the desk and stared down at her. She gave him a big smile, turned round and walked calmly out of the room. Fortunately he didn't hear the ripple of applause that greeted her as she walked through the outer office, or several other employees might have ended up having to join her.

Armstrong picked up a phone and dialled an internal number.

'Security. How can I help you?'

'It's Dick Armstrong. Mrs Carr will be leaving the building

in the next few minutes. Do not under any circumstances let her drive off in her company car, and be sure that she is never allowed back on the premises again. Do I make myself clear?'

'Yes, sir,' said a disbelieving voice on the other end of the line.

Armstrong slammed down the phone and immediately picked it back up again, then dialled another number.

'Accounts department,' said a voice.

'Put me through to Fred Preston.'

'He's on the phone at the moment.'

'Then get him off the phone.'

'Who shall I say is calling?'

'Dick Armstrong,' he bawled, and the line went dead for a moment. The next voice he heard was the head of the accounts department.

'It's Fred Preston here, Dick. I'm sorry that . . .'

'Fred, Sally has just resigned. Cancel her monthly cheque and send her P45 to her home address without delay.'

There was no response. Armstrong shouted, 'Did you hear me?'

'Yes, Dick. I assume she is to receive the bonuses that are due, as well as the appropriate long-term severance pay?'

'No. She is to receive nothing other than what she is entitled to under the terms of her contract and by law.'

'As I'm sure you're aware, Dick, Sally's never had a contract. In fact she's the longest-serving member of the company. Don't you feel in the circumstances . . .'

'Say another word, Fred, and you'll be collecting your P45 as well.' Armstrong slammed the phone down again and picked it up a third time. This time he dialled a number he knew off by heart. Although it was answered immediately, nobody spoke.

'It's Dick,' he began. 'Before you put the phone down, I've just sacked Sally. She's already left the building.'

'That's wonderful news, darling,' said Sharon. 'When do I begin?'

'Monday morning.' He hesitated. 'As my secretary.'

'As your personal assistant,' she reminded him.

'Yes, of course. As my PA. Why don't we discuss the details over the weekend? We could fly down to the yacht . . .'

'But what about your wife?'

'I rang her first thing this morning and told her not to expect me home this weekend.'

There was a long pause before Sharon said, 'Yes, I'd love to spend the weekend on the yacht with you, Dick, but if anyone should bump into us in Monte Carlo, you will remember to introduce me as your PA, won't you?'

─◦─

Sally waited in vain for her final paycheque, and Dick made no attempt to contact her. Friends at the office told her that Miss Levitt – as she insisted on being called – had moved in, and that the place was already in complete chaos. Armstrong never knew where he was meant to be, his letters remained unanswered, and his temper was no longer mercurial, simply perpetual. No one was willing to tell him that he had it in his power to resolve the problem with one phone call – if he wanted to.

Over a drink at her local pub, a barrister friend pointed out to Sally that under new legislation she was, after twenty-one years of unbroken service, in a strong position to sue Armstrong for unfair dismissal. She reminded him that she didn't have a contract of employment, and no one knew better than she what tactics Armstrong would employ were she to serve him with a writ. Within a month she would find she couldn't afford her legal fees, and would be left with no choice but to abandon the case. She had seen these tactics used to good effect on so many others who'd dared to retaliate in the past.

Sally had just arrived home one afternoon from a temping job when the phone rang. She picked up the receiver and was asked, over a crackling line, to hold on for a call from Sydney. She wondered why she didn't simply put the phone down, but after a few moments another voice came on the line. 'Good evening, Mrs Carr, my name is Keith Townsend and I'm . . .'

'Yes, Mr Townsend, I am well aware who you are.'

'I was calling to say how appalled I was to hear how you've been treated by your former boss.'

Sally made no comment.

'It may come as a surprise to you that I'd like to offer you a job.'

'So you can find out what Dick Armstrong has been up to, and which paper he's trying to buy?'

There was a long silence, and only the crackling convinced her that the line hadn't gone dead. 'Yes,' said Townsend eventually. 'That's exactly what I had in mind. But then at least you could take that holiday in Italy you've made the downpayment on.' Sally was speechless.

Townsend continued, 'I would also make good any compensation you should have been entitled to after twenty-one years of service.'

Sally said nothing for a few moments, suddenly aware why Dick considered this man such a formidable opponent. 'Thank you for your offer, Mr Townsend, but I'm not interested,' she said firmly, and put the phone down.

Sally's immediate reaction was to contact the accounts department at Armstrong House to try and find out why she hadn't received her final paycheque. She was kept waiting for some time before the senior accountant came on the line.

'When can I expect last month's paycheque, Fred?' she asked. 'It's more than two weeks overdue.'

'I know, but I'm afraid I've been given instructions not to issue it, Sally.'

'Why not?' she asked. 'It's no more than I'm entitled to.'

'I realise that,' said Fred, 'but . . .'

'But what?'

'It seems there was a breakage during your final week which you've been billed for. A fine bone china Staffordshire coffee set, I was told.'

'The bastard,' said Sally. 'I wasn't even in the room when he smashed it.'

'And he's also deducted two days' wages for taking time off during office hours.'

'But he knows very well that he told me to keep out of the way himself, so that he could . . .'

'We all know that, Sally. But he's no longer prepared to listen.'

'I know, Fred,' she said. 'It's not your fault. I appreciate the risk you're taking by even speaking to me, so thank you.' She hung up, and just sat at the kitchen table staring into space. When she picked up the telephone again an hour later she asked to be put through to the international operator.

In Sydney, Heather put her head round the door. 'There's a reverse-charge call for you from London,' she said. 'A Mrs Sally Carr. Will you take it?'

—◦—

Sally flew into Sydney two days later. Sam picked her up from the airport. After a night's rest the debriefing began. At a cost of $5,000, Townsend had employed a former head of the Australian Security Intelligence Organisation to conduct the interview. By the end of the week Sally was drained, and Townsend wondered if there was anything else he could possibly know about Richard Armstrong.

On the day she was due to fly back to England, he offered her a full-time job in his London office. 'Thank you, Mr Townsend,' she replied as he handed her a cheque for $25,000, but added, with the sweetest of smiles, 'I've spent almost half my life working for one monster, and after a week with you, I don't think I want to spend the rest of it working for another one.'

After Sam had taken Sally to the airport, Townsend and Kate spent hours listening to the tapes. They agreed on one thing: if he was to have any chance of purchasing the remaining shares in the *Globe*, he had to get to Margaret Sherwood before Armstrong did. She was the key to gaining control of 100 per cent of the company.

Once Sally had explained why Armstrong had bid a million francs for an egg at an auction in Geneva, all Townsend needed to discover was the equivalent of Peter Carl Fabergé for Mrs Margaret Sherwood.

Kate jumped out of bed in the middle of the night, and started playing tape number three. A drowsy Keith raised his head from the pillow when he heard the words 'the senator's mistress'.

25

Ocean Times

6 JUNE 1967

Welcome Aboard!

Keith landed at Kingston airport four hours before the liner was due to dock. He checked through customs and took a taxi to the Cunard booking office on the dockside. A man in a smart white uniform, with a little too much gold braid for a booking clerk, asked if he could be of assistance.

'I'd like to reserve a first-class cabin on the *Queen Eliza-beth*'s voyage to New York,' said Townsend. 'My aunt is already on board taking her annual cruise, and I was wondering if there might be a cabin available somewhere near her.'

'And what is your aunt's name?' asked the booking clerk.

'Mrs Margaret Sherwood,' Townsend replied.

A finger ran down the passenger list. 'Ah, yes. Mrs Sherwood has the Trafalgar Suite as usual. It's on level three. We only have one first-class cabin still available on that level, but it's not far from her.' The booking clerk unrolled a large-scale layout of the ship and pointed to two boxes, the second of which was considerably larger than the first.

'Couldn't be better,' said Townsend, and passed over one of his credit cards.

'Shall we let your aunt know that you'll be joining the ship?' the booking clerk asked helpfully.

'No,' said Townsend, without missing a beat. 'That would spoil the surprise.'

'If you would like to leave your bags with me, sir, I'll see they are taken to your cabin as soon as the ship docks.'

'Thank you,' said Townsend. 'Can you tell me how to get to the centre of town?'

As he strolled away from the dockside he began to think about Kate, and wondered if she had managed to place the article in the ship's paper.

He dropped into three newsagents on the long walk into Kingston, and purchased *Time*, *Newsweek* and all the local newspapers. He then stopped at the first restaurant he came across with an American Express sign on its door, took a quiet table in the corner and settled down for a lengthy lunch.

Other people's newspapers always fascinated him, but he knew he would leave the island without the slightest desire to be the owner of the *Jamaica Times*, which, even with nothing else to do, was only a fifteen-minute read. In between articles about how the agriculture minister's wife spent her day and why the island's cricket team had been losing so consistently, his mind kept returning to the information Sally Carr had recorded in Sydney. He found it hard to believe that Sharon could be quite as incompetent as she claimed, but if she was, he also had to accept her judgement that she must be remarkable in bed.

Having paid for a lunch best forgotten, Townsend left the restaurant and began to stroll around the town. It was the first time he had spent like a tourist since his visit to Berlin back in his student days. He kept checking his watch every few minutes, but it didn't help the time pass any quicker. Eventually he heard the sound of a foghorn in the distance: the great liner was at last coming into dock. He immediately began walking back towards the dockside. By the time he arrived, the crew were lowering the gangplanks. After the passengers had flooded down onto the quay, looking grateful for a few hours of escape, Townsend walked up the gangway and asked a steward to direct him to his cabin.

As soon as he had finished unpacking, he began to check the layout on level three. He was delighted to discover that Mrs

Sherwood's stateroom was less than a minute away from his cabin, but he made no attempt to contact her. Instead he used the next hour to find his way around the ship, ending up in the Queen's Grill.

The chief steward smiled at the slight, inappropriately-dressed man as he entered the large, empty dining room being set up for the evening meal. 'Can I help you, sir?' he asked, trying not to sound as if he felt that this particular passenger must have strayed onto the wrong deck.

'I hope so,' said Townsend. 'I've just joined the ship, and wanted to find out where you've placed me for dinner.'

'This restaurant is for first-class passengers only, sir.'

'Then I've come to the right place,' said Townsend.

'Your name, sir?' asked the steward, sounding unconvinced.

'Keith Townsend.'

He checked the list of first-class passengers who were joining the ship at Kingston. 'You're on table eight, Mr Townsend.'

'Is Mrs Margaret Sherwood on that table, by any chance?'

The steward checked again. 'No, sir, she's on table three.'

'Would it be possible for you to find me a place on table three?' asked Townsend.

'I'm afraid not, sir. No one from that table left the ship at Kingston.'

Armstrong took out his wallet and removed a hundred-dollar bill.

'But I suppose if I were to move the archdeacon onto the captain's table, that might solve the problem.'

Townsend smiled and turned to leave.

'Excuse me, sir. Were you hoping to sit next to Mrs Sherwood?'

'That would be most considerate,' said Townsend.

'It's just that it might prove a little awkward. You see, she's been with us for the whole trip, and we've had to move her twice already because she didn't care for the passengers at her table.'

Townsend removed his wallet a second time. He left the dining room a few moments later, assured that he would be sitting next to his quarry.

By the time he had returned to his cabin, his fellow-passengers were beginning to come back on board. He showered, changed for dinner and once again read the profile of Mrs Sherwood that Kate had compiled for him. A few minutes before eight he made his way down to the dining room.

One couple were already seated at the table. The man immediately stood up and introduced himself. 'Dr Arnold Percival from Ohio,' he said, shaking Townsend by the hand. 'And this is my dear wife, Jenny – also from Ohio.' He laughed raucously.

'Keith Townsend,' he said to them. 'I'm from . . .'

'Australia, if I'm not mistaken, Mr Townsend,' said the doctor. 'How nice that they put you on our table. I've just retired, and Jenny and I have been promising ourselves we'd go on a cruise for years. What brings you on board?' Before Townsend could reply, another couple arrived. 'This is Keith Townsend from Australia,' said Dr Percival. 'Allow me to introduce you to Mr and Mrs Osborne from Chicago, Illinois.'

They had just finished shaking hands when the doctor said, 'Good evening, Mrs Sherwood. May I introduce Keith Townsend?'

Keith knew from Kate's profile that Mrs Sherwood was sixty-seven, but it was clear that she must have spent a considerable amount of time and money trying to deny the fact. He doubted if she had ever been beautiful, but the description 'well preserved' certainly came to mind. Her evening dress was fashionable, even if the hem was perhaps an inch too short. Townsend smiled at her as if she was twenty-five years younger.

When Mrs Sherwood first heard Townsend's accent, she was barely able to hide her disapproval, but then two other passengers arrived within moments of each other and distracted her. Townsend didn't catch the name of the general, but the woman introduced herself as Claire Williams, and took the seat next to

Dr Percival on the far side of the table. Townsend smiled at her but she didn't respond.

Even before Townsend had taken his seat, Mrs Sherwood demanded to know why the archdeacon had been moved.

'I think I see him on the captain's table,' said Claire.

'I do hope he'll return tomorrow,' said Mrs Sherwood, and immediately began a conversation with Mr Osborne, who was seated on her right. As she resolutely refused to speak to Townsend during the first course, he began chatting to Mrs Percival while trying to listen to Mrs Sherwood's conversation at the same time. He found it quite difficult.

Townsend had hardly spoken a dozen words to Mrs Sherwood by the time the main course was being cleared away. It was over coffee that Claire enquired from the other side of the table if he had ever visited England.

'Yes, I was up at Oxford just after the war,' Townsend admitted for the first time in fifteen years.

'Which college?' demanded Mrs Sherwood, swinging round to face him.

'Worcester,' he replied sweetly. But that turned out to be the first and last question she addressed to him that evening. Townsend stood as she left the table, and wondered if three days was going to be enough. When he had finished his coffee, he said good night to Claire and the general before returning to his cabin to go over the file again. There was no mention of prejudice or snobbery in the profile, but then, to be fair to Sally, she had never met Margaret Sherwood.

When Townsend took his seat for breakfast the following morning the only vacant place was on his right, and although he was the last to leave, Mrs Sherwood never appeared. He glanced at Claire as she left the table and just wondered whether to follow her, but then decided against it, as it wasn't part of the plan. For the next hour he strolled around the ship, hoping to bump into her. But he didn't see her again that morning.

When he appeared a few minutes late for lunch, he was disconcerted to find that Mrs Sherwood had moved to the other side of the table, and was now sitting between the general and Dr Percival. She didn't even look up when he took his seat. When Claire arrived a few moments later, she had no choice but to take the place next to Townsend, although she immediately began a conversation with Mr Osborne.

Townsend tried to listen to what Mrs Sherwood was saying to the general, in the hope that he could find some excuse to join in their conversation, but all she was saying was that this was her nineteenth world cruise, and that she knew the ship almost as well as the captain.

Townsend was beginning to fear that his plan wasn't going at all well. Should he approach the subject directly? Kate had strongly advised against it. 'We mustn't assume she's a fool,' she had warned him when they parted at the airport. 'Be patient, and an opportunity will present itself.'

He turned casually to his right when he heard Dr Percival ask Claire if she had read *Requiem for a Nun*.

'No,' she replied, 'I haven't. Is it any good?'

'Oh, I have,' said Mrs Sherwood from the other side of the table, 'and I can tell you it's far from his best.'

'I'm sorry to hear that, Mrs Sherwood,' said Townsend, a little too quickly.

'And why is that, Mr Townsend?' she asked, unable to hide her surprise that he even knew who the author was.

'Because I have the privilege of publishing Mr Faulkner.'

'I had no idea you were a publisher,' said Dr Percival. 'How exciting. I'll bet there are a lot of people on this ship who could tell you a good story.'

'Possibly even one or two at this table,' said Townsend, avoiding Mrs Sherwood's stare.

'Hospitals are an endless source for stories,' continued Dr Percival. 'I should know.'

'That's true,' said Townsend, now enjoying himself. 'But having a good story isn't enough. You must then be able to commit it to paper. That's what takes real talent.'

'Which company do you work for?' asked Mrs Sherwood, trying to sound casual.

Townsend had cast the fly and she had leapt right out of the water. 'Schumann & Co., in New York,' he replied, equally casually.

At this point the general began to tell Townsend how many people had urged him to write his memoirs. He then proceeded to give everyone at the table a flavour of how the first chapter might turn out.

Townsend wasn't surprised to find that Mrs Sherwood had replaced Claire at his side when he appeared for dinner. Over the smoked salmon he spent a considerable time explaining to Mrs Percival how a book got onto the best-seller list.

'Can I interrupt you, Mr Townsend?' asked Mrs Sherwood quietly, as the lamb was being served.

'With pleasure, Mrs Sherwood,' said Townsend, turning to face her.

'I'd be interested to know which department you work in at Schumann's.'

'I'm not in any particular department,' he said.

'I'm not sure I understand,' said Mrs Sherwood.

'Well, you see, I own the company.'

'Does that mean you can override an editor's decision?' asked Mrs Sherwood.

'I can override anyone's decision,' said Townsend.

'It's just that . . .' She hesitated so as to be sure no one else was listening to their conversation – not that it really mattered, because Townsend knew what she was going to say. 'It's just that I sent a manuscript to Schumann's some time ago. Three months later all I got was a rejection slip, without even a letter of explanation.'

'I'm sorry to hear that,' said Townsend, pausing before he delivered his next well-prepared line. 'Of course, the truth is that many of the manuscripts we receive are never read.'

'Why's that?' she asked incredulously.

'Well, any large publishing house can expect to receive up to a hundred, possibly even two hundred, manuscripts a week. No one could afford to employ the staff to read them all. So you shouldn't feel too depressed.'

'Then how does a first-time novelist like myself ever get anyone to take an interest in their work?' she whispered.

'My advice to anyone facing that problem is to find yourself a good agent – someone who will know exactly which house to approach, and perhaps even which editor might be interested.'

Townsend concentrated on his lamb as he waited for Mrs Sherwood to summon up the necessary courage. 'Always let her lead,' Kate had warned, 'then there will be no reason for her to become suspicious.' He didn't look up from his plate.

'I don't suppose,' she began diffidently, 'that you would be kind enough to read my novel and give me your professional opinion?'

'I'd be delighted,' said Townsend. Mrs Sherwood smiled. 'Why don't you send it over to my office at Schumann's once we're back in New York. I'll see that one of my senior editors reads it and gives me a full written report.'

Mrs Sherwood pursed her lips. 'But I have it on board with me,' she said. 'You see, my annual cruise always gives me a chance to do a little revision.'

Townsend longed to tell her that thanks to her brother-in-law's cook he already knew that. But he satisfied himself with, 'Then why don't you drop it round to my cabin so I can read the first couple of chapters, which will at least give me a flavour of your style.'

'Would you really, Mr Townsend? How very kind of you. But then, my dear husband always used to say that one mustn't assume all Australians are convicts.'

Townsend laughed as Claire leaned across the table. 'Are you the Mr Townsend who is mentioned in the article in the *Ocean Times* this morning?' she asked.

Townsend looked surprised. 'I've no idea,' he said. 'I haven't seen it.'

'It's about a man called Richard Armstrong – ' neither of them noticed Mrs Sherwood's reaction ' – who's also in publishing.'

'I do know a Richard Armstrong,' admitted Townsend, 'so it's quite possible.'

'Won an MC,' said the general, butting in, 'but that was the only good thing the article had to say about him. Mind you, can't believe everything you read in the papers.'

'I quite agree,' said Townsend, as Mrs Sherwood rose and left them without even saying good night.

As soon as she had gone, the general began regaling Dr Percival and Mrs Osborne with the second chapter of his autobiography. Claire rose and said, 'Don't let me stop you, General, but I'm also off to bed.' Townsend didn't even glance in her direction. A few minutes later, as the old soldier was being evacuated from the beach at Dunkirk, he also made his apologies, left the table and returned to his cabin.

He had just stepped out of the shower when there was a knock on the door. He smiled, put on one of the towelling dressing-gowns supplied by the ship, and walked slowly across the room. At least if Mrs Sherwood delivered her manuscript now, he would have a good excuse to arrange a meeting with her the following morning. He opened the cabin door.

'Good evening, Mrs Sherwood,' he was about to say, only to find Kate standing in front of him, looking a little anxious. She hurried in and quickly closed the door.

'I thought we agreed not to meet except in an emergency?' said Keith.

'This is an emergency,' answered Kate, 'but I couldn't risk telling you at the dinner table.'

'Is that why you asked me about the article when you were meant to bring up the subject of what was playing on Broadway?'

'Yes,' replied Kate. 'Don't forget, I've had an extra couple of days to get to know her, and she's just phoned my cabin to ask me if I really believed that you were in publishing.'

'And what did you tell her?' asked Keith, as there was another knock on the door. He put a finger to his lips and pointed in the direction of the shower. He waited until he had heard the curtain pulled across, and then opened the door.

'Mrs Sherwood,' said Keith. 'How nice to see you. Is everything all right?'

'Yes, thank you, Mr Townsend. I thought I'd drop this in for you tonight,' she said, handing over a thick manuscript. 'Just in case you had nothing else to do.'

'How very thoughtful of you,' said Keith, taking the manuscript from her. 'Why don't we get together sometime after breakfast tomorrow? Then I can give you my first impressions.'

'Oh, would you really, Mr Townsend? I long to know what you think of it.' She hesitated. 'I trust I didn't disturb you.'

'Disturb me?' said Keith, puzzled.

'I thought I heard voices as I was coming down the passageway.'

'I expect it was just me humming in the shower,' said Keith rather feebly.

'Ah, that would explain it,' said Mrs Sherwood. 'Well, I do hope you'll find time to read a few pages of *The Senator's Mistress* tonight.'

'I most certainly will,' said Keith. 'Good night, Mrs Sherwood.'

'Oh, do call me Margaret.'

'I'm Keith,' he said with a smile.

'I know. I've just read the article about you and Mr Armstrong. Most interesting. Can he really be that bad?' she asked.

Keith made no comment as he closed the door. He turned round to find Kate stepping out of the shower, wearing the other dressing-gown. As she walked towards him, the cord fell to the ground, and the robe came slightly open. 'Oh, do call me Claire,' she said as she slipped a hand around his waist. He pulled her towards him.

'Can you really be that bad?' she laughed as he guided her across the room.

'Yes, I am,' he said as they fell on the bed together.

'Keith,' she whispered, 'don't you think you ought to start reading the manuscript?'

◄○►

It was only a matter of hours after Sharon had moved from the bedroom into the office that Armstrong realised Sally hadn't been exaggerating about her secretarial skills. But he was too proud to call her and admit it.

By the end of the second week his desk was piled high with unanswered letters or, worse, replies he couldn't consider putting his signature to. After so many years with Sally, he had forgotten that he rarely spent more than a few minutes each day checking over her work before simply signing everything she put in front of him. In fact the only document he had put his signature to that week had been Sharon's contract, which it was clear she had not drawn up herself.

On Tuesday of the third week, Armstrong turned up at the House of Commons to have lunch with the minister of health, only to discover that he wasn't expected until the following day. He arrived back at his office twenty minutes later in a furious temper.

'But I told you that you were having lunch with the chairman of NatWest today,' Sharon insisted. 'He's just rung from the Savoy asking where you were.'

'Where you sent me,' he barked. 'At the House of Commons.'

'Am I expected to do everything for you?'

'Sally somehow managed it,' said Armstrong, barely able to control his anger.

'If I hear that woman's name again, I swear I'll leave you.'

Armstrong didn't comment, but stormed back out of the office and ordered Benson to get him to the Savoy as quickly as possible. When he arrived at the Grill, Mario told him that his guest had just left. And when he got back to the office, he was informed that Sharon had gone home, saying she had a slight migraine.

Armstrong sat down at his desk and dialled Sally's number but no one answered. He continued to call her at least once a day, but all he got was a recorded message. At the end of the following week he ordered Fred to pay her monthly cheque.

'But I've already sent her a P45, as you instructed,' the chief accountant reminded him.

'Don't argue with me, Fred,' said Armstrong. 'Just pay it.'

In the fifth week temps began coming and going on a daily basis, some lasting only a few hours. But it was Sharon who opened the letter from Sally, to find a cheque torn in half and a note attached that read: 'I have already been amply paid for last month's work.'

◄○►

When Keith woke the following morning, he was surprised to find Kate already in his dressing-gown, reading Mrs Sherwood's manuscript. She leaned across and gave him a kiss before handing over the first seven chapters. He sat up, blinked a few times, turned to the opening page and read the first sentence: 'As she stepped out of the swimming pool, the bulge in his trunks started to grow.' He looked across at Kate, who said, 'Keep reading. It gets steamier.'

Keith had finished about forty pages when Kate leaped out of bed and headed off towards the shower. 'Don't bother with much more,' she said. 'I'll tell you how it ends later.'

By the time she reappeared, Keith was halfway through the third chapter. He dropped the remaining pages on the floor. 'What do you think?' he asked.

She walked across to the bed, pulled back the sheets and stared down at his naked body. 'Judging from your reaction, either you still fancy me or I'd say we've got a best-seller on our hands.'

When Townsend went into breakfast about an hour later, only Kate and Mrs Sherwood were at the table. They were deep in conversation. They stopped talking immediately he sat down. 'I don't suppose . . .' Mrs Sherwood began.

'Suppose what?' asked Townsend innocently.

Kate had to turn away to avoid Mrs Sherwood seeing the look on her face.

'That you might have dipped into my novel?'

'Dipped?' said Townsend. 'I've read it from cover to cover. And one thing is clear, Mrs Sherwood: no one at Schumann's could possibly have looked at the manuscript, or they would have snapped it up immediately.'

'Oh, do you really think it's that good?' said Mrs Sherwood.

'I certainly do,' said Townsend. 'And I can only hope, despite our unforgivably offhand response to your original submission, that you'll still allow Schumann's to make an offer.'

'Of course I will,' said Mrs Sherwood enthusiastically.

'Good. However, may I suggest that this is not the place to discuss terms.'

'Of course. I quite understand, Keith,' she said. 'Why don't you join me in my cabin a little later?' She glanced at her watch. 'Shall we say around 10.30?'

Townsend nodded. 'That would suit me perfectly.' He rose as she folded her napkin and left the table.

'Did you learn anything new?' he asked Kate as soon as Mrs Sherwood was out of earshot.

'Not a lot,' she said, nibbling on a piece of raisin toast. 'But I don't think she really believes you read the entire manuscript.'

'What makes you say that?' asked Townsend.

'Because she's just told me that you had a woman in your cabin last night.'

'Did she indeed?' said Townsend. He paused. 'And what else did she have to say?'

'She discussed the article in the *Ocean Times* in great detail, and asked me if . . .'

'Good morning, Townsend. Good morning, dear lady,' said the general as he took his seat. Kate gave him a broad smile and rose from her place.

'Good luck,' she said quietly.

'I'm glad to have this opportunity of a quiet word with you, Townsend. You see, the truth of the matter is that I have already written the first volume of my memoirs, and as I happen to have it with me on board, I wondered if you'd be kind enough to read it and give me your professional opinion.'

It took another twenty minutes for Townsend to escape a book he didn't want to read, let alone publish. The general hadn't left him much time to prepare for the meeting with Mrs Sherwood. He returned to his cabin and went over Kate's notes one final time before heading off for Mrs Sherwood's stateroom. He knocked on her door just after 10.30, and it was opened immediately.

'I like a man who's punctual,' she said.

The Trafalgar Suite turned out to be on two levels, with its own balcony. Mrs Sherwood ushered her guest towards a pair of comfortable chairs in the centre of the drawing room. 'Would you care for some coffee, Keith?' she asked as she sat down opposite him.

'No, thank you, Margaret,' he replied. 'I've just had breakfast.'

'Of course,' she said. 'Now, shall we get down to business?'

'Certainly. As I told you earlier this morning,' said Townsend, 'Schumann's would consider it a privilege to publish your novel.'

'Oh, how exciting,' said Mrs Sherwood. 'I do wish my dear husband were still alive. He always believed I would be published one day.'

'We would be willing to offer you an advance of $100,000,' continued Townsend, 'and 10 per cent of the cover price after the advance has been recouped. Paperback publication would follow twelve months after the hardcover, and there would be bonus payments for every week you're on the *New York Times* best-seller list.'

'Oh! Do you really think my little effort might appear on the best-seller list?'

'I would be willing to bet on it,' said Townsend.

'Would you really?' said Mrs Sherwood.

Townsend looked anxiously across at her, wondering if he had gone too far.

'I happily accept your terms, Mr Townsend,' she said. 'I do believe this calls for a celebration.' She poured him a glass of champagne from a half-empty bottle in the ice bucket beside her. 'Now that we have come to an agreement on the book,' she said a few moments later, 'perhaps you'd be kind enough to advise me on a little problem I'm currently facing.'

'I will if I possibly can,' said Townsend, staring up at a

painting of a one-armed, one-eyed admiral who was lying on a quarterdeck, dying.

'I have been most distressed by an article in the *Ocean Times* that was brought to my attention by . . . Miss Williams,' said Mrs Sherwood. 'It concerns a Mr Richard Armstrong.'

'I'm not sure I understand.'

'I'll explain,' said Mrs Sherwood, who proceeded to tell Townsend a story he knew rather better than she did. She ended by saying, 'Claire felt that as you were in publishing, you might be able to recommend someone else who would want to buy my shares.'

'How much are you hoping to be offered for them?' asked Townsend.

'Twenty million dollars. That is the sum I agreed with my brother Alexander, who has already disposed of his stock to this Richard Armstrong for that amount.'

'When is your meeting with Mr Armstrong?' asked Townsend – another question he knew the answer to.

'He's coming to see me at my apartment in New York on Monday at 11 a.m.'

Townsend continued to gaze up at the picture on the wall, pretending to give the problem considerable thought. 'I feel sure that my company would be able to match his offer,' he said. 'Especially as the amount has already been agreed on.' He hoped she couldn't hear his heart pounding away.

Mrs Sherwood lowered her eyes and glanced down at a Sotheby's catalogue that a friend had sent her from Geneva the previous week. 'How fortunate that we met,' she said. 'One couldn't get away with this sort of coincidence in a novel.' She laughed, raised her glass and said, 'Kismet.'

Townsend didn't comment.

After she had put her glass down, she said, 'I need to give the problem a little more thought overnight. I'll let you know my final decision before we disembark.'

'Of course,' said Townsend, trying to hide his disappointment. He rose from his chair and the old lady accompanied him to the door.

'I must thank you, Keith, for all the trouble you've gone to.'

'My pleasure,' he said as she closed the door.

Townsend immediately returned to his cabin to find Kate waiting for him.

'How did it go?' were her first words.

'She hasn't finally made up her mind, but I think she's nearly hooked, thanks to your bringing the article to her attention.'

'And the shares?'

'As the price has already been settled, she doesn't seem to care who buys them, as long as her book gets published.'

'But she wanted more time to think about it,' said Kate, who remained silent for a few moments before adding, 'Why didn't she question you more closely on why you would want to buy the shares?'

Townsend shrugged.

'I'm beginning to wonder if Mrs Sherwood wasn't sitting on board waiting for us, rather than the other way round.'

'Don't be silly,' said Townsend. 'After all, she's going to have to decide if it's more important to get her book published, or to fall out with Alexander, who's been advising her to sell to Armstrong. And if that's the choice she has to make, there's one thing in our favour.'

'And what's that?' asked Kate.

'Thanks to Sally, we know exactly how many rejection slips she's had from publishers over the past ten years. And having read the book, I can't imagine any of them gave her much cause for hope.'

'Surely Armstrong is also aware of that, and would be just as willing to publish her book?'

'But she can't be sure of that,' said Townsend.

'Perhaps she can, and is far brighter than we gave her credit for. Is there a phone on board?'

'Yes, there's one on the bridge. I tried to place a call to Tom Spencer in New York so that he could start amending the contract, but I was told the phone can't be used unless it's an emergency.'

'And who decides what's an emergency?' asked Kate.

'The purser says the captain is the sole arbiter.'

'Then neither of us can do anything until we reach New York.'

Mrs Sherwood arrived late for lunch, and took the seat next to the general. She seemed content to listen to a lengthy summary of chapter three of his memoirs, and never once raised the subject of her own book. After lunch she disappeared back into her cabin.

When they took their places at dinner, they found that Mrs Sherwood had been invited to sit at the captain's table.

After a sleepless night Keith and Kate arrived early at breakfast, hoping to learn her decision. But as the minutes passed and Mrs Sherwood failed to appear, it became clear that she must be taking breakfast in her suite.

'Probably fallen behind with her packing,' suggested the ever helpful Dr Percival.

Kate didn't look convinced.

Keith returned to his cabin, packed his suitcase and then joined Kate on deck as the liner steamed towards the Hudson.

'I have a feeling we've lost this one,' said Kate, as they sailed past the Statue of Liberty.

'I think you might be right. I wouldn't mind so much if it weren't at the hands of Armstrong again.'

'Has beating him become that important?'

'Yes, it has. What you have to understand is . . .'

'Good morning, Mr Townsend,' said a voice behind them. Keith swung round to see Mrs Sherwood approaching. He hoped she hadn't spotted Kate before she melted into the crowd.

'Good morning, Mrs Sherwood,' he replied.

'After some considerable thought,' she said, 'I have come to a decision.'

Keith held his breath.

'If you have both contracts ready for me to sign by ten o'clock tomorrow morning, then you have, to use that vulgar American expression, "got yourself a deal".'

Keith beamed at her.

'However,' she continued, 'if my book isn't published within a year of signing the contract, you will have to pay a penalty of one million dollars. And if it fails to get on the *New York Times* best-seller list, you will forfeit a second million.'

'But . . .'

'You did say when I asked you about the best-seller list that you would be willing to bet on it, didn't you, Mr Townsend? So I'm going to give you a chance to do just that.'

'But . . .' repeated Keith.

'I look forward to seeing you at my apartment at ten tomorrow morning, Mr Townsend. My lawyer has confirmed that he will be able to attend. Should you fail to turn up, I shall simply sign the contract with Mr Armstrong at eleven.' She paused and, looking straight at Keith, said, 'I have a feeling he would also be willing to publish my novel.'

Without another word she began walking towards the passenger ramp. Kate joined him at the railing and they watched her slow descent. As she stepped onto the quay, two black Rolls-Royces swept up, and a chauffeur leaped out of the first one to open the back door for her. The second stood waiting for her luggage.

'How did she manage to speak to her lawyer?' said Keith. 'Calling him about her novel could hardly be described as an emergency.'

Just before she stepped into the car, Mrs Sherwood looked up and waved to someone. They both turned and stared in the direction of the bridge.

The captain was saluting.

26

Daily Mail

10 JUNE 1967

End of Six-Day War: Nasser Quits

Armstrong double-checked the flight times for New York. He then looked up Mrs Sherwood's address in the Manhattan telephone directory, and even phoned the Pierre to be sure the Presidential Suite had been booked. This was one meeting he couldn't afford to be late for, and for which he couldn't turn up on the wrong day or at the wrong address.

He had already deposited $20 million at the Manhattan Bank, gone over the press statement with his public relations adviser and warned Peter Wakeham to prepare the board for a special announcement.

Alexander Sherwood had phoned the previous evening to say that he had called his sister-in-law before she went on her annual cruise. She had confirmed that the agreed figure was $20 million, and was looking forward to meeting Armstrong at eleven o'clock at her apartment on the day after her return. By the time he and Sharon stepped onto the plane, Armstrong was confident that within twenty-four hours he would be the sole proprietor of a national newspaper second only in circulation to the *Daily Citizen*.

They touched down at Idlewild a few hours before the *Queen Elizabeth* was due to dock at Pier 90. After they had checked into the Pierre, Armstrong walked across to 63rd Street to be sure he knew exactly where Mrs Sherwood lived. For $10 the doorman confirmed that she was expected back later that day.

Over dinner in the hotel that night he and Sharon hardly spoke. He was beginning to wonder why he had bothered to bring her along. She was in bed long before he headed for the bathroom, and asleep by the time he came out.

As he climbed into bed, he tried to think what could possibly go wrong between now and eleven o'clock the next morning.

◄◌►

'I think she knew what we were up to all along,' said Kate as she watched Mrs Sherwood's Rolls disappear out of sight.

'She can't have,' said Townsend. 'But even if she did, she still accepted the terms I wanted.'

'Or was it the terms *she* wanted?' said Kate quietly.

'What are you getting at?'

'Just that it was all a little bit too easy for my liking. Don't forget, she's not a Sherwood. She was just clever enough to marry one.'

'You've become too suspicious for your own good,' said Townsend. 'Try not to forget, she isn't Richard Armstrong.'

'I'll only be convinced when you have her signature on both contracts.'

'Both?'

'She won't part with her third of the *Globe* unless she really believes you're going to publish her novel.'

'I don't think there'll be any problem convincing her of that,' said Townsend. 'We mustn't forget that she's desperate – she had fifteen rejection slips before she bumped into me.'

'Or did she see you coming?'

Townsend looked down to the quayside as a black stretch limousine pulled up by the gangplank. A tall, thickset man with a head of unruly black hair jumped out of the back and looked up towards the passengers standing on the deck. 'Tom Spencer's just arrived,' said Townsend. He turned back to Kate. 'Stop worrying. By the time you're back in Sydney, I'll own 33.3 per cent of the *Globe*. And I couldn't have done it without you. Call me the moment you land at Kingsford-Smith, and I'll bring you up to date.' Townsend gave her a kiss and held her in his arms before they returned to their separate cabins.

He grabbed his bags and made his way quickly down to the quayside. His New York attorney was pacing rapidly around the car – a throwback from his days as a cross-country runner, he had once explained to Townsend.

'We've got twenty-four hours, counsellor,' said Townsend, as they shook hands.

'So Mrs Sherwood fell in with your plan?' said the attorney, guiding his client towards the limousine.

'Yes, but she wants two contracts,' said Townsend as he climbed into the back of the car, 'and neither of them is the one I asked you to draw up when I called from Sydney.'

Tom removed a yellow pad from his briefcase and rested it on his knees. He had long ago realised that this was not a client who spent any time indulging in small talk. He began to make notes as Townsend gave him the details of Mrs Sherwood's terms. By the time he had heard what had taken place over the past few days, Tom was beginning to have a sneaking admiration for the old lady. He then asked a series of questions, and neither of them noticed when the car drew up outside the Carlyle.

Townsend leaped out and pushed his way through the swing doors into the lobby to find two of Tom's associates waiting for them.

'Why don't you check in?' suggested Tom. 'I'll brief my colleagues on what you've told me so far. When you're ready, join us in the Versailles Room on the third floor.'

After Townsend had signed the registration form, he was handed the key to his usual room. He unpacked before taking the lift down to the third floor. When he entered the Versailles Room he found Tom pacing around a long table, briefing his two colleagues. Townsend took a seat at the far end of the table while Tom continued circling. He stopped only when he needed to ask for more details of Mrs Sherwood's demands.

After walking several miles, devouring pile after pile of freshly cut sandwiches and consuming gallons of coffee, they had outline drafts prepared for both contracts.

When a maid came in to draw the curtains just after six, Tom sat down for the first time and read slowly through the drafts. After he had finished the last page, he stood up and said, 'That's as much as we can do for now, Keith. We'd better get back to the office and prepare the two documents ready for engrossing. I suggest we meet up at eight tomorrow morning so you can go over the final text.'

'Anything I ought to be thinking about before then, counsellor?' asked Townsend.

'Yes,' replied Tom. 'Are you absolutely certain we should leave out those two clauses in the book contract that Kate felt so strongly about?'

'Absolutely. After three days with Mrs Sherwood, I can assure you that she knows nothing about book publishing.'

Tom shrugged his shoulders. 'That wasn't how Kate read it.'

'Kate was being overcautious,' said Townsend. 'There's nothing to stop me printing 100,000 copies of the damn book and storing every one of them in a warehouse in New Jersey.'

'No,' said Tom, 'but what happens when the book fails to get onto the *New York Times* best-seller list?'

'Read the relevant clause, counsellor. There's no mention of a time limit. Anything else you're worried about?'

'Yes. You'll need to have two separate money orders with you for the ten o'clock meeting. I don't want to risk cheques with Mrs Sherwood – that would only give her an excuse not to sign the final agreement. You can be sure of one thing: Armstrong will have a draft for $20 million in his hand when he turns up at eleven.'

Townsend nodded his agreement. 'I transferred the money from Sydney to the Manhattan Bank the day I briefed you on the original contract. We can pick up both drafts first thing in the morning.'

'Good. Then we'll be on our way.'

When Townsend returned to his room, he collapsed onto

the bed exhausted, and immediately fell into a deep sleep. He didn't wake until five the next morning, and was surprised to find that he was still fully dressed. His first thoughts were of Kate and where she might be at that moment.

He undressed and stood under a warm shower for a long time before ordering an early breakfast. Or should it be a late dinner? He studied the twenty-four-hour menu and settled for breakfast.

As he waited for room service, Townsend watched the early-morning newscasts. They were dominated by Israel's crushing victory in the Six-Day War, although no one seemed to know where Nasser was. A NASA spokesman was being interviewed on the *Today* show about America's chances of putting a man on the moon before the Russians. The weather man was promising a cold front in New York. Over breakfast he read the *New York Times*, followed by the *Star*, and he could see exactly what changes he would make to both papers if he were the proprietor. He tried to forget that the FCC was continually badgering him with questions about his expanding American empire, and reminding him of the cross-ownership regulations that applied to foreigners.

'There's a simple solution to that problem,' Tom had told him on several occasions.

'Never,' he had always replied firmly. But what would he do if that became the only way he could ever take over the *New York Star*? 'Never,' he repeated, but not with quite the same conviction.

For the next hour he watched the same newscasts and reread the same newspapers. By seven-thirty he knew everything that was happening around the world, from Cairo to Queen's, and even in space. At ten to eight he took the lift down to the ground floor, where he found the two young lawyers waiting for him. They appeared to be wearing the same suits, shirts and ties as on the previous day, even if they had somehow found time to shave. He didn't ask where Tom was: he knew he would be pacing around the lobby, and would join them as soon as he completed his circuit.

'Good morning, Keith,' Tom said, shaking his client by the hand. 'I've reserved a quiet table for us in a corner of the coffee room.'

After three black coffees and one white had been poured, Tom opened his briefcase, took out two documents and presented them to his client. 'If she agrees to sign these,' he said, '33.3 per cent of the *Globe* will be yours – as will the publishing rights for *The Senator's Mistress*.'

Townsend was taken through the documents slowly, clause by clause, and began to realise why the three of them had been up all night. 'So what's next?' he asked, as he handed the contracts back to his lawyer.

'You have to pick up the two money drafts from the Manhattan Bank, and be sure that we're outside Mrs Sherwood's front door by five to ten, because we're going to need every minute of that hour if these are to be signed before Armstrong turns up.'

—◇—

Armstrong also began reading the morning papers only moments after they had been dropped outside the door of his hotel room. As he turned the pages of the *New York Times*, he too kept seeing changes he would make if only he could get his hands on a New York daily. When he had finished the *Times* he turned to the *Star*, but it didn't hold his attention for long. He threw the papers to one side, switched on the television and began flicking between the channels to pass the time. An old black-and-white movie starring Alan Ladd took precedence over an interview with an astronaut.

He left the television on when he disappeared into the bathroom, not giving a thought as to whether it might wake Sharon.

By seven he was dressed and becoming more restless by the minute. He switched to *Good Morning America* and watched the mayor explaining how he intended to deal with the firemen's union and their demand for higher redundancy pay. 'Kick the bastards where it hurts!' he shouted at the screen. He finally flicked it off after the weather man informed him that it was going to be another hot, cloudless day with temperatures in the high seventies – in Malibu. Armstrong picked up Sharon's powder puff from the dressing table and dabbed his forehead, then put it in his pocket. At 7.30 he ate breakfast in the room, not having bothered to order anything for Sharon. By the time he left their suite at 8.30 to join his lawyer, she still hadn't stirred.

Russell Critchley was waiting for him in the restaurant. Armstrong began ordering a second breakfast before he sat down. His lawyer extracted a lengthy document from his brief-case and began to take him through it. While Critchley sipped coffee, Armstrong devoured a three-egg omelette followed by four waffles covered in thick syrup.

'I can't foresee any real problems,' said Critchley. 'It's virtually the same document as her brother-in-law signed in Geneva – although of course she has never requested any form of under-the-counter payment.'

'And she has no choice but to accept $20 million in full settlement if she is to keep to the terms of Sir George Sherwood's will.'

'That is correct,' said the lawyer. He referred to another file before adding, 'It seems that the three of them signed a binding agreement when they inherited the stock that if they were ever to sell, it must be at a price agreed by at least two of the parties. As you know, Alexander and Margaret have already settled on $20 million.'

'Why would they do that?'

'If they hadn't, they would have inherited nothing under the terms of Sir George's will. He obviously didn't want the three of them to end up squabbling over the price.'

'And the two-thirds rule still applies?' asked Armstrong, spreading syrup over another waffle.

'Yes, the clause in question is unambiguous,' Critchley said, flicking over the pages of yet another document. 'I have it here.' He began reading:

If any person or company becomes entitled to be registered as the owner of at least 66.66 per cent of the issued shares, that person or company shall have the option to purchase the balance of the issued shares at a price per share equal to the average price per share paid by that person or company for its existing shares.

'Bloody lawyers. What the hell does that mean?' asked Armstrong.

'As I told you over the phone, if you are already in possession of two-thirds of the stock, the owner of the remaining third – in this case Sir Walter Sherwood – has no choice but to sell you his shares for exactly the same price.'

'So I could own 100 per cent of the stock before Townsend even finds out the *Globe* is on the market.'

Critchley smiled, removed his half-moon spectacles and said, 'How considerate it was of Alexander Sherwood to bring that fact to your attention when you met him in Geneva.'

'Don't forget it cost me a million francs,' Armstrong reminded him.

'I think it may turn out to be money well spent,' said Critchley. 'As long as you can produce a money order for $20 million in favour of Mrs Sherwood . . .'

'I've arranged to pick it up from the Bank of New Amsterdam at ten o'clock.'

'Then as you already own Alexander's shares, you'll be entitled to buy Sir Walter's third for exactly the same amount, and he won't be able to do a thing about it.'

Critchley checked his watch, and as Armstrong plastered syrup over another order of waffles, he allowed the hovering waiter to pour him a second cup of coffee.

◄◦►

At 9.55 precisely, Townsend's limousine drew up outside a smart brownstone on 63rd Street. He stepped onto the pavement and headed for the door, his three lawyers following a pace behind him. The doorman had obviously been expecting some guests for Mrs Sherwood. All he said when Townsend gave him his name was 'The penthouse,' and pointed in the direction of the lift.

When the lift doors on the top floor slid open, a maid was waiting to greet them. A clock in the hall struck ten as Mrs Sherwood appeared in the corridor. She was dressed in what Townsend's mother would have described as a cocktail dress, and seemed a little surprised to be faced with four men. Townsend introduced the lawyers, and Mrs Sherwood indicated that they should follow her through to the dining room.

As they passed under a magnificent chandelier, down a long corridor littered with Louis XIV furniture and Impressionist paintings, Townsend was able to see how some of the *Globe*'s profits had been spent over the years. When they entered the dining room, a distinguished-looking elderly man with a head of thick grey hair, wearing horn-rimmed spectacles and a double-breasted black suit, rose from his chair on the other side of the table.

Tom immediately recognised the senior partner of Burlingham, Healy & Yablon, and suspected for the first time that his task might not prove that easy. The two men shook hands warmly, then Tom introduced Yablon to his client and his two associates.

Once they were all seated and the maid had served tea, Tom opened his briefcase and handed over the two contracts to Yablon. Aware of the time restriction placed on them, he began to take Mrs Sherwood's lawyer through the documents as quickly as he could. As he did so, the old man asked him a number of questions. Townsend felt his lawyer must have dealt with them all satisfactorily, because after they had reached the last page, Mr Yablon turned to his client and said, 'I am quite happy for you to sign these two documents, Mrs Sherwood, subject to the drafts being in order.'

Townsend looked at his watch. It was 10.43. He smiled as Tom opened his briefcase and removed the two money orders. Before he could pass them over, Mrs Sherwood turned to her lawyer and asked, 'Does the book contract stipulate that if

Schumann's fail to print 100,000 copies of my novel within one year of this agreement being signed, they will have to pay a penalty of $1 million?'

'Yes, it does,' said Yablon.

'And that if the book fails to make the *New York Times* best-seller list, they will have to forfeit a further million?'

Townsend smiled, knowing that there was no clause about the distribution of the book in the contract, and no mention of a time limit by which the novel had to appear on the best-seller list. As long as he printed 100,000 copies, which he could do on any of his American presses, the whole exercise need only cost him around $40,000.

'That is all covered in the second contract,' Mr Yablon confirmed.

Tom tried to conceal his astonishment. How could a man of Yablon's experience have overlooked two such glaring omissions? Townsend was proving to be right – they seemed to have got away with it.

'And Mr Townsend is able to supply us with drafts for the full amounts?' asked Mrs Sherwood. Tom slid the two money orders across to Yablon, who passed them on to his client without even looking at them.

Townsend waited for Mrs Sherwood to smile. She frowned.

'This is not what we agreed,' she said.

'I think it is,' said Townsend, who had collected the drafts from the senior cashier of the Manhattan Bank earlier that morning and checked them carefully.

'This one,' she said, holding up the draft for $20 million, 'is fine. But this one is not what I requested.'

Townsend looked confused. 'But you agreed that the advance for your novel should be $100,000,' he said, feeling his mouth go dry.

'That is correct,' said Mrs Sherwood firmly. 'But my under-standing was that this cheque would be for two million one hundred thousand dollars.'

'But the $2 million was to be paid at some later date, and

then only if we failed to meet your stipulations concerning the publication of the book,' said Townsend.

'That is not a risk I am willing to take, Mr Townsend,' she said, staring at him across the table.

'I don't understand,' he said.

'Then let me explain it to you. I expect you to lodge with Mr Yablon a further $2 million in an escrow account. He will be the sole arbiter as to who should receive the money in twelve months' time.' She paused. 'You see, my brother-in-law Alexander made a profit of a million Swiss francs, in the form of a Fabergé egg, without bothering to inform me. It is therefore my intention to make a profit of over $2 million on my novel, without bothering to inform him.'

Townsend gasped. Mr Yablon leaned back in his chair, and Tom realised that he wasn't the only person who'd been working flat out all night.

'If your client's confidence in his ability to deliver proves well-founded,' said Mr Yablon, 'I will return his money in twelve months' time, with interest.'

'On the other hand,' said Mrs Sherwood, no longer looking at Townsend, 'if your client never had any real intention of distributing my novel and turning it into a best-seller . . .'

'But this isn't what you and I agreed yesterday,' said Townsend, staring directly at Mrs Sherwood.

She looked sweetly across the table, her cheeks not colouring, and said, 'I'm sorry, Mr Townsend, I lied.'

'But you've left my client with only eleven minutes to come up with another $2 million,' said Tom, glancing at the grandfather clock.

'I make it twelve minutes,' said Mr Yablon. 'I have a feeling that clock has always been a little fast. But don't let's quibble over a minute either way. I'm sure Mrs Sherwood will allow you the use of one of her phones.'

'Certainly,' said Mrs Sherwood. 'You see, my late husband always used to say: "If you can't pay today, why should one believe you'll be able to pay tomorrow?"'

'But you have my draft for $20 million,' said Townsend, 'and another one for $100,000. Isn't that proof enough?'

'And in ten minutes' time I will have Mr Armstrong's draft for the same amount, and I suspect that he will also be happy to publish my book, despite Claire's – or should I say Kate's – well-planted article.'

Townsend remained silent for about thirty seconds. He considered calling her bluff, but when he looked at the clock he thought better of it.

He rose from his place and walked quickly over to the phone on the side table, checked the number at the back of his diary, dialled seven digits and, after what seemed an interminable wait, asked to be put through to the chief cashier. There was another click, and a secretary came on the line.

'This is Keith Townsend. I need to speak to the chief cashier urgently.'

'I'm afraid he's tied up in a meeting at the moment, Mr Townsend, and has left instructions that he's not to be disturbed for the next hour.'

'Fine, then you can handle it for me. I have to transfer $2 million to a client account within eight minutes, or the deal he and I discussed this morning will be off.'

There was a moment's pause before the secretary said, 'I'll get him out of the meeting, Mr Townsend.'

'I thought you might,' said Townsend, who could hear the seconds ticking away on the grandfather clock behind him.

Tom leaned across the table and whispered something to Mr Yablon, who nodded, picked up his pen and began writing. In the silence that followed, Townsend could hear the old lawyer's pen scratching across the paper.

'Andy Harman here,' said a voice on the other end of the line. The chief cashier listened carefully as Townsend explained what he required.

'But that only gives me six minutes, Mr Townsend. In any case, where is the money to be deposited?'

Townsend turned round to look at his lawyer. As he did so

Mr Yablon finished writing, tore a sheet off his pad and passed it over to Tom, who handed it on to his client.

Townsend read out the details of Mr Yablon's escrow account to the chief cashier.

'I will make no promises, Mr Townsend,' he said, 'but I will call you back as soon as I can. What's your number?'

Townsend read out the number on the phone in front of him and replaced the receiver.

He walked slowly back to the table and slumped into his chair, feeling as if he had just spent his last cent. He hoped Mrs Sherwood wouldn't charge him for the call.

No one round the table spoke as the seconds ticked noisily by. Townsend's eyes rarely left the grandfather clock. As each old minute passed, he grew to recognise the familiar click. Each new one made him feel less confident. What he hadn't told Tom was that the previous day he had transferred exactly twenty million, one hundred thousand US dollars from his account in Sydney to the Manhattan Bank in New York. As it was now a few minutes before two in the morning in Sydney, the chief cashier had no way of checking if he was good for a further two million.

Another click. Each tick began to sound like a time bomb. Then the piercing sound of the phone ringing drowned them. Townsend rushed over to the sideboard to pick it up.

'It's the hall porter, sir. Could you let Mrs Sherwood know that a Mr Armstrong and another gentleman have arrived, and are on their way up in the lift.'

Beads of sweat appeared on Townsend's forehead, as he realised that Armstrong had beaten him again. He walked slowly back to the table as the maid headed down the corridor to welcome Mrs Sherwood's eleven o'clock appointment. The grandfather clock struck one, two, three, and then the phone rang once again. Townsend rushed over and grabbed it, knowing it was his last chance.

But the caller wanted to speak to Mr Yablon. Townsend turned towards the table and handed the phone over to Mrs

Sherwood's lawyer. As Yablon took the call, Townsend began to look around the room. Surely there was another way out of the apartment? He couldn't be expected to come face to face with a gloating Armstrong.

Mr Yablon replaced the phone and turned to Mrs Sherwood. 'That was my bank,' he said. 'They confirm that $2 million has been lodged in my escrow account. As I have said for some time, Margaret, I believe that clock of yours is a minute fast.'

Mrs Sherwood immediately signed the two documents in front of her, then revealed a piece of information concerning the late Sir George Sherwood's will that took both Townsend and Tom by surprise. Tom gathered up the papers as she rose from the table and said, 'Follow me, gentlemen.' She quickly led Townsend and his lawyers through to the kitchen, and out onto the fire escape.

'Goodbye, Mr Townsend,' she said as he stepped out of the window.

'Goodbye, Mrs Sherwood,' he said, giving a slight bow.

'By the way – ' she added.

Townsend turned back, looking anxious.

'Yes?'

'You know, you really ought to marry that girl – whatever her name is.'

◄○►

'I'm so sorry,' Mr Yablon was saying as Mrs Sherwood walked back into the dining room, 'but my client has already sold her shares in the *Globe* to Mr Keith Townsend, with whom I understand you are acquainted.'

Armstrong couldn't believe what he was hearing. He turned to his lawyer, a look of fury on his face.

'For $20 million?' Russell Critchley asked the old attorney calmly.

'Yes,' replied Yablon, 'the exact figure that your client agreed with her brother-in-law earlier this month.'

'But Alexander assured me only last week that Mrs Sherwood had agreed to sell her shares in the *Globe* to me,' said Armstrong. 'I've flown to New York specially . . .'

'It was not your flight to New York that influenced me, Mr Armstrong,' said the old lady firmly. 'Rather the one you made to Geneva.'

Armstrong stared at her for some time, then turned and marched back to the lift he had left only a few minutes earlier, and whose doors were still open. As he and his lawyer travelled down he cursed several times before asking, 'But how the hell did he manage it?'

'I can only assume he joined Mrs Sherwood at some point on her cruise.'

'But how could he possibly have found out that I was involved in a deal to take over the *Globe* in the first place?'

'I have a feeling that you won't find the answer to that question on this side of the Atlantic,' said Critchley. 'But all is not lost.'

'What the hell do you mean?'

'You are already in possession of one third of the shares.'

'So is Townsend,' said Armstrong.

'True. But if you were to pick up Sir Walter Sherwood's holding, you would then be in possession of two-thirds of the company, and Townsend would be left with no choice but to sell his third to you – at a considerable loss.'

Armstrong looked across at his lawyer, and the hint of a smile broke out across his jowly face.

'And with Alexander Sherwood still supporting your cause, the game's far from over yet.'

27

The GLOBE

1 JUNE 1967

Your Decision!

'Can you get me on the next flight to London?' barked Armstrong when the hotel's travel desk came on the line.

'Certainly, sir,' she said.

His second call was to his office in London, where Pamela – his latest secretary – confirmed that Sir Walter Sherwood had agreed to see him at ten o'clock the following morning. She didn't add, reluctantly.

'I'll also need to speak to Alexander Sherwood in Paris. And make sure Reg is at the airport and Stephen Hallet is in my office when I get back. This all has to be sorted before Townsend gets back to London.'

When Sharon walked into the suite a few minutes later, weighed down by shopping, she was surprised to find Dick was already packing.

'Are we going somewhere?' she asked.

'We're leaving immediately,' he said without explanation. 'Do your packing while I pay the bill.'

A porter took Armstrong's bags down to a waiting limousine, while he picked up the airline tickets from the travel desk and then went to reception to settle his bill. He checked his watch – he could just make the flight, and would be back in London early the following morning. As long as Townsend didn't know about the two-thirds rule, he could still end up owning 100 per cent of the company. And even if Townsend did know, he was confident Alexander Sherwood would press his claim with Sir Walter.

As soon as Sharon stepped into the back of the limousine, Armstrong ordered the driver to take them to the airport.

'But my bags haven't been brought down from the room yet,' said Sharon.

'Then they'll have to be sent on later. I can't afford to miss this flight.'

Sharon didn't say another word on the journey to the airport. As they drove up to the terminal, Armstrong fingered the two tickets in his inside pocket to be sure he hadn't left them behind. They stepped out of the limousine, and he asked the Skycap to check his bags straight through to London, then began running towards passport control with Sharon in his wake.

They were ushered quickly in the direction of the exit gate, where a stewardess was already checking passengers on board. 'Don't worry, sir,' she said. 'You've still got a couple of minutes to spare. You can both catch your breath.'

Armstrong removed the tickets from his pocket and gave one to Sharon. A steward checked his ticket, and he hurried off down the long corridor to the waiting plane.

Sharon handed over her ticket. The steward looked at it and said, 'This ticket is not for this flight, madam.'

'What do you mean?' said Sharon. 'I'm booked first class on this flight along with Mr Armstrong. I'm his personal assistant.'

'I'm sure you are, madam, but I'm afraid this ticket is economy, for Pan Am's evening flight. I fear you're going to have rather a long wait.'

◄○►

'Where are you phoning from?' he asked.

'Kingsford-Smith airport,' she replied.

'Then you can turn straight round and book yourself back on the same plane.'

'Why? Did the deal fall through?'

'No, she signed – but at a price. A problem has arisen over Mrs Sherwood's novel, and I have a feeling you're the only person who can solve it for me.'

'Can't I grab a night's sleep, Keith? I'd still be back in New York the day after tomorrow.'

'No, you can't,' he replied. 'There's something else we need to do before you get down to work, and I've only got one afternoon free.'

'What's that?' asked Kate.

'Get married,' replied Keith.

There was a long silence on the other end of the line before Kate said, 'Keith Townsend, you must be the least romantic man God ever put on earth!'

'Does that mean "yes"?' he asked. But the line had already gone dead. He put the phone down and looked across the desk at Tom Spencer.

'Did she accept your terms?' the lawyer asked with a grin.

'Can't be absolutely certain,' Townsend replied. 'But I still want you to go ahead with the arrangements as planned.'

'Right, then I'd better get in touch with City Hall.'

'And make sure you're free tomorrow afternoon.'

'Why?' asked Tom.

'Because, counsellor, we'll need a witness to the contract.'

–◦–

Sir Walter Sherwood had sworn several times that day, well above his average for a month.

The first string of expletives came after he had put the phone down on his brother. Alexander had called from Paris just before breakfast to tell him that he had sold his shares in the *Globe* to Richard Armstrong, at a price of $20 million. He recommended Walter to do the same.

But everything Sir Walter had heard about Armstrong only convinced him that he was the last man alive who should control a newspaper that was as British as roast beef and Yorkshire pudding.

He had calmed down a little after a good lunch at the Turf

Club, but then nearly had a heart attack when his sister-in-law called from New York to say that she had also sold her shares, not to Armstrong, but to Keith Townsend, a man Sir Walter considered gave colonials a bad name. He would never forget being stuck in Sydney for a week and having to endure the daily views of the *Sydney Chronicle* on the subject of 'the so-called Queen of Australia'. He had switched to the *Continent*, only to discover that it was in favour of Australia becoming a republic.

The final call of the day came from his accountant just before he sat down to dinner with his wife. Sir Walter didn't need to be reminded that sales of the *Globe* had been falling every week for the past year, and that he would therefore be wise to accept an offer of $20 million from whatever quarter. Not least because, as the bloody man so crudely put it, 'The two of them have stitched you up, and the sooner you get your hands on the money the better.'

'But which one of the bounders should I close a deal with?' he asked pathetically. 'Each seems to me just as bad as the other.'

'That is not a matter on which I'm qualified to advise,' replied the accountant. 'Perhaps you should settle on the one you dislike least.'

Sir Walter arrived in his office unusually early the following morning, and his secretary presented him with a thick file on each of the interested parties. She told him they had both been delivered by hand, within an hour of each other. He began to dip into them, and quickly realised that each must have been sent by the other. He procrastinated. But as the days passed, his accountant, his lawyer and his wife regularly reminded him about the continued drop in sales figures, and that the easy way out had been presented to him.

He finally accepted the inevitable, and decided that so long as he could remain as chairman of the board for another four years – which would take him up to his seventieth birthday – he could learn to live with either Armstrong or Townsend. He felt it was important for his friends at the Turf Club to know that he had been kept on as chairman.

The following morning, he asked his secretary to invite the rival suitors to lunch at the Turf Club on successive days. He promised he would let them know his decision within a week.

But after having had lunch with them both, he still couldn't decide which he disliked most – or, for that matter, least. He admired the fact that Armstrong had won the MC fighting for his adopted country, but couldn't abide the thought of the proprietor of the *Globe* not knowing how to hold a knife and fork. Against that, he rather enjoyed the idea of the proprietor of the *Globe* being an Oxford man, but felt ill whenever he recalled Townsend's views on the monarchy. At least both of them had assured him that he would remain as chairman. But when the week was up, he was still no nearer to reaching a decision.

He began to take advice from everyone at the Turf Club, including the barman, but he still couldn't make up his mind. It was only when his banker told him that the pound was strengthening against the dollar because of President Johnson's continuing troubles in Vietnam that he finally came to a decision.

Funny how a single word can trigger a stream of unrelated thoughts and turn them into action, mused Sir Walter. As he put the phone down on his banker, he knew exactly who should be entrusted to make the final decision. But he also realised that it would have to be kept secret, even from the editor of the *Globe*, until the last moment.

On the Friday afternoon, Armstrong flew to Paris with a girl called Julie from the advertising department, instructing Pamela that he was not to be contacted except in an emergency. He repeated the word 'emergency' several times.

Townsend had flown back to New York the previous day, having been given a tip that a major shareholder in the *New York Star* might at last be willing to sell their stock in the paper. He told Heather he didn't expect to return to England for at least a fortnight.

Sir Walter's secret broke on the Friday evening. The first person in Armstrong's camp to hear the news rang his office immediately, and was given his secretary's home number. When it was explained to Pamela what Sir Walter was planning, she was in no doubt that this was an emergency by any standards and immediately phoned the George V. The manager informed her that Mr Armstrong and his 'companion' had moved hotels after he had come across a group of Labour ministers, who were in Paris to attend a NATO conference, sitting in the bar. Pamela spent the rest of the evening systematically ringing every first-class hotel in Paris, but it wasn't until a few minutes after midnight that she finally ran Armstrong to ground.

The night porter told her emphatically that Mr Armstrong had said he was not to be disturbed under any circumstances. Remembering the age of the girl who was with him, he felt that he wouldn't get much of a tip if he disobeyed that order. Pamela lay awake all night and phoned again at seven the following morning. But as the manager didn't come on duty until nine on a Saturday, she received the same frosty reply.

The first person to tell Townsend what was going on was Chris Slater, the deputy features editor of the *Globe*, who decided that for the trouble it took to make an overseas call, he might well secure his future on the paper. In fact it took several overseas calls to track Mr Townsend down at the Racquets Club in New York, where he was eventually found playing squash with Tom Spencer for $1,000 a game.

Townsend was serving with a four-point lead in the final set when there was a knock on the glass door and a club servant asked if Mr Townsend could take an urgent telephone call. Trying not to lose his concentration, Townsend simply asked, 'Who?' As the name Chris Slater meant nothing to him, he said, 'Tell him I'll call back later.' Just before he served, he added, 'Did he say where he was calling from?'

'No, sir,' replied the messenger. 'He only said he was with the *Globe*.'

Townsend squeezed the ball as he considered the alternatives.

He was currently $2,000 up against a man he hadn't beaten in months, and he knew that if he left the court, even for a few moments, Tom would claim the match.

He stood staring at the front wall for another ten seconds, until Tom said sharply, 'Serve!'

'Is that your advice, counsellor?' he asked.

'It is,' replied the lawyer. 'Get on with it or concede. The choice is yours.' Townsend dropped the ball, ran out of the court and chased after the messenger. He reached him just before he put the phone down.

'This had better be good, Mr Slater,' said Townsend, 'because so far you've cost me $2,000.'

He listened in disbelief as Slater told him that in the following day's edition of the *Globe*, Sir Walter Sherwood would be inviting the paper's readers to vote on who they felt should be its next proprietor.

'There will be balanced full-page profiles on both candidates,' Slater went on to explain, 'with a voting slip at the bottom of the page.' He then read out the last three sentences of the proposed editorial.

> The loyal readers of the *Globe* need have no fear for the future of the best-loved paper in the kingdom. Both candidates have agreed that Sir Walter Sherwood shall remain as chairman of the board, guaranteeing the continuity that has been the hallmark of the paper's success for the better part of a century. So register your vote, and the result will be announced next Saturday.

Townsend thanked Slater, and assured him that if he became proprietor he would not be forgotten. His first thought after he had put the phone down was to wonder where Armstrong was.

He didn't return to the squash court, but immediately rang Ned Brewer, his bureau chief in London. He briefed him on exactly what he expected him to do during the night, and ended by telling him that he would be in touch again as soon as he landed at Heathrow. 'In the meantime, Ned,' he said, 'make sure you have at least £20,000 in cash available by the time I reach the office.'

As soon as he had put the phone down, Townsend went to the front desk and picked up his wallet from security, walked out onto Fifth Avenue and hailed a taxi. 'The airport,' he said. 'And you get $100 if we're there in time for the next flight to London.' He should have added 'alive'.

As the cab weaved in and out of the traffic, Townsend suddenly remembered that Tom was still waiting for him on the court, and that he was meant to be taking Kate out to dinner that night so she could bring him up to date on her progress with *The Senator's Mistress*. Every day that passed, Townsend thanked a God he didn't believe in that Kate had flown back from Sydney. He felt he had been lucky enough to find the one person who could tolerate his intolerable lifestyle, partly because she had accepted the situation long before they were married. Kate had never once made him feel guilty about the hours he kept, the turning up late or not turning up at all. He only hoped Tom would phone to let her know he had disappeared. 'No, I have no idea where,' he could hear him saying.

When he landed at Heathrow the following morning, the cabbie didn't feel it was his place to ask why his fare was dressed in a tracksuit and carrying a squash racket. Perhaps all the courts in New York were booked.

He arrived at his London office forty minutes later, and took over the operation from Ned Brewer. By ten o'clock every available employee had been sent to all corners of the capital. By lunchtime no one within a twenty-mile radius of Hyde Park Corner could find a copy of the *Globe* at any price. By nine that evening Townsend was in possession of 126,212 copies of the paper.

Armstrong arrived back at Heathrow on the Saturday afternoon, having spent most of the morning in Paris barking out orders to his staff all over Britain. By nine o'clock on Sunday morning, thanks to a remarkable trawl from the West Riding area, he was in possession of 79,107 copies of the *Globe*.

He spent the Sunday ringing the editors of all his regional papers and ordering them to write front-page stories for the following morning's editions, urging their readers to dig out

Saturday's *Globe* and vote Armstrong. On Monday morning he talked himself on to the *Today* programme and as many news slots as possible. But each of the producers decided it was only fair that Townsend should be allowed the right of reply the following day.

By Thursday, Townsend's staff were exhausted from signing names; Armstrong's sick from licking envelopes. By Friday afternoon both men were phoning the *Globe* every few minutes, trying to find out how the count was going. But as Sir Walter had called in the Electoral Reform Society to count the votes, and they were more interested in accuracy than speed, even the editor wasn't told the result until just before midnight.

'The Dodgy Dingo Beats the Bouncing Czech' ran the banner headline in the first editions of Saturday's paper. The article that followed informed the *Globe*'s readers that the voting had been 232,712 in favour of the Colonial, to 229,847 for the Immigrant.

Townsend's lawyer arrived at the *Globe*'s offices at nine o'clock on Monday morning, bearing a draft for $20 million. However much Armstrong protested, and however many writs he threatened to issue, he could not stop Sir Walter from signing his shares over to Townsend that afternoon.

At the first meeting of the new board, Townsend proposed that Sir Walter should remain as chairman, on his present salary of £100,000 a year. The old man smiled and made a flattering speech about how the readers had unquestionably made the right choice.

Townsend didn't speak again until they reached Any Other Business, when he suggested that all employees of the *Globe* should automatically retire at the age of sixty, in line with the rest of his group's policy. Sir Walter seconded the motion, as he was keen to join his chums at the Turf Club for a celebratory lunch. The motion went through on the nod.

It wasn't until Sir Walter climbed into bed that night that his wife explained to him the significance of that final resolution.

28

The Citizen

15 APRIL 1968

Minister Resigns

'One hundred thousand copies of *The Senator's Mistress* have been printed and are stacked in the warehouse in New Jersey, awaiting Mrs Sherwood's inspection,' said Kate, looking up at the ceiling.

'That's a good start,' said Townsend. 'But they're not going to return a penny of my money until they see them in the shops.'

'Once her lawyer has verified the numbers and the invoiced orders, he'll have no choice but to return the first million dollars. We will have fulfilled that part of the contract within the stipulated twelve-month period.'

'And how much has this little exercise cost me so far?'

'If you include printing and transport, around $30,000,' replied Kate. 'Everything else was done in-house, or can be set against tax.'

'Clever girl. But what chance do I have of getting my second million back? For all the time you've spent rewriting the damn book, I still can't see it making the best-seller lists.'

'I'm not so sure,' said Kate. 'Everybody knows that only eleven hundred shops report their sales to the *New York Times* each week. If I could get a sight of that list of booksellers, I'd have a real chance of making sure you get your second million back.'

'But knowing which shops report doesn't make customers buy books.'

'No, but I think we could nudge them in the right direction.'

'And how do you propose doing that?'

'First by launching the book in a slow month – say, January or February – and then by only selling in to those outlets that report to the *New York Times*.'

'But that won't make people buy them.'

'It will if we only charge the bookshop fifty cents a copy, with a cover price of $3.50, so the bookseller shows a 700 per cent mark-up on every copy sold, instead of the usual one hundred.'

'But that still won't help if the book is unreadable.'

'It won't matter in the first week,' said Kate. 'If the bookshops stand to make that sort of return, it will be in their interest to put the book in the window, on the counter, by the till, even on the best-seller shelves. My research shows that we'll only have to sell ten thousand copies in the first week to hit the number fifteen slot on the best-seller list, which works out at less than ten copies per shop.'

'I suppose that might just give us a fifty-fifty chance,' said Townsend.

'And I can lower those odds even further. In the week of publication we can use our network of newspapers and magazines across America to make sure the book gets favourable reviews and front-page advertisements, and put my article on "The Amazing Mrs Sherwood" in as many of our journals as you think we can get away with.'

'If it's going to save me a million dollars, that will be every one of them,' said Townsend. 'But that still only makes the odds a shade better than fifty-fifty.'

'If you'll let me go one step further, I can probably make it odds-on.'

'What are you proposing? That I buy the *New York Times*?'

'Nothing quite as drastic as that,' said Kate with a smile. 'I'm recommending that during the week of publication our own employees buy back 5,000 copies of the book.'

'Five thousand copies? That would just be throwing money down the drain.'

'Not necessarily,' said Kate. 'After we've sold them back to the shops at fifty cents apiece a second time, for an outlay of $15,000 you'll be virtually guaranteed a week on the best-seller list. And then Mr Yablon will have to return your second million.'

Townsend took her in his arms. 'We just might pull it off.'

'But only if *you* get hold of the names of the shops that report to the *New York Times* best-seller list.'

'You're a clever girl,' he said, pulling her closer.

Kate smiled. 'At last I've found out what turns you on.'

—◁◦▷—

'Stephen Hallet is on line one, and Ray Atkins, the minister for industry, on line two,' said Pamela.

'I'll take Atkins first. Tell Stephen I'll call him straight back.'

Armstrong waited for the click on his latest toy, which would ensure that the whole conversation was recorded. 'Good morning, Minister,' he said. 'What can I do for you?'

'It's a personal problem, Dick. I wondered if we could meet?'

'Of course,' Armstrong replied. 'How about lunch at the Savoy some time next week?' He flicked through his diary to see who he could cancel.

'I'm afraid it's more urgent than that, Dick. And I'd prefer not to meet in such a public place.'

Armstrong checked his appointments for the rest of the day. 'Well, why don't you join me for lunch today in my private dining room? I was due to see Don Sharpe, but if it's that urgent, I can put him off.'

'That's very kind of you, Dick. Shall we say around one?'

'Fine. I'll see that there's someone to meet you in reception and bring you straight up to my office.' Armstrong put the phone down and smiled. He knew exactly what the minister of industry wanted to see him about. After all, he had remained a loyal supporter of the Labour Party over the years – not least by donating a thousand pounds per annum to each of fifty key marginal seats. This small investment ensured that he had fifty close friends in the parliamentary party, several of them ministers, and gave him an entrée into the highest levels of government whenever he needed it. Had he wanted to exert the same influence in America, it would have cost him a million dollars a year.

His thoughts were interrupted by the phone ringing. Pamela had Stephen Hallet on the line.

'Sorry to have to call you back, Stephen, but I had young Ray Atkins on the line. Says he needs to see me urgently. I think we can both work out what that's about.'

'I thought the decision on the *Citizen* wasn't expected until next month at the earliest.'

'Perhaps they want to make an announcement before people start speculating. Don't forget that Atkins was the minister who referred Townsend's bid for the *Citizen* to the Monopolies and Mergers Commission. I don't think the Labour Party will be ecstatic about Townsend controlling the *Citizen* as well as the *Globe*.'

'It's the MMC who'll decide in the end, Dick, not the minister.'

'I still can't see them allowing Townsend to gain control of half of Fleet Street. In any case, the *Citizen* is the one paper that's consistently supported the Labour Party over the years, while most of the other rags have been nothing more than Tory magazines.'

'But the MMC will still have to appear even-handed.'

'Like Townsend has been with Wilson and Heath? The *Globe* has become a daily love letter to Teddy the sailor boy. If Townsend were to get his hands on the *Citizen* as well, the Labour movement would be left without a voice in this country.'

'You know it and I know it,' said Stephen. 'But the MMC isn't made up only of socialists.'

'More's the pity,' said Armstrong. 'If I could get my hands on the *Citizen*, for the first time in his life Townsend would discover what real competition is all about.'

'You don't have to convince me, Dick. I wish you luck with the minister. But that wasn't the reason I was calling.'

'Whenever you phone, Stephen, it's a problem. What is it this time?'

'I've just received a long letter from Sharon Levitt's solicitor, threatening you with a writ,' said Stephen.

'But I signed a settlement with her months ago. She can't expect another penny out of me.'

'I know you did, Dick. But this time they're going to serve a paternity order on you. It seems that Sharon has given birth to a son, and she's claiming that you're the father.'

'It could be anyone's, knowing that promiscuous little bitch . . .' began Armstrong.

'Possibly,' said Stephen. 'But not with that birthmark below its right shoulderblade. And don't forget there are four women on the MMC, and Townsend's wife is pregnant.'

'When was the bastard born?' asked Armstrong, quickly leafing backwards through his diary.

'4 January.'

'Hold on,' said Armstrong. He stared down at the entry in the diary for nine months before that date: Alexander Sherwood, Paris. 'The bloody woman must have planned it all along,' he boomed, 'while pretending that she wanted to be my personal assistant. That way she knew she'd end up with two settlements. What are you recommending?'

'Her solicitors will be aware of the battle that's going on for the *Citizen*, and therefore they know that it would only take one call to the *Globe* . . .'

'They wouldn't dare,' said Armstrong, his voice rising.

'Perhaps not,' replied Stephen calmly. 'But she might. I can only recommend that you let me settle on the best terms I can get.'

'If you say so,' said Armstrong quietly. 'But make sure you warn them that if one word of this leaks out, the payments will dry up the same day.'

'I'll do my best,' said Stephen. 'But I'm afraid she's learned something from you.'

'And what's that?' asked Dick.

'That it doesn't pay to hire a cheap solicitor. I'll phone you back as soon as we've agreed terms.'

'Do that,' said Armstrong, slamming the phone down.

'Pamela!' he bellowed through the door. 'Get me Don Sharpe.' When the editor of the *London Evening Post* came on the line, Armstrong said, 'Something's come up. I'm going to have to postpone our lunch for the time being.' He put the phone down before giving Sharpe a chance to respond. Armstrong had long ago decided that this particular editor needed replacing, and he had even approached the man he wanted for the job, but the minister's phone call had caused that decision to be delayed for a few more days.

He wasn't too worried about Sharon and whether she might blab. He had files on every editor in Fleet Street, even thicker ones on their masters, and almost an entire cabinet devoted to Keith Townsend. His mind drifted back to Ray Atkins.

After Pamela had gone through the morning mail with him, he asked her for a copy of *Dod's Parliamentary Companion*. He wanted to remind himself of the salient facts of Atkins's career, the names of his wife and children, the ministries he'd held, even his hobbies.

Everyone accepted that Ray Atkins was one of the brightest politicians of his generation, as was confirmed when Harold Wilson made him a shadow minister after only fifteen months. Following the 1966 general election Atkins became Minister of State at the Department of Trade and Industry. It was generally agreed that if Labour were to win the next election – a result that Armstrong didn't consider likely – Atkins would be invited to join the Cabinet. One or two people were even talking of him as a future leader of the party.

As Atkins was a member for a northern constituency covered by one of Armstrong's local papers, the two men had become more than casual acquaintances over the years, often having a meal together at the party conference. When Atkins was appointed minister of industry, with special responsibilities for takeovers, Armstrong made even more of an effort to cultivate him, hoping that might tip the balance when it came to deciding who should be allowed to take over the *Citizen*.

Sales of the *Globe* had continued their steady decline after Townsend had bought out Sir Walter Sherwood. Townsend had intended to sack the editor, but he shelved his plans when a few months later Hugh Tuncliffe, the proprietor of the *Citizen*, died, and his widow announced she would be putting the paper up for sale. Townsend spent several days convincing his board that he should put in an offer for the *Citizen* – an offer which the *Financial Times* described as 'too high a price to pay', even though the *Citizen* boasted the largest daily circulation in Britain. After all the bids had been received, his turned out to be the highest by far. There was an immediate outcry from the chattering classes, whose strongly held views were reported on the front page of the *Guardian*. Day after day, selected columnists trumpeted their disapproval of the prospect of Townsend owning the two most successful dailies in the land. In a rare display of broadsheet solidarity *The Times* thundered its views in a leader on behalf of the Establishment, condemning the idea of foreigners taking over national institutions and thus exerting a powerful influence over the British way of life. The following morning several letters landed on the editor's desk pointing out that *The Times*'s own proprietor was a Canadian. None of them was published.

When Armstrong announced that he would match Townsend's offer, and agreed to retain Sir Paul Maitland, the former ambassador to Washington, as chairman of the board, the government were left with no choice but to recommend that the matter be referred to the Monopolies and Mergers Commission. Townsend was livid at what he described as 'nothing more than a socialist plot', but he didn't gain much sympathy from those who had followed the decline in the journalistic standards of the *Globe* over the past year. Not that many people came out in favour of Armstrong either. The cliché about having to choose the lesser of two evils had appeared in several papers during the past month.

But this time Armstrong was convinced he had Townsend

on the run, and that the biggest prize in Fleet Street was about to fall into his lap. He couldn't wait for Ray Atkins to join him for lunch and have the news officially confirmed.

Atkins arrived at Armstrong House just before one. The proprietor was having a conversation in Russian when Pamela ushered him into the office. Armstrong immediately put the phone down in mid-sentence and rose to welcome his guest. He couldn't help noticing as he shook Atkins's hand that it was a little damp.

'What would you like to drink?' he asked.

'A small Scotch and a lot of water,' Atkins replied.

Armstrong poured the minister a drink and then led him through to the adjoining room. He switched on an unnecessary light and, with it, a concealed tape recorder. Atkins smiled with relief when he saw that only two places had been laid at the long dining table. Armstrong ushered him into a chair.

'Thank you, Dick,' he said nervously. 'It's most kind of you to see me at such short notice.'

'Not at all, Ray,' said Armstrong, taking his place at the top of the table. 'It's my pleasure. I'm only too delighted to see anyone who works so tirelessly for our cause. Here's to your future,' he added, raising his glass, 'which everyone tells me is rosy.'

Armstrong noticed a slight tremble of the hand before the minister responded. 'You do so much for our party, Dick.'

'Kind of you to say so, Ray.'

During the first two courses they chatted about the Labour Party's chances of winning the next election, and both of them admitted that they weren't over-optimistic.

'Although the opinion polls are looking a little better,' said Atkins, 'you only have to study the local election results to see what's really happening out there in the constituencies.'

'I agree,' said Dick. 'Only a fool would allow the opinion polls to influence him when it comes to calling an election. Although I believe Wilson regularly gets the better of Ted Heath at Question Time in the House.'

'True, but only a few hundred MPs see that. If only the

Commons was televised, the whole nation could see that Harold's in a different class.'

'Can't see that happening in my lifetime,' said Dick.

Atkins nodded, then fell into a deep silence. When the main course had been cleared away, Dick instructed his butler to leave them alone. He topped up the minister's glass with more claret, but Atkins only toyed with it, looking as if he was wondering how to broach an embarrassing topic. Once the butler had closed the door behind him, Atkins took a deep breath. 'This is all a bit awkward for me,' he began hesitantly.

'Feel free to say anything you like, Ray. Whatever it is will go no further than this room. Never forget, we bat for the same team.'

'Thank you, Dick,' the minister replied. 'I knew straight away that you'd be the right person with whom to discuss my little problem.' He continued to toy with his glass, saying nothing for some time. Then he suddenly blurted out, 'The *Evening Post* has been prying into my personal life, Dick, and I can't take much more of it.'

'I'm sorry to hear that,' said Armstrong, who had imagined that they were going to discuss a completely different subject. 'What have they been doing that's so disturbed you?'

'They've been threatening me.'

'Threatening you?' said Armstrong, sounding annoyed. 'In what way?'

'Well, perhaps "threatening" is a little strong. But one of your reporters has been constantly calling my office and my home at weekends, sometimes two or three times a day.'

'Believe me, Ray, I knew nothing about this,' said Armstrong. 'I'll speak to Don Sharpe the moment you've gone. You can be assured that's the last you'll hear of it.'

'Thank you, Dick,' he said. This time he did take a gulp of wine. 'But it's not the calls I need stopped. It's the story they've got hold of.'

'Would it help if you were to tell me what it's all about, Ray?'

The minister stared down at the table. It was some time

before he raised his head. 'It all happened years ago,' he began. 'So long ago, in fact, that until recently I'd almost been able to forget it ever took place.'

Armstrong remained silent as he topped up his guest's wine glass once again.

'It was soon after I'd been elected to the Bradford city council.' He took another sip of wine. 'I met the housing manager's secretary.'

'Were you married to Jenny at the time?' asked Armstrong.

'No, Jenny and I met a couple of years later, just before I was selected for Bradford West.'

'So what's the problem?' said Armstrong. 'Even the Labour Party allows girlfriends before you're married,' he added, trying to lighten the tone.

'Not when they become pregnant,' said the minister. 'And when their religion forbids abortion.'

'I see,' said Armstrong quietly. He paused. 'Does Jenny know anything about this?'

'No, nothing. I've never told her, or anyone else for that matter. She's the daughter of a local doctor – a bloody Tory, so the family never approved of me in the first place. If this ever came out, among other things I'd have to suffer the "I told you so" syndrome.'

'So is it the girl who's making things difficult?'

'No, God bless her, Rahila's been terrific – although her family regard me with about as much affection as my in-laws. I pay her the full maintenance, of course.'

'Of course. But if she isn't causing you any trouble, what's the problem? No paper would dare to print anything unless she corroborated the story.'

'I know. But unfortunately her brother had a little too much to drink one night and began shouting his mouth off in the local pub. He didn't realise there was a freelance journalist at the bar who works as a stringer for the *Evening Post*. The brother denied everything the following day, but the journalist just won't stop digging, the bastard. If this story gets out, I'd be left with no choice but to resign. And God knows what that would do to Jenny.'

'Well, it hasn't reached that stage yet, Ray, and you can be sure of one thing: you'll never see it referred to in any paper I own. On that you have my word. The moment you leave I'll call Sharpe and make it clear where I stand on this. You won't be contacted again, at least not on this subject.'

'Thank you,' said Atkins. 'That's a great relief. Now all I have to pray is that the journalist doesn't take it anywhere else.'

'What's his name?' asked Armstrong.

'John Cummins.'

Armstrong scribbled the name down on a pad by his side. 'I'll see that Mr Cummins is offered a job on one of my papers in the north, somewhere not too near Bradford. That should dampen his ardour.'

'I don't know how to thank you,' said the minister.

'I'm sure you'll find a way,' said Armstrong as he rose from his place, not bothering to offer his guest a coffee. He accompanied Atkins out of the dining room. The minister's nervousness had been replaced by the voluble self-assurance more usually associated with politicians. As they passed through Armstrong's office, he noticed that the bookshelf contained a full set of *Wisden*. 'I didn't know you were a cricket fan, Dick,' he said.

'Oh yes,' said Armstrong. 'I've loved the game from an early age.'

'Which county do you support?' asked Atkins.

'Oxford,' replied Armstrong as they reached the lift.

Atkins said nothing. He shook his host warmly by the hand. 'Thank you again, Dick. Thank you so much.'

The moment the lift doors had slid closed, Armstrong returned to his office. 'I want to see Don Sharpe immediately,' he shouted as he passed Pamela's desk.

The editor of the *Evening Post* appeared in the proprietor's office a few minutes later, clutching a thick file. He waited for Armstrong to finish a phone conversation in a language he didn't recognise.

'You asked to see me,' he said once Armstrong had put the phone down.

'Yes. I've just had Ray Atkins to lunch. He says the *Post* has been harassing him. Some story that you've been following up.'

'Yes, I have had someone working on a story. In fact we've been trying to get in touch with Atkins for days. We think the minister may have fathered a love child some years ago, a boy called Vengi.'

'But this all took place before he was married.'

'That's true,' said the editor. 'But . . .'

'So I can hardly see how it could be described as in the public interest.'

Don Sharpe appeared somewhat surprised by the proprietor's unusual sensitivity on the matter – but then, he was also aware that the MMC's decision on the *Citizen* was due to be made within the next few weeks.

'Would you agree or not?' asked Armstrong.

'In normal circumstances I would,' replied Sharpe. 'But in this case the woman in question has lost her job with the council, been abandoned by her family, and is surviving – just – in a one-bedroom flat in the minister's constituency. He, on the other hand, is being driven around in a Jaguar and has a second home in the south of France.'

'But he pays her full maintenance.'

'Not always on time,' said the editor. 'And it could be regarded as being in the public's interest that when he was an under-secretary of state in the Social Services Department, he was responsible for piloting the single-parent allowance through its committee stage on the floor of the House.'

'That's irrelevant, and you know it.'

'There's another factor that might interest our readers.'

'And what's that?'

'She's a Moslem. Having given birth to a child out of wedlock, she can never hope to marry. They're a little stricter on these matters than the Church of England.' The editor removed a photograph from his file and placed it on Armstrong's desk. Armstrong glanced at the picture of an attractive Asian mother with her arms around a little boy. The child's resemblance to his father would have been hard to deny.

Armstrong looked back up at Sharpe. 'How did you know I was going to want to discuss this with you?'

'I assumed you hadn't cancelled our lunch because you wanted to chat to Ray Atkins about Bradford City's chances of being relegated this season.'

'Don't be sarcastic with me,' snapped Armstrong. 'You'll drop this whole enquiry, and you'll drop it immediately. If I ever see even a hint of this story in any one of my papers, you needn't bother to report to work the next morning.'

'But . . .' said the editor.

'And while you're at it, you can leave that file on my desk.'

'I can what?'

Armstrong continued to glower at him until he meekly placed the heavy file on the desk. He turned and left without another word.

Armstrong cursed. If he sacked Sharpe now, the first thing he would do would be to walk across the road and give the story to the *Globe*. He had made a decision that was likely to cost him a great deal of money either way. He picked up the phone. 'Pamela, get me Mr Atkins at the Department of Trade and Industry.'

Atkins came on the line a few moments later. 'Is this a public line?' asked Armstrong, aware that civil servants often listened in on conversations in case their ministers made commitments that they would then have to follow up.

'No, you've come through on my private line,' Atkins assured him.

'I have spoken to the editor in question,' said Armstrong, 'and I can assure you that Mr Cummins won't be bothering you again. I also warned him that if I see any reference to this incident in any one of my papers, he can start looking for another job.'

'Thank you,' said the minister.

'And it may interest you to know, Ray, that I have on my

desk Cummins's file concerning this matter, and will be shredding it as soon as we've finished speaking. Believe me, no one will ever hear a word of this again.'

'You're a good friend, Dick. And you've probably saved my career.'

'A career worth saving,' said Armstrong. 'Never forget, I'm here if you need me.' As he replaced the phone Pamela put her head round the door.

'Stephen called again while you were on the phone to the minister. Shall I get him back?'

'Yes. And after that, there's something I want you to do for me.' Pamela nodded and disappeared into her own office. A moment later one of the phones on his desk rang. Armstrong picked it up.

'What's the problem, Stephen?'

'There's no problem. I've had a long discussion with Sharon Levitt's solicitors, and we've come up with some preliminary proposals for a settlement – subject of course to both parties agreeing.'

'Fill me in,' said Armstrong.

'It seems that Sharon has a boyfriend living in Italy, and . . .' Armstrong listened intently as Stephen outlined the terms that had been negotiated on his behalf. He was smiling long before his lawyer had finished.

'That all seems very satisfactory,' he said.

'Yes. How did the meeting with the minister go?'

'It went well. He's facing roughly the same problem that I am, but he has the disadvantage of not having someone like you to sort it out for him.'

'Am I meant to understand that?'

'No,' replied Armstrong. As soon as he had put the phone down, he called for his secretary.

'Pamela, when you've typed up the conversation that took place over lunch today, I want you to put a copy of it in this file,' he said, pointing to the pile of papers Don Sharpe had left on his desk.

'And then what do I do with the file?'

'Lock it in the large safe. I'll let you know if I need it again.'

—◇—

When the editor of the *London Evening Post* requested a private meeting with Keith Townsend, he received an immediate response. It was well understood in Fleet Street that Armstrong's staff had a standing invitation to see Townsend if they had any interesting information about their boss. Not many of them had taken advantage of the offer, because they all knew that if they were caught, they could clear their desks the same day, and would never work for any of Armstrong's newspapers again.

It had been some time since anyone as senior as Don Sharpe had contacted Townsend direct. He suspected that Mr Sharpe already knew his days were numbered, and had calculated that he had nothing to lose. But like so many others before him, he had insisted that the meeting should take place on neutral ground.

Townsend always hired the Fitzalan Suite at the Howard Hotel for such purposes, as it was only a short distance from Fleet Street, but wasn't a haunt of prying journalists. One phone call from Heather to the head porter and all the necessary arrangements were made with complete discretion.

Sharpe told Townsend in detail about the conversation that had taken place between himself and Armstrong following the proprietor's lunch with Ray Atkins the previous day, and waited for his reaction.

'Ray Atkins,' said Townsend.

'Yes, the minister for industry.'

'The man who will make the final decision as to who takes control of the *Citizen*.'

'Precisely. That's why I thought you would want to know immediately,' said Sharpe.

'And Armstrong kept the file?'

'Yes, but it would only take me a few days to get duplicates of everything. If you broke the story on the front page of the

Globe, I'm sure that under the circumstances the Monopolies and Mergers Commission would have to remove Armstrong from their calculations.'

'Perhaps,' said Townsend. 'Once you've put the documentation together, send it to me direct. Make sure you put my initials, K.R.T., on the bottom left-hand corner of the package. That will ensure that no one else opens it.'

Sharpe nodded. 'Give me a week, a fortnight at the most.'

'And should I end up as proprietor of the *Citizen*,' said Townsend, 'you can be sure that there will be a job for you on the paper if ever you want it.'

Sharpe was about to ask him what job he had in mind when Townsend added, 'Don't leave the hotel for another ten minutes.' As he stepped out onto the street, the senior porter touched the rim of his top hat. Townsend was driven back to Fleet Street, confident that the *Citizen* must now surely fall into his hands.

A young porter, who had seen the two men arrive separately and leave separately, waited for his boss to take a tea break before he made a phone call.

―◇―

Ten days later two envelopes arrived in Townsend's office with 'K.R.T.' printed boldly in the bottom left-hand corners. Heather left them on his desk unopened. The first was from a former employee of the *New York Times*, who supplied him with the full list of shops that reported to the best-seller list. For $2,000 it had been a worthwhile investment, thought Townsend. He put the list on one side, and opened the second envelope. It contained pages and pages of research supplied by Don Sharpe on the extra-curricular activities of the minister for industry.

An hour later, Townsend felt confident not only that he would retrieve his second million, but also that Armstrong would live to regret suppressing the minister's secret. He picked up a phone and told Heather that he needed to send a package to New York by special delivery. When she had taken one of the sealed envelopes away, he picked up the phone and asked the editor of the *Globe* to join him.

'When you've had a chance to read through this,' he said, pushing the second envelope across his desk, 'you'll know what to lead on tomorrow.'

'I already have a lead story for tomorrow,' said the editor. 'We have evidence that Marilyn Monroe is alive.'

'She can wait for another day,' said Townsend. 'Tomorrow we lead on the minister for industry and his attempt to suppress the story of his illegitimate child. Make sure I have a dummy front page on my desk by five this afternoon.'

⊷⊶

A few minutes later Armstrong received a call from Ray Atkins.

'How can I help you, Ray?' he asked, as he pressed a button on the side of his phone.

'No, Dick, this time it's my turn to help you,' said Atkins. 'A report has just landed on my desk from the Monopolies and Mergers Commission, outlining their recommendations for the *Citizen*.'

It was Armstrong's turn to feel a slight sweat on his hands.

'Their advice is that I should rule in your favour. I'm simply ringing to let you know that I intend to take that advice.'

'That's wonderful news,' said Armstrong, standing up. 'Thank you.'

'Delighted to be the one to let you know,' said Atkins. 'As long as you've got a cheque for £78 million, the *Citizen* is yours.'

Armstrong laughed. 'When does it become official?'

'The MMC's recommendation will go before the Cabinet at eleven o'clock this morning, and I can't imagine you'll find anyone round that table objecting,' said the minister. 'I'm scheduled to make a statement in the House at 3.30 this afternoon, so I'd be obliged if you said nothing before then. After all, we don't want to give the commission any reason to reverse their decision.'

'Not a word, Ray, of that I can promise you.' He paused. 'And I want you to know that if there is anything I can do for you in the future, you only have to ask.'

―◦―

Townsend smiled as he checked the headline once again:

Minister's Moslem Love Child Mystery

He then read the proposed first paragraph, inserting one or two small changes.

> Last night Ray Atkins, the minister for indus-
> try, refused to comment when asked if he was
> the father of little Vengi Patel (see picture),
> aged seven, who lives with his mother in a
> dingy one-room flat in the minister's constitu-
> ency. Vengi's mother Miss Rahila Patel, aged
> thirty-three . . .

'What is it, Heather?' he asked, looking up as his secretary entered the room.

'The political editor is on the phone from the press gallery at the House of Commons. It seems there's been a statement concerning the *Citizen*.'

'But I was told there would be no announcement for at least another month,' said Townsend as he grabbed the phone. His face became grimmer and grimmer as the details of the state-ment Ray Atkins had just made to the House were read out to him.

'Not much point in running that front-page story now,' said the political editor.

'Let's just set and hold,' said Townsend. 'I'll have another look at it this evening.' He stared gloomily out of the window. Atkins's decision meant that Armstrong would now control the one daily in Britain that had a larger circulation than the *Globe*. From that moment he and Armstrong would be locked in battle for the same readers, and Townsend wondered if they could both survive.

◄○►

Within an hour of the minister delivering his statement in the Commons, Armstrong had called Alistair McAlvoy, the editor of the *Citizen*, and asked him to come across to Armstrong House. He also arranged to have dinner that evening with Sir Paul Maitland, the chairman of the *Citizen*'s board.

Alistair McAlvoy had been editor of the *Citizen* for the past decade. When he was briefed on the minister's decision, he warned his colleagues that no one, including himself, should be confident they would be bringing out the next day's edition of the paper. But when Armstrong put his arm around McAlvoy's shoulder for a second time that afternoon, describing him as the greatest editor in the street, he began to feel that perhaps his job was safe after all. As the atmosphere became a little more relaxed, Armstrong warned him that they were about to face a head-on battle with the *Globe*, which he suspected would begin the following morning.

'I know,' said McAlvoy, 'so I'd better get back to my desk. I'll call you the moment I discover what the *Globe* is leading on, and see if we can find some way of countering it.'

McAlvoy left Armstrong's office as Pamela walked in with a bottle of champagne.

'Who did that come from?'

'Ray Atkins,' said Pamela.

'Open it,' said Armstrong. Just as she uncorked the bottle, the phone rang. Pamela picked it up and listened. 'It's the junior porter at the Howard Hotel – he says he can't hang on for much longer, or he'll be caught.' She placed her hand over the mouthpiece. 'He tried to speak to you ten days ago, but I didn't put him through. He says it's about Keith Townsend.'

Armstrong grabbed the phone. When the porter told him who Townsend had just had a meeting with in the Fitzalan Suite, he immediately knew what the *Globe*'s front-page story would be the following morning. All the boy wanted for this exclusive piece of information was £50.

He put the phone down and blasted out a series of orders before Pamela had even finished filling his glass with champagne. 'And once I've seen Sharpe, put me through to McAlvoy.'

The moment Don Sharpe walked back into the building, he was told that the proprietor wanted to see him. He went straight to Armstrong's office, where the only words he heard were 'You're fired.' He turned round to find two security guards standing by the door waiting to escort him off the premises.

'Get McAlvoy for me.'

All Armstrong said when the editor of the *Citizen* came on the line was, 'Alistair, I know what's going to be on the front page of the *Globe* tomorrow, and I'm the one person who can top it.'

As soon as he put the phone down on McAlvoy, Armstrong asked Pamela to dig the Atkins file out of the safe. He began sipping his champagne. It wasn't vintage.

—◦—

The following morning the *Globe*'s headline read: 'Minister's Secret Moslem Love Child: Exclusive'. There followed three pages of pictures, illustrating an interview with Miss Patel's brother, under the byline 'Don Sharpe, Chief Investigative Reporter'.

Townsend was delighted, until he turned to the *Citizen* and read its headline:

Love Child Minister Reveals All to the *Citizen*

There followed five pages of pictures and extracts from a tape-recorded interview given exclusively to the paper's unnamed special affairs correspondent.

The lead story in the *London Evening Post* that night was that the prime minister had announced from 10 Downing Street that he had, with considerable regret, accepted the resignation of Mr Ray Atkins MP.

FIFTH EDITION

The *Citizen* v the *Globe*

29

The Citizen

21 AUGUST 1978

Not Many People Inhabiting
the New Globe

When Townsend had cleared customs he found Sam waiting outside the terminal to drive him into Sydney. On the twenty-five-minute journey, Sam brought the boss up to date with what was happening in Australia. He left him in no doubt as to what he felt about the prime minister, Malcolm Fraser – out of date and out of touch – and the Sydney Opera House – a waste of money, and already out of date. But he gave him one piece of information which was fresh, and not out of date.

'Where did you pick that up, Sam?'

'The chairman's driver told me.'

'And what did you have to tell him in exchange?'

'Only that you were coming back from London on a flying visit,' replied Sam, as they pulled up outside Global Corp's headquarters on Pitt Street.

Heads turned as Townsend pushed his way through the revolving doors, walked across the lobby and into a waiting lift which whisked him straight up to the top floor. He called for the editor even before Heather had a chance to welcome him back.

Townsend paced up and down his office as he waited, stopping occasionally to admire the opera house, which, like

Sam, all his papers with the exception of the *Continent* had been quick to condemn. Only half a mile away was the bridge that had until recently been the city's trademark. In the harbour, colourful dinghies were sailing, their masts glowing in the sun. Although its population had doubled, Sydney now seemed terribly small compared to when he had first taken over the *Chronicle*. He felt as if he was looking down on a Lego town.

'Good to have you back, Keith,' said Bruce Kelly as he walked through the open door. Townsend swung round to greet the first man he had ever appointed to be editor of one of his newspapers.

'And it's great to be back, Bruce. It's been too long,' he said as they shook hands. He wondered if he had aged as much as the balding, overweight man who stood in front of him.

'How's Kate?'

'She hates London, and seems to spend most of her time in New York, but I'm hoping she'll be joining me next week. What's happening over here?'

'Well, you'll have seen from our weekly reports that sales are slightly up on last year, advertising is up, and profits are at a record level. So I guess it must be time for me to retire.'

'That's exactly what I came back home to talk to you about,' said Townsend.

The blood drained out of Bruce's face. 'Are you serious, chief?'

'Never been more serious,' said Townsend, facing his friend. 'I need you in London.'

'Whatever for?' asked Bruce. 'The *Globe* is hardly the sort of paper I've been trained to edit. It's far too traditional and British.'

'That's exactly why it's losing sales every week. For one thing, its readers are so old that they're literally dying on me. If I'm going to tackle Armstrong head-on, I need you as the next editor of the *Globe*. The whole paper has to be reshaped. The first thing to be done is to turn it into a tabloid.'

Bruce stared at his boss in disbelief. 'But the unions will never wear it.'

'I also have plans for them,' said Townsend.

—◁◇▷—

BRITAIN'S BEST-SELLING DAILY

Armstrong was proud of the strapline that ran below the *Citizen*'s masthead. But although the sales of the paper had remained steady, he was beginning to feel that Alistair McAlvoy, Fleet Street's longest-serving editor, might not be the right man to carry out his long-term strategy.

Armstrong remained puzzled as to why Townsend had flown off to Sydney. He couldn't believe that he would allow the circulation figures of the *Globe* to keep on dropping without even putting up a fight. But as long as the *Citizen* was outselling the *Globe* by two to one, Armstrong didn't hesitate to remind its loyal readers every morning that he was the proprietor of Britain's best-selling newspaper. Armstrong Communications had just declared a profit of seventeen million pounds for the previous year, and everyone knew that its chief executive was now looking west for his next big acquisition.

He must have been told a thousand times, by people who imagined they were in the know, that Townsend had been buying up shares in the *New York Star*. What they didn't realise was that he had been carrying out exactly the same exercise himself. He had been warned by Russell Critchley, his New York attorney, that once he was in possession of more than 5 per cent of the stock he would, under the rules of the Securities and Exchange Commission, have to go public and state whether he intended to mount a full takeover.

He was now holding just over 4½ per cent of the *Star*'s stock, and suspected that Townsend was in roughly the same position. But for the moment each was content to sit and wait for the other to make the first move. Armstrong knew that Townsend controlled more city and state newsprint in America

447

than he did, despite his own recent acquisition of the Milwaukee Group and its eleven papers. Both knew that as the *New York Times* would never come up for sale, the ultimate prize in the Big Apple would be to take control of the tabloid market.

While Townsend remained in Sydney, going over his plans for the launching of the new *Globe* on an unsuspecting British public, Armstrong flew to Manhattan to prepare for his assault on the *New York Star*.

◄o►

'But Bruce Kelly knew nothing about it,' said Townsend, as Sam drove him from Tullamarine airport into Melbourne.

'I wouldn't expect him to,' said Sam. 'He's never even met the chairman's driver.'

'Are you trying to tell me that a driver knows something that no one else in the newspaper world has heard about?'

'No. The deputy chairman also knows, because he was discussing it with the chairman in the back of the car.'

'And the driver told you that the board are meeting at ten o'clock this morning?'

'That's right, chief. In fact he's taking the chairman to the meeting right now.'

'And the agreed price was $12 a share?'

'That's what the chairman and deputy chairman settled on in the back of the car,' said Sam as he drove into the centre of the city.

Townsend couldn't think of any more questions to ask Sam that could prevent him from making a complete fool of himself. 'I don't suppose you'd care to take a wager on it?' he said as the car turned into Flinders Street.

Sam thought about the proposition for some time before saying, 'OK by me, chief.' He paused. 'A hundred dollars says I'm right.'

'Oh no,' said Townsend. 'Your wages for a month, or we turn round and go straight back to the airport.'

Sam ran through a red light and just managed to avoid

hitting a tram. 'You're on,' he said finally. 'But only if Arthur gets the same terms.'

'And who in hell's name is Arthur?'

'The chairman's driver.'

'You and Arthur have got yourselves a deal,' said Townsend, as the car drew up outside the *Courier*'s offices.

'How long do you want me to wait?' asked Sam.

'Just as long as it takes you to lose a month's wages,' Townsend replied, slamming the car door behind him.

Townsend stared up at the building in which his father had begun his career as a reporter in the 1920s, and where he himself had carried out his first assignment as a trainee journalist while he was still at school, which his mother later told him she had sold to a rival without even letting him know. From the footpath he could pick out the room his father had worked in. Could the *Courier* really be up for sale without any of his professional advisers being aware of it? He had checked the share price that morning before taking the first flight out of Sydney: $8.40. Could he risk it all on the word of his driver? He began to wish Kate was with him, so that he could seek her opinion. Thanks to her, *The Senator's Mistress* by Margaret Sherwood had spent two weeks at the bottom of the *New York Times* best-seller list, and the second million had been returned in full. To the surprise of both of them, the book had also received some reasonable reviews in the non-Townsend press. Keith had been amused to receive a letter from Mrs Sherwood asking if he'd be interested in a three-book contract.

Townsend walked through the double doors and under the clock above the entrance to the foyer. He stood for a moment in front of a bronze bust of his father, remembering how as a child he had stretched up and tried to touch his hair. It only made him more nervous.

He turned and walked across the foyer, joining a group of people who stepped into the first available lift. They fell silent when they realised who it was. He pressed the button and the doors slid closed. He hadn't been in the building for over thirty years, but he could still remember where the boardroom was – a few yards down the corridor from his father's office.

The doors slid open on circulation, advertising and then editorial, until he was finally left alone in the lift. At the executive floor he stepped cautiously out into the corridor, and looked in both directions. He couldn't see anyone. He turned to the right and walked towards the boardroom, his pace slowing as he passed his father's old office. It then became slower and slower until he reached the boardroom door.

He was about to turn back, leave the building and tell Sam exactly what he thought of him, and his friend Arthur too, when he remembered the wager. If he hadn't been such a bad loser, he might not have knocked on the door and, without waiting for a response, marched in.

Sixteen faces turned and stared up at him. He waited for the chairman to ask him what the hell he thought he was doing, but no one spoke. It was almost as if they had been anticipating his arrival. 'Mr Chairman,' he began, 'I am willing to offer $12 a share for your stock in the *Courier*. As I leave for London tonight, we either close the deal right now or we don't close it at all.'

Sam sat in the car waiting for his boss to return. During the third hour he rang Arthur to tell him to invest next month's wages in *Melbourne Courier* shares, and to do it before the board made an official announcement.

◄○►

When Townsend flew into London the following morning, he issued a press release to announce that Bruce Kelly would be taking over as editor of the *Globe* in its run-up to becoming a tabloid. Only a handful of insiders appreciated the significance of the appointment. During the next few days, profiles of Bruce appeared in several national newspapers. All of them reported that he had been editor of the *Sydney Chronicle* for twenty-five years, was divorced with two grown-up children, and though Keith Townsend was thought not to have any close friends, he was the nearest thing to it. The *Citizen* jeered when he wasn't granted a work permit, and suggested that editing the *Globe* couldn't be considered work. Beyond that there wasn't a lot of information on the latest immigrant from Australia. Under the headline 'R.I.P.', the *Citizen* went on to inform its readers that Kelly was nothing more than an undertaker who had been brought in to bury something everyone else accepted had been dead for years. It went on to say that for every copy the *Globe* sold, the *Citizen* now sold three. The real figure was 2.3, but Townsend was becoming used to Armstrong's exaggeration when it came to statistics. He had the leader framed, and hung it on the wall of Bruce's new office to await his arrival.

As soon as Bruce landed in London, even before he'd found somewhere to live, he began poaching journalists from the tabloids. Most of them didn't seem to be concerned by the *Citizen*'s warnings that the *Globe* was on a downward spiral, and might not even survive if Townsend was unable to come to terms with the unions. Bruce's first appointment was Kevin Rushcliffe, who, he had been assured, was making a reputation as deputy editor on the *People*.

The first time Rushcliffe was left to edit the paper on Bruce's day off, they received a writ from lawyers representing Mr Mick Jagger. Rushcliffe casually shrugged his shoulders and said, 'It was too good a story to check.' After substantial damages had been paid and an apology printed, the lawyers were instructed to check Mr Rushcliffe's copy more carefully in future.

Some seasoned journalists did sign up to join the editorial staff. When they were asked why they had left secure jobs to join the *Globe*, they pointed out that as they had been offered three-year contracts, they didn't care much either way.

In the first few weeks under Kelly's editorship sales continued to slide. The editor would have liked to have spent more time discussing the problem with Townsend, but the boss seemed to be continually locked into negotiations with the print unions.

On the day of the launch of the *Globe* as a tabloid, Bruce held a party in the offices to watch the new paper coming off the presses. He was disappointed when many of the politicians and celebrities he had invited failed to turn up. He learned later that they were attending a party thrown by Armstrong to celebrate the *Citizen*'s seventy-fifth anniversary. A former employee of the *Citizen*, now working at the *Globe*, pointed out that it was actually only their seventy-second year. 'Well then, we'll just have to remind Armstrong in three years' time,' said Townsend.

A few minutes after midnight, when the party was drawing to a close, a messenger strolled into the editor's office to let him know that the presses had broken down. Townsend and Bruce ran down to the print room to find that the workforce had downed tools and already gone home. They rolled up their sleeves and set about the hopeless task of trying to get the presses started again, but they quickly discovered that a spanner had literally been thrown in the works. Only 131,000 copies of the paper appeared on the streets the following day, none of them delivered beyond Birmingham, as the train drivers had come out in support of their brothers in the print unions.

Not Many People Inhabiting the New Globe, ran the headline in the *Citizen* the following morning. The paper went on to devote the whole of page five to suggesting that the time had come to bring back the old *Globe*. After all, the 'illegal immigrant' – as they kept referring to Bruce – had promised new sales records, and had indeed achieved them: the *Citizen* now outsold the *Globe* by thirty to one. Yes, thirty to one!

On the opposite page, the *Citizen* offered its readers a hundred to one against the *Globe* surviving another six months. Townsend immediately wrote out a cheque for £1,000 and sent it round to Armstrong's office by hand, but he received no acknowledgement. However, one call to the Press Association from Bruce made sure that the story was released to every other newspaper.

On the front page of the *Citizen* the following morning, Armstrong announced that he had banked Townsend's cheque for £1,000, and that as the *Globe* had no hope of surviving for another six months, he would be giving a donation of £50,000 to the Press Benevolent Fund and a further £50,000 to any charity of Mr Townsend's choice. By the end of the week, Townsend had received over a hundred letters from leading charities explaining why he should select their particular cause.

During the next few weeks the *Globe* rarely managed to print more than 300,000 copies a day, and Armstrong never stopped reminding his readers of the fact. As the months passed, Townsend accepted that eventually he would have to take on the unions. But he knew it wouldn't be possible while the Labour Party remained in power.

30

The GLOBE

4 MAY 1979

Maggie Victorious!

Townsend left the television in his office on all night so he could watch the election results coming in from around the country. Once he was certain Margaret Thatcher would be moving in to 10 Downing Street, he hastily wrote a leader assuring readers that Britain was about to embark on an exciting new era. He ended with the words 'Fasten your seatbelts.'

As he and Bruce staggered out of the building at four o'clock in the morning, Townsend's parting words were, 'You know what this means, don't you?'

—◇—

The following afternoon Townsend arranged a private meeting with Eric Harrison, the general secretary of the breakaway print union, at the Howard Hotel. When the meeting broke up, the head porter knocked on the door and asked if he could see him privately. He told Townsend what he had overheard his junior saying on the telephone when he had arrived back early from his tea break. Townsend didn't need to be told who must have been on the other end of the line.

'I'll sack him at once,' said the head porter. 'You can be sure it will never happen again.'

'No, no,' said Townsend. 'Leave him exactly where he is. I may no longer be able to meet people I don't want Armstrong to know about here, but that doesn't stop me from meeting those I do.'

-<o>-

At the monthly board meeting of Armstrong Communications, the finance director reported that he estimated the *Globe* must still be losing around £100,000 a week. However deep Townsend's pockets were, that sort of negative cash-flow would soon empty them.

Armstrong smiled, but said nothing until Sir Paul Maitland moved on to the second item on the agenda, and called on him to brief the board on his latest American trip. Armstrong brought them up to date on his progress in New York, and went on to tell them that he intended to make a further trip across the Atlantic in the near future, as he believed it would not be long before the company was in a position to make a public bid for the *New York Star*.

Sir Paul said he was anxious about the sheer scale of such an acquisition, and asked that no commitments should be made without the board's approval. Armstrong assured him that it had never crossed his mind to do otherwise.

Under Any Other Business, Peter Wakeham brought to the attention of the board an article in the *Financial Times* which reported that Keith Townsend had recently purchased a large block of warehouses on the Isle of Dogs, and that a fleet of unmarked lorries were regularly making late-night deliveries to it.

'Has anyone any idea what this is all about?' asked Sir Paul, his eyes sweeping the table.

'We know,' said Armstrong, 'that Townsend got himself landed with a trucking company when he took over the *Globe*. As his papers are doing so badly, perhaps he's having to diversify.'

Some members of the board laughed, but Sir Paul was not among them. 'That wouldn't explain why Townsend has set up such tight security around the site,' he said. 'Security guards, dogs, electric gates, barbed wire along the tops of the walls – he's up to something.'

Armstrong shrugged his shoulders and looked bored, so Sir Paul reluctantly brought the meeting to a close.

Three days later, Armstrong took a call from the Howard Hotel, and was told by the junior porter that Townsend had spent the whole afternoon and most of the evening locked in the Fitzalan Suite with three officials from one of the leading print unions, who were refusing to carry out any overtime. Armstrong assumed they were negotiating for improved pay and conditions in exchange for getting their members back to work.

The following Monday he flew to America, confident that as Townsend was preoccupied with his problems in London, there couldn't be a better time to prepare a takeover bid for the *New York Star*.

—◇—

When Townsend called a meeting of all the journalists who worked on the *Globe*, most of them assumed that the proprietor had finally reached a settlement with the print unions, and the get-together would be nothing more than a public relations exercise to prove he had got the better of them.

At four o'clock that afternoon, over seven hundred journalists crammed onto the editorial floor. They fell silent as Townsend and Bruce Kelly walked in, clearing a path to allow the proprietor to walk to the centre of the room, where he climbed up onto a table. He looked down on the group of people who were about to decide his fate.

'For the past few months,' he began quietly, 'Bruce Kelly and I have been involved in a plan which I believe will change all our lives, and possibly the whole face of journalism in this country. Newspapers cannot hope to survive in the future if they continue to be run as they have been for the past hundred years. Someone has to make a stand, and that person is me. And this is the time to do it. Starting at midnight on Sunday, I intend to transfer my entire printing and publishing operation to the Isle of Dogs.'

A small gasp was audible.

'I have recently come to an agreement,' Townsend continued, 'with Eric Harrison, the general secretary of the Allied Printworkers, which will give us a chance once and for all to rid ourselves of the stranglehold of the closed shop.' Some people began to applaud. Others looked uncertain, and some downright angry.

The proprietor went on to explain to the journalists the logistics of such an immense operation. 'The problem of distribution will be dealt with by our own fleet of trucks, making it unnecessary in future for us to rely on the rail unions, who will undoubtedly come out on strike in support of their comrades in the print unions. I can only hope that you will all back me in this venture. Are there any questions?' Hands shot up all around the room. Townsend pointed to a man standing directly in front of him.

'Are you expecting the unions to picket the new building, and if so, what contingency measures have you put in place?'

'The answer to the first part of your question has to be yes,' said Townsend. 'As far as the second part is concerned, the police have advised me not to divulge any details of what they have planned. But I can assure you that I have the backing of the prime minister and the Cabinet for this whole operation.'

Some groans could be heard around the room. Townsend turned and pointed to another raised hand.

'Will there be compensation for those of us who are unwilling to join this crazy scheme?'

That was one question Townsend had hoped someone would ask.

'I advise you to read your contracts carefully,' he said. 'You'll find in them exactly how much compensation you'll get if I have to close the paper down.'

A buzz began all around him.

'Are you threatening us?' asked the same journalist.

Townsend swung back to him and said fiercely, 'No, I'm not. But if you don't back me on this one, you'll be threatening the livelihood of everyone who works for the *Globe*.'

A sea of hands shot up. Townsend pointed to a woman standing at the back.

457

'How many other unions have agreed to back you?'

'None,' he replied. 'In fact, I'm expecting the rest of them to come out on strike immediately following this meeting.' He pointed to someone else, and continued to answer questions for over an hour. When he finally stepped off the table, it was clear that the journalists were divided on whether to go along with his plan, or to join the other print unions and opt for an all-out strike.

Later that evening, Bruce told him that the National Union of Journalists had issued a press release stating their intention to hold a meeting of all Townsend employees at ten o'clock the next morning, when they would decide what their response would be to his demands. An hour later Townsend issued his own press release.

Townsend spent a sleepless night wondering if he had embarked on a reckless gamble that would in time bring the whole of his empire to its knees. The only good news he had received in the past month was that his youngest son, Graham, who was in New York with Kate, had spoken his first word, and it wasn't 'newspaper'. Although he had attended the child's birth, he had been seen boarding a plane at Kennedy three hours later. He sometimes wondered if it was all worthwhile.

The following morning, after being driven to his office, he sat alone awaiting the outcome of the NUJ meeting. If they decided to call a strike, he knew he was beaten. Following his press release outlining his plans, Global Corp's shares had fallen four pence overnight, while those of Armstrong Communications, the obvious beneficiaries if there was to be any fall-out, had risen by two.

A few minutes after one o'clock, Bruce charged into his office without knocking. 'They backed you,' he said. Townsend looked up, the colour rushing back into his cheeks. 'But it was a damn close thing. They voted 343 to 301 to make the move. I think your threat to close the paper down if they didn't support you was what finally tilted it in your favour.'

Townsend rang Number Ten a few minutes later to warn the prime minister that there was likely to be a bloody confrontation which could last for several weeks. Mrs Thatcher promised her full backing. As the days passed, it quickly became clear that he hadn't exaggerated: journalists and printers alike had to be escorted in and out of the new complex by armed police; Townsend and Bruce Kelly were given twenty-four-hour protection after they received anonymous death threats.

That didn't turn out to be their only problem. Although the new site on the Isle of Dogs was unquestionably the most modern in the world, some of the journalists were complaining about the life they were expected to endure, pointing out that there was nothing in their contracts about having abuse, sometimes even stones, hurled at them by hundreds of trades unionists as they entered Fortress Townsend each morning and left at night.

The journalists' complaints didn't stop there. Once they were inside, few of them cared for the production-line atmosphere, the modern keyboards and computers which had replaced their old typewriters, and in particular the ban on alcohol on the premises. It might have been easier if they hadn't been stranded so far from their familiar Fleet Street watering holes.

Sixty-three journalists resigned in the first month after the move to the Isle of Dogs, and sales of the *Globe* continued to fall week after week. The picketing became more and more violent, and the financial director warned Townsend that if it went on for much longer, even the resources of Global Corp would be exhausted. He went on to ask, 'Is it worth risking bankruptcy to prove a point?'

Armstrong watched with delight from the other side of the Atlantic. The *Citizen* kept picking up sales, and his share price soared. But he knew that if Townsend was able to turn the tide he would have to return to London and quickly put a similar operation in motion.

But no one could have anticipated what would happen next.

31

4 MAY 1982

Gotcha!

On a Friday night in April 1982, while the British were fast asleep, Argentinian troops invaded the Falkland Islands. Mrs Thatcher recalled Parliament on a Saturday for the first time in forty years, and the House voted in favour of despatching a task force without delay to recapture the islands.

Alistair McAlvoy contacted Armstrong in New York and persuaded him that the *Citizen* should toe the Labour Party line – that a jingoistic response was not the solution, and that the United Nations should sort the problem out. Armstrong remained unconvinced until McAlvoy added, 'This is an irresponsible adventure which will cause the downfall of Thatcher. Believe me, the Labour Party will be back in power within weeks.'

Townsend, on the other hand, was in no doubt that he should back Mrs Thatcher and wrap the Union Jack round the *Globe*. 'Argy Bargy' was the headline on Monday's edition, with a cartoon depicting General Galtieri as a cut-throat pirate. As the task force headed out of Portsmouth and on towards the South Atlantic, sales of the *Globe* rose to 300,000 for the first time in months. During the first few days of skirmishing even Prince Andrew was praised for his 'gallant and heroic service' as a helicopter pilot. When the British submarine HMS *Conqueror* sunk the *General Belgrano* on 2 May, the *Globe* told the world 'BULLSEYE!', and sales rose again. By the time the

British forces had retaken Port Stanley, the *Globe* was selling over 500,000 copies a day, while sales of the *Citizen* had dipped slightly for the first time since Armstrong had become proprietor. When Peter Wakeham called Armstrong in New York to let him know the latest circulation figures, he jumped on the first flight back to London.

By the time the triumphant British troops were sailing back home, the *Globe* was selling over a million copies a day, while the *Citizen* had dipped below four million for the first time in twenty-five years. When the fleet sailed into Portsmouth, the *Globe* launched a campaign to raise money for the widows whose gallant husbands had made the ultimate sacrifice for their country. Day after day, Bruce Kelly ran stories of heroism and pride alongside pictures of widows and their children – all of whom turned out to be readers of the *Globe*.

◄◦►

On the day after the remembrance service at St Paul's Cathedral, Armstrong called a council of war on the ninth floor of Armstrong House. He was reminded quite unnecessarily by his circulation manager that most of the *Globe*'s gains had been at the expense of the *Citizen*. Alistair McAlvoy still advised him not to panic. After all, the *Globe* was a rag; the *Citizen* remained a serious radical newspaper with a great reputation. 'It would be foolish to lower our standards simply to appease an upstart whose paper is not fit to be wrapped around a self-respecting serving of fish and chips,' he said. 'Can you imagine the *Citizen* ever involving itself in a bingo competition? Another one of Kevin Rushcliffe's vulgar ideas.'

Armstrong made a note of the name. Bingo had put the *Globe*'s circulation up by a further 100,000 copies a day, and he could see no reason why it shouldn't do the same for the *Citizen*, But he also knew that the team McAlvoy had built up over the past ten years was still fully behind its editor.

'Look at the *Globe*'s front-page lead this morning,' Armstrong said in a last desperate effort to make his point. 'Why don't we get stories like that?'

'Because Freddie Starr wouldn't even make page eleven of the *Citizen*,' said McAlvoy. 'And in any case, who cares a damn about his eating habits? We get offered stories like that every day, but we don't get the handful of writs that usually go with them.' McAlvoy and his team left the meeting believing that they had persuaded the proprietor not to go down the same path as the *Globe*.

Their confidence lasted only until the next quarter's circulation figures landed on Armstrong's desk. Without consulting anyone, he picked up a phone and made an appointment to see Kevin Rushcliffe, the deputy editor of the *Globe*.

Rushcliffe arrived at Armstrong Communications later that afternoon. He couldn't have been in greater contrast to Alistair McAlvoy. He addressed Dick at their first meeting as if they were old friends, and talked in rapid-fire soundbites that the proprietor didn't begin to understand. Rushcliffe left him in no doubt as to the immediate changes he would make if he were given a chance to edit the *Citizen*. 'The editorials are too bland,' he said. 'Let them know what you feel in a couple of sentences. No words with more than three syllables, and no sentences with more than ten words. Don't ever try to influence them. Just make sure you demand what they already want.' An unusually subdued Armstrong explained to the young man that he would have to start as the deputy editor, 'Because McAlvoy's contract has another seven months to run.'

Armstrong nearly changed his mind about the new appointment when Rushcliffe told him the package he expected. He wouldn't have given way so easily had he known the terms of Rushcliffe's contract with the *Globe*, or the fact that Bruce Kelly had no intention of renewing it at the end of the year. Three days later he sent a memo down to McAlvoy telling him that he had appointed Kevin Rushcliffe as his deputy.

McAlvoy considered protesting at having the *Globe*'s deputy editor foisted upon him, until his wife pointed out that he was due for retirement in seven months on a full pension, and that this was not the time to sacrifice his job on the altar of principle. When he arrived in the office the next morning, McAlvoy simply ignored his new deputy and his idea-a-minute for tomorrow's front page.

When the *Globe* put a nude on page three and sold two million copies for the first time, McAlvoy declared at morning conference, 'Over my dead body.' No one felt able to point out that two or three of his best reporters had recently left the *Citizen* to join the *Globe*, while only Rushcliffe had made the journey in the opposite direction.

As Armstrong continued to spend a great deal of his time preparing for a takeover battle in New York, he reluctantly continued to accept McAlvoy's judgement, not least because he didn't want to sack his most experienced editor only weeks before a general election.

When Margaret Thatcher was returned to the Commons with a majority of 144, the *Globe* claimed the victory as theirs, and declared that this would surely hasten the downfall of the *Citizen*. Several commentators were quick to point out the irony of this particular statement.

When Armstrong returned to England the following week for the monthly board meeting, Sir Paul raised the subject of the fall in the paper's circulation figures.

'While the *Globe*'s continue to rise every month,' Peter Wakeham interjected from the other end of the table.

'So what are we going to do about it?' asked the chairman, turning to face his chief executive.

'I have already put some plans in hand,' said Armstrong.

'Are we to be privy to these plans?' asked Sir Paul.

'I will brief the board fully at our next meeting,' said Armstrong.

Sir Paul didn't look satisfied, but made no further comment.

The next day, Armstrong called for McAlvoy without bothering to consult anyone on the board. When the editor of the *Citizen* entered the proprietor's office, Armstrong didn't stand to greet him, and made no suggestion that he should take a seat.

'I'm sure you've worked out why I've asked to see you,' he said.

'No, Dick, I haven't the slightest idea,' replied McAlvoy innocently.

'Well, I've just seen the JICNAR figures for the past month. If we continue at this rate, the *Globe* will be selling more copies than we are by the end of the year.'

'And you will still be the proprietor of a great national newspaper, while Townsend will still be publishing a rag.'

'That may well be the case. But I have a board and shareholders to consider.'

McAlvoy couldn't recall Armstrong ever mentioning a board or shareholders in the past. The last refuge of a proprietor, he was about to say. Then he recalled his lawyer's warning that his contract still had five months to run, and that he would be unwise to provoke Armstrong.

'I assume you've seen the *Globe*'s headline this morning?' said Armstrong, holding up his rival's paper.

'Yes, of course I have,' said McAlvoy, glancing at the thick, bold print: 'Top Pop Star Named in Drugs Scandal'.

'And we led on "Extra Benefits for Nurses".'

'Our readers love nurses,' said McAlvoy.

'Our readers may well love nurses,' said Armstrong, flicking through the paper, 'but in case you haven't noticed, the *Globe* had the same story on page seven. It's fairly clear to me, even if it isn't to you, that most of our readers are more interested in pop stars and drug scandals.'

'The pop star in question,' countered McAlvoy, 'has never had a record in the top hundred, and was smoking a joint in the privacy of his own home. If anyone had ever heard of him, the *Globe* would have put his name in the headline. I have a filing cabinet full of such rubbish, but I don't insult our readers by publishing it.'

'Then perhaps it's time you did,' said Armstrong, his voice rising with every word. 'Let's start challenging the *Globe* on its own ground for a change. Maybe if we did that, I wouldn't be looking for a new editor.'

McAlvoy was momentarily stunned. 'Am I to assume from this outburst that I'm fired?' he asked eventually.

'At last I've got through to you,' said Armstrong. 'Yes, you're fired. The name of the new editor will be announced on Monday. See that your desk is cleared by this evening.'

'Can I assume that after ten years as editor of this paper I will receive my full pension?'

'You will receive no more and no less than you are entitled to,' shouted Armstrong. 'Now get out of my office.' He glared at McAlvoy, waiting for him to unleash one of the tirades for which he was so famous, but the sacked editor simply turned and left without uttering another word, closing the door quietly behind him.

Armstrong slipped into the adjoining room, towelled himself down and changed into a fresh shirt. It was exactly the same colour as the previous one, so no one would notice.

Once McAlvoy was back at his desk, he quickly briefed a handful of his closest associates on the outcome of his meeting with Armstrong and on what he planned to do. A few minutes later he took the chair at the afternoon conference for the last time. He looked down the list of stories vying for the front page.

'I'm putting down a marker for tomorrow's splash, Alistair,' said a voice. McAlvoy looked up at his political editor.

'What do you have in mind, Campbell?' he asked.

'A Labour councillor in Lambeth has gone on hunger strike to highlight the unfairness of the government's housing policy. She's black and unemployed.'

'Sounds good to me,' said McAlvoy. 'Anyone else pushing for the lead?' No one spoke as he looked slowly round the room. His eyes finally rested on Kevin Rushcliffe, to whom he hadn't addressed a word for over a month.

'How about you, Kevin?'

The deputy editor looked up from his place in the corner of the room and blinked, unable to believe that the editor was addressing him. 'Well, I've been following up a lead on the foreign secretary's private life for some weeks, but I'm finding it hard to make the story stand up.'

'Why don't you knock out three hundred words on the

subject, and we'll let the lawyers decide if we can get away with it.'

Some of the older hands began to shuffle in their chairs.

'And what happened to that story about the architect?' asked McAlvoy, still addressing his deputy editor.

'You spiked it,' said Rushcliffe, looking surprised.

'I thought it was a bit dull. Can't you spice it up a little?'

'If that's what you want,' said Rushcliffe, looking even more surprised.

As McAlvoy never had a drink until he had read the first edition from cover to cover, one or two of those present wondered if he was feeling well.

'Right, that's settled then. Kevin gets the front page and Campbell gets the second lead.' He paused. 'And as I'm taking my wife to see Pavarotti tonight, I'll be leaving the paper in Kevin's hands. Do you feel comfortable with that?' he asked, turning to face his deputy.

'Of course,' said Rushcliffe, looking delighted that he was at last being treated as an equal.

'Then that's settled,' said McAlvoy. 'Let's all get back to work, shall we?'

As the journalists began to drift out of the editor's office muttering to each other, Rushcliffe came across to McAlvoy's desk and thanked him. 'Not at all,' said the editor. 'You know this could be your big chance, Kevin. I'm sure you're aware that I saw the proprietor earlier this afternoon, and he told me that he'd like to see the paper challenging the *Globe* on its own ground. In fact, those were his exact words. So when he reads the *Citizen* tomorrow, be sure it has your stamp on it. I won't be sitting in this chair forever, you know.'

'I'll do my best,' promised Rushcliffe as he left the office. If he'd stayed a moment longer, he would have been able to help the editor clear his desk.

Later that afternoon McAlvoy made his way slowly out of the building, stopping to speak to every member of staff he bumped into. He told all of them how much he and his wife were looking forward to seeing Pavarotti, and when they asked who would be bringing out the paper that night, he told them, even the doorman. Indeed, he double-checked the time with the doorman before he headed off towards the nearest underground station, aware that his company car would already have been clamped.

Kevin Rushcliffe tried to concentrate on writing his front-page story, but he was constantly interrupted by a stream of people who wanted his input for their copy. He cleared several pages he just didn't have time to check carefully. When he finally handed his piece in, the print room was complaining about running late, and he was relieved when the first edition came off the stone a few minutes before eleven.

◄○►

Armstrong picked up the phone by his bed a couple of hours later to have the front page read out to him by Stephen Hallet. 'Why the hell didn't you stop it?' he demanded.

'I didn't see it until the first edition hit the streets,' replied Stephen. 'By the time the second edition came off the stone, we were leading on a Lambeth councillor who's gone on a hunger strike. She's black and . . .'

'I don't give a damn what colour she is,' shouted Armstrong. 'What the hell did McAlvoy imagine he was up to?'

'McAlvoy didn't edit the paper last night.'

'Then who in heaven's name did?'

'Kevin Rushcliffe,' the lawyer replied.

Armstrong didn't get back to sleep that night. Nor did most of Fleet Street, who were frantically trying to contact the foreign secretary and/or the actress/model. By the time their final editions came out, most of them had established that he had never actually met Miss Soda Water Syphon 1983.

The story was so widely discussed the following morning that few people spotted a little item tucked away on page seven of the *Citizen* under the headline 'Bricks but no Mortarboard', which claimed that one of Britain's leading architects was designing council houses which kept falling down. A hand-delivered letter from his equally distinguished solicitor pointed out that Sir Angus had never designed a council house in his life. The solicitor enclosed a copy of the apology he expected to be published on the front page of the following day's paper, and a note stating the size of the donation that should be sent to the architect's favourite charity.

On the food pages a leading restaurant was accused of poisoning a customer a day, while the travel section named the tour company alleged to have left the most holiday-makers stranded in Spain without a hotel room. On the back page the England football manager was said to have . . .

McAlvoy made it clear to everyone who called him at home that morning that he had been sacked by Armstrong the previous day and told to clear his desk immediately. He had left Armstrong House at 4.19, leaving the deputy editor in charge. 'That's Rushcliffe with an e,' he added helpfully.

Every member of staff who was approached confirmed McAlvoy's story.

Stephen Hallet rang Armstrong five times during the day, telling him on every occasion that he had received a writ, and recommending that each of them be settled, and settled quickly.

The *Globe* reported on page two the sad departure of Alistair McAlvoy from the *Citizen* after a decade's devoted service. They went on to describe him as the doyen of Fleet Street editors, who would be sadly missed by all true professionals.

◄◇►

When the *Globe* sold three million copies for the first time, Townsend held a party to celebrate. This time most of the leading politicians and media personalities did attend – despite Armstrong's rival party to celebrate the *Citizen*'s eightieth anniversary.

'Well, at least he got the date right this time,' said Townsend.

'Talking about dates,' said Bruce, 'when can I hope to return to Australia? I don't suppose you've noticed, but I haven't been home for five years.'

'You don't go home until you've removed the words "Britain's Best-Selling Daily" from the *Citizen*'s masthead,' replied Townsend.

Bruce Kelly didn't book a flight to Sydney for another fifteen months, when the audit commission announced that the *Globe*'s daily sales for the previous month had averaged 3,612,000 against the *Citizen*'s 3,610,000. The *Globe*'s banner headline the following morning was 'GET 'EM OFF', above a picture of the twenty-two-stone Armstrong in boxer shorts.

When the *Citizen*'s boast remained firmly in place, the *Globe* informed 'the world's most discerning readers' that the proprietor of the *Citizen* still hadn't honoured his debt of £100,000 from his lost bet, and was 'not only a bad loser, but also a welcher'.

Armstrong sued Townsend for libel the following day. Even *The Times* felt this was worthy of comment: 'Only the lawyers will benefit,' it concluded.

The case reached the High Court eighteen months later, and lasted for over three weeks, regularly making every front page except that of the *Independent*. Mr Michael Beloff QC, on behalf of the *Globe*, argued that the official audit figures proved his client's case. Mr Anthony Grabiner QC pointed out for the *Citizen* that the audited figures did not include the sales of the *Scottish Citizen*, which when combined with those of the *Daily* kept its circulation comfortably ahead of the *Globe*.

The jury retired for five hours to consider their verdict, and by a majority of ten to two came down in favour of Armstrong. When the judge asked what damages they were recommending, the foreman stood up and declared without hesitation, 'Twelve pence, m'Lud,' – the price of a copy of the *Citizen*.

The judge told leading counsel that in the circumstances he felt both sides should pay their own costs, which were conservatively estimated at one million pounds each. Counsel nodded their acquiescence and began gathering up their briefs.

The following day the *Financial Times*, in a long article on the two press barons, predicted that one of them must eventually cause the other's downfall. However, the reporter went on to reveal that the trial had helped to increase the sales of both papers, which in the case of the *Globe* had passed four million copies for the first time.

Next day both groups' shares rose by a penny.

◄○►

While Armstrong was reading about himself in the acres of column inches devoted to the trial, Townsend was concentrating on an article in the *New York Times* which had been faxed over to him by Tom Spencer.

Although he had never heard of Lloyd Summers, or the art gallery that was coming to the end of its lease, when he reached the last line of the fax he realised why Tom had written boldly across the top: FOR IMMEDIATE ATTENTION.

After he had read the piece for a second time, Townsend asked Heather to get Tom on the line, and after she had done that, to book him onto the earliest possible flight to New York.

Tom wasn't surprised that his client rang back within minutes of the fax being placed on his desk. After all, he had been looking for an opportunity to get his hands on a substantial shareholding in the *New York Star* for over a decade.

Townsend listened intently as Tom told him everything he had found out about Mr Lloyd Summers and why his art gallery was looking for new premises. When he had exhausted all his questions, he instructed his lawyer to arrange a meeting with Summers as quickly as possible. 'I'll be flying to New York tomorrow morning,' he added.

'No need for you to come all this way, Keith. I can always see Summers on your behalf.'

'No,' Townsend replied. 'With the *Star* it's personal. I want to close this particular deal myself.'

'Keith, you do realise that if you succeed you'll have to become an American citizen,' said Tom.

'As I've told you many times, Tom, never.'

He put the phone down and jotted some notes on a pad. Once he had worked out how much he was willing to offer, he picked up the receiver and asked Heather what time his flight was. If Armstrong wasn't on the same plane, he could close a deal with Summers before anyone realised that a lease on an art gallery in SoHo could hold the key to his becoming the owner of the *New York Star*.

—◦—

'My bet is that Townsend will be on the first flight to New York,' said Armstrong, once Russell Critchley had finished reading the article out to him.

'Then you'd better be on the same plane,' said his New York attorney, sitting on the end of his bed.

'No way,' said Armstrong. 'Why alert the bastard to the fact that we know as much as he does? No, my best bet is to make a move even before his plane touches down. Set up an appointment to see Summers as soon as possible.'

'I doubt if the gallery opens much before ten.'

'Then make sure you're outside waiting for him at five to ten.'

'How much leeway have I got?'

'Give him anything he wants,' said Armstrong. 'Even offer to buy him a new gallery. But whatever you do, don't let Townsend get anywhere near him, because if we can convince Summers to back us, that will open the door to his mother.'

'Right,' said Critchley, pulling on a sock. 'I'd better get moving.'

'Just make sure you're outside the gallery before it opens,' said Armstrong. He paused. 'And if Townsend's lawyer gets there before you, run him over.'

Critchley would have laughed, but he wasn't entirely sure that his client was joking.

—◦—

Tom was waiting outside the customs hall when his client came through the swing doors.

'The news isn't good, Keith,' were his first words after they had shaken hands.

'What do you mean?' said Townsend as they headed towards

the exit. 'Armstrong couldn't have got to New York ahead of me, because I know he was still at his desk at the *Citizen* when I flew out of Heathrow.'

'He may still be at his desk right now, for all I know,' said Tom, 'but Russell Critchley, his New York attorney, had an appointment with Summers earlier this morning.'

Townsend stopped in the middle of the road, ignoring the screeching of brakes and the immediate cacophony of taxi horns.

'Did they sign a deal?'

'I have no idea,' said Tom. 'All I can tell you is that when I got into my office, Summers's secretary had left a message on my machine saying that your appointment had been cancelled.'

'Damn. Then our first stop has to be the gallery,' said Townsend, finally stepping onto the sidewalk. 'They can't have signed a contract yet. Damn. Damn,' he repeated. 'I should have let you see him in the first place.'

—◆—

'He's agreed to pledge you his 5 per cent share in the *Star* if you'll put up the money for a new gallery,' said Critchley.

'And what's that going to cost me?' asked Armstrong, putting down his fork.

'He hasn't found the right building yet, but he thinks around three million.'

'How much?'

'You would of course own the lease on the building . . .'

'Of course.'

'. . . and as the gallery is registered as a non-profit-making charity, there are some tax advantages.'

There was a long silence on the other end of the line before Armstrong said, 'So how did you leave it?'

'When he reminded me for the third time that he had an appointment with Townsend later this morning, I said yes, subject to contract.'

'Did you sign anything?'

'No. I explained that you were on your way over from London, and I didn't have the authority to do so.'

'Good. Then we still have a little time to . . .'

'I doubt it,' said Russell. 'Summers knows only too well that he's got you by the balls.'

'It's when people think they've got me by the balls,' said Armstrong, 'that I most enjoy screwing them.'

32

WALL STREET JOURNAL

12 SEPTEMBER 1986

New York Stocks Dive Record 86.61 Points

'Ladies and gentlemen,' Armstrong began. 'I have called this press conference to announce that I informed the Securities Exchange Commission this morning that it is my intention to make an official takeover bid for the *New York Star*. I am delighted to report that a major shareholder in the paper, Mrs Nancy Summers, has sold her stock to Armstrong Communications at a price of $4.10 per share.'

Although some journalists continued to write down Armstrong's every word, this piece of news had been flagged up in most papers for over a week. Most of the journalists' pencils remained poised as they waited for the real news.

'But I am especially proud to announce today,' continued Armstrong, 'that Mr Lloyd Summers, the son of Mrs Summers and the director of the foundation which bears her name, has also pledged the 5 per cent of the company held in trust to my cause.

'It will come as no surprise to you that it is my intention to continue to support the outstanding work the Summers Foundation does in promoting the careers of young artists and sculptors who would not normally be given the chance to exhibit in a major gallery. I have, as many of you will know, had a lifelong involvement with the arts, in particular with young artists.' Not one journalist present could remember a single artistic event Armstrong had ever attended, let alone supported. Most of the pencils remained poised.

'With Mr Summers's backing, I am now in control of 19 per cent of the *Star*'s stock, and I look forward in the near future to becoming the majority shareholder and taking over as chairman of the paper at the AGM next month.'

Armstrong looked up from the statement that had been prepared for him by Russell Critchley, and smiled at the sea of faces. 'I shall now be happy to answer your questions.'

Russell felt that Dick handled the first few questions well, but then he pointed to a woman seated in the third row.

'Janet Brewer, *Washington Post*. Mr Armstrong, may I ask for your reaction to the press release issued this morning by Keith Townsend?'

'I never read Mr Townsend's press releases,' said Armstrong. 'They're about as accurate as his newspapers.'

'Then allow me to enlighten you,' she said, looking down at a sheet of paper. 'It seems that Mr Townsend has the backing of the bankers J. P. Grenville, who have pledged 11 per cent of their portfolio stock in support of his bid to take over the *Star*. With his own shareholding, that gives him over 15 per cent.'

Armstrong looked straight at her and said, 'As chairman of the *Star*, I shall look forward to welcoming Mr Townsend to next month's AGM – as a minority shareholder.'

This time the pencils wrote down his every word.

─◦─

Sitting in his newly acquired apartment on the thirty-seventh floor of Trump Tower, Armstrong read over Townsend's press release. He chuckled when he came to the paragraph in which Townsend praised the work of the Summers Foundation. 'Too late,' he said out loud. 'That 5 per cent belongs to me.'

He immediately gave instructions to his brokers to buy up any *Star* stock that came on the market, whatever the price. The shares rocketed as it became clear that Townsend had given the same order. Some financial analysts suggested that because of 'a strong personal animosity', both men were paying well above the real value.

For the next four weeks Armstrong and Townsend, accompanied by a battery of lawyers and accountants, spent every waking hour in planes, trains and cars as they zigzagged across America, trying to convince banks and institutions, trusts and even the occasional wealthy widow to support them in the battle to take over the *Star*.

The chairman of the paper, Cornelius J. Adams IV, announced that he would hand over the reins of power at the AGM to whichever contender controlled 51 per cent of the shares. With only two weeks to go before the *Star*'s AGM, the financial editors were still unable to agree on who had the largest shareholding in the company. Townsend announced that he now controlled 46 per cent of the stock, while Armstrong claimed that he had 41 per cent. The analysts therefore concluded that whichever one of them was able to capture the 10 per cent held by the Applebaum Corporation must surely carry the day.

Vic Applebaum was determined to enjoy his fifteen minutes of fame, and declared to anyone who cared to listen that it was his intention to see both would-be proprietors before he came to a final decision. He chose the Tuesday before the AGM to conduct the interviews which would decide on whom he should bestow his favour.

The two rivals' lawyers met on neutral ground, and agreed that Armstrong should be allowed to see Applebaum first, which Tom Spencer assured his client was a tactical error. Townsend agreed, until Armstrong emerged from the meeting clutching the share certificates which proved he was in possession of Applebaum's 10 per cent.

'How did he manage that?' Townsend asked in disbelief.

Tom didn't have an answer until he read the first edition of the *New York Times* at breakfast the following morning. Its media correspondent informed readers on the front page that Armstrong had not spent a great deal of time explaining to Mr

Applebaum how he would manage the *Star*, but had concentrated more on telling him in Yiddish that he had never really recovered from losing his entire family in the Holocaust, and that he had ended their meeting by disclosing that the proudest moment in his life had been when the prime minister of Israel had appointed him as the country's roving ambassador to the USSR, with a special brief to assist Russian Jews who wished to emigrate to Israel. At this point Applebaum apparently broke down in tears, handed over the stock and refused to see Townsend.

Armstrong announced that as he now controlled 51 per cent of the company, he was therefore the new owner of the *New York Star*. The *Wall Street Journal* concurred, declaring that the *Star*'s AGM would be nothing more than an anointing ceremony. But it added a postscript pointing out that Keith Townsend shouldn't be too depressed about having lost the paper to his great rival. Because of the huge rise in the share price, he would make a profit in excess of $20 million.

The *New York Times* arts section reminded its readers that the Summers Foundation would be opening an avant-garde exhibition on Thursday evening. After the press barons' claims of support for Lloyd Summers and the foundation's work, it said, it would be interesting to see if either of them bothered to turn up.

Tom Spencer advised Townsend that it might be wise to drop in for a few minutes, as Armstrong was certain to be there, and you never knew what you might pick up on such occasions.

◄○►

Townsend regretted his decision to attend the exhibition moments after he arrived. He circled the room once, glanced at the selection of paintings chosen by the trustees and concluded that they were, without exception, what Kate would have described as 'pretentious rubbish'. He decided to leave as quickly as possible. He had successfully negotiated a route to the door when Summers tapped a microphone and called for silence. The director then proceeded to 'say a few words'.

Townsend checked his watch. When he looked up he saw Armstrong, firmly clutching a catalogue, standing next to Summers and beaming at the assembled guests.

Summers began by saying how sad he was that his mother was unable to be with them because of a prolonged illness, and delivered a lengthy disquisition extolling the virtues of the artists whose works he had selected. He declared twenty minutes later how delighted he was that the *New York Star*'s new chairman had been able to find the time to attend 'one of our little *soirées*'.

There was a smattering of applause, hampered by the holding of wine glasses, and Armstrong beamed once again. Townsend assumed that Summers had come to the end of his speech and turned to leave, but he added, 'Unhappily, this will be the last exhibition to be held at this venue. As I'm sure you all know, our lease is coming to an end in December.' A sigh went up around the room, but Summers raised his hands and said, 'Fear not, my friends. I do believe I have, after a long search, found the perfect site to house the foundation. I hope that we will all meet there for our next exhibition.'

'Though only one or two of us really know why that particular site was chosen,' someone murmured *sotto voce* behind Townsend. He glanced round to see a slim woman who must have been in her mid-thirties, with short-cropped auburn hair and wearing a white blouse and a floral-patterned skirt. The little label on her blouse announced that she was Ms Angela Humphries, deputy director.

'And it would be a wonderful start,' continued Summers, 'if the first exhibition in our new building were to be opened by the *Star*'s next chairman, who has so generously pledged his continued support for the foundation.'

Armstrong beamed and nodded.

'Not if he's got any sense, he won't,' said the woman behind Townsend. He took a pace back so that he was standing next to Ms Angela Humphries, who was sipping a glass of Spanish champagne.

'Thank you, my dear friends,' said Summers. 'Now, do please continue to enjoy the exhibition.' There followed another round of applause, after which Armstrong stepped forward and shook the director warmly by the hand. Summers began moving among the guests, introducing Armstrong to those he considered important.

Townsend turned to face Angela Humphries as she finished her drink. He quickly grabbed a bottle of Spanish champagne from the table behind them and refilled her glass.

'Thank you,' she said, looking at him for the first time. 'As you can see, I'm Angela Humphries. Who are you?'

'I'm from out of town.' He hesitated. 'Just visiting New York on a business trip.'

Angela took a sip before asking, 'What sort of business?'

'I'm in transport, actually. Mainly planes and haulage. Though I do own a couple of coalmines.'

'Most of these would be better off down a coalmine,' said Angela, her free arm gesturing towards the pictures.

'I couldn't agree more,' said Townsend.

'Then what made you come in the first place?'

'I was on my own in New York and read about the exhibition in the *Times*,' he replied.

'So, what sort of art do you like then?' she asked.

Townsend avoided saying 'Boyd, Nolan and Williams,' who filled the walls of his house at Darling Point, and told her 'Bonnard, Camoir and Vuillard,' who Kate had been collecting for several years.

'Now they really could paint,' Angela said. 'If you admire them, I can think of several exhibitions that *would* have been worth giving up an evening for.'

'That's fine if you know where to look, but when you're a stranger and on your own . . .'

She raised an eyebrow. 'Are you married?'

'No,' he replied, hoping she believed him. 'And you?'

'Divorced,' she said. 'I used to be married to an artist who was convinced he had a talent second only to Bellini's.'

'And how good was he really?' asked Townsend.

'He was rejected for this exhibition,' she replied, 'which may give you a clue.'

Townsend laughed. People had begun steadily drifting towards the exit, and Armstrong and Summers were now only a few paces away. As Townsend poured Angela another glass of champagne, Armstrong suddenly came face to face with him. The two men stared at each other for a moment, before Armstrong grabbed Summers by the arm and dragged him quickly back to the centre of the room.

'You notice he didn't want to introduce me to the new chairman,' Angela said wistfully.

Townsend didn't bother to explain that he thought it was more likely that Armstrong didn't want him to meet the director.

'Nice to have met you, Mr . . .'

'Are you doing anything for dinner?'

She hesitated for a moment. 'No,' she said. 'I had nothing planned, but I do have an early start tomorrow.'

'So do I,' said Townsend. 'Why don't we have a quick bite to eat?'

'OK. Just give me a minute to get my coat, and I'll be with you.'

As she walked off in the direction of the cloakroom, Townsend glanced around the room. Armstrong, with Summers in tow, was now surrounded by a crowd of admirers. Townsend didn't need to be any closer to know that he would be telling them all about his exciting plans for the future of the foundation.

A moment later Angela returned, wearing a heavy winter coat that stopped only inches from the ground. 'Where would you like to eat?' Townsend asked as they began to climb the wide staircase that led from the basement gallery up to the street.

'All the halfway decent restaurants will already be booked up by this time on a Thursday night,' said Angela. 'Where are you staying?'

'The Carlyle.'

'I've never eaten there. It might be fun,' she said, as he held open the door for her. When they stepped out onto the sidewalk they were greeted by an icy New York gale, and he almost had to hold her up.

The driver of Mr Townsend's waiting BMW was surprised to see him flag down a taxi, and even more surprised when he saw the girl he was with. Frankly, he wouldn't have thought she was Mr Townsend's type. He turned on the ignition and trailed the cab back to the Carlyle, then watched them get out on Madison and disappear through the revolving door into the hotel.

Townsend guided Angela straight to the dining room on the first floor, hoping that the maître d' wouldn't remember his name.

'Good evening, sir,' he said. 'Have you booked a table?'

'No,' Townsend replied. 'But I'm resident in the hotel.'

The head waiter frowned. 'I'm sorry, sir, but I won't be able to fit you in for at least another thirty minutes. You could of course take advantage of room service, if you wish.'

'No, we'll wait at the bar,' said Townsend.

'I really do have an early appointment tomorrow,' Angela said. 'And I can't afford to be late for it.'

'Shall we go in search of a restaurant?'

'I'm quite happy to eat in your room, but I'll have to be away by eleven.'

'Suits me,' said Townsend. He turned back to the maître d' and said, 'We'll have dinner in my room.'

He gave a slight bow. 'I'll have someone sent up immediately. What room number is it, sir?'

'712,' said Townsend. He guided Angela back out of the restaurant. As they walked down the corridor they passed a room in which Bobby Schultz was playing.

'Now he really does have talent,' Angela said as they headed towards the elevator. Townsend nodded and smiled. They joined a group of guests just before the doors closed, and he pressed the button for the seventh floor. When they stepped out she gave him a nervous smile. He wanted to tell her that it wasn't her body he was interested in.

Townsend slipped his pass-key into the lock and pushed open the door to let Angela in. He was relieved to see the complimentary bottle of champagne, which he hadn't bothered to open, was still in its place on the centre table. She took off her coat and placed it over the nearest chair as he removed the gold wrapping from the neck of the bottle, then eased the cork out and filled two glasses up to the brim.

'I mustn't have too much,' she said. 'I drank quite a lot at the gallery.' Townsend raised his glass just as there was a knock on the door. A waiter appeared holding a menu, a pad and a pencil.

'Dover sole and a green salad will suit me just fine,' Angela said, without looking at the proffered menu.

'On or off the bone, madam?' asked the waiter.

'Off, please.'

'Why don't you make that two?' said Townsend. He then took his time selecting a couple of bottles of French wine, ignoring his favourite Australian chardonnay.

Once they were both seated, Angela began to talk about other artists who were exhibiting in New York, and her enthusiasm and knowledge of her subject almost made Townsend forget why he had invited her to dinner in the first place. As they waited for the meal to arrive, he slowly guided the conversation round to her work at the gallery. He agreed with her judgement of the current exhibition, and asked why she, as the deputy director, hadn't done something about it.

'A grand title that carries little or no influence,' she said with a sigh as Townsend refilled her empty glass.

'So Summers makes all the decisions?'

'He certainly does. I wouldn't waste the foundation's money on that pseudo-intellectual rubbish. There's so much real talent out there, if only someone would take the trouble to go and look for it.'

'The exhibition was well hung,' said Townsend, trying to push her an extra yard.

'Well hung?' she said in a tone of disbelief. 'I'm not discussing the hanging – or the lighting, or the framing, for that matter. I was referring to the pictures. In any case, there's only one thing in that gallery that ought to be hung.'

There was a knock on the door. Townsend rose from his chair and stood aside to allow the waiter to enter, pushing a laden trolley. He set up a table in the centre of the room and laid out dinner for two, explaining that the fish was in a warming drawer below. Townsend signed the check and handed him a ten-dollar bill. 'Shall I come back and clear up later, sir?' the waiter asked politely. He received a slight but firm shake of the head.

Angela was already toying with her salad when Townsend took the seat opposite her. He uncorked the chardonnay and filled both their glasses. 'So you feel that Summers possibly spent more than was strictly necessary on the exhibition?' he prompted.

'More than was strictly necessary?' said Angela, as she tasted the white wine. 'He fritters away over a million dollars of the foundation's money every year. We have nothing to show for it other than a few parties, the sole purpose of which is to boost his ego.'

'How does he manage to get through a million a year?' asked Townsend, pretending to concentrate on his salad.

'Well, take tonight's exhibition. That cost the foundation a quarter of a million for a start. Then there's his expense account, which runs second only to Ed Koch's.'

'So how does he get away with it?' asked Townsend, topping up her glass of wine. He hoped she hadn't noticed he'd hardly touched his.

'Because there's no one to check on what he's up to,' said Angela. 'The foundation is controlled by his mother, who holds the purse strings – until the AGM, at least.'

'Mrs Summers?' prompted Townsend, determined to keep the flow going.

'No less,' said Angela.

'Then why doesn't she do something about it?'

'How can she? The poor woman's been bedridden for the past two years, and the one person who visits her – daily, I might add – is none other than her devoted only son.'

'I've got a feeling that could change as soon as Armstrong takes over.'

'Why do you say that? Do you know him?'

'No,' said Townsend quickly, trying to recover from his mistake. 'But everything I've read about him would suggest that he doesn't care much for hangers-on.'

'I only hope that's right,' said Angela, pouring herself another glass of wine, 'because that might give me a chance to show him what I could do for the foundation.'

'Perhaps that's why Summers never let Armstrong out of his sight this evening.'

'He didn't even introduce him to me,' said Angela, 'as I'm sure you noticed. Lloyd isn't going to give up his lifestyle without a fight, that's for sure.' She stuck her fork into a slice of courgette. 'And if he can get Armstrong to sign the lease on the new premises before the AGM, there will be no reason for him to do so. This wine really is exceptional,' she said, putting down her empty glass. Townsend filled it again, and uncorked the second bottle.

'Are you trying to get me drunk?' she asked, laughing.

'The thought hadn't even crossed my mind,' said Townsend. He rose from his place, removed two plates from the warming drawer and set them on the table. 'Tell me,' he said, 'are you looking forward to moving?'

'Moving?' she said, as she put some Hollandaise sauce on the side of her plate.

'To your new premises,' said Townsend. 'It sounds as if Lloyd has found the perfect location.'

'Perfect?' she repeated. 'At $3 million it should be perfect. But perfect for whom?' she said, picking up her knife and fork.

'Still, as he explained,' said Townsend, 'you weren't exactly left with a lot of choice.'

'No, what you mean is that the board weren't left with a lot of choice, because he told them there wasn't an alternative.'

'But the lease on the present building was coming to an end, wasn't it?' said Townsend.

'What he didn't tell you in his speech was that the owner would have been quite happy to renew the lease for another ten years with no rent increase,' said Angela, picking up her wine glass. 'I really shouldn't have any more, but after that rubbish they serve at the gallery, this is a real treat.'

'Then why didn't he?' asked Townsend.

'Why didn't he what?'

'Renew the lease.'

'Because he found another building that just happens to have a penthouse apartment thrown in,' she said, putting down her wine glass and concentrating once again on her fish.

'But he has every right to live on the premises,' said Townsend. 'He's the director, after all.'

'True, but that doesn't give him the right to have a separate lease on the apartment, so that when he finally decides to retire they won't be able to get rid of him without paying vast compensation. He's got it all worked out.' She was beginning to slur her words.

'How do you know all this?'

'We once shared a lover,' she said rather sadly.

Townsend quickly refilled her glass. 'So where is this building?'

'Why are you so keen to know all about the new building?' she said, sounding suspicious for the first time.

'I'd like to look you up when I'm next in New York,' he replied without missing a beat.

Angela put her knife and fork down on the plate, pushed her chair back and said, 'You don't have any brandy, do you? Just a small one, to warm me up before I face the blizzard on my way home.'

'I'm sure I do,' said Townsend. He walked over to the fridge, extracted four miniature brandies of different origins and poured them all into a large goblet.

'Won't you join me?' she asked.

'No, thank you. I haven't quite finished my wine,' he said,

picking up his first glass, which was almost untouched. 'And more important, I don't have to face the blizzard. Tell me, how did you become deputy director?'

'After five deputies had resigned in four years, I think I must have been the only person who applied.'

'I'm surprised he bothers with a deputy.'

'He has to.' She took a sip of brandy. 'It's in the statutes.'

'But you must be well qualified to have been offered the job,' he said, quickly changing the subject.

'I studied the history of art at Yale, and did my PhD on the Renaissance 1527–1590 at the Accademia in Venice.'

'After Caravaggio, Luini and Michelangelo, that lot must be a bit of a come-down,' said Townsend.

'I wouldn't mind even that, but I've been deputy director for nearly two years and haven't been allowed to mount one show. If only he would give me the chance, I could put on an exhibition the foundation could be proud of, at about a tenth of the cost of this current show.' She took another sip of brandy.

'If you feel that strongly, I'm surprised you stick around,' said Townsend.

'I won't for much longer,' she said. 'If I can't convince Armstrong to change the gallery's policy, I'm going to resign. But as Lloyd seems to be leading him around on a leash, I doubt if I'll still be around when they open the next exhibition.' She paused, and took a sip of brandy. 'I haven't even told my mother that,' she admitted. 'But then, sometimes it's easier to talk to strangers.' She took another sip. 'You're not in the art world, are you?'

'No, as I said, I'm in transport and coalmines.'

'So what do you actually do? Drive or dig?' She stared across at him, drained her glass and tried again. 'What I mean is . . .'

'Yes?' said Townsend.

'To start with . . . what do you transport, and to where?' She picked up her glass, paused for a moment, then slowly slid off her chair onto the carpet, mumbling something about fossil fuels in Renaissance Rome. Within a few seconds she was curled up on the floor, purring like a contented cat. Townsend picked her up gently and carried her through to the bedroom. He pulled back the top sheet, laid her down on the bed and covered her slight body with a blanket. He had to admire her for lasting so long; he doubted if she weighed more than eight stone.

He returned to the sitting room, closing the bedroom door quietly behind him, and set about looking for the statute book of the *New York Star*. Once he had found the thin red volume tucked in the bottom of his briefcase, he sat on the sofa and began to read slowly through the company statutes. He had reached page forty-seven before he nodded off.

◄o►

Armstrong couldn't think of a good excuse for turning Summers down when he suggested they should have dinner together after the exhibition. He was relieved that his lawyer hadn't gone home. 'You'll join us, won't you, Russell?' he boomed at his attorney, making it sound more like a command than an invitation.

Armstrong had already expressed privately to Russell his thoughts on the exhibition, which he had just managed to conceal from Summers. He had been trying to avoid a meeting from the moment Summers announced he'd found the perfect site for the foundation to move into. But Russell had warned him that Summers was becoming impatient, and had even begun threatening, 'Don't forget, I still have an alternative.'

Armstrong had to admit that the restaurant Summers had chosen was quite exceptional, but over the past month he had become accustomed to the man's extravagant tastes. After the main course had been cleared away, Summers reiterated how important it was to sign the lease for the new building as quickly as possible, or the foundation wouldn't have a home. 'I made it clear on the first day we met, Dick, that my condition for pledging the trust's shares was that in return you would purchase a new gallery for the foundation.'

'And it is still my intention to do so,' said Armstrong firmly.

'And before the AGM.' The two men stared across the table

at each other. 'I suggest you have the lease drawn up immediately, so it's ready for signing by Monday.' Summers picked up a glass of brandy and drained it. 'Because I know someone else who'd be only too happy to sign it if you don't.'

'No, no, I'll have it drawn up immediately,' said Armstrong.

'Good. Then I'll show you round the premises tomorrow morning.'

'Tomorrow morning?' said Armstrong. 'I'm sure I'll be able to fit that in.'

'Shall we say nine o'clock, then?' said Summers, as a decaffeinated coffee was placed in front of him.

Armstrong gulped down his coffee. 'Nine o'clock will be fine,' he said eventually, before calling for the bill. He settled another of Summers's extravagances, threw his napkin on the table and rose from his place. The director of the foundation and Russell followed suit, and accompanied him in silence to his waiting stretch limousine.

'I'll see you at nine tomorrow morning,' Summers said, as Armstrong climbed into the back of the car.

'You most certainly will,' muttered Armstrong, not looking back.

On their way to the Pierre, Armstrong told Russell that he wanted answers to three questions. The lawyer took a small leather notepad from his inside pocket.

'First, who controls the foundation? Second, how much of the *Star*'s profits does it eat up each year? And third, is there any legal obligation on me to spend three million on this new building he keeps going on about?'

Russell scribbled away on his little notepad.

'And I want the answers by tomorrow morning.'

The limousine dropped Armstrong outside his hotel, and he nodded good night to Russell, then got out of the car and took a stroll around the block. He picked up a copy of the *New York Star* on the corner of Sixty-first and Madison, and smiled when he saw a large photo of himself dominating the front page, with the headline 'Chairman' underneath. It didn't please him that

Townsend's photo was also on the same page – even if it was considerably smaller, and below the fold. The caption read: 'A $20 million profit?'

Armstrong tucked the paper under his arm. When he reached the hotel, he stepped into a waiting lift and said to the bellboy, 'Who cares about $20 million, when you can be the owner of the *Star*?'

'Excuse me, sir?' said the puzzled bellboy.

'Which would you rather have,' Armstrong asked. 'The *New York Star* or $20 million?'

The bellboy looked up at the giant of a man, who seemed perfectly sober, and said hopefully, '$20 million, sir.'

◄○►

When Townsend woke the following morning he had a stiff neck. He stood up and stretched. Then he noticed the *New York Star*'s statutes lying at his feet. And then he remembered.

He walked across the room and cautiously opened the bedroom door. Angela was still fast asleep. He closed the door quietly, returned to his chair and rang through to room service. He ordered breakfast and five papers, and asked them to clear away the dinner table.

When the bedroom door opened the second time that morning, Angela stepped out gingerly to find Townsend reading the *Wall Street Journal* and sipping coffee. She asked the same question as she had when they met in the gallery. 'Who are you?' He gave her the same reply. She smiled.

'Can I order you some breakfast?'

'No thanks, but you could pour me a large black coffee. I'll be back in a moment.' The bedroom door closed and didn't open again for another twenty minutes. When Angela sat down in the chair opposite Townsend, she looked very nervous. He poured her a coffee, but she made no attempt at conversation until she had taken several large gulps.

'Did I do anything foolish last night?' she asked eventually.

'No, you didn't,' said Townsend with a smile.

'It's just that I've never . . .'

'There's nothing to worry about,' he assured her. 'You fell asleep and I put you to bed.' He paused. 'Fully dressed.'

'That's a relief.' She looked at her watch. 'Good heavens, is that really the time, or did I put my watch on upside down?'

'It's twenty past eight,' said Townsend.

'I'll have to grab a cab immediately. I've got a site meeting in SoHo with the new chairman at nine, and I must make a good impression. If he refuses to buy the new building, it could be my one chance.'

'Don't bother with a cab,' said Townsend. 'My driver will take you wherever you want to go. You'll find him parked out front in a white BMW.'

'Thank you,' she said. 'That's really generous of you.'

She quickly drained her coffee. 'It was a great dinner last night, and you were very thoughtful,' she said as she rose from her chair. 'But if I'm to be there ahead of Mr Armstrong, I really must leave now.'

'Of course.' Townsend stood up and helped her on with her coat.

When they reached the door she turned and faced him again. 'If I didn't do anything foolish last night, did I say anything I might regret?'

'No, I don't think so. You just chatted about your work at the foundation,' he said as he opened the door for her.

'It was kind of you to listen. I do hope we meet again.'

'I have a feeling we will,' said Townsend.

She leaned forward and gave him a kiss on the cheek. 'By the way,' she said, 'you never did tell me your name.'

'Keith Townsend.'

'Oh shit,' she said, as the door closed behind her.

—◇—

When Armstrong arrived outside 147 Lower Broadway that morning, he was greeted by the sight of Lloyd Summers waiting on the top step standing next to a rather thin, academic-looking woman, who was either very tired or simply bored.

'Good morning, Mr Armstrong,' said Summers as he stepped out of the car.

'Good morning,' he replied, forcing a smile as he shook the director's hand.

'This is Angela Humphries, my deputy,' he explained. 'You may have met her at the opening last night.'

Armstrong could recall her face, but didn't remember meeting her. He nodded curtly.

'Angela's speciality is the Renaissance period,' said Summers, opening the door and standing to one side.

'How interesting,' said Armstrong, making no attempt to sound interested.

'Let me start by showing you round,' said the director, as they entered a large empty room on the ground floor. Armstrong put a hand in his pocket and flicked on a switch.

'So many wonderful walls for hanging,' enthused the director.

Armstrong tried to appear fascinated by a building he had absolutely no intention of buying. But he knew that he couldn't admit as much until he had been confirmed as the *Star*'s chairman on Monday, and that wouldn't be possible without Summers's 5 per cent. He somehow managed to punctuate the director's effusive monologue with the occasional 'Wonderful,' 'Ideal,' 'Perfect,' 'I do agree,' and even 'How clever of you to find it,' as they entered each new room.

When Summers took him by the arm and started to lead him back down to the ground floor, Armstrong pointed to a staircase that led up to another floor. 'What goes on up there?' he asked suspiciously.

'It's just an attic,' replied Summers dismissively. 'It might prove useful for storage, but not much else.' Angela said nothing, and tried to remember if she had told Mr Townsend what was on the top floor.

By the time they arrived back at the ground floor, Armstrong couldn't wait to escape. As they stepped out onto the sidewalk, Summers said, 'Now you'll understand, chairman, why I consider this to be the ideal spot for the foundation to continue its work into the next century.'

'I couldn't agree with you more,' Armstrong said. 'Absolutely ideal.' He smiled with relief when he saw who was waiting for him in the back of the limousine. 'I'll deal with all the necessary paperwork just as soon as I get back to my office.'

'I'll be at the gallery for the rest of the day,' said Summers.

'Then I'll send the documents round for you to sign this afternoon.'

'Any time – today,' said Summers, offering his hand.

Armstrong shook hands with the director and, without bothering to say goodbye to Angela, stepped into the car. He found Russell, yellow pad on lap, pen poised. 'Do you have all the answers?' he asked, before the driver had even turned the key in the ignition. He turned to wave at Summers as the car moved away from the kerb.

'Yes, I do,' Russell replied, looking down at his pad. 'First, the foundation is currently chaired by Mrs Summers, who appointed her son director six years ago.' Armstrong nodded. 'Second, they spent a little over a million dollars of the *Star*'s profits last year.'

Armstrong gripped the armrest. 'How in hell's name did they manage that?'

'Well, to start with, Summers is paid a salary of $150,000 a year. But more interestingly,' said Russell, referring to his notes, 'he's somehow managed to get through $240,000 a year in expenses – for each of the past four years.'

Armstrong could feel his pulse-rate increasing. 'How does he get away with it?' he asked, as they passed a white BMW he could have sworn he'd seen somewhere before. He turned and stared at it.

'I suspect his mother doesn't ask too many questions.'

'What?'

'I suspect his mother doesn't ask too many questions,' Russell repeated.

'But what about the board? Surely they have a duty to be more vigilant. Not to mention the shareholders.'

'Someone did raise the subject at last year's AGM,' said Russell, referring to his notes. 'But the chairman assured them

– and I quote – that "the *Star*'s readers thoroughly approve of the paper being involved with the advancement of culture in our great city".'

'The advancement of what?' said Armstrong.

'Culture,' said Russell.

'And what about the building?' demanded Armstrong, pointing out of the back window.

'No future management is under any obligation to purchase another building once the lease on the old one runs out – which it does on December quarter day.'

Armstrong smiled for the first time that morning.

'Though I must warn you,' said Russell, 'that I believe Summers will need to be convinced that you have purchased the building before the AGM takes place on Monday. Otherwise, as director of the trust, he could still switch his 5 per cent at the last moment.'

'Then send him two copies of a lease prepared for signature. That will keep him quiet until Monday morning.'

Russell didn't look convinced.

–◆–

When the BMW arrived back at the Carlyle, Townsend was already waiting on the sidewalk. He climbed in next to the driver and asked, 'Where did you drop the girl off?'

'SoHo, Lower Broadway,' the driver replied.

'Then that's where I want to go,' Townsend said. As the driver joined the Fifth Avenue traffic, he remained puzzled by what Mr Townsend saw in the girl. There had to be an angle he hadn't worked out. Perhaps she was an heiress.

When the BMW turned into Lower Broadway, Townsend couldn't miss the stretch limousine parked outside a building with a 'For Sale' sign in the front window. 'Park on this side of the road, about fifty yards short of the building where you dropped the lady earlier this morning,' he said.

As the driver pulled on the handbrake, Townsend squinted over his shoulder and asked, 'Can you read the phone numbers on those signs?'

'There are two signs, sir, with different numbers on them.'

'I need both,' Townsend said. The driver read the numbers out, and Townsend wrote them on the back of a five-dollar bill. Then he picked up the car phone and dialled the first number.

When the line was answered with, 'Good morning, Wood, Knight & Levy. How may I assist you?' Townsend said he was interested in the details of 147 Lower Broadway.

'I'll put you through to Offices, sir,' he was told. A click followed and a second voice asked, 'How may I assist you?' Townsend repeated his query, and was put through to a third voice.

'Number 147 Broadway? Ah, yes, I'm afraid we already have a prospective buyer for that property, sir. We've been instructed to draw up a lease, with a view to closing on Monday. However, we do have other properties in the same locality.'

Townsend pressed the END button without saying another word. Only in New York would no one be surprised by such bad manners. He immediately dialled the second number. While he waited to be connected to the right person, he became distracted by a taxi drawing up outside the building. A tall, elegantly-dressed middle-aged man jumped out and walked over to the stretch limousine. He had a word with the driver, and then climbed into the back as a voice came onto the line.

'You'll have to move quickly if you're interested in number 147,' said the agent. 'Because I know the other firm involved with the property already has a party interested who is close to nailing a deal, and that's no bullshit. In fact they're looking over the building right now, so I couldn't even take you round before ten.'

'Ten will suit me just fine,' said Townsend. 'I'll meet you outside the building then.' He pressed the END button.

Townsend had to wait only a few more minutes before Armstrong, Summers and Angela came out onto the sidewalk. After only a short exchange and a handshake, Armstrong stepped into the back of the limousine. He didn't seem at all surprised to find someone waiting there for him. As the car moved off, Summers waved effusively until Armstrong was out of sight. Angela stood a pace behind him, looking fed up. Townsend ducked as the limousine passed him, and when he looked back up, he saw Summers hailing a Yellow Cab. He and Angela got in, and Townsend watched them as they disappeared in the opposite direction to the limousine.

Once the cab had turned the corner, Townsend got out of his car and walked across the road to study the building from the outside. After a few moments he walked a little further down the pavement, and found that there was a similar property up for sale a few doors away, the number of which he also wrote down on the back of the five-dollar bill. He then returned to the car.

One more phone call, and he had discovered that the price of number 171 was $2.5 million. Not only was Summers getting an apartment thrown in, but it also looked as if he was making a handsome profit on the side.

The driver tapped on the internal window and pointed towards number 147. Townsend looked up and saw a young man climbing the steps. He put the phone down and went across to join him.

After an extensive viewing of all five floors, Townsend had to agree with Angela that at $3 million it was perfect – but for only one person. As they stepped back out onto the sidewalk he asked the agent, 'What's the minimum deposit you would require on this building?'

'Ten per cent, non-returnable,' he replied.

'With the usual thirty days for completion, I assume?'

'Yes, sir,' said the agent.

'Good. Then why don't you draw up a lease immediately,' Townsend said, handing the young man his card. 'Send it round to me at the Carlyle.'

'Yes, sir,' the agent repeated. 'I'll make sure it's with you by this afternoon.'

Townsend finally extracted a hundred-dollar bill from his wallet and held it up so that the young man could see which

THE FOURTH ESTATE

president was on it. 'And I want the other agent who's trying to sell this property to know that I will be putting down a deposit first thing on Monday morning.'

The young man pocketed the hundred-dollar bill, and nodded.

◄○►

When Townsend arrived back in his room at the Carlyle, he immediately called Tom at his office. 'What have you got planned for the weekend?' he asked his lawyer.

'A round of golf, a little gardening,' said Tom. 'And I was also hoping to watch my youngest pitch for his high school. But from the way you phrased that question, Keith, I have a feeling I won't even be taking the train back to Greenwich.'

'You're right, Tom. We've got a lot of work to do before Monday morning if I'm going to be the next proprietor of the *New York Star*.'

'Where do I start?'

'With a lease that needs checking over before I sign it. Then I want you to close a deal with the one person who can make this all possible.' When Townsend eventually put the phone down, he leaned back in his chair and gazed at the little red book that had kept him awake the previous night. A few moments later he picked it up, and turned to page 47.

For the first time in his life he was grateful for an Oxford education.

33

NEW YORK TIMES

11 OCTOBER 1986

Star Wars

Armstrong signed the lease, then passed his pen to Russell, who witnessed the signature.

Lloyd Summers hadn't stopped grinning since he'd arrived at Trump Tower that morning, and he almost leaped out of his chair when Russell added his signature to the lease on 147 Lower Broadway. He thrust out his hand at Armstrong and said, 'Thank you, chairman. I can only say how much I'm looking forward to working with you.'

'And I with you,' said Armstrong, shaking his hand.

Summers bowed low in Armstrong's direction, then gave a slightly lesser bow to Russell. He gathered up the lease and the draft for $300,000 before turning to leave the room. When he reached the door, he looked back and said, 'You'll never regret it.'

'I fear you might, Dick,' said Russell the moment the door was closed. 'What made you change your mind?'

'I didn't have a lot of choice once I discovered what Townsend was up to.'

'So that's $3 million down the drain,' said the lawyer.

'Three hundred thousand,' said Armstrong.

'I don't understand.'

'I may have paid the deposit, but I have absolutely no intention of buying the bloody building.'

'But he'll issue a writ against you if you fail to complete within the thirty days.'

'I doubt it,' said Armstrong.

'What makes you so sure?'

'Because in a couple of weeks' time you will phone his lawyer and tell him how horrified I was to discover that his client had signed a separate lease on a penthouse apartment above the gallery, having described it to me as an attic.'

'That will be almost impossible to prove.'

Armstrong removed a small cassette from an inside pocket and handed it over to Russell. 'It may be easier than you think.'

'But this could well be inadmissible,' said Russell, taking the tape.

'Then you may just have to ask what would have happened to the $600,000 the agents were going to pay Summers over and above the original asking price.'

'He'll simply deny it, especially as you won't have completed the contract.'

Armstrong paused for a moment. 'Well, there's always a last resort.' He opened a drawer in his desk and withdrew a dummy front page of the *Star*. The headline read: 'Lloyd Summers Indicted for Fraud'.

'He'll just issue another writ.'

'Not after he's read the inside pages.'

'But by the time the trial comes around it will all be ancient history.'

'Not as long as I'm proprietor of the *Star*, it won't.'

—◇—

'How long will it all take?' asked Townsend.

'About twenty minutes would be my guess,' Tom replied.

'And how many people have you signed up?'

'Just over two hundred.'

'Will that be enough?'

'It's all I could manage at such short notice, so let's hope so.'

'Do they know what's expected of them?'

'They sure do. I took them through several rehearsals last night. But I still want you to address them before the meeting begins.'

'And how about the lead player? Has she been rehearsing?' Townsend asked.

'She didn't need to,' said Tom. 'She's been understudying the part for some time.'

'Did she agree to my terms?'

'Didn't even haggle.'

'What about the lease? Any surprises there?'

'No, it was just as she said it would be.'

Townsend stood up, walked across to the window and stared out over Central Park. 'Will you be proposing the motion?'

'No, I've asked Andrew Fraser to do that. I'm going to stick with you.'

'Why did you pick Fraser?'

'He's the senior partner, which will ensure that the chairman realises just how serious we are.'

Townsend swung round and faced his attorney. 'So what can go wrong?'

◄○►

When Armstrong walked out of the offices of Keating, Gould & Critchley, accompanied by the senior partner, he was faced with a battery of cameramen, photographers and journalists, all hoping to get the same questions answered.

'What changes do you intend to make, Mr Armstrong, when you are the chairman of the *Star*?'

'Why change a great institution?' he replied. 'In any case,' he added, as he marched down the long corridor and out onto the sidewalk, 'I'm not the sort of proprietor who interferes with the daily running of a paper. Ask any of my editors. They'll tell you.'

One or two of the journalists who were chasing after him had already done so, but Armstrong had reached the relative safety of his limousine before they could follow up with any supplementaries.

'Bloody hacks,' he said, as the car set off in the direction of the Plaza Hotel where the Annual General Meeting of the *Star* shareholders was to be held. 'You can't even control the ones you own.'

Russell didn't comment. As they proceeded down Fifth Avenue, Armstrong began glancing at his watch every few moments. Lights seemed to turn red just as they approached them. Or did you only ever notice such things when you were in a hurry? Armstrong looked out at the busy sidewalk and watched the natives of Manhattan streaming back and forth at a pace he now took for granted. As the lights turned green, he touched his breast pocket to check his acceptance speech was still in place. He had once read that Margaret Thatcher would never allow an aide to carry her speeches, because she had a dread of arriving on a platform without the script. He understood her anxiety for the first time.

The nervous conversation between Armstrong and his attorney stopped and started, as the car passed the General Motors building. Armstrong took a large powder puff out of his pocket and dabbed his forehead. Russell continued to stare out of the window.

'So what can go wrong?' asked Armstrong, for the tenth time.

'Nothing,' repeated Russell, tapping the leather briefcase on his knees. 'I have shares and pledges totalling 51 per cent of the stock, and we know Townsend has only 46 per cent. Just relax.'

More cameramen, photographers and journalists were waiting on the steps of the Plaza as the limousine drew up. Russell glanced across at his client who, despite his protests to the contrary, seemed to be enjoying every moment of the attention. As Armstrong stepped out of the car, the manager of the Plaza took a pace forward to greet him as if he were a visiting head of state. He guided the two men into the hotel, across the lobby and on towards the Lincoln Room. Armstrong failed to notice Keith Townsend and the senior partner of another distinguished law firm step out of the elevator as he and his party swept by.

Townsend had arrived at the Plaza an hour earlier.

Unnoticed by the manager, he had checked out the room where the meeting would be held, and then made his way to the State Suite, where Tom had assembled a team of out-of-work actors. He briefed them on the role they would be expected to play, and why it was necessary for them to sign so many transfer forms. Forty minutes later he returned to the lobby.

Townsend and Tom Spencer walked slowly towards the Lincoln Room in Armstrong's wake. They could easily have been mistaken for two of his minor acolytes.

'What if she doesn't turn up?' asked Townsend.

'Then a lot of people will have wasted a great deal of time and money,' said Tom as they entered the Lincoln Room.

Townsend was surprised to find how crowded the room was; he had imagined that the five hundred chairs he had watched the staff putting out earlier that morning would prove far more than were needed. He was wrong – there were already people standing at the back. About a third of the way down the room, a red rope prevented anyone other than stockholders from taking a place in the twenty rows nearest the stage. The press, employees of the paper and the simply curious were packed into the back of the room.

Townsend and his lawyer walked slowly down the centre aisle, the occasional flashbulb popping, until they came to the red rope, where both were asked to produce proof that they were stockholders of the company. An efficient woman ran her finger down a long list of names that covered several pages. She made two little ticks, gave them a smile, and unhooked the rope.

The first thing Townsend noticed was the amount of media attention being focused on Armstrong and his entourage, who seemed to be occupying most of the front two rows. It was Tom who spotted them first. He touched Townsend on the elbow. 'Far left-hand side, about the tenth row.' Townsend looked to his left, and let out an audible sigh when his eyes settled on Lloyd Summers and his deputy, who were seated next to each other.

Tom guided Townsend to the other side of the room, and

they took two vacant seats halfway back. As Townsend looked nervously around, Tom nodded in the direction of another man walking down the centre aisle. Andrew Fraser, the senior partner of Tom's law practice, slipped into an empty seat a couple of rows behind Armstrong.

Townsend turned his attention towards the stage, where he recognised some of the *Star* directors he had met during the past six weeks, milling around behind a long table covered in a green baize cloth which had printed on it in bold red letters the legend 'The New York Star'. Armstrong had promised several of them they would remain on the board if he became chairman. None of them believed him.

The clock on the wall behind them indicated that it was five to twelve. Townsend glanced over his shoulder, and noticed that the room was becoming so crowded that it would soon be difficult for anyone else to find a place. He whispered to Tom, who also looked back, frowned and said, 'If it's still a problem when they start coming in, I'll deal with it personally.'

Townsend turned back to the stage and watched the members of the board beginning to take their places behind the long table. The last person to occupy his seat was the chairman, Cornelius J. Adams IV, as a smartly printed card placed in front of him reminded the less well-informed. The moment he took his place, the cameras switched their attention from the front row of the audience to the stage. The buzz that had been filling the hall became distinctly subdued. As the clock behind him struck twelve, the chairman banged his gavel several times, until he had gained everyone's attention.

'Good afternoon, ladies and gentlemen,' he began. 'My name is Cornelius Adams, and I am chairman of the board of the *New York Star*.' He paused. 'Well, at least for a few more minutes.' He looked in Armstrong's direction. A little laughter broke out for what Townsend suspected had been a well-rehearsed line. 'This,' he declared, 'is the annual general meeting of the greatest newspaper in America.' This statement was greeted with enthusiastic applause by large sections seated at the front of the hall, and with silent indifference by most of those behind the red rope.

'Our main purpose today,' he continued, 'is to appoint a new chairman, the man who will have the responsibility of leading the *Star* into the next century. As I am sure you all know, a takeover bid for the paper was launched earlier in the year by Mr Richard Armstrong of Armstrong Communications, and a counter-bid was made on the same day by Mr Keith Townsend of Global Corp. My first task this afternoon is to guide you through the procedure which will ensure that a transfer of power takes place smoothly.

'I am able to confirm that both parties concerned have presented to me, through their distinguished counsel, proof of their entitlement or control over the company's stock. Our auditors have double-checked all these claims and found them to be in order. They show,' he said, referring to a clipboard that he picked up from the table, 'that Mr Richard Armstrong is in possession of 51 per cent of the company's stock, while Mr Keith Townsend has control over 46 per cent. Three per cent of stockholders have not made their preference known.

'As the majority shareholder, Mr Armstrong is *ipso facto* in control, so there is nothing left for me to do other than hand over the chair to his stewardship – unless, as the marriage service states, anyone can show just cause or impediment for me not so to do.' He beamed at the audience like a priest standing in front of the bride and groom, and remained silent for a moment.

A woman immediately jumped up in the third row. 'Both of the men who have been bidding to take over the *Star* are foreigners,' she said. 'What recourse do I have if I don't want either of them as chairman?'

It was a question that the company secretary had anticipated, and for which Adams had an answer prepared. 'None, madam,' came back the chairman's immediate reply. 'Otherwise any group of stockholders would be in a position to remove American directors from British and Australian companies throughout the world.' The chairman was satisfied that he had dealt with the woman politely and effectively.

The questioner obviously did not agree. She turned her back on the stage and stalked out of the room, followed by a CNN camera and one photographer.

There followed several more questions in the same vein, which Russell had warned Armstrong was likely. 'It's simply stockholders exercising their goddamn rights,' he had explained.

As each question was answered, Townsend turned round and looked anxiously towards the door. Every time there were more people blocking it. Tom could see how nervous his client had become, so he slipped out of his seat and went to the back of the room to have a word with the chief usher. By the time the chairman was satisfied he had answered every question from the floor, several of them twice, Tom had returned to his place. 'Don't worry, Keith,' he said. 'Everything's under control.'

'But when will Andrew . . .'

'Patience,' said Tom, as the chairman announced, 'If there are no more questions from the floor, I am left only with the pleasant task of inviting Mr Richard . . .' He would have completed the sentence if Andrew Fraser hadn't risen from his place a couple of rows behind Armstrong and indicated that he wished to speak.

Cornelius J. Adams frowned, but nodded curtly when he saw who it was wanting to ask a question.

'Mr Chairman,' Fraser began, as one or two groans went up around the room.

'Yes?' said Adams, unable to disguise his irritation.

Townsend looked back towards the entrance once again, and saw a trickle of people making their way down the centre aisle towards the shareholders' seats. As each of them reached the red rope barrier, they were stopped by the efficient woman who checked their names on the long list before unhooking the rope and allowing them through to fill up the few remaining places.

'I wish to bring to your attention,' continued Tom's colleague, 'rule 7B of the company's statutes.' Conversations started up around the room. Few people on either side of the rope had ever read the company's statutes, and certainly none had any idea what rule 7B referred to. The chairman leaned down to allow the company secretary to whisper in his ear the words he had just looked up on page forty-seven of the rarely consulted little red leather book. This was one question he had not anticipated, and for which he did not have a prepared answer.

Townsend could see from the frenzy of activity in the front row that the man he had first seen climbing into the back of the limousine outside 147 Lower Broadway was trying to explain the significance of rule 7B to his client.

Andrew Fraser waited for the furore around him to settle before he attempted to continue, allowing more time for the steady stream of people entering the room to take their places beyond the red rope. The chairman found it necessary to bang his gavel several more times before the room was quiet enough for him to inform everyone: 'Rule 7B allows any shareholder attending the annual general meeting' – he was reading directly from the little red book – '"to propose a nominee for the position of any office-holder of the company". Is that the rule to which you are referring, sir?' he asked, looking directly at Andrew Fraser.

'It is,' responded the elderly lawyer firmly. The company secretary tugged the sleeve of his chairman. Once again Adams leaned over and listened. Andrew Fraser remained in his place. A few moments later, the chairman drew himself up to his full height and stared down at Fraser. 'You are of course aware, sir, that you are unable to propose an alternative nominee for chairman without giving thirty days' notice in writing. Rule 7B, subsection a,' he said, with some degree of satisfaction.

'I *am* aware of that, sir,' said Fraser, who had remained standing. 'It is not the position of chairman for which I wish to propose a nominee.'

Uproar broke out in the hall. Adams had to bang his gavel several times before Fraser could continue.

'I wish to propose a nominee for the position of director of the Summers Foundation.'

Townsend kept his eye on Lloyd Summers, who had turned white. He was staring at Andrew Fraser and dabbing his forehead with a red silk handkerchief.

'But we already have an excellent director in Mr Summers,' said the chairman. 'Or are you merely wishing to confirm his position? If that is so, I can assure you that Mr Armstrong intends . . .'

'No, sir. I propose that Mr Summers be replaced by Ms Angela Humphries, the current deputy chairman.'

The chairman bent down and tried to ascertain from the company secretary if the motion was in order. Tom Spencer stood up in his place and began checking to make sure that all his recruits were safely in front of the red rope. Townsend could see that every seat had been taken, and several late arrivals had to be content with standing at the side or sitting in the aisles.

Having been told by the company secretary that the motion was in order, the chairman asked, 'Do I have a seconder?' To his surprise, several hands shot up. Adams selected a woman in the fifth row. 'May I have your name, please, for the record?'

'Mrs Roscoe,' she said.

The company secretary turned to another page in the little red book, which he passed up to the chairman.

'It is my duty to inform you that a ballot will now take place under rule 7B, which allows any shareholders present to cast their votes,' he read directly from the red book. 'Ballot papers will be distributed, as directed by the statutes, and you may place a cross in one of the boxes provided, indicating whether you are for or against the motion to replace Mr Lloyd Summers as director of the Summers Foundation with Ms Angela Humphries.' He paused and looked up. 'I feel it appropriate at this juncture to let you know that it is your board's intention to vote as one against this motion, as we believe that the trust has been well served by its present director, Mr Summers, and that he should be allowed to continue in that position.' Summers looked nervously towards Adams, but seemed to be reassured when he saw the board members nodding in support of their chairman.

Attendants began moving up and down the aisles, handing out voting slips. Armstrong placed his cross in the square marked 'AGAINST'. Townsend placed his in the square marked 'FOR', and dropped the slip into the tin box provided.

As the voting continued, some people in the room began to stand and stretch. Lloyd Summers remained silently slumped in his chair, occasionally mopping his forehead with his red silk handkerchief. Angela Humphries didn't once look in his direction.

Russell advised his client to remain cool and use the time to go over his acceptance speech. He was confident that, after the board's clear lead, the motion would be heavily defeated.

'But shouldn't you have a word with Ms Humphries, just in case it isn't?' whispered Armstrong.

'I think that would be most unwise in the circumstances,' said Russell, 'especially in view of who she is sitting next to.'

Armstrong glanced in their direction, and scowled. Surely Townsend couldn't have . . .

While the counting was taking place somewhere behind the stage, Lloyd Summers could be seen angrily trying to ask his deputy a question. She glanced in his direction and smiled sweetly.

'Ladies and gentlemen,' said Cornelius Adams as he rose again from his place. 'Can I now ask you to return to your seats, as the counting has been completed.' Those who had been chatting in the gangways went back to their places and waited for the result of the ballot to be declared. The chairman was passed a folded slip of paper by the company secretary. He opened it and, like a good judge, gave no clue from his expression as to the verdict.

'Those voting for the motion, 317,' he declared in senatorial tones.

Townsend took a deep breath. 'Is it enough?' he asked Tom, trying to calculate how many people were sitting in front of the red rope.

'We're about to find out,' said Tom calmly.

'Those voting against, 286. I therefore declare the motion

carried by thirty-one votes.' He paused. 'And Ms Angela Humphries to be the new director of the foundation.'

A gasp went up around the room, followed by uproar, as it seemed that everyone in the audience had a view to express.

'Closer than I'd expected,' shouted Townsend.

'But you won, and that's all that matters,' Tom replied.

'I haven't won yet,' said Townsend, his eyes now firmly fixed on Angela.

People were now looking round the room trying to discover where Ms Humphries was seated, though not many of them had any idea what she looked like. One person remained standing in his place.

On the stage, the chairman was having a further consultation with the secretary, who was once again reading directly to him from the little red book. He eventually nodded, turned back to the audience and banged his gavel.

Looking directly down at Fraser, the chairman waited for the gathering to return to some semblance of order before asking, 'Is it your intention to propose another motion, Mr Fraser?' He did not attempt to hide the sarcasm in his voice.

'No, sir, it is not. But I do wish to know who the newly elected director will be supporting with the foundation's 5 per cent shareholding in the company, as that will affect the identity of the next chairman of the board.'

For a second time everybody in the room began chattering or looking around the room, searching for the new director. Mr Fraser sat down, and Angela rose from her place, as if she was on the other end of the seesaw.

The chairman switched his attention to her. 'Ms Humphries,' he said, 'as you now control 5 per cent of the company's shares, it is my duty to ask who you will be supporting as chairman.'

Lloyd Summers continued to mop his brow, but couldn't bring himself to look in Angela's direction. She herself appeared remarkably calm and composed. She waited until there was total silence.

'Mr Chairman, it will come as no surprise to you that I wish to support the man who I believe will serve the foundation's best interests.' She paused as Armstrong stood up and waved in her direction, but the glare of the television arc-lights made it impossible for her to see him. The chairman appeared to relax.

'The trust casts its 5 per cent in favour of – ' she paused again, obviously enjoying every moment ' – Mr Keith Townsend.'

A gasp went up around the room. For the first time, the chairman was speechless. He dropped his gavel on the floor and stared open-mouthed at Angela. A moment later he recovered it as well as his composure, and began calling for order. When he felt he could be heard, he asked, 'Are you aware, Ms Humphries, of the consequences of switching the foundation's vote at this late stage?'

'I mostly certainly am, Mr Chairman,' she replied firmly.

A bevy of Armstrong's lawyers were already up on their feet protesting. The chairman banged his gavel on the table again and again. Once the noise had subsided, he announced that as Ms Humphries had pledged the foundation's 5 per cent of stock in favour of Mr Townsend, thus giving him 51 per cent to Mr Armstrong's 46, he was therefore left with no choice under standing order 11A, subsection d, but to declare Mr Keith Townsend the new chairman of the *New York Star*.

The two hundred shareholders who had arrived in the hall late rose and cheered on cue like well-rehearsed film extras as Townsend made his way up onto the stage. Armstrong stormed out of the room, leaving his lawyers to carry on with their protests.

Townsend began by shaking hands with Cornelius Adams, the former chairman, and each of the members of the board, though none of them looked particularly pleased to see him.

He then took his place at the front of the stage and looked down into the noisy hall. 'Mr Chairman, ladies and gentlemen,' he said, tapping the microphone, 'may I begin by thanking you, Mr Adams, and the board of the *Star*, for the service and inspired leadership you have all given the company over the years, and may I wish every one of you success in whatever it is you choose to do in the future.'

Tom was glad that Townsend couldn't see the expressions on the faces of the men seated behind him.

'Let me assure the shareholders of this great paper that I will do everything in my power to continue to uphold the traditions of the *Star*. You have my word that I will never interfere in the editorial integrity of the paper, other than to remind every journalist of the words of the great *Manchester Guardian* editor C. P. Scott, which have been the benchmark of my professional life: "Comment is free, but facts are sacred."'

The actors rose from their places again and began applauding on cue. When the noise finally died down, Townsend ended by saying, 'I look forward to seeing you all again in a year's time.' He banged the gavel and declared the AGM closed.

Several people in the front row leaped up again to continue their protest, while two hundred others carried out their instructions. They rose and began to make their way towards the exit, talking loudly among themselves. Within minutes, the room was cleared of all but a handful of protesters addressing an empty stage.

As Townsend left the room, the first thing he asked Tom was, 'Have you drawn up a new lease on the foundation's old building?'

'Yes, it's in my office. All it requires is your signature.'

'And there will be no increase in rent?'

'No, it's fixed for the next ten years,' said Tom. 'As Ms Humphries assured me it would be.'

'And her contract?'

'Also for ten years, but at a third of Lloyd Summers's salary.'

As the two men stepped out of the hotel, Townsend turned to his lawyer and said, 'So all I have to do now is decide whether to sign it or not.'

'But I've already made a verbal agreement with her,' said Tom.

Townsend grinned at his attorney as the hotel manager and several cameramen, photographers and journalists pursued them to their waiting car.

'My turn to ask you a question,' said Tom as they slipped into the back seat of the BMW.

'Go ahead.'

'Now it's all over, I'd just like to know when you came up with that masterstroke to defeat Armstrong.'

'About forty years ago.'

'I'm not sure I understand,' said the lawyer, looking puzzled.

'No reason why you should, Brother Tom, but then, you weren't a member of the Oxford University Labour Club when I failed to become chairman simply because I had never read the statute book.'

34

12 JUNE 1987

Maggie the Third:
Tories Romp it 'by 110 Seats'

As Armstrong stormed out of the Lincoln Room, unwilling to suffer the humiliation of having to sit through Townsend's acceptance speech, few of the press bothered to follow him. But two gentlemen who had travelled down from Chicago did. Their client's instructions could not have been clearer. 'Make an offer to whichever one of them fails to become chairman of the *Post*.'

Armstrong stood alone on the sidewalk, having dispatched one of his expensive lawyers to go and find his limousine. The manager of the hotel was no longer to be seen. 'Where is my bloody car?' shouted Armstrong, staring at a white BMW parked on the opposite side of the road.

'It should be with us in a few moments,' said Russell as he arrived by his side.

'How did he fix the vote?' Armstrong demanded.

'He must have created a large number of shareholders in the past twenty-four hours, who wouldn't show up on the register for at least another two weeks.'

'Then why were they allowed into the meeting?'

'All they had to do was present the person checking the list with evidence of the minimum required shareholding and their identity. A hundred shares each for, say, a couple of hundred of them, would be all that was needed. They could have bought the stock from any broker on Wall Street, or Townsend could have allotted them 20,000 of his own shares as late as this morning.'

'And that's legal?'

'Let's say that it's within the letter of the law,' said Russell. 'We could challenge its legality in the courts. That might take a couple of years, and there's no saying which side the judge would come down on. But my advice would be that you should sell your shares and satisfy yourself with a handsome profit.'

'That's exactly the sort of advice you would give,' said Armstrong. 'And I don't intend to take it. I'm going to demand three places on the board and harry the damned man for the rest of his days.'

Two tall, elegantly-dressed men in long black coats hovered a few yards away from them. Armstrong assumed they must be part of Critchley's legal team. 'So how much are those two costing me?' he demanded.

Russell glanced at them and said, 'I've never seen them before.'

This seemed to act as a cue, because one of the men immediately took a pace forward and said, 'Mr Armstrong?'

Armstrong was about to answer when Russell stepped forward and said, 'I'm Russell Critchley, Mr Armstrong's New York attorney. Can I be of assistance?'

The taller of the two men smiled. 'Good afternoon, Mr Critchley,' he said. 'I'm Earl Withers of Spender, Dickson & Withers of Chicago. I believe we have had the pleasure of dealing with your firm in the past.'

'On many occasions,' said Russell, smiling for the first time.

'Get on with it,' said Armstrong.

The shorter of the two men gave a slight nod. 'Our firm has the honour to represent the Chicago News Group, and my colleague and I are eager to discuss a business proposition with your client.'

'Why don't you contact me at my office tomorrow morning?' said Russell, as a limousine drew up.

'What business proposition?' asked Armstrong, as the driver jumped out and opened the back door for him.

'We have been invested with the authority to offer you the opportunity to purchase the *New York Tribune*.'

'As I said . . .' Russell tried again.

'I'll see you both back at my apartment in Trump Tower in fifteen minutes,' said Armstrong, climbing into the car. Withers nodded as Russell ran round to the other side of the vehicle and joined his client in the back. He pulled the door closed, pressed a button, and said nothing until the glass had slid up between them and the driver.

'Dick, I could not under any circumstances recommend . . .' the lawyer began.

'Why not?' said Armstrong.

'It's quite simple,' said Russell. 'Everyone knows that the *Tribune* is in hock for $200 million, and is losing over a million a week. Not to mention that it's locked into an intractable trade union dispute. I promise you, Dick, no one is capable of turning that paper around.'

'Townsend managed it with the *Globe*,' said Armstrong. 'As I know to my cost.'

'That was a quite different situation,' said Russell, beginning to sound desperate.

'And I'll bet he does it again with the *Star*.'

'From a far more viable base. Which is precisely why I recommended that you should mount a takeover bid in the first place.'

'And you failed,' said Armstrong. 'So I can't think of any reason why we shouldn't at least give them a hearing.'

The limousine drew up in front of the Trump Tower. The two lawyers from Chicago were standing there waiting for them. 'How did they manage that?' asked Armstrong, pushing himself out of the car and onto the sidewalk.

'I suspect they walked,' said Russell.

'Follow me,' said Armstrong to the two lawyers, as he marched off towards the lifts. None of them said another word until they had reached the penthouse suite. Armstrong didn't ask if they would like to take off their coats, or to have a seat, or offer them a cup of coffee. 'My attorney tells me that your paper is bankrupt and that it is most unwise of me even to agree to speak to you.'

'Mr Critchley's advice may well turn out to be correct. Nevertheless, the *Tribune* remains the *New York Star*'s only competitor,' said Withers, who seemed to be acting as spokesman. 'And despite all its current problems, it still commands a far higher circulation than the *Star*.'

'Only when it's on the streets,' said Russell.

Withers nodded but said nothing, obviously hoping that they would move on to another question.

'And is it true that it's in debt for $200 million?' said Armstrong.

'Two hundred and seven million, to be precise,' said Withers.

'And losing over a million a week.'

'Around one million three hundred thousand.'

'And the unions have got you by the balls.'

'In Chicago, Mr Armstrong, we would describe it as over a barrel. But that is precisely why my clients felt we should approach you, as we do not have a great deal of experience in handling unions.'

Russell hoped his client realised that Withers would happily have exchanged the name of Armstrong for Townsend if half an hour earlier the vote had gone the other way. He watched his client closely, and began to fear that he was slowly being seduced by the two men from Chicago.

'Why should I be able to do something you've failed so lamentably to achieve in the past?' Armstrong asked, as he looked out of the bay window over a panoramic view of Manhattan.

'My client's long-term relationship with the unions has, I fear, become unsustainable, and having the *Tribune*'s sister paper, as well as the group's headquarters, based in Chicago doesn't help matters. I'm bound to add that it's going to take a big man to sort this one out. Someone who is willing to stand up to the trade unions the way Mr Townsend did so successfully in Britain.'

Russell watched for Armstrong's reaction. He couldn't believe his client would be beguiled by such sycophantic flattery. He must surely turn round and throw them out.

He turned round. 'And if I don't buy it, what's your alternative?'

Russell leaned forward in his chair, put his head in his hands and sighed loudly.

'We will have no choice but to close the paper down and allow Townsend to enjoy a monopoly in this city.'

Armstrong said nothing, but continued to stare at the two strangers, who still hadn't taken off their coats.

'How much are you hoping to get for it?'

'We are open to offers,' said Withers.

'I'll bet you are,' said Armstrong.

Russell willed him to make them an offer they could refuse.

'Right,' said Armstrong, avoiding his lawyer's disbelieving stare. 'Here's my offer. I'll take the paper off your hands for twenty-five cents, the current cover price.' He laughed loudly. The lawyers from Chicago smiled for the first time, and Russell's head sank further into his hands.

'But you will carry the debt of $207 million on your own balance sheet. And while due diligence is being carried out, any day-to-day costs will continue to be your responsibility.' He swung round to face Russell. 'Do offer our two friends a drink while they consider my proposition.'

Armstrong wondered just how long it would take them to bargain. But then, he had no way of knowing that Mr Withers had been instructed to sell the paper for a dollar. The lawyer would have to report back to his clients that they had lost seventy-five cents on the deal.

'We will return to Chicago and take instructions,' was all Withers said.

Once the two lawyers from Chicago had left, Russell spent the rest of the afternoon trying to convince his client what a mistake it would be to buy the *Tribune*, whatever the terms.

By the time he left Trump Tower a few minutes after six – having sat through the longest lunch of his life – they had agreed that if Withers rang back accepting his offer, Armstrong would make it clear that he was no longer interested.

◄o►

When Withers called the following morning to say that his clients had accepted the offer, Armstrong told him he was having second thoughts.

'Why don't you visit the building before you commit yourself?' suggested Withers.

Armstrong could see no harm in that, and even felt it would give him an easy way out. Russell suggested that he should accompany him, and after they had seen over the building, he would phone Chicago and explain that his client no longer wished to proceed.

When they arrived at the *New York Tribune* building later that afternoon, Armstrong stood on the sidewalk and stared up at the art deco skyscraper. It was love at first sight. When he walked into the lobby and saw the seventeen-foot globe marked with the distance in miles to the world's capital cities, including London, Moscow and Jerusalem, he proposed. When the hundreds of staff who had crammed into the hall to await his arrival began cheering, the marriage was consummated. However much the best man tried to talk him out of it, he couldn't stop the signing ceremony taking place.

Six weeks later Armstrong took possession of the *New York Tribune*. The headline on the paper's front page that afternoon told New Yorkers, 'DICK TAKES OVER!'

◄o►

Townsend first heard of Armstrong's offer to purchase the *Tribune* for twenty-five cents on the *Today* show, just as he was about to step into a shower. He stopped and stared down at his rival, slumped in an armchair and wearing a red baseball cap with 'The N.Y. Tribune' emblazoned on it.

'I intend to keep New York's greatest newspaper on the

streets,' he was telling Barbara Walters, 'whatever the personal cost to me.'

'The *Star* is already on the streets,' said Townsend, as if Armstrong were in the room.

'And keep the finest journalists in America in a job.'

'They're already working for the *Star*.'

'And perhaps, if I'm lucky, make a small profit,' Armstrong added, laughing.

'You'll have to be very lucky,' said Townsend. 'Now ask him how he intends to deal with the unions,' he added, glaring at Barbara Walters.

'But isn't there a massive overmanning problem which has beleaguered the *Tribune* for the past three decades?'

Townsend left his shower running as he waited to hear the reply. 'That may well have been the case in the past, Barbara,' said Armstrong. 'But I have made it abundantly clear to all the trade unions concerned that if they won't accept my proposed cuts in the workforce, I will be left with no choice but to close the paper down once and for all.'

'How long will you give them?' demanded Townsend.

'And just how long are you willing to go on losing over a million dollars a week before you carry out that threat?'

Townsend's eyes never left the screen.

'I couldn't have made my position clearer with the trade union leaders,' Armstrong said firmly. 'Six weeks at the outside.'

'Well, good luck, Mr Armstrong,' said Barbara Walters. 'I look forward to interviewing you again in six weeks' time.'

'An invitation I'll be happy to accept, Barbara,' said Armstrong, touching the peak of his baseball cap. Townsend flicked off the television, threw off his dressing-gown and headed for the shower.

From that moment he didn't need to employ anyone to tell him what Armstrong was up to. For an investment of a quarter a day he could be brought up to date by reading the front page of the *Tribune*. Woody Allen suggested that it would take a plane crash in the middle of Queens to remove Armstrong from the front page of the paper – and even then it would have to be Concorde.

Townsend was also having his problems with the unions. When the *Star* came out on strike, the *Tribune* almost doubled its circulation overnight. Armstrong began to appear on every television channel that would take him, telling New Yorkers that 'If you know how to negotiate with the unions, strikes become unnecessary.' The trade union leaders quickly sensed that Armstrong enjoyed being on the front page of the paper and regularly appearing on television, and that he would be loath to close the *Tribune* down or admit he had failed.

When Townsend finally settled with the unions, the *Star* had been off the streets for over two months, and had lost several million dollars. It took him a great deal of his time to rebuild the circulation. The *Tribune*'s figures, however, weren't helped by a series of banner headlines telling New Yorkers that 'Dick Bites the Big Apple', 'Dick Pitches for Yankees' and 'Magic Dick Shoots a Basket for the Nicks'. But these appeared humble when the troops came back from the Gulf and the city gave the returning heroes a tickertape parade all the way down Fifth Avenue. The front page of the *Tribune* was given over to a picture of Armstrong standing on the podium between General Schwarzkopf and Mayor Dinkins; the inside story, covering the event in detail, mentioned Captain Armstrong's MC on four different pages.

But as the weeks went by, Townsend was unable to find any mention of Armstrong reaching a settlement with the print unions, search as he might through the columns of the *Tribune*. When Barbara Walters did invite him back on the programme six weeks later, Armstrong's press secretary told her that there was nothing he would have enjoyed more, but that he had to be in London to attend a board meeting of the parent company.

That at least was true – but only because Peter Wakeham had called to warn him that Sir Paul was on the warpath, and demanding to know how much longer he intended to keep the *New York Tribune* on the streets while it was still losing over a million dollars a week.

'Who does he imagine allowed him to stay on as chairman in the first place?' asked Armstrong.

'I couldn't agree with you more,' said Peter. 'But I thought I ought to let you know what he's been telling everyone.'

'Then I'll just have to come back and explain a few home truths to Sir Paul, won't I?'

◄○►

The limousine drew up outside the district court in Lower Manhattan a few minutes before 10.30 that morning. Townsend, accompanied by his lawyer, stepped out of the car and walked swiftly up the courthouse steps.

Tom Spencer had visited the building the previous day to deal with all the legal formalities, so he knew exactly where his client needed to go, and guided him through the maze of corridors. Once they had entered the courtroom, the two of them squeezed onto one of the overcrowded benches near the back and waited patiently. The room was packed with people chattering away in different languages. They sat in silence between two Cubans, and Townsend wondered if he had made the right decision. Tom had kept pointing out that it was the only way left open for him if he wished to expand his empire, but he knew that his countrymen, not to mention the British Establishment, would be scathing about his reasons. What he couldn't tell them was that there was no form of words which would ever make him feel he was anything other than an Australian.

Twenty minutes later, a judge in a long black gown entered the court and everyone rose. Once he had taken his seat on the bench, an immigration officer stepped forward and said, 'Your Honour, I ask permission to present one hundred and seventy-two immigrants for your consideration as American citizens.'

'Have they all carried out the correct procedure as demanded by the law?' the judge asked solemnly.

'They have, Your Honour,' replied the court officer.

'Then you may proceed with the Oath of Allegiance.'

Townsend and 171 other would-be Americans recited in

unison the words he had read for the first time in the car on the way to the court.

'I hereby declare, on oath, that I absolutely and entirely renounce and abjure all allegiance and fidelity to any foreign prince, potentate, state or sovereignty, of whom or which I have heretofore been a subject or citizen; that I will support and defend the Constitution and laws of the United States of America against all enemies, foreign and domestic; that I will bear true faith and allegiance to the same; that I will bear arms on behalf of the United States when required by law; that I will perform noncombatant service in the armed forces of the United States when required to do so by the law; that I will perform work of national importance under civilian direction when required by the law; and that I take this obligation freely without any mental reservation of purpose or evasion: So help me God.'

The judge smiled down at the joyful faces. 'Let me be the first to welcome you as full citizens of the United States,' he said.

◂◦▸

As eleven o'clock struck, Sir Paul Maitland coughed slightly and suggested that perhaps the time had come to bring the meeting to order. 'I would like to begin by welcoming our chief executive back from New York,' he said, glancing to his right. There were murmurs of assent from around the table. 'But it would be remiss of me not to admit to a little anxiety caused by some of the reports coming out of that city.' The murmurs were repeated, and if anything were slightly louder.

'The board backed you, Dick, when without seeking its approval you purchased the *New York Tribune* for twenty-five cents,' continued Sir Paul. 'However, we now feel you should let us know for how much longer you are willing to tolerate losses in the region of nearly one and a half million dollars a week. Because the present situation,' he said, referring to a row of figures in front of him, 'is that the group's profits in London are only just covering the losses we are sustaining in New York.

In a few weeks' time we will have to face our shareholders at the annual general meeting – ' he looked up at his colleagues seated round the table – 'and I am not convinced that they will approve our stewardship if this state of affairs continues for much longer. As you are all aware, our share price has fallen from £3.10 to £2.70 in the last month.' Sir Paul leaned back in his chair and turned to Armstrong, indicating that he was ready to listen to his explanation.

Armstrong looked slowly around the boardroom table, aware that almost everyone present was there because of his patronage.

'I am able to tell the board, Mr Chairman,' he began, 'that my negotiations with the New York unions, which I must admit have been keeping me up most nights, are finally reaching their conclusion.' He paused as one or two smiles appeared on the faces around the table.

'Seven hundred and twenty members of the print union have already agreed to take early retirement, or to accept a redundancy package. I shall be announcing this officially as soon as I return to New York.'

'But the *Wall Street Journal* has estimated,' said Sir Paul, referring to an article he had extracted from his briefcase, 'that we need to reduce the workforce by between fifteen hundred and two thousand.'

'What do that lot know, sitting in their cosy air-conditioned offices downtown?' said Armstrong. 'I am the person who has to deal with these men face to face.'

'Nevertheless . . .'

'The second tranche of sackings and redundancies will take place in the next few weeks,' continued Armstrong. 'I remain confident that I will have concluded those negotiations by the time of the next board meeting.'

'And how many weeks do you imagine it will be before we see the benefits of these negotiations?'

Armstrong hesitated. 'Six weeks. Eight weeks at the most, Chairman. But naturally I will be doing everything in my power to speed the process up.'

'How much is this latest package going to cost the company?' asked Sir Paul, returning to a typewritten sheet of paper in front of him. Armstrong could see he had been ticking off a list of questions one by one.

'I don't have an exact figure to hand, chairman,' replied Armstrong.

'I would be content, for the purposes of this meeting,' said Sir Paul, looking up from his notes, 'with what I think the Americans call "a ballpark figure".' A little laughter broke the tension round the table.

'Two hundred, perhaps as much as two hundred and thirty million,' said Armstrong, aware that the accountants in New York had already warned him it could be nearer three hundred million. No one round the table offered an opinion, although one or two of them began writing down the figures.

'It may have escaped your notice, chairman,' added Armstrong, 'that the *New York Tribune* building is on the books, and is conservatively valued at $150 million.'

'As long as it's producing a newspaper,' said Sir Paul, now turning the pages of a glossy document supplied to him by a legal firm from Chicago called Spender, Dickson & Withers. 'But in a closing-down situation, I'm reliably informed it is worth no more than fifty million.'

'We are not in a closing-down situation,' said Armstrong, 'as everyone will soon come to appreciate.'

'I only hope you're right,' said Sir Paul quietly.

Armstrong remained silent as the board moved on to discuss the rest of the agenda item by item. He sat there wondering why he was treated so badly in his own country while he was hailed as a hero in the States. His mind drifted back to the proceedings when he caught Eric Chapman, the company secretary, saying '. . . and we have a satisfactory surplus in that account at the present time, Mr Chairman.'

'As is quite right and proper,' said Sir Paul. 'Perhaps you'd be kind enough to take us through the figures, Mr Chapman.'

The company secretary bent down, lifted an old-fashioned leather-bound ledger up onto the table and slowly turned its pages. 'The pension fund,' he began, 'is financed, as members of the board are aware, by joint contributions. The employees pay 4 per cent of their wages into the fund, and management tops it up with an equal contribution. On a year-on-year basis, we are currently paying our former employees approximately £34 million, while we receive in income from present employees the sum of £51 million. Thanks in part to a shrewd investment programme carried out by our merchant bankers, the account's balance currently stands at a little over £631 million, against a requirement properly to fulfil our legal obligation to former employees of around £400 million.'

'Most satisfactory,' purred Sir Paul. Armstrong continued to listen intently.

'Though I must inform the board,' continued Chapman, 'that I have taken actuarial advice, and that although this may appear a large surplus on paper, it is, with life expectancy rising every year, no more than a necessary cushion.'

'We take your point,' said Sir Paul. 'Any other business?'

No one spoke, and the directors began placing pens into pockets, closing files and opening briefcases.

'Good,' said Sir Paul. 'Then I declare the meeting closed, and we can all adjourn for lunch.'

The moment they left the boardroom and entered the dining room Armstrong took over. He marched straight to the head of the table, sat down and began attacking the first course before anyone else had taken their place. He waved at Eric Chapman as he entered the room, indicating that he wanted him to sit on his right, while Peter Wakeham took the seat on his left. Sir Paul found a vacant place halfway down the table on the right-hand side.

Armstrong allowed the company secretary to chatter on about his golf handicap, the state of the government and the economy. He didn't take a lot of interest in his views on Nick Faldo, Neil Kinnock or Alan Walters. But when Chapman moved on to his greatest passion, the pension fund, he listened intently to his every word.

'To be fair, Dick, it's you we have to thank,' Chapman admitted. 'You were the one who spotted what a goldmine they were handing over to us. Not that it's ours really, of course. But the surpluses always make for good reading on the balance sheet, not to mention the audited accounts that have to be presented at the AGM.'

After five slices of prime roast beef had been placed on Armstrong's plate and he had covered them with gravy, he turned his attention to Peter, who still accorded him the hound-like devotion he had become used to since they had served together in Berlin.

'Why don't you fly over to New York and join me for a few days, Peter?' he suggested, as a waitress went on piling potatoes onto his side plate. 'That way you'll be able to see what I'm up against with the unions – and, more importantly, what I've achieved. Then, if for any reason I can't make it back in time for next month's meeting, you could report to the board on my behalf.'

'If that's what you want,' said Peter, enjoying the thought of a visit to New York, but rather hoping that it would still be Dick who reported back to the board the following month.

'Take Concorde over next Monday,' said Armstrong. 'I have a meeting scheduled with Sean O'Reilly, one of the paper's most important trade union leaders, that afternoon. I'd like you there to see how I handle him.'

After lunch, Armstrong returned to his office to find a mountain of mail on his desk. He made no attempt even to sift through it. Instead he picked up a telephone and asked to be connected to the accounts department. When the call was answered he said, 'Fred, can you let me have a chequebook? I'm only in England for a few hours, and . . .'

'It's not Fred, sir,' came back the reply. 'It's Mark Tenby.'

'Then put me through to Fred, will you?'

'Fred retired three months ago, sir,' the chief accountant said. 'Sir Paul appointed me in his place.'

Armstrong was just about to say 'With whose authority?'

when he changed his mind. 'Fine,' he said. 'Then perhaps you would send me up a chequebook immediately. I'm leaving for the States in a couple of hours.'

'Of course, Mr Armstrong. Personal or company?'

'The pension fund account,' he said evenly. 'I'll be making one or two investments on behalf of the company while I'm in the States.'

There followed a longer silence than Armstrong had expected. 'Yes, sir,' said the chief accountant eventually. 'You will of course require the signature of a second director for that particular account, as I'm sure you know, Mr Armstrong. And I should remind you that it's against company law to invest pension fund money in any company in which we already have a majority shareholding.'

'I don't need a lecture on company law from you, young man,' shouted Armstrong, and slammed the phone down. 'Bloody cheek,' he added to the empty room. 'Who does he imagine pays his wages?'

Once the chequebook had been sent up, Armstrong abandoned any pretence of going through his post, and slipped out of the room without even saying goodbye to Pamela. He took the elevator to the roof and ordered his helicopter pilot to take him to Heathrow. As they took off, he looked down on London with none of the affection he now felt for New York.

He landed at Heathrow twenty minutes later, and quickly made his way through to the executive lounge. While he was waiting to board his flight, one or two Americans came over to shake him by the hand and thank him for all he was doing for the citizens of New York. He smiled, and began to wonder what would have happened to his life if the boat on which he had escaped all those years ago had docked at Ellis Island rather than Liverpool. Perhaps he might have ended up in the White House.

His flight was called, and he took his place at the front of the aircraft. After an inadequate meal had been served, he slept intermittently for a couple of hours. The nearer they came to the east coast of the United States, the more confident he became that he could still pull it off. A year today the *Tribune* would not only still be outselling the *Star*, but would be declaring a profit that even Sir Paul Maitland would have to acknowledge he had achieved single-handed. And with the prospect of a Labour government in power, there was no saying what he might achieve. He scribbled on the menu, 'Sir Richard Armstrong', and then, a few moments later, put a line through it and wrote underneath, 'The Rt Hon the Lord Armstrong of Headley'.

When the wheels touched down on the tarmac at Kennedy he felt like a young man again, and couldn't wait to get back to his office. As he strode through the customs hall, passengers pointed at him, and he could hear murmurs of 'Look, it's Dick Armstrong.' Some of them even waved. He pretended not to notice, but the smile never left his face. His limousine was waiting for him in the VIP section, and he was quickly whisked off in the direction of Manhattan. He slumped in the back seat and turned on the television, flicking from channel to channel until a familiar face suddenly caught his attention.

'The time has come for me to retire and concentrate on the work of my foundation,' said Henry Sinclair, the chairman of Multi Media, the largest publishing empire in the world. Armstrong was listening to Sinclair and wondering what price he would consider selling up for when the car came to a halt outside the *Tribune* building.

Armstrong heaved himself up out of the car and waddled across the pavement. After he had pushed his way through the swing doors, people in the lobby applauded him all the way to the elevator. He smiled at them as if this were something that happened wherever he went. A trade union official watched as the elevator doors closed, and wondered if the proprietor would ever find out that his members had been instructed to applaud whenever and wherever he appeared. 'Treat him like the president and he'll start to believe he is the president,' Sean O'Reilly had told the packed meeting. 'And go on applauding until the money runs out.'

At each floor on which the elevator doors opened the

applause started afresh. When he reached the twenty-first floor, Armstrong found his secretary standing waiting for him. 'Welcome home, sir,' she said.

'You're right,' he replied as he stepped out of the elevator. 'This is my home. I only wish I'd been born in America. If I had, by now I'd be the president.'

'Mr Critchley arrived a few minutes ahead of you, sir, and is waiting in your office,' the secretary said as they walked down the corridor.

'Good,' said Armstrong, striding into the largest room in the building. 'Great to see you again, Russell,' he said as his lawyer stood up to greet him. 'So, have you sorted out the union problem for me?'

'I'm afraid not, Dick,' said Russell, as they shook hands. 'In fact, the news is not good from this end. I'm sorry to report that we're going to have to start over.'

'What do you mean, start over?' said Armstrong.

'While you were away the unions rejected the $230 million redundancy package you proposed. They've come back with a demand for $370 million.'

Armstrong collapsed into his chair. 'I only have to go away for a few days, and you let everything fall apart!' he screamed. He looked towards the door as his secretary entered the room and placed the first edition of the *Tribune* on the desk in front of him. He glanced down at the headline: 'WELCOME HOME DICK!'

FINAL EDITION

Double or Quits

35

NEW YORK TRIBUNE

4 FEBRUARY 1991

Captain Dick in Command

'Armstrong has made a bid of $2 billion for Multi Media,' said Townsend.

'What? That's like a politician declaring war when he doesn't want people to realise how bad his problems are at home,' said Tom.

'Possibly. But like those same politicians, if he pulls it off, it just might sort out his problems at home.'

'I doubt it. After going through those figures over the weekend, if he stumps up $2 billion it's more likely to end up as yet another disaster.'

'Multi Media is worth far more than two billion,' said Townsend. 'It owns fourteen newspapers stretching from Maine to Mexico, nine television stations, and the *TV News*, the biggest-selling magazine in the world. Its turnover alone touched a billion last year, and the company declared an overall profit of over $100 million. It's a cash mountain.'

'For which Sinclair will expect to be given Everest in return,' said Tom. 'I can't see how Armstrong can hope to make a profit at $2 billion, especially if he has to borrow heavily to get it.'

'Simply by generating more cash,' said Townsend. 'Multi Media has been on autopilot for years. To start with, I'd sell off several of the subsidiaries that are no longer profitable and revitalise others that should be making far more. But my main efforts would concentrate on building up the media side, which has never been properly exploited, using the turnover and profits from the newspapers and magazines to finance the whole operation.'

'But you have more than enough to worry about at the moment without getting involved in another takeover,' said Tom. 'You've only just settled the strike at the *New York Star*, and don't forget that the bank recommended a period of consolidation.'

'You know what I think of bankers,' said Townsend. 'The *Globe*, the *Star* and all my Australian interests are now in profit, and I may never have an opportunity like this again. Surely you can see that, Tom, even if the bank can't.'

Tom didn't speak for some time. He admired Townsend's drive and innovation, but Multi Media dwarfed anything they had ever attempted in the past. And however hard he tried, he just couldn't make the figures add up. 'There's only one way I can see it working,' he said eventually.

'And how's that?' asked Townsend.

'By offering him preference shares – our stock in exchange for his.'

'But that would simply be a reverse takeover. He'd never agree to it, especially if Armstrong has already offered him two billion in cash.'

'If he has, God knows where he's getting it from,' said Tom. 'Why don't I have a word with their lawyers and see if I can find out if Armstrong really has made a cash offer?'

'No. That's not the right approach. Don't forget that Sinclair owns the entire company himself, so it makes a lot more sense to deal with him direct. That's what Armstrong will have done.'

'But that's hardly your usual style.'

'I realise that. But it's become rare for me lately to be able to deal with anyone who owns their own company.'

Tom shrugged his shoulders. 'So, what do you know about Sinclair?'

'He's seventy,' said Townsend, 'which is why he's retiring. In his lifetime he's built up the most successful privately-owned media corporation in the world. He was the Ambassador to the Court of St James's when his friend Nixon was president, and in his spare time he's put together one of the finest private collections of Impressionist paintings outside a national gallery. He's also chairman of a charitable foundation which specialises in education, and somehow he still finds time to play golf.'

'Good. And what do you imagine Sinclair knows about you?'

'That I'm Australian by birth, run the second-largest media company in the world, prefer Nolan to Renoir, and don't play golf.'

'So how do you intend to approach him?'

'Cut out the bullshit, call him direct and make an offer. At least that way I won't spend years wondering if I might have pulled it off.' Townsend looked across at his lawyer, but Tom made no comment.

Townsend picked up the phone. 'Heather, get me Multi Media headquarters in Colorado. And when they come on, connect me to the operator.' He replaced the receiver.

'Do you really believe that Armstrong has put in a bid for two billion?' asked Tom.

Townsend considered the question for some time. 'Yes, I do.'

'But where would he find that amount of cash?'

'Wherever he found the money to pay off the unions would be my guess.'

'And how much do you intend to offer?'

The phone on the desk rang before he could answer.

'Is that Multi Media?'

'Yes, sir,' replied a deep Southern voice.

'My name is Keith Townsend,' he said. 'I'd like to speak to Mr Sinclair.'

'Does Ambassador Sinclair know you, sir?'

'I hope so,' said Townsend. 'Otherwise I'm wasting my time.'

'I'll put you through to his office.'

Townsend made a sign to his lawyer that he should listen in on the extension. Tom picked up the phone on the side table next to him.

'Ambassador Sinclair's office,' said another Southern voice.

'It's Keith Townsend. I was rather hoping I might be able to have a word with Mr Sinclair.'

'The Ambassador is at his ranch, Mr Townsend, and I know he's due at the country club in twenty minutes for his weekly golf lesson. But I'll see if I can catch him before he leaves.'

Tom put his hand over the mouthpiece and said quietly, 'Call him Ambassador. It's obvious that everyone else does.'

Townsend nodded as a voice came on the line and said, 'Good morning, Mr Townsend. Henry Sinclair here. How can I help you?'

'Good morning, Ambassador,' said Townsend, trying to remain calm. 'I wanted to have a word with you in person, so as not to waste unnecessary time dealing through lawyers.'

'Not to mention unnecessary expense,' suggested Sinclair. 'What is it that you felt you had to speak to me about, Mr Townsend?'

For a moment Townsend wished he'd spent a little more time discussing tactics with Tom. 'I want to make a bid for Multi Media,' he said eventually, 'and it seemed sensible to deal with you direct.'

'I appreciate that, Mr Townsend,' said Sinclair. 'But remember that Mr Armstrong, with whom I believe you are acquainted, has already made me an offer I was able to refuse.'

'I'm aware of that, Ambassador,' said Townsend, wondering how much Armstrong had really offered. He paused for a moment, not looking in Tom's direction.

'Would it be too much to ask the figure you have in mind, Mr Townsend?' said Sinclair.

When Townsend replied, Tom nearly dropped the phone on the floor.

'And how would you intend to finance that?' asked Sinclair.

'In cash,' said Townsend, without any idea how he would raise the money.

'If you can come up with that amount of cash within thirty days, Mr Townsend, you have yourself a deal. In which case perhaps you would be kind enough to ask your lawyers to get in touch with mine.'

'And the name of your lawyers . . . ?'

'Forgive me for cutting this conversation short, Mr Townsend, but I'm due on the driving range in ten minutes, and my pro charges by the hour.'

'Of course, Ambassador,' said Townsend, relieved that Sinclair couldn't see the look of disbelief on his face. He put the phone down and looked across at Tom.

'Do you know what you've just done, Keith?'

'The biggest deal of my life,' replied Townsend.

'At three billion dollars, it's possibly the last,' said Tom.

―◦―

'I'll close the damn paper down,' shouted Armstrong, thumping his fist on the desk.

Russell Critchley, who stood one pace behind his client, felt the words might have carried a little more conviction if Sean O'Reilly hadn't heard them every day for the past three months.

'It will cost you a whole lot more if you do,' replied O'Reilly, his voice quiet and gentle as he stood facing Armstrong.

'What do you mean by that?' hollered Armstrong.

'Just that by the time you put the paper up for sale, there might not be anything left worth selling.'

'Are you threatening me?'

'I guess you might interpret it that way.'

Armstrong rose from his chair, placed the palms of his hands on the desk and leaned forward until he was only a few inches away from the trade union leader's face; but O'Reilly didn't even blink. 'You expect me to settle for $320 million, when only last night I found eighteen names listed on the checking-in sheets who have retired from the company, one of them over ten years ago?'

'I know,' said O'Reilly. 'They get so attached to the place they just can't stay away.' He tried to keep a straight face.

'At $500 a night,' shouted Armstrong, 'I'm not surprised.'

'That's why I'm offering you a way out,' said O'Reilly.

Armstrong grimaced as he looked down at the latest work sheets. 'And what about Bugs Bunny, Jimmy Carter and O. J. Simpson, not to mention another forty-eight other well-known personalities who signed on for yesterday's late shift? And I'll bet the only finger any of them lifted all night was to stir their coffee between hands of poker. And you expect me to agree that every one of them, including George Bush, has to be included in your redundancy package?'

'Yes. It's just our way of helping him with his campaign contributions.'

Armstrong looked towards Russell and Peter in desperation, hoping to get some support from them, but for different reasons neither of them opened his mouth. He turned back to face O'Reilly. 'I'll let you know my decision later,' he shouted. 'Now get out of my office.'

'Were you still hoping that the paper will hit the streets tonight?' asked O'Reilly innocently.

'Is that another threat?' asked Armstrong.

'Sure is,' said O'Reilly. 'Because if you are, I suggest you settle before the evening shift comes on at five o'clock. It doesn't make a lot of difference to my men if they're paid for working or not working.'

'Get out of my office,' Armstrong repeated at the top of his voice.

'Whatever you say, Mr Armstrong. You're the boss.' He nodded to Russell and turned to leave.

Once the door had closed behind him, Armstrong swung round to face Peter. 'Now you can see what I'm up against. What do they expect me to do?' He was still shouting.

'To close the paper down,' said Russell calmly, 'as you should have done on the first day of the seventh week. By now they would have settled at a far lower price.'

'But if I'd taken your advice, we'd have no paper.'

'And we'd all be getting a night's sleep.'

'If you want a night's sleep, you have one,' said Armstrong. 'I'm going to settle. In the short term it's the only way out.

We'll win them round in the end, nothing's more certain. O'Reilly is about to crack. I'm sure you agree with me, Peter.'

Peter Wakeham didn't say anything until Armstrong turned to face him, when he began to nod vigorously.

'But where are you going to find another $320 million?' asked Russell.

'That's my problem,' said Armstrong.

'It's mine too. I'll need the money within minutes of O'Reilly putting his signature to the agreement, otherwise they'll come out on strike just as we're about to print the next edition.'

'You'll have it,' said Armstrong.

'Dick, it's still not too late . . .' said Russell.

'Settle, and settle now,' shouted Armstrong.

Russell nodded reluctantly and left the room as Armstrong picked up a phone that would put him directly through to the editor. 'Barney, it's good news,' he boomed. 'I've managed to convince the unions that they should settle on my terms. I want a front-page story saying it's a victory for common sense and a leader on how I've achieved something no one else has ever done in the past.'

'Sure, if that's what you want, boss. Would you like me to print the details of the settlement?'

'No, don't bother with the details. The terms are so complicated that even the readers of the *Wall Street Journal* wouldn't understand them. In any case, there's no point in embarrassing the unions,' he added before putting the phone down.

'Well done, Dick,' said Peter. 'Not that I was in any doubt that you'd win in the end.'

'At a price,' said Armstrong, opening the top drawer of his desk.

'Not really, Dick. O'Reilly caved in the moment you threatened to close the paper. You handled him quite brilliantly.'

'Peter, I need a couple of cheques signed,' said Armstrong, 'and as you're the only other director in New York at the moment . . .'

'Of course,' said Peter. 'Only too happy to oblige.'

Armstrong placed the pension fund chequebook on his desk

and flicked open the cover. 'When are you returning to London?' he asked as he waved Peter into his chair.

'Tomorrow's Concorde,' Peter replied with a smile.

'Then you'll have to explain to Sir Paul why I can't make the board meeting on Wednesday, much as I'd like to. Just tell him that I've finally settled with the unions on excellent terms, and that by the time I report to the board next month we should be showing a positive cash flow.' He placed his hand on Peter's shoulder.

'With pleasure, Dick,' said Peter. 'Now, how many of these cheques do you need signed?'

'You may as well do the lot while you're at it.'

'The whole book?' said Peter, shifting uneasily in his chair.

'Yes,' replied Armstrong, handing him his pen. 'They'll be quite safe with me. After all, none of them can be cashed until I've countersigned them.'

Peter gave a nervous laugh as he unscrewed the top of the pen. He hesitated until he felt Armstrong's fingers tightening round his shoulder.

'Your position as deputy chairman comes up for renewal in a few weeks' time, doesn't it?' said Armstrong.

Peter signed the first three cheques.

'And Paul Maitland won't go on for ever, you know. Eventually someone will have to take his place as chairman.'

Peter continued signing.

36

DAILY EXPRESS

8 FEBRUARY 1991

Cabinet Escapes as IRA Bomb Explodes in Garden of No. 10

'Bitten off More than They Can Chew' was the headline on the article in the *Financial Times*. Sir Paul Maitland, sitting by the fire at his home in Epsom, and Tom Spencer, travelling in from Greenwich, Connecticut, on a commuter train, both read the article a second time, although only half the contents were of any real interest to them.

> The press barons Keith Townsend and Richard Armstrong appear to have made the classic mistake of leveraging their borrowings on far too high a ratio against their assets. They both look destined to become case studies for future generations of students at Harvard Business School.
>
> Analysts have always agreed that Armstrong initially appeared to have pulled off a coup when he purchased the *New York Tribune* for only twenty-five cents while all the paper's liabilities were underwritten by the former owners. The coup might have turned into a triumph had he carried out his threat to close the paper down within six weeks if the unions failed to sign a binding agreement.

But he did not, and then he compounded his mistake by eventually giving such a generous redundancy settlement that union leaders stopped calling him 'Captain Dick' and started referring to him as 'Captain Santa'.

Despite that settlement, the paper continues to lose over a million dollars a week, although agreement on a second package of redundancies and early retirements is thought to be imminent.

But while interest rates continue to rise and the vogue for cutting the cover price of newspapers continues, it cannot be long before the profits of the *Citizen* and the rest of the Armstrong Communications group will no longer be able to sustain the losses of its American subsidiary.

Mr Armstrong has not yet informed his shareholders how he intends to finance the second settlement of $320 million recently agreed with the New York print unions. His only reported statement on the subject is to be found in the columns of the *Tribune*: 'Now that the second package has been accepted by the unions, there is no reason to believe that the cash flow of the *Tribune* shouldn't prove positive.'

The City remained sceptical of this claim, and shares in Armstrong Communications fell yesterday by a further nine pence to £2.42.

Keith Townsend's mistake . . .

The phone rang, and Sir Paul put the paper down, rose from his chair and went into his study to answer it. When he heard the voice of Eric Chapman, he asked him to wait for a moment while he closed the door. This was somewhat unnecessary, as there was no one else in the house at the time; but when you've been the British Ambassador in Beijing for four years, some habits die hard.

'I think we ought to meet immediately,' said Chapman.

'The *Financial Times* article?' said Sir Paul.

'No, it's potentially far more damaging than that. I'd rather not say too much over the phone.'

'I quite understand,' said Sir Paul. 'Shall I ask Peter Wakeham to join us?'

'Not if you want the meeting to remain confidential.'

'You're right,' said Sir Paul. 'Where shall we meet?'

'I could drive over to Epsom straight away. I should be with you in about an hour.'

—◦—

Tom Spencer skimmed through the first half of the article as his train headed past Mamaroneck on its journey into New York. He only began to concentrate fully when he reached the words:

> Keith Townsend's mistake was to want something so badly that he failed to keep to the basic rules of closing a deal.
>
> Every schoolboy knows that if you hope to exchange old conkers for an unopened packet of crisps, not only must you never blink, you must also wait for your opponent to make the opening bid. But it seems that Townsend was so determined to own Multi Media that he never stopped blinking, and without asking how much Henry Sinclair might be willing to sell the company for, he made an unsolicited offer of $3 billion. He then compounded his problems by agreeing to pay the full amount in cash.
>
> Just as the print unions in New York refer to Mr Armstrong as 'Captain Santa', Mr Sinclair could be forgiven for thinking Christmas had come early this year – especially when it was common knowledge that he had been on the point of closing a deal with Armstrong for

$2 billion, and even that, it is now thought, would have been too high a price.

Having agreed terms, Mr Townsend found it extremely difficult to raise the cash within the thirty days stipulated by Mr Sinclair. And by the time he had finally done so, it was on such exorbitant terms that keeping to the punitive repayment schedule may in the end prove terminal for the rest of Global International. Throughout his life Mr Townsend has been a gambler. With this deal he has proved that he is willing to risk everything on a single throw of the dice.

On reporting their half-year forecast yesterday, Global shares fell a further eight pence to £3.19.

Over and above any problems the two press barons are currently facing, both of them will be particularly hard hit by the steady rise in the price of paper and the dollar's current weakness against the pound. If the combination of these trends continues for much longer, even their cash cows will run out of milk.

The future of both companies now rests in the hands of their bankers, who must be wondering – like the creditors of a Third World nation – if they will ever see the interest, let alone the long-term debt, being repaid. Their alternative is to cut their losses and agree to participate in the biggest fire sale in history. The final irony is that it would only take one bank to break the link in the lending chain and the whole edifice will come crashing down.

As one insider put it to me yesterday, if either man were to present a cheque at the moment, their bank would bounce.

Tom was the first person off the train when it pulled in to Grand Central station. He ran to the nearest phone booth and dialled Townsend's number. Heather put him straight through. This time Townsend listened attentively to his lawyer's advice.

◄○►

When Armstrong finished reading the article he picked up an internal phone and instructed his secretary that if Sir Paul Maitland should call from London, he was out. No sooner had he replaced the receiver than the phone rang.

'Mr Armstrong, I've got the chief dealer at the Bank of New Amsterdam on the line. He says he needs to speak to you urgently.'

'Then put him through,' said Armstrong.

'The market is being flooded with sell orders on Armstrong Communications stock,' the dealer informed him. 'The share price is now down to $2.31, and I wondered if you had any instructions?'

'Keep buying,' said Armstrong without hesitation.

There was a pause. 'I must point out that every time the shares drop a cent, you lose another $700,000,' said the chief dealer, quickly checking the number of shares that had been traded that morning.

'I don't care what it costs,' said Armstrong. 'It's a short-term necessity. Once the market has settled again, you can release the shares back onto the floor and gradually recoup the losses.'

'But if they continue to fall despite . . .'

'You just keep on buying,' said Armstrong. 'At some point the market is bound to turn.' He slammed down the phone and stared at the photograph of himself on the front page of the *Financial Times*. It wasn't flattering.

◄○►

The moment Townsend had finished reading the article, he took Tom's advice and called his merchant bankers before they called him. David Grenville, the chief executive of the bank, confirmed that Global shares had fallen again that morning. He felt it would be a good idea if they met as soon as possible, and Townsend agreed to reschedule his afternoon appointments to fit in a meeting at two o'clock. 'You might find it worthwhile to have your lawyer present,' Grenville added ominously.

Townsend instructed Heather to cancel all his afternoon appointments. He spent the rest of the morning being briefed on a seminar that the company was due to hold the following month. Henry Kissinger and Sir James Goldsmith had already agreed to be the keynote speakers. It had been Townsend's idea that all his senior executives throughout the world should get together in Honolulu to discuss the development of the corporation over the next ten years, where Multi Media fitted into the overall company structure, and how they could best take advantage of their new acquisition. Would the seminar end up having to be cancelled too, he wondered? Or would it turn out to be a funeral service?

It had taken twenty-seven frantic days to put together the financial package to acquire Multi Media, and many more sleepless nights wondering if he had made a disastrous mistake. Now it appeared as if his worst fears had been confirmed by a hack on the *Financial Times*. If only he had failed to make the deadline, or had listened to Tom in the first place.

His driver turned into Wall Street a few minutes before two and drew up outside the offices of J. P. Grenville. As Townsend stepped out onto the pavement, he remembered how nervous he had been when he had first been summoned to his headmaster's study almost fifty years before. The huge plate-glass door was opened by a man in a long blue coat. He touched the rim of his top hat when he saw who it was. But for how much longer would he do that, Townsend wondered.

He nodded and walked on towards the reception desk, where David Grenville was deep in conversation with Tom Spencer. The moment they saw him both men turned and smiled. They had obviously been confident that this was one appointment he would not be late for. 'Good to see you, Keith,' said Grenville as they shook hands. 'And thank you for being so prompt.' Townsend smiled. He couldn't remember his headmaster ever saying that. Tom put an arm round his client's shoulder as they walked towards a waiting elevator.

THE FOURTH ESTATE

'How's Kate?' asked Grenville. 'When I last saw her she was editing a novel.'

'It was such a success she's now working on one of her own,' said Townsend. 'If things don't work out, I might end up living off her royalties.' Neither of his two companions made any comment on his gallows humour.

The lift doors slid open at the fifteenth floor, and they walked down the corridor and into the chief executive's office. Grenville ushered the two men into comfortable chairs, and opened a file on the blotter in front of him. 'Let me begin by thanking you both for coming in at such short notice,' he said.

Townsend and his lawyer both nodded, although they knew they hadn't been left with a lot of choice.

'We have had the privilege,' said Grenville, turning to Townsend, 'of acting on behalf of your company for over a quarter of a century, and I would be sorry to see that association come to an end.'

Townsend's mouth went dry, but he made no attempt to interrupt.

'But it would be foolish for any of us to underestimate the gravity of the situation we are now facing. On a superficial study of your affairs, it looks to us as if your borrowings may well exceed your assets, possibly leaving you insolvent. If you wish us to remain as your investment bankers, Keith, then we will do so only if we are guaranteed your full co-operation in trying to solve your current dilemma.'

'And what does "full co-operation" mean?' asked Tom.

'We would begin by attaching to your company a financial team under one of our most senior banking officers, who would be given complete – and I mean complete – authority to investigate any aspect of your dealings we felt necessary in order to ensure the company's survival.'

'And once that investigation has been completed?' asked Tom, his eyebrows rising.

'The banking officer would make recommendations which we would expect you to carry out to the letter.'

'When can I see him?' asked Townsend.

'Her,' the bank's chief executive replied. 'And the answer to your question is immediately, because Ms Beresford is in her office on the floor below us waiting to meet you.'

'Then let's get on with it,' said Townsend.

'First I must know if you agree to our terms,' said Grenville.

'I think you can assume that my client has already made that decision,' said Tom.

'Good, then I'll take you down to meet E.B. so she can brief you on the next stage.'

Grenville rose from behind his desk, and led the two men down a flight of stairs to the fourteenth floor. When they arrived outside Ms Beresford's office, he stopped and gave an almost deferential knock.

'Come in,' said a woman's voice. The chief executive opened the door and led them into a large, comfortably furnished room overlooking Wall Street. It gave an immediate impression of being occupied by someone who was neat, tidy and efficient.

A woman Townsend would have guessed was around forty, perhaps forty-five, stood up and came from behind the desk to greet them. She was about the same height as Townsend, with neatly cropped dark hair and an austere face almost hidden by a rather large pair of spectacles. She wore a smartly-cut dark blue suit and a cream blouse.

'Good afternoon,' she said, thrusting out her hand. 'I'm Elizabeth Beresford.'

'Keith Townsend,' he said, shaking her hand. 'And this is my legal counsel, Tom Spencer.'

'I'll leave you to get on with it,' David Grenville said. 'But do drop into my office on the way out, Keith.' He paused. 'If you still feel up to it.'

'Thank you,' said Townsend. Grenville left the room, closing the door quietly behind him.

'Please have a seat,' said Ms Beresford, ushering them into two comfortable chairs on the opposite side of her desk. As she returned to her own seat, Townsend stared at the dozen or more files laid out in front of her.

'Would either of you care for coffee?' she asked.

'No, thank you,' said Townsend, desperate to get on with it. Tom also shook his head.

'I am a company doctor,' began Ms Beresford, 'and my task, Mr Townsend, is quite simply to save Global Corp from a premature death.' She leaned back in her chair and placed the tips of her fingers together. 'Like any doctor who diagnoses a tumour, my first task is to discover whether it is malignant or benign. I have to tell you at the outset that my success rate in such operations is about one in four. I should also add that this is my most difficult assignment to date.'

'Thank you, Ms Beresford,' said Townsend. 'That's most reassuring.'

She showed no reaction as she leaned forward and opened one of the files on her desk.

'Though I've spent several hours this morning going over your balance sheets, and despite the additional research of my excellent financial team, I am still in no position to judge if the *Financial Times*'s assessment of your company is accurate, Mr Townsend. That paper has satisfied itself with an educated guess that your liabilities exceed your assets. It is my job to be far more exacting.

'My problems have been compounded by several outside influences. Firstly, having gone through your files, it is clear for anyone to see that you suffer from a disease common among self-made men – when you're closing a deal you're fascinated by the distant horizon, so long as you can leave it to others to worry about how you get there.'

Tom tried not to smile.

'Secondly, you appear to have made the classic error which the Japanese so quaintly describe as "the Archimedes principle" – namely that your latest deal is often greater than the sum of all your other deals put together.

'Specifically, you went ahead and borrowed $3 billion from a number of banks and institutions for the purpose of taking over Multi Media, without ever considering if the rest of the group could produce the cash flow to sustain such a vast loan.' She paused and placed the tips of her fingers together again.

'I find it hard to believe that this was a transaction on which you took professional advice.'

'I did take professional advice,' said Townsend. 'And Mr Spencer tried to talk me out of it.' He glanced towards his lawyer, who remained impassive.

'I see,' said Ms Beresford. 'If I fail, it will be the reckless gambler in you that will have been the cause of your downfall. Reading through these files last night and into the early hours of this morning, I came to the conclusion that the only reason you have survived so far is that over the years you have just about won more than you have lost, and your bankers, although often nearly driven to distraction, have – sometimes against their better judgement – retained their confidence in you.'

'Is there going to be any good news?' asked Townsend.

She ignored the question and continued, 'My first responsibility will be to go over your books with the clichéd fine-tooth comb, study every one of your companies and its commitments – whatever their size, in whatever country, in whatever currency – and try to make some sense of the overall picture. If, when that is done, I conclude that Global Corp is still solvent in the legal sense of the word, I will move on to the second stage, which will undoubtedly mean selling off some of the company's most treasured assets, to many of which I feel sure you will have a personal attachment.'

Townsend didn't even want to think about which treasures she had in mind. He just sat there, listening to her mortician's diagnosis.

'Even assuming that process is satisfactorily completed, as a contingency plan we will then have to draft a press release setting out why Global Corp is filing for voluntary liquidation. Should it prove necessary, I would release it to Reuters without delay.'

Townsend gulped.

'But if that step proves unnecessary, and we are still working together, I will go on to stage three. This will require me to visit every bank and financial institution with which you are involved, in order to try to convince them to give you a little more time to repay your outstanding loans. Though I must say that if I were in their position, I would not do so.'

She stopped for a moment, then leaned forward and opened another file. 'It appears,' she said, reading from a handwritten note, 'that I would have to visit thirty-seven banks and eleven other financial institutions based in four continents, most of which have already been in touch with me this morning. I only hope I've been able to stall them long enough for us to make sense of all this.' Her hands swept the air above the files on her desk. 'If, by some miracle, stages one, two and three can be completed, my final task – and by far the most difficult – will be to convince those same banks and institutions, currently so apprehensive about your future prospects, that you should be allowed to put together a financial package to ensure the long-term survival of the company. I will not be able to reach that stage unless I can prove to them, with independently audited figures, that their loans are secured on real assets and a positive cash flow. On that subject, you will not be surprised to learn, I still need to be convinced myself. And don't imagine for one moment that should you be fortunate enough to reach stage four, you can relax. Far from it, because that is when you'll be told the details of stage five.'

Townsend could feel the sweat beginning to trickle down onto his nose.

'In one respect the *Financial Times* was accurate,' she continued. 'If one of the banks takes it upon itself to be bloody-minded, then, I quote, "the whole edifice will come crashing down". If that is the eventual outcome, then I shall pass this case on to a colleague of mine who works on the floor below this one, and who specialises in liquidations.

'I will conclude by saying, Mr Townsend, that if you hope to avoid the fate of your fellow-countrymen Mr Alan Bond and Mr Christopher Skase, you must not only agree to co-operate with me fully, but you must also give me your assurance that from the moment you leave this office you will not sign a cheque, or move any monies from any account under your control, other than those which are absolutely necessary to cover your day-to-day expenses. And even then they must not, under any circumstances, exceed $2,000 without it being referred to me.' She looked up and waited for his response.

'Two thousand dollars?' Townsend repeated.

'Yes,' she said. 'You will be able to reach me at all times, night or day, and you will never have to wait more than an hour for my decision. If, however, you feel unable to adhere to these conditions,' she said, closing the file, 'then I am not willing to continue representing you, and in that I include this bank, whose reputation, needless to say, is also on the line. I hope I have made my position clear, Mr Townsend.'

'Abundantly,' said Townsend, who felt as if he had gone ten rounds with a heavyweight boxer.

Elizabeth Beresford leaned back in her chair. 'You may of course wish to take professional advice,' she said. 'In which case I will be happy to offer you the use of one of our consultation rooms.'

'That won't be necessary,' said Townsend. 'If my professional adviser had disagreed with any part of your assessment, he would have said so long before now.'

Tom allowed himself a smile.

'I will co-operate fully with your recommendations.' He turned to glance at Tom, who nodded his approval.

'Good,' said Ms Beresford. 'Perhaps you could start by handing over your credit cards.'

Three hours later Townsend rose from his chair, shook hands with Elizabeth Beresford again and, feeling utterly exhausted, left her to her files. Tom returned to his office as Townsend made his way unsteadily up the staircase to the floor above and along the corridor to the chief executive's room. He was about to knock when the door swung open and David Grenville stood in front of him holding a large glass of whisky.

'I had a feeling you might need this,' he said, handing it to Townsend. 'But first tell me, did you survive the opening rounds with E.B.?'

'I'm not sure,' he replied. 'But I'm booked in every afternoon from three to six for the next fortnight, including weekends.' He took a large gulp of whisky and added, 'And she's taken away my credit cards.'

'That's a good sign,' said Grenville. 'It shows that she hasn't given up on you. Sometimes E.B. simply sends the files down a floor as soon as the first meeting is concluded.'

'Am I supposed to feel grateful?' asked Townsend when he had drained his whisky.

'No, just temporarily relieved,' said Grenville. 'Do you still feel up to attending the bankers' dinner tonight?' he asked as he poured Townsend a second whisky.

'Well, I was hoping to join you,' replied Townsend. 'But she,' he said, pointing down at the floor, 'has set me so much homework to be completed by three tomorrow afternoon that . . .'

'I think it would be wise if you were to put in an appearance tonight, Keith. Your absence might easily, in the present circumstances, be misinterpreted.'

'That may be true. But won't she send me home even before they've served the entrée?'

'I doubt it, because I've placed you on her right-hand side. It's all part of my strategy to convince the banking world that we're 100 per cent behind you.'

'Hell. What's she like socially?'

The chairman considered the question only briefly before saying, 'I must confess, E.B. doesn't have a great deal of small talk.'

37

Daily Mail

2 JULY 1991

Charles and Diana:
'Cause for Concern'

'There's a call from Switzerland on line one, Mr Armstrong,' said the temporary secretary whose name he couldn't remember. 'He says his name is Jacques Lacroix. I'm also holding another call from London on line two.'

'Who's calling from London?' asked Armstrong.

'A Mr Peter Wakeham.'

'Ask him to hold, and put the call from Switzerland straight through.'

'Is that you, Dick?'

'Yes, Jacques. How are you, old friend?' Armstrong boomed.

'A little disturbed, Dick,' came the softly-spoken reply from Geneva.

'Why?' asked Armstrong. 'I deposited a cheque for $50 million with your New York branch last week. I even have a receipt for it.'

'I am not disputing the fact that you deposited the cheque,' said Lacroix. 'The purpose of this call is to let you know that it has been returned to the bank today, marked "Refer to drawer".'

'There must be some mistake,' said Armstrong. 'I know that account still has more than enough to cover the sum in question.'

'That may well be the case. But someone is nevertheless refusing to release any of those funds to us, and indeed has made it clear, through the usual channels, that they will not in future honour any cheques presented on that account.'

'I'll ring them immediately,' said Armstrong, 'and call you straight back.'

'I would be grateful if you did,' said Lacroix.

Armstrong rang off and noticed that the light on top of the phone was flashing. He remembered that Wakeham was still holding on line two, grabbed the receiver and said, 'Peter, what the hell is going on over there?'

'I'm not too sure myself,' admitted Peter. 'All I can tell you is that Paul Maitland and Eric Chapman visited me at home late last night, and asked if I had signed any cheques on the pension fund account. I said exactly what you told me to say, but I got the impression that Maitland has now given orders to stop any cheques that have my signature on them.'

'Who the hell do they think they are?' bawled Armstrong. 'It's my company, and I'll do as I see fit.'

'Sir Paul says he's been trying to get in touch with you for the past week, but you haven't been returning his calls. He said at a finance committee meeting last week that if you fail to turn up at next month's board meeting, he will be left with no choice but to resign.'

'Let him resign – who gives a damn? As soon as he's gone I can appoint anyone I like as chairman.'

'Of course you can,' said Peter. 'But I thought you'd want to know that his secretary told me he's spent the last few days drafting and redrafting a press release to coincide with his resignation.'

'So what?' said Armstrong. 'No one will bother to follow it up.'

'I'm not so sure,' said Peter.

'What makes you say that?'

'After his secretary had left for the evening, I hung around and managed to bring up the statement on her console.'

'And what does it say?'

'Among other things, that he will be asking the Stock Exchange to suspend our shares until a full inquiry can be carried out.'

'He doesn't have the authority to do that,' shouted Armstrong. 'It would have to be sanctioned by the board.'

'I think he plans to ask for that authority at the next board meeting,' said Peter.

'Then make it clear to him that I will be present at that meeting,' hollered Armstrong down the phone, 'and that the only press release that will be issued will be the one from me setting out the reasons why Sir Paul Maitland has had to be replaced as chairman of the board.'

'Perhaps it would be better if you told him that yourself,' said Peter quietly. 'I'll just let him know that you intend to be there.'

'Say what you damn well like. Just make sure that he doesn't issue any press statements before I get back at the end of the month.'

'I'll do my best Dick, but . . .' Peter heard a click on the other end of the line.

Armstrong tried to collect his thoughts. Sir Paul could wait. His first priority was somehow to get his hands on fifty million before Jacques Lacroix let the whole world in on his secret. The *Tribune* still hadn't turned the corner, despite all his efforts. Even after the second settlement with the unions, the company was showing a disastrously negative cash flow. He had already removed over £300 million from the pension fund without the board's knowledge, to get the unions off his back and keep the share price as steady as he could by buying up massive amounts of stock in his own company. But if he failed to pay back the Swiss in the next few days, he knew there would be a further run on the stock, and this time he wouldn't have such a ready source of funds with which to shore them up.

He glanced round at the international clock on the wall behind his desk to check what time it was in Moscow. Just after six o'clock. But he suspected that the man he needed to speak to would still be in his office. He picked up the phone and asked the secretary to get him a number in Moscow.

He put the receiver down. No one had been more delighted than Armstrong when Marshal Tulpanov was appointed head of the KGB. Since then he had made several trips to Moscow, and a number of large Eastern European contracts had come his way. But recently he had found that Tulpanov hadn't been quite so readily available.

Armstrong began to sweat as he waited for the call to be put through. Over the years he had had a number of meetings with Mikhail Gorbachev, who appeared to be quite receptive to his ideas. But then Boris Yeltsin had taken over. Tulpanov had introduced him to the new Russian leader, but Armstrong had come away from the meeting with a feeling that neither of them appreciated how important he was.

While he waited to be put through, he began to leaf through the pages of his Filofax, searching for any names that might be able to help with his present dilemma. He'd reached C – Sally Carr – when the phone rang. He picked it up to hear a voice in Russian asking who wished to speak to Marshal Tulpanov.

'Lubji, London sector,' he replied. There was a click, and the familiar voice of the head of the KGB came on the line.

'What can I do for you, Lubji?' he asked.

'I need a little help, Sergei,' began Armstrong. There was no immediate response.

'And what form is this help expected to take?' Tulpanov eventually enquired in a measured tone.

'I need a short-term loan of $50 million. You'd get it back within a month, that I can guarantee.'

'But, comrade,' said the head of the KGB, 'you are already holding $7 million of our money. Several of my station commanders tell me that they haven't received their royalties from the publication of our latest book.'

Armstrong's mouth went dry. 'I know, I know, Sergei,' he pleaded. 'But I just need a little more time, and I'll be able to return everything in the same package.'

'I'm not sure I want to take that risk,' said Tulpanov after another long silence. 'I believe the British have a saying about throwing good money after bad. And you'd be wise to remember, Lubji, that the *Financial Times* is read not only in London and New York, but also in Moscow. I think I shall wait until I have seen my seven million deposited in all the correct accounts before I consider lending you any more. Do I make myself clear?'

'Yes,' replied Armstrong quietly.

'Good. I will give you until the end of the month to fulfil your obligations. Then I fear we may have to resort to a less subtle approach. I think I pointed out to you many years ago, Lubji, that at some time you would have to make up your mind about which side you were on. I remind you only because at the moment, to quote another English saying, you seem to be playing both sides against the middle.'

'No, that's not fair,' protested Armstrong. 'I'm on your side, Sergei, I've always been on your side.'

'I hear what you are saying, Lubji, but if our money is not returned by the end of the month, I will be powerless to help. And after such a long friendship, that would be most unfortunate. I am sure you appreciate the position you have put me in.'

Armstrong heard the line go dead. His forehead was dripping with sweat; he felt queasy. He put down the receiver, took a powder puff from his pocket and began dabbing his forehead and cheeks. He tried to concentrate. A few moments later he picked up the phone again. 'Get me the prime minister of Israel.'

'Is that a Manhattan number?' asked the temp.

'Damn it, am I the only person left in this building who can carry out a simple task?'

'I'm sorry,' she stammered.

'Don't bother, I'll do it myself,' shouted Armstrong.

He checked his Filofax and dialled the number. While he waited to be connected, he continued to turn the pages of his Filofax. He had reached H – Julius Hahn – when a voice on the end of the line said, 'The prime minister's office.'

'It's Dick Armstrong here. I need to speak to the prime minister urgently.'

'I'll see if I can interrupt him, sir.'

Another click, another wait, a few more pages turned. He reached the letter L – Sharon Levitt.

'Dick, is that you?' enquired Prime Minister Shamir.

'Yes it is, Yitzhak.'

'How are you, my old friend?'

'I'm just fine,' said Armstrong, 'and you?'

'I'm well thank you.' He paused. 'I've got all the usual problems, of course, but at least I'm in good health. And how's Charlotte?'

'Charlotte's fine,' said Armstrong, unable to remember when he had last seen her. 'She's in Oxford looking after the grandchildren.'

'So how many do you have now?' asked Shamir.

Armstrong had to think for a moment. 'Three,' he said, and nearly added, 'or is it four?'

'Lucky man. And are you still keeping the Jews of New York happy?'

'You can always rely on me to do that,' said Armstrong.

'I know we can, old friend,' said the prime minister. 'So tell me. What is it I can do for you?'

'It's a personal matter, Yitzhak, that I hoped you might be able to advise me on.'

'I'll do everything I can to help; Israel will always be in your debt for the work you have done for our people. Tell me how I can assist you, old friend.'

'A simple request,' replied Armstrong. 'I need a short-term loan of $50 million, no more than a month at the most. I wondered if you could help in any way?'

There was a long silence before the prime minister said, 'The government does not involve itself in loans, of course, but I could have a word with the chairman of Bank Leumi if you thought that would be helpful.'

Armstrong decided not to tell the prime minister that he already had an outstanding loan of $20 million with that particular bank, and they had made it clear that no more would be forthcoming.

'That's a good idea, Yitzhak. But don't you bother, I can contact him myself,' he added, trying to sound cheerful.

'By the way, Dick,' said the prime minister, 'while I've got you on the line, about your other request . . .'

'Yes?' he said, his hopes rising for a moment.

'Without sounding too morbid, the Knesset agreed last week that you should be buried on the Mount of Olives, a privilege afforded only to those Jews who have done a great service to the State of Israel. My congratulations. Not every prime minister can be sure of making it, you know.' He laughed. 'Not that I anticipate you will be taking advantage of this offer for many years to come.'

'Let's hope you're right,' said Armstrong.

'So, will I see you and Charlotte in London for the Guildhall Banquet next month?'

'Yes, we're looking forward to it,' said Armstrong. 'I'll see you then. But don't let me detain you any longer, prime minister.'

Armstrong put the phone down, suddenly aware that his shirt was soaked through and clinging to his body. He heaved himself out of his chair and made his way to the bathroom, taking off his jacket and unbuttoning his shirt as he went. When he had closed the door behind him, he towelled himself down and pulled on his third clean shirt that day.

He returned to his desk and continued flicking through his list of phone numbers until he reached S – Arno Schultz. He picked up the phone and asked the secretary to get his lawyer on the line.

'Do you have his number?' she asked.

After another outburst he slammed down the receiver and dialled Russell's number himself. Without thinking, he turned a few more pages of his Filofax until he heard the attorney's voice on the other end of the line. 'Have I got $50 million hidden away anywhere in the world?' he asked.

'What do you need it for?' asked Russell.

'The Swiss are beginning to threaten me.'

'I thought you'd settled with them last week.'

'So did I.'

'What's happened to that endless source of funds?'

'It's dried up.'

'I see. How much did you say?'

'Fifty million.'

'Well, I can certainly think of one way you could raise at least that amount.'

'How?' asked Armstrong, trying not to sound desperate.

Russell hesitated. 'You could always sell your 46 per cent stake in the *New York Star*.'

'But who could come up with that sort of money at such short notice?'

'Keith Townsend.' Russell held the phone away from his ear and waited for the word 'Never' to come booming down the line. But nothing happened, so he carried on. 'My guess is that he'd agree to pay above the market price, because it would guarantee him complete control of the company.'

Russell held the phone away from his ear again, expecting a tirade of abuse. But all Armstrong said was, 'Why don't you have a word with his lawyers?'

'I'm not sure that would be the best approach,' said Russell. 'If I were to phone them out of the blue, Townsend would assume that you were short of funds.'

'Which I am not!' shouted Armstrong.

'No one's suggesting you are,' said Russell. 'Will you be attending the bankers' dinner tonight at the Four Seasons?'

'Bankers' dinner? What bankers' dinner?'

'The annual get-together for the principal players in the financial world and their guests. I know you've been invited, because I read in the *Tribune* that you'd be sitting between the governor and the mayor.'

Armstrong checked the printed day-sheet which was lying on his desk. 'You're right, I'm supposed to be going. But so what?'

'I have a feeling that Townsend will make an appearance, if

only to let the banking world know he's still around after that unfortunate article in the *Financial Times*.'

'I suppose the same could apply to me,' said Armstrong, sounding unusually morose.

'It might be the ideal opportunity to bring up the subject casually and see what sort of reaction you get.'

Another phone began to ring.

'Hold on a moment, Russell,' Armstrong said, as he picked up the other phone. It was his secretary on the end of the line. 'What do you want?' Armstrong bellowed out the words so loudly that Russell wondered for a moment if he was still talking to him.

'I'm sorry to interrupt you, Mr Armstrong,' she said, 'but the man from Switzerland has just phoned again.'

'Tell him I'll call straight back,' said Armstrong.

'He insisted on holding, sir. Shall I put him through?'

'I'll have to call you back in a moment, Russell,' said Armstrong, switching phones.

He looked down at his Filofax, which was open at the letter T.

'Jacques, I think I may have solved our little problem.'

38

NEW YORK STAR

20 AUGUST 1991

Mayor Tells Police Chief: 'The Cupboard's Bare'

Townsend hated the idea of having to sell his shares in the *Star*, and to Richard Armstrong of all people. He checked his bow tie in the mirror and cursed out loud yet again. He knew that everything Elizabeth Beresford had insisted on that afternoon was probably his only hope of survival.

Perhaps Armstrong might fail to turn up to the dinner? That would at least allow him to bluff for a few more days. How could E.B. begin to understand that of all his assets, the *Star* was second only to the *Melbourne Courier* in his affections? He shuddered at the thought that she hadn't yet told him what she felt would have to be disposed of in Australia.

Townsend rummaged around in the bottom drawer, searching for a dress shirt, and was relieved to find one neatly wrapped in a cellophane packet. He pulled it on. Damn! He cursed as the top button flew off when he tried to do it up, and cursed again when he remembered that Kate wouldn't be back from Sydney for another week. He tightened his bow tie, hoping that it would cover the problem. He looked in the mirror. It didn't. Worse, the collar of his dinner jacket was so shiny that it made him look like a 1950s band leader. Kate had been telling him for years to get a new DJ, and perhaps the time had come to take her advice. And then he remembered: he no longer had any credit cards.

When he left his apartment that evening and took the elevator down to the waiting car, Townsend couldn't help noticing for the first time that his chauffeur was wearing a smarter suit than anything he had in his entire wardrobe. As the limousine began its slow journey to the Four Seasons, he sat back and tried to work out just how he might bring up the subject of selling his shares in the *Star* should he get a moment alone with Dick Armstrong.

—<o>—

One of the good things about a well-cut double-breasted DJ, Armstrong thought, was that it helped to disguise just how overweight you really were. He had spent more than an hour that evening having his hair dyed by his butler and his hands manicured by a maid. When he checked himself in the mirror, he felt confident that few of those attending the bankers' dinner that night would have believed he was nearly seventy.

Russell had phoned him just before he left the office to say that he calculated the value of his shares in the *Star* must be around sixty to seventy million dollars, and he was confident that Townsend would be willing to pay a premium if he could buy the stock in one block.

All he needed for the moment was fifty-seven million. That would take care of the Swiss, the Russians and even Sir Paul.

As his limousine drew up outside the Four Seasons, a young man in a smart red jacket rushed up and opened the back door for him. When he saw who it was trying to heave himself out, he touched his cap and said, 'Good evening, Mr Armstrong.'

'Good evening,' Armstrong replied, and handed the young man a ten-dollar bill. At least one person that night would still believe he was a multi-millionaire. He climbed the wide staircase up to the dining room, joining a stream of other guests. Some of them turned to smile in his direction, others pointed. He wondered what they were whispering to each other. Were they predicting his downfall, or talking of his genius? He returned their smiles.

Russell was waiting for him at the top of the stairs. As they walked on towards the dining room, he leaned over and whispered, 'Townsend's already here. He's on table fourteen as a guest of J. P. Grenville.' Armstrong nodded, aware that J. P. Grenville had been Townsend's merchant bankers for over twenty-five years. He entered the dining room, lit up a large Havana cigar and began to weave his way through the packed circular tables, occasionally stopping to shake an outstretched hand, and pausing to chat for a few moments to anyone he knew was capable of loaning large sums of money.

Townsend stood behind his chair on table fourteen and watched Armstrong make his slow progress towards the top table. Eventually he took his place between Governor Cuomo and Mayor Dinkins. He smiled whenever a guest waved in their direction, always assuming it was him they were interested in.

'Tonight could well turn out to be your best chance,' said Elizabeth Beresford, who was also looking towards the top table.

Townsend nodded. 'It might not be quite that easy to speak to him privately.'

'If you wanted to buy his shares, you'd find a way quickly enough.'

Why was the damned woman always right?

The master of ceremonies thumped the table with a gavel several times before the room fell quiet enough for a rabbi to deliver a prayer. Over half the people in the room put khivas on their heads, including Armstrong – something Townsend had never seen him do at a public function in London.

As the guests sat down, a band of waiters began serving the soup. It didn't take long for Townsend to discover that David Grenville had been right in his assessment of E.B.'s small talk, which came to an end long before he had finished the first course. As soon as the main course had been served, she turned towards him, lowered her voice and began to ask a series of questions about his Australian assets. He answered every one of them as best he could, aware that even the slightest inaccuracy would be picked up and later used in evidence against him. Making no concessions to the fact that they were at a social occasion, she then moved on to how he intended to raise the subject of selling his shares in the *Star* to Armstrong.

The first opportunity to escape E.B.'s interrogation – Townsend's answers having already filled the back of two menu cards – arrived when a waiter came between them to top up his wine glass. He immediately turned to Carol Grenville, the bank chairman's wife, who was seated on his left. The only questions Carol wanted answering were 'How are Kate and the children?' and 'Have you seen the revival of *Guys and Dolls*?'

'Have you seen the revival of *Guys and Dolls*, Dick?' the governor asked.

'I can't say I have, Mario,' replied Armstrong. 'What with trying to run the most successful newspapers in New York and London, I just don't seem to find the time for the theatre nowadays. And frankly, with an election coming up, I'm surprised you can either.'

'Never forget, Dick, that voters go to the theatre as well,' said the governor. 'And if you sit in the fifth row of the stalls, three thousand of them see you at once. They're always pleased to discover that you have the same tastes they do.'

Armstrong laughed. 'I'd never make a politician,' he said, putting a hand up. A few moments later a waiter appeared by his side. 'Can I have a little more?' Armstrong whispered.

'Certainly, sir,' said the top-table waiter, although he could have sworn that he had already given Mr Armstrong a second helping.

Armstrong glanced to his right at David Dinkins, and noticed that he was only picking at his food – a habit common among after-dinner speakers, he had found over the years. The mayor, head down, was checking his typewritten text, making the occasional change with a Four Seasons ballpoint pen.

Armstrong made no attempt to interrupt him, and noticed

that when Dinkins was offered a *crème brûlée* he waved it away. Armstrong suggested to the waiter that he should leave it on one side, in case the mayor changed his mind. By the time Dinkins had finished going over his speech, Armstrong had devoured his dessert. He was delighted to see a plate of *petits fours* placed between them a few moments after the coffee had been poured.

During the speeches that followed, Townsend became distracted. He tried not to dwell on his current problems, but when the applause had died down after the President of the Bankers' Association had given his vote of thanks, he realised he could barely recall anything that had been said.

'The speeches were excellent, didn't you think?' said David Grenville, from the other side of the table. 'I doubt if a more distinguished line-up will address an audience in New York this year.'

'You're probably right,' said Townsend. His only thought now was how long he would have to hang around before E.B. would allow him to go home. When he glanced to his right, he saw that her eyes were fixed firmly on the top table.

'Keith,' said a voice from behind him, and he turned to receive the bearhug for which the mayor of New York was famous. Townsend accepted that there had to be some disadvantages in being the proprietor of the *Star*.

'Good evening, Mr Mayor,' he said. 'How good to see you again. May I congratulate you on your excellent speech.'

'Thank you, Keith, but that wasn't why I came to have a word with you.' He jabbed a finger at Townsend's chest. 'Why do I have the feeling that your editor has got it in for me? I know he's Irish, but I want you to ask him how I can be expected to give the NYPD another pay increase, when the city's already run out of money for this year. Does he want me to raise taxes again, or just let the city go bankrupt?'

Townsend would have recommended that the mayor employ E.B. to sort out the problem of the police department, but when David Dinkins finally stopped talking, he agreed to have a word with his editor in the morning. Though he did point out that it had always been his policy not to interfere in the editorial input of any of his papers.

E.B. raised an eyebrow, which indicated just how meticulously she must have been through his files.

'I'm grateful, Keith,' said the mayor. 'I was sure that once I'd explained what I'm up against, you'd appreciate my position – although you can hardly be expected to know what it's like not to be able to pay your bills at the end of the month.'

The mayor looked over Townsend's shoulder, and announced at the top of his voice, 'Now there's a man who never gives me any trouble.'

Townsend and E.B. turned round to see who he was referring to. The mayor was pointing in the direction of Richard Armstrong.

'I assume you two are old friends,' he said, holding his arms out to them both. One of them might have answered the question if Dinkins hadn't walked off to continue his milk round. Elizabeth retreated discreetly, but not so far that she couldn't hear every word that passed between them.

'So, how are you, Dick?' asked Townsend, who had not the slightest interest in Armstrong's well-being.

'Never better,' Armstrong replied, turning to blow a mouthful of cigar smoke in Elizabeth's direction.

'It must be quite a relief for you to have finally settled with the unions.'

'They were left with no choice in the end,' said Armstrong. 'Either they agreed to my terms, or I would have closed the paper down.'

Russell walked quietly over and hovered behind them.

'At a price,' said Townsend.

'A price I can well afford,' said Armstrong. 'Especially now that the paper has begun showing a profit every week. I only hope you'll eventually find that possible at Multi Media.' He drew deeply on his cigar.

'That's never been a problem for Multi Media since day one,' said Townsend. 'With the sort of cash flow that company generates, my biggest worry is to make sure we have enough staff to bank the money.'

'I have to admit that coughing up three billion for that cowboy outfit showed you've got balls. I only offered Henry Sinclair one and a half billion, and then not until my accountants had gone over his books with a magnifying glass.'

In different circumstances Townsend might have reminded him that at the Lord Mayor's Dinner at the Guildhall the previous year, Armstrong had told him that he had offered Sinclair two and a half billion, despite the fact that they wouldn't let him even see the accounts – but not while E.B. was only a couple of paces away.

Armstrong sucked deeply on his cigar before delivering his next well-rehearsed line. 'Do you still have enough time to keep an eye on my interests at the *Star*?'

'More than enough, thank you,' Townsend replied. 'And although it may not have the circulation figures of the *Tribune*, I'm sure you'd be happy to exchange them for the *Star*'s profits.'

'By this time next year,' said Armstrong, 'I can assure you that the *Tribune* will be ahead of the *Star* on both counts.'

It was Russell's turn to raise an eyebrow.

'Well, let's compare notes at next year's dinner,' said Townsend. 'By then it should be clear for anyone to see.'

'As long as I control 100 per cent of the *Tribune* and 46 per cent of the *Star*, I'm bound to win either way,' said Armstrong.

Elizabeth frowned.

'In fact, if Multi Media is worth three billion dollars,' Armstrong continued, 'my shares in the *Star* must be worth at least a hundred million of anyone's money.'

'If that's the case,' said Townsend, a little too quickly, 'mine must be worth well over a hundred million.'

'So perhaps the time has come for one of us to buy the other out,' said Armstrong.

Both men fell silent. Russell and Elizabeth glanced at each other.

'What did you have in mind?' Townsend eventually asked.

Russell turned his attention back to his client, not quite sure how he would react. This was a question for which they hadn't rehearsed a reply.

'I'd be willing to sacrifice my 46 per cent of the *Star* for . . . let's say one hundred million.'

Elizabeth wondered how Townsend would have responded to such an offer if she hadn't been there.

'Not interested,' he said. 'But I tell you what I'll do. If you think your shares are worth a hundred million, I'll let mine go for exactly the same amount. I couldn't make you a fairer offer.'

Three people tried not to blink as they waited for Armstrong's reaction. Armstrong inhaled once again before leaning across the table and stubbing out the remains of his cigar in Elizabeth's crème brûlée. 'No,' he finally said as he lit up another cigar. He puffed away for a few seconds before adding, 'I'm quite happy to wait for you to put your stock on the open market, because then I'll be able to pick it up for a third of the price. That way I'd control both tabloids in this city, and there are no prizes for guessing which one I'd close down first.' He laughed, and turning to his lawyer for the first time said, 'Come on, Russell, it's time we were on our way.'

Townsend stood there, barely able to control himself.

'Let me know if you have a change of heart,' said Armstrong loudly as he headed in the direction of the exit. The moment he felt sure he was out of earshot, he turned to his lawyer and said, 'That man's so strapped for cash he was trying to sell me his shares.'

'It certainly looked that way,' said Russell. 'I must confess that was one scenario I hadn't anticipated.'

'What chance do I now have of selling my stock in the *Star*?'

'Not much of one,' said Russell. 'After that conversation it won't be long before everyone in this city knows he's a seller. Then any other potential buyer will assume that you're both trying to offload your stock before the other gets the chance to.'

'And if I were to put mine on the open market, what do you think they might fetch?'

'If you placed that quantity of shares on the market in one tranche, it would be assumed you were dumping them, in which case you'd be lucky to get twenty million. In a successful sale there has to be a willing buyer and a reluctant seller. At the moment this deal seems to have two desperate sellers.'

'What alternatives am I left with?' asked Armstrong as they walked towards the limousine.

—◦—

'He's left us with virtually no alternative,' E.B. replied. 'I'm going to have to find a third party who's willing to buy your shares in the *Star*, and preferably before Armstrong's forced to dump his.'

'Why go down that route?' asked Townsend.

'Because I have a feeling that Mr Armstrong is in even worse trouble than you.'

'What makes you say that?'

'My eyes never left him, and once the speeches were over the first thing he did was to head straight for this table.'

'What does that prove?'

'That he had only one purpose in mind,' replied E.B. 'To sell you his shares in the *Star*.'

A thin smile appeared on Townsend's face. 'So why don't we buy them?' he said. 'If I could get my hands on his holding, I might . . .'

'Mr Townsend, don't even think about it.'

39

FINANCIAL TIMES

1 NOVEMBER 1991

Newspaper Groups' Shares in Free Fall

By the time Townsend boarded the plane for Honolulu, Elizabeth Beresford was already halfway across the Atlantic. During the past three weeks he had been put through the toughest examination of his life – and, like all examinations, it would be some time before the results were known.

E.B. had questioned, probed and investigated every aspect of every deal he had ever been involved in. She now knew more about him than his mother, wife, children and the IRS put together. In fact Townsend wondered if there was anything she didn't know – other than what he had been up to in the school pavilion with the headmaster's daughter. And if he'd paid for that, she would doubtless have insisted on being told the precise details of the transaction.

When he arrived back at the apartment each night, exhausted, he would go over the latest position with Kate. 'I'm certain of only one thing,' he often repeated. 'My chances of survival now rest entirely in the hands of that woman.'

They had completed stage one: E.B. accepted that the company was technically solvent. She then turned her attention to stage two: the disposal of assets. When she told Townsend that Mrs Summers wanted to buy back her shares in the *New*

York Star, he reluctantly agreed. But at least E.B. allowed him to retain his controlling interest in the *Melbourne Courier* and the *Adelaide Gazette*. He was however made to sell off the *Perth Sunday Monitor* and the *Continent* in exchange for keeping the *Sydney Chronicle*. He also had to sacrifice his minority interest in his Australian television channel and all the non-contributing subsidiary companies in Multi Media, so that he could go on publishing *TV News*.

By the end of the third week she had completed the striptease, and left him all but naked. And all because of one phone call. He began to wonder how long those words would haunt him:

'Would it be too much to ask the figure you have in mind, Mr Townsend?'

'Yes, Ambassador. Three billion dollars.'

E.B. didn't have to remind him that there was still the contingency plan to be considered before she could move on to stage three.

However many times they wrote and rewrote the press release, its conclusion was always the same: Global Corp was filing for Chapter Eleven, and would be going into voluntary liquidation. Townsend had rarely spent a more distasteful couple of hours in his life. He could already see the stark headline in the *Citizen*: 'Townsend Bankrupt'.

Once they had agreed on the wording of the press release, E.B. was ready to move on to the next stage. She asked Townsend which banks he felt would be most sympathetic to his cause. He immediately identified six, and then added a further five whose long-term relationship with the company had always been amicable. But as for the rest, he warned her, he had never dealt with any of them before he set about raising the three billion for the Multi Media deal. And one of them had already demanded their money back, 'come what may'.

'Then we'll have to leave that one till last,' said E.B.

She began by approaching the senior loan officer of the bank with the largest credit line, and told him in detail of the rigours she had put Townsend through. He was impressed and agreed to support her plan – but only if every other bank involved also accepted the rescue package. The next five took a little longer to fall into line, but once she had secured their co-operation, E.B. began to pick off the others one by one, always able to point out that to date every institution she had talked to had agreed to go along with her proposals. In London she had appointments with Barclays, Midland Montagu and Rothschilds. She intended to continue her journey to Paris, where she would see Crédit Lyonnais, and then flights were booked for Frankfurt, Bonn and Zurich, as she tried to weld each link in the chain.

She had promised Townsend that if she was successful in London she would phone and let him know immediately. But if she failed at any stage, her next flight would be to Honolulu, where she would brief the assembled Global delegates not on the company's long-term future, but on why, when they returned to their own countries, they would be looking for new jobs.

E.B. left for London that evening, armed with a case full of files, a book of plane tickets and a list of telephone numbers that would allow her access to Townsend at any time of the day or night. Over the next four days she planned to visit all the banks and financial institutions which would, between them, decide Global's fate. Townsend knew that if she failed to convince just one of them, she wouldn't hesitate to return to New York and send his files down to the thirteenth floor. The only concession she agreed was to give him an hour's notice before she issued the press release.

'At least if you're in Honolulu you won't be doorstepped by the world's press,' she had said just before she left for Europe.

Townsend had given her a wry smile. 'If you issue that press release it won't matter where I am,' he said. 'They'll find me.'

◄○►

Townsend's Gulfstream landed in Honolulu just as the sun was setting. He was picked up at the airport and driven straight to the hotel. When he checked in, he was handed a message which read simply, 'All three banks in London have agreed to the package. On my way to Paris. E.B.'

He unpacked, took a shower and joined his main board directors for dinner. They had flown in from all over the world for what he had originally intended to be an exchange of ideas on the development of the company over the next ten years. Now it looked as if they might be talking about how to dismantle it in the next ten days.

Everyone around the table did their utmost to appear cheerful, although most of them had been summoned to the presence of E.B. at some time during the past few weeks. And all of them, after they had been released, immediately shelved any ideas they might have had for expansion. The most optimistic word that ever passed E.B.'s lips during those cross-examinations had been 'consolidation'. She had asked the company secretary and the group's chief financial officer to prepare a contingency plan which would involve suspending the company's shares and filing for voluntary liquidation. They were finding it particularly difficult to look as if they were enjoying themselves.

After dinner Townsend went straight to bed, and spent another sleepless night that couldn't be blamed on jetlag. He heard the message being pushed under his door at around three in the morning. He leaped out of bed and tore it open nervously. 'The French have agreed – reluctantly. On my way to Frankfurt. E.B.'

At seven, Bruce Kelly joined him in his suite for breakfast. Bruce had recently returned to London to become managing director of Global TV, and he began by explaining to Townsend that his biggest problem was getting the sceptical British to buy the hundred thousand satellite dishes that were presently being stored in a warehouse in Watford. His latest idea was to give them away free to every reader of the *Globe*. Townsend just nodded between sips of tea. Neither of them mentioned the one subject that was on both their minds.

After breakfast they went down to the coffee room together, and Townsend moved among the tables, chatting to his chief executives from around the world. By the time he had circled the room, he came to the conclusion that they were either very good actors or they had no idea how precarious the situation really was. He hoped the latter.

The opening lecture that morning was given by Henry Kissinger, on the international significance of the Pacific Rim. Townsend sat in the front row, wishing that his father could have been present to hear the words of the former secretary of state as he talked of opportunities no one would have thought possible a decade before, and in which he believed Global would be a major player. Townsend's mind drifted back to his mother, now aged over ninety, and her words when he had first returned to Australia forty years earlier: 'I have always had an abhorrence of debt in any form.' He could even remember the tone of her voice.

During the day, Townsend dropped into as many of the seminars as he could manage, leaving each one with the words 'commitment', 'vision' and 'expansion' ringing in his ears. Before he climbed into bed that night, he was handed the latest missive from E.B.: 'Frankfurt and Bonn have agreed, but extracted tough terms. On my way to Zurich. Will phone as soon as I know their decision.' He had another sleepless night as he lay waiting for the phone to ring.

Townsend had originally suggested that, following Zurich, E.B. should fly straight to Honolulu so that she could brief him personally. But she didn't think that was a good idea. 'After all,' she reminded him, 'I'm hardly going to boost morale by chatting to the delegates about my job description.'

'Perhaps they'd think you're my mistress,' said Townsend.

She didn't laugh.

After lunch on the third day, it was Sir James Goldsmith's turn to address the conference. But as soon as the lights were lowered, Townsend began checking his watch, anxiously wondering when E.B. might call.

Sir James walked onto the platform to enthusiastic applause from the delegates. He placed his speech on the lectern, looked out into an audience he could no longer see and began with the words: 'It is a great pleasure for me to be addressing a group of people who work for one of the most successful companies in the world.' Townsend became engrossed by Sir James's views on the future of the EC, and why he had decided to stand for the European Parliament. 'As an elected member I will have the opportunity to . . .'

'Excuse me, sir.' Townsend looked up to see the hotel manager hovering beside him. 'There's a call from Zurich for you. She says it's urgent.' Townsend nodded and quickly followed him out of the darkened room and into the corridor.

'Would you like to take it in my office?'

'No,' Townsend said. 'Put it through to my room.'

'Of course, sir,' said the manager, as Townsend headed for the nearest lift.

In the corridor he passed one of his secretaries, who wondered why the boss was leaving Sir James's lecture when he was down on the programme to give the vote of thanks.

When Townsend let himself into his suite, the phone was already ringing. He walked across the room and picked up the receiver, glad she couldn't see how nervous he was.

'Keith Townsend,' he said.

'The Bank of Zurich have agreed to the package.'

'Thank God for that.'

'But at a price. They're demanding three points above base rate, for the entire ten-year period. That will cost Global a further $17.5 million.'

'And what was your response?'

'I accepted their terms. They were shrewd enough to work out that they were among the last to be approached, so I didn't have many cards to bargain with.'

He took his time before he asked the next question. 'What are my chances of survival now?'

'Still no better than fifty-fifty,' she said. 'Don't put any money on it.'

'I don't have any money,' Townsend said. 'You even took away my credit cards, remember?'

E.B. didn't respond.

'Is there anything I can still do?'

'Just be sure that when you deliver your closing speech this evening, you leave them in no doubt that you're the chairman of the most successful media company in the world, not that you're possibly only a few hours away from filing for voluntary liquidation.'

'And when will I know which it is?'

'Sometime tomorrow would be my guess,' said E.B. 'I'll call you the moment my meeting with Austin Pierson is over.' The line went dead.

◄◦►

Armstrong was met off Concorde by Reg, who drove him through the drifting sleet from Heathrow into London. It always annoyed him that the civil aviation authorities wouldn't allow him the use of his helicopter over the city during the hours of darkness. Back at Armstrong House, he took the lift straight up to the penthouse, woke his chef and ordered him to prepare a meal. He took a long, hot shower, and thirty minutes later he appeared at the dining room table in a dressing-gown, smoking a cigar.

A large plate of caviar had been laid out for him; he had scooped up the first mouthful with his fingers even before he sat down. After several more handfuls, he lifted his briefcase up onto the table and extracted a single sheet of paper which he placed in front of him. He began to study the agenda for the next day's board meeting, between mouthfuls of caviar and glass after glass of champagne.

After a few minutes he pushed the agenda to one side, confident that if he could get past item one he had convincing answers to anything else Sir Paul might come up with. He lumbered into the bedroom and propped himself up in bed with a couple of pillows. He switched on the television and began flicking from channel to channel in search of something to distract him. He finally fell asleep watching an old Laurel and Hardy movie.

◄◦►

Townsend picked up his speech from a side table, left the suite and walked across the corridor to the lift. At the ground floor, he made his way quickly over to the conference centre.

Long before he reached the ballroom he could hear the relaxed chattering of the waiting delegates. As he entered the room, a thousand executives fell silent and rose from their places. He walked down the centre aisle onto the stage and placed his speech on the lectern, then looked down at his audience, a group of the most talented men and women in the media world, some of whom had served him for over thirty years.

'Ladies and gentlemen, let me begin by saying that Global has never been in better shape to face the challenges of the twenty-first century. We now control forty-one television and radio stations, 137 newspapers and 249 magazines. And of course we have recently added a jewel to our crown: *TV News*, the biggest-selling magazine in the world. With such a portfolio, Global has become the most powerful communications empire on earth. Our task is to remain the world leaders, and I see before me a team of men and women who are dedicated to keeping Global in the forefront of communications. During the next decade . . .' Townsend spoke for another forty minutes on the future of the company and the roles they would all be playing in it, finishing with the words: 'It has been a record year for Global. When we meet next year, let's confound our critics by delivering an even better one.'

They all stood and cheered him. But as the applause died down, he couldn't help remembering that another meeting would be taking place in Cleveland the following morning, at which only one question would be answered, and it certainly wouldn't be followed by applause.

As the delegates broke up, Townsend strolled round the room, trying to appear relaxed as he said goodbye to some of his chief executives. He only hoped that when they returned to their own territories, they wouldn't be met by journalists from rival newspapers wanting to know why the company had gone into voluntary liquidation. And all because a banker from Ohio had said, 'No, Mr Townsend, I require the fifty million to be repaid by close of business this evening. Otherwise I will be left with no choice but to place the matter in the hands of our legal department.'

As soon as he could get away, Townsend returned to his suite and packed. A chauffeur drove him to the airport, where the Gulfstream was waiting to take off. Would he be travelling economy class tomorrow? He was unaware of how much the conference had taken out of him, and within moments of fastening his seatbelt he fell into a deep sleep.

◄o►

Armstrong had planned to rise early and give himself enough time to destroy various papers in his safe, but he was woken by the chimes of Big Ben, foreshadowing the seven o'clock television news. He cursed jetlag as he heaved his legs over the side of the bed, aware of what still needed to be done.

He dressed and went into the dining room to find his breakfast already laid out: bacon, sausages, black pudding and four fried eggs, which he washed down with half a dozen cups of steaming black coffee.

At 7.35 he left the penthouse and took the lift down to the eleventh floor. He stepped out onto the landing, switched on the lights, walked quickly down the corridor past his secretary's desk, and stopped to jab a code into the pad by the side of his office door. When the light turned from red to green he pushed the door open.

Once inside, he ignored the pile of correspondence waiting for him on his desk and headed straight for the massive safe in the far corner of the room. There was another longer and more complicated code to complete before he could pull back the heavy door.

The first file he dug out was marked 'Liechtenstein'. He went over to the shredder and began to feed it in, page after page. Then he returned to the safe and removed a second file marked 'Russia (Book Contracts)', and carried out the same process. He was halfway through a file marked 'Territories for

Distribution' when a voice behind him said, 'What the hell do you think you're doing?' Armstrong swung round to find one of the security guards shining a torch into his face.

'Get out of here, you fool,' he shouted. 'And close the door behind you.'

'I'm sorry, sir,' said the guard. 'No one told me you were in the building.' When the door had closed, Armstrong continued to shred documents for another forty minutes until he heard his secretary arrive.

She knocked on the door. 'Good morning, Mr Armstrong,' she said cheerfully. 'It's Pamela. Do you need any help?'

'No,' he shouted above the noise of the shredder. 'I'll be out in a few moments.'

But it was another twenty-five minutes before he eventually opened the door. 'How much time have I got before the board meeting?' he asked.

'Just over half an hour,' she replied.

'Ask Mr Wakeham to join me immediately.'

'The deputy chairman is not expected in today, sir,' said Pamela.

'Not expected? Why not?' bellowed Armstrong.

'I think he's caught the 'flu bug that's been going around. I know he's already sent his apologies to the company secretary.'

Armstrong went over to his desk, looked up Peter's number in his Filofax and began dialling. The phone rang several times before it was answered by a female voice.

'Is Peter there?' he boomed.

'Yes, but he's in bed. He's been rather poorly, and the doctor said he needed a few days' rest.'

'Get him out of bed.'

There was a long silence, before a reedy voice asked, 'Is that you, Dick?'

'Yes, it is,' replied Armstrong. 'What the hell do you mean by missing such a crucial board meeting?'

'I'm sorry, Dick, but I've got rather a bad dose of 'flu, and my doctor recommended a few days' rest.'

'I don't give a damn what your doctor recommended,' said

Armstrong. 'I want you at this board meeting. I'm going to need all the support I can get.'

'Well, if you feel it's that important,' said Peter.

'I most certainly do,' replied Armstrong. 'So get here, and get here fast.'

Armstrong sat behind his desk, aware of the buzz emanating from the outer offices that showed the building was coming to life. He checked his watch: only about ten minutes before the meeting was due to begin. But not one director had dropped in for their usual chat, or to ensure that they had his support for whatever proposal they were recommending to the board. Perhaps they just didn't realise he was back.

Pamela entered his office nervously and handed him a thick briefing file on the agenda for the morning's meeting. Item number one, as he had read the previous night, was 'The Pension Fund'. But when he checked in the file, there were no briefing notes for the directors to consider – the first such notes were attached to item number two: the fall in circulation of the *Citizen* after the *Globe* had cut its cover price to ten pence.

Armstrong continued reading through the file until Pamela returned to tell him that it was two minutes to ten. He pushed himself up from the chair, tucked the file under his arm and walked confidently into the corridor. As he made his way towards the boardroom, several employees who passed him said 'Good morning.' He gave them each a warm smile and returned their greeting, though he wasn't always certain of their names.

As he approached the open door of the boardroom, he could hear his fellow directors muttering among themselves. But the moment he stepped into the room there was an eerie silence, as if his presence had struck them dumb.

◄o►

Townsend was woken by a stewardess as the plane began its descent into Kennedy.

'A Ms Beresford phoning from Cleveland. She says you'll take the call.'

'I've just come out of my meeting with Pierson,' said E.B. 'It lasted over an hour, but he still hadn't made up his mind by the time I left him.'

'Hadn't made up his mind?'

'No. He still needs to consult the bank's finance committee before he can come to a final decision.'

'But surely now that all the other banks have fallen into place, Pierson can't – '

'He can and he may well. Try to remember that he's the president of a small bank in Ohio. He's not interested in what other banks have agreed to. And after all the bad press coverage you've been getting in the past few weeks, he only cares about one thing right now.'

'What's that?'

'Covering his backside.'

'But doesn't he realise that all the other banks will renege if he doesn't go along with the overall plan?'

'Yes, he does, but when I put that to him he shrugged his shoulders and said, "In which case I'll just have to take my chance along with all the others."'

Townsend began to curse.

'But he did promise me one thing,' said E.B.

'What was that?'

'He'll call the moment the committee has reached its decision.'

'That's big of him. So what am I expected to do if it goes against me?'

'Release the press statement we agreed on,' she said.

Townsend felt sick.

Twenty minutes later he dashed out of the terminal. A limousine was waiting for him, and he climbed into the back before the driver could open the door for him. The first thing he did was to dial his apartment in Manhattan. Kate must have been waiting by the phone, because she answered immediately.

'Have you heard anything from Cleveland yet?' was her first question.

'Yes. E.B.'s seen Pierson, but he still hasn't made up his mind,' replied Townsend, as the car joined the bumper-to-bumper traffic on Queen's Boulevard.

'What do you think the odds are on him extending the loan?'

'I asked E.B. the same question yesterday, and she said fifty-fifty.'

'I just wish he'd put us out of our misery.'

'He will soon enough.'

'Well, the moment he does, be sure I'm the first person you call, whatever the outcome.'

'Of course you'll be the first person I call,' he said, putting the phone down.

Townsend's second call, as the limousine crossed the Queensboro Bridge, was to Tom Spencer. He hadn't heard anything either. 'But I wouldn't expect to until after E.B. has briefed you,' he said. 'That's just not her style.'

'As soon as I know what Pierson's decided, we'd better get together to discuss what has to be done next.'

'Sure,' said Tom. 'Just give me a call the moment you hear anything and I'll come straight over.'

The driver swung into Madison Avenue and eased the limousine into the right-hand lane before pulling up outside the headquarters of Global International. He was taken by surprise when Mr Townsend leaned forward and thanked him for the first time in twenty years. But he was shocked when he opened the door and the boss said, 'Goodbye.'

The chairman of Global International strode quickly across the sidewalk and into the building. He headed straight for the bank of elevators and entered the first one that returned to the ground floor. Although the lobby was full of Global employees, none of them attempted to join him, except a bellhop who jumped in and turned a key in a lock next to the top button. The doors slid closed and the elevator began to accelerate towards the forty-seventh floor.

When the lift doors opened again, Townsend stepped out into the thickly carpeted corridor of the executive floor and walked straight past a receptionist who looked up and smiled at him. She was about to say 'Good morning, Mr Townsend,' when she saw the grim expression on his face and thought better of it.

Townsend's pace never faltered as the glass doors that led to his office area slid open.

'Messages?' was all he said as he passed his secretary's desk and headed towards his office.

40

^{The} GLOBE

5 NOVEMBER 1991

Search for Missing Tycoon

'Good morning, gentlemen,' Armstrong said in a loud, cheerful voice, but he received only the odd murmur in response. Sir Paul Maitland gave a slight nod as Armstrong took the vacant place on his right. Armstrong looked slowly round the boardroom table. Every seat was filled except for the deputy chairman's.

'As everyone is present other than Mr Wakeham,' said Sir Paul, checking his fob watch, 'who has already tendered his apologies to the company secretary, I suggest we begin. Can I ask if you all accept the minutes which have been circulated of last month's board meeting as a true and accurate record?'

Everyone nodded except Armstrong.

'Good. Then the first item on the agenda is the one we discussed at great length during our recent finance meeting,' continued Sir Paul, 'namely the current position of the pension fund. On that occasion Mr Wakeham did his best to brief us following his short trip to New York, but I fear several questions still remain unanswered. We came to the conclusion that only our chief executive could properly bring us up to date on what was actually taking place in New York. I am relieved to see that he has found it possible to join us on this occasion, so perhaps I should begin by . . .'

'No, perhaps it is I who should begin,' interrupted Armstrong, 'by giving you a full explanation of why it was impossible for me to attend last month's board meeting.' Sir Paul pursed his lips, folded his arms and stared at the unoccupied chair at the other end of the table.

'I remained at my desk in New York, gentlemen,' continued Armstrong, 'because I was the only person with whom the print unions were willing to negotiate – as I am sure Peter Wakeham confirmed at last month's board meeting. Because of this, not only did I pull off what some commentators described as a miracle – ' Sir Paul glanced down at a leader that had appeared in the *New York Tribune* the previous week, which did indeed use the word 'miracle' – 'but I am now able to confirm to the board something else I asked Mr Wakeham to pass on to you, namely that the *Tribune* has finally turned the corner, and for the past month has been making a positive contribution to our P and L account.' Armstrong paused before adding, 'And what's more, it is doing so for the first time since we took the paper over.' Several members of the board seemed unable to look in his direction. Others who did were not indicating approval. 'Perhaps I deserve some praise for this monumental achievement,' Armstrong said, 'rather than the continual carping criticism I get from a chairman whose idea of enterprise is to feed the ducks on Epsom Downs.'

Sir Paul looked as if he was about to protest, but Armstrong waved a hand in the air and, raising his voice, said, 'Allow me to finish.' The chairman sat bolt upright, his fingers gripping the arms of his chair, his gaze still fixed rigidly ahead of him.

'Now, as far as the pension fund is concerned,' continued Armstrong, 'the company secretary will be in a better position than I am to confirm that we are holding a considerable surplus in that account, a little of which I used – quite legitimately – for investments in the United States. It may also interest the board to know that I have recently been in confidential negotiations with Keith Townsend, with a view to taking over the *New York Star*.' Most of the directors looked stunned by the announcement, and this time all of them turned to face him.

'It's no secret,' continued Armstrong, 'that Townsend is in

deep financial trouble following his foolhardy takeover of Multi Media, for which he paid three billion dollars. The board will recall that only last year I recommended we should offer no more than one and a half billion for that particular company, and in hindsight it turns out that my judgement was correct. I have now been able to take advantage of Townsend's disastrous mistake and make him an offer for his shares in the *Star* that would not have been thought possible only six months ago.'

Now he had everyone's attention.

'That coup will make Armstrong Communications the most powerful newspaper presence on the east coast of America.' Armstrong paused for effect. 'It will also ensure an even larger contribution to our bottom line than we presently enjoy from Britain.'

One or two of the faces round the table brightened up, but the chairman's was not among them. 'Are we to understand that this deal with Townsend has been concluded?' he asked quietly.

'It is in its final stages, Chairman,' replied Armstrong. 'But I wouldn't dream of committing the company to an undertaking of such importance without first seeking the board's approval.'

'And what exactly does "final stages" mean?' enquired Sir Paul.

'Townsend and I have had an informal meeting on neutral ground, with both our professional advisers present. We were able to come to an agreement on the sort of figure that would be acceptable to both parties, so now it's simply up to the lawyers to draw up the contracts for signature.'

'So we don't yet have anything in writing?'

'Not yet,' said Armstrong. 'But I am confident that I will be able to deliver all the necessary documentation in time for the board's approval at next month's meeting.'

'I see,' said Sir Paul drily, as he opened a file in front of him. 'Nevertheless, I wonder if we might now return to the first item on the agenda, and in particular to the current state of the pension fund.' He checked his notes and added, 'Which has recently had withdrawals totalling over four hundred and . . .'

'And I can assure you that the money has been well

invested,' said Armstrong, once again not allowing the chairman to finish his sentence.

'In what, may I ask?' enquired Sir Paul.

'I don't have the precise details to hand at the moment,' said Armstrong. 'But I have requested that our accountants in New York produce a detailed and comprehensive report, so that members of the board are in a position to make a full appraisal of the situation before the next board meeting.'

'How interesting,' said Sir Paul. 'When I spoke to our accounts department in New York only last night, they had no idea what I was talking about.'

'That's because a small inner team has been chosen for this particular exercise, and they've been instructed not to release any details, owing to the sensitivity of one or two of the deals I am currently involved in. I cannot therefore . . .'

'Damn it,' said Sir Paul, his voice rising with every word. 'I am the chairman of this company, and I have the right to be informed of any major development that may affect its future.'

'Not if that might jeopardise my chances of closing a major deal.'

'I am not a rubber stamp,' said Sir Paul, turning to face Armstrong for the first time.

'I didn't suggest you were, Chairman, but there are times when decisions have to be made when you are tucked up in bed fast asleep.'

'I would be quite happy to be woken,' said Sir Paul, still looking directly at Armstrong, 'as I was last night by a Monsieur Jacques Lacroix from Geneva, who rang to tell me that unless an outstanding loan to his bank of $50 million is repaid by close of business tonight, they will find it necessary to place the matter in the hands of their lawyers.'

Several of the directors bowed their heads.

'That money will be in place by tonight,' said Armstrong, without flinching. 'Of that I can assure you.'

'And where do you propose to get it from this time?' asked Sir Paul. 'Because I have issued clear instructions that nothing more can be withdrawn from the pension fund as long as I remain chairman. Our lawyers have advised me that if that cheque for $50 million had been cashed, every member of this board would have been liable to criminal prosecution.'

'That was a simple clerical error made by a junior clerk in the accounts department,' said Armstrong, 'who foolishly deposited the cheque with the wrong bank. He was sacked the same day.'

'But Monsieur Lacroix informed me that you had delivered the cheque personally, and he has a signed receipt to prove it.'

'Do you really believe that I spend my time in New York going around depositing cheques?' Armstrong said, staring back at Sir Paul.

'Frankly, I have no idea what you get up to when you're in New York – though I am bound to say that the explanation Peter Wakeham gave to last month's meeting of how money withdrawn from the pension fund ended up in accounts at the Bank of New Amsterdam and the Manhattan Bank was just not credible.'

'What are you suggesting?' shouted Armstrong.

'Mr Armstrong, we are both aware that the Manhattan is the bank which represents the print unions in New York, and that BNA were given instructions by you to purchase over $70 million of our shares during the past month – this despite the fact that Mark Tenby, our chief accountant, pointed out when he issued you with a pension fund chequebook that to purchase shares in one of our own companies was a criminal offence.'

'He said no such thing,' shouted Armstrong.

'Is that just another example of "a simple clerical error",' said Sir Paul, 'which can no doubt be solved by sacking the chief accountant?'

'This is absolutely preposterous,' said Armstrong. 'BNA could have been purchasing those shares for any one of their customers.'

'Unfortunately not,' said Sir Paul, referring to another file. 'The chief dealer, who was willing to return my call, confirmed that you had given clear instructions,' he glanced at his notes, 'to "prop up" – in your words – the share price, because you couldn't afford to let the stock fall any further. When the implications of such an action were pointed out to you, you apparently told him' – once again Sir Paul checked his notes – '"I don't give a damn what it costs."'

'It's his word against mine,' said Armstrong. 'If he repeats it, I'll take out a writ for slander against him.' He paused. 'In both countries.'

'That might not be a wise course of action,' said Sir Paul, 'because every call which goes through to that department at BNA is recorded and logged, and I have requested that a transcript of the conversation should be sent to me.'

'Are you accusing me of lying?' shouted Armstrong.

'If I were to do so,' asked the chairman, 'would you then issue a writ for slander against me?'

For a moment Armstrong was stunned.

'I can see that you have no intention of answering any of my questions candidly,' continued Sir Paul. 'I am therefore left with no choice but to resign as chairman of the board.'

'No, no,' cried a few muted voices round the table.

Armstrong realised for the first time that he had overplayed his hand. If Sir Paul were to resign now, within days the whole world would become aware of the precarious state of the company's finances. 'I do hope you will find it possible to remain as chairman until the AGM in April,' he said quietly, 'so that we can at least expedite an orderly handover.'

'I fear it has already gone too far for that,' said Sir Paul.

As he rose from his place, Armstrong looked up and said, 'Do you expect me to beg?'

'No, sir, I do not. You are about as capable of that as you are of telling the truth.'

Armstrong immediately rose from his place, and the two men stared at each other for some time before Sir Paul turned and left the room, leaving his papers on the desk behind him.

Armstrong slipped across into the chairman's place, but didn't speak for some time as his eyes slowly scanned the table. 'If there is anyone else who would care to join him,' he said finally, 'now's your chance.'

There was a little shuffling of papers, some scraping of chairs and the odd staring down at hands, but nobody attempted to leave.

'Good,' said Armstrong. 'Now, as long as we all behave like grown-ups, it will soon become clear that Sir Paul was simply jumping to conclusions without any grasp of the real situation.'

Not everyone around the table looked convinced. Eric Chapman, the company secretary, was among those whose heads remained bowed.

'Item number two,' said Armstrong firmly. The circulation manager took some time explaining why the figures for the *Citizen* had fallen so sharply during the past month, which he said would have an immediate knock-on effect on our advertising revenue. 'As the *Globe* has slashed its cover price to ten pence, I can only advise the board that we should follow suit.'

'But if we do that,' said Chapman, 'we'll just suffer an even greater loss of revenue.'

'True . . .' began the circulation manager.

'We just have to keep our nerve,' said Armstrong, 'and see who blinks first. My bet is that Townsend won't be around in a month's time, and we'll be left to pick up the pieces.'

Although one or two of the directors nodded, most of them had been on the board long enough to remember what had happened the last time Armstrong had suggested that particular scenario.

It took another hour to go through the remaining items on the agenda, and it became clearer by the minute that no one around the table was willing to confront the chief executive directly. When Armstrong finally asked if there was any other business, no one responded.

'Thank you, gentlemen,' he said. He rose from his place, gathered up Sir Paul's files and quickly left the room. As he strode down the corridor towards the lift, he saw Peter Wakeham rushing breathlessly towards him. Armstrong smiled at the deputy chairman, who turned and chased after him. He caught up just as Armstrong stepped into the lift. 'If only you had arrived a few minutes earlier, Peter,' he said, looking down at him. 'I could have made you chairman.' He beamed at Wakeham as the lift doors closed.

He pressed the top button and was whisked up to the roof, where he found his pilot leaning on the railing, enjoying a cigarette. 'Heathrow,' he barked, without giving a thought to clearance by air-traffic control or the availability of take-off slots. The pilot quickly stubbed out his cigarette and ran towards the helicopter landing pad. As they flew over the City of London, Armstrong began to consider the sequence of events that would take place during the next few hours unless the $50 million were somehow miraculously to materialise.

Fifteen minutes later, the helicopter landed on the private apron. He lowered himself onto the ground and walked slowly over to his private jet.

Another pilot, this one waiting to receive his orders, greeted him at the top of the steps.

'Nice,' said Armstrong, before making his way to the back of the cabin. The pilot disappeared into the cockpit, assuming that 'Captain Dick' would be joining his yacht in Monte Carlo for a few days' rest.

The Gulfstream took off to the south. During the two-hour flight Armstrong made only one phone call, to Jacques Lacroix in Geneva. But however much he pleaded, the answer remained the same: 'Mr Armstrong, you have until close of business today to repay the $50 million, otherwise I will be left with no choice but to place the matter in the hands of our legal department.'

41

NEW YORK STAR

6 NOVEMBER 1991

SPLASH!

'I have the President of the United States on line one,' said
Heather, 'and a Mr Austin Pierson from Cleveland, Ohio on
line two. Which will you take first?'

Townsend told Heather which call he wanted put through.
He picked up the phone nervously and heard an unfamiliar
voice.

'Good morning, Mr Pierson, how kind of you to call,'
Townsend said. He listened intently.

'Yes, Mr Pierson,' he said eventually. 'Of course. I fully
understand your position. I'm sure I would have responded in
the same way, given the circumstances.' Townsend listened
carefully to the reasons why Pierson had come to his decision.

'I understand your dilemma, and I appreciate your taking
the trouble to call me personally.' He paused. 'I can only hope
that you won't regret it. Goodbye, Mr Pierson.' He put the
phone down and buried his head in his hands. He suddenly felt
very calm.

When Heather heard the cry she stopped typing, jumped
up and ran through to Townsend's office. She found him leaping
up and down, shouting, 'He's agreed! He's agreed!'

'Does that mean I can finally order another dinner jacket
for you?' asked Heather.

'Half a dozen, if you want to,' he said, taking her in his arms.

'But first you'll have to get my credit cards back.' Heather laughed, and they both started to jump up and down.

Neither of them noticed Elizabeth Beresford enter the room.

'Am I to assume that this is some form of cult worship practised in the more remote parts of the Antipodes?' asked E.B. 'Or could there be a more simple explanation, involving a decision made by a banker in a mid-western state?'

They abruptly stopped and looked towards her. 'It's cult worship,' Townsend said. 'And you're its idol.'

E.B. smiled. 'I'm gratified to hear it,' she said calmly. 'Perhaps, Heather, I could have a word with Mr Townsend in private?'

'Of course,' said Heather. She put her shoes back on and left the room, closing the door quietly behind her.

Townsend put a hand through his hair and returned quickly to his chair. Once he had sat down, he tried to compose himself.

'Now I want you to listen, Keith, and listen carefully,' E.B. began. 'You have been incredibly lucky. You were within a whisker of losing everything.'

'I realise that,' said Townsend quietly.

'I want you to promise me that you will never make a bid for anything ever again without first consulting the bank – and by the bank, I mean me.'

'You have my solemn oath on it.'

'Good. Because you've now got ten years in which to consolidate Global and make it into one of the most conservative and respected institutions in its field. Don't forget, that was stage five of our original agreement.'

'I will never forget,' said Townsend. 'And I shall be eternally grateful to you, Elizabeth, not only for saving my company, but me along with it.'

'It's been a pleasure to help,' said E.B., 'but I won't feel my job has been completed until I hear your company described, especially by your detractors, as blue chip.'

He nodded solemnly as she bent down, flicked open her briefcase and removed a stack of credit cards. She passed them across to him.

'Thank you,' he said.

A flicker of a smile appeared on her lips. She rose from her chair and offered an outstretched hand across the table. Townsend shook it. 'I hope we'll meet again soon,' he said as he accompanied her to the door.

'I hope not,' said E.B. 'I don't think I want to be put through that particular mangle a second time.'

When they reached Heather's office, E.B. turned to face him. For a moment Townsend considered kissing her on the cheek, but then thought better of it. He remained by Heather's desk as E.B. shook hands with his secretary in the same formal way. She glanced in Townsend's direction, nodded and left without another word.

'Some lady, that,' said Townsend, staring at the closed door.

'That's for sure,' said Heather wistfully. 'She even taught me one or two things about you.'

Townsend was about to ask what they could possibly be when Heather added, 'Shall I call the White House back?'

'Yes, straight away. I'd completely forgotten. When I've finished with him, get me Kate.'

As Townsend returned to his office, Elizabeth stood in the corridor, waiting for one of the six lifts to arrive at the top floor. She was in a hurry to get to the bank and clear her desk – she hadn't spent a weekend at home for the past month, and had promised her husband that she would be back in time to see their daughter perform the role of Gwendolen in the school play. When a lift finally reached the executive level, she stepped inside and pressed the button for the ground floor just as another lift door opened on the other side of the corridor. But the doors closed before she could see who it was who had leaped out and run off in the direction of Townsend's office.

The lift stopped at the forty-first floor, and E.B. was joined by three young men who continued their animated conversation as if she wasn't there. When one of them mentioned Armstrong's name, she began to pay closer attention. She couldn't believe what they were saying. Every time the lift stopped and new people came in, she picked up a fresh piece of information.

A breathless Tom came rushing into Heather's office. All he said was, 'Is he in?'

'Yes, Mr Spencer,' she replied. 'He's just finished speaking to the President. Why don't you go straight through?'

Tom walked towards the executive suite and threw open the door just as Townsend completed dialling a number on his private phone. 'Have you heard the news?' he gasped.

'Yes,' said Townsend, looking up. 'I was just phoning Kate to let her know that Pierson's agreed to extend the loan.'

'I'm delighted to hear it. But that's not news, it's history,' said Tom, falling into the seat E.B. had recently vacated.

'What do you mean?' asked Townsend. 'I only heard it myself a few minutes ago.'

A voice came on the line and said, 'Hello, Kate Townsend.'

'I mean, have you heard about Armstrong?'

'Armstrong? No, what's he been up to now?' asked Townsend, ignoring the phone.

'Hello,' Kate repeated. 'Is anyone there?'

'He's committed suicide,' said Tom.

'Is that you, Keith?' said Kate.

'He's done what?' said Townsend, dropping the receiver back in place.

'It seems he was lost at sea for several hours, and some fishermen have just picked up his body off the coast of Sardinia.'

'Armstrong dead?' Townsend swivelled his chair round, and for a few moments just stared out of the window over Fifth Avenue. 'And to think my mother outlived him,' he said eventually.

Tom looked bemused by this statement.

'I can't believe it was suicide,' said Townsend.

'Why do you say that?' asked Tom.

'It's just not his style. The damned man always believed he could survive anything.'

'Whatever it was, London's leaking like a sieve,' said Tom. 'It seems that Armstrong's endless flow of cash came from the company's pension fund, which he was not only using to buy up his own shares, but also to pay off the unions in New York.'

'The company's pension fund?' said Townsend. 'What are you talking about?'

'Apparently Armstrong discovered there was far more cash in the fund than was legally necessary, so he began siphoning it off at a few million a time, until his chairman found out what he was up to and handed in his resignation.'

Townsend picked up an internal phone and pressed three digits.

'What are you doing?' asked Tom.

'Shh,' said Townsend, placing a finger up to his lips. When he heard a voice on the other end of the line, he asked, 'Is that the accounts department?'

'Yes, sir,' said someone who immediately recognised the Australian accent. 'It's Hank Turner, I'm the company's deputy chief accountant.'

'You're exactly the man I need, Hank. First, tell me, does Global have a separate pension fund account?'

'Yes, of course it does, sir.'

'And how much are we holding in that account at the present time?' he asked.

He hung on and waited for the answer. E.B.'s lift had reached the ninth floor on the way back up by the time the deputy chief accountant was able to inform Townsend, 'As of nine o'clock this morning, sir, that account is showing a balance of $723 million.'

'And how much are we required to hold by law in order to fulfil our pension fund obligations?'

'A little over $400 million,' came back the accountant's reply. 'Thanks to our fund manager's shrewd investment policy, we've been able to keep well ahead of inflation.'

'So we're carrying a surplus of more than $300 million over and above our statutory obligation?'

'That is correct, sir, but the legal position is that at all times we must . . .'

Townsend replaced the receiver and looked up to find his lawyer staring at him in disbelief.

E.B. stepped out of the lift and into the corridor.

'I hope you're not thinking what I think you're thinking,' said Tom, as E.B. walked into Heather's office.

'I need to see Mr Townsend urgently,' she said.

'Don't tell me Pierson has changed his mind?' said Heather.

'No, it's nothing to do with Pierson. It's Richard Armstrong.'

'Armstrong?'

'He's been found dead at sea. The first reports are suggesting that he committed suicide.'

'Good heavens. You'd better go in immediately, Mrs Beresford. He's got Tom Spencer with him at the moment.'

E.B. headed towards Townsend's room. Tom had left the door open when he had rushed in, so before she reached the office, E.B. was aware that a heated discussion was taking place. When she heard the words 'pension fund' she froze on the spot, and listened in disbelief to the conversation taking place between Townsend and his lawyer.

'No, hear me out, Tom,' Townsend was saying. 'My idea would still fall well within any legal requirements.'

'I hope you'll allow me to be the judge of that,' said Tom.

'Let's assume that trading in Armstrong Communications shares will be suspended later today.'

'That's a fair assumption,' agreed Tom.

'So it would be pointless at this stage for me to try and lay my hands on any of their stock. All we know at present is that Armstrong was bleeding the pension fund dry, so when the shares come back on the market, they're certain to be at an all-time low.'

'I still can't see how that helps you,' said Tom.

'Because, like the crusaders of old, dressed in the armour of righteousness, I shall ride in and save the day.'

'And how do you propose to do that?'

'Simply by merging the two companies.'

'But they would never agree to that. To start with, the trustees of the *Citizen*'s pension fund wouldn't risk a further . . .'

'They might when they discover that the surplus in our pension fund more than covers the losses in theirs. It would conveniently solve two problems at the same time. First, the

British government wouldn't have to dip into its special reserve fund.'

'And second?' said Tom, still looking highly sceptical.

'The pensioners themselves could sleep secure in the knowledge that they would not be spending the rest of their lives facing penury.'

'But the Monopolies and Mergers Commission would never agree to you owning both of the two biggest tabloids in Britain,' said Tom.

'Perhaps not,' said Townsend, 'but they couldn't object to my taking over all of Armstrong's regional publications – which should have been mine in the first place.'

'I suppose they just might wear that,' said Tom, 'but the shareholders wouldn't . . .'

'. . . they wouldn't give a damn about Armstrong's 46 per cent stockholding in the *New York Star*.'

'It's a bit late to be worrying about that,' said Tom. 'You've already lost overall control of that paper.'

'Not yet, I haven't,' said Townsend. 'We're still going through the process of due diligence. I'm not required to sign the completion documents until next Monday.'

'But what about the *New York Tribune*?' asked Tom. 'Armstrong may be dead, but you'd simply inherit all his problems. Whatever he claimed to the contrary, that paper is still losing over a million dollars a week.'

'But it won't be if I do what Armstrong should have done in the first place, and close the paper down,' said Townsend. 'That way I'd create a monopoly in this city which no one would ever be able to challenge.'

'But even if you squared the British government and the Monopolies and Mergers Commission, what makes you think the board of Armstrong Communications will fall in with your cosy little plan?'

'Because not only will I be replenishing their pension fund, but I would also allow the management to retain control of the *Citizen*. And we wouldn't be breaking the law, because the surplus in our pension fund more than covers the shortfall in theirs.'

'I still think they'd put up one hell of a fight to prevent you,' said Tom.

'Not when the *Globe* reminds the *Citizen*'s 35,000 former employees every morning that there's a simple solution to their pension problem. Within days they'll be demonstrating outside Armstrong House, demanding that the board go along with the merger.'

'But that also assumes Parliament will wear it,' said Tom. 'Think of those Labour members who detest you even more than they did Armstrong.'

'I'll just have to make sure that those same members receive sackfuls of letters from their constituents, reminding them that they are only months away from an election, and that if they expect them to vote . . .'

Keith looked up to see E.B. standing in the doorway. She stared at him in the same way she had on the first day they met.

'Mr Townsend,' she said, 'less than fifteen minutes ago, you and I came to an agreement, an agreement on which you gave your solemn oath. Or does your memory not stretch back that far?'

Keith's cheeks reddened slightly, and then a smile slowly appeared on his face. 'I'm sorry, E.B.,' he said, 'I lied.'

extracts reading groups
competitions books new
discounts extracts
competitions extracts
books new
events extracts
events books
interviews reading groups
discounts events
events new books events
events new
discounts extracts discounts

extracts events reading groups
competitions books extracts new